RIVERSIDE COMMUNITY COLLEGE
1916

P9-DWY-772

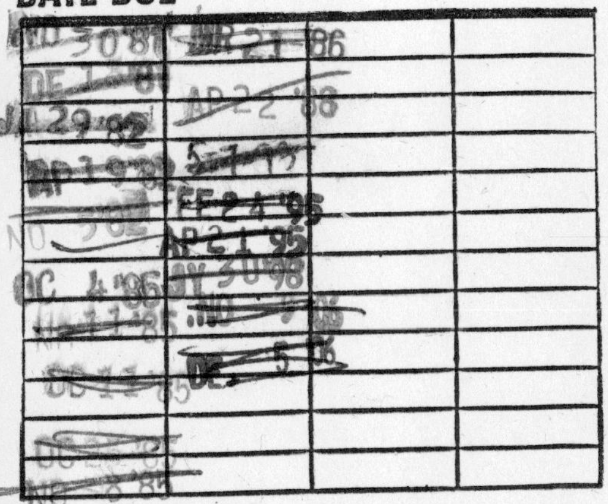
DATE DUE

By Alexandra Ripley

CHARLESTON

WHO'S THAT LADY IN THE PRESIDENT'S BED?

By Alexandra Ripley
Ninette Beaver & Patrick Trese

CARIL

CHARLESTON

CHARLESTON

Alexandra Ripley

1981
DOUBLEDAY & COMPANY, INC.
GARDEN CITY, NEW YORK

With the exception of historical political and military figures, all of the characters in this book are fictitious, and any resemblance to actual persons, living or dead, is purely coincidental.

Library of Congress Cataloging in Publication Data
Ripley, Alexandra.
Charleston.
I. Title.
PS3568.I597C47 813'.54
ISBN: 0-385-14572-1
Library of Congress Catalog Card Number 79-8568

PRINTED IN THE UNITED STATES OF AMERICA
FIRST EDITION

This book is dedicated to

JANE CLARK TWOHY

in grateful acknowledgment of
her Medici view of banking.

Boastful and braggart Charleston . . .
Terrible is the self-inflicting retribution
which an All-Wise Providence has decreed
against this cockatrice's den . . .
O fallen Babylon! . . .

New York *Independent*, February 1865

If ever a people deserved extermination and
banishment, it was the unprincipled, obstinate,
ignorant and treacherous ruling class of
South Carolina . . .

Chicago *Tribune*, April 1865

BOOK ONE

1863-1865

1

The wide street was quiet and deserted under the scorching sun. The leaves on the vines and trees in its gardens hung limply; even the birds had no strength to sing in the heavy, sticky air.

Then the silence was broken by the rise and fall of chimes, repeated four times. A deep bell sounded four strokes, and a strong voice called out: "Four of the clock, and all's well."

A short time later, there was a distant noise of galloping hooves. The watchman in the church steeple looked intently as the gray-uniformed rider approached then passed beneath him. It was all right. He recognized the young officer. It was Andrew Anson, hurrying to his house farther down Meeting Street.

"August 8, 1863," wrote Major William Ellis in his small pocket journal. His handwriting was precise, neatly formed and even. "We have succeeded in our efforts to remain undetected," the words marched exactly across the thin page, "and we are prepared to defend ourselves against the aroused Rebels when they learn of our presence. There will be many of them, to our few, but we trust in God to help us, because our cause is just. The Parrott gun we have brought from the ship is aimed at the very heart of the Rebellion. It will be our privilege to bring down in dust the arrogant seed of the so-called Confederacy. God grant that the wound be mortal."

"Andrew!" Lucy Anson's arms reached for her husband. He kissed her, hurried kisses on her face, eyes, lips, hair, until Lucy began to gasp. Then he took both her hands in his and held them to his face. His eyes were glowing.

"You're so beautiful," he whispered.

Lucy's wide gray eyes filled with happy tears. "How long is your leave?" she said. "You should have told me you were coming so I could have everything ready. No, I take that back. The surprise was wonderful."

She rubbed her cheek against his chest and breathed in the smell of him. It was intoxicating. At first she did not realize what Andrew was saying. He had no leave. He had volunteered to carry an urgent dispatch from Wilmington to Savannah just so that he could pass through Charleston and see his wife and baby. He'd have to get a fresh horse and be on his way immediately. Maybe on the way back, he could stay one night . . .

"No, I can't bear it!" Lucy wrapped her arms around his neck. "It's not fair. I won't let you go."

"Shhh. Hush, love. Don't make things hard for me." His voice was stern, the voice of a soldier.

"I'll be good," she whispered. "Come see your son."

Little Andrew was sleeping in a net-shrouded cradle next to Lucy's bed. It was the first time Andrew had seen him. He looked with wonder at the tiny figure. "I guess I'm the happiest man in the world," he said quietly. Lucy slid her arms around his waist.

"I could be the happiest woman," she whispered. "Hold me. Oh, dearest, it's only four o'clock. It won't get dark until almost ten. You don't have to leave yet awhile." She brought his hand to her breast.

Major Ellis read what he had written, then nodded with satisfaction. He closed the book, put it in the pocket of his sweat-stained, muddy breeches, then put on the scratchy wool tunic of his uniform. Gloves and hat followed. He could barely breathe in the near-tropical heat, but the Major had a sense of history, and he wanted to be dressed for destiny. He raised his sword; the gun crew moved into position, igniting torch flaming. Ellis took one last look through his field glass. Across the calm wide waters of the harbor, the old city of Charleston shimmered in heat-haze like a mirage, its tall, narrow houses shuttered against the sun, their pastel walls pale and insubstantial-looking. Rising above the steep tiled roofs and chimney pots, the delicate spire of Saint Michael's church was a whiter arrow against the background of towering white clouds that promised a thunderstorm to cool the heavy air.

The spire was the Major's target. He lowered his sword in a chopping signal.

The cannonball was painted a dull black. It rose over the wide waters like a carrion bird, hung motionless for an instant at the top of its trajectory, then fell lazily toward the city. It was 4:12 P.M.

The shot was wide. It fell into the marsh that edged the city on the west and was swallowed by the thick blue-black mud of low tide. Major Ellis cursed and made calculations.

In the belfry of Saint Michael's, Edward Perkins rubbed his eyes. He had been a day watchman for almost twenty years, and he had expected to work for at least twenty more. At thirty-eight, his eyes were "keener than an eagle's," as the Charleston *Mercury* had written in a story about him. His main duty was to look for smoke, not the thin white smoke that rose constantly from the chimneys of kitchen buildings, but the dark plumes that meant fire. The crowded old city had been destroyed five times by fire since its beginning in 1670; its inhabitants carried the memory and the terror in their blood. But with eagle eyes on constant watch and the two shiny red pumper wagons in the firehouse near the docks, Charlestonians could laze away the hot summer afternoons, secure in their shuttered houses.

There it was. Another one. Edward Perkins strained forward, shading his eyes with his hand. The dark speck rose from James Island, grew larger as it crossed the water. When it began to fall, Edward Perkins ran, stumbling, to the thick knotted rope that hung from the biggest bell in the steeple. His thin arms swelled as he pulled, then stretched when the huge bronze bell tipped back, lifting him from the platform. The deep clang of alarm rang out over the city.

Mary Ashley Tradd was "having a little talk" with her ten-year-old son Stuart. It was not going well. When Stuart's father and his older brother, Pinckney, left for Virginia at the beginning of the War, they told him he'd have to be the man of the house. Stuart interpreted that to mean that he could make all his own decisions without asking his mother's permission or opinion.

Mary looked at Stuart's stubborn freckled face and felt despair. He was like a miniature of his father, Anson Tradd. Even his hair is mulish, she thought. Secretly she had always hated the wiry, copper-gold hair of the Tradd family and hoped that her children would look like her. Not one of them, she mourned internally. They just as well not be my children at all. They look like Anson, even baby Lizzie, and they're as reckless and stubborn as Anson and they won't listen to a thing anybody tells them except Anson and now Anson's dead and gone, out of pure pigheadedness, leading a cavalry charge at his age, and I'm all alone with a bunch of do-nothing servants and talk-back children and nobody to help me. Her big dark eyes filled slowly with becoming tears and her little plump hand rose to touch the mourning brooch she wore. Stuart moved his feet restlessly. Like men of any age, he was incapable of handling a crying woman. When the alarm bell began to ring, he leapt to his feet, reprieved.

"Hurricane!" he shouted joyfully.

"Fire!" Mary's voice was a terrified squeak.

They hurried onto the long, columned second-story porch that stretched the length of the house.

On the opposite side of Meeting Street Andrew Anson lifted his head. "What's that?"

"Nothing, darling," Lucy murmured, "just old Ed Perkins thinking he sees a fire." She grabbed Andrew's thick hair and pulled his mouth down to meet hers.

All over the city, shutters opened and heads popped out. People sniffed the air and looked up at the sky. There was nothing out of the ordinary. The shutters closed.

Except on Meeting Street. The shot had fallen into one of the walled gardens, splintering a huge magnolia tree. The big leaves were falling over half a block, turning in spirals of dark green and tan as the upper and under sides showed.

"What on earth?" Mary Tradd clutched her son's sleeve. Up and down the street, ladies and old men began to fill the piazzas. Below them, house doors opened. Servants spilled out onto the smooth granite blocks of the sidewalks and the rounded cobblestones of the street, sent to find out what was going on. "Stuart, tell Elijah to go see what's happening."

"I'll go, Mama."

"No you will not. Send Elijah."

But Stuart was gone.

On James Island, Major Ellis lowered his field glass and smiled for the first time in a week. "That one almost got there, boys. A little more powder behind the next one and we might just take the top off that steeple." A bullet hissed past his ear and he ducked instinctively. The fighting had begun at the walls his men had built around the emplacement. The Major listened intently. Behind the sharp cracking noise of gunfire, he could hear the deep booming of ships' cannons. Good for the Admiral, he thought. As long as he keeps up a steady shelling on Fort Johnson, the Rebs can't send too many of their men after us.

At the firehouses, the captains were shouting orders to the firemen, who were hitching up horses and checking the equipment on the pumpers.

The youngest of them rode on the fastest horse to Saint Michael's. "Where is it?" he shouted through cupped hands. Edward Perkins waved his arms wildly and went back to his rope. The boy shouted again. Then, getting no answer, he slid off the horse and ran through the door to the narrow spiral of iron stairs.

Farther along Meeting, a crowd had gathered. They milled in front of a tall, intricately patterned wrought-iron gate, peering through the arabesques. "Lightning, must be," the ones in front said, holding their places against the pushing from the rear. Behind the gate, the neat geometrics of the garden were almost intact. Paths of pale pink brick intersected to make five lozenges. The pattern was repeated on the rear wall by espaliered peach trees. Late summer roses crowded the raised beds by the south wall.

The four corner lozenges were of grass, each with a towering magnolia tree in the center. Except that in one, only a broken trunk remained, with huge limbs tumbled around it, some extending over crushed hedges onto the paths.

The alarm bell continued to peal, but the city did not know why. In several houses, the sound woke children, who added their cries to the noise. In others, people went back to their windows to look again for the cause.

There was nothing to see. On James Island, Major Ellis' men were hard pressed by attacking Confederates. One of the gunners had been shot. He fell across the breech, and everything stopped until he could be carried away. Finally a frightened replacement took his position. The Major's face was apoplectic. "Fire!" he shouted.

While the shot was still in the air, the small old city came to life. The young fireman burst through the door in the side wall of Saint Michael's yelling. "Yankees!" he bellowed. "Yankee shells." His voice was lost in the sound of the bell. He ran toward the crowd that was aimlessly moving away from the garden's gate. His excitement caught everyone's attention. "Yankees," he gasped and pointed upward. Then he sped away to spread the news.

Some boys in the crowd looked up in time to see the cannonball just before it hit a stable on Church Street, one block east. They leapt from foot to foot, half terrified, half wild with the excitement of it all. "Yankees," they howled. Within seconds, someone in the crowd made out the word and passed it on with embellishment. "The Yankees are coming. They've got past the forts." People scattered in all directions, bumping into each other, pushing and yelling in panic.

One of the carriage horses in the Church Street stable had colic. His groom had started preparing a hot mash only seconds before the cannonball shattered the tile roof. The tiny flame under the cauldron was fanned into a tongue of fire by the sudden whoosh of air. It touched off fresh-laid straw on the floors of the stalls. The horses, crazed, reared and struck at the doors to the stalls, but they were firmly latched. The groom could not free them; he had been struck in the head by the missile.

The heartbreaking cries of the burning horses brought servants running, but it was already too late. Huge gouts of flame were bursting from every door and window of the stables. Clumps of burning straw shot up through the opening in the roof and scattered across the narrow street, falling on people who had run out of their houses when they heard the terrible sounds.

The acrid smell of burning wood was overlaid by the sickening odor of charred animal flesh. It hung heavy in the narrow street, pressed down by the billowing smoke. Everywhere, there was the sound of neighing horses. Stableboys at every house on the street were trying to lead them out to safety, but the terrified animals fought the ropes. Their hooves slashed the air dangerously.

"Where is the blasted pumper?" bellowed a white-bearded man from his doorway. "What do I pay that fire company for anyhow?"

The pumper was hitched up, its matched team restlessly ready in the traces. But the boy who had gone for directions to locate the fire—before there was a fire—was a half mile away, galloping from street to street shouting "Yankees" at the heads that appeared in windows along his way.

Behind him, he left a wake of panic. People, black and white, dashed out of their houses, shouting questions at the disappearing rider and then, when he did not answer, at each other.

The fire was spreading. The pumpers, mired in the frantic crowds, could not get to it. "Stuart!" Mary Tradd leaned out over the piazza railing, searching for the bright head of her son in the maelstrom below her. "Stuart!" Behind her, three-year-old Lizzie squirmed in the relentless grip of her nurse, Georgina. She had been wakened from her nap, and she was frightened by the unearthly commotion. She began to cry, and Georgina pulled her to her pillowlike bosom.

A collective moan of fear rose from the mob on Meeting Street. All faces turned up to look at the black ball falling toward them. Then, screaming, the crowd scattered. The shot plowed a furrow in the cobblestones and came to rest, a larger darker mound among the gray hemispheres.

Andrew Anson nearly tripped on it when he ran out of his house. He tried to stop one of the running, whimpering black girls who were passing, but she pushed him away savagely. Andrew plunged into the crowd.

Opposite, Mary Tradd momentarily forgot her fear. "I didn't know Andrew Anson was home," she said to Georgina. "You remember Andrew. His father is second cousin to Mr. Tradd. Pinckney was best man when Andrew married Lucy Madison." Across the street Lucy appeared on the upstairs piazza. She was wearing a ruffled dressing gown. Mary giggled and rolled her eyes at Georgina, who did not respond. Then she waved at Lucy. But Lucy, too, was unresponsive. She was following Andrew with her eyes.

A loud rumbling filled the air. Everyone looked up. The sky was obliterated by the thick, nauseating smoke of the fire a block away. No one could see the flashes of lightning. They heard artillery in the thunder.

Mary Tradd paced furiously on her porch. "Where is that Stuart?" Suddenly he appeared, walking the wall above the carriage drive. He saw his mother and grinned, his smile very white in his smudged face. "False alarm, Mama," he shouted cheerfully. "The Yankees haven't broken through at all; they've just got one gun on James Island, and they won't have that long." He balanced himself with windmill arms as he walked the length of the wall to Meeting Street. Then he sat, legs dangling, and bellowed the news to the scurrying people below his feet.

"What about the fire?" Lucy Anson yelled. "Stuart! Hey, look over here. What about the fire?"

"Oh, hello, Lucy. How are you?"

"The fire, Stuart."

"It's wonderful. I was over there. Boy, sparks shooting up like the Fourth of July. But the pumpers have got through. They'll have it out soon." Stuart was obviously disappointed.

Lucy relaxed her grip on the porch railing. There, she said to herself, you see, you silly, you were all upset over nothing. Andrew won't be captured by any Yankees, his precious dispatch is safe and he'll hardly even be late. Even if he is, he'll have more news than just his old papers. He'll be able to tell all about the gun the Yankees got into the swamp. That's certainly worth waiting an hour for.

She looked with contempt at the agitation on the street. Everyone was ignoring Stuart's shouts. Geese, she thought. All that milling around. They should just go home where they belonged. Then she spied Andrew a half block away. He was pushing people aside, heading for home. Lucy's hands felt her hair, arranging the rumpled curls around her smiling face.

When Andrew got close, he made a megaphone of his hands. "Don't worry," he shouted, "everything's all right." Lucy nodded comprehension.

The people near him stopped, approached him, questioning. His uniform carried credibility. Andrew became the center of a small, then a large group. Soon they dispersed, shaking their heads with relief and rueful shame for their panic. There was a clap of thunder. Rain suddenly fell in tropical deluge. The departing people began to run for home.

So did Andrew. Lucy, protected by the roof of the piazza, laughed at his spurt toward the shelter of the trees that lined the sidewalk. She did not see the cannonball. Black against the suddenly dark sky, its fall went unobserved by the scuttling people fleeing the rain.

It made a tearing, crashing noise when it landed on the marble portico of the Clay house. Lucy looked away from Andrew for a moment, afraid of lightning. Chips of white marble were thrown outward, like a halo for the doorway under the portico. Then, slowly, it seemed so slowly, the two Doric columns leaned away from each other. "No!" Lucy screamed. "Andrew!"

His head bowed against the rain, Andrew looked up at his wife, still running. He felt, more than saw, the shadow of the column. He tried to run faster. But an overpowering weight struck his back, throwing him forward. Then his face was in a puddle. He tried to roll over, but he couldn't move.

Georgina had shepherded Lizzie and her mother indoors as soon as the first sheets of rain came down. Stuart, enjoying the excitement, sat heedless, looking like a laughing, red-haired Pan. When the pillar fell on Andrew, his face froze in forgotten mirth. He leapt to the ground and ran for the alley between houses that led to Church Street. Dr. Perigru had been there only a little earlier, tending the burns of the firemen.

He returned with the doctor, the old man puffing from the haste of the short journey. Lucy was sitting in a puddle with Andrew's head in her lap. Her body, bent over him, sheltered him from the worst of the rain. At his feet, the men were tying ropes around the marble column that lay across his legs. They were servants from neighboring houses, led by Andrew's butler, Jeremiah. Tears mingled with the rain on Jeremiah's face.

Dr. Perigru felt Andrew's heartbeat and looked closely at his ashen face. "You in much pain, son?"

Andrew shook his head and tried to smile. "I'm pretty scared, though."

"We'll take good care of you." The doctor moved off to supervise the lifting of the pillar.

"Oh, Andrew, are you suffering much? Do you hurt?"

"No, love, I really don't. I'm awful wet, that's all. So are you. You shouldn't be out in this rain."

Sobs shook Lucy's body. She turned her face into her shoulder.

"Hush, now, hush. No crying. Do you want me to tell you something funny?"

Lucy gulped, took a deep breath. She nodded.

Dr. Perigru's voice was muted, but clear. "I'm going to count. When I say 'three,' pull up on those ropes. And I mean up. Don't drag it."

Andrew held Lucy's hand tighter. "I bet you don't know what they're calling the cannon," he said. "I don't know who started it, but it's typical soldiers' humor. They've named it 'The Swamp Angel.' "

"Three!"

Andrew and Lucy clung to each other.

Dr. Perigru's head appeared above them. "Nothing like as bad as it could have been, my boy." There was unmistakable relief in his voice. Lucy felt as if her heart had been released from a vise. "Now, it may hurt like hell—sorry, Lucy—when we go to move you. If it does, holler. No need to be a hero about it." The old man knelt by Andrew's head. He slipped his arm under his shoulders and lifted them enough to release Lucy. "You go in the house, young lady, and get some hot soup started.

Get out the brandy, too. Your husband and I are both going to need some.

"Jeremiah, you get hold in the middle," Dr. Perigru ordered, "and you, Jubilo, get his legs. When I say 'lift,' pick him up nice and gentle . . . Lift . . . now let's take him in the house. How you doing, Andrew?"

"Doctor, I don't feel anything. Nothing at all."

On James Island, Major Ellis stamped furiously through the water that filled the center of the emplacement. "Damn rain. We can't do anything with wet powder. Just keep those Rebs away, boys, and we'll try again tomorrow. One paltry fire. Damn. We didn't do any real damage at all." Across the harbor, a flash of lightning illuminated Saint Michael's spire.

"Goddamn it all," said the Major.

2

The Swamp Angel began shelling again at daybreak, but by now the city was prepared. All evening Confederate officers had gone from house to house, reassuring the inhabitants and advising them about precautions against fire and falling timbers. When the bombardment recommenced, it was viewed with anger and curiosity, but no panic. Piazzas and rooftops were soon filled with people, watching the succession of massive iron balls that rose, halted, then fell onto the area around Saint Michael's. When, in midmorning, the overworked Swamp Angel exploded while firing its thirty-seventh round, the bright glare was seen by all the spectators. The sound of the explosion rolled across the water to the city, where it was echoed by the cheers of the crowds.

Within an hour, the familiar figures of the Brewtons' houseboys in their red-and-black-striped vests were hurrying all over town. Sally Brewton's nearly illegible handwriting sprawled over the notes they were carrying. "Tea alfresco in the drawing room, four o'clock, do come."

Sally Brewton was a petite woman in her thirties. She had a figure like a boy's and a tiny, monkey-like face. Her flashing eyes and inexhaustible good spirits had won Miles Brewton's heart when every great beauty had tried and failed. Later, on their many trips to Europe, Asia and Africa, she had captivated everyone she met. Her parties were famous for the special imprint of the hostess, who was described, with admiration, as an "original." Every lady in Charleston who was not in deep mourning set out for the Brewton house shortly before four o'clock, curious about Sally's latest innovation. Carriages and buggies clogged King Street for blocks, depositing their passengers in turn. The delays only heightened the guests' anticipation.

They were not disappointed. When they entered the severely beautiful eighteenth-century drawing room, they discovered Sally seated behind a large tea table near the center. A thick spotlight of sunshine fell on her through a hole in the ceiling. It wrapped her in a radiant nimbus, reflected off the Georgian silver tea service and danced among the glittering prisms of the crystal chandelier that hung dangerously near the opening. Sally was wearing a white lawn dress to heighten the effect. Its huge skirts seemed to gather the light. Her tiny feet, which were her chief vanity, were outrageous in red-satin slippers with diamond buckles. They rested side by side on the dark mound of the cannonball imbedded in the parquet under the table.

"Come in," Sally called as each guest appeared in the door. "We're celebrating history. I've always said it was boring, with all that repetition. Now I find it more interesting."

The ladies exclaimed, admired and laughed. Everyone knew that during the War of Independence a British shell had fallen through the Brewton house, barely missing the Waterford chandelier that was one of its treasures. The Yankee shell had followed the exact path of its predecessor.

Every guest went home from Sally Brewton's tea feeling better than she had for a long time. Sally's high spirits were always contagious, but the party also had a deeper and longer lasting effect. Everyone there was related by blood or by marriage to the Charleston families who had settled in the city before the Revolution. All of them knew bits of family history from those days, passed down, like the silver and portraits, through the generations. It was good to be reminded that Charleston had been besieged before. It had even been captured and occupied. But the British were defeated, the damage repaired, the old life restored. Except for transitory inconvenience, the city had maintained its highly civilized, individualistic minuet through time. There was really nothing to worry about. This War, too, would be over one day. The Brewton's house, and all the other damaged houses, would have patches in one place or another, but after a few years, they would be unnoticeable.

Sally's red slippers were better than a regiment.

In the months that followed, the Charlestonians needed every reassurance they could muster. The respite after the Swamp Angel's death was brief. Having discovered the vulnerability of the islands that ringed the harbor, Union forces moved cannon emplacements onto one after another. James, Johns, Yonges, Wadmalaw, Folly—each island became a threat to the city. Newer cannonballs, with explosive centers, fell in place of the Swamp Angel's iron shot. Then explosive shells were added, with a power to damage a hundred times greater than anything Charleston had ever known.

The modern cannon also had a longer range. Families moved uptown above Broad Street to escape bombardment. Then they had to move again, above Calhoun. Some left for towns inland, where they had friends or relatives to take them in. By the end of November, everyone remaining in Charleston was crowded into an area a quarter mile square at the northernmost edge of the city. The largest part of Charleston was deserted, left to the day and night screaming of the shells.

Andrew Anson's imposing mother, Emma, sent her carriage to bring him "home" the day after his accident. Lucy was left to follow in her own buggy with the baby and nursemaid. Emma turned her big house on Charlotte Street into an extended sickroom. Proper care, she said, would heal him and restore the use of his legs. When the exodus from downtown began, she refused to take in any of her numerous cousins. She even turned away her brother's family. Andrew needed peace and quiet.

Her next door neighbor, Julia Ashley, had no such excuse. Julia was a spinster in her mid-forties. She lived alone in the big brick mansion which she had inherited when her adored father died ten years earlier. She had worn mourning ever since that day. Julia had no brothers. Her only sister was Mary Tradd, eight years younger and her opposite in every way.

Mary was the pretty one; tiny, plump, feminine, with dark curling hair and large blue eyes. The house had been crowded with her beaux from the moment she made her debut until the day she chose Anson Tradd from the many. It had also rung with Mary's laughter, shrieks of joy and outbursts of tears. To Julia, bitterly resigned to her single future, those two years of Mary's romances had been agony.

After Mary moved into her own home, Julia became her own person for the first time. Without Mary's softness for comparison, Julia's tall, thin body and strong bony features looked almost handsome. Her quiet, infrequent comments could be heard and appreciated. She developed a circle of her own friends, who were interested in literature, science and natural history; she traveled; she was a sponsor of the symphony orchestra and had the best box at the theater. By the time she reached forty, Julia was a distinguished woman and a happy one.

Now Julia's orderly existence was shattered by the noisy arrival of her sister, her sister's children and her sister's servants. Mary opened up the dust-sheeted rooms on the third floor for Lizzie, Stuart and Georgina, moved back into her old room and dominated the house as she had always done. Julia began to have migraine headaches.

Throughout the neighborhood, other families were also opening closed rooms and making adjustments, but for most of them it was easy, even normal. The Christmas season was approaching, and they always had a house full of guests at that time of year.

Charleston was a social town; people enjoyed a constant round of large and small parties. From Christmas to the end of January was the busiest time of all. In normal years it offered concerts by orchestras from London, plays at the Dock Street Theater performed by imported companies with world-famous stars, elaborate balls and suppers three or four nights a week and, in January, excitement at the luxurious clubhouse overlooking the racecourse, when owners bet thousands on the horses wearing their colors. For five weeks every year, the gayest city in America was at its extravagant, expansive best.

The War had curtailed the elaborate, organized entertainments. The Dock Street was closed; so was the racetrack; and there would be no Saint Cecelia Ball, where young girls were presented to society. But the air of festivity was as strong as ever. Perhaps stronger. It was important to keep up spirits in spite of the interruption of war.

On December twentieth, Mary Tradd looked in on the scene in the drawing room and felt a glow of satisfaction. The Yankees had sunk three blockade runners that month, but the fourth narrow, fast ship had gotten past their guns. By great good luck, it was the one with the cargo that interested her most. The children's Christmas presents made brightly wrapped pyramids on the deep windowsills.

"Miz Tradd," Mary started. She had been so engrossed that she had not heard Elijah's footsteps. When she saw his face, she put her hand to her heart. His lip was trembling, his eyes wide with fear. His hand held a telegram. It was all exactly like the time, eighteen months earlier, when the news came of her husband's death. Mary moaned. She snatched the flimsy paper from Elijah's hand and tore it open.

Then she burst into tears. "It's all right," she sobbed, "I was just so frightened. It's just fine, Elijah. It's from Mr. Pinckney. He'll be home before Christmas. Tell everybody."

Before the end of the day, everyone in town had heard the good news, and everyone was delighted. Pinckney Tradd was a universal favorite.

As a boy, he had been wild, but never mean. His red-gold hair served as a beacon for other boys, who followed his lead in exploits of climbing, swimming, exploring, racing boats and horses, and experimenting with cigars and liquor. His tutors had torn their hair because he would not apply his good mind to his studies, preferring the stables to the schoolroom, but they always succumbed to his laughing apologies. Pinckney was disobedient, but never devious. He admitted his sins and took his canings without excuses.

Foremost among his sins was his quick, hot temper. It faded as quickly as it flared, but it was awesome while it lasted. As he grew older, he learned to control it; layers of gallant good manners insulated him from his emotions. He could bow and laugh when he met obstacles, and only his closest friends recognized the storm behind his suddenly pale face and darkened blue eyes. He became a thoroughly civilized animal, still physically daring, but with an overlay of fashionable smiling languor. His lithe, muscular body could lift a fallen tree or the thin length of a fencing foil with equal effectiveness. He was the best rider and the best dancer in all of South Carolina.

To his mother's intense delight, Pinckney grew up handsome. He was perpetually tanned from his outdoor life, and unlike most redheads, he did not freckle. His browned skin added a romantic, gypsylike air to his narrow, fine-boned face. It was clean-shaven. To Pinckney's horror, his facial hair was brown, not red, and he could not have a beard, as most men did, without looking ridiculous.

When he smiled, which was often, his rather small, thin-lipped mouth stretched astonishingly to reveal large white teeth with a tiny gap in the center; his bright eyes flashed wickedly. Sally Brewton called him Apollo, and all the ladies in Charleston agreed.

His father was relieved to observe that it made no difference to the boy.

The summer he was seventeen, Pinckney was sent to Oxford. It was expected that, like other Charleston boys and their fathers and grandfathers before them, he would manage to get a decent degree without any serious scandals and then make the Grand Tour. Instead, South Carolina seceded from the Union the following year. Pinckney came home. He had learned a smattering of Shakespeare, made dozens of friends and unconsciously picked up an English accent mixed with his Southern drawl. In May 1861 he rode off at his father's side to join Wade Hampton's volunteers. He had not been home since.

In almost every house, people reminisced fondly about Pinckney's boyhood escapades and shared accounts they had heard about his daring in battle. He had earned command of his own troop of cavalry; it was said that General Lee called him "the centaur."

In many houses, mothers looked critically at their daughters' dresses, complexions and posture. Pinckney was twenty now; he had inherited the Tradd plantation and fortune. And everyone knew that a hero returned from the horrors of battle was susceptible to a soft, sympathetic voice and pretty face. There was at least one furlough wedding every month.

At Emma Anson's, Andrew's cheerfulness was genuine for the first time when he heard the news. He and Pinckney had grown up together, inseparable best friends. He had even had second thoughts about asking Lucy to marry him, because it meant not going to Oxford with Pinckney. But Lucy's adoring gray eyes were more appealing than education. In anticipation of Pinckney's arrival at the house next door, Andrew had the furniture moved in his room. The couch where he spent his days was put next to the window that overlooked the entrance to Julia's house.

In her room next door, Andrew's seventeen-year-old sister, Lavinia, rubbed her cheeks with a dampened bit of red flannel. She had worshiped Pinckney for as long as she could remember. Hidden under the embroidered handkerchiefs in her dressing table, Lavinia's most precious talisman was a napkin that Pinckney had used. Sometimes she locked her door and held it to her lips while she wondered what it felt like to be kissed.

At Julia's, Mary was a tornado, giving conflicting orders to the servants, opening the trunks where Pinckney's clothes were stored and dashing to the kitchen building to remind Julia's cook that Mr. Pinckney liked salt in his butter and preferred tea to coffee.

Stuart, like Andrew, posted himself by a window. Pinckney was his idol.

Even Julia lost her composure. Pinckney, then only six, had won her heart for all time when he had suggested that his mother should give Julia all her rings because his aunt's hands were long and graceful whereas Mary's were pudgy. She aired her father's room, always kept locked, and told Elijah to prepare it the way Pinckney liked his room to be.

The only person who was not pleased was Lizzie. She was confused by all the turmoil. Try as she might, she could remember neither her brother nor her father. All she knew was that Georgina pulled harder than usual when she brushed her hair and that no one seemed to have time to admire the doll she had gotten for her fourth birthday the month before. The doll had shiny black boots, which Lizzie could lace up by herself. After four days of being told to keep out of the way while the preparations for Pinckney were made, Lizzie decided to run away from home. She marched bravely through the front gate and down the street to the corner. There she crouched behind a holly bush that grew next to the sidewalk in the Wilsons' garden and thought about where to go.

A shadow fell on her, and a deep voice said hello. Lizzie shrank into the holly.

The stranger stooped, then sat on the sidewalk. "How do you do, madam," he said. "I'm looking for the home of Miss Elizabeth Tradd."

Lizzie scowled suspiciously. "I'm not allowed to talk to strangers."

"That's a very sensible rule," the man said, "but we aren't exactly strangers . . . Do you like guessing games?"

The little girl crept out from the screen of holly. She loved to play games. Only, everyone had been too busy to play with her lately. She eyed the stranger warily. "What kind of guessing game?" she said.

The man smiled. "Not such a hard one. You have to look at me and try to figure what redheaded, dirty-faced man would be calling on Miss Elizabeth Tradd, hoping for a tea party."

Lizzie backed away and stared. Then some dim memory clarified. "Pinny!" Her arms locked around his neck. "I like you."

"I'm so glad. I adore you." With one smooth movement, Pinckney stood, holding Lizzie on one arm. He began to walk toward Julia's.

"Stop," Lizzie cried. He stopped. There was a moment of silence. "I was running away," Lizzie confessed.

"I'm glad you changed your mind."

"You won't tell?"

"I won't tell. But you'll have to give me a party in the nursery."

"Oh, I will, Pinny. Let's hurry."

Pinckney began to run. Lizzie screamed with joy. When he turned into Julia's gate, he swung Lizzie around in a circle; she was ecstatic.

"Pinny!" Andrew's shout was booming. Pinckney turned and grinned at the yellow head sticking out of the window next door.

"Halloo, Andrew. I have an engagement with this lady, and then I'll be over."

3

Inside the house Pinckney was besieged by his family and servants. "Hello, hello," he shouted, laughing. "Let a fellow get his breath, won't you? Merry Christmas."

In spite of Mary's protests, he insisted on having tea in the playroom. Mary, Julia and Stuart found themselves sitting on the floor while Lizzie passed walnut-sized cups filled with tea brought up by Georgina.

When the pot was empty and everyone had had a chance to talk, Pinckney stretched and yawned. "What I want more than anything in the world is a bath and some clean clothes. That train was a converted cattle car, I think."

He took his mother's hand in his. "Then I have to go see Andrew. How is he?"

Mary held Pinckney's hand tightly. "Andrew's just fine, just wonderful," she said. "Always so cheerful and happy."

"I see," said Pinckney quietly. He squeezed his mother's hand and then withdrew his. "Let's see about that bath."

"It's ready, Mist' Pinckney. In Mist' Ashley's room."

"Thank you, Georgina. And thank you, Aunt Julia. I've wanted to sleep in Grandpapa's big bed ever since I could remember."

"Don't go, Pinny." The sound was a wail.

Pinckney kissed his little sister. "I'll be back soon. And then I'll read you a story."

When he finished bathing and dressing, Pinckney felt ready for anything. Even the visit to Andrew. His mother had written him about the accident, and he had tried to write Andrew, but the words wouldn't come. He had seen many men wounded, even killed, but he never got used to it. And Andrew was his best friend. He filled a silver case with thin cheroots, slipped it into the pocket made to fit it and ran down the stairs. "I'll be back soon," he called to whoever might be listening.

He knocked on the front door of the Anson house, trying to

remember the name of Emma Anson's butler. When the door was opened, his eyes widened.

He remembered Lavinia in pigtails with unpleasant red pimples on her face. The girl before him now was a breathtaking beauty. Shining hair fell from a center part into long coils of spun gold. It framed a heart-shaped face with a tiny, saucy nose, full red lips and widely separated eyes the color of the sky on a brisk winter day. Her skin was like porcelain, the color of milk except where a flush of pink stained her cheeks. "Come in," she said, and stepped back into a curtsy.

Pinckney walked into the hall and bowed. "Lavinia? Merry Christmas."

Lavinia rose from her curtsy and smiled. A small crescent dimple appeared at one corner of her mouth. "It's nice to see you, Pinny." She spoke in a soft near-whisper. "Andrew's expecting you. I'll take you up."

Pinckney followed her up the stairs, noticing her tiny waist wrapped in a gauze-like sash of iridescent silk stripes. When she was two steps above him, her head was on a level with his. The scent of jasmine floated from her hair.

She glided along the hall to Andrew's room with a swish of skirts, then opened the door. "Andrew, darling, Pinny's here." When she stepped back, she flattened her hoops to make room for Pinckney to enter. The front of her dress tilted upward, revealing a froth of lace petticoats and small velvet slippers below trim silk-clad ankles.

"Oh, my goodness," she exclaimed and pushed her skirt down. Then she ran off, her long eyelashes lowered to hide her embarrassment.

Pinckney dropped into a chair, shaking his head. "I can't believe that's really little Lavinia. Last time I saw her, she was in pinafores."

Andrew chuckled. "Last time you saw her, you weren't looking, Pinny. It was at my wedding and you were too worried about keeping the ushers sober until we got to the church. But Lavinia saw you all right. Don't you remember her catching the bouquet and putting a flower in your buttonhole? She already had her eye on you."

Pinckney laughed. "Of course. Damn thing oozed all over the coat I'd just got. I wanted to wring her neck. I didn't realize that was Lavinia."

"I won't tell her. It would break her heart. She's got her cap set for you."

"More like a baby bonnet."

"All right. Don't say I didn't warn you."

Pinckney smiled. Then he became serious. He glanced at the door, saw that it was firmly closed and pulled his chair close to Andrew's couch. "How is it really, Drew?"

Andrew looked down at his hands. They were neatly folded across the border of his woolen lap robe. "There's no pain," he said. Then he was silent for a long moment. He looked up at Pinckney and his eyes were bleak. "You'll think I'm crazy, but I think it would be easier if there was some pain. Then I'd know I was hurt. I forget. God help me, Pinny, I wake up in the morning, and the sun's shining, and I'm in a clean bed instead of some muddy tent, and I think how lucky I am—as if I had a furlough—and I go to jump out of bed . . . and my legs don't move.

"It happens over and over. You'd think I'd learn . . . There's nothing to fight. If I had some enemy, I could be a man and overcome it. I could beat pain. But this . . . nothing." His right hand made a fist and began to pound the dead thighs under the robe.

"Hey, that's not smart." Pinckney seized Andrew's wrist. For an ugly moment, Andrew fought him, his mouth twisted in rage. Then he relaxed. Pinckney dropped Andrew's arm. "That's the first time you didn't flatten me Indian wrestling. Want to try two out of three?"

Five minutes later, Lavinia knocked gently and came in carrying a tray with glasses and a decanter. She was horrified at the sight of the two men, hands locked, faces red, muscles straining. "What are you doing?" she screamed. "You're hurting Andrew."

They ignored her. She ran down the hall, still holding the tray, glasses tinkling dangerously. When she returned with Lucy, Pinckney's arm lay flat on the couch. Andrew's hand still gripped his, pressing it into the horsehair upholstery. They were grinning like young boys. "You sure you didn't let me win?"

"Don't be a jackass. I'll beat you next time."

Before they could start, the two women rushed to the couch. Lavinia scolded Pinckney archly, her dimple flashing, while Lucy mopped Andrew's forehead with her tiny lace-edged handkerchief.

In gentlemanly tradition, the men submitted. Pinckney took the tray from Lavinia and poured whiskey into the glasses. Andrew forced a smile for Lucy. The color faded from his face.

"Lucy," he said, "you know we men can't drink in front of you ladies."

With a last anxious look at Andrew, Lucy herded Lavinia from the room. Pinckney offered a glass. Andrew drained it and passed it back for a refill.

"They're going to kill me," he said heavily. "They'll smother me to death."

Pinckney set his glass down. "I still want revenge. Two out of three we said."

Andrew shook his head. "Maybe tomorrow. If the women go out someplace. I don't like to upset Lucy." His glass was empty again. Pinckney put the decanter on the table by the couch.

"I'll be over about four," he said. "If the ladies go out, send one of the boys to tell me, and I'll come whip your tail. You owe me a chance to get even." He winked at Andrew and left. As he expected, Lucy was hovering outside Andrew's room. He bowed and said good-bye. Lucy managed a pale smile before she darted through Andrew's door.

Pinckney paused in the gate before Julia's house. In the west, the sunset was a subdued deep red with streaks of purple. The thunder of the siege guns had stopped during the afternoon for an unannounced Christmas truce. It was very quiet. He took out a long, thin cigar and smoked it slowly. One by one the windows of the house glowed as servants lit the gas lamps in the rooms. Then the light narrowed and disappeared when curtains were drawn. When the house and the sky were dark, he shrugged off his depressed spirits and went in.

Christmas Eve was a quiet family time. With a pinecone fire snapping and shooting sparks in the fireplace, Pinckney sat in a deep wing chair and settled Lizzie on his knees. Mary, Julia and Stuart selected chairs.

When everyone was in place, Pinckney cleared his throat and opened the leather-bound book that was waiting on the table by his chair.

"'Twas the night before Christmas, and all through the house . . .'"

When the story was over, Lizzie reluctantly agreed that she had to go to bed so that Saint Nicholas could come. She went as slowly as possible from adult to adult, saying good night and making her curtsy.

When she was gone, Pinckney emptied a basket of pinecones on the fire and returned to his chair, his long legs stretched out to the warmth. Mary began to tell him all the gossip of the two years he had been away. The deep wings on the chair's back made a cave of shadow. His eyes closed.

Stuart woke him. "Mama said for me to shake you. You just have time for supper before we leave for church."

"What time is it?"

"After ten. You've been sleeping for three hours. We went ahead and ate without you. Aunt Julia said you needed rest more than food."

Pinckney rose and stretched. "Ouch. I've got a crick in my neck. And a hole in my stomach. Come talk to me while I eat."

Between mouthfuls of chicken pilau, he fended off Stuart's eager questions about what it was like to fight a war. He talked mostly about horses, and he ate quickly. Then he went up to change his wrinkled clothes.

When he came down, everyone was in the hall, ready to leave. Lavinia was standing close to Mary. "I hope you don't mind me intruding on you-all like this," she said. "Mama and Lucy are staying with Andrew, so I begged Cousin Mary to let me go to church with you-all. It seems awfully mean to make Jeremiah drive me, just one."

The Episcopal Church of Saint Paul on Ann Street was filled beyond capacity. Its congregation had invited the members of the downtown churches to join with them as soon as the bombardment started.

This Christmas Eve, the older churchgoers crowded into the family pews. The young people were relegated to the galleries where they shared the space with the slaves for whom they had been built.

After the service, the cold air outdoors was a welcome tonic. The masses of candles and the press of bodies made the interior stupefyingly close. Everyone lingered on the steps and path to the church door, exchanging Christmas greetings. Pinckney was a center of attention, answering questions about sons and husbands and giving encouraging reports about conditions in Virginia. Several young ladies urged their mothers to push through the crowd around him to "ask after Papa"; they were surprised and annoyed when they saw Lavinia at his side. She smiled brilliantly at everyone, looked with wide eyes at Pinckney when he spoke and, from time to time rested her hand momentarily on his arm in a proprietary butterfly touch. It was so light that Pinckney, engrossed in conversation, was not conscious of it.

On Christmas Day, everyone in the house got up at first light. Lizzie was a whirlwind of excitement. Her piping voice could be heard by everyone. "When can I go downstairs, Georgina? Did Saint Nicholas come yet?" The adults smiled and hurried to dress.

After the intriguing bulges in the stockings were extracted one by one down to the tangerine in the toe, everyone except Lizzie went in to breakfast. "I'll feed Miss Lizzie later," Georgina said decidedly. "Ain't nothing going to stay on that stomach until she settle down."

Clear, thin winter sunlight fell in steep rays through the tall windows of the dining room. It caught in the red hair of the man and the boy and brought a deeper red glow from the mahogany table. Under Elijah's supervision, white-gloved house boys moved in orderly procession around the table. They carried silver serving bowls and platters offering eggs—scrambled, fried, boiled, poached—and towers of crisp bacon, ranks of plump sausage, mounds of tiny, sweet shrimp, pyramids of fried oysters and mountains of glistening white hominy. In front of each place setting, there was a filigreed boat-shaped tray. The linen napkin inside it was folded over an assortment of steaming hot corn muffins, yeast rolls and buttermilk biscuits. Porcelain ramekins heaped with butter stood nearby. It was the usual Charleston breakfast.

While the ladies chattered, Stuart boasted to Pinckney about his own heroism. Together with the other Charleston boys who were too young to go to war, Stuart was assigned after-school duties in support of the new Confederate artillery battery that was being built on the bank of the Ashley River.

"It's sort of dog work, really," he said, pretending humility. "We carry messages and haul water and count the numbers of shells and sandbags and such. See, if the Yankees manage to get one of their batteries put up on this side of Waccamaw Creek, they'll be able to knock out the bridge to the Savannah road. So of course we've got to be ready to get shells into the area where they might try to build."

"Stuart, put down that bacon and use your fork." Mary interrupted. Stuart frowned and obeyed.

"Fingers were made before forks," he muttered. Pinckney raised his napkin to hide a smile.

"How close is the emplacement to the racetrack?"

"Right on it. The oval gives plenty of room for the supply wagons to get around and dump things, and the stables are right there for the horses." Stuart was enthusiastic as he described the ingenuity of General Beauregard's alterations.

Pinckney hardly heard him. His mother's letters had told him about the destruction downtown, the burnt-out houses, the streets full of broken glass, the gardens given over to weeds; but he had still not really thought of Charleston as being seriously wounded. Buildings could be repaired, or replaced. And Mary's lamentations about the lack of ballrooms made no impression on him. Life seemed very much the same as it always was. The transformation of the racecourse, however, made him feel sick. The biggest thing in his life before the war had been Race Week. He loved discussing the fine points of the animals with their owners, many of them from Saratoga, England and Ireland. And the excitment of betting, even though his wagers were much smaller than those of the older men, was more thrilling than any other experience in his life. Even including the visits his father arranged to the luxurious perfumed house on Chalmers Street which restricted its clientele to "gentlemen only."

He had not yet won a cup of his own to match the many his father had accumulated, but he had had high hopes for a colt named Mary's Pride. The war had cut off those hopes. Mary's Pride was now somewhere in Virginia, one of the hundreds of thoroughbreds given by Charlestonians to the Confederate cavalry. He had managed not to think about the reality of what was happening in Charleston. Now it swept over him. The war was mutilating everything that he had gone away to fight for.

"Are you ready, Pinny?" Julia's voice brought him out of his somber reverie. "People will be calling."

"Oh, certainly, Aunt Julia." Pinckney dropped his napkin onto the table and followed the others into the drawing room.

At all times of the year, the people of Charleston kept busy by a constant round of paying and receiving calls. They called to congratulate new mothers, to welcome brides to new homes, to share news of children and relatives, to exchange gossip, to admire each other's gardens, to share each other's grief. Before the annual move to the country, they called to say good-bye. When they returned from the plantations, they called to announce their return and to discuss the events of the months out of the city. Everyone knew which days different families were "at home" and expecting callers. On a special day, like Christmas, the crisscross of activity was less organized. Some people paid calls in the morning and received them in the afternoon. Others reversed the schedule. Where callers found no one at home, they left their cards and handwritten Christmas notes, confident that the call would be returned. If not that day, then the next, or the day after that.

Christmas morning, the Tradds and Miss Ashley received. For three hours, people came and went. At times, there were more than thirty callers in the great double drawing room having tea or sherry and small cheese biscuits. The distinctive flat vowels of Charleston speech mounted into a well-bred bedlam, punctuated by Pinckney's curious overlay of British accent.

Dinner was at the usual time, two-thirty. Lizzie was allowed to eat with the adults because it was Christmas, but her treat did not last long. She watched Pinckney adoringly as he popped her paper snapper while she held her hands over her ears. The prize in it was a pretend pearl bracelet, which he helped her put on. His snapper had a matching necklace. When he gave it to her, her gratitude was so noisy that her mother threatened to send her to her room. "Ladies say 'thank you,' Lizzie. They don't screech like owls."

Dinner proceeded. As always in Charleston, each course offered a choice. And as always there was rice, the backbone of the planter economy. All Charlestonians ate rice every day, sometimes twice in a day.

Pinckney shook his head when the houseboys entered with souffle, fruit cake and pecan pie. "I'll save my sweet tooth for supper," he said. "I need to consult you ladies about my schedule. Can I regret the Walkers' dance tomorrow night?"

"Oh, no." Mary was adamant. "It's really a coming out for Louise, and I promised her mother you'd be there. There just aren't enough men to dance with, and she needs you, Pinny."

"Well, then, I'll have to leave right now to ride out to the plantation. I had planned to go tomorrow, but I'd never get back in time."

Mary began to offer pressing reasons why Pinckney had to accompany her on her afternoon calls, but Julia's voice overrode her.

"Stop gabbling, Mary. I have something to talk to Pinckney about."

She glanced toward the door to the serving pantry. "We'll go into the library. Just the two of us."

In the tall, book-lined room, Julia sat herself behind the leather-topped kneehole desk and unlocked one of the drawers. Pinckney's admiration for his aunt grew as she showed him the documents she took out of the drawer.

They were itemized receipts and expenses for Carlington, the Tradd plantation. Julia explained the major points: with the port blockaded, it was impossible to ship the tons of rice that were the plantation's source of income. But the cost of operation was higher than ever. "To sum up, Pinckney, you're living on principal. To date, it's been my principal; I've been selling railroad bonds when necessary. Here is the account of what you owe me. And a power of attorney. You'll have to trust me to manage your affairs.

"I've already instructed your overseer, Ingram, to omit a rice crop next year. I'm doing the same. There's no sense planting a crop you have no use for. All the warehouses are already full. Also, your people are infected with all this freedom talk. Let them try not working and see how tired they get with nothing to do."

By "your people," Julia meant the Carlington slaves. Charlestonians never used the ugly word, preferring to think of the black men and women as a sort of extended family and to ignore the implications of one man's owning another. It had always been that way. They did not question.

Julia recounted the stories of trusted house servants running away when the bombardment began. She was impassive, but Pinckney could sense and understand her fear. With the black population outnumbering the whites by five to one in the city and a hundred to one on the plantations, fear of a slave uprising was constant, though never acknowledged. There had been two slave revolts in Charleston's history, each put down with losses among both races. Many of the families with French names had fled to Charleston from the bloody massacres in Haiti. There were some things it did not do to think about.

"John Ingram is doing fine running the place for you, Pinny. He sees to the food crops and sends boats down with plenty of supplies for us. My man at the Barony does the same. I sent Ingram everything he needed to do the Christmas gifts for your people. No point in you going out to Carlington."

Pinckney remonstrated. He could vividly remember riding with his father from cabin to cabin, talking to each of their people, admiring growing children, listening to complaints and congratulating successes. "There's no fertilizer like the owner's boot," he said.

Julia's nostrils flared. "Well, go on if you're determined. But your mother will have a seizure."

"Aunt Julia, that's not fair."

"True, nonetheless."

Pinckney shrugged, defeated. "Where did you learn to be such a good manager?" he asked, shifting to safer ground.

"From your grandfather. When your mother was born, the doctors told him he'd have to give up hoping for a son. So he trained me to be one. When he died and I inherited, I learned by doing. It wasn't hard. I've always had a good white overseer. And then I have Isaiah who knows more than the overseer does. I send instructions to both of them."

"How? Isaiah can't read."

"Yes, he can. I taught him to read and write. He's more reliable than anybody else. Except Solomon, my carpenter. I taught him, too. He reports on the condition of the buildings."

"But, Aunt Julia, it's against the law to teach a darky to read."

Julia laughed one of her rare laughs. It sounded like a bark. "My dear nephew," she said, "what have laws to do with me? I'm an Ashley . . . and you're a Tradd. The head of the family now that your father's gone. You've got to start thinking about yourself that way, not like a carefree boy."

"I'll tell you the truth, Aunt Julia. It scares me. The Barony is ten times the size of Carlington, and you don't turn a hair about running it. But I'm worried about how I'll be able to manage."

Julia fingered the papers on the desk. "You'll do just fine," she said flatly. "For one thing, you're a man and people won't try to treat you like an idiot. For another, you'll have all the help I can give you. If you want it."

Pinckney lifted one of her hands and kissed it. "I'd be grateful," he said. "Now where's a pen? I'll make out a draft on the bank for you, and I want to sign that power of attorney before you change your mind."

4

Mary was overjoyed when Pinckney told her that he was at her disposal as an escort to any and all events. The schedule for the season was as busy as ever. Although the big clubhouse ballrooms were all downtown and therefore unavailable, people were moving furniture out of drawing rooms, dining rooms and hallways, and the orchestra supported by the clubs would be playing for dancing at someone's house every night. Sally Brewton, who was living with cousins on Elizabeth Street, had invited three hundred and fifty people for New Year's Eve. "She's sent cards to every single soul in town," Mary marveled. "Where's she going to put them?"

"Unless Sally has lost her touch, Mama, she'll manage. What's more important right now is the problem of my dancing shoes. They have a hole in the bottom."

"Don't worry. Elijah can fix it. He can use the leather from one of those dusty books in the library."

Pinckney laughed.

"So much for Aristotle," he said later, reporting the conversation to Andrew. "I adore my dear mama, but she has all the brains of a flea."

"Well, you wouldn't want a lady to be too smart. Your mama's as pretty as a girl, and that's what counts. It's no surprise Miss Julia never caught herself a husband."

"I guess you're right. I'll tell you this much, though. After just one day at home with the ladies, I really sympathize with you. Want a little toddy?"

"A big toddy, friend. I told Lavinia to leave us a decanter and some decent-sized glasses. Since it was for you, she was meek as a lamb." Pinckney poured four fingers of whiskey into each glass, passed one to Andrew and sprawled in his chair.

"Ah, that's good," he said.

"Good enough for more," Andrew replied. As the week passed, the two phrases became the opening ritual for Pinckney's daily visits. Both men managed to sustain a blur of perception, in which Andrew did not think about his useless body, and Pinckney did not consider the likelihood that he would be killed or crippled when he returned to the War.

The women noticed the ever-present aroma of whiskey but did not speculate about the reasons. Southern men always drank. You could tell a gentleman by how well he held his liquor.

And it did not interfere with Pinckney's role of gallant escort. Every afternoon he took his mother to a tea, every evening to a dance. Sometimes Julia accompanied them. More frequently, Lavinia asked if there was room for her in the carriage. Andrew teased Pinckney about Lavinia's transparent ruses. He also thanked him for acting as a substitute father and big brother. "I want you to know that I'm grateful."

"Shut up, will you? It gives me good practice for when Lizzie grows up."

Lavinia's pretty mouth formed a disfiguring pout. She tiptoed away from her listening post on the other side of Andrew's door. When she reached her room, she fell on the bed and sobbed.

On New Year's Eve, Pinckney made one hopeless attempt to persuade his mother to stay home. "I have to leave tomorrow, Mama, and I'd really rather spend the time with the family."

"But, Pinny, it's Sally Brewton's party."

Pinckney shrugged. When he went to his room to change, he carried a decanter with him.

Sally Brewton never let her friends down. When they arrived at her cousins' house, where Sally was living, they were directed through the center hall to the back door. There they found a long path made up of overlapping Persian carpets. Liveried servants stood at intervals, holding blazing torches to light the way to the carriage house and stables. Sally stood inside the stable door with her cousins, an elderly couple who had the dazed expressions of survivors of a cataclysm.

The interior of the stable was warm and welcoming. Fires roared in the two enormous fireplaces that had been built into the end walls. The interior was freshly whitewashed. Two lines of posts marched down the center of the long building. They were covered with garlands of holly and ivy. The partitions that had formed the stalls were gone, and groups of brocaded chairs and sofas stood where the horses had slept. The iron hay racks along the walls were piled with masses of flaming red poinsettias. Red candles filled the tall silver candelabra on tables along the wall, and the rich red of oriental rugs covered the floor.

The adjoining carriage house had become a fairy ballroom. Six tall gold-framed mirrors hung on each wall. They reflected the shimmering lights of gilded candles in four crystal chandeliers that hung from the high peaked rafters. Between the mirrors, the walls were painted to look like climbing flowering vines. Along the rafters, fresh smilax continued the sinuous line and clusters of gardenias sent out a heady fragrance. The brick floor had been painted green and covered with layer after layer of wax. The room seemed to be paved with emeralds.

In one corner an orchestra played. The men were concealed by a flower-studded screen of pungent pine boughs so that the music seemed to come magically from the air. The other three corners held serving tables with mammoth bowls of ice studded with the gold-foil necks of champagne bottles. The waiters passing trays of champagne were clad in white knee breeches and green-satin tailcoats the color of the floor.

Sally's guests were overcome. She enjoyed the compliments but denied accusations of lavishness. "My dears, I had no choice. When I had to move uptown, I went through the attic of the King Street house and found all these things stored up there. I couldn't leave them. Suppose another cannonball broke all those mirrors? I'd have bad luck forever. And as for those miles of green satin, I don't know which one of Miles's grandmothers bought it, but I certainly would never use it. Too gaudy. I took just a tiny bit, for fun." And Sally lifted her pink silk skirts just enough to show the toes of her bright satin slippers.

The fantasy ballroom evoked a magic evening. Everyone danced. General Beauregard himself led Sally out to open the ball, and it seemed that he had brought every officer in his command with him. For the first time since the War began, there were enough men to partner every lady. Girls became dizzy from excitement as crowds of men begged to put their names on dance cards. When the first rush was over, it was the mothers and grandmothers who had their heads turned. Ladies of seventy found themselves being whirled to the latest waltz tune.

Pinckney watched from a corner within reach of the champagne. In the middle of the second waltz, he was joined by a distant cousin, Bill Ashley. Pinckney hardly knew him; Bill was eight years older and Pinckney had always been beneath his notice. He was pleased when Bill spoke. "Standing this one out?"

"Standing them all out. After the past week, I find it a welcome relief."

Bill grunted. "I can't say the same. I just got home today and I can't get a word with the girl I want to see. Who are all those uniforms, anyhow?"

Pinckney grinned. "Who knows? My charming, feather-brained mama, who is shrewder than she looks, has a theory. She figures that Sally Brewton told General Beau he couldn't come unless he brought every man in his Army. Hero or no, he didn't dare refuse her. Mrs. Beau wouldn't let him back in New Orleans if he missed a chance to go to one of Sally Brewton's parties."

Bill choked on his champagne. "She's probably right," he sputtered.

"When I was in Paris in fifty-nine, the first thing people asked me was if I knew Sally Brewton. When I said I did, every door was open to me."

"Same thing in London. A toast to our Sally." The men touched glasses, drained them and picked up replacements.

At ten-thirty the orchestra took a needed rest while the guests ate supper in the stables. Pinckney was looking for Mary and Julia when he felt a tug on his sleeve.

It was Lavinia. "Pinny, could I please sit with you and Cousin Mary? I don't mind dancing with all these strangers, but I wouldn't know what to say to them over supper, and there are about twenty of them arguing over who's going to eat with me."

Lavinia's upturned face looked very young. Her cheeks were flushed; a tendril of hair had escaped from the ringlets piled high on her head; it was clinging to a damp spot of perspiration on her white throat. Her upper lip was also beaded. Pinckney smiled. "Of course," he said, "but I have to tidy you up first." He mopped her face with his handkerchief then offered her his arm.

Even Julia had been dancing, although she was quick to say that none of the officers was anyone that anyone knew. Mary was as flushed as Lavinia and chattered with her as if she were the same age. Pinckney tuned them out and concentrated on obtaining a steady supply of refills for his glass. When the music began again, partners came to claim the ladies. They were strangers to Pinckney, officers in Beauregard's troop. Julia watched closely as Pinckney stood and bowed to the introductions. He was perfectly steady.

When everyone had gone into the ballroom, Pinckney stayed in the stables. A waiter put a bottle of champagne on the table near him. After twenty minutes, it was empty. Pinckney rested his elbow on the table next to the bottle. He felt very sleepy. "Too hot in here," he said aloud. He stood and walked easily to the ballroom. On the opposite side, he saw his mother in animated conversation with General Beauregard. He started edging around the dancers to join them.

While dancing, Lavinia had been watching the door. When she saw Pinckney, her smile became brighter and her dimple deepened, but he did not see her. Lavinia scowled, then remembered to smooth her forehead. She must look pretty. And she must get his attention. He would be leaving the next day, and then she'd never have a chance to make him notice her. She had managed to be with him every day that he was home, and he still looked on her only as Andrew's little sister. Couldn't he see that she was grown up? He had to see; she'd make him pay attention. Her cheeks colored and her eyes flashed with anger.

Pinckney walked nearer, about to pass by without a word. Lavinia turned her eyes up to her partner and smiled flirtatiously.

"I declare, Miss Anson, you're the prettiest girl I ever saw in my life," said the clumsy boy from Tennessee who was dancing with her. To his amazement, Lavinia pulled on his arm and swung him around, her body pressed to his.

"You mustn't say things like that," she said loudly, "and you mustn't hold me so close. Let me go." Her words ended in a small, choked sob.

The boy felt a hand grip his shoulder. "Back off, soldier," said a low voice behind him. "We don't treat ladies that way here." Lavinia pushed him away; he turned to face Pinckney.

"I didn't do nothing, mister. This little girl grabbed me all of a sudden . . ."

"Quiet. You needn't insult the lady further by making a scene. You can apologize and leave her with me." Pinckney forced a grim smile so that they would seem to be having a friendly conversation.

The boy stiffened. He had all the hair-trigger sensitivity of the frontier. "I've got nothing to apologize for," he barked, "and no high-and-mighty dandy is going to tell me different."

Pinckney's eyes darkened. "You have offended my cousin, and now you have offended me. Will you meet me, sir?"

"Name the time and place."

"I'll have a friend notify you within the hour."

Lavinia had been watching. Her breath was coming in fast puppyish pants. Pinckney took her arm and led her toward Mary.

"Good evening, sir," he said to the General. "I hope you'll forgive me for intruding. My cousin is feeling a little faint from the closeness in here, and I thought my mother would know how to help her."

Lavinia drooped against Pinckney's arm. "My poor child," Mary crooned. "here, take my fan. I've got some salts in my bag. Pinny, find a seat for Lavinia."

General Beauregard lifted his hand infinitesimally. An aide appeared at once and was sent for a chair. In less than a minute, Lavinia was the center of a concerned group. Pinckney slipped away to find Bill Ashley.

"I need someone to serve as my second," he told him. "If you don't want to do it, I won't be offended."

"Don't be an ass. Of course I'll do it. Who's your man? If it's one of these foreigners, I'll be honored."

While Bill was making arrangements with a friend of the Tennessean, Pinckney took Lavinia and Julia home. The ride was silent. Julia communicated disapproval by her tight lips. Lavinia was so awed by the results of her impetuous scheme to get Pinckney's attention that she was incapable of speech. Pinckney was distracted by the dull ache which had taken possession of his head.

When he returned to the ball for his mother, his sanguine belief that the incident had gone unnoticed was shattered. Every eye looked in his direction, then turned quickly away, pretending civilized indifference. When he paid his respects to Sally Brewton before leaving, she broke all protocol by whispering "Good luck" near his bowed head.

Mary began to talk the moment the carriage pulled away. "Please, Mama," Pinckney begged, "I have a crashing headache."

"Then you'd better try to get some sleep," Mary said. "Although I don't suppose it makes any difference. A country boy like that probably doesn't know any more about pistols than he does about shoes.

"Pinny, you must tell me everything that happened. It's all so exciting. And so romantic. I had no idea that you were really courting Lavinia. Will you be able to extend your furlough or will you come back for the wedding? We'll have to go through my jewel box the minute we get home so you can pick out a ring for her. I think maybe a sapphire, don't you? So pretty with that pale hair. Too bad her eyes are so wash-water looking. The sapphire might just make them look paler. Mind you, I'm not criticizing when I notice her eyes. Lavinia is a darling girl, and she's already almost like one of the family."

Pinckney felt sick. He had been thinking of Lavinia as he would have thought of Lizzie. Mary's monologue made him realize his position. Lavinia was not his sister, and she was not a child. Only a brother or a father or a husband had the right to fight for a lady. In challenging the Tennessean, he had announced that he was Lavinia's protector and had assumed the role of a husband. He was bound by the code of honor to marry her.

If he wasn't killed. Pinckney knew, even if his mother did not, the reputation of the sharpshooting Tennessee mountain men.

5

The duel began in monotone. In the gray false light of predawn, there was no color. The wide, slow-moving river was a metallic blur, barely seen through thin floating shreds of gray morning mist. A few wisps crept from the river up onto the bank, where they hid the feet and ankles of the men standing there, blending with the gray of their uniformed legs. Over their heads, gray beards of Spanish moss hung motionless from wide branches of live oaks, heavy with moisture from the raw, cold morning air. The two seconds stood close together, talking quietly. Nothing was moving. The scene might have been an engraving.

Pinckney was thinking about death. It would not be a bad way to die, a clean shot through the heart or head, and his body falling onto the soft grass. He compared it with the death he had seen on the battlefields, the twisted piles of men and horses, their blood pulsing into the thick red clay of Virginia, their screams robbing them of the dignity that should accompany a man to whatever lay beyond the grave. There had been so many—his father, friends from his youth, new friends he had made in that fresh spring when all the South's best and bravest had ridden forth under their banners, confident of victory.

There would be, Pinckney knew now, no victory. They would continue fighting and bleeding and dying until there was no one left, and then the War would be over. The world as he knew it was already over, in spite of the oasis of Julia's well-run household.

Revulsion gripped him, twisting his heart and lungs and bowels. He felt icy sweat at his temples and at the nape of his neck. He had accepted the fact that he would probably die, but suddenly he could not bear the thought of the slimy mud of Virginia in his mouth and nostrils. His entire soul cried out for the rich black lowcountry soil of his homeland. It was dark, as a grave should be, and smelled sweetly of a gentle decay that would be restful and welcoming.

A stir of movement caught his attention. Bill Ashley was wading through the mist toward him, offering the open case with its remaining pistol. Behind Bill's head, the first streaks of apricot on the horizon announced the coming day. While Pinckney watched Bill's progress, the mist on the river warmed to a soft peach tint. Light's magic touched the black mass of shrubbery at Pinckney's elbow, transforming it into the thick dark green of a camellia bush studded with less dense shadows that would glow like jewels when the sun rose and defined their rich red petals and golden stamens.

Pinckney shrugged off his morbid mood, ashamed of the weakness that had gripped him. Hell, he was twenty years old. Death would have to run a fast race to catch him. He examined the load and wadding of the pistol with an expert eye. This was not his first duel. He and his friends had been settling arguments on the "field of honor" ever since they were seventeen, but his friends had been taught the same rules he had; the solemn ceremony always ended with a gentlemanly discharge of pistols in the air. He couldn't expect the same masquerade from this stranger. This was the real thing, a meeting of men, not boys. A surge of dangerous excitement made his heart race. When he took his designated place, he was grinning with youthful exuberance.

His obvious delight so unnerved the boy opposite that his shot went wild and took off the hat of his second. Pinckney's grazed the boy's shoulder, which was exactly what he had aimed for. He laughed joyously and pulled the silver brandy flask from his pocket for them all to share.

The camaraderie was so pleasurable that Pinckney almost missed his train. He had barely time to stop at Julia's for his luggage and good-byes and at the Ansons' to ask Andrew officially for his sister's hand in marriage. Lavinia was still trying to decide which of her dresses was the most becoming when she heard the front door slam behind Pinckney. She ran to the window and raised it.

"Pinny!" He turned and blew a kiss. Then he was gone. Lavinia stood, gaping, until the chilly air reminded her that she was wearing nothing but her shimmy. She ran to the bed and burrowed under the covers; then she cried for her departed hero.

Before dinner time, the story of the engagement and the duel was all over town. In all of the houses with unmarried daughters, there were sounds of sympathetic urgings to eat more of the traditional New Year's mixture of black-eyed peas and rice, called, no one knew why, "Hoppin' John." It was said that the amount of Hoppin' John consumed on New Year's would govern the amount of good luck in the year ahead. Some people believed the legend and claimed personal experience of its truth; everyone was superstitious enough to fear defying it. At the Ansons', Lucy teased Lavinia about the number of platefuls she must have had the year before.

Lavinia was radiant. She had pushed her chair away from the table so that she could look at her left hand, which was properly resting on the napkin in her lap. Her skin seemed as white as the linen, a dramatic contrast to the deep blue of the oval sapphire in the ring Mary Tradd had brought over. Engaged! And to Pinckney Tradd, the most eligible man in Charleston, which meant in South Carolina, in the world, probably. Lavinia could barely wait for the afternoon when people would call. They would be so jealous.

Next door, the atmosphere was less festive. Mary prattled happily about the party she was planning to give for Lavinia, but she spoke into a heavy silence. Julia's face was set in disapproval; she refused to enter into Mary's delight about the romantic drama. Stuart and Lizzie were, of course, not allowed to speak unless spoken to, and they wanted nothing more than to be ignored. When Julia announced that they were excused, they walked sedately to the door. Then Stuart ran outside to join his friends in the New Year's pastime of shooting off firecrackers. Lizzie climbed the long flights to the playroom to tell her dolls that Pinny was marrying a princess and that he had fought a dragon to win her hand.

"My dearest husband-to-be," read the letter Lavinia wrote that night, "my heart is full of an inexpressible joy because of the honor you have done me in asking me to be your wife. It beats within my breast like a frightened but exultant small bird, frightened by the awesome richness of its cage, which is your love, and exultant because of the emotion that makes it sing. When we are together again, it will, I fear come near to death with happiness too great to be contained, but I am confident that your strong arms will encompass my weak form and restrain the too rapid beating of the lark heart which wants only to sing to you a heavenly melody of bliss, of shared love and shared lives . . ."

Her graceful handwriting, with its elegant loops, covered four pages before she was done. She had copied it from her favorite novel, a story of romance and danger in the days of Bonnie Prince Charlie. The shelves above her escritoire were full of similar books, and she was able to write a new, throbbing love letter to Pinckney every night. He received them in batches of a dozen or more when the mail courier caught up with the hard-pressed men of Hampton's cavalry as they moved across the rolling Virginia countryside.

As in every war, letters from home were precious to the men at the front. Lavinia's extravagant pages and sentiments were a richness to Pinckney. As the months passed, his thoughts mingled memories of her soft, scented hair with his longing for home and the long, golden hours of the life he had known. She became the embodiment of all that was lost, and he yearned for her.

When spring came, he found a dogwood tree that had miraculously survived the artillery battle near Fredericksburg, and he pressed a blossom between the cherished pages which he carried in his saddle bags. In the back cover of his watch, he had a miniature of her, sent by Mary, which he often looked at, trying to remember the girl it portrayed. Even to himself, he never admitted that the single letter he received from Julia Ashley was more important to him, although he read it again and again. It reached him at the end of June.

> 11 May, 1864. Charleston. Have returned to city after usual season at plantation. Crops well up on Barony and Carlington. All buildings in prime condition. Excellent hay from pea vines. 14 births 3 deaths among Carl. people. Promising colt from your old chestnut mare. Sire unknown. All good horses with Hampton. Slaughtered, salted, sent ⅔ cattle, swine, sheep to Army. Remaining stock sound. Carl. overseer fool and thief. Hired wounded veteran from hill country to replace. Expect rash of light brown babies next winter. Woods sickly from deer eating bark. Am encouraging poaching by servants. Enough venison for us all. Good sport when you return. Huge boar seen near cypress swamp on Barony. Family well. Provisions plentiful. Siege heavier but Charlotte St. untouched. God keep you. Julia Ashley.

Pinckney ate his scanty evening meal as he reread Julia's letter by the light of the campfire. The leatherlike salt beef which was his only ration that day tasted almost good to him when he thought it might be from Carlington. Although his teeth hurt and his gums were bleeding from prolonged malnutrition, he smiled as he chewed.

"Is that tabakky you got there, Cap'n?"

Pinckney started, then turned in a rage. All fighting men knew better than to sneak up behind each other. It was an unwritten law to approach from the front or to make plenty of noise.

His anger faded somewhat when he saw the owner of the voice. He was just a boy, and a pitiful specimen of boy, one of the new recruits who had been waiting for the troop when they returned to camp. "What's your name soldier?"

"Joe Simmons, sir." The boy threw his bony shoulders back and saluted. Pinckney let him stand uncomfortably at attention while he studied him. Tow hair, dead-white skin, protruding ribs, elbows, collar bones, thin bowed legs. He was short and would have been stocky if he had ever had good food, but his coloring, deformed legs and pasty skin all spoke of pellagra and rickets, and the classic poor-white diet of fatback and corn mush. Also an indication of the boy's back-country origin was the murderous, proud anger that was growing in him, showing in his pale, amber-brown eyes.

"At ease, Joe Simmons. Squat down here and let me teach you something."

The boy slouched but remained standing. "Can't see no use in cozying up to no fire in the summer time."

"As you please. But if you don't want your head shot off, better listen to what I tell you. Don't ever Indian walk up behind a man with a pistol and ask him what he's chewing. I nearly killed you."

Joe grinned. "I shoulda thought of that." He dropped easily to the ground near Pinckney. "Me and my paw was waiting for a buck once, and my brother come up on us real quiet. Paw let go both barrels. Only reason Sam wasn't killed was Paw's a positive thinker. He aimed for a big buck, and Sam was a real small fellow."

Pinckney recognized the accent. "You from around Fort Mill, Joe?"

"Yep. Calhoun country."

"Good old John C. We can thank him we're here right now. I suppose you couldn't wait to get in the War. You don't look very old to me."

Joe spit into the coals. "I'm old enough to kill a man and old enough to burn in Hell. So I run off to kill me a Yankee, otherwise I would most likely have killed my paw. There's a commandment about that, but the Bible don't mind you killing Yankees."

"Why isn't your paw fighting?"

Joe laughed. "Hell, Cap'n, what's this War to folks like us? We never had no niggers, just us kids to hoe our patch of cotton and Paw's strap to see we done it right. I'm the biggest, so I got beat the most. My paw'll fight fast enough if anybody takes to come on his land, and he don't care what color suit he's wearing, but he says he can't see getting killed so's those high-toned gentry in Charleston can keep their field hands.

"All this talking's making my mouth awful dry, Cap'n. How about a share of that chaw you got?"

Pinckney offered the remaining beef jerky. Joe put a corner in his mouth, then pulled it out.

"That ain't tabakky."

"I never said it was."

"Then how come you're over here by yourself roasting your bones? I figured you was guarding something good."

"I needed the light from the fire to read by."

Joe stared at Pinckney as if he had said he could walk on water. Then his eyelids dropped, and he squinted suspiciously. "Lemme see you read."

Pinckney obligingly read several sentences.

Joe stared. "Who are you?" he demanded.

"I'm one of those 'Charleston gentry' your paw won't fight for."

Joe stood and walked slowly in a circle around Pinckney and the fire, studying his ragged clothing and the calm smile on his neatly shaven face. "My paw's wrong again," he said at last. "Ain't the first time, neither. I'll fight for you Cap'n."

From that moment, the boy never left Pinckney's side. He stayed always at his right, and a little behind. The other men made fun of him at first, calling him "Shadow," but Joe ignored them. After a few months, the odd twosome became commonplace. Joe's nickname was shortened to "Shad"; after a time, he was the only person who remembered that he had ever been called anything else.

The Christmas of sixty-four in Charleston bore a surface resemblance to the Christmases before the War. The hospitable houses were crammed to overflowing with guests; meals had to be served in two or more sittings, because the dining room tables, even with all their leaves inserted, could not accommodate more than thirty at a time. Food, brought by river from the plantations, was still plentiful, and course followed course with little apparent scantiness. The sharp sweetness of evergreen garlands filled the air, mantels were piled high with pine boughs, long vines of smilax were twined around stair banisters, and huge silver bowls of camellia blossoms rested on every table. In spite of incessant rain, ladies and their children still went from house to house paying calls and greeting cousins, and cousins of cousins, whom they had not seen for years. But the animated conversation had a shrillness of fear, not celebration. The visitors were refugees from the relentless march of Sherman's Army and its torches. After taking Atlanta, Sherman and his men had begun, in mid-November, to move southeast through Georgia. They burned and looted as they went, leaving behind them a scorched trail sixty miles wide and an ever-increasing terror. Everyone knew that when he reached the coast, Sherman would turn north and blaze his way through the Carolinas to join Grant's Army in Virginia.

Charleston's visitors hovered for a few days, taking comfort from the pretense of normality, then moved on to other havens, leaving a residue of panic. The Confederate troops in Charleston attempted to reassure them, but they could not lie, and they knew that they, too, would be retreating before the Union advance sometime soon. They advised the city's residents to accompany their relatives when they left.

Julia Ashley found her sister in tears, surrounded by colorful piles of ballgowns on the floor of her bedroom. "Oh, Julia, I don't know what to do," Mary wailed. "If I don't take these dresses, I won't have anything to wear when I get out of mourning, but there are too many for me to pack. I've got space on the train, but they won't let me take more than two trunks."

Julia groaned. "You are God's own idiot, Mary. Where do you think you're going?"

"Columbia, of course. Everybody's going to Columbia. They've already taken up Mr. Calhoun's coffin, and they're sending it to Columbia. Saint Michael's bells, too."

"And you think Sherman will be afraid of John C. Calhoun's ghost?"

"Well, I am. It's going to be on the same train with us." Mary looked fearfully at her sister. "I hope you don't mind, Julia. I left room for your things in a corner of the children's trunk. I really need all of this one for myself. And you never cared much about clothes and all."

Julia shook her head. "It doesn't matter. I'm not such a fool as to go to Columbia. Sherman will head right for it on his way North. I'm going to the Barony. I won't allow those ruffians to burn my house or terrorize my people."

"Julia! You must be crazy. You can't do it."

"Don't say 'can't' to me, Mary Ashley. I'm going. And you'd be smart to come with me if you won't stay here. Every ninny in Charleston is going to be crowding into Columbia like sitting ducks."

"You think you know everything. I've already sent a telegram to Cousin Eulalie Pinckney telling her we're coming. She has plenty of room; it won't be crowded at all."

Julia sighed. "Nobody ever could talk sense to you, Mary. No point trying to start now. If your so-called mind is made up, at least take some food with you. You can't eat corset covers." Secretly, she was relieved that Mary was leaving. She did not know what would face her at the plantation, and Mary's hysteria would have been just one more thing to cope with.

Mary Tradd, Stuart, Lizzie, Lizzie's "dah," Georgina, Mary's personal maid, Sophy, and three trunks were loaded onto the derelict train that left the next day. As soon as they were gone, Julia began the task of sorting out the few valuables she would take with her in the boat to the Barony. The Charlotte Street house, she knew, would probably be destroyed. She had heard, if Mary had not, about Sherman's telegram to Lincoln delivering Savannah for a Christmas present and about the promise to sow the streets of Charleston with salt like a modern day Carthage. She had, of course, a full complement of servants who stayed permanently at the plantation, but she promised to send the boat back for all the city servants, both hers and Mary's, who wanted to leave. When it arrived at the plantation, she was not surprised to find so few. Freedom fever was infectious in Charleston, and many blacks were waiting for Sherman's men as if they were a band of angels. She settled down in the country at the end of January to wait and to make plans. No one looking at her proud, impassive face would have known that she was not still confident that being an Ashley would overcome all opposition.

6

Had Julia Ashley been able to see what was happening in Charleston, she would have thanked God that she was not there. On February 18 the Union Army entered the city from the south after the Confederate Army evacuated to the north. Sherman's main force bypassed it, striking directly up through the center of the state toward Columbia. But he had promised vengeance to the arrogant Charleston that had started the War, and he delivered it. He sent Kilpatrick's raiders and bummers to burn all the outlying plantations and played on the deep-seated racial terrors of the white population by spearheading the occupation troops with a shining display of immaculately uniformed black troops. The famous all-Negro 54th Massachusetts marched smartly through Meeting Street carrying a silk banner that read "Liberty" and singing "John Brown's Body." When they reached the lower city, their voices were almost inaudible because of the noise of their booted feet on the masses of broken window glass that covered the streets. But their faces were smiling with the joy of liberation, and they were surrounded by mobs of dancing, laughing men and women who had been slaves that morning.

After the march, their officers, all white, ordered the soldiers to carry out their next assignment. Into each and every building they went, houses, offices, warehouses, stores. Any Negroes they found were told the good news of liberation and embraced. All firearms were confiscated and any "abandoned" property was seized. Lucy Anson watched fearfully from Andrew's window as a troop of soldiers entered Julia's house next door. None of the Ansons had evacuated. Andrew could not be moved, and his mother forbade anyone's leaving him. Lavinia had hidden herself in the attic behind an old storage wardrobe; she crouched there, muffling the whimpers she could not control by stuffing her mouth full of an old silk shirtwaist. Andrew had been drugged with laudanum in a glass of brandy so that he would not risk all their lives by trying to defend his home and family. Mrs. Anson and Lucy supported each other wordlessly, standing erect in Andrew's room between the door and the bed where he slept.

The noise outside drew Lucy to the window. She stared at the procession of soldiers carrying silver, mirrors and casks of wine from Julia's house. Then they were halted by the arrival of a stout, epauletted officer on a huge bay gelding. She could not hear what he said, but the antlike activity reversed itself, and the blue-coated men began to return everything they had removed. "Miss Emma," she whispered, "they're not stealing. There's a white General, and he's making them stop. Oh, maybe he'll make them leave us alone. Miss Emma, I'm going down to speak to him."

"You cannot speak to a Yankee soldier, General or not," snapped her mother-in-law.

"But it might save us. They'll be coming here next, and if these soldiers see Andrew, and the General isn't there to stop them, who knows what they might do?"

Mrs. Anson moved ponderously across the room to the window. She would not bend her head, but looked down her prominent nose at the scene below. Suddenly she laughed, a sound she had not made since Andrew's injury. "Praise the Lord, that's Dan Sickles. I used to see him every summer at Saratoga. Why, we practically grew up together. He took it very hard when I got engaged to Andrew's father. Everything's going to be all right." Tears of relief rolled down her face, and she almost ran from the room.

Lucy watched, unconsciously holding her breath, as Emma Anson stalked down her front walk and approached the commanding figure on the big horse. She gasped with premature joy when the General saw Mrs. Anson, dismounted and bowed. Mrs. Anson's manner was an embarrassing parody of her daughter's most flirtatious bellishness. She actually furled and unfurled a lace fan and peeped at the General over it while she spoke. His response caused an immediate change; Mrs. Anson dropped the fan and stuck her head forward like an old turtle. Her lips moved rapidly. The General spread his hands, seemingly beseeching her for something. Then, as she continued talking and began to shake her fist, he drew himself away from her and assumed a stiff military stance. Now it was Sickles who was talking. Emma Anson grabbed at his sleeve, but he eluded her and turned his back. It was like a wall. He called out to a curious officer standing by the gate to the Ashley house, mounted his horse and rode away without looking back.

Mrs. Anson stood like a statue. Then she noticed the officer looking at her. She threw her head back in the haughty angle that was characteristic of her and walked slowly to her own house. Lucy ran to meet her, frightened more by the scene she had witnessed than by the prospect of what the invaders might do. She had always been intimidated by Andrew's mother. Now she felt sorry for her, and it was a terrifying emotion.

"Were you watching, Lucy?"

"Yes, ma'am." Lucy looked at the floor.

"Thank God Andrew didn't see his mother humiliate herself and him. It is the last time I will ever ask any Yankee for anything. Nor will any member of my household."

Lucy longed to give Mrs. Anson the privacy she knew the older woman needed, but her own need was greater. She had to know what was going to happen to Andrew and her baby. "I'm sorry, Miss Emma, but what did he say?"

Mrs. Anson snapped out of her trancelike stare. "Say? He said that he would tell his mother that he had seen me and that I was looking well. Then he said that he was taking Julia Ashley's house for his headquarters. Then he said that the Army would confiscate my house for another officer. Then, when I told him Andrew could not be disturbed, he said that he had lost a brother and his father in the War. Then he laughed an awful laugh and quoted his commander. 'War is Hell,' he said. And he said that he would order a group of white soldiers to help me pack our clothing and to move Andrew. We have to leave everything else in the house for some damyankee to use."

"What are we going to do?"

"What we have to. We'll send the servants downtown to clean up your little house on Meeting Street, and we'll take Andrew there." She began to mount the stairs. "That is, if we have any servants. If not, you and Lavinia and I will do it. I'm going to my room for a few minutes now, Lucy. I want to go over every disgraceful moment of what has happened. I want to be sure I remember it all. Then, when the War is over, I will exact retribution for every single second."

Lucy's cry stopped her climb. "What do you mean, 'When the War is over?' Charleston has fallen. We are done in."

Emma Anson turned to look down. "Nonsense. In the Revolution, Charleston was occupied for over two years before we won. History always repeats itself. Except that the British were gentlemen. I'll certainly never go to Saratoga again. I don't care to associate with parvenu rabble." Majestically, she moved upstairs. Lucy crumpled onto the bottom step and cried into her crooked elbow.

A sharp "hsst" brought her head up. It was Jeremiah. "What's happening, Miss Lucy? Is the Yankees going to take Mist' Andrew away?"

"Oh, Jeremiah, I'm so glad to see you. I thought you were gone."

The tall black man walked out from the shadows of the hallway. "I just went to see the parade, ma'am. Most of the others are cavorting around in the White Point Gardens. They's fireworks and all. But I couldn't leave Mist' Andrew for too long. I raised that boy from a puppy, you know that. I can't leave him now when the blue soldiers is after him."

Lucy dried her face on her hem. "Thank you, Jeremiah," she said, "you're a real friend. Mr. Andrew is going to need you more than ever now. We all are. We're going home to Meeting Street as soon as we can. The Yankees are going to be living on Charlotte Street, and we don't want to be in the same neighborhood. If you'll get some trunks down from the attic, we'll start to pack Mr. Andrew's things." She crossed the hall and took down a painting of Andrew as a young boy that hung over a small console table. "I'll pack this first. They'll have no part of Mr. Andrew. Not even a likeness."

Within a half hour, Andrew, still unconscious, was carried down to Emma Anson's carriage in Jeremiah's cradling arms. Lucy and Lavinia held him steady while Jeremiah drove them slowly down Meeting Street past the shell-scarred brick homes and burnt-out skeletons of once-grand frame houses. Emma Anson remained alone to supervise the loading of their trunks in the wagon which General Sickles provided. She stood, immobile, in the warmth of the drawing room and waited for the wagon to take her and her allowed possessions to her son's house. She was in a state of shock, so stunned by events that she could not will her eyes to close. They stared at the laughing, shouting black soldiers who gathered all the small decorative objects from the tables into their caps. When the T'ang porcelain vases fell from the mantel and shattered, she did not react at all.

Twelve miles away, up the wide, winding track of the Ashley River, Julia was looking out of an attic window with a telescope. There was no sign of movement on the river nor on the corduroy road at the end of the long carriage drive from the house on the other side. She ground her teeth. Sherman was on the move. It was just a matter of time before his arsonists reached the Barony. But how much time? There was no way to tell. Waiting was hard for her.

She closed the telescope with a snap and left the window. She had already walked around the house that morning, but she decided to allow herself to do it again. She had a definite sense of farewells. Even if her plan worked, she would not have many more opportunities to go through the beautiful, orderly rooms and gardens. Tranquillity, she knew, would soon be a stranger to Ashley Barony.

The servants had been well-trained. As they heard Julia's firm step approach, they melted away out of sight, available if called, but not in her way. She moved slowly, touching a delicate bisque figurine from time to time, adjusting errant blossoms in the vases of hot-house lilies that filled every room, stopping before the portraits of her mother and father, her grandparents, great-grandparents, herself and Mary as children seated at their beautiful mother's feet, and—her favorite—the rakish younger son who had founded the Barony with a grant from King Charles in 1675. Julia had an especial fondness for him. He looked slightly wild in his elaborate wig and satin knee breeches. There was a definite glint to his eye. No wonder nothing had been able to stop him from carving an Empire out of the Carolina wilderness. Her chin lifted. Nothing would stop her from keeping it. She walked briskly through the great wide hall that ran from front to back of the house, across the deep columned veranda, and down the wide white steps. She did not even look back at the majestic mansion.

She marched past the brick kitchens and smokehouse, past the stables and barns, and down the middle of the road between the rows of slave cabins. In the small pine wood at the end of the row, she opened the wrought-iron gate to the family graveyard. She hurried past the marble catafalque, then through the gate on the far side, and slowed only when she reached the tiny crumbling cottage made of the ground oyster-shell material called tabby that the first settlers had used for fire-resistant building. The mansion reflected the grandeur of the eighteenth-century Ashleys, but at this moment she wanted the determination that had carried that first Carolina Ashley through hardship to arrive at that grandeur.

She pressed her cheek to the rough wall of the cottage. It was durable and strong. She would be, too. She turned and retraced her steps until she reached a gate into the gardens. There, she walked methodically up and down the paths, noting that the azaleas were almost ready to bloom and that the gardeners had not yet clipped the topiary boxwood, although she had instructed them about it the day before.

She took a small pad of paper from her pocket and made a note. The fountains needed scrubbing, too. Another note. Before she finished her tour, three pages were covered with her small, meticulous printing. As long as she could manage it, life at the Barony would continue as normal.

As long as she could manage it. She knew that it would not be more than days. Or hours. In the meantime, she had to keep herself busy or she might break down. And that was unthinkable. Her people were depending on her strength. They had to be reassured. Even the ones who were not depending on her, those who were eager to meet the Yankees—they had to be restrained from infecting the others, restrained by the force of her personality. A white woman alone with hundreds of black slaves could exhibit no fear or weakness. Julia walked deliberately up the steps and into the house. There was work to be done.

She was checking the linens with the maid Pansy when she heard the cries from the yard. Her face remained calm; she had been preparing herself for this moment, and she was ready. Thank heaven the waiting was almost over. She stared at Pansy and stopped the woman's trembling by the force of her will. "Those sheets will see us through two more years," she said, "and then we can open some of the attic trunks." She closed and locked the door to the big armoire. "You may go, Pansy. Tell Jefferson I'm on my way down." Pansy lifted her skirts and ran for the stairs.

The yard looked like a revival meeting when Julia got there. In the center, his eyes staring, stood Jonah, the head teamster of the Middletons, who owned the plantation next to the Barony. He was shouting lamentations, moaning and crying. "Burning," he howled, "and killing all the beasts, and firing the crops and the house. Toby, he sass one, and the soldier, he split Toby head with he sword, same like a muskmelon. They's blue devils, laughing in hellfire."

All around him, Julia's slaves were on their knees, rocking back and forth, their arms raised up to the pale winter sky. "Burning," they echoed, "Burning." Their shrill wails ended in piercing shrieks.

Julia looked downriver toward Middleton Place. Clouds of black smoke were beginning to stain the thin blue air. There wasn't much time. She struck the iron triangle that hung near the back door. In the sudden silence that surrounded its fading vibrations, she spoke sharply and clearly. "The Yankees will not burn the Barony. I won't allow it. And they won't hurt you or leave you hungry. Jessie, you gather all the children and take them in the dining room. They can sit on the floor under the table. Give them some candy and tell them to be quiet as possums . . . Griffin . . . Dinah . . . Snippy . . . Ezekiel . . . Solomon . . . Jupiter . . ."

Julia called the best trained and bravest of the servants from the crowd and issued orders to carry out the strategy she had devised to fight the Yankees. Small animals and poultry were taken into the house and given an unexpected meal, doctored with whiskey to make them sleep. Large animals and equipment were driven into hiding in the woods and swamps. The smokehouse and ice house were already emptied of their food, with hams and cheeses stacked in the corners of the ballroom.

Julia's lieutenants selected their helpers and hurried away to carry out the commands. Their terror had been replaced by excitement. If Miss Julia said she wouldn't let the Yankees hurt them, then there was nothing to fear, and the disruption of routine was thrilling. Few of them wondered how Julia proposed to stand off an Army by herself. They were so in awe of her that they believed her capable of anything.

When the yard emptied, Julia turned to the injured boy from Middleton Place. "Go in the kitchen and tell Willie to fetch my medicine box. I'll be there in a minute to dress those burns and scratches. What's your name?"

"Jonah, ma'am."

"Don't you worry, Jonah. You'll be all right. Now scoot. And tell Dinah to get four jars of strawberry preserves out of the store house. Can you remember that?"

"Yes'm."

"Then get going."

Julia stood for a moment, surveying the empty orderliness of the kitchenyard, preparing herself for the ordeal ahead. Then she lifted her bony chin higher and stalked into her house.

The kitchen was a bedlam. All the house servants were there, shouting at each other. Julia grabbed a long tin spoon and beat it on a copper cauldron. "Stop it," she commanded. There was instant silence. "Dinah," she said, "give me those preserves and a spoon. And I want one of your old aprons. One with plenty of stains on it."

"Miss Julia, you gone crazy? You must disremember. Strawberry give you the rash."

"I remember very well. Give them to me; find that apron."

Later, Julia leaned against the wall near the front door, looking through the tiny panes of the glass panels at its side. She felt as if she had been there forever. Where were the damn Yankees?

She was a shockingly ugly sight. Her angular body was covered with a faded old calico dress, property of Pansy. The skirt and bodice was blotched with grease spots, spooned earlier from a pan of frying chicken. They smelled stale and rank. Dinah's stained apron had been twisted into wrinkles, then rubbed with ashes. It covered most of the calico dress. Julia's hair was a rat's nest. She had taken it from its smooth bun and tangled it, then dotted it with grease and soot. Every visible inch of her was dirty, except for her face and hands.

The hands were tied behind her back. Like her face, and all of her body, they were covered with throbbing red eruptions, product of her severe allergy to strawberries. The itching was driving her insane. She had ordered her hands tied so that she could not claw at herself.

The early twilight of winter was falling, made earlier by the pall of smoke that had rolled upriver from the burning buildings of Middleton Place. Soon she would be able to see nothing, and all her preparations would be wasted.

"Pansy," she said, "light that kerosene lamp and put it under the wastebasket for a screen." The effort of speaking made her gag. The hall smelled like an open grave. Three haunches of spoiled venison hung from the chandelier. The nauseating sweet odor of putrefying flesh was accented by the sharp aroma of turpentine, which was sprinkled on the rugs and curtains.

The scratching sound of the match striking almost made Julia jump. Control, she said fiercely inside her head. Then she heard another scratching sound, fainter. She leaned closer to the window. Yes, it was horses on the gravel of the long drive. Her heart was racing. Now that the moment had arrived, Julia felt no itching, no fear. She was a gambler, staking everything on one card; her body was flooded with adrenalin and a high, singing excitement.

"Pansy," she whispered, "they're coming. Untie me."

The band of cavalry drew up on the wide graveled carriage drive before the house. They were led by Kilpatrick himself, the infamous officer known as Sherman's most brutal junior commander. "Looks deserted," he said. "The hands must have run off."

"They'll come out of the woods when we start cooking," laughed his aide. He hawked and spit on the white marble steps.

"They always do. Go back to the column and tell them to move up. We'll camp here tonight and burn it in the morning."

The aide turned his tired mare. Before he could sink his spurs in, the great door to the house flew open, and a haggard scarecrow of a woman staggered out holding a lamp ahead of her.

"Thank God," Julia croaked. "Do you have a doctor in your Army? I've got sixty darkies in here with smallpox, and I can't nurse them anymore." She raised the lantern, swinging it. The flickering light poured over her swollen, blotched face and hands, then left them in darkness, then swung back to illuminate them again. Behind her, invisible in the shadows of the hall, Pansy waved two wide palmetto fans, pushing the rotten air toward the door.

Kilpatrick and his men jerked on their reins, backing their horses. "We can't help," one shouted. "Keep away from us."

Julia lurched forward, one puffy hand reaching for the reins of Kilpatrick's horse. "But you must help," she groaned. "Four of them are dead, and we're all too weak to bury them. Help me." She was surrounded by a rancid odor.

It hit Kilpatrick like a blow. "Jesus God," he bellowed, "let's get out of here." The horsemen galloped away to join the other soldiers. Behind them, they could hear Julia's cries. "Help, help me." Then there was only the noise of drumming hoofbeats.

When that, too, faded, Julia Ashley's laughter rang out. She sat on the steps, weak from reaction, and laughed until the tears rolled down her swollen cheeks. "Pansy," she called, "get me some camomile. I itch like fire."

BOOK TWO

1865

7

Shad Simmons rowed the leaking boat down the Cooper River, cursing the tide that had begun to run against him in the past half hour. He turned from time to time to look anxiously at Pinckney's slumped figure in the bow. He hoped Pinny was only sleeping; their trip from Virginia had pushed them both far past the limits of exhaustion.

But now they were at the end. On Shad's right, the remains of the piers and warehouses of Charleston jutted into the river. The acrid odor of their charred wood blended grotesquely with the heavy sweet fragrance of jasmine and wisteria from the overgrown gardens of the city beyond them.

Suddenly the twilight sky flashed a brilliant red. It was exactly like the flash of an exploding mortar shell. Shad threw himself into the filthy water in the bottom of the boat. The rocking motion he caused woke Pinckney; he raised his head.

"What the hell?" he muttered.

Shad sat up. "It can't be shelling. The Goddamn War's over." They had gotten the news of Lee's surrender from Union soldiers who surprised them sleeping in an abandoned railroad car.

While they looked apprehensively at the sky, it lit up again, this time in a pattern of greens and yellows. They were fireworks.

"I don't believe it," said Pinckney. He began to laugh. "Do you suppose it's a welcome-home celebration?"

His laughter was rusty, but genuine. There had been long days when he had doubted that he would ever get home; now, the inexplicable skyrockets illuminated Saint Michael's white spire in carnival colors. He was in Charleston. He sniffed the sweetly rancid odor of the blue-black mud flats exposed by low tide. Pluff mud. An abomination to visitors, but a sulphurous perfume of belonging to those who had known it since birth. A wave of happiness warmed his weary heart.

"Pull over right there, Shad," he said, gesturing. "There are some steps if we can find them. When we climb up over that rubbish, we'll be at the foot of Tradd Street."

They had only three blocks to walk from the river to Pinckney's home, but it took them a long time. Shad was slowed by the rapid-fire succession of impressions he had to digest; he had never seen a city before. The tall houses on both sides of narrow Tradd Street loomed close above them; to Shad it felt like being in a mountain pass, closed in, vulnerable. He looked up repeatedly, unconsciously watching for snipers on the cliffs. Above the uneven, jagged line of the roofs, the heavens lit and darkened erratically from the unseen sky rockets. The noise of their explosions was muffled but audible. Shad's jaws moved rapidly and he shifted the wad of tobacco from cheek to cheek in nervous agitation.

Pinckney, too, was looking around him. The near-dark was cosmetic. He could see little of the damage inflicted by the siege. To him, the familiar houses in their age-old places were immensely comforting. His step was unsteady on the brick sidewalk; he bumped into the walls of the houses on his left from time to time. He had not yet learned the new sense of balance he would need for the rest of his life. His right sleeve was half empty, flapping from the elbow down, unable to give counterweight to his body.

When they emerged onto Meeting Street, Shad was able to relax somewhat. It was wide, with, directly in front of them, a double-domed church set in the ample open space of its gardens and graveyard. Both men walked faster; "We're home, Shad!"

The Tradd house was tightly shuttered, but chinks of light gleamed through jagged shrapnel holes in the panels. They hurried past the front door and tall brick wall to an iron gate, one half sagging on bent hinges. "We'll go round to the back," Pinckney said under his breath. "Better clean up before we see the ladies." A burst of green stars overhead gave ghastly illumination to his bearded face and matted hair.

"Guess you're right, Cap'n." Shad spat a stream of tobacco juice into the street, looked again at the tall, ghostly white columns of the piazzas, shrugged and expelled the wad, too.

They walked the length of the brick-paved carriage drive to a bare-earth yard behind the weed-choked garden. A young black woman was there, her back to them, hanging wet clothes on a thin rope strung taut between two trees. In the dim light, her calico dress and bandanna were the only vivid note of color. The buildings in the yard were made of the unique grayish-rose brick manufactured in pre-War Charleston; their edges blurred imperceptibly into the gray dusk, with its sporadic rose reflection from the red fireworks.

"Sophy? Is that you?" Pinckney could not be sure.

The woman dropped the voluminous folds of a wet nightdress and spun on her heel. "Praise lawd! Mist' Pinckney!" She clasped her hands over her heart. When he got closer to her, she moved them to hold the sides of her head. "What I see?" she moaned. "Skin and bone. And lacking." She emitted a thin, keening note of grief.

"Sophy, stop that howling. Is that any welcome for two heroes?" He could not sustain the false jocularity. "Sophy, I implore you," he cried. He had steeled himself not to be hurt by the reactions of his family when they learned about his arm. He had gotten himself completely under control. But that was in Virginia, in the Army. Now that he was, at last, home again, he felt his control slipping away. Too many emotions were battering his heart. He wanted to fall on the earth of the familiar yard and embrace it. He wanted to throw his head back and howl with the pain of seeing the patched holes in the walls of the house and the fear of what lay in the future. None of his turmoil showed on his thin face. He smiled at Sophy and patted her shoulder. "It's all right," he said. "Everything's all right."

The woman stuffed her fist in her mouth until she was quiet.

"That's better," said Pinckney. He gestured to Shad, who joined him. "This is Sophy, Shad. She used to take care of my mama and her clothes, but from all this washing, it looks like she's taking care of the whole family now . . ."

"Yessir," Sophy grumbled, "and Miss Julia, she particular for sure."

"Miss Julia? Is she living here?"

"Yessir. The Yankee General, he on Charlotte Street in Miss Julia house."

"I see. Well . . . This is Mr. Simmons, Sophy. He'll be living here, too. But don't worry. He's not too particular about the washing, and neither am I. Do you still have a wash kettle boiling?"

"The fire out, but I ain't empty the water yet."

"Then add some wood and light it, please, Sophy. Mr. Simmons and I need to take a scrub brush and some lye soap to ourselves first, and then you'd better boil these things we're wearing."

"Yessir, Mist' Pinckney. I'll tell Solomon to take a bathtub to your room."

"Don't do that. I'm wearing some passengers in these clothes, and I don't want to take them in the house. We'll wash out here in the yard. And you—no peeking, do you understand?"

"Oh, Mist' Pinckney." Sophy giggled extravagantly.

"All right, get to it. And Sophy—we'll need a razor and some clothes to put on. I left things in my clothes press. Are they still there?"

"Yessir."

"I'd be glad to see you hurry."

"Yessir . . . Mist' Pinckney? I is going, but I just want to tell you we is all going to be glad to have you home. This house sure need a man in it."

"Thank you, Sophy. A clean man would be better, don't you think?"

"Yessir. I done gone." She ran for the kitchen building.

Pinckney held a kerosene lamp high and led Shad up to the drawing room. They were clean, and that was about all that could be said for them. Pinny's pre-War clothes hung loosely on his emaciated form and all but obliterated Shad. "My Aunt Julia is a gorgon, Shad," he warned. "Don't let anything she says upset you." He knocked on the side of the open door.

Julia looked up from her embroidery frame. She was darning a shirt of Stuart's with the same exquisite satin stitch that she used for decorative work. "Good evening, Pinckney," she said calmly. "Don't just stand there; come in and sit down."

For a long moment, Pinckney could not force his legs to move. His eyes jumped from place to place in the room that he had known from birth, cataloguing the damage and pillage of war. Gone were the silver bowls that once held fragrant potpourri on gleaming mahogany tables. Gone, too, the carved crystal vases that had always had fresh flowers. And the porcelain temple dogs that had sat sentinel on the hearth. All the porcelains had disappeared—the Dresden shepherd and shepherdess whose simpers had always annoyed him, the little Chinese dancer with the miniature flowered tree painted on her tiny fan, the lidded boxes that had been crammed with his mother's bonbons. Everything else that he remembered, too. All the frivolous bits of beauty were no more.

The silvery-blue silk that covered the walls was stained, the draperies gone. On one wall, a picture hung awkwardly low. From the water marks around it, its role as covering for a patched shell hole was apparent. It was the only picture left in the room. Darker rectangles marked the places where delicate, light-filled landscapes had been.

Less than half the furniture remained, all of it scarred. Deep gouges marked the legs of the chairs, souvenirs of men in boots with spurs. Neat squares of Julia's delicate needlework showed the careful repair of torn upholstery. The battered floor had been polished, but splinters still poked up from grooves made when the heavy secretary and consoles were dragged out. There were no longer any soft, faded Persian carpets to hide the wounds.

Pinckney forced himself to enter the room. He set his feet gently on the bare, bruised floor. Julia's eyes widened briefly at the sight of his pinned-up sleeve. "Dear boy. I'm so sorry. Do you have much pain?"

"Not anymore, thank God. Aunt Julia, may I present my friend Shad Simmons. I lost my arm and Shad saved my life."

Julia looked at Shad. She did not attempt to hide her distaste. Pinckney felt an invigorating surge of anger. He looked at his aunt from challenging, steel-blue eyes. "In that case, Mr. Simmons is certainly welcome," Julia said. She did not try to sound convincing.

Pinckney turned to Shad, still hovering in the hallway. "I told you so," he muttered. "Come on in. She barks, but she doesn't bite. I'm sorry, Shad."

"I've faced worse," the boy replied. He walked into the room, with a hint of swagger. "Howdy, ma'am," he said to Julia. Then he settled himself in a tall wing chair whose sides hid him from her view. And her from his.

Pinny took a stool near his aunt's chair. His anger had brought color to his cheeks. He wished desperately that he could say what he was thinking; but Julia was his aunt, his elder and a lady. "I thank you for the firework display," he said, instead.

The irony did not escape Julia; nor did it disturb her sour arrogance. Without looking up from her work, she explained the occasion. It was the fourth anniversary of the surrender of Fort Sumter and the beginning of the War. Ever since the occupation of Charleston in February, the primary objective of the Union troops had been the restoration of the fort for its reopening. The tiny bit of land in the harbor, once a symbol for the South, had become a symbol for the North. For this anniversary rededication, steamers had come down from New York and Boston carrying triumphant figures of the Abolitionist movement, led by Henry Ward Beecher. Major—now Colonel—Anderson, who had surrendered in April 1861, was in Charleston to raise the flag he had lowered four years earlier.

"They had guns firing salutes all day. It gave me quite a headache. Now this display. It entertains all the drunk darkies at White Point Gardens and reminds all of us what those eighteen months of siege were like. I closed all the shutters, of course. I will have no part of it, not even as a witness."

Pinckney found his aunt's irritation a comfort. Julia was exactly the same as she had always been. And she had made only the one, perfunctory reference to his missing arm. Her indifference was strangely healing, and her sharp, aggrieved voice made him feel truly at home, in spite of all the changes.

"What about Stuart and Mama and Lizzie?" he asked. "Surely they're not out watching the fireworks."

"Certainly not. Lizzie was put to bed right after tea as usual. Stuart is your mother's reluctant escort for a party. Gentlemen are in short supply, so even a twelve-year-old has to do his duty."

Pinckney chuckled. "Poor Stuart. Twelve isn't the age for admiring ladies. But where did dear Mama manage to find a party in these days?"

"There is one every Friday. Sally Brewton—who else—got everyone together and invented a thing called the 'starvation' party. Every house that still has a piano takes its turn. In the afternoon, the boys move any furniture and rugs that are left and wax the floors. Then in the evening the girls take turns playing the piano while the young dance. They have punch cups full of water for refreshments. Someone suggested that they call them 'water dances' instead of 'tea dances,' but Sally didn't think that was dramatic enough."

Pinckney glanced at his aunt's gaunt body. "And are people starving?"

Julia grimaced. "Pretty near. The Yankees have all the food. They give tickets for supplies from their commissary—rice flour, vinegar, salt pork, corn grist—and the darkies line up for supplies. Pansy and Solomon and Hattie waste half the day there getting dinner."

"But can't white people go to the commissary, too?"

Julia's laugh was like a curse. "They could, but they don't. We wouldn't give the blue devils the satisfaction. The War may be over in Virginia, Pinckney, but it's just begun here. It's us against them."

With an occasional question from Pinckney, Julia gave an emotionless detailed report on the events in Charleston since his last time home and on the conditions under which they now had to live.

In the days immediately following the occupation, the Union soldiers had taken possession of all the undamaged buildings above Calhoun Street and moved the Charlestonians down into the Old City. They had also fired the warehouses full of stored cotton and rice, which destroyed the docks. For a while, it looked as if the exuberant enlisted men might torch the whole city, but the officers managed to keep them under control. The only house lost was the one belonging to the French Consul, where some of Charleston's Huguenots had stored valuables for international safekeeping.

Freed slaves from city houses and from the plantations formed a never-ending procession into town, sleeping in ruined houses, in the parks, in the streets. Under Sherman's Field Order Number 15, all land from Beaufort to Charleston for thirty miles inland had been confiscated, to be redistributed to the freed slaves who had followed his Army through Georgia. That included the Barony. One of Sherman's Generals, a man named Saxon, was supposed to allocate 485,000 acres. He made a speech in Charleston: "I came to tell you to get the land," which most blacks understood to mean any land they wanted. On street corners all over town, sharp operators set up booths selling numbered wooden stakes for a dollar each. All a black man had to do, they said, was drive the stake into any piece of land he fancied, and the forty acres surrounding it was his.

"I understand," said Julia, "that a number of the claimants tried successfully to kill each other. They were not too happy with their benefactors, either."

Angry, feeling betrayed, the freed slaves poured back into town where they began to attack any white man they saw, even Union officers. Julia smiled. "A certain Colonel Gurney thought he had the solution. He told them to go back to the plantations north of the city and work for the whites for wages. The confiscated land south was just for the Georgia blacks. Any able-bodied man who wouldn't leave was put to work cleaning the streets of all the debris from the bombardment. The riots were very noisy. It was almost impossible to get any sleep at night. So then the officers went all around town offering to arm all the white men with clubs if they would help the Yankees control the laborers. They even paid them something. Another influx was a lot of riff-raff poor whites from up-country." Her eyes flicked over Joe, sitting in a chair behind Pinckney's. "They were happy to have a chance to break a few heads for pay. Naturally, no one we know would do it, although Stuart wanted to. He thought he could club a few Yankees and no one would notice. I had to speak very severely to him."

"Stuart? But Stuart's just a child."

"Wait until you see him." She took up her narrative. The Army had two separate groups trying to control things: the regular occupation troops and an office called The Bureau of Freedmen, Refugees and Abandoned Lands. "For which, read 'confiscated.'" The Bureau had taken all the school buildings, including the South Carolina Hall next door, and had opened up nine schools for black children and adults. "Of course, there weren't nine school buildings in the whole town. Most people had tutors or private classes for their children. So they converted what they needed. St. Luke's was sacked, down to the last altar cloth, and now it's a school for black girls."

Pinckney thought about the Christmas Eve service there and Lavinia's smiling face near his shoulder. How would she react to the empty sleeve below that shoulder now? He forced his attention back to what his aunt was saying.

". . . an honest dollar at least. And it's a lot easier to teach a little darky her ABC's than it is to teach her to set a table properly."

"I'm sorry, Aunt Julia. I didn't hear all you said."

"I'm not speaking for my own amusement, Pinckney. Pay attention." Her sharp tone was a curious comfort to Pinny. At least some things at home had not changed. "I said that most of the teachers are ladies you know." She named a dozen. "The jackass Yankees sent down about nine or ten do-gooders, which wasn't nearly enough. So they've had to hire more than seventy local teachers. Old men for the boys' schools, and ladies for the girls. Annabelle Marion is teaching reading, which is surprising; I always considered her illiterate. She says there are over three thousand students all told. Your mother wanted to offer herself as a teacher, but I told her they weren't scraping that deep in the bottom of the barrel."

"Mama?" Pinckney shouted with laughter. "She can't spell 'cat.' Why on earth did she want to be a teacher?"

"It's all part of her latest lunacy. She has become a religious fanatic."

"Mama?"

"Your empty-headed mama. When people moved back downtown, Saint Michael's started services again right away. The very first Sunday, Mr. Sanders droned on the way he always does, but some clever Yankee sitting in the gallery was paying too much attention. He noticed that Mr. Sanders skipped the prayer for the President. He had been leaving it out for years; none of us thought much of Davis, you know. But the Yankee reported it, and it became a big hoohaw. General Sickles insisted that we all had to pray for Lincoln, Mr. Sanders refused, and they took his house and furniture and even his vestments and replaced him with a man from Rhode Island. Edwards is his name, Adam Edwards. A real hell-fire and damnation preacher. I refer to him as Jonathan, which drives your mother crazy, even if she doesn't get the reference."

"I don't understand."

"You will when you see him. The Episcopal Church has done the one thing that might really destroy Charleston. The man is as handsome as Gabriel, has a voice like an organ, and is a widower. Half the females in Charleston are besotted with him, and they go through all manner of contrivances to get his attention. I don't think many of them are as absurd as your mother. They just act holy, but she really believes his message: Charleston is Sodom and Gomorrah combined, and the War was God's punishment for our sins. She's like a parrot, too, and I find it extremely tedious. The only amusement is watching the middle-aged belles in church on Sunday. Such soulful looks. When Edwards gives communion, he positively has to wrench the chalice away so that he can move on to the next one.

"The reason for the longing to teach is that the romantic field is so crowded that Mary has been making no mark at all. But this Edwards has a daughter, and she is teaching at the school they've put in next door. Your darling mother had visions of dropping into the rectory every ten minutes to discuss school business with Prudence. Then she could loiter until she saw Prudence's papa."

8

Pansy slipped into the room and waited for Julia to acknowledge her. Then she said, quietly, "Supper's ready for Mist' Pinckney and the other gennilman, ma'am." She flashed a smile at Pinckney. "Clothes is cooked, too." With a giggle she sped into the hall.

Two places were set on the long table. Pinckney pulled out an extra chair for his aunt, but she looked at Shad, who was cramming hot biscuits into his mouth whole, and refused to join them. "I'll be in the book room when you finish. If you're not too tired, I'd be happy to have you join me."

The two young men spoke little while they ate. They were both near starvation, and the hot food seemed ambrosial. It was an austere menu, hominy, bacon and biscuits, but the quantities were generous. Elijah served it as if it were a pre-War banquet, wearing his velvet tailcoat and breeches with white-silk stockings in which the darned places were barely perceptible. When the butler's magnificent form first appeared in the doorway, Shad's eyes goggled. But Pinckney did not notice. He was busy struggling up from his chair to embrace the black man. "'Lijah, I'm so happy to see you!"

"Yessir, me too, Mist' Pinny, but if you spills this here hominy, they'se gonna kill me in the kitchen. It's all we got." He set the tray down on the table and folded his two strong arms around Pickney's thin form. Tears glistened in his eyes.

Pinckney submitted to Elijah's firm maneuvering and found himself back in his chair. "You needs to eat, boy, you ain't got as much meat on you as a stray cat." Elijah picked up the tray, found that Shad had already reached across the table for the food and that the bowl and platter were half-empty. He scowled horribly.

"Shad, this is Elijah. He runs the family," said Pinckney rapidly. "'Lijah, this is Mr. Simmons. He saved my life when I lost my arm. I'm hoping he'll stay with us for a while."

"Yessir," Elijah said. The scowl disappeared. He offered the tray on

Pinckney's right side. "Ole Miz Ashley, she always told us ahead of time which guests was left-handed," he said gently, "and I knows what to do. Anything needs cutting, I'll do it in the kitchen and bring it special. I give you a extra spoon till you gets practiced with a fork." His brown eyes met Pinckney's for a long moment, sharing the pain in the blood-shot blue ones, saying everything there was to be said about loss and love and regret and courage. Pinckney smiled, looking very young.

"Thank you, 'Lijah," he murmured.

"I'm glad Elijah is still with us," he said to Julia after supper.

His aunt snorted. "Old hypocrite," she said. "He'll tell you he stayed to 'look out for the ladies,' but don't pay any attention. He ran off to the Yankees just like the rest of them. Your mother never could manage her servants. They came straggling back after a few days when they found out the Yankees weren't offering quarters like the ones here and that we were going to have to provide the same room and board and clothing as before, plus pay wages. I had to turn most of them away. I don't know how we're going to afford to keep the ones we have."

"Who's here?"

"Elijah and Sophy from your house. Pansy and Solomon from the Barony, and my cook, Dilcey, from the Charlotte Street house. Solomon's working as gardener and general repairman. Elijah's too grand for anything so menial. I'd send him packing tomorrow, but your mother won't hear of it. He walks behind us to church, dressed to the nines and carrying her prayer book. It does make her noticeable, I'll say that."

"Aunt Julia, you have an adder's tongue."

Julia smiled. "I like to think so."

The street door banged. "Stuart, how many times do I have to tell you not to slam doors?" The party-goers were home.

Unprepared for the meeting, Mary Tradd screamed and burst into tears when she saw Pinckney's worn face and empty sleeve. Then she apologized abjectly through her sobs, making everything worse.

Stuart's first reaction was to throw his arms around his brother's neck. But then he remembered that he was too old for such childish behavior and extended his hand for a manly greeting. Pinckney felt helpless. No matter what he did, it would be wrong. He tried to meet Stuart's right hand with his left. As he feared, the action only emphasized the awkward situation. Stuart jerked his hand away, blushed and scowled. His wrists hung exposed from the too-short sleeves of his outgrown jacket; even they were blotched with red. The half hour that followed was miserable for them all. Shad's introduction was met by hastily covered shocked faces; then a glutinous silence fell. No one could think of what to say. Stuart tried to rescue them by an excited account of the Club he had organized with his closest friend Alex Wentworth.

"We were all on the Ashley River bridge together every day. All eight of us. When the Yankee shells would start fires, we'd dip up water in buckets on ropes and put them out. Our Colonel said we were as much soldiers as if we'd been in the Army. It was in the *Messenger* and everything. We took a solemn blood oath not to quit fighting, even when our Army had to pull out, and the orders came to burn the bridge so the Yankees couldn't get it. And we never will. They think we're just children, but we'll grow up. We're making our plans. The day'll come when we can run the damn Yankees out . . ."

"Stuart!"

"Mama, 'damn' for Yankees isn't the same as cussing."

"There'll be no profanity in this house."

"But it isn't . . ."

Pinckney was bone weary. He stood up. "If nobody minds," he said, "I'm going to go to bed. Good night, Mama; good night, Aunt Julia; good night, Stuart. Come along, Shad. I told 'Lijah to make up a cot for you in my room."

Shad bobbed his head at the ladies and mumbled. He was happy to escape the tension, bickering and surreptitious glances his way. He could feel sweat rolling down his spine. He followed Pinckney up the stairs at a near run. The light from the kerosene lamp in Pinny's hand flickered erratically.

He stopped on the third floor landing. Shad nearly ran into him. "This is my baby sister's room," Pinny whispered. "I'm going to see if she's grown six inches, too. Want to come?"

"I might scare her. A stranger and all."

"Not Lizzie. She's the most loving little thing in the world. Besides, she's asleep." He opened the door carefully and tiptoed into the dark space.

Lizzie was curled into a ball on a narrow trundle bed. The uneven light revealed that she was dangerously thin. Dark shadows hollowed her cheeks and the area under her closed eyes. "Dear God," said Pinckney with horror.

The child's eyes flew open, looking up into the lamp. She covered them with her skeletal fists and screamed.

Pinckney thrust the lamp into Shad's hand and dropped to his knees. "Hush, Lizzie, hush, sweetheart, hush, baby." He tried to put his arm around her, but she kicked and hit at him, still screaming. "Lizzie, it's Pinny. Baby Sister, this is your Pinny."

The screaming stopped. There was an instant's silence; then a terrifying gasping, choking noise from the little girl's throat. Her hands clutched at the air as if to capture the breath that her shaking body needed. Pinckney tried frantically to soothe her, talking, patting her.

"Get away from her!" It was Julia. "Do you want to scare her to death?" She pulled on Pinckney's good arm.

He allowed himself to be drawn into the hallway. "She always chokes like that when she's frightened. It sounds worse than it is."

Pinny tried not to listen to the agonizing choking sounds. "Shouldn't we get a doctor?"

"Dr. Perigru has seen her. He says she'll outgrow it. And it won't kill her."

"Aunt Julia, that's heartless."

"Maybe so. But it's the way things are. Listen. It's getting better."

Pinny strained his ears. Yes, the choking sounds were interspersed with rasping inhalations. "Thank you, Aunt Julia."

"Go to bed. It's late. You're going to have to harden yourself, Pinckney. There'll be a lot for you to get used to, lots of things that we just can't do anything about."

The sun was almost at its zenith when Pinckney woke from his exhausted sleep. For a few half-dreaming moments, the familiar surroundings allowed him to feel like the eager, life-loving young man who had awakened in that bed with the same sweet scent of spring from that room's open windows in the days before the War.

Then he was crushed by the realization of all that had happened since and by apprehension of all that lay ahead. His body felt too heavy to move.

"Pinny! Wake up. Good news." Stuart burst into the room, capering with glee. Pinckney sat up abruptly.

The happy boy he saw was a vastly changed person from the Stuart of the night before. Except for his added inches, he was the noisily exuberant younger brother Pinny had left more than a year earlier.

"What is it? I'd be glad for some good news."

"Old Abe is dead! Shot last night in Washington while his friends were celebrating in Charleston. I wish we could shoot off fireworks tonight. See how they like it."

Pinckney felt a bitter satisfaction. "I think we should drink a toast to the departure of Honest Abe. Do you know if there's anything in the house?"

"'Lijah'll find something. He has things hid all over the place. Can I have one, too?"

"Damn right. You're a soldier, aren't you? Find Shad. I'll get my clothes on, and we three Confederate veterans will honor the good news. Meet me in the dining room. And tell Elijah I want some food and a bottle on the table when I get down there."

Stuart snapped a salute. "Yes, sir, Captain Tradd, sir." He tore out of the room, slamming the door behind him, and clattered down the stairs screaming the banshee wail of a Rebel yell.

Lincoln's assassination loosed a week-long outbreak of violence in the streets of Charleston. Sticks and pieces of broken bricks crashed against the barred doors and locked shutters of the city's houses, thrown by the shouting crowds of Negro Union soldiers and despairing former slaves. The Charlestonians waited out the siege, grateful for the Union officers who galloped their horses from one outbreak to another, bringing order with their swords and pistols. When the worst was over, they continued to patrol the streets. No one was permitted to be on them without an urgent, provable reason.

During that week of enforced seclusion, the disparate personalities in the Tradd house rubbed against each other, clashed, retreated, advanced and slowly settled into a pattern which had Pinckney as its central focus. He became in fact what his father's death had made him in title. He was head of the family.

He was too busy to take time to resent the demands on his patience and inexperience. He had to lead, as he had done in the easier battles on the fields of Virginia. He had to go over the house and yard, assessing the damage done by bombardment and neglect; he had to cajole Elijah into uncovering all the things he had managed to conceal from the occupying forces; he had to allocate his father's clothes to Stuart and Shad and persuade his aunt to instruct Pansy to alter them; he had to show Solomon what he meant by a whittled arm and hand which he could strap on and wear in a sling so that his mother would not cry every time she looked at him; he had to take valuable moments to sit silently in Lizzie's room while she rocked in her little chair and got used to his non-demanding, unthreatening presence; he had to question his aunt about the last reports she had had from Carlington before Sherman's Army came; he had to restrain Stuart from running out to fight the dangerous crowds in the street; he had to wonder if Lavinia was looking over at the shutters which hid him as he looked through their cracks at the Anson house across the street and its covered windows; he had to act as a buffer between Shad and the family, especially the servants and their ostentatious condescension; he had to be strong and confident, postponing his gut-wrenching worry until the quiet darkness of the sleeping house could hide it from all those who depended on him.

With Shad in the same room, Pinckney did not even have the freedom to pace back and forth while his mind and heart struggled with the turbulence that beset him. He had to keep himself still, forcing the slow, regular breathing that pretended sleep. While all the time, he longed to cry out in anger and fear. Nothing in his young life had prepared him to face what was before him now. Not the carefree, extravagant years of his youth; they had taught him how a dashing young man of unlimited fortune should behave in civilized society; now he had no fortune, and the ruling class that he had been a part of was reduced to hiding behind locked doors from a threatening new world of violence and anarchy.

Not even the danger and privation of the battlefield had been as bad as what he was going through now. There, he had been able to fight back, to meet violence with violence. Now he had to swallow the humiliation of being protected by his enemies. He was not allowed to fight. A battle was something he understood. It was a challenge, a dare, a gamble against death, and the heart rose to meet it, exulting in the wild excitement. It swept a man along, took all his fevered concentration, then it was over. But this new life would never be over, and Pinckney did not understand it.

What do they expect of me? he demanded silently, knowing that there was no one to answer. He felt like a bewildered, frightened child, and he longed for his father. Anson Tradd's death had been a hero's death; Pinckney's pride in his father had outweighed his sense of loss. Now it swept over him, and he grieved for the man who had meant all the world to him, without his ever realizing it. He saw the tall, elegant figure, heard the slow voice, so full of laughter and compassion, felt the warm, loving strength of his father's presence. Help me, Papa, his heart cried. I need you so.

But he was alone.

He had been raised to be a planter, to take over at Carlington with the guidance of his father and the experienced overseer. He would have had time to learn and an established order to follow. Now there was no time, and the old order was no more. Pinckney realized that he did not know how to run a plantation. It was in his blood—the rhythm of the seasons, the unbreakable bonds to the land and the river, the respect for the God who gave death and renewal and who humbled with His storms. But that was not enough. Aunt Julia would help. She had promised. That was not enough, either. Carlington had not been confiscated; it was north of the city and did not come under Sherman's Order. It still belonged to him. But how much destruction had there been? Julia had been able to learn nothing except that the overseer she had hired was gone. His last message had said that the servants were running away and taking everything with them.

I don't care, Pinckney thought. I'll do it alone. A one-armed man can learn to plow and to plant. I can feed my family at least. His mind filled with hope, remembering the fertile rows of black earth and the abundant game in the acres of woods. Then bitter reality punctured the dream. He had no mules, no seed, no rifle, no shells, no plow. And no money. The food on the table came from the Yankee handouts to the servants. Carlington, he thought, and his heart turned over. He put it out of his mind. He could not afford to use his energy in mourning.

He would have to find work in the city. He was not the only man in the world who had had to learn a trade, and he was not afraid of hard work. As soon as the riots were over, as soon as the streets were open, he'd go looking. There had to be something he could do.

There has to be something, his mind said. And his heart cried: What? I'll find something, he told himself. I have to. They're all depending on me—Mama, Aunt Julia, Stuart, baby Lizzie, the servants, even Shad. I can't let them down. A man isn't a man unless he can take care of his family.

. . . And his wife. Dear God, what about Lavinia? He thought of her passionate letters, and his body quickened. He tried to remember her face, but he could recapture only a blurred memory of soft hair and a sweet scent. She was more a symbol than a person, the essence of femininity, to be cherished and protected.

I don't even know her, he thought with a stab of fear. I lost my temper, and I won a wife. Who is she? She'll have to stand by me, even though I'm a penniless cripple. Those are the rules, and Lavinia is a lady. She's bound by them, the same as I am.

He imagined the solace of a sweet, young wife who would share the new, unknown life that he had to find. She would comfort him in his sorrow and take pride in his courage. He would not be alone.

No. It was asking too much. He would have to release her from their engagement . . . But she might not want to be released. Those letters . . . His loins ached, demanding an outlet for the passions that had been suppressed for the long years of the War.

He concentrated all his will on thinking, not feeling. There must be something he could hold on to, in the midst of his confusion and the chaos of the world outside. He had to have a fixed star to steer by.

Then, so clearly that he looked for him in the room, Pinckney heard his father speaking. "A man has to guard his honor, son. It's worth more than his life." Anson Tradd had said the words a thousand times, whenever Pinny wanted to know the why of all the rules and regulations that constricted his young life. He had almost forgotten them as he grew older; they had become a part of him and no longer needed to be said. Now they came back, in the voice he trusted above all others. "Always do the right thing, no matter what it costs. You'll know, even if no one else does. And then you can hold your head high, the way the Tradds always have."

Thank you, Papa, Pinckney said silently. That's what I needed to know. I'm still scared, but there's no dishonor in fear. As long as I go ahead and do what I have to do. I'll find out what that is, and I'll keep my head high.

His innate optimism began to grow. Hell, the Tradds had been through worse than poverty in their time. And they had always come through. He'd find a way.

9

When the week was over and an uneasy calm settled on the city, Pinckney steeled himself for the moment he had been dreading and anticipating.

In the late morning he sent Elijah to the Ansons' to warn them that he would call after dinner, at four o'clock. Then he laid out his clothes and lost himself in searching with Solomon and Shad for the source of the leak in the roof over Stuart's bedroom. During the bath that followed, he scrubbed every inch of his body and head. Then, shaved and dressed in his finest, he sat down at the head of the long table and pretended to eat while he went over and over the speech he had composed in his mind. He was still rehearsing when he marched across the street, unaware of the determined set to his jaw.

Lavinia, peeping out from behind the curtains, felt her heart pounding. She knew, of course, about his arm. Elijah had managed to bring the news across the street. When she heard about it, she ran to the garden door and got sick; then she suffered from a terrible headache when her mother lectured her about her bad behavior. She didn't care if Pinckney Tradd was a hero; the idea of being engaged to a man with a stump for an arm still made her feel queasy . . .

Why, it didn't look bad at all. It was in a sling. Elijah must have been wrong. Pinny's arm wasn't shot off at all; it was just broken. The sun glinted on his golden-red hair. She had forgotten how extremely handsome he was. Even though he was awfully thin.

At his knock, she ran to open the door.

"Welcome home, Pinckney." Lavinia curtsied deeply, and the wide pink ruffles of her skirt encircled her like the petals of a flower, sending up tiny puffs of sweetness from the bags of sachet pinned to her hidden petticoats.

She moved before him into the sitting room, her great hoop swaying.

Pinckney stopped in the doorway, anxious to deliver his speech before the tantalizing vision of her drove it from his mind. When he spoke, his voice was hoarse with strain.

"I have something to say, Lavinia, and you must be silent until I've got it out," he blurted. "I tried to find the right way to put what I'm feeling. I guess I've been a soldier too long. I can't find any graceful expressions." He wished desperately that he could mop his brow. Lavinia's big eyes were fastened on his face expectantly. Pinckney took a quick, rasping breath and struggled on.

"I'm not the man I was, Lavinia. I've lost a piece of myself, and it's done something to me. I've also lost the world I knew. We all have . . ." His mind raced, trying to remember the words he had selected, unable to catch them.

Lavinia's lashes trembled. So it was true. It must be a wooden arm in that sling. Her mouth felt acid. But, she reminded herself, it doesn't show. I don't have to look at it. I can pretend it's broken and not think about the rest. Poor Pinny. I guess it is sad. A tear glimmered in the corner of one eye; she touched it with her tiny handkerchief. Pinny hurried to the conclusion of his speech.

"I intended to offer you a release from our engagement, but I cannot do that. I dare not. I know how brave your heart is; I know you would refuse. And I would rejoice in your refusal, even though it might be wrong for your happiness. I won't allow your courage to bind you without time for thought . . . Your father will be coming home soon. I will speak with him about the alteration in my prospects, and he will be the best person to give you advice. Then, when you are ready, you can decide whether you will still want to throw yourself away on a penniless old soldier." He breathed deeply, glad that it was over.

Lavinia, her eyes still lowered, sighed. What a beautiful speech. Just like Count Roderigo in one of her novels. If she didn't look at him, she could imagine that he was wearing a brocade coat and plumed hat, like the illustration in the frontispiece. She lifted her eyes slowly, looking into space over his shoulder and swayed toward him with her mouth formed for kissing.

"Oh, my God," Pinny groaned. He crushed her body to him and kissed her in a way that none of the books had mentioned. Lavinia was too shocked to protest.

"Forgive me," Pinckney mumbled in her hair. "So long away from you, and the softness of you, and the smell . . ." He broke away. Lavinia thought he was breathing very strangely. "I must go," he said, "I'm sorry." She held her hand out to be kissed, but he did not even notice. After he had gone, Lavinia went to a mirror and examined her swollen lips and disordered hair. Her eyes flamed. Imagine Pinckney Tradd getting so flustered. She tasted her own power and found it delicious.

Shad was repairing the bedframe he had found in the attic when Pinckney returned from the Ansons'.

"You ever have a woman, Shad?" Pinckney was very pale.

"Nope. Can't say as I have," said Shad.

"Then it's time. Come on with me." Shad put the priceless nails and hammer away quickly.

Pinckney set a brisk pace up Meeting Street. "It's only a few blocks to where we're going," he said. "Chalmers Street. My father took me there before I left for England in 'sixty. I was seventeen then and pretty wild. Pretty ignorant, too. Thought I was already a man because I knew how to ride a horse and shoot a gun." He smiled reflectively. "When Papa told me where we were going, I all of a sudden felt very young. I didn't let on, of course. Acted like a real man of the world. At least I thought I did. I'm sure I didn't fool Papa for a minute.

"Anyhow, he had it all arranged. There's a house, very small, very elegant, very sweet-smelling, very, very private. Just for gentlemen. I suppose it's still there. That's one trade that war doesn't hurt."

Shad's usual diffidence slipped. "They got many girls, Cap'n?"

"I really don't know, Shad. The way it works, you give your card to the butler at the door, he shows you into a little drawing room, brings you a glass of Madeira, then Madame Dupuis comes in with a woman, introduces her, stays a few minutes making conversation about the weather and leaves. I guess she and my father had made the decision for me. I never had cause to change it. Lily, her name is."

"You reckon she's still there?"

"I'm counting on it. I sure don't have any money to make friends with a stranger."

"Costs pretty high, huh?"

"I don't know that, either, Shad. My father handled it. And whatever he paid, it was worth it. She knew everything there was to know about men and women together. I fell crazy in love with her, spent every minute I could manage in her bed. God, I was as randy as a goat. When I had to leave, it nearly killed me. Swore my heart was broken. Fortunately, I had introductions to some places in London, and I found out Lily's talents weren't unique to her."

"Well, Cap'n, I don't mean to be discouraging, but it ain't likely this Lily has been waiting all by her lonesome for you to get back. And your paw ain't here to pay."

"True on both counts. I have an optimistic nature, though. And if she's here, I think she'll be glad to see me, even with my pockets empty.

She liked me a lot, too; it wasn't just on my side." Pinny winked. "Besides, I gave her a spectacular present as a memento. Biggest damn ruby ring the jeweler had in his safe. A memory like that should be good for at least a little welcome home for a brave soldier and his friend. Come on. We turn here."

Chalmers Street was teeming with people. Just a few steps from Meeting, a crowd of soldiers were stamping their feet and clapping to the music of a sweating, grinning banjo player. Farther along, a larger group of whites and blacks shouted comments and bids at the hoarse, florid auctioneer on the platform before a squat, shell-pocked building. Behind the platform, armed men guarded untidy pyramids of candlesticks, silver trays, clocks and mirrors.

"Three dollars once . . . twice . . . sold!" The purchaser, a stout man with a bushy black beard and bald head, held out his money then took the tall, shining pair of candelabra from the platform.

Pinckney stared. "What's happening here?" he asked an officer lounging against a buggy.

"Rebs' stuff, mister. Spoils of war. Makes a nice little gift to send home. And gives our brave boys that it belongs to a little pocket money. The auction company only keeps half."

Shad dragged Pinckney away. "I know I recognized that silver," Pinny insisted. "I know it was from Lavinia's mother's house. I've seen those candelabra on the dinner table."

"Don't think about it, Cap'n. Nothing you can do."

"But I ought to do something."

"You can't. That's the truth of that. Think about something else. Tell me more about this Lily, for instance." His strong grip propelled Pinckney along the street through the crowds. At the corner of Church Street they had to stop to allow a closed carriage to cross in front of them.

When it had passed, they had a clear view of the block ahead. "Christ!" said Pinckney. Shad echoed him. The remaining length of Chalmers was like a scene of bacchanalia. Drunken men, black and white, staggered back and forth across the uneven cobblestones, holding bottles of whiskey. Many of them had their arms around elaborately gowned, laughing women with skin in every shade of brown. Others shouted to other women in the windows of the houses and taverns that lined the street. A cacophony of laughter, shouts, screams and piano music poured into the confusion every time a door opened to admit or release anyone. While Pinckney and Shad watched, a white boy in a lieutenant's uniform poured champagne into the low décolletage of the woman with him; she seized the bottle and tried to hit him, then dropped it and led him through a nearby door.

"Let's get out of here," said Pinckney. "The place I knew must be gone." The rowdy vulgarity repelled him.

Shad hardly heard him. He was hypnotized by the rampant sexuality before his eyes. "No call to leave, Cap'n. Don't they say dark meat's the sweetest?"

Pinny pulled at his arm. "This is sickening. Come on."

Shad shook his head. "You got my mind running on women; I mean to have one. Don't need no favors, neither; a feller back yonder lost his money pouch in the crowd, and I kinda found it in my pocket. Feels like enough gold for both of us to have anything we want."

"It's no good, Shad. I'm leaving."

"Suit yourself, Cap'n. I ain't so finicky as you. I'll be home by curfew." He darted across the street and joined the maelstrom of figures. Pinckney hesitated, then walked rapidly away down Church Street.

During the following weeks, Charleston's veterans came home, some alone, some in pairs, some in groups. For all of them, the entrance to their fallen city and the slow progress through scarred streets and jeering loungers was an agony greater than any wound, greater than the pain they had known when a friend or a son or a brother fell at their sides in battle.

Josiah Anson was turned away from the door of his home by his former coachman, now elevated to the position of butler for the family of the Union Colonel living there. He refused the assistance of the sergeant stationed at the gate, then apologized for his curtness and mounted his foam-flecked horse. His back and shoulders were straight. No one could have known how near he was to collapse.

His legs almost buckled under him when he climbed the steps to Andrew's door. Emma Anson was on the piazza picking dead leaves off the potted hydrangeas. When Jeremiah did not respond to the knock, she clucked angrily and stalked the length of the porch to open the door.

Lucy heard the knock also. She came running from Andrew's room where Jeremiah was bathing him. The scene that met her eyes stopped her short. Her mother-in-law, that terrifying, imposing, middle-aged woman was on her knees, crying like a small child. The sprawled form of Josiah Anson lay half in her lap, his head cradled to her breast.

"My darling," Mrs. Anson said, "I thought I would never see you again." Her husband did not respond. He had lost consciousness.

Lucy backed away silently; she was ashamed to have intruded on such a private moment but glad to have learned the astonishing fact that Emma Anson had a heart. She loves him, Lucy thought, amazed. More than Lavinia, more than Andrew, even. All the love she has she saves for Mr. Josiah.

During the next days and weeks, Lucy also discovered that Josiah Anson was deeply in love with his stout, unbeautiful wife. His emotions were not, however, as exclusive as hers. Outside of their moments alone together, she remained as forbidding as ever, but he was a steady source of warmth and affection to everyone in his family. Which included the children and the wife of his cousin, Anson Tradd.

He was thinking about them now, particularly about Pinckney. The boy had tried to deliver a stilted speech about his engagement to Lavinia almost as soon as Mr. Anson had recovered from his journey, but the older man had stopped him. "Later," he had said, "we'll talk later. We all have a lot of adjusting to do, then we can think about the future. Right now, let's all get to know each other again. You come see Lavinia and all of us as much as you can. Take her to those sad little parties and be as happy as you can. I have work to do, and you have work to find. We'll talk later."

Now a month had passed. It was already the end of May. Josiah Anson had pulled together the remnants of the law practice he had left when he went to war. And he had watched Pinny's determined cheerfulness in spite of the succession of failures in his attempts to find work. Josiah and Emma Anson had visited the Tradd house. He had seen the conditions there; he could imagine the weight on Pinny's shoulders. Mr. Anson looked again at the stack of papers on the desk before him. And he shuddered.

He had been Anson Tradd's lawyer ever since he had hung out his shingle, and he knew more about Pinckney's situation than Pinckney did. He found himself, for the first time in his fifty-two years, experiencing cowardice. The whole world had fallen apart for him, his friends and his beloved city; he felt profound sorrow for them all. But for his godson, this boy of twenty-two, he felt anguish and despair, and he dreaded having to tell him what he knew Pinckney had to hear.

Still, it had to be done. He straightened his coat and picked up his hat and gloves.

". . . So you see, Pinny, you'll probably have to sell Carlington. I can sell the undeveloped land you own on the Wappoo River, but that will bring in just enough to pay the bequests your father left in his will and tide you over for a few months. If you're going to support the Meeting Street house, you can't afford to keep the plantation, too. There'll be taxes to pay and no crops to bring in any money. A lot of people are in the same fix. Some of them are selling the town house and counting on rebuilding their plantations. But they're people with fewer responsibilities . . ."

"And two hands."

"I understand your feelings, son, believe me. I remember Carlington. It was a paradise. But it's no place for one lone man with two women to keep off each other's throats and two children to educate. I wouldn't dare to be isolated with Julia Ashley in the Garden of Eden itself."

Pinckney was startled. It showed.

Josiah Anson smiled. "You're not a boy anymore, Pinny. You're going to have to get used to the fact that gentlemen occasionally have distinctly ungentlemanly thoughts about ladies. And express them among themselves. There aren't more than three men in Charleston who aren't terrified of Julia Ashley. Furthermore, I'm not one of them." Good. The boy was smiling. Josiah Anson stood. "Well, then, that's it. I'm always relieved when bad news is delivered and done with. I'll be on my way."

Pinckney cleared his throat. "There is one more thing, Cousin Josiah. I mean, about Lavinia and me."

Mr. Anson sat down slowly. He did not want to talk about Lavinia. He did not even want to think about Lavinia, because when he did, he remembered the words he had inadvertently overheard her speak, words that revealed the heartlessness hidden by her sweet smile and ingenuous ways. He loved her, she was his own flesh, but she was cruel, and he could not allow Pinckney to become a victim of that cruelty. He loved the boy, too. He forced himself to concentrate on what Pinckney was saying.

"You know what a spot I'm in, Cousin Josiah. I don't know that there's any way that I'll ever be able to take care of her. But I'm willing to work at anything honest I can find, and I believe I'll find something somehow. I offered to release Lavinia, but she refused. If you'll permit us, sir, we're willing to wait. After all, we're both young enough."

"Yes," Josiah Anson said, "you have youth." He debated silently with himself. This was the time to tell Pinckney he could not marry Lavinia. Delay would be unconscionable. But how could he? He had just told the boy he would have to give up the land where the Tradds had lived for almost two hundred years. Could he add another blow?

Also, the boy needed him, whether he knew it or not. He was Pinckney's godfather, and he meant to act in his father's place as much as Pinckney would allow. If he forbid the marriage, without telling Pinny the real reason, he would cause a breach that would prevent his ever doing any good for the boy. And cut Andrew off from his closest friend when he badly needed his friends.

You should tell him, his conscience warned. You owe it to him. The engagement must be broken.

But not now, said his heart. As he just said, they are young and willing to wait. Later, it will be easier. When he is not so thin, so tired, facing such burdens.

He had been silent too long. Pinckney wore a look of defeat. It decided Josiah. Not now.

"Forgive me, Pinny, I was remembering what it was like to be your age. I wouldn't go through it again for all the tea in China. Too energetic. Of course you have my blessing. Provided you're willing, as you say, to wait until I agree for the marriage to take place."

Pinckney held out his hand. "Thank you, Cousin Josiah." Mr. Anson clasped it briefly. "Thank you," Pinny repeated.

Then his face was transformed by a youthful grin. "Just one more thing, Cousin Josiah. I mean to keep Carlington, too. Somehow."

Mr. Anson laughed. "If anyone could do it, my friend, I believe it would be you. I'll help you any way I can."

He astonished the pair of officers patrolling Meeting Street by greeting them cheerfully as he crossed in front of them. By God, the boy just might do it. He thought for a self-indulgent moment how good it would be to have Pinckney Tradd for a son-in-law, to have grandchildren with that flaming hair and flaming spirit.

Then he sighed and went into his son's house. The soft voices of his daughter and daughter-in-law floated down from the upstairs piazza. Josiah Anson's shoulders sagged. They sounded so sweet, like music, like sleepy birds in early morning, like life before the War. That was why he had sat silent in the dark corner that night, half-sleeping, breathing in the perfume of the moonlike waxy blossoms on the magnolia tree that grew near the house. He should have called attention to himself, let them know he was there. Instead, he had let their light young voices be an additional sweetness. Until he realized what he was hearing.

"You can't mean that, Lavinia."

"But I do. If Mikell Johnson so much as looked at me, I'd pick a fight with Pinny and drop him in a minute. But Mikell can't even see anybody except Sarah Leslie. I guess I'm stuck with Pinny."

Lucy remonstrated, but Lavinia was adamant. "I've looked at everybody at every party. They're all home now, whoever's coming home, and they're all a sad, shabby, damaged lot. Mikell Johnson's the only one halfway decent. And with Papa too poor to send me to Saratoga or Newport to catch me a rich husband, I'll settle for what I've got. When that's my house, though, there's not going to be any room for that white trash Shad or that old horror Miss Ashley. Or those children. Any children in my house will be my children. Cousin Mary can stay, though. She adores me."

10

Somehow by the end of June the city had found an equilibrium. After the years of turbulence, it returned gratefully to the age-old rhythms of Charleston life with its adjustments to the demands and bounties of climate. In the early hours, people stirred without waking at the hollow minor-key notes blown from conch shells, the black boatmen's warnings to each other of their presence in the predawn darkness. As the sun rose, its first weak light picked out the tips of the masts, then bathed the sails in a cool wash of pink. Inside the boats, baskets filled with vegetables, fish, oysters, crabs and flowers glowed with color and pearl-like drops of moisture. The wealth of James Island's rich earth was on its way to market, as always in the summer months, and what did it matter to the season that the land might have a new owner.

At five o'clock, the Market opened; sleepy black housemen and cooks began to arrive with empty palmetto baskets to be filled from the bright mounds and pyramids arranged on long tables beneath the arches of the long covered block. It was a social as well as a commercial occasion. The long, nasal vowels and heavy accented syllables of Gullah mixed with laughter and shouting in a music incomprehensible to outsiders, intoxicating to the participants of the milling, shifting minuet of buying and selling. On the roof-tree of the arcade, dozens of turkey buzzards side-stepped, opening and closing their wide, sail-like wings. Theirs was the duty of garbage collectors for the old city; the Market, when it closed at seven A.M., was the first and freshest stop of their day.

There were fewer of them than there had been. The profligate waste of plantation times was past. At seven, the abundant excess produce was no longer left to rot. Instead, black entrepreneurs loaded it into mule-drawn wagons and began their rounds through the city, going through the streets behind the push-barrow peddlers of shrimp brought in by the boats which had trawled through the rosy dawn Atlantic outside the protecting islands. The still-fresh air of morning carried the sounds of creaking wheels and singing through the open windows of the old houses.

"Swimp. Who buy me raw swimp . . . Got de fine vegetibbel . . . Strawberry . . . She-crab . . ."

Soon the windows were closed and the shutters drawn, to hold in the cool night air, while the sun rose overhead and made its path across the impossibly blue near-tropical sky. They would open again in late afternoon when the southwest breeze came in off the sea bringing salt-scented relief to the houses set at an angle in their gardens to receive it. The wind was the city's blessing and ruler, unchanging throughout peace, war, prosperity, poverty. It had determined the location of the first settlement and the lives of its descendants ever since, lulling them to sleep in their tall rooms, bringing the great sailing ships to their busy docks, shaking their complacency with demonstrations of its power.

The officers of Sickles' occupying army sweated and suffered in their uniforms, cursed the heat, scorned the Charlestonians as lazy Southerners, kept at their work all day and collapsed by the dozens. The black soldiers were tougher and wiser. With little supervision over their activities, they abandoned work and drifted into the hedonistic alleys and streets near the docks they were supposed to be repairing. A city within the city was there, throbbing with life and music, a city without whites or white rules, a city where the black man was truly free. Where the main street was renamed "Do As You Choose Alley" and the talk was about a pale-skinned youth newly arrived from the country around the Ashepoo River; he called himself "Daddy Cain," and his forum was the Union League. He spoke what was in his heart and put it into the hearts of others: torch the white houses with everyone in them, the whites and the renegade niggers who worked for them. Join the Union League. When enough were joined together, they would be unstoppable.

The relentless rise of the thermometer affected the Charlestonians more than their captors could see. Behind their shuttered windows, they were fighting the hardest battle of the War. There were no more crises, no heroic occasions to rise to. There were only want and worry and unaccustomed poverty. The enemy was no longer Sickles and his men, it was their own nervous irritability under the accumulation of small problems that they had been too busy to notice before.

The Tradd house was no exception. Pinckney dreaded coming home every day. He was occupied from first light with the Charleston Light Dragoons Rifle Club, and by dinner time he was tired, hot and discouraged. He wanted peace and a good meal; he got squabbling and complaints.

It was Sickles who had asked Charleston's veterans to form the Clubs. He needed their help to deter the potential violence brewing near the docks. Each area of the city had its Club, with its own arsenal guarded twenty-four hours a day by members on eight-hour shifts. The General did not worry about the Club members turning their weapons on him and his men; they were ex-soldiers and gentlemen, and they had all sworn the oath of allegiance required of all defeated citizens of the South.

Not so Julia Ashley. She refused. At least once a week, a Union officer appeared at the Meeting Street house and demanded that she take the oath. Each week, Julia received him in the drawing room, sitting like an Empress in a tall-backed chair, her face like carved ivory. She stared at his lips while he stammered his instructions; then she snapped "No" and stood in dismissal. If the messenger was so foolish as to argue, she left the room without a word.

The charade soon became the talk of the neighborhood. Mary was humiliated because Adam Edwards had asked her to intercede, and she had failed to change her sister's mind. Stuart was ferociously proud of his aunt. He had not been asked to take the oath because he was too young. It galled him; he would have refused, too, even if they hung him for it, he said. And said again, until Pinckney wearily told him to be quiet.

He could not silence the servants the same way. They waylaid him individually, complaining that they had too much work to do, telling tales of the shortcomings of the others, pointing out their need for clothes, for money, for settlement of disputes. Elijah was the worst. His dignity required authority that he did not have over Julia's servants, and his way to retaliate was to disappear for hours, explaining when he returned that he had been at school learning to read. Pinckney had no reason to believe him, but he could not deny the old man the chance to improve himself. And he could not discharge him. Elijah belonged to the Tradds, and he was their responsibility. He had chosen to be loyal to the family; the family had no alternative but to repay that loyalty.

Like Elijah, Shad was absent for many hours without explanation. Pinckney knew that he was working occasionally as a driver of the labor gangs. He disapproved but admitted that he had no right, so he never mentioned it. Nor did he refer to the probability that Shad was spending the money he earned in the brothels on Chalmers Street, now nicknamed "Mulatto Alley." He tried once to warn Shad about the dangers of the pox, but when Shad's pale eyes disappeared into the network of wrinkles around them, he gave up. The sudden springing out of those creases around the eyes was the only indication that Shad was smiling. He kept his mouth closed to hide his crooked, tobacco-stained teeth.

At least Shad was quiet. Pinckney blessed him for it. At the dinner table, he ate his food methodically, taking no part in the arguments that flowed back and forth. It was as if he wasn't even there. When he was not away on his own business, he usually found some work to do in the carriage house or the garden, repairing the old things he found in the attics or patiently clearing away the weeds that Solomon missed. He talked to no one, but chewed his tobacco and spat the juice on the ground near the rose bushes, which thrived on it.

Little Lizzie was another quiet one, but her quiet alarmed Pinckney even more than the noisy conflict of the others in his family. She stayed in her room alone, except for meals and the two trips to church on Sunday, which Pinckney refused to join. At the table, she struggled mightily with her knife and fork under Julia's constant correction, cleaning her plate as she was told. She answered politely when she was spoken to, remembered her curtsy and "thank you" when she was excused. But she was still grotesquely thin, and she flinched when anyone came near her. Pinckney managed to spend a little time with her every day, but he could think of nothing to talk about to a child of five, and Lizzie helped him not at all.

He put off doing anything about it until the Fourth of July ordeal was over. The constant drilling of the Rifle Clubs had been largely in preparation for that day. Sickles had been warned that Daddy Cain was preaching an Independence Day that meant complete independence, wiping out every white in Charleston. The General countered brilliantly, offering an all-day feast at White Point Gardens with fireworks to follow. "Bread and circuses," he said dryly to his staff. "It worked for the Caesars; let's hope it works for the U. S. Army." The Rifle Clubs were posted unobtrusively at the entrances to all the residential streets; Union officers led the parade that opened the festivities and kept a watchful eye on their men and the celebrating throng after the parade was over, breaking up fist fights and shouting matches before they could turn into a riot. It was a grueling long, hot day and night, but it passed peacefully.

And now Pinckney had to present himself for duty at the Dragoons only twice a week. He had time to do something about the friction at home. He joined his mother and aunt on the piazza in the early evening. They were arguing about God, as they so often did, Mary quoting Dr. Edwards and Julia quoting Voltaire. Pinckney declined the invitation to join in. "I'll just have a cigar, if you ladies will permit, and enjoy the breeze." He tilted his chair back against the railing and crossed one long leg over the other, his eyes closed.

The argument lost momentum and died. There was a brief oasis of quiet. Then Mary sniffed. "Your papa used to sit just like that, Pinny. Sometimes we'd come out after supper so that he could smoke, and we'd just sit quiet until good dark. It was very restful . . . I miss him."

"We all do, Mama."

"I wish things could be like they used to be."

"Wishing won't dress those children," Julia snapped. She stood. "I'm going to go turn the collars on Stuart's good shirts."

"Please don't leave, Aunt Julia. I want you ladies to help me with something."

Julia returned to her chair.

"I'm worried about Lizzie. She's so quiet and fearful. It doesn't seem natural to me, but I don't know anything about children. I'm only a man, and you ladies will have to be the experts for me."

Mary fluttered her hands. "I do the best I can, Pinny, but those children just defeat me. What am I supposed to do? Stuart's tutor left even before the War started because he was from Massachusetts. A nice family, too. I had no choice but to let Stuart study with Alex Wentworth. There was no getting anybody, and at least the Wentworths' man was too old to go in the War. I know he's wild. So is Alex. The old man just can't control them."

"I wasn't talking about Stuart, Mama. He's just like any other boy his age. I was talking about Lizzie."

"But Lizzie is a perfect child, no trouble at all."

"That's just it, Mama. She's no trouble so nobody pays any attention to her. She used to be such a happy little thing, and now she's like a scared mouse."

"She's learning how to behave, that's all. Little girls have to be little ladies."

"But Mama, she never leaves her room. That can't be good for her. And she looks so sad."

"She needs a dah, that's all. I asked Sophy to start taking her to the gardens to play, but she doesn't have time. All little children need a dah. I think Lizzie's still grieving for Georgina."

"Nonsense," said Julia. "The child's too old for a dah. She'll be six in November. She needs to go to school. Pinckney, you will have to find the money to send her to Mme. Talvande."

"Julia," said Mary, "I told you that I'm not ready to talk to Mme. Talvande yet. Eleanor Allston is going to open a school in her house, and Lizzie might do better there. Eleanor is a lovely person and a good example."

"Eleanor Allston knows absolutely nothing about teaching. Mme. Talvande has had a school for years. Her accent isn't pure, but at least she is French. A young lady has to learn French in her earliest years."

"I never learned a word, no matter what our Mademoiselle did. I don't see that French is so important."

"That's because you're an imbecile. All civilized people speak French."

"I just don't know . . ."

Pinckney paid no attention. He was thinking about what his mother had said. Of course. Lizzie should have a dah and she should go play with other children her age. No wonder she was sad. She was in a house full of older people. Stuart must seem an adult to her. She was lonely. "Mama," he said, "I will tell Sophy that she is to take Lizzie out every day after dinner. Don't let her talk you around." He felt as if a weight had lifted from his heart.

"Miz Tradd, supper's served," said Elijah from the shadows in the hall.

"Thank you, 'Lijah, we'll be right down." Mary sighed. "I never know what time it is anymore. Do you suppose Saint Michael's bells will ever be back?"

"Ask the Archangel Gabriel. It was his Yankee friends who broke them to bits in Columbia." Julia had found a new, more irritating soubriquet for the Reverend Doctor Edwards. It infuriated her sister. Pinckney hastened to intervene.

"Ladies, ladies. The northern Episcopalians did pay for shipment to England for recasting. We can't blame the Church for the Army."

Mary sobbed like a mourning dove. "I can't bear it when you blaspheme."

"Mama, what I said was hardly blasphemy."

"But Julia . . ."

"Don't bring me into this taradiddle, Mary. I go to service every Sunday as I have all my life. I don't have to like what I find there these days."

"Julia! Dr. Edwards is a truly inspired man."

"Inspired, my foot. How inspired would you find him if he had a hare lip?"

Mary began to cry in earnest. Pinckney put his arm around her plump shoulders. Like many men older and wiser than he, he would do anything to stop a woman's crying. "Don't be upset, Mama," he said desperately. "I'll take you to church next Sunday. Does that make you feel better?"

Beginning the next day, Sophy walked Lizzie the two long blocks to White Point Gardens every afternoon. She was sullen at first, but when she joined the rows of nursemaids sitting on the benches and discovered several old friends, she cheered up immediately. The other women complimented her on Lizzie's appearance in her stiffly starched white pinafore. At the end of the afternoon, Sophy congratulated herself. Unlike the other children, Lizzie was still clean. While they ran and played and fell on the grass under the wide branches of the park's ancient live oaks, Lizzie sat by herself near an oleander bush, making little piles of the leaves and flowers it had dropped. She was no trouble at all.

Pinckney was waiting when they got home. "Did you have a good time, Baby Sister?"

Lizzie nodded mechanically. "Yes, sir."

Pinny's face fell. "Take time Mist' Pinckney, for children to get accustom," Sophy said with authority.

"Yes, I suppose so. Thank you, Sophy." He smiled at Lizzie, who made a smiling face in return. It was a pitiful counterfeit.

Pinckney went to the Ansons'. The house across the street had become a refuge. He was expected to call on Lavinia daily; engaged men always did. Because the term of the engagement was, of necessity, indefinite, the other rules that governed engagements were altered to fit the special circumstances. Pinckney would escort Lavinia to parties, and at home he could sit with her on the settee, holding her hand. But they had a chaperone at all times; Mary Tradd for parties and Lucy Anson at the house. Josiah Anson had produced the formula. "You might not find the means to marry, Pinny; we cannot tell what will happen in this world. You wouldn't want Lavinia to be compromised."

Indeed he would not, Pinckney replied. And meant it with all his heart. He deeply regretted having lost control of himself when he kissed her that first time, and he was grateful that the temptation was removed by their never being alone. Lavinia could have no idea, he thought, of the danger of flirting with him the way she did. She was so beautiful and so trusting, tucking her soft little hand into his and leaning against his shoulder when Lucy's eyes were on the mending she always had with her.

Lucy always looked tired, thought Pinckney. Poor thing. Taking care of Andrew couldn't be an easy job. Pinckney went up to his room every day after his hour with Lavinia and Lucy. Andrew was drinking less, which made him look healthier, but he was more morose than ever without the anesthetic whiskey. Josiah Anson was teaching him the law; a lawyer didn't need to walk. But Andrew was a poor student, and he knew it.

"Hell, Pinny, I never did anything really well except ride a horse and waltz. My tutor had to beat the times tables into my head. What can I do with all these 'whereases' and 'parties of the second part'? I try my damnedest. Lucy coaches me by the hour, and Papa has the patience of a saint, but it's no good."

Pinckney had no answers. Not for Andrew, not for himself. All either of them could do was to get through each day as best he could. Sometimes the "best" was to fall back on the decanter in Andrew's room. At least it helped a man forget. Forget that the land on the Wappoo River had sold for very little money. Forget that the little dwindled to less every day, in spite of scrimping on everything. Forget, most of all, that the time was coming when he would have to sell Carlington.

His heart cried out for Carlington. He dreamed of it, sleeping and waking. But he did not have the courage to travel the short distance to his heart's home. It was too precious to him. Only Shad knew how he felt. He had noticed Pinckney's unwillingness to talk about the plantation when his mother mentioned it. "What's wrong, Cap'n?" he had asked softly. "Fraid old Sherman got it?"

Pinckney blurted out his fears, grateful for the release of being able to tell the silent, unobtrusive younger man.

"If the house is gone," he told Shad, "it will be as if I never existed, or my father or his father before him. The Yankees probably burnt it, but I don't know that. I don't want to know. I need to think that it's there just as it was when Papa and I left to go to Virginia. There's a big difference between understanding that the life we had is gone and knowing it. I have to understand, but I don't have to know. I'm not ready to know."

11

Mary's hands fluttered in the cascade of cobwebby lace at the throat of her gray gown. "Oh, Pinny," she said when he walked into the dining room, "do you think this neckpiece is too frivolous? My, you do look handsome. I hope Stuart won't disgrace us. He's growing like a weed and nothing fits him anymore. I don't want to look worldly. I *feel* meek and humble the way one should for going into God's house, and if I try to take this lace out, the whole bodice may fall apart. It's a very old one, like everything else. Will it be all right, do you think?"

"Fine, Mama."

"After all, I'm not wearing any jewelry. That would be vainglorious." She twittered on. Pinckney felt the ache behind his eyes spread up to the top of his head. He should not have stayed so late with Andrew last night, and they should not have had so much to drink. Most of all, he should never have promised his mother that he would escort her to church.

"It's only seven-thirty, Mary, stop fidgeting." Julia took the chair Elijah pulled out for her. She was followed by Stuart and Lizzie, who took their places quietly. Stuart was glum, Lizzie pale and withdrawn. Shad's place was set, but he did not appear. Pinny explained that he had left the house early on an errand of his own.

Mary's agitation sped them through breakfast. By seven forty-five, the family was already walking the block and a half to Saint Michael's. Mary led the procession, her hand proudly on her son's left arm. He did look splendid. Dilcey's meals had filled out his body so that his gray frock coat and black weskit hung properly from his broad shoulders to trim waist. His right sleeve looked normal with the clever artificial arm and gloved hand that Solomon had made, cradled in a black-silk sling.

As always, there was a crowd in the porch of the church, exchanging greetings before entering. Pinckney ushered his mother to the Tradds' pew and opened the door for her. While Lizzie and Stuart filed in, Mary held a whispered conference with Julia. "Come on, Pinny," his aunt said audibly, "you follow me and let your mother sit next the aisle." Mary's face assumed a saintly expression; she waited until her son entered before her. Then she stepped into the square box pew and sank gracefully onto the petit point prayer stool. Pinckney reached across her bent head and closed the door.

The organ thumped, then emitted the first note of the processional hymn. Everyone rose. Pinny heard the Reverend Adam Edwards' voice from the back of the church. It was deep, rich and loud, soaring over the voices of the choir and the notes of the organ. When the cross passed, he bowed his head and looked backward. Edwards was magnificent. The full white surplice fell from his arms like the wings of an angel. His hair was equally full and white. It swept back from what could only be called a noble forehead above a large face with wide cheekbones, a prominent thin nose as straight as a ruler, and a closely shaven square jaw with a deep cleft in the chin. Pinckney faced forward again. He did not dare meet his aunt's eye for fear he might laugh. She had not exaggerated. A soft rustle of silk skirts swept after Edwards' figure when the ladies in the congregation turned, drawn as if by a magnetic lode.

When the hymn was over, Adam's voice rang from the pulpit even before everyone was seated. "The sacrifices of God," he shouted, "are a broken spirit: a broken and a contrite heart, O God, thou wilt not despise." Then, he lifted his arm, looking up as if into the heavens. The people knelt. He waited, they waited, until there was no sound of settling bodies or clothing. Silence stretched, taut. And then the golden voice poured down on their bent heads. "Dearly beloved brethren," the words were like a caress, "the Scripture moveth us in sundry places," the rhythm mounted, "to acknowledge and confess our manifold sins and wickedness." Pinckney felt the vibration of the words throughout the whole of his own body. It was an experience he had known only once before, when he had heard Patti sing *Lakme* in London. He had come with a mixture of curiosity and amusement about Edwards. All that was now forgotten; he was spellbound. He chanted with the people around him, following the lead of Adam's commanding voice. ". . . We have followed too much the devices of our own hearts. We have offended against thy holy laws . . ." The familiar service continued, transformed. It was as if it were new-minted by Edwards. When he opened the Bible on the lectern before him, every face turned upward, waiting.

In the pew nearest the lectern, Prudence Edwards tilted her head as if she were looking intently at her father's profile. She liked sitting there, because the overhanging gallery created a strange acoustic dead spot; she could hear only every tenth word. Her father's astounding voice held no marvels for her; she had heard it every day of her life. She looked from the corner of her eye at the congregation. As always they were mesmerized. It was safe for her to turn her head a fraction to look for the woman. Yes, there she was. Nothing had changed. The thin woman with the arrogant face was obviously bored. In all the years and all the churches, she was the only woman who had not been drawn into Adam Edwards' spell. Prudence's heart lifted. Each Sunday she worried that this woman would be like all the rest. There had been others, in other churches, immune at first but eventually succumbing.

She noticed something different. The girl and the boy were with the woman as usual. Prudence liked to watch the way the sun, rising higher during the service, would eventually send a ray slanting through the clerestory onto those copper-gold heads. Today there was a taller head with them, already touched with an aureole. She forgot her caution and turned her head too far so that she could see better. Her father's hand lifted, calling her back to attention. But not before she filled her mind with the beautiful head and face of the man with the halo. She followed the service automatically, making the responses and singing the hymns without conscious effort. Outwardly, she appeared totally concentrated. In fact, she was counting the moments until the end. When the recessional reached the midpoint of the aisle, she could slip out the side door, run through the graveyard and stand in the shadow of one of the entrance pillars to watch the people leave. If they all stopped to talk, and they always did, she might hear the man speak; perhaps he would even smile. He looked as if he hadn't smiled for too long a time.

Shad's absence that Sunday was not because of a casual restlessness. Nor were his many previous absences. He had not been in the Tradd house for many weeks before he understood as a certainty that something outside Pinckney's experience was needed. He set out to identify it, find it and get it.

He was a silent person, both outwardly and inwardly. Without education, he had no words to express himself to others or to formulate his thinking. He had, instead, an unconscious sensitivity to the atmosphere surrounding him and unexamined emotions that were stronger for being unquestioned. He was, therefore, incapable of expressing his gratitude for Pinckney's championship and for the home he had been given. Nor did he question that it was up to him to protect that home for Pinckney. He never doubted that he could do it. He sensed that the ruthlessness he had learned in order to survive the brutality of his early life would be the current coin in the chaotic post-War South. As soon as the major repairs on the Meeting Street house were completed, he began to wander about the city, scenting the currents, observing the actors, until he located his field of operations; then he moved in.

The Charleston Hotel was the biggest building he had ever seen. It stretched for a full city block and was three stories tall. On each level, wide porches laid with green and yellow marble squares ran from the huge Doric columns to the twenty-foot-tall arched doors and windows of the hotel. The facade was a gleaming white, painted by Sickles' troops for the Fort Sumter celebration. The sides and back were still scarred from shell damage. The original brick shouted through scabrous white paint.

Almost daily, Shad sauntered into the cavernous, ill-lit lobby. All around the edges, groups of men were talking, some in conspiratorial undertones, others in stentorian braggadoccio. This was the center of business in the city now. The hotel housed the influx of predators whom history would call "carpetbaggers." The lobby was their communal office. Throughout the day and evening, groups formed, split, shifted and regrouped. Through the huge, open front doors, men came and went, many in uniform.

Shad wandered, without apparent purpose, among the shadows near the men. He wore cut-down, threadbare pants and shirt and a faintly dim-witted expression. His pale eyes moved aimlessly, seemingly awestruck by the magnificent setting and self-important inhabitants.

But there was nothing aimless about him. His eyes and ears took in everything and everyone, recording faces, voices, meetings, handshakes, conversations.

"Railroads, that's where the money is," a bent, heavily bearded man shouted to the circle around him. "There's three ready to fall like ripe fruit soon as these Charlestonians feel the pinch some more. The tracks are gone; the right-of-way will sell for a song."

"And you're just the man to write the tune, eh?" his cohorts guffawed. Shad moved on.

". . . so Al, he gets the contract to supply the schoolbooks to all the Bureau schools. The Senator, he makes a big splash talking about how many grateful pickaninnies are reading Shakespeare, the Congress votes the money, then a couple hundred old McGuffeys net Al more than a hundred thousand."

"How much did he have to give the Senator?"

"Not a nickel." The narrator winked. "But somebody sent his wife a new buggy with a pair of bays in silver-plated harness." Shad slid away.

". . . get cotton land for a dollar an acre soon as the tax bills go out. Hire some poor whites to farm it. Cotton's going to go sky high . . . You're crazy. The money's in factoring, not owning . . . Souvenirs are bringing top dollar in New York. Anything with a rebel flag or a coat of arms, makes no difference, long's it's Old South. You can buy the coat of arms for a penny on the dollar. They're not hungry enough yet to sell the flags, but the day will come . . . I hear Harry's got a deal working to supply lumber to rebuild four warehouses . . . Naw, that's going to old

Ardsley. Harry's got the bricks . . . Say, anybody got any pipeline into Sickles' office? I need to know if that adjutant can be bought . . ." Shad joined the exodus. He never stayed very long; he did not want to be noticed.

After a month, he knew more about the deals being made than the men who made them. After two months, he had identified the few who could be trusted—up to a point. Then he was ready to become actor instead of spectator.

He got Pansy to alter the linen suit Pinckney had given him, and on the Sunday that Pinckney took his mother to church, Shad borrowed his watch and chain, took a walking stick from the coatstand and made his debut as a businessman.

His back-country twang made the man he approached smile and turn away. Shad kept talking. Soon the man turned back. "Did you say 'Tradd'? Like 'Tradd Street' Tradd?"

"You heard me. And every other nabob in Charleston."

"How can you get to them?"

"That's no matter to you, mister. Long's I deliver."

"Let's go into the dining room, son. Look's like you could use a good meal."

"I ain't your son, so don't call me that. But I ain't too proud to eat your food."

Shad left with a full belly and a pocketful of peppermints for Lizzie. He also had a deal.

Behind him, his host shifted the toothpick in his mouth. Goddamn, he thought, he's a better deal-maker than I am. And I don't believe he's even started shaving yet.

When Shad got home, he returned Pinckney's watch, then reported what he had done. "Cap'n, your Charleston friends have been sending their niggers to sell things so they can buy food. They'se getting robbed. I lined up a fellow who'll give the best price going."

Pinckney was furious. He bit back the words on his tongue and turned his back to get himself under control. Then he heard what Shad was saying and slowly turned again. His shoulders hunched with his head hanging between them. He hated the truth of what Shad was saying.

"Somebody's got to do business with them. I ain't from Charleston, so I got no pride to save. It ain't like you'd be doing it. All you got to do is help your own kind. They give the stuff to you, you to me, and I do the selling. For gold. I can't read or write, Cap'n, but I can count. Nobody's going to get cheated.

"It's already started, Cap'n. Little things, silver spoons and bowls and such. You saw that auction place. It's still going strong. People need money. You want them cheated worse than they have to be?"

Pinckney nodded his head. "You're right, Shad. And I should be grateful. It's just—so sad." He blinked. "I think I'm crying."

This time it was Shad who turned away. "I got to put this suit away," he said. He decided not to tell Pinckney now about the commission they would earn.

12

For the rest of the summer, they did business in a small way. Pinckney discussed it with Josiah Anson first. He agreed totally with Shad and set up record books for the enterprise. "I'll keep them for you until that left hand can manage a pen, son. And I'll charge you for the service. You've got to learn that a man's time is worth money, same as a man's rice. What you're doing is a service, too, just as much as my keeping your books is a service. There's no shame in getting paid for it. Now, I happen to know that Eleanor Allston needs money to buy desks for her school. She was talking about mortgaging the house. She'd be a damn sight better off selling that monstrosity of a marble nymph in the garden. It's naked, too; should appeal to a certain type of art collector. Go see her. And take the commission that boy must be collecting for you. Where did you find him, anyhow?"

And to his godfather alone, Pinckney told the full story of Shad, his attachment and how he had killed the Yankee who shot from ambush and half-severed Pinckney's arm. "He used a knife he carried in his coat. Another shot would have called attention to us. Then he tore his coat to make a tourniquet and carried me on his back until we were away from the enemy lines. I hardly remember the rest. He built a fire and put the knife in it, knocked me out with a sock to the jaw, and the next thing I knew I was in the medical tent with a clean bandage on a clean stump. I'm a head taller and twenty pounds heavier, and he must have hauled me close to five miles. He won't let me thank him."

"So you brought him home."

"No, he brought me home. I was pretty weak. I wish I knew what I could do to repay him."

"Pinny, there's no payment for a man's life. The only thing you can do is what you're doing. Give him a home, because it sounds like he never had one. And if you're really generous, let him take care of you some. He's a man who needs to be taking care of somebody. He can't be much more than sixteen, but he's a man who never was a boy, I guess. I'd be proud to be his friend if he'd let me."

"That's an honor, Cousin Josiah. I'll tell him."

"Better not. There's nobody touchier than a poor white. I saw that in the circuit courts plenty of times. You just let your friend Shad have all the room and all the time he wants. Maybe one day he'll be able to receive as well as give. Now get on down the street to Eleanor's. She's been worrying herself sick about money."

Pinckney saw Mrs. Allston that day and other old friends whom Josiah Anson recommended at the rate of two or three a week. He also accepted the money Shad brought him with as good grace as he could manage.

He could not keep his activities a secret. Charleston was too small for word not to get back to his family. He told his mother, his face pale and his manner defensive, after his visit to Mrs. Allston, whom he did not name. He was astonished by her reaction. Mary clapped her hands and smiled broadly at him and at Shad.

"What a good idea. I must have something around here that the Yankees didn't get. Then we can buy Lizzie and Stuart some things. They're practically barefoot now. I can't believe how fast their feet grow. I didn't dare mention it before because you've been so cranky, Pinny. Now let me think. There's the big silver punchbowl that your father used to call 'the bathtub.' It's in the roof of the carriage house. It's hideous, but it's very valuable. Your great grandmother Marshall used it when they entertained Lafayette."

Shad cleared his throat. "No offense, ma'am, but there's enough silver for sale to pave the streets with. If you happened to have anything kind of sparkly, I know just the customer for it."

"You mean jewels. Oh, dear. My jewel case was stolen in Columbia."

Shad shrugged. "Well, that's that. Maybe if I said the punchbowl *was* a bathtub. Is there any engraving on it?"

Pinckney interrupted. "What were you doing in Columbia, Mama? Don't tell me you evacuated there. You never mentioned anything."

"I don't want to talk about it, Pinckney. It was too horrible. Let's talk about something nice." Her smile was almost natural.

Shad stared incredulously at Pinckney's mother. There must be more courage to her than a person could see. Or else she was the silliest woman God ever made. Not to think to mention it. Everyone in the South knew about Columbia. Of all the horrors of Sherman's war on civilians, the death of Columbia was the most bestial. He accepted the surrender of the city from the mayor in a formal, dignified ceremony, then withdrew with his honor guard to the place outside the city where the Army had set up camp. Three hours later, Union soldiers stationed around the edge used kerosene to start a ring of fire. There was no escape. If a break in the circle occurred, new fires were started. The smoke darkened the skies early, adding to the terror of the thousands who discovered they were trapped in the city. When night came, the flames lit the streets where the panicked crowds ran, screaming, trampling the weak who fell in the rush. The circle narrowed in leaps, cutting off the old and the injured who could not move fast enough. The lucky ones ended up huddled desperately in the wide park in the center of the city. They used hats, bonnets, boots and shoes to dip water from the lake in the park which they poured on themselves to put out falling brands of fire. Embers still glowed two days later when the soot-stained survivors straggled out of the ruined capital city of South Carolina. No one would ever forget Columbia.

Shad looked again at Mary Tradd; he felt the effort she was making to keep from breaking down. She don't want the Cap'n to see the scars, he thought, and a new respect for this spoiled, childlike woman was added to his store of impressions. "Where's that bowl at?" he said to break the taut silence.

"You have to climb up in the roof. Stuart did it, of course. He's always been like a monkey that boy. Oh! Wait a second. What luck. I just remembered. Stuart. Where's Stuart? He put my wedding necklace in a hole way up in the pecan tree where he had his tree house. Remember that tree house, Pinny? That you and Andrew had your club in when you were little. Stuart fixed it all up, he and Alex Wentworth. Then, when we had to move up to Julia's, he took it down so the Yankees couldn't climb the tree. I thought it was real clever of him. He'd put my necklace up there, you see. Julia always criticized my necklace. I didn't dare take it to her house. She was always so jealous that your papa fell in love with me." She discovered that she was talking to the air. Pinny and Shad were already in the yard, shouting for Stuart and looking up at the high limbs of the tree.

Stuart shinnied up to the highest branches and threw three padded chamois pouches down to Shad who turned them over to Pinckney. "Better take these to your mama," he said, "I'll watch out for Stuart."

"Good work," he said to the boy when he reached the ground.

"You don't know how good. I knew how forgetful Mama is, so I put a bunch of her other stuff up there when I hid the necklace. Let's go look."

"In a minute. Say, I just heard you was in Columbia, is that so?"

"Is it? I'll say. Let me tell you—" Stuart started a minute-by-minute account of his experiences. He had found a pistol and was going to kill some Yankees, but it was unloaded. Still, he had managed some genuine heroics while protecting his mother in their scramble for safety. He was not reluctant to tell about them.

"Was the baby there, too?"

"Lizzie? She nearly got us all killed. When we ran out of Cousin Eulalie's house, Lizzie forgot her silly old stuffed bear. Halfway to the park, she started screaming for it. She wanted to go back, and she was pulling on Mama one way while I was pulling the other. That was bad enough; Georgina picked her up and carried her, crying and kicking, so we kept going. Then we got separated, and Mama started screaming for Lizzie. I had a time, I'll tell you."

"But you all made it, that's what counts. How did you find Georgina?"

"We never did. Mama figures she died in the fire, but I'll bet she just hid. Mama would have killed her for losing Lizzie."

"She left her?"

"She must have. We didn't see Lizzie again until we were waiting at the depot for the train the Yankees lent for everybody to leave in. She was with the Hutchinson ladies. They had seen her wandering around, calling for that dumb bear, and they grabbed her up. Boy, was Mama mad. She had been half crazy with worry. Lizzie was always running away, you know, any time she didn't get her way. Mama spanked her right there in the depot. I'll bet you Lizzie never runs away again."

Shad thought about the silent little girl. "No, I don't think she will."

Mary was waltzing around the dining room table when they entered the house. She held her arms out to catch the sunlight in the diamonds and rubies of the bracelets and rings on both wrists and hands. Long diamond earrings swayed next to her neck. And circling it was a dazzle of brilliance that made Shad's eyes blink.

The necklace was a cascade of diamonds; row after row of matched stones tapered down to a point low on the bodice of Mary's dull gray dress. An enormous single diamond, cut in a pear shape, dangled from the point, lying heavily between her full breasts. Pinckney was grinning. "Mama, it really staggers the imagination. What was Papa thinking of?"

Mary stopped whirling. Her wide bell skirt continued to sway around her. She put her glittering hands over her face to cover the blush that stained her cheeks, and giggled. "He was thinking something very naughty that I won't tell you. He said sometimes even vulgarity had its place. It was his private wedding present to me. He gave me pearls to show other people as his gift."

"I think our money problems are solved," said Pinckney. "Shad's businessman will never find anything gaudier in a million years."

Shad looked at their laughing faces without comprehension. He thought the necklace the most beautiful thing in the world.

It took some time for Shad to negotiate the sale of Mary Tradd's jewels. He kept competing bidders on tenterhooks of waiting until his instinct told him they had reached their limits of patience and money. He realized a small fortune, for the hardship conditions under which he was working.

When he poured the gold coins onto the table in the dining room, Pinckney was overwhelmed. Carlington was saved. "My God, Shad, we can live like kings," he said. "New shoes for all of us. A bonnet for Mama to wear to church that will capture the elusive Dr. Edwards' eye and heart and maybe even a horse. Solomon can polish up the buggy, and we can go out in style."

"Cap'n—they's going to be taxes coming up. You might better think about keeping the house 'stead of keeping a horse."

Pinckney clapped him on the shoulder. "I'm so relieved to have this gold I'm not even angry at you for being right. We'll just buy what we have to have and save the rest for the rainy day that's bound to come . . . what's this?" He took the box Shad was holding out to him and eyed the lumpy paper-wrapped parcel Shad put on the table.

"It's something you and me both need."

Pinny lifted the top to reveal a stack of schoolroom slates and a box of chalk. Under them he could see an alphabet book. "You told me Mr. Anson said you should work on writing with your left hand. I was hoping you'd show me how, too. I mean to get me some learning."

Pinny was too touched to speak. He looked mutely at Shad, who avoided his eyes.

Instead, he went on talking as if nothing had happened. "I brung a present for the baby, too. You give it to her, Cap'n." He unwrapped the parcel on the table. A plump stuffed bear stared up at them from its black shoe-button eyes. Pinny found his voice.

"How kind of you, Shad. You thought of it; you give it to her. She hasn't had a new toy for a very long time."

"It'd be better coming from you. She don't hardly know me, and she's such a shy little critter I don't want to scare her."

Pinny picked up the toy. "Perhaps you're right," he said, "but you should get credit. Come along, we'll both go find her." A toy, he thought, starting up the stairs. If I believed a toy would make her happy, I'd sell this house and everything in it to buy all the toys in creation. Still, Shad means well. He's an odd, silent sort, almost as shy as Lizzie. Hope he doesn't take it hard when she doesn't react. She's like a little puppet, making all the motions she's supposed to, but made of wood. It's hard, her losing Georgina. I hope to God she gets over it soon. He knocked gently on Lizzie's door then opened it, hiding the toy behind his back. Shad followed him into the room.

She was sitting in her little rocking chair near the window. The staves creaked as she moved rhythmically back and forth. Pinckney knew that the meter never changed. He heard the steady creak, creak every time he came upstairs to his own room. "Hello, Lizzie," he said. "Shad brought you a wonderful present." Lizzie put her feet neatly side by side on the floor and stood up. "Thank you, Mr. Simmons," she said, then she curtsied and stood quietly.

"Come now, Lizzie, doesn't he get a smile?"

She moved her face obediently, stretching her mouth upward. But her eyes were dull. Pinckney had the familiar sensation of desperation that came with his daily attempts to reach his little sister. "Don't you want to know what it is? Look." He swung the animal from its hiding place with a flourish. Please God, he thought, let her remember to smile again. He forced a smile on his own face as a model for her. Then his mouth dropped open in amazement. Lizzie was running to him, her arms stretched out, her eyes bright and alive.

"Bear!" she shouted. Pinckney kneeled just in time to receive the embrace that hugged him and the toy. Lizzie sat on the floor with a thump and clutched the bear to her shoulder. She laughed joyfully and began to kiss it. Then she held it away from her and frowned, first at the toy, then at Pinny.

"This isn't Bear," she said.

Pinckney shook his head in confusion. First the laughter, now anger. At least she was reacting, but what had gone wrong?

Shad sat down near the door. "Oh, that's Bear, all right," he said, "leastways, he claims that's his name. Stopped me on the street he did, bold as brass. Said he'd been on a trip, working in a circus. Folks gave him so much candy to eat, he got kinda fat. But he got a fancy new coat to fit him, and then he looked so fine he decided to come home and show off. Thinks a lot of himself, that Bear does." He looked at Lizzie. His face was grave.

She looked at the toy, then at Pinckney. "He's making that up." Her voice was flat. Pinckney tried smiling.

Lizzie glared at him, then at Shad. "You made that up."

For a long moment, their direct stares met. Neither moved a muscle. Then Shad spoke. "That's up to you, missy. Do you want it to be a made-up story?"

Lizzie's eyebrows came together as she thought. Her gaze was still locked with Shad's. Pinckney held his breath. He knew something important was happening. Then Lizzie's brow unknotted. "No," she said. She held the bear and shook it. "You won't get any candy here," she shouted, "you greedy old fat Bear, you." Then she wrapped her arms around it and buried her face in its woolen neck.

Shad stood up and crooked his finger at Pinckney. They tiptoed out of the room.

When they were halfway down the stairs, Lizzie's face appeared over the banister railing above them. Bear's head was next to hers. "Mr. Simmons," she whispered. Shad and Pinckney looked up. "I have a loose tooth," she said. She grinned and wiggled one of the tiny teeth with her tongue. Then she and Bear disappeared.

"I need a drink," Pinckney muttered. He led the way to the library.

"What happened up there, Shad?"

"Some good luck, that's all. Stuart mentioned that the baby had lost her stuffed bear in that mess in Columbia and took it hard. I always noticed younguns seem to get specially attached to some one play toy. Figured maybe she missed that bear more than the nigger you worried about. Damn black bitch. Leaving a little baby like that when hell's burning all around her."

Pinny's face told him that he hadn't known. Shad touched his hand. "No sense brooding. Only God knows what that little girl went through that night, Cap'n, and there's no way to change it now." He downed his whiskey and held out his glass. "I could use a partner to that." Pinckney went to fill it.

Behind him, Shad chuckled. "She's a smart one, that Lizzie. She knew that wasn't the bear she lost, but she decided to tell herself it was. Thought it over, then made up her mind. I admire a person that faces facts."

Pinny gave him his glass. "I'm grateful to you, Shad."

"No need."

Pinckney lifted his own glass in unacknowledged salute, and both men drank.

13

Shad's inspired gift-giving marked a turning point in Lizzie's life. She was still very quiet and overly polite with everyone in the family, but she seemed to regard Shad as another child, and she offered a wary friendship to him even though she did not establish any contact with the children at the Gardens. Pinckney was happy to see her coming out of the frightening shell she had been in, but he was, he admitted to himself, jealous that she was not as free with him.

It was an accident that provided him the way to get a little closer to Lizzie. In August, the seasonal thunderstorms sent the children and nurses running home early from the Gardens. One day, Sophy looked at the sky and decided not to go at all. Lizzie, at loose ends, surprised Pinckney and Shad at the secret work they did while the ladies were napping and Stuart was at his Club and Lizzie out with Sophy. Pinny was teaching Shad his letters and practicing writing with his left hand. "Oh, Pinny," she squealed. "Me, too, Pinny, please, let me, too." In her excitement she actually touched his arm. It was the first contact she had made since the dramatic entrance of Bear.

Wordlessly, Shad offered her a slate. "This here is a C," he said to no one in particular. "Shouldn't take some folks long to catch up to me." Lizzie sighed happily.

"Pinny can teach me real fast," she said. "Pinny's the smartest person in the whole world."

Unfortunately for Pinckney, he was not smart enough to extricate himself from the web of feminine intrigue his mother was spinning. It had not taken long for Julia's sharp eye to notice Prudence Edwards' covert interest in Pinckney, and she did not miss the opportunity to taunt her sister about her son's allure for the Edwards family. Mary went to work at once.

It was common knowledge that the Edwards girl behaved outrageously even for a Yankee. She did not wear hoop skirts or stays, and she walked with long strides like a boy so that one could actually see that her legs were moving. Furthermore, she walked alone, unchaperoned, the block from the rectory to the South Carolina Hall where she taught at the black school. And she walked back home again, alone. It was a situation ripe for exploitation.

The first time, Pinckney did not know that the meeting was not accidental. His mother asked him to escort her to Dr. Trott's pharmacy on Broad Street so that she could examine a new kind of smelling salt that Sally Brewton had recommended. When he helped her down the step from the front door, she moved very slowly, saying that she had caught her heel in the hem of her dress. Somehow it righted itself just as Prudence Edwards emerged from the portico next door. Mary ran up to her and chattered charmingly for a minute, then introduced Pinckney. "You must let us escort you home, Miss Edwards. There's no telling what ruffians are on the streets." And, naturally, when they reached the rectory, Miss Edwards invited them in for tea. She and her father took their tea at very odd hours, she said. Mary accepted instantly. "It would be terribly rude to refuse," she whispered to Pinckney while Prudence was bringing her father from his study.

A miserable half hour followed for Pinckney. His mother and Dr. Edwards talked seriously about the deplorable condition of the choir's robes while Prudence looked fixedly at her hands in her lap and he attempted not to fidget.

The next time it happened, he glared furiously at Mary when she agreed to have tea and at both Edwardses while he was in their house. Dr. Edwards seemed oblivious. Prudence returned a malevolent stare. "This won't do, Mama," Pinckney said sternly when they were walking home. "You are being obvious. It embarrasses me, and it puts a burden on Miss Edwards. Clearly, she doesn't like having the Tradds as guests."

Mary pouted, accused him of disrespect, and changed her tactics. As a woman, she knew the real meaning of Prudence Edwards' display of hostility. "She's absolutely mad about Pinny," she confided to her friend Caroline Wragg. "It's as plain as day. I've already sent her a note saying that she should stop over at the house after school whenever the weather is too bad for her to get home. And you know very well, Caroline, that it storms every day."

"Mary, that's not only devious and unladylike, it's also dim-witted. You don't want to see the daughter."

"Her papa will call for her. You'll see. The girl has a crafty look about her. She can recognize a bargain when one comes her way."

"But what about poor Pinny? You're throwing him into her clutches."

"Oh, piffle, Pinny's all right. He's engaged to Lavinia. The Edwards girl can mope after him all she pleases; it won't do her any good."

"And you call yourself a Christian! It's shocking."

"What's shocking is that a man of God has been here for six months, and not one soul in his congregation has opened a door to him. Even the vestrymen cut him once he's outside the church."

"That's the men. There are plenty of ladies who'd open their doors quick enough."

"But they can't. Even I couldn't give him a cup of tea without a man from the family there. It should be very comforting to the poor man to have a little sociability in his life."

And thus it turned out. Adam Edwards had found life in Charleston very lonely. He was accustomed to the usual way of life for a prominent clergyman, where his presence was expected at every major social occasion and was sought after for dinners, teas and even all-male shooting parties. In addition, he had been a leading figure among the abolitionists of New England, with a constant demand for his speeches at meetings and rallies. His harsh religious sentiments were sincere and his sense of calling genuine. Mary Tradd's piety gave him a warm feeling of fulfillment in his difficult duties in alien, hostile territory. Her soft voice and chirruping solicitude warmed him, too. She was an extremely comfortable little lady.

Soon the Edwardses were guests for tea every Tuesday and Friday, regardless of the weather. Pinckney complained bitterly at his required attendance. Mary cried. Pinckney was there.

His manners were faultless, so he was attentive to the conversation, which usually consisted of a series of monologues in Adam Edwards' glorious voice. Prudence contributed little. Pinckney was used to girls who chattered and made a man feel important. Prudence Edwards made him feel peculiar.

Mary glowed. She also hummed when she bustled around getting ready to receive her guests. It made Julia more sour than ever. She refused acquaintance with the Edwardses as contemptuously as she refused the oath.

"Damn," Pinckney muttered. It was the first sound, other than the click-screech of chalk on slate, that had broken the silence in the dining room for a long time.

Lizzie and Shad looked up from their work. "Sorry," said Pinckney. "I broke my chalk." He flexed his cramped fingers. "I think I'll call it a day." He pushed away from the table, almost upsetting his chair, and left, slamming the door behind him.

Lizzie's little fingers closed more tightly around her chalk. She concentrated fiercely on the uneven rows of W's she was making. Her hand was shaking.

Shad looked up at the chandelier, lit against the darkness of the rainstorm outside. The gas service had been restored and the bright light was cruel to the glued repairs and dusty prisms of the once magnificent crystal confection. "Ever tried writing with your left hand? It's mighty hard." The words drawled slowly. Lizzie kept working. "Course, I have a mighty hard time writing with my right hand because I never had no learning. You ain't no bigger'n June bug, but you write better'n me already."

Lizzie stopped writing. "You're making that up," she mumbled, eyes on her letters.

"No I ain't. Look here." Shad held out his slate. The little girl peered suspiciously at it. A melange of V's, M's and W's crowded the smudged surface.

"You got three," she exclaimed.

"Three what?"

"Three different letters."

"Those ain't W's?"

"Not all of them. Those are." She touched them with her index finger. Her hand had stopped shaking.

"How about that one?" He indicated an M. "Same, only turned round. What's wrong with that? Upend the slate, you'll see what I mean."

Lizzie turned the slate. Her eyes widened. Then her eyebrows moved together in a frown of concentration. "I'll have to think about it," she announced. Shad waited. The sound of tree toads came through the window.

"I know!" She looked into his face with a gap-tooth smile of delight. "See here, the ones you had wrong before are right now, but that makes the ones you had right before wrong now. It's only a W if you make it right and leave it that way. Otherwise it's a M, no matter what you think."

Shad made a humming noise and scratched his nose. Lizzie stared anxiously at him. Finally, his eyes crinkled. "I'll be! You're right, missy. I get it."

Lizzie beamed. Then she tugged at his sleeve. Her big eyes were sparkling with mischief. "If you don't stand on your head," she said, collapsing into giggles.

Shad watched her fondly. He never questioned his affection for the little girl or wondered why the pale, frightened figure in the shadows had touched his heart at first meeting. He was satisfied that the growing bond between them existed, that the child was beginning to trust him even though she still feared her own brothers and mother, without cause. Her terror of Julia was completely understandable to him; he was terrified of her, too.

"Mr. Simmons?"

"What is it, baby?"

"Why's Pinny so mad at me?"

"He ain't mad at you, honey. He's mad at the Yankee what shot off his arm. Now he's got to start all over learning things with the other one. Not just writing, but everyday things like eating and getting dressed and turning the pages in the newspaper."

"He can still read, though."

"Oh, yes. You don't need arms to read."

"Can you read?"

"No, I can't. I count on you to learn it to me."

"Me? That's silly. I can't read. Just picture books because I make up the stories." In fact, Lizzie spent most of her time now in a shaded corner of the downstairs piazza, turning the pages of a book that Stuart had scornfully discarded. Bear sat on her lap, listening with bright eyes to her hushed voice while she "read."

"But you'll be going to school soon, and they'll learn you there. Then you can learn me."

"I suppose. You really want me to?"

"I'd be real obliged."

"Then I will." She clapped her hands. "We can play I'm the teacher and you and Bear are the children. I might make you stand in the corner. Teachers do that." She smiled wickedly.

Shad showed alarm. Lizzie chortled. Then her face darkened. "Mr. Simmons?"

"Hm?"

"I don't especially want to go to school."

"Why's that, baby?"

"It's awful crowded. Lots of people."

Shad longed to take her thin hand in his big warm one, but he had observed her fear of being touched. He chose his words carefully. "They don't mean no harm, Lizzie. If somebody bumps you, it's only because they didn't look where they was going. Ain't nobody going to hurt you."

She was obviously unconvinced.

"Another thing, baby, a big grown-up thing, is this. Every single soul has got to do things he don't want to do. When I went to Virginny, I didn't want to go. I was scared half to death. But I had to. Now it's over, I see it wasn't no joyride, but it wasn't so bad as I thought it was going to be."

"You were scared?"

"Half to death. Everybody has things they're scared of."

"Even Pinny?"

Shad's voice was sorrowful. "Even Pinny."

Lizzie's face took on its thinking look. Shad waited. At last, she spoke firmly. "It doesn't show. I can do that, I think. I can go to school and not show."

"Shoot, baby, sure you can. You do anything you put your mind to."

After much dithering, Mary decided to send Lizzie to Mrs. Allston's school. "After all," she said, "she does have a French lady, even though I don't know who she is. And say what you will, Eleanor Allston is family. Her grandmother's sister married a Pinckney. In times like these, that's all you can depend on."

A week later, she crowed triumphantly over Julia. Mme. Talvande's was closed. "Can you imagine?" Mary said, with delighted horror, "General Sickles put up the notice himself. Madame refused to let his daughter enroll, and he closed the whole school. I don't know what Caroline Wragg is going to do. Eleanor Allston won't have room for little Caroline."

But Mrs. Allston found room for Caroline. And also for the Sickles child. Mary Tradd descended upon her in a rage. "Eleanor, I cannot believe what people are saying. I thought I could depend on you. How *can* you let that man force his daughter in? To mingle with Charleston girls! The day that girl sets foot in your door, I'm going to withdraw my Lizzie."

The elegant, tired widow looked stern. "Stop, and think for once in your life, Mary. Whatever the Yankees may have done, we are not the kind of people who make war on children."

Mary attempted argument, but Mrs. Allston cut her off. "I shall miss having Lizzie," she said. Mary backed down. When she arrived home, she quoted Eleanor Allston as if the thought had been her own, adding her comments.

"We don't make war on children. Only a Yankee would burn Columbia. Poor Mme. Talvande, you can't expect her to understand. She's not from Charleston."

"Only since eighteen-five," Julia commented.

Mary pretended she hadn't heard. She went to talk to Sophy about Lizzie's dresses. If the hems couldn't be let down again, she'd have to find some things of her own to cut down. School started October the first, and that was only a week away.

14

"Stupid fools!" Pinckney crumpled the newspaper in his fist.

Julia muttered "redundant" and went on with her sewing.

"What is it, Pinny?"

"Politics, Mama, you wouldn't be interested."

"Oh." His answer satisfied Mary. "I'm sorry, dear. Why don't you talk it over with Andrew? You men understand those things so much better."

Her perpetual cooing was more than Pinckney could bear. He left the room. Shad gave him a few minutes then joined him on the piazza. "Smoke, Cap'n?" Pinny took the cigar, growled a thanks.

"So you know what happened? It'll ruin us."

"Yep." Shad had known it was coming; he had been listening to the talk of the men involved. The military government had allowed the state legislature to reopen, with a group of South Carolinians who were sure to do precisely what the newspaper reported. With fervid oratory, they had passed a series of laws, the "Black Code," outlawing voting by Negroes and setting up separate courts and laws for black and white.

"What next, Shad? You always know."

"There'll be a new bunch in Columbia. And the only ones born in South Carolina will be black show pieces. The ones who'll really be running things are at the Hotel. They been packed and ready to go all week."

His forecast was accurate, as always. Within a week, an Army Colonel had replaced James Orr, the provisional governor. Before the end of October, new legislators had been elected, two thirds of them black. Most of the whites were former agents of the Freedmen's Bureau. Radical Reconstruction had come in.

The official forms used by the Military Government were sent out in flimsy yellow envelopes. On the first Monday in November, uniformed brigades marched through every street, halted, and stood at attention while junior officers delivered the Notice of Property Assessments and

Taxes Due announcements, neatly folded inside their canary coverings. Charlestonians had until the end of the month to pay.

On Tuesday, the speculators came. In person, if they could get past whoever opened the door to their knocks; if not in person, then by a note under the door or by shouted harangues from the sidewalk. They would help the widows, the orphaned, the wounded who had managed to get home. They would buy the house for a hundred, three hundred, five hundred dollars. Then they would be responsible for the taxes, not the penniless owner.

"Vultures!" Julia snorted. "How do they know who to torment? They fasten on the weakest, like Susannah Addison, all alone with those three children. You notice not one of them has dared come here. I'd shut off that caterwauling fast enough."

"It's a judgment on us, Julia. God is punishing us for all our sins and vanities."

"Just stop that driveling nonsense, Mary, or I'll slap you." After a look at her sister's face, Mary decided to return to reading the Book of Job. She had already discovered several passages that she needed to have explained by Dr. Edwards.

Julia went to find Pinckney. There must be some way the Dragoons could act against the outrage of disturbance.

There was, in fact, little that the men could do about the noise the speculators made. But there was some action that the citizens could take. In that month, there were meetings in houses all over the city. The most frightened and helpless were comforted by visits from friends with clearer heads and stronger minds. Lawyers examined deeds, wills and titles. Women made inventories of things that might be sold. People prayed together and for each other. The spontaneous solidarity of the city was put into words, crystallized into comfort and a hope for the future.

Many were able to delay ruin by giving Pinckney heirloom jewelry to sell. His role in the transactions made him wild with anger and despair. But he continued to carry out his repugnant duties, delivering anonymous packages to Shad and painfully small amounts of money to the friends he represented. He could bear the knowledge that they were being shamefully cheated by the buyers. Reality was bitter, but at least it was impersonal. What drove him to near-madness was the genuine gratitude that he had to accept. It angered him almost past bearing that he could do no more than to reduce the cheating marginally, and it broke his heart to see the stoic graciousness of Charleston's women, thanking him with as much warmth as if he had given them the jewels instead of taken them away.

Throughout the desperate days until December, Pinckney continued to pay his expected daily tribute to Lavinia. She prattled gaily about little Andrew's newest accomplishments, the plans for the next starvation party, the clever ideas Lucy had for redoing a dress for Lavinia to wear, and the gossip about her friends and their flirtations. Pinckney's abstraction irritated her. After all, she spent all day making herself pretty for him and thinking up things to say to amuse him. When, inevitably, he excused himself to go talk to Andrew, she was always furious, but relieved.

Being engaged was not as easy as she had expected. The alternative was worse, though. Many girls were already showing the faded, pinched look of resignation that was the hallmark of the old maid. There were not enough men to go around, even including those damaged by the War. As for Mikell Johnson, she had been right about him. He had asked Sarah Leslie to marry him. Pinny was all that she could hope for. She'd just have to manage somehow. Let Andrew cope with Pinckney's moods. She didn't care.

Andrew's hospitality was as silent as Lavinia's was talkative. The two men shared the decanter by Andrew's bed until it was empty or Andrew fell asleep, whichever came first. Then Pinny went home to bed, to stare for hours at the darkness of his bedroom, longing for sleep.

December came in time to save him. If he had had many more days of sharing the desperation of his friends, he would have broken. But the day of reckoning passed, the taxes were met or, in the worst cases, the evictions were over and shelter found for the homeless. Charleston had adapted and survived this crisis, as it had done so many times before, rising from the ashes of fires, the shambles of hurricanes, the devastations of epidemics, the assaults of the Indians and the Spanish in the early days and, less than a century before, the British, twice in forty years. On December first, the starvation party was the largest ever held, and they danced late into the night, defying the curfew and the government that had imposed it.

The numbers of the Charlestonians had diminished, but their solidarity had become impenetrable. They were strong in their survival.

"I sure am glad you're your old self again, Pinny," Lavinia said. "Now that that awful taxes business is over, everybody's planning parties for the Christmas season. We'll have a wonderful time."

Shad looked at the small orange globe in his hand. He did not know what it was, nor did he understand why Pinckney had made such a to-do when he found one just like it in the toe of his stocking. For that matter, he didn't understand the whole business of driving nails into the mantelpiece of the study and hanging those moth-eaten old stockings on them. The one they had given him was the only one in good shape. He hadn't questioned the ceremony; it was his practice to learn by looking. When, after breakfast, the family had come in and carried on over the stuffed stockings, he had realized that this was what they did for Christmas. This and go to church a lot, once last night and now they were planning to go again before dinner. At least they didn't expect him to go with them. Even Pinckney's mother, churchy as she was, knew better than that.

"I don't know what this is." Lizzie's thin voice was trembling. She held up her mysterious treasure. "It smells sharp. Is it medicine?"

"Dummy!" Stuart was scornful. "It's a tangerine. We always have tangerines in our toes."

Lizzie bit her lip.

"That's no way for a gentleman to address a lady," said Julia.

Mary put her arms around Lizzie. "Poor baby," she crooned, "she doesn't remember." The little girl froze in her mother's embrace.

Pinckney gently pulled his mother away. "Let me show her," he said. "This is a treat we always had at Christmas, Lizzie. Until Santa Claus couldn't get through the blockade." He paused, wondering how he could explain presents during the War years.

"I know there's no Santa Claus," Lizzie said solemnly. "Stuart told me."

The boy retreated from the angry looks of his mother and brother.

Pinckney looked back at Lizzie. "Tangerines are very good. Sweet. And already made into little bites. All you have to do is peel it. See." He thrust his thumb through the puckered end of his fruit and stripped it neatly. The hard-won dexterity was seemingly effortless. "Taste a piece of mine, baby. I promise you'll like it."

With everyone's attention on Lizzie, Shad quickly peeled his fruit. The neatness of the segments fascinated him. He inhaled the exotic aroma released when the tangerine was opened. Suddenly his heart was filled with a sensation he could not name. These people, these Tradds, with all their differences from any people he had ever known, with their fussiness about rules and their talk about ladies do this and gentlemen don't do that—they had included him as naturally as if he was not what they knew, and he knew, he was. Poor white trash. What their servants called po' buckra, without caring that he heard them. He could not understand it. I'll have to do like the baby, he said to himself. I'll have to think about it.

"Don't you like tangerines, Shad?" Pinckney said. "If you don't, Lizzie and I will eat it."

"I like 'em fine, Cap'n." Shad put a piece in his mouth. He was relieved to discover that he did, in fact, like it very much.

In the week that followed Christmas, Charlestonians managed to arrange a round of festivities that matched the pre-War years in number, if not in splendor. Josiah Anson's aged horse and buggy were in perpetual transit carrying Ansons and Tradds to and from a ceaseless round of social engagements. Shad knew that, although he was on special terms with the Tradds, he would not be welcome in the houses of their myriad relations and friends. He quietly refused any invitations to accompany them. He did not in any way want to go; he had plans of his own.

Every day, he went out to explore the city. Not as he had done before, looking for the center of action; this time he was looking for understanding of the family around him. His paw had always told him Charlestonians were different from other people. He had said it with hate. But then he had hated everything and everybody, so Shad had not paid attention. Now he thought that perhaps his paw was right. Not about the hate. About the difference. Shad sorted through the observations he had stored in his mind. And as he tried to find the sense of them, he walked slowly along the narrow streets of the old city, seeking the quiet ones where there were no people coming and going, no parties, no business activity, nothing but the tall quiet trees and houses. Somehow it was fitting to let his feet ramble with his thoughts.

And just as his walking always took him back to the house on Meeting Street, so also his mind always ended up on Pinckney. He did not think about the unequivocal loyalty he had given him at their first meeting. That was a fact and required no examination. That was done. That was the Cap'n.

But Pinckney wasn't the Cap'n. That is, he was and he wasn't. The Cap'n was a flamboyant cavalry officer. Pinckney Tradd was more. This man had many other sides to him; he was head of his family, and at the same time a respectful son and nephew; he was a dandy, squiring his ladies to parties in the evening, and yet he was a sweating laborer in the daytime, giving clumsy assistance to Solomon's repair work; he took tea like a sissy from the eggshell-thin cups that terrified Shad to touch, and then he put down enough hard liquor to kill a normal man without showing any effect; he got blazingly angry over small things and didn't turn a hair about big ones; he had rules that made no sense to Shad together with the same reckless spirit that had driven him into battle against impossible odds and brought him out triumphant time and time again. And with all of these contradictions, with his many moods—gaiety, depression, tenderness, rage, frustration, apathy, friendliness, cold disapproval—he was somehow all of a piece. There was a bedrock of immutable oneness to Pinckney. In all his different ways, he was somehow, deep down, always the same essential person. It was a puzzle.

It had something to do with this place, Shad had decided. This place was a puzzle, too. He was long past his first awe-struck reaction, when the sheer size of the towering houses had made him feel insignificant and belligerent. Now he observed how the town was put together, how this oldest part of the city differed from the rest, and how every structure in it was distinct and at the same time part of an indefinable unified being. It was like a person, a complex person, difficult to understand and full of surprises. Always the unexpected. What kind of place would paint houses blue and pink and green for no reason, jumbling them in with brick ones and white ones. And then, on top of it, would have the grumpiest old man Shad had ever seen—including his paw—living in the palest pink, sweetest, most candy-box-looking house.

He stopped briefly to look at the massive lion's head door knocker on the house nearest him. It was polished to a fare-thee-well. They were mighty fussy about the little things, these Charlestonians. You'd think they'd try not to call attention to the door; its paint was chipped and peeling.

The door, he knew, would open onto the piazza, not into the house. They didn't even have porches like other people, to sit on and visit with people passing by. No, theirs had doors downstairs and lowered half-blinds upstairs to close them off from the street. They were almighty protective about their privacy. Big brick walls to close off their gardens. And putting the houses sideways, with the skinny end facing the street. By God, it worked, too. Only this morning he had come upon a Yankee lieutenant who looked around him at the silent houses and cursed. "Even they give you the cold shoulder."

But Shad had noticed him later, loitering by one of the elaborate wrought-iron gates in the walls, sneaking a peek into the wreckage of the garden. And he had looked sad, not triumphant, about the ruin. There was an overpowering seductiveness about the place, an irresistable "look but don't touch." If cities were like people, Charleston was—no two ways about it—a woman.

He crossed Legare Street to take a close look at the gates that the Cap'n had told him about. Lots of people said they were the best in town. Shad looked them up and down, running his finger along the swooping spirals and then testing the edges of the heavy swords that made the iron crosspieces. He decided that he didn't think so much of them. Kind of nasty it was, big swords on your gate. He looked at the weather-stained notice tied to the gate. He could barely make out the letters: Closed By Order of the Military Authorities. The old French woman lived here. He was glad that the baby hadn't had to go to school behind those swords.

She was really something, that little girl. He could see how hard it was for her to go to school every day, even if no one else noticed. But she did it, and no complaining, either. Worked hard on her lessons at home, too. And on teaching him. At least she got to laugh some at that part. His mistakes delighted her. She was a good little teacher, too, more than she knew. At the dinner table, he'd watch her and copy what she did. When her mother and her aunt corrected her, like they did all the time, he'd also learn from that. Too bad it was Lizzie that had to bear the brunt, but there was nothing he could do about that. Except make her laugh once in a while. It appeared he was the only one she laughed with. She was too scared of the others, even the Cap'n. Seems like she'd be able to know that he'd die for her if need be. Nothing to be scared of in him.

Shad heard the sound of shod hoofs on the cobbles of the street and resumed his casual strolling pace. The Yankee patrols weren't too friendly to stray whites on the streets any more than they were to stray blacks. Besides, it was almost dinner time. He hoped they'd have those fried oysters again soon. Once you stopped thinking about what you were eating, they tasted awfully good.

BOOK THREE

1866-1867

15

"Mama, that big vase of dogwood looks beautiful. You do have a magic touch for flower arranging. Good morning, Aunt Julia. I've brought you the *Messenger*. There's a rumor in it should interest you." Pinckney's attempt to placate the ladies did not work. Mary continued to pout; Julia's expression was hard as granite. He rolled his eyes at Shad, and they took their places at the breakfast table. He was not daunted. The sun was shining, the flowers were blooming, the birds were singing, spring was working its alchemy. No matter what, a man could feel happy and hopeful on a day like this.

His mother began to sniffle behind her napkin.

"Stop that, Mary. I have never once asked for any consideration of the inconvenience to me when you have that Bible-thumper in the drawing room. Today you can repay my forbearance by postponing your absurd pursuit of the Reverend Gentleman for twenty-four hours. Pinckney, you will not be dismayed, I am sure, by learning that you need not lend respectability to your mother's assignation this afternoon. I shall need an escort to Sally Brewton's."

"Sally's? I wasn't invited. I'll have to join a monastery. I certainly couldn't hold my head up in public after being cut off Sally's list."

"It is a ladies' party. You will escort and call for. The rest of your time is your own."

Pinckney could have shouted for joy. This was no day to be indoors. "Gladly," he said. He turned to his mother and smiled engagingly. "None of that, Mama. You can see the Edwardses any time, but a party at Sally's is an event."

"I can't go," Mary wailed.

"Whyever not?"

Julia sniffed. "Because she's a sanctimonious jackass, that's why not."

Mary threw her napkin on the floor, stamped on it and ran from the room. Julia rose majestically and moved to Mary's chair. "I'll ring for breakfast," she said. "And pour the coffee." She was irritatingly calm.

"Your mother regretted Sally's invitation. It's a whist party, and we will be playing for sugar and salt. Gambling, the Archangel says, is an abomination in the eyes of the Lord, so of course your mother can't go. She's in a snit because she hates to miss it." Her lips twitched.

Pinckney laughed aloud.

There were eight tables of cards. Sally assigned the ladies to places with a discerning eye for levels of skill and degrees of friendship. Her own table was made up of herself, Emma Anson, Julia Ashley and Eleanor Allston. While most of the room was a babble of chatter, they played with fierce concentration and daring competition. Except for their bids and stakes, they said almost nothing until two maids brought in the tea.

Julia stacked the cards in a corner of the table and smiled. "A good game, ladies. I thank you." The others agreed. Julia was like a different person from the carping, acid woman in the Tradd house. Her table companions were her closest friends, equals in intelligence, in experience with the world and in dedication to the subtleties of gambling for high stakes. In the past, each of them had risked fortunes on the turn of a card at Baden-Baden. They found the same satisfaction in wagering their hoarded household staples. The game was what counted.

And the pleasure of conversation. They rarely had an opportunity to meet as a group; usually they saw each other at parties where convention demanded constant circulation and abbreviated snatches of talk. Also, a determined cheerfulness. In a world of hardship, it was a luxury to admit discouragement.

"How is the school going, Eleanor?" Julia asked. "You are certainly doing marvels with Lizzie. She reads everything she can get her hands on, whether she understands it or not. I'm becoming positively fond of her."

"She's a good student. I wish I had more like her. Most of them, I'm afraid, have heads of finest Carrara marble. Still, I can't complain. I'm paying my bills with a little left over to buy the Madeira I need when I'm correcting papers."

"Madeira. You're such a lady, Eleanor," Sally scoffed. "Brandy, that's what carries me. When Miles gets home, he'll find his precious cellar as dry as Sahara."

"What's the news from Miles?"

"The same as ever. He's still careening around London like a shuttlecock, trying to find somebody kind enough or bribeable enough to slip the gold under our government's noses in the diplomatic pouch or some duke's valise. If it were our little bit only, I think he'd have come home months ago, but he's representing everybody in South Carolina who had any investments in England. Poor darling, he's dreadfully homesick. I wrote him, of course, that things were far from madly gay here, but that was no comfort at all. He says the Queen has spread a virulent boringness throughout the entire populace."

Emma Anson expressed her opinion that what England needed was another Restoration, which reminded Julia that she still had Josiah's copy of *The Country Wife*. "I'll send it back by Pinckney this evening, else Lizzie might get at it, and I believe in encouraging precosity only to a point."

Eleanor chuckled. "The older girls want to put on a play for May Day. I've been trying to think of something suitable. Perhaps I'll censor some Wycherley for them."

They discussed literature with friendly acrimony for several minutes, then Sally confessed that she was planning to disguise herself and go to the opera series that General Sickles was sponsoring.

Julia's lips thinned. "You cannot do that, Sally."

"Come, now, Julia, why not? We cannot pretend that the Yankees don't exist. Why shouldn't we take advantage of whatever we can? It's all very well for Eleanor's girls to do amateur theatrics; their families are satisfied if they remember their lines. But I cannot be expected to enjoy an evening of arias sung by my friends' children. And that's all the entertainment we have to go to."

Emma bridled. "We've started the Lyceum Society again. I sent you an announcement."

"Dearest Emma, I know you did. And I mean to come, really I do. But I need amusement much more than edification. What was the program for the last meeting?"

Mrs. Anson's stout body quivered.

"Come on, Emma, it's not disloyal to laugh." Julia and Eleanor began to smile. "Come on, Emma." Sally was relentless.

Emma Anson laughed until tears rolled down her face. The others joined her. When they regained their calm, Eleanor Allston supplied the answer. Mrs. Anson had sent announcements to them all.

"Descriptions of Mount Vesuvius," she sputtered, then gave in to giggles.

". . . and the Aurora Borealis," Julia contributed.

". . . by Professor Francis S. Holmes," Sally concluded.

Emma Anson was shaking again. "How could you all bear to miss it?" Her deep, baritone laugh rolled across the room and was lost in the high chattering voices from the other tables.

"But," said Eleanor quietly, "Julia's right. We cannot fraternize with the Army and the carpetbaggers."

"I agree," said Emma. "We have to find our amusement in watching them struggle with the mess they've made for themselves. I can hardly wait for summer. They all had prickly heat last year."

"That's the Army. Those odious men with the toothpicks didn't suffer."

"No, but they weren't too happy. They're all scared to death of the darkies. One black face is just the same as another to them."

"They wanted to free them, didn't they? What are they complaining about?"

"I don't think they knew that Negroes eat. They didn't count on having all those hungry black faces looking to the new Massahs for their dinners."

"And breakfasts and suppers. Josiah tells me they've put up a lot of money for something called the African Colonization Society. They're sending anyone who'll go, free passage, to Liberia."

"That's terrible. The poor souls won't know how to survive."

"At least somebody's getting some good out of it. Josiah charged a whopping big fee for drawing up the papers."

Julia frowned. "I don't see how Josiah can do business with those people," she said.

"Don't be a goose, Julia. Who else is there to do business with? Josiah has a crippled son and a fat old wife and an empty-headed daughter to support."

"And Lucy," Sally added.

Emma sighed. "And Lucy. I'm a mean old woman. That girl is as meek as a lamb, devoted to Andrew, respectful to me, patient with Lavinia and a better daughter to Josiah than his own flesh and blood. And I just can't like her."

Eleanor was comforting. "I despise little Eleanor's husband. Just because he has a mole on his neck. I can't take my eyes off it, it has the longest hair in the world growing out of it, and it fascinates me like a snake with a rabbit. It makes me hate him."

Sally surpassed her. "I can't stand my one and only grandchild. Baby looks like a toad. Colicky, too."

"Your turn, Julia. Who do you hate?"

"Everybody in Washington, D.C. And almost everybody any place else."

It was agreed that Julia had won the contest.

"What's the time?" said Emma. "Can we play another rubber? I've eaten everything except the cups and saucers."

Sally looked at the watch pinned to her shirtwaist. "We can play at least two. By then I'll have lost all my salt unless my luck changes."

Julia shuffled the cards. While Emma dealt, they extracted a promise from Sally that she would forget the opera.

"All right," she said, "but I'm not going to let you talk me out of riding the streetcars they're putting in."

Eleanor looked at her hand and grimaced, fooling no one. "That's different," she said. "It's the least they can do, giving us transportation. They've priced slippers so high no one can afford to walk."

Sally opened the bidding.

When Pinckney left his aunt at the entrance to the Brewtons', he walked on down to the end of King Street and the promenade along the harbor. He stood facing the water, with a brisk wind in his face and the afternoon sun warm on his shoulders. Behind him, the shrill voices of the children in the Gardens were faint, blown away by the salt air. In front of him, four seagulls hovered, then swooped on a bit of refuse in the water. When they discovered it was inedible, they cried to each other, circled upward and caught a current of air for an effortless, soaring ride. Pinckney smiled as he watched, losing himself in vicarious enjoyment of their grace and freedom.

A tug on his coattails brought him out of his reverie. It was Lizzie. "Will you walk me home, Pinny? Sophy's talking to her friends, so she won't leave the park, and I want to finish the book I'm reading before I have to do my schoolwork."

Pinckney bowed. "I'd be honored, Miss Tradd. But you'd best tell Sophy we're leaving. You run tell her, and I'll catch you up at South Battery. Don't cross the street till I get there."

So much for his afternoon to himself. The wind seemed chilly all of a sudden. "Stop that," he said aloud. "You've got no cause to feel sorry for yourself on a glorious spring day." He walked through the gardens, inhaling the scents of tea olive and wisteria, and then took Lizzie home past the sweetness of the hidden gardens along their way.

At the house, Lizzie remembered to thank him; then she ran up the stairs. She knew Julia wasn't home.

Elijah brought him a note that had been delivered in his absence. "What time did Mama go out?" Pinckney asked after he read it.

"Shortly after you, Mist' Pinckney. She got Mist' Stuart to walk her. She and he both look mighty put out."

"Thank you, 'Lijah. I'll be back in awhile." As he walked up Meeting Street, he scowled at his feet. The note was from Mary; he should call for her at the Edwards', she instructed. Maybe Julia was right. Maybe his mother was making a spectacle of herself. It was bad enough entertaining Edwards as a caller at her own home so frequently; it was humiliating to drag Stuart to call on him. He knocked loudly on the door of the rectory.

It was not a servant who opened the door, but Prudence Edwards. "Good day, Mr. Tradd, come in." She led the way up to the drawing room.

Pinckney stopped in the doorway. His mother was not in the room. Nor was Mr. Edwards. He assumed immediately that Mary had maneuvered Edwards into his study under the guise of looking for spiritual guidance, and his jaw stiffened. She had no right to embarrass everyone by her behavior, not even foreigners like the Edwardses. "I'll go find my mother," he said.

The girl's words stopped him. "Don't bother. She's not here."

"But I had a note—"

"I sent it. Your dear mother and my sainted father are both attending a meeting about starting a Youth Fellowship. Your reluctant brother is one of the youths."

Pinckney waited for an explanation.

"Come sit down," said Prudence. She sank into a corner of a brocade settee and patted the spot at the other end. "I probably won't bite you." She was smiling, but her eyes were angry.

He obeyed. "If you propose to discuss our respective parents, Miss Edwards, I'll tell you right now I won't do it."

"I can think of nothing duller. If we must discuss anything, let it be our respective selves. Why do you avoid me, Pinckney? It's not because I bore you. I can tell you don't find me boring."

"Miss Edwards, I—"

"And don't call me 'Miss Edwards.' For heaven's sake, I've tricked you into coming here, I'm entertaining you in an empty house without a chaperone. You're not so dim-witted that you think you need to be formal." Her angry eyes challenged him.

Pinckney felt a matching anger mount in him. "I don't know what to think," he snapped.

"Then don't. Kiss me." She turned her face up to him, taunting him with the invitation of half-closed eyes and parted lips.

"You're acting—"

"Like the biblical whore of Babylon?" Prudence opened her eyes and laughed. "Shocked, are you? Ladies don't say words like 'whore.' But then I'm not really a lady, am I? I'm a Yankee, and everyone knows that the only ladies are your pale Southern flowers. So dainty. Fainting at the sound of an Anglo-Saxon word. Do you know why they faint? Because they can't breathe in those stupid iron corsets they wear to pull their waists in. Oh, oh, there's another bad word. 'Corset.' Too intimate to be mentioned. How about 'legs'? You'd never know they had any under those absurd skirts. Maybe they don't, maybe they have wheels. But you know I have legs, don't you? I've seen you looking at them when the wind blew my skirts. Are you going to deny it? Go ahead."

"I'm going to leave now." He stood, found his stance unsteady.

"Coward," Prudence hissed. "You know you want to kiss me, to touch a real woman's body that's not wrapped in metal. What's it like, kissing your dimpled darling? A wooden doll to match your arm."

Her vicious whispers attacked Pinckney like stinging hornets. "Stop that," he shouted. "Be quiet."

She was panting with rage. Her cheeks glowed with perspiration, and her breasts moved fluidly with each breath. Pinckney stared. The high-buttoned brown dress was molded to her body. He could see the outline of her nipples. She had nothing on under the thin cotton.

"Afraid?" She was laughing at him.

He fell onto the settee and caught her head in his hand. His lips attacked her mouth. She closed her arms across his back and pulled herself against him. As they explored each other's face and eyes and mouth with unrestrained kisses, his fingers pulled the pins from the tight coils of her hair. It fell over her shoulders, thick and silken and smelling of chalk dust. Pinckney released her. He pushed on the back of the settee to free himself. Prudence dropped her arms. He looked down at her. Her face was shining, flushed, desirable, yielding. The mass of shining hair spread behind her over the glowing satin brocade.

Her fingers flew expertly along her bodice, then pulled it open. She caught his head and brought it down to her bare breasts.

"Help me find my hairpins, damn you. There's not much time." Prudence was on her knees behind the settee where Pinckney sat slumped, unhearing, conscious only of his own shame and despair. They had copulated wantonly, like wild animals, rolling over the sinuous pattern of the Turkey carpet. He had released all his pent-up need and frustration and anger in her, using her in a way that he had never used a prostitute. He had been brutally uncaring and rough. There were no words he could say, nothing he could do to repair the appalling injury.

Prudence arranged her hair quickly, checked it in the mirror over the mantel and turned to face him. "You'd better get out of here," she said briskly. "We'd never be able to think of an excuse for your being here."

Pinny brought his attention back from the depths of his anguish. "What?"

"I said 'get out of here.'"

"Yes, yes." He struggled to his feet. "I'll make arrangements tomorrow," he said.

"Arrangements for what?"

"For our marriage. Lavinia will have to release me. Then I'll talk to your father."

Prudence pushed him toward the door. "You'll do nothing of the sort. Now go. Meet me at the school at three o'clock tomorrow, and don't let anyone see you come in. We'll talk about things then. Don't say a word about this."

"Of course not. Prudence, I don't—"

"Get going, Pinckney. Hurry."

She watched through the blinds of the study window until he was safely down the street. Then she allowed herself to laugh.

Julia was in excellent spirits when Pinckney called for her at the Brewton house. She had won a great deal of sugar, enough for one of the Huguenot tortes she missed so much. "I found the piece in this morning's paper very interesting," she said. "Perhaps I'll go to the Ansons' with you this evening and talk to Josiah about it. What time are you going?"

"What? I'm sorry, Aunt Julia. I'm not feeling quite myself."

"Spring fever, no doubt. You're old enough to be past that. I asked what time you were planning to call on Lavinia."

Pinckney turned so pale that Julia was convinced he was really ill. She insisted that he go straight home and to bed. He was happy to comply.

When his head touched the pillow, he fell into a deep, peaceful sleep, escaping everything including the agonies of guilt that he had expected would keep him awake all night.

Julia sent a note to Emma Anson excusing Pinckney. She was annoyed that she couldn't talk to Josiah about the newspaper story. But there was probably nothing in it anyhow. It reported an act before the Congress in Washington which would restore the lands confiscated by Sherman to their former owners. Julia would not allow herself to hope. The previous October a General Howard had come from Washington with a proclamation restoring the land. It had been nothing more than a piece of paper and an evidence of President Johnson's ineffectuality. He could proclaim, but he couldn't enforce. Nothing was changed.

She decided that she didn't really want the torte after all. Her excellent spirits had disappeared.

16

As Pinckney mounted the wide, shallow steps of the South Carolina Hall, his mind and his body were in turmoil. He had difficulty adjusting his stride. For three years, from thirteen to sixteen, he had reluctantly climbed those stairs every Friday night for five months of every year to go to dancing school. His legs were much longer now.

And he could not drug himself with memories. The smell of chalk brought him vividly back to the present and to his dreadful dilemma. He was expected at the Ansons' at five. What could he say to Lavinia?

The pervasive odor also triggered body-memory. He felt an unwelcome excitement tighten his loins, and shame stabbed his heart. He forced his feet to move upward.

The familiar ballroom was shabby, with dirty windows and the marks of many heels on the once-shining wide floor boards. It was filled with rows of new pine desks, still fresh with varnish. He noticed that the one nearest him had a single initial carved into its sloping surface.

"At least that one is learning to write." Behind him, Prudence's voice was crisp. Pinny spun to face her.

She put ink-stained fingers over his mouth to keep him from speaking. "You're pale as a ghost. Sit down on that excellent B and listen to me. I can guess everything you mean to say, and I do not care to hear any of it." Pinny obeyed.

Prudence paced back and forth, talking, biting off the words. She did not look at him. Her tone was flat, without emotion. "You can forget apologies and guilt, Pinckney. You did me no injury. I seduced you in the easiest possible way. You were not the first, and I am sure that you will not be the last. There's nothing like being raised on a steady diet of the sinfulness of man to make a girl curious. I lost my virtue at thirteen, and I've never regretted it. The first time I saw you, I knew I wanted you. I put myself in front of you at every opportunity, but you were too much the gentleman to admit that you wanted me. Even to yourself. Finally, I got tired of waiting.

"In spite of your missish reluctance, you were, in the end, everything I expected. I suppose an animal recognizes its own kind. If you will shed your Charleston rules and restrictions, you will admit the same thing. I don't want to have to rape you again." She stopped in front of him. "Well?"

Pinckney put his mouth on hers. She bit his lower lip, then took his arm and led him to the couch in the cloak room. They came together in a frenzy.

In the warm lassitude that followed, Pinckney felt a protectiveness and gratitude that he almost mistook for love. He cradled her to his chest and murmured endearments. When she responded with expert hands, rousing his body again with practiced ease, he accepted her the way she presented herself, as a harlot.

The basin of water and clean towel that she offered him afterward were not warmed and scented as Lily's had been, but they were, for Pinckney, a confirmation of Prudence's status. He left her then, after arranging to meet again in two days. He almost whistled when he ran down the stairs. Later, he greeted Lavinia with a chaste kiss on the brow and found her transparent innocence enchanting instead of frustrating. He felt no guilt at all.

Or so he told himself.

Pinckney Tradd was not a man who could lie to himself about his weaknesses. He had been raised by a father and in a society that placed the code of honor highest on the ladder of values in a man's life. The goal might be impossible to achieve, but it must be striven for throughout a man's days, and when he violated that code, he could not excuse himself.

His affair with Prudence was wrong. No matter that she had initiated it and that she portrayed herself as no more than one of the women on Chalmers Street. He was wronging her. And Lavinia—he owed his future wife fidelity. He was betraying his own mother by risking a scandal that would destroy the happiness she had managed to build from the chilly comfort in Adam Edwards and his view of God. And Edwards himself. Pinckney was committing an offense against this man that defiled the laws of man and of the God whom Edwards represented. Edwards had every right to kill him, except that he deserved worse.

Yet, he could not stop. Prudence Edwards was like a powerful drug in his system. She dominated his mind and his body. He was obsessed with her.

In Pinckney, emotions had always been dangerously strong. Also, he was young and hot-blooded and had been deprived of sexual activity for the long years of the War and the longer months of chaotic peace that had followed. And then, not by chance, Prudence had offered herself to him at a time when the very air he breathed was voluptuous with the fecundity of a Charleston spring. Masses of flowering trees, vines, shrubs poured forth an inescapable perfumed richness that made a man drunk from their excess. Everywhere he looked, fresh green growth and bright satiny flowers shouted that life was for the living, and the earth itself proclaimed the sensuality owing to the season.

During the days and weeks that followed his seduction, Pinckney struggled with himself in a hidden, exhausting conflict that drained his days and tormented his dreams. The Edwardses continued to come for tea twice a week. Prudence was as she had always been, a silent, composed, well-bred young woman. Mary twittered and fluttered. Adam Edwards spoke interminably. And Pinckney was in Hell. He dared not look at Prudence, yet could not prevent his eyes touching every part of her and reminding his body of its guilty knowledge. He silently cursed Edwards for a fool and then had to fight the impulse to shout his sin and plead for Edwards' punishment.

On Sundays, it was worse. His nerves vibrated to Edwards' mighty voice, pulling him toward the solitary figure in the pew nearest the pulpit. The majestic words of the litany stirred his heart with overwhelming fear and guilt and pain. They struck his head like thunderbolts from Adam Edwards' lips: " 'From all evil and mischief; from sin, from the crafts and assaults of the devil; from thy wrath, and from everlasting damnation.' "

Pinckney made the responses with all the tortured pain of his soul. " 'Good Lord, deliver us.' "

" 'From fornication and all other deadly sin; and from all the deceits of the world, the flesh, and the devil.' "

" 'Good Lord, deliver us.' "

And all the time that he was praying with all the strength in his body, he was burning with the knowledge that under the cushion on which he knelt, there was a note from Prudence telling him when their next meeting would be.

He hid the turmoil well, marveling that no one noticed any change in him. The only outward signs were the purple shadows under his eyes and his constant fatigue. In the mornings, he walked for miles, releasing some of his tension by exercise so that he could appear calm at dinner. In the afternoons, if he was not meeting Prudence, he retired to the study, ostensibly to work on the account books that recorded the steady depletion of the family's financial reserve. Actually, he usually sat in the big chair behind the desk and gave in to the wild, despairing conflict that possessed him.

One day, he heard the click of the knob turning and felt a surge of murderous irritation. Couldn't he expect at least an hour's freedom from worry about money, about the friction in the kitchens, about his failures in every aspect of his life. He looked fixedly at the pages before him. Perhaps they'd go away.

Then Pinckney felt eyes on him. He turned his head slowly. His anger disappeared. Lizzie's solemn face was extended past the partially open library door like a free-floating pale moon. "May I come in, please?"

"Of course. I'm happy to see you. What can I do for you?" The little girl's thin body slipped through the narrow opening.

"I'm looking for my book," she said. "The one you gave me to practice with. I had it in my room, but now it's gone. If I lost it, Mama'll be awful mad."

With a tiny mew of joy, she ran to the desk and picked up the tattered red book on top. "Here it is. Pansy must've put it here after she cleaned my room. Oh, thank goodness." Her face was shining.

"You didn't say why you wanted it. Is it a good story?"

"I don't read it, Pinny." She was amazed at his ignorance.

"What do you do with it, eat it?" Pinckney's eyes laughed at her.

Lizzie frowned, then realized that he was joking. "I'm going to put it on my head and walk up and down stairs. Want to see?" she offered.

"I'd like to, but I'm too tired to stand in the hall. Can't you walk around in here?"

"I suppose so." She balanced the book and began to take tiny careful steps across the room.

"What's that for?" Pinny asked.

"Deportment." As she spoke, the book slid off her head onto the floor. "Now look what you made me do. A person can't talk and do deportment at the same time. Don't ask me any more questions." She bent over to pick up her burden. It lay halfway in the cold ashes of the fireplace. "Oh, shoot," Lizzie exclaimed. Then she grimaced. "I've got to stop saying that. Aunt Julia washes my mouth out with laundry soap when I say it. I got it from Mr. Simmons. I like him, Pinny."

"So do I. Is Aunt Julia making you carry that book on your head?"

"No, we have it at school. We're learning to walk right and sit right and stand up right like a lady. You've got to hold your head real still. I do pretty well, but Caroline Wragg does better. So I practice."

"I see. Is it fun, this walking and sitting right?"

Lizzie frowned. "Not really. I expect it will be when I learn to be the best. I mean, being best must be fun. I don't think holding your head up like some turkey buzzard is ever going to be much." She looked at the mantel above her head. "That's what I'd like," she said softly.

"What is that, Baby Sister?"

She pointed with a sooty finger. "To be like them. Didn't you ever look at them? They're beautiful, I think. I make up stories about them all the time."

Pinny stood up and joined her by the fireplace. He looked at the carved graceful nymphs that danced across the width of the mantelpiece. They were barefoot and clad in floating-free robes. Their outflung arms and tilted heads were the very expression of joy.

"Very pretty," he said. "I see what you mean. You know, sweetheart, there's plenty of room in here for you to dance."

"Oh, I couldn't. I'd look silly."

"Not to me. I like seeing a little girl having some fun. Go on. Just throw your arms out and jump around. Here. Sit down and let me help you with your boots."

She began timidly, as rigid as if the book were still on her head. Then, when Pinckney did not laugh, she became more adventurous. Soon she was whirling rapturously, then leaping, then spinning.

He watched, fondly nodding encouragement. Then Lizzie tripped. Before he could move to help her, she crashed into the desk, cried out and fell to the floor, her hands going to cup her knee. Pinckney moved just fast enough to catch the tottering lamp. He didn't get to the funny old inkwell. It poised for an instant on the edge of the desk, tipped, then fell into the copper wastepaper basket.

"Are you all right? Tell Pinny where it hurts."

Lizzie looked terrified. "Did anything break?"

"No, not a thing. The ink spilled, but it went right into the basket." He reached in. His fingers touched the inkwell. It had lost a piece.

Lizzie read his face. "It broke," she said hopelessly. She began to sob, then to choke.

"Now stop that, Lizzie. It's nothing some glue won't fix," Pinckney felt frantic. She would strangle if he didn't do something. "Solomon has a glue pot. But I can't fix it with one hand. I'll need some help." Please, Lord, let it work, he prayed silently. He bent protectively over the little girl, cursing his own helplessness.

Her body shuddered with the effort to breathe. Slowly, it became less tortured. Finally she was able to speak. "I'm so awful sorry, Pinny."

"I know. It doesn't matter. Really."

"Really truly?"

"Cross my heart." Lizzie's frightened face made him want to cry. Damn. Just when some sort of bridge of trust was being built, this had to happen. "Let me help you up. Does your knee pain you much?" If he could just hug her, comfort her a little. It would comfort him so much.

But she scrambled quickly to her feet alone. "It doesn't hurt a bit," she said. It was an obvious lie. "I'll go ask Solomon for some glue." She evaded Pinckney's outstretched hand and hurried out of the room.

"Damn," he said aloud.

Lizzie brushed the glue on the pieces and matched them together with shaking, awkward fingers. "Solomon said I had to hold it until it set.

Do you think that takes very long? I have to wash my face and hands before Aunt Julia sees me."

"Just a few minutes. Would you like me to tell you the story about that inkwell?"

"A story? Oh, yes, would you please?"

"All right. Let's see. Once upon a time . . ."

Lizzie sighed happily, her fears almost forgotten.

"Once upon a time there was a little boy named Anson Tradd."

"Papa?"

"Right. Our papa. You don't remember him, I suppose."

"No. I wish I did."

"I wish you did, too, Baby Sister. He was a fine man, very brave and full of laughter. Well, when Papa was very little, littler than you are now, his papa, our grandfather, gave him a pony for his birthday."

"Which birthday?"

"Fifth. Or maybe fourth. I don't really know. Anyhow, Papa really loved that pony."

"What was his name?"

"Prince. Do you want me to tell this story or not?"

"I do, I do. I won't interrupt anymore."

"That's a good girl. So Papa loved Prince. Every single day, he'd be out at the stables before breakfast pestering the grooms to saddle Prince and let him go riding. When the family came into town, nothing would do but to bring Prince, too. And then a terrible thing happened. Papa grew but Prince didn't. After a while, Papa's feet nearly dragged the ground. He started riding horses. And that made Prince sad, because he loved Papa, too."

"Poor Prince."

"Yes, and poor Papa. He hated to see his old friend feeling bad. So he visited him every time he went to the stables. And on easy rides, he'd take Prince with him, trotting alongside the horse that carried Papa. He still brought him to town, too. He'd put a lead line on him and take him for walks down Meeting Street to White Point Gardens."

Lizzie giggled.

"Right. Everybody laughed. But Papa didn't care. Prince was his friend. Finally, Prince got to be too old to go running alongside when Papa rode. He even got too old to go for walks. All he liked to do was to eat his mash and sleep in the shade of a tree."

"He died."

"Yes. He was very old for a pony. Papa was almost a grown man. He told me that, big as he was, he cried like a baby. They buried Prince under the tree he liked the best, and Papa kept his hoof to remember him by. He got the plantation woodworker to make a little lid for it and kept it on his desk all the time to use for his inkwell."

Lizzie wrinkled her nose. "I wouldn't want somebody to keep my foot on their desk. I think that's sad and mean."

"Ponies are different from people, Lizzie. Papa did it out of love and loyalty. There's more story, do you want to hear it?"

"If it's not sad."

"No, I think it'll make you laugh. Now, time went on. Papa met a beautiful lady and got married . . ."

"Mama?"

"Mama. And they had a little baby boy named—" He waited.

"Pinckney!"

"Pinckney. And he was very wicked."

Lizzie smiled ecstatically. "No," she whispered.

"Oh, yes. He was the wickedest little boy in South Carolina."

"What did he do?"

"All sorts of terrible things. I won't tell you what all because it might put mischievous ideas in your head. The wickedest of all was that he'd shinny out of the window when he was supposed to be doing his lessons."

"At school?"

"No, they didn't have school then. Boys had tutors and girls had governesses; they lived in the house. I'll take you to Carlington one day and show you the schoolroom. Well, this terrible Pinny, as soon as the tutor turned his back, he'd be off out the window. Papa talked to him, hollered at him, even caned him. And it did no good at all. So then he began to scheme . . . There was one thing Pinny really coveted. The inkwell."

"Why?"

"I don't remember. It was a long time ago. Maybe because Papa prized it so much. Whyever, I wanted that inkwell for my very own, wanted it more than anything. So Papa made a deal with me. When I got good enough at my lessons to write them in ink, he'd give it to me."

"And did you?"

"Yes. It took a while. Sometimes the window called to me louder than the inkwell did. But I wanted it a lot. And, wicked as I was, I still wanted to please Papa."

"So he gave it to you."

"Yes, he did. When you get big enough for a pen, I'll give it to you."

"Will you, Pinny? Really truly? I'll try real hard at my lessons."

"Really truly, Baby Sister." Pinckney studied her happy, excited face and took a chance. "Will you give me something, too?"

Lizzie's face clouded. "I don't have anything," she said. "Except Bear. I don't know if I could get along without Bear, Pinny. I could try."

Pinckney's eyes stung. What kind of world was this, where a man couldn't find money to buy anything for a child except some food and the cheapest boots. "I don't want Bear, baby. I would be proud to have a hug."

Lizzie took a long breath. Then, her face pale with determination, she deposited the inkwell on the desk and approached Pinckney. Her little hands touched his knee tentatively, then his chest. He held himself very still, barely breathing. Her arms crept around his neck. He could feel her wraithlike body trembling. Suddenly she tightened her arms convulsively and rested her head against his cheek. "This is my Pinny," she whispered to herself.

Pinckney moved his arm slowly to encircle her thin form. He held her for a long moment then freed her gently, as if she were one of the tiny harmless wild creatures he used to find in the snares set for predatory animals in Carlington's woods.

Lizzie stepped back and placed her arms at her sides. She had a look of exhausted peace, like a traveler who has won through a desperate storm. "I believe," she said in a very small voice, "that I would like some lap, please."

Pinckney swallowed. "I believe I'd like that very much." He managed a smile. Lizzie climbed onto his knees and snuggled against him. Pinckney held her quietly while the room slowly faded into twilight and the tears a man could not shed gathered in his throat and his heart.

17

Lizzie's return to the affectionate child of the past had a dramatic effect on everyone in the Tradd house. For Pinckney it brought a deep, clean happiness and a respite from his pervasive sense of failure. For Mary, it was a proof of the power of prayer and the abiding love of God. For Shad it meant deposition from his spot closest to Lizzie, and he experienced jealousy for the first time in his life. He also discovered humility and gratitude when Lizzie used his lap as a throne, just as she did Pinckney's, and put her little arms around his neck. Love was a gift Shad had never before been offered.

When she recaptured trust, Lizzie also returned to her old, impulsive behavior. The house became a battlefield, with Julia complaining constantly about the noise of Lizzie's laughter and running feet. The dinner table was dominated by a recital of "Ladies don't: slouch . . . talk with their mouths full . . . kick their chairs . . . interrupt . . . gobble their food . . . spill their milk . . . play with their pudding . . . forget their napkins . . . wiggle . . . put their elbows on the table . . . speak unless spoken to . . . make faces . . . drop spoons . . ."

For Stuart, the attention to Lizzie meant a welcome obscurity for his own sins of torn, dirty clothes and unfavorable reports from his tutor. He was free to spend all of his energies on the activities of the Club. They were mapping the walls and rooftops of the blocks around them, creeping along the best routes and spying on the patrolling enemy. Soon they would enter the exciting time when their plans would come to fruition with sneak attacks of water bombs and rotten fruit, then escape to the Clubhouse in Alex's yard. They already had a notebook which they had stolen from the schoolroom. They would record all their missions in the code they had invented.

He was also pleased to see Lizzie happy. In the few moments he had that were not taken up by the self-importance typical of a thirteen-year-old boy, he was fond of his little sister.

As the days became warmer, increasing household tensions began to repeat the previous summer's pattern. Then relief came from the least likely source—the Yankees.

In June the government in Washington changed its collective mind again, deciding after all to restore to its owners the appropriated land from Charleston to Beaufort. Pinckney congratulated Julia with a toast.

"They're probably lying again," she commented. "They're incapable of honesty, those jackals."

"No, Aunt Julia, not this time. Shad heard about it from people who know."

Julia favored Shad with a glare.

"Is that so, young man?"

"Yes, ma'am. With a few conditions."

"Hah! I might have known. There's a trick in everything they do." She obviously included Shad in the word "they."

Pinny tried to rescue him. "It's nothing unreasonable, Aunt Julia. You have to prove title, that's all, and, um, take the oath." He waited for the explosion.

To his amazement, his aunt smiled. "They think that will stop me, no doubt. If so, they are grievously mistaken. As Henry of Navarre said, 'Paris is worth a mass.' How do we proceed?"

"There's no hurry, Julia. It's three months before it's safe to go to the country." Mary smiled placidly. Charleston's planters had learned centuries before that white men had to leave their plantations before the tenth of May and not return until October. The night air was full of disease in the summer.

"Nonsense. Every day that passes is another day of damage to my property. I'm not afraid of swamp fever. My old overseer had his house in that patch of pine woods at the north end, and he never had any trouble. I can move in there until first frost. As long as I get back there every night before it gets dark, I'll be fine. And I'll have all day to work.

"Now Pinckney. And you, too, Mr. Simmons. I want you to go out immediately after dinner and do whatever must be done. I imagine I shall need a military escort. See to it that they are armed. The place must be full of black roosters.

"Lizzie, stop goggling and eat your dinner. We can't wait all day for you.

"Stuart, you can go out with Solomon this afternoon. He'll find out if any Barony darkies are in the city. Write their names down. I'll want to hire the good workers and take them with me. Eat, boy, don't dawdle. There are things to do." She rode over their attempts to speak, impatient and imperious.

"Aunt Julia!" Pinckney managed to say when she paused for an instant.

"Well?"

"I'm sorry, but we don't have enough money for you to start hiring hands and repairing the Barony. If we did, I'd have gone to Carlington long before now."

Her response stunned them all. "I have money," she said. Her manner was regal.

Mary was the first to react. "You stood by and let me sell my jewelry when you had money? How could you be so mean?"

"It is Barony money, and I kept it for the Barony."

Mary was silenced. She could not believe what she had heard. Pinckney controlled himself with evident effort. The room was thick with tension. After a time, he pushed his chair back and stood.

"Please excuse me, ladies," he said, "I suddenly have a lot to do. Stuart will not go with Solomon, it's too dangerous. I will. After I get a firearm from the Arsenal. Everything will be arranged as quickly as possible, Aunt Julia. You may wish to begin packing."

Shad mumbled his excuses and followed him from the room.

And so it was that four days later Julia Ashley stood in the drawing room of her house on Charlotte Street facing its occupant, General Daniel Sickles. He held a Bible in his hand. Julia put her hand on it, looked directly into his eyes and repeated the words he told her to speak.

"'I do solemnly swear or affirm, in the presence of Almighty God, that I will henceforth faithfully support, protect and defend the Constitution of the United States and the union of states thereunder, and that I will in like manner abide by and faithfully support all laws and proclamations made during the existing rebellion with reference to the emancipation of slaves.

"'So help me God.'"

A week afterward, she set out with the tide for the trip up the Ashley River to Ashley Barony. She was immaculately gowned in shining black bombazine. A haughty hat of glossy black feathers sat on her head, protected by the big silk umbrella she held in her gloved hand. A little thing like a rainstorm had no power to stop Julia Ashley. She rode in the cypress canoe as if it were a royal barge. Behind it, four flatboats carried her trunks, her servants and a company of dripping Union soldiers.

Pinckney turned away from the dock. "I wouldn't care if lightning struck her," he said.

"God wouldn't dare," drawled Shad.

Pinny whooped. "I bet you're right. Let's get out of this damned rain."

In the succeeding months, Pinckney received laconic notes from Julia, delivered by Solomon when he came to the city to carry out various errands for her. These mostly consisted of delivering orders for materials. Pinckney refused to give in to his curiosity and ask Solomon how much she was buying or how she arranged to pay for it. The big suppliers of tools, seed, and farm equipment were all strangers now. The Ashley name would get no special treatment from them. And certainly not credit. Before the War, planters had settled their accounts every January when they were in town for Race Week. Now it was payment in advance of delivery or else interest charges of 15 or 20 percent.

To preserve tranquillity, her name was rarely mentioned in the house. Mary Tradd had recovered from her shock and was now eloquent on the subject of her sister's selfishness. The only person willing to listen was Adam Edwards. He prayed with Mary that she would be cleansed of the sin of anger and that Julia would be vouchsafed an understanding of her sinful materialism. Mary found the spiritual counseling very helpful. Her anger diminished every time she was with the Reverend Doctor.

Julia's departure brought a much needed tranquillity to the Tradds. Elijah found a cook named Clara and a maid named Hattie to replace Dilcey and Pansy. Solomon was irreplacable, but a boy called Billy was willing to do anything he was told to do, and he had a green thumb. The kitchen became a peaceful kingdom ruled by Elijah. Pinckney found that he could look forward to being with his family, that his home was a place of repose again, as he had remembered it. The constant worry about taking care of them all was still there, but the everyday happiness in the house, especially Lizzie's bubbling gaiety, restored the optimism that had always been part of his basic nature. He began to believe that he might conquer the exterior enemy of poverty and his inability to find acceptable work. He was sure that he could make up for the damage he had done to Prudence and to his own honor. He admitted to himself that he did not love Lavinia and that he had never loved her, only his image of her. He also realized that his lust for Prudence was being transformed into something much more important. Perhaps it started with her easy acceptance of his exposed stump, which no one else had ever seen except Shad. Having nothing to hide about his body, he gradually ceased hiding the interior of his mind. To her alone, he could talk about the hatred he felt for his weakness in not ending their liaison. He could berate her in the same breath. And she did not say soothing things the way women always did. She laughed at him and herself and sorrowed at the waste of life that she considered his guilt to be. She argued with him, made him question his demands on himself. In time, he found himself talking to her about everything, even about his inability to go to Carlington and face whatever he found there. Prudence did not sympathize. She understood. The hard intelligence that she never attempted to disguise fascinated and challenged him. She became essential to him as a friend; she was already indispensable to his need for a lover. He decided to ask Lavinia to let him go. He never doubted that Prudence would marry him even though he was close to penniless. Nor did he doubt that she was strong enough to face whatever lay in the future.

Lavinia refused. "You must be crazy," she yelled. Her frightened anger made her incautious, and she revealed herself with a burst of honesty that shocked Pinckney to the root of his being. "I wouldn't let you go if you begged me on your knees," she said in a cold voice. "Not because I love you so much. I don't. Your nasty wooden arm makes me sick to my stomach, and the idea of looking at you without it makes my flesh crawl. But I'd rather have to vomit every hour of my life than be a shriveled up old maid. You're stuck with me, Pinny, same as I'm stuck with you. So make the best of it. You'll never jilt me because you care too much about Papa's good opinion of you. And I won't jilt you because there's nobody to jilt you for. You can quit coming over here every day. It bores me anyhow. But you'll take me to every party, and you'll hop when I call on you to hop. And you'll be a gentleman and I'll be a lady and we'll make do with each other. You'll never mention this subject to me again, either."

When he slipped and told Prudence that Lavinia would not set him free to marry her, her response was an even greater shock because it made no sense. "I'd never marry you, my love. I care for you too much."

He could only try to accept a situation that was in every way intolerable. His innate resilience won out over his urge to admit defeat and retreat into an unfeeling apathy. He learned to live with deceit and self-loathing, sustaining himself with the hours when he could forget the world, lost in his absorption with his duties at the Arsenal or his delight in Lizzie's company or his fulfilling sharing of his total self with Prudence. He did not tell himself that he was happy, but he managed to find a balance of near-peace.

Shad was an unexpected source of strength. He was at home much more these days. It was, he admitted, a lot easier for him with Pinckney's aunt gone. He spent many hours sitting with Lizzie in her corner of the piazza "playing school." He spent many more with Pinckney, talking little, asking a question from time to time about the city's history, for the most part just sharing a comfortable silence. His unspoken admiration and confidence were subtle healers. Pinckney returned affection and acceptance and a growing respect which meant all the more to Shad because he knew that he deserved them. His place in the Tradd family convinced him of his own value. Mary ignored him, as she did her children. Stuart boasted to him and to Pinckney interchangeably. Lizzie pestered him constantly to join her and Bear with a book.

The only things denied to him were a share in the social life—which he did not want—and a share in the responsibility—which he wanted very much. Pinckney had never allowed him to contribute to the expenses of running the house. Shad's portion of the commissions they had earned were his to keep, Pinckney insisted. His pride could not bear obligation, and Shad realized it, so he did not argue.

Instead, he invested his money in a newly organized firm of factors. He knew that he would be cheated, but he also knew that the profits would be so enormous that it would hardly be worth the trouble to cheat him of very much.

Factoring was a business that he knew all about from its dark side. It preyed on small farmers like Shad's father, advancing them seed and money for them to live on until their crops were in, then buying the crop at the price set by the factor. The farmer stayed in debt all his life, in constant fear of the lien on his land that he had to give as security. The crop, usually cotton, was sold at a profit of 500 to 600 percent after it had been ginned. The seeds that were the by-product of the ginning were then sold for cotton-seed oil, except for the small amount saved to advance to the farmer for the start of the same yearly cycle again. It was a vulture's profession.

Shad did not tell Pinckney that he was involved in it. He banked his money and waited until it would be needed.

In November 1866, it seemed that the time had come. Although Mary's jewels had sold for what seemed a fortune a year ago, there was barely enough money in the Tradd accounts now to pay this year's property taxes. And there was nothing left in Charleston to be sold for commissions.

"I'll have to sell Carlington," Pinckney said. "I'd rather lose my other arm." He was frantic with desperation. "Don't talk to me, Shad. Get out of here."

Shad grunted. He knew that Carlington was Pinckney's touchstone. His moment had come. For Carlington, Pinckney would have to accept his money. His heart would win out over his pride. "Let me go mosey around some, Cap'n," he said casually, "and see if I can drum up some answers."

He left with a light heart, walking to the Hotel to find his business partners.

What he heard there took his breath away.

18

Shad entered the library and spoke with unusual animation. "Say, Cap'n, what's this thing people call 'marl'?"

Pinckney looked up from the account books. He was ashamed of his outburst earlier. "You're home early. How about a glass of wine?"

"No, thanks. How about what I asked you?"

Pinny laughed. "You'll never be accused of idle conversation. 'Marl' is a chalky sort of deposit you find in the soil some places. Fascinating stuff. It's full of fossils. People have come across bones of prehistoric animals and fish and maybe even men. Why do you want to know? Don't tell me they've got archeologists at the Charleston Hotel now."

Shad handed Pinckney the Madeira he had poured. "They're saying it's good fertilizer," he said. He was so tense that he vibrated.

"Then they're crazy. Nothing grows on land with marl near the top. We've got a big stretch of it at Carlington. Not even poison oak will grow there. If it's far enough below the surface, it's all right. But not especially productive."

Shad relaxed. "That's what I was hoping. When you was—were—in the hospital, you were talking a lot about some little horse."

"Did I? I don't remember. I must have been half-dreaming. Funny, the things that come to you in a fever. Yes, when I was a boy, they started digging for an extra icehouse. That chalky ground is good for that, keeps the cold in somehow. When they got down about three or four feet, they came across a perfect skeleton of an eohippus. It scared the darkies half to death, so they came running to my father. He was very excited about it.

"The darkies wouldn't go near it. Papa and I got down in the hole and cleared away the rest of the chalk covering it. Then he sent me in for the encyclopedia, and I had to read it aloud to him. 'Eohippus.' Had a time pronouncing that, I'll tell you. It's the progenitor of our modern horses, you see, but there hasn't been one on earth for—"

Shad cleared his throat. "That's very interesting, Professor."

Pinny grinned. "Actually, it is. But I get the feeling you're not fascinated."

"Let me fascinate you some. This here—this—marl is full of what they call phosphates. And all the land that's planted in wheat needs to be fed phosphates all the time. Some fellows from Philadelphia just come into town to set up a company with a local who's got the same kind of land as you. They've brought one million dollars with them. Nobody invests that kind of money unless they're figuring to earn back fifty dollars for every one they put in."

"Phosphates? I don't know anything about that."

"Well, Cap'n, you'd best look it up in your encyclopedia. It's a damn sight more interesting than dead horses. You might just have the answer to all your troubles lying out there in the icehouse. Like picking up money off the ground."

The battered skiff rocked and skipped water. "Scuse me, Mist' Pinckney," said Billy, with a grin. "Must be caught a crab." Pinckney nodded and smiled mechanically. All his attention was on the succession of landmarks on the riverbank.

The twisted oak with the wisteria vine should be just around the next bend in the river. They had already passed the boathouse where the heavy barges used to be kept. The building was nothing now but rotting stumps, but he was sure it was the boathouse. The marsh grass, golden brown in the autumn sunlight, swayed with the invisible tide, hypnotic in its undulating progression of slow, rhythmic folding and unfolding upon itself. It had reclaimed the tidelands, then. The dikes that had put the print of man's will on the river, claiming it for his use when he chose to flood the rice fields, must have worn down and returned the fields to wildness. No matter. The natural marsh was beautiful to Pinckney's eye. And, if Shad was right, there would be no more rice on Carlington. But the grasses would remain forever, part of the river, home for nesting birds and food for the great seasonal migrations of duck.

They were near the point now. Pinckney's mind repeated the senseless bargain it had struck with the Fates. If you'll let the tree still be there, I won't mind if the house is gone, it said soundlessly, again and again, in time with the oars rising from the water on "let" and "mind." The river carried them closer. Pinckney could hear his heart beating.

Soon. Any minute now. How could so much scrub pine have grown up; he couldn't see through it. Maybe he was wrong. Maybe it was a different bend—no. There it was, his tree. He stared, his heart full of memory and pain and thankfulness. The huge gnarled wisteria vine still cloaked limbs where he had climbed. There was the long branch that stretched off alone, where he had put a rope bridle and ridden its springing motion as if it were an ungaited horse. When he was very small, it had felt as if he would be flung up into the sky, weightless, flying, able to rope and ride the very clouds. A little older, and he had discovered the indestructible strength of the heavy vine, scorning the heavy sweetness of the purple panicles in spring bloom, ripping them off the one special part of it, then wrapping arms and legs around it, pushing off and swinging with a delicious, dangerous swoop over the river, to jump into the scream-making chill of the water, still holding its winter cold.

"Home," he said. Then, greedy, he forgot his bargain and began to pray. Please, God, let it be there. The house, my home, my life, Carlington. He did not bargain. There was nothing he could promise that was big enough to equal his yearning for the avenue of mulberry trees and the sprawling old house beyond. Just a little farther. The oars splashed, pulled, rose, splashed, pulled . . .

The dock. The dock was still there. Pinckney pounded Shad on the shoulder. And the tall, spreading trees, already beginning to brown. Mulberries had been a poor choice for an avenue. Oaks or magnolias stayed green in the winter. But some long-ago Tradd had believed that he could add silk-worms to the produce of Carlington, and he had planted mulberries. The trees hung heavy with Spanish moss. Pinckney waited impatiently until they passed the gray, waving screen.

And let out a screeching Rebel yell. "It's there! Billy, Shad, there's the house. Hallelujah—that's Carlington. Haul on those oars, now. Let's get landed."

Built for winter living, the house was lower than the tall Charleston dwellings that Shad's eye had got accustomed to. It was only two floors high. In the center, a huge semicircular veranda on both floors had peeling white-painted columns of cypress. To each side stretched a simple wing with ten windows above, five windows and five doors below. The walls were of the grayish-red brick made in Charleston, with window trim in carved limestone. Sturdy green shutters still hung at a few of the windows. Three were crooked; one hinge gone. Most of the windows were bare, with many broken panes. Ivy climbed the walls; it had invaded some of the windows.

Pinckney noticed none of the damage. To him, it was home, and he saw it with his heart's eye. He ran ahead of the others, oblivious of the weed-grown avenue and lawns.

The front door was jammed. He needed Shad's help to get it open. Inside, it was bare, except for cobwebs and piles of blown dead leaves in corners of the rooms with broken windows. Pinckney led the way through every room in the house. Shad kept his usual place behind him, watching him through half-closed eyes. When they returned to their starting place, Pinckney sighed once, then shrugged. "Picked us clean, the bastards," he said. There was no emotion in his voice.

"Come on, Shad, I'll show you the fossil pit." He walked away without looking back.

The excavation was about ten feet square by three feet deep. The two men sat on its edge and let their feet dangle. As Pinckney had promised, the sides of the hole were studded with rough nodules of various sizes. Shad broke one off and studied it. It contained a long triangle of bone.

"Shark's tooth," Pinckney explained. "I used to collect them when I was a child. They'd work up to the surface, turn up in plowed fields, and the servants would send for me so that I could search the furrows and find them. I must have had two hundred of them. The prize specimen was eight inches long.

"There were bones, too, but nothing as perfect as the little horse." The bottom of the pit was full of dead leaves, so they could not see it. Without speaking, they agreed to leave it undisturbed.

"What do you think, Shad?"

"Looks good to me, Cap'n. I'll break off a few more pieces and we'll get it analyzed. Why don't you take this tooth?"

"No, thanks. I said good-bye to my young self in there. I don't want to start collecting souvenirs."

"Can I keep it?"

"Sure. Let's get going. The tide'll be turning."

"Ready, Cap'n."

They were getting in the boat when they heard a voice hailing them. Pinckney peered upriver at the hollowed-out cypress canoe that was approaching. When it came nearer, they could see that an incredibly old black man was rowing it. He grinned toothlessly when Pinny recognized him.

"It's Cudjo," Pinny shouted, "Daddy Cudjo!" He climbed up on the dock and reached out toward the white-wooled, shriveled old man.

"Bless Gawd, Mist' Pinckney. I never thought to set eye on you again." Cudjo scrambled nimbly onto the dock and was lost in Pinckney's embrace.

They did not have long to talk. The tide would not wait. Pinny learned that Cudjo was still living in the cabin that had been his home for fifty years and that his grandsons, his "boys," provided him with ample food and firewood. Then Pinny had to leave. "I'll be back, Cudjo," he promised.

"I'll be waiting, Mist' Pinckney."

In the boat going home to the city, Pinny told Shad and Billy about the old man. "He was head man at the stables for as long as anyone can remember. Taught my papa to ride. And me. And Stuart. And did he ever love horses. He could talk to them in some special language, and they understood every word he said. Everybody said that Cudjo *was* the Carlington stud. He hand-raised every horse we ever raced . . . Also, he managed to wear out four wives and father more than thirty children. What a grand old man. Seeing him is the happiest thing that could have happened. Shad, life is looking better all the time. We'll be winners yet, you'll see."

The next day, Shad learned where to send the samples for testing. He waited until no one was near the Exchange Building and slipped unobserved into the Post Office. Then he performed the same maneuver at his bank. He returned to the house with a draft made out to Pinckney. "Found a fellow willing to gamble," he said. "We'll hear from the testers in a couple of months. This'll tide us over till then."

He did not name the gambler.

19

"Emma, how are your feet?"

"Josiah Anson! What kind of question is that? Next thing you'll ask me how is my liver."

Her husband bowed low before her. "Will you do me the honor of favoring me with the next waltz, Mistress Anson?"

"Have you taken leave of your senses? Go on about your business, Josiah. I have mending to do."

Mr. Anson's sudden wide smile made his face young. His wife's heart missed a beat. It was the first real smile she had seen on his face since he came home after Appomattox. "Emma, my dear," he said, "we've decided that it's time to revive the Society. We had a meeting this morning—all of us who're left—and made all the arrangements. Six weeks from today, there'll be a Saint Cecelia Ball."

Emma Anson gasped. Her husband did not need to explain the importance of his announcement. The Saint Cecelia Society represented the essence of the lost world of Charleston as it had been. Founded when the city itself was still a tiny, walled enclave, it had always been a symbol of the gaiety and lavish elegance of Charleston. The Ball held every January during the racing season was the highlight of social activity. Invitations were coveted by visitors from every major city in Europe and America. For Charlestonians, a young girl's major step into the world came when she was presented at the Saint Cecelia. The loss of land, money, slaves, family jewels—none of them had the impact of the loss of the treasured tradition of the Saint Cecelia. Its restoration would invigorate the shrinking ranks of survivors as nothing else could. "Josiah," Emma breathed. They clasped hands in unspoken communication.

Then she had a hundred questions. How would they find the materials for the punch—the Saint Cecelia Punch—where would they get food, an orchestra—the Society had had its own orchestra, made of the finest musicians from Europe—the money to pay for it all?

"You let the Managers worry about all that."

Mrs. Anson bit her lip. Only men were members of the Society. Always had been and always would be. They arranged everything, even to the names on the ladies' dance cards.

"You'll let me choose my own gown, I hope."

"Not even that, my dear. For this Ball, I want you to wear exactly what you did at the last one. I used to remember you in it all through the War. It reminded me what I was fighting for."

"Oh, Josiah." Mrs. Anson's lips began to tremble.

"Particularly that silly blue feather fan. Damn thing got in my nose." He peered, eyes bright, at his wife. Yes, she was all right. He always could make Emma laugh when she was threatening to cry; that, mercifully, had not changed.

"It's molted some," she said now, "but I know where it is. Even the Yankees didn't take it, it's so shabby."

"You carry it anyhow."

"Proudly."

". . . There is one thing that only you ladies can do for the Ball, Emma."

"But of course. What is it? The flowers, decorations? We'll do anything."

"You must be gracious to General Sickles." Emma Anson looked stricken. "I know," her husband said gently, "believe me, my dear, I know. You ladies will never forgive the Yankees for beating us. Any more than you will ever blame your men for losing. We don't deserve you.

"I hate to ask you this, Emma, but I am depending on you. The invitation to General and Mrs. Sickles is a condition of his permission to us to restore the Society. I want you to tell me what ladies will dance with him. I'll get their husbands to agree."

"But, Josiah, this is insufferable. The man's effrontery knows no limits. It would be better to have no Ball at all than to have those vultures preying on our private lives."

"Emma. Think. Think what the Ball will mean to everyone. And there will be at least five hundred. Surely we can lose two outsiders in the crowd. If you and the others will help."

"No. Absolutely not. It would spoil everything."

Josiah Anson was astounded. It was the first time in twenty-eight years of marriage that his wife had defied him.

"Emma, I beg of you."

And his wife was shocked. Never had Josiah Anson used those words to her. She thought of how Dan Sickles had shamed her. Worse, how she had humiliated herself. Suppose he said something about it to someone at the Ball. Suppose he had already said something to her husband. She looked at Mr. Anson through tear-drowned eyes. Oh, dear God, he looked so defeated. And only a few minutes earlier, he had been so proud and happy.

"Josiah, please forgive me. I'm a cantankerous old woman."

"I was just thinking that." He laughed, convincing neither of them.

"I know Sally Brewton will do it. I'll call on her tomorrow, and we'll make a list."

"Emma." He put his arms around her. "Thank you."

"What are you thinking of, Josiah Anson? Someone might walk in any minute. Now let me go before you muss my hair." Things were back to normal.

Pinckney waved the bankdraft like a flag. His eyes glowed with a reckless fire. Shad knew that look. It had always preceded a cavalry charge.

"If some stranger can gamble, so can we. We'll have a Christmas this year like Christmases should be." Pinckney threw his flaming head back and began the yell. Shad joined in.

The Tradds had a dozen friends to Christmas dinner but no invitations went out. Widows who had prepared themselves for a chicken wing so that their children could fill their stomachs found a ribbon-tied ham inside their doors with notes from Santa Claus attached to toys for the children and the basket of fruit and cakes.

Lizzie and Mary wore their new velvet dresses to their own dinner table, which was set for six courses. Stuart checked his new silver pocket watch every ten minutes and then returned it carefully to the pocket of his waistcoat. He had a man's suit. Pinckney introduced Shad to the strange taste of champagne. And all the servants found an odd little leather-covered notebook with their gifts of new clothing. They were now possessors of savings accounts at the National Freedman's Savings Bank and Trust Company. The U. S. Government-sponsored bank would open an account for any Negro with five cents to deposit. Elijah's subjects had five dollars recorded in their bankbooks, plus a shiny penny to take a ride on the streetcars which had just started operating from White Point Gardens to the far edge of the city at Shepard Street.

Julia Ashley contributed a haunch of vension and bushel basket of holly and pine boughs to decorate the house. She had come down from the Barony the week before, thinner than ever, uncommunicative about her life on the plantation, but with a warmth and air of quiet happiness that transformed her.

When she went out with Emma Anson to call on her friends, Mary and Pinckney speculated on what had happened to her. Shad's comment decided it. "Miss Ashley's been looking for trouble as long as I've known her," he said. "I expect she's got plenty of it now trying to run her place. Some folks need to be fighting to be happy."

The first post-War Saint Cecelia Ball had—as all good parties always must have—a swirl of unexpressed currents, undercurrents and crosscurrents. At the most evident level, it was a joy-filled reunion for the Charlestonians who had had to move away; almost without exception, they found a way to get back to the city for the special occasion, to greet old friends and relations, to exchange news of the missing months or years, to feel at home again as if the War had never been, as if there had been no break in the long tradition of the annual event.

Less evident but even more vital was the presentation of the debutantes. All those who had missed "their" year were dressed in white and made the Grand March with their fathers or brothers or grandfathers. All participants held their heads high with a proud smile, as did the spectators, in an unstated conspiracy: no one would notice how many men were missing, nor find anything unusual in the couples made of a tall girl escorted by a brother who was still amost a child. Mr. Anson escorted Lavinia, even though she was engaged. A girl should not be deprived of her coming out; she would remember it all her life. Of course, Pinckney was on her card for the sixteenth dance. It was always reserved for sweethearts and wives.

The great ball skirts swayed, dipped in deep curtsies, flourished laces rescued from attics and white gardenias newly gathered for decoration. Every mother watching surreptitiously compared the whiteness of her daughter's long kid gloves to the others'. They had been bleaching in corn meal ever since the Ball was announced. If anyone in Charleston had money enough to buy new ones, she would not embarrass her friends by doing so. Mrs. Sickles had the decency to be obviously uncomfortable in her dazzlingly fresh gown, slippers and gloves. The ladies of Charleston had the grace to hide the enormous gratification they felt when they saw her unease.

Before the dancing began, the young girls had already stolen glances at the dance cards given them. There was the same reaction that there had been at the Ball for over a hundred years. Elation at some names, despair at others, horror at at least one. Yet still, it was a real ball, the first most of these white-gowned girls had known. The music was thrilling; the men and boys looked universally romantic in their dress suits; the excitement of everyone there was contagious. They would, indeed, remember it all their lives.

Mr. Anson bowed low before a diminutive girl in white satin. General Sickles started to step forward, but a small, determined hand grabbed his arm. "You are not planning to make a scene, General," Sally Brewton murmured. It was a statement, not a question.

"He should invite my wife to dance first," Sickles whispered in a harsh tone.

"But, General," Sally looked up at him with her enchanting smile, "then you would not be at the Saint Ceceila. The most recent bride is *always* honored by wearing her wedding gown and opening the Ball with the president of the Society. I've known of girls who would marry anybody just as long as it was timed right. And the unfortunate ministers of our churches! The scheduling of weddings in the season requires a diplomacy that, I fear, has driven more than one Godly man straight to the bottle."

Sickles smiled.

The crisis was past.

Throughout the long, giddy evening, General Daniel Sickles, hero of Gettysburg, was treated to an ordeal that made the War seem a picnic. There was no insult, not the slightest show of disrespect to him or his wife. On the contrary, the gentlemen and ladies of Charleston were so cordial, so charming, so solicitous of their comfort and enjoyment that even Mrs. Sickles, a woman of remarkable obtuseness, finally began to feel that something elusive was not quite right. The unfortunate General, who had insisted on the invitation only because his wife tormented him into the demand, discovered that he had unaccountably become clumsy, almost oafish. He repeatedly stepped on the feet of his dancing partners, even Sally Brewton who was legendary for her gossamer waltzing. The ladies all refused to accept his apologies, with such vehement claims to responsibility that he knew that he was at fault. Before an hour had passed, he was sweating horribly. After two, he wanted to throttle his wife. By the time supper was served, he wished whole-heartedly that he was dead.

For the citizens of Charleston, the presence of their oppressors sharpened their wits and added exquisite spice to their pleasure. "Only the very civilized," said Julia Ashley to her nephew, "recognize the value of subtlety. I understand that the Chinese have knives so finely honed that a man can be in ribbons before he realizes that he's bleeding. I haven't enjoyed myself so much in twenty years."

For the final dance, the orchestra played "The Blue Danube Waltz." Emma Anson's chin quivered when she heard it, but she willed herself into dry eyes. That had been the final dance at the last Saint Cecelia, the one before the War. The music had been new then, like the finery of the Charlestonians who heard it again this night, six years later. Nothing had changed, nothing that mattered. She spread the battered blue feather fan across the lower half of her face until she gained control of it. "I'm flirting with you, Josiah Anson," she said when her husband bowed before her.

"My dear, you ravish my heart. Shall we show these young people what real waltzing looks like?"

Emma Anson rose, curtsied deeply, then stepped into the firm embrace of her husband. She no longer felt any sadness.

The following month, the bells of Saint Michael's came home from recasting in England. The customs official appointed by Sickles set a duty of two thousand dollars on them, but everyone contributed willingly from their lean purses. The chimes had marked the passing hours for all of them since their births, and the births of their fathers and grandfathers. When the bells returned so did the watchman who sang out after the hour struck. ". . . of the clock, and all's well." With the familiar deep bell still reverberating in the air, the people of the old city could believe that it was true. They still had their heritage.

And so, another tradition, the Cotillion Club, was reborn with a Ball planned for March. It was a much younger organization than the Saint Cecelia, because it had started only in 1800 and by its very nature had a less stable form. The members were Charleston's bachelors. Membership terminated with marriage, and the officers were elected for one year only. In the Saint Cecelia, the President was elected for his lifetime, and the other officers were usually renamed every year unless they asked to be excused. The Cotillion Club was a sort of proving ground. Pinckney was a member, but he was not nominated for any duties, for which he was grateful. The report on the sample of marl came back in February, and it plunged him into a whirl of activity.

The chemical analysis meant nothing to him or to Shad. Someone had to decipher the list of symbols and numbers before they could tell whether the news was good or bad. Clearly, it was Pinckney's job. Shad's progress in basic education was astounding, but he was not up to the task of learning a whole new science. Pinckney was not at all sure about his own abilities, but Shad's confidence in him was absolute. He would have to deliver.

It was a challenge he invited Prudence to share. She was, after all, a teacher. And a regular guest in the Tradd home. Here at last was an acceptable bond between them. Besides, as Pinckney admitted, he wanted to share everything with her.

The nightmare of deception that had been necessary when the Edwardses came to the Tradds' was over at last. Pinckney and Prudence could be openly interested in each other, at least as scholars. While Mary cooed admiration of Adam Edwards' opinions, the younger man and woman huddled over the books and papers they spread on a table in the corner of the room. It did not take many weeks for them to learn what they needed to know. The deposit of minerals at Carlington was 60 percent phosphate of lime, a high concentration. It yielded phosphoric acid, the essential ingredient for manufacturing chemical fertilizer, at just under 6.00 on the scale used for calibration. In all the world, there were only four major known sources of phosphate: Germany, England, the Bordeaux region of France and an almost inaccessible undeveloped dot on the map named Raza Island. Carlington's deposit was richer than any of the European sources, more available than Raza's.

Pinckney and Shad were euphoric. "I told you," Shad chortled. "Picking up money off the ground, I said." Prudence was genuinely happy for Pinckney's sake. She knew, better than anyone, how he had agonized about his need to support his family. But his preoccupation with the development of the find at Carlington had diminished the hold she had over him. He no longer needed her or her body to give meaning and happiness in his life. He had a new, consuming interest to absorb his energies, to give him scope for his daring impulses, to fill his active mind. And his love for Carlington was of a degree that love for a woman could never equal. The clandestine meetings in the schoolroom became more and more widely separated. And a seed of anger was planted in her wild heart.

When the representatives of the Cotillion Club came to tell her they wanted to use the Hall for their dance, the seed sent out an unfelt tiny shoot. Pinckney could have arranged to be the one who would speak for the club. Then they would have had another hour alone together. She forced herself not to think about him with Lavinia at his side, surrounded by music and laughter and all the people in Charleston who barely tolerated the Edwardses for a few hours on Sunday. Jealousy was ignoble and childish, she reminded herself.

But when Pinckney told her that he had invited Shad to the Ball, she almost wept. Why could a man who was an outsider cross lines that were like high walls to a woman? It was no comfort to her that Shad wanted very much not to go.

"You must be crazy, Cap'n," he said when Pinckney presented him with his guest card.

"Maybe so, Shad, but not about this. You'll have a good time."

"You bet I will. Somewhere else."

Pinny would not be denied. He nagged and bullied for days. Finally he found the soft spot in Shad's resistance. He laid Anson Tradd's dress suit on Shad's bed. It had already been altered to fit him. Shad knew that Pinckney idolized his lost father. The gift of the suit might have been refused; the gift of its alteration could not. In a way, Pinny had already given up a bit of his memory of his father so that his friend could have some pleasure. Shad had to accept. He hid his apprehensions and went out for a haircut, shave and manicure. On the night of the dance, he looked at himself in the long mirror in the drawing room without recognition. He had gained weight. The still-handsome swallow-tailed coat called for a prouder stance; he straightened from his customary slouch without effort. His tow hair was sleek and darkened by the barber's oil to almost blonde. His new straggly moustache had been trimmed to geometric sharpness, and his sparse chin whiskers were gone. He looked like a gentleman.

Pinckney's face appeared over his shoulder. "What do you think?" He smiled proudly.

Shad's eyes crinkled. "I'd be lying if I said I wasn't taken with myself . . . Long's I don't say nothing to nobody, who's to know I ain't a drop of blue blood?"

"Stop that kind of talk. Let's get moving. I have to call for Lavinia and Lucy across the street. When you see us crossing back over, meet us next door. Until then, you can let the strange creature behind that chair over there come out and admire you." Lizzie giggled and emerged from hiding.

20

"How can they do that, Cap'n?"

"How can who do what, Shad?"

"All them—those—ladies. Waving their fans and rolling their eyes and dancing around chattering like they didn't have a care in the world. Hardly a one but I sold more than half what she owned, but you'd think they wasn't bothered atall."

Pinckney surveyed the scene before him. The long ballroom of the South Carolina Hall had been cleared of desks and chairs, and the floor waxed to the point of danger. At the far end of the room, a band of eight musicians in formal dress were seated on a flower-bordered platform, playing waltzes nonstop. The windowsills were heaped with masses of peach blossoms, which dropped a few creamy petals every time a breeze blew through the open windows. Just inside the tall french doors, tail-coated black butlers served fruit punch from huge bowls at each end of a long banquet table. Platters of tiny sandwiches filled the space between them. Out on the deep, columned porch where he and Shad were, formally dressed gentlemen stood in groups around the smaller table where Elijah presided with a broad grin over a single punchbowl. Pinckney lit a thin cheroot.

"I'll tell you, Shad, as well as I can. It's more something you feel in your bones than something you understand in your head. Every year since I can remember, the Cotillion Club always had a Ball in this place. Now they're having another. The orchestra's smaller, the refreshments are pitiful, the ladies have old dresses and no jewels, but everybody's having a good time. Part of it is because Charleston always has been a place where people believed in pleasure—none of the Puritan business the New England settlements had—and part of it is because tradition is important to us—we're almighty proud of our ancestors—and part of it is because we've learned the past two years that when the Yankees took away our things, we were left with something very valuable we hadn't even noticed we had—good manners. In history books, it's called 'civilization'; here right now, it's called nobody eating more than one of those fingernail-sized sandwiches so that it will look like there are more refreshments than needed. In the old days, three or four hams, and a couple of hundred biscuits and a few gallons of oyster stew and a half-dozen turkeys would have been just the beginning. Does that make any sense to you?"

Shad's watchful eyes crinkled, his way of smiling. "I can't say it makes much sense, but I kind of admire it." He gestured behind him with his thumb. "I don't suppose that hurts none, neither." In the street below, groups of soldiers and flashily dressed civilians stood with their faces turned up toward the sound of the music.

Pinckney grinned. "It galls the hell out of them to know we're enjoying ourselves. It's a great added pleasure. Speaking of which, let's get a little something from 'Lijah. Out here on the porch, the gentlemen are allowed to smoke, and the punch has a stick in it. Then we'd better do our duty and go join the ladies."

As Pinny expected, Shad ignored all the expectant debutantes who were stealing glances at Pinckney Tradd's interesting looking friend. He had learned to trust Shad's instincts about the invisible boundaries of his relationships with the Charlestonians he met at the Tradd house or when he was out with Pinckney. Josiah Anson was one species; Emma Anson was another. Debutantes were not for him. Pinckney did not think that he might be putting too much weight on Shad. He wanted his friend to share as much as possible of what he valued most about his city. They both knew that the possible was severely limited. Shad walked directly to Lucy Anson and bowed awkwardly.

"Shad! How kind of you to come talk to me. Won't you sit down?" Pinny made his bow then responded to Lavinia's call. Shad settled himself gingerly on the narrow gilded chair next to Lucy's.

"Do you think this thing will hold me?"

Lucy patted his arm. "They're a lot stronger than they look. My mother-in-law can't break them."

Shad blinked. He would never have suspected that Lucy could say anything sharp about anyone. He had not seen her often, and when she had been in evidence, she had hardly spoken a word. Lucy was the kind of lady who unobstrusively made sure that there were enough cups and saucers while another lady made a ceremony out of pouring the tea.

"Are you enjoying yourself, Shad?"

Somehow he understood that she really wanted to know. "Half and half," he replied.

"Which is the good half?"

"The pretty part. I never heard this kind of music before. And I never looked so pretty myself." He was amazed at his own words.

Lucy smiled warmly. "I thank you for confiding in me," she said quietly. "I know a confidence when I hear one. Now I'll trade you one if you'll let me." Shad didn't know what to say.

"Why, sure," he stammered.

"I want you to do me a big favor. I want you to act as if I'm fascinating you right out of your collar."

"Truth is, Mistress Anson, you are."

Lucy giggled. She sounded as young as Lizzie. "Please don't call me that. Miss Emma is Mistress Anson. I don't call you Mr. Simmons. You must call me Lucy." They compromised on "Miss Lucy." She responded to Shad's quiet attentiveness like a wilted garden in a rain shower, talking with unaccustomed animation and indiscretion. "I never expected to be here," she said, "but Mr. Josiah insisted. I'll be grateful for the rest of my life. I didn't realize how much I missed parties and people. You know, one minute I was like all those girls, flirting and dancing, and the next minute I was a married lady and a mother. Andrew and I were both so young. And then the War and then— It's selfish of me to miss dancing when Andrew can't even walk. But I do. How old are you, Shad?"

"I don't rightly know."

"You can tell me. I won't tell anybody."

"I don't mind you knowing. It's just that I ain't—I'm not sure myself. Near's I can figure, I must be pretty near eighteen one way or the other."

"Good grief. And I thought I was young. I'm twenty-one tomorrow." She grimaced. "Feeling sorry for myself because I have to be a grown-up, too. That's silly. Sitting here talking up a storm with a handsome young man, causing a little scandal, that's too much fun to put a cloud on."

"Scandal? Miss Lucy, I don't want you to get in trouble."

"Pooh! You're being nice to me. I can trust you, Shad, and feel naughty and flirtatious at the same time. I can, can't I?"

"Yes, ma'am. I wouldn't know flirting if I saw it anyhow."

"You and Pinckney. He's just as bad. Just look at all the girls—and plenty of the ladies, too—cutting their eyes at him. He doesn't notice a thing."

"But he's engaged."

"Don't be a simpleton, Shad. Look at Lavinia. Is that a girl about to be married to a man she loves? Pinny should either horsewhip her or jilt her tomorrow."

In fact, if there was a scandal brewing at the ball, it was in Lavinia Anson's behavior. Her father's and mother's eyes were not on her, as they had been at the Saint Cecelia. She was giddy with freedom and with the heady reactions of all the boys and men to the secret she had learned from Pinckney. She had something they all wanted. Even though she did not know exactly what it was, the knowledge that it existed and was in her possession made her seductive in a way that the debutantes could not match. Lavinia's flirtation was not innocent, even though she was ignorant. Even older men responded unconsciously. The younger ones clustered around her like the proverbial moths when exposed to a candle. Pinckney alone was immune. And Shad. The elderly female chaperones were horrified.

It made the Ball a much greater success than it would otherwise have been. There was nothing Charlestonians liked better than a good scandal, and they had not had the luxury of one for a long time. In all the excitement, Pinckney Tradd's unacceptable protégé was forgotten, and Shad had the luxury of making a friend.

That did not, however, blur his two perceptions of the evening. He was neither comfortable nor welcome among the aristocracy, no matter what Pinckney might persuade himself to believe. And excellent clothing changed a man, both outside and in. He made a silent vow to himself that he would accept no more invitations from Charlestonians and that someday he would have the finest suits money could buy.

Pinckney and Shad did not sleep at all that night. After they escorted Lavinia and Lucy to the Anson house, they changed their clothes and left on hired horses to ride to Carlington by moonlight. A cold drizzle began when they were halfway there, but nothing could dampen their spirits. It was daylight when they arrived, a very dim, wet daylight. They sat on the edge of the excavation with the rain dripping off their hat brims and drank the whiskey in their flasks, toasting the beginnings of the Tradd-Simmons Phosphate Company. The division of labor was according to the pattern they had already established. Pinckney would produce the material; Shad would sell it. "Hard times are almost over," Pinny shouted to the sky. "Nothing can stop us now."

It was as if he had defied heaven itself. The rain that began that morning continued with only brief respites for the next three months. No one in Charleston could remember weather like it. The crops planted before the rains rotted in seas of mud that had been fields of pea vines and rows of pole beans. Later crops could not be planted. The city drains were unable to handle the volume of water. The earth banks along the promenade and the edges of the city overflowed at full moon, and people had to use boats on some streets. There was no possible way to start organizing work at Carlington. It was inaccessible by roads waist-deep in mud, and the swollen Cooper River was full of perilous snags where whole trees had fallen in when the riverbanks washed away. Pinckney was confined to the city, although he was too restless to stay in the house. He spent much of his time at the old Powder Magazine on Cumberland Street. It was the Arsenal for the Light Dragoons, and he could count on finding friends there, escapees from their own homes and their feelings of being caged. Frequently he let Stuart accompany him. The Clubhouse in Alex Wentworth's yard was washed out, and Mrs. Wentworth would not allow the boys to meet in the house. Nor would the mothers of any of the other members, including Mary Tradd. Eight boys were too many, too big, too noisy.

Thus it was that Stuart was able to trail along behind when the Dragoons were called out to put down a riot. It made him the envy of all his friends.

One of the hardest hit areas of town was the network of alleys near the docks. The Negroes there lived four and five to a room in the deteriorating buildings that had never been repaired. The crowding did not seem to matter very much when life was lived primarily in the courtyards and streets. It was intolerable when week after week people had to huddle under leaking roofs. Like their white neighbors, they began by praying for relief. But then the adherents of older, more primitive religions began to make themselves heard. The conjure women, terrifying crones who practiced ancient arts of herbalism and witchcraft, had the answer. The reason for the rain was the mermaid that was in captivity in Trott's Pharmacy. Before the rumor was an hour old, twenty people swore that they had seen her, that she was alive and kept in a glass tank filled with water. Men and women seized lengths of wood to use as clubs, and a raging mob poured into the streets and splashed through the water toward the pharmacy. They had to release the water creature or else the water would rise so high that she would be freed by her own element.

The Dragoons arrived too late to prevent the destruction of all the jars and bottles in the pharmacy. They did stop the mob from killing Dr. Trott and each other when they finally found that the mermaid was a small sea horse in a bottle of alcohol. Stuart enjoyed every minute of it.

Of all the inhabitants of the Tradd house, Shad was most affected by the rain and showed it least. He joked with Lizzie when he carried her to and from school on the days that Meeting Street was flooded. In the afternoons, he let her bully him into reading aloud from the Waverley novels while she rocked Bear on her lap. He sat for hours with Pinckney making plans and sketches for the exploration of the marl deposits. And all the time, he was worried sick. The rain was not as heavy or persistent in the country away from Charleston. But it was bad enough to be a threat to the cotton crop. And if there was no cotton, there would be nothing to factor and no money to invest in developing Carlington. He was determined to allow no outsider to invest. He knew that they would treat Tradd-Simmons Phosphate Company with as much mercy as his factoring business showed to the cotton farmers. The only thing he could do was wait.

In June, the sun came out. The streetcars' bells rang again, the streets steamed, and roses which should have drowned long ago bloomed overnight. While the Army and the carpetbaggers complained about the prices of the food shipped in on the new shining rails of the three railroads they had built, the Charlestonians took a grim pride in their ability to survive yet another disaster and the tough bitter collard greens that were usually considered Negro food. Nothing could kill collard greens, not even a biblical deluge. Just as nothing could kill Charleston. Collards became a regular part of the city's diet, black and white, even when the seasons returned to normal.

Shad resisted Pinckney's pleas that they take their chances on either the roads or the river. He claimed a sudden desire to see his father, packed a small valise and a pouch of cornbread and took the train upstate to see for himself what had happened to cotton.

The hasty trip was one of the major turning points in his life. He discovered that the crops were poor, but not a total loss. He also learned about the new towns that had been born during the winter.

They resulted from the three-way mating of the new railroad, the age-old Edisto River, and the mills built by men with shrewd eyes and war profits to invest. There was no need to ship cotton to the coast then to England where it was spun into thread and woven into cloth. The spinning mills could take the cotton directly from the gin and ship compact spools, a thousand times the value of the same tonnage in cotton bales.

It cost almost nothing to produce. Poor whites, weary of fighting the soil and the skies to produce a crop for the factors' profit, were lining up for jobs in the mills. To them, a ten-hour day was idleness in comparison with farming. Besides, they were given a fresh pine two-room shack to live in, and they had neighbors to celebrate with on Saturday night and to sing with in church on Sunday. They did not have to work on the Sabbath, not even milk a cow. There was plenty of milk at the town store that the mill operated. And they could put what they wanted to buy on their accounts. Their salaries were paid to the store manager to cover their bills. Anything left over was theirs to do with as they pleased. They did not recognize their bondage, and if a few did realize it, they did not care. There was plenty of "white lightning" to buy from the moonshiners on Saturday night and salvation on Sunday.

Shad Simmons extended his trip by two days. In overalls, on a borrowed mule, he roamed up and across the river until he found what he wanted. The land was flat, the river straight and swift, and a spur track could be laid without any hills to detour it. He bought three twenty-acre farms for two dollars an acre and generously allowed the families on them to stay, rent-free, until he told them to move. He would learn about the mill machinery when he had enough money from factoring to buy it. He returned to Charleston with empty pockets and a gallon jug of corn likker.

He told Pinckney about the mill towns he had seen. He did not mention his intention to build one as soon as he could; he knew that the rice planters of Charleston looked down their patrician noses at red-clay cotton and everything associated with it, except the fees the cotton brokers had charged in the days before the War when brokerage was an acceptable occupation for gentlemen who never saw the country that produced the cotton or even the interiors of the warehouses that held it on the Bay Street docks. Instead, he painted a Garden of Eden of happiness for the workers who had every comfort provided without the burden of worrying about how to manage their wages. To Pinckney, who had been raised on the paternalistic slave-owner views of his father, it sounded like the perfect system for the labor he would hire for Carlington. Shad agreed solemnly. Later he would find a white man to run the store, he said. Pinny agreed impatiently. He had many of the prejudices of his class, without knowing that he had them or that they were prejudices. Of course, they would need a white man to run the store; darkies couldn't be expected to learn bookkeeping or to work long hours. And Shad would have to locate him among the new people in Charleston whom he knew at the Hotel; no one Pinckney knew would go into trade, even if he had to starve first. Besides, Pinckney didn't want to think about details. He wanted to get to Carlington.

21

Pinckney's departure totally disrupted the routine that had developed in the Tradd house. The twice weekly visits by the Edwardses had to stop. Mary bemoaned the gap in her life. Prudence suffered more silently and more deeply. She and Pinckney had exchanged roles. Now it was she who was obsessed and he who determined the clandestine rendezvous. During the months of rain, his increasing tension had escalated their frequency, and Prudence had existed in a perpetual fever of hidden excitement. Then he was gone.

Pinny was missed in the Anson household, too. His calls on Lavinia had decreased to near extinction, but he had remained faithful to his friend Andrew, seeing him for at least a few minutes every second or third day. He had encouraged Andrew to perservere in his laborious studies. With Pinckney gone, Andrew gave up. It was a body blow to his father and to his wife. Josiah and Lucy were unable to rally Andrew or to make him believe in himself. "Selfish," Emma Anson said about Pinckney, hiding her worry about Andrew in her anger.

Lizzie was tearful and disobedient. Shad might have filled in the void for her, but he was almost never home, out "on business," which was all he would say. When Sophy took her to the Gardens, Lizzie delighted in getting as dirty as possible to irritate her.

One hot afternoon, Sophy offered her a forbidden treat. Instead of staying at the park, they would ride the streetcar. Lizzie had been on the exciting red cars only once, with Pinckney, and then only for the five blocks from the start of the line at the park to Broad Street. She climbed aboard with Sophy and squealed with excitement when the driver rang the bell and slapped the reins on the horses' backs. The car stopped at Broad Street and Lizzie sighed. But Sophy told her to stay seated. They weren't getting off. Lizzie's eyes widened. What an adventure. She hadn't been above Broad Street, which was the limit of the purely residential district, since they had moved down from Julia's house on Charlotte Street more than two years earlier.

Her wonder grew as the car moved slowly up Meeting. Everywhere there was an air of hurry, of busy activity. The sidewalks were crowded with people walking fast. On all sides, new buildings were going up, and the sound of hammering made her cover her ears. Men and women boarded the car and left it, always in a hurry. Except for two women with extremely pink cheeks and gowns trimmed in feathers and beads. They took their time. Lizzie was admiring them when Sophy's rough hand clamped over her eyes and stayed there while the car proceeded for three more stops.

At the next corner, the car turned to the left. Lizzie stared, awe-struck, at the crenelated walls and towers of The Citadel. On the parade ground in front of it, one of the Army regiments headquartered there marched in drill, with drums to set the beat. It was a display of authority and power meant to impress the knots of loungers who thronged the edges of the square. It terrified Lizzie. She made herself as small as she could and moved nearer to Sophy. On the far corner, the car stopped and Sophy told her to get off. "No, I don't want to," Lizzie cried. Sophy held her by the upper arm and pulled her along down the step onto the crowded sidewalk.

Pushing with one hand, clutching Lizzie in a cruel vise with the other, Sophy battered a path through the masses of men and women. Lizzie could hardly keep up, and she could see nothing except blurred color through the tears pouring from her eyes. She felt the press of hot bodies and smelled the rank odors of stale sweat and cheap whiskey. Hands pulled the sash of her pinafore and the ribbons on her straw hat. Loud voices exclaimed about her red hair and white face. She couldn't breathe.

Sophy dragged her away from the people, across the uneven bricks of King Street and along an almost empty sidewalk. Then she stopped. "Look at there," she said in a frightening whisper. She pointed Lizzie toward the street. On the other side, a tall brick wall surrounded a square of sunburnt grass. Huge iron gates with a frieze of pointed spears stood open. Through them, Lizzie could see an enormous stone building. She did not appreciate the beauty of its proportions and rhythmic repetition of pillared porches. It looked monolithic and overpoweringly threatening to her. Her breath rasped in her throat, and she began to choke. Sophy shook her roughly. "Stop that badness," she hissed. "You is a bad girl and I done bring you here to show you what happen to bad girls like you. That there is the Orphan Asylum where they puts bad children. Do you want to know what they gets to eat? I tell you. They gets to eat once a day and what they eats is cold hominy and water. Lessen they is real bad. Then they don't gets nothing at all. They sleeps on the floor, them bad girl like you, with cockroach biting they toe. And that's where your mama going to send you if you don't stop dirtying your pinafore and start minding what I tells you to do. You hear me?"

Lizzie gasped for air. Sophy twisted her arm. "I says do you hear me?" Lizzie nodded. "Then let's go home. And don't you tell nobody I took you on the streetcar or the soldiers will come get you and lock you up in the Asylum." The child's body crumpled in a faint.

"Do, Jesus," Sophy moaned. She picked Lizzie up in her arms and hurried back to King Street. She held her on her lap on the streetcar, rocking the trembling body back and forth, praying aloud. Before they got home, Lizzie regained consciousness. When the car crossed Broad Street, and she saw the familiar houses and trees, her breathing eased.

"I'll be good, Sophy," she said. "Please don't take me to that place ever. I'll be good, I promise."

A few days later, Mary Tradd noticed that the house was more peaceful than it had been. "I think Pinny spoiled Lizzie dreadfully," she said to her callers. "Lizzie is ever so much better behaved now that he's away."

He stayed away for over four months. Mary sent frantic written and verbal entreaties to come home every time Shad went to Carlington to view progress and report on his own activity about supplies and sales; every time Pinckney sent back polite written and verbal refusals.

His mother wanted to lean on his strength; conditions were straining the courage of the Charlestonians to the breaking point. For many, the money realized by the sale of their land and possessions was running out. For everyone, poverty's grip was tightening because of the inflated prices that resulted from the crop failures and the increasing numbers of carpetbaggers with fat purses. The weakest women—whose men had not returned from the War—had no way of surviving if their relatives could not take them in or if they were too proud themselves to be a burden on their struggling kin. As it had always done, the close-knit community found a way to survive. Everyone made do with less of everything, except a brave gaiety. Then the Mistresses Snowden, who were widows themselves, mortgaged their home to pay the rent on a beautiful, sound building on Broad Street. It had been a comfortable small hotel; it became The Confederate Home for Mothers, Widows and Daughters of Confederate Soldiers. And everyone managed on even less, to contribute to the maintenance of the Home.

In September, Sickles was replaced by General E. R. S. Canby, whose rule was harsher and more humiliating. He instructed his men to enforce the nine o'clock curfew with no exceptions; even ladies and their escorts leaving a starvation party were arrested and taken before a military judge at the Guardhouse and jail on the corner of Broad and Meeting streets. He issued orders to the Rifle Companies instead of requesting their assistance; Charleston's men had to comply or leave the residential streets unguarded, and their protection was needed more than ever before because the Union League was growing stronger with each passing day. Finally,

Canby unwittingly struck a terrible blow to the morale of everyone. He inspected Sickles' living arrangements in Julia Ashley's house and decided that they were not adequately luxurious. For himself and his wife, he took Miles Brewton's house; the military guard in front was a constant reminder that even the old town did not really belong to its citizens. And Sally Brewton went to England to join her husband.

"I need you, Pinny," Mary Tradd lamented, but he could not respond. He had to get operations at Carlington underway for the survival of them all. He had to do it in solitude, so that no one would know the despair it caused him to tear apart the earth that had always nurtured the Tradds and given them a silent final home. And he had to hide from them all the violent attacks of swamp fever that had begun in midsummer.

They occurred regularly every third day, so he was able to schedule Shad's visits for his good days. On the bad days, he would start work at dawn and then when, in the afternoon, the chills attacked his lower spine, he had time to get to his camp bed in the house before his body was shaking too much for him to move. Cudjo stayed with him then, covering his shivering form with rough blankets and, when the chills reversed to dry heat, bathing his dry skin and holding a gourd of water to his thirsty lips. When the sweating began, Cudjo's dark face would lose its worry lines, and he would fall asleep on the bed he had put near Pinckney's. Soon after, his snores would blend with the regular, feverless breathing of Pinckney's exhausted sleep.

One day in November, Shad made an unannounced visit, bringing the contract he had completed after two months of negotiations, and a bottle of champagne. The preliminaries were over. First they'd celebrate, then they'd go into production.

He heard the eerie spasmodic rattling before he passed the front door. Cudjo ran out to stop him in the hall, but Shad pushed past him and stepped into the long, shadowy room where once Anson Tradd had bargained with his son about an inkwell. Pinckney saw him and tried to sit up, but the muscle tremors were stronger than his will. He fell back on his stained canvas cot, and the sound of his chattering teeth echoed grotesquely as he abandoned the effort to control his weak body. His face was ghostly white, with dark rings around sunken eyes. The skin seemed to be stretched too tightly over it; his thin nose and high cheekbones stood out like knives. Shad knelt by him and took his hand. It was bleached and bony like his face; the nails were blue. "Christ!" Shad groaned, "he's dying."

"No, sir, Mist' Shad, he ain't," said Cudjo. "Be all right for breakfast, don't you fret yourself none."

Shad did not believe him. He stayed on his knees by Pinckney until the bed stopped shaking. Then he paced the lamp-lit room in an agony of worry while Cudjo ministered expertly to Pinny's delirious cries for water. When the fever broke, Pinckney was weak but lucid. "What the hell did you come today for?" he demanded.

Shad rushed to his side. The sweat poured from every pore of Pinckney's body, soaking his clothes and his hair. "See why I gave up sheets and pillows?" he said with a smile. "Don't look like an old granny, I'm all right. Just a little ague."

"You sure?"

"Sure. I just need a little rest. Tell Cudjo to find you a bed and a blanket." He closed his eyes and went immediately into a deep sleep. Shad held the lantern close. Pinckney's color was healthy, his skin moist and cool to the touch. Nevertheless, Shad sat on the floor by him all night.

In the morning his eyes were scratchy and his cramped muscles ached. Pinckney woke at daybreak full of vitality, which Shad found irritating. "What the hell have you done to yourself, anyhow?" he asked.

Pinny laughed. "Just what I always do to get myself in trouble," he said. "Act first, pay for it later. Somehow I never thought the fever would get me. I know it gets any white man who stays in the country in the summer, but I couldn't wait to get started, so I didn't. And it got me."

"Can't you take something for it?"

"Yes. Peruvian bark cuts the pain and the fever. I had some, but I ran out."

"You don't have the sense of a crawfish. I'm taking you back with me." And in spite of Pinckney's outraged objections, that is what he did. In fact, there was little left for Pinckney to do. The excavation in the surface patch of marl had been extended by Cudjo's boys in radiating spokelike trenches, which followed the deposit as it moved deeper under the surface. They knew now that it tailed off on its western perimeter and extended for acres to the north and south. The house was not far from its eastern edge; Pinckney did not want to dig there, although the deposit continued under its foundations.

They had also repaired thc old street of slave cabins and had caulked walls and replaced windows in three rooms of the house. The former dining room was now outfitted with a counter and shelves, waiting the supplies for the workers with which it would be stocked before the first of January. They could hire no workers until then. The low country had developed a new tradition to add to its collection. New Year's Day was now known as Emancipation Day by all the Negroes. On that morning they would accept or refuse to hire on at the jobs offered to them. And after doing business, the employer was expected to provide food, drink and fireworks for festivities that lasted the rest of the day.

Shad had already bought the picks, shovels, ropes, wheelbarrows and nets they would need. They would be held in Charleston warehouses until the last minute while Cudjo and his boys built barges for their transport.

"You're going to have to give your store manager something more comfortable than a camp cot to live with," Shad said. "Maybe Miss Ashley will spare you a bed and a table."

"Aunt Julia? She wouldn't spare anybody a kind word."

"She might. She's got her house in town back now, and Stuart says there's enough furniture in it for a hotel. You can ask her nice. She's coming to town next week."

"Dear heaven. Now I know I'm staying here."

"Then you know wrong."

Dr. Trott of mermaid fame was able to supply Pinckney with a high quality quinine. "No more than thirty grains a day," he said, "or you'll poison yourself." Pinny agreed. He took fifty, and the attacks stopped.

All his days were, in truth, extremely busy. He wanted to see the stored equipment for Carlington and his friends and his family. He had to see his aunt and Lavinia. Both of them had shocks in store for him.

Lavinia wanted to set the date for their wedding. "After all, Pinny," she said demurely, "we've been engaged four years this Christmas. I understand why it had to be so long. Papa explained to me that you had to get your feet on the ground and be able to take care of a family and all. I respect you for it, really I do, and it just makes me love you more. But it's been awful hard, Pinny, watching you work yourself to the absolute bone and everybody taking advantage of you and leaning on you and you being so brave and strong. When all the time I was just longing to be there at your side, sharing your burdens and caring for you and all. It just ate at me and ate at me. That's what made me so mean and horrid. You know I didn't mean any of those terrible things I said." Her wide blue eyes looked up at him imploringly. The long lashes were wet. Pinckney stammered unintelligibly. Lavinia threw her soft bare arms around his neck and placed a virginal kiss on his cheek. "Oh, my angel husband," she whispered into his ear, "I knew you wouldn't be mad at me. And I'll never, never be mad at you no matter what." She released him and nestled against his shoulder, looking up, smiling, her dimple like a beauty spot. "Papa says you're going to do real well with that bone stuff, whatever it is. You're so smart to have thought of selling some old rocks to the Yankees. And that means there's nothing to stop us getting married. I guess I'm the happiest girl in the whole world."

Pinckney clutched at the only straw he could see. "I'll have to talk to your father," he said.

"Of course you will. But not right this minute, darling. He and Mama have just finished moving back to Charlotte Street, and he's mad as a hornet about the damage the Yankees did. I absolutely tiptoe when he's around; he's grouchy as an old bear."

Delay seemed reprieve to Pinckney. He agreed to wait awhile before approaching Josiah Anson, not realizing that he was, in effect, agreeing to marry Lavinia at the same time.

A few days later he saw Josiah Anson, but there was no opportunity to talk to him. The two of them were only uneasy spectators at a fight between Emma Anson and Julia Ashley. Pinckney had escorted his aunt to Charlotte Street to see her house the same day she arrived from the Barony. On the drive uptown, she told him the news that later enraged her old friend and neighbor. She was going to rent her house, not as a house, but by the room. "I made a trip in to see it when the Yankees turned it back over to me," she said, "and I decided then. For one thing, the rain ruined my rice this year, and I need money; for another, the Barony takes all my time year around; and mainly, the whole city is changing. No one wants to live uptown except darkies and white trash. If I'm going to rent it, I might as well rent to the kind that want it. I hired a commission agent who'll see that they pay. A family to a room, white in the house and black in the outbuildings."

When she repeated this to Emma Anson, the battle was joined, and the men were helpless. Mr. Anson could not argue with his wife. "Josiah built me this house for a wedding present," she said. "We lived here every day of our lives until the Yankees stole it. Now that they've given it back, I mean to spend every day I have left right here in my home."

Nor could Pinckney have argued with his aunt, even if he had been so foolhardy. The city was changing. Julia Ashley was not the first to turn her home into a slum. Under the constant attack of hardship and insult, the Charlestonians were slowly closing in on themselves, a physical and emotional tightening. The old city, which had survived every attack man or nature could devise, was becoming their refuge. Without conscious choice, they were withdrawing behind the line where the first settlers had built Charleston's wall of defense. Broad Street. The area north of it could be abandoned to the outsiders. South of Broad was and always would be the real Charleston. They would never be defeated as long as they had their traditions; they could keep them best where they had begun.

Pinckney closed the account book he had been studying and put it away in the desk drawer. The Tradd-Simmons Phosphate Company had a balance that would cover wages for the first three months of the New Year. Across the room, Lizzie closed the book she had been reading and opened another. Pinny sighed quietly. He blamed the depression that he felt on the large doses of quinine he was taking. He had, he told himself, a great deal to be happy about. Soon Carlington would be producing a regular income, and his chief worry would be over. Granted, Lizzie was not as affectionate as she used to be, but she was not frighteningly withdrawn, just quiet and extremely well-behaved. And Stuart more than made up for Lizzie's lack of interest; he dogged his brother's footsteps every time Pinckney went to the Arsenal to talk to his friends; sometimes he was there waiting for hours in the hope that Pinckney would come. Julia was not the abrasive element he had feared she would be. She discounted the disaster to the Barony's rice and was already talking optimistically about the '68 planting. She was enjoying the social busyness of town after her solitude on the plantation, and she was good company. Pinny had almost forgotten how intelligent and interesting his aunt could be. They shared memories of London and of books he hardly remembered having read and enjoyed until Julia mentioned them. Best of all, she was amazingly knowledgeable about the cultivation of rice, and she would talk about it for hours. Pinckney had always known that his future was to be a rice planter at Carlington. Now that would never be. He listened avidly to Julia's accounts of the Barony and the age-old rhythms of the planter's life, seeing Carlington as it had been when he was too young to appreciate what was before his eyes.

As for Mary, she was radiant with happiness. Her handsome favorite child was home, and he was handsomer than ever, bronzed by the sun and with muscles as hard as the rock he had been digging. She hung proudly on his arm whenever they went out. And when they were at home, she could entertain the Edwardses.

Both Adam and Prudence had changed. She was defensively distant and reserved; her father was touchingly happy to be back at the Tradd home. His eyes glowed warmly at Mary; Prudence's glittered oddly at no one at all.

Pinckney felt the sudden cold touch of fever at the base of his spine. Damn, he thought. I must have forgotten my medicine. He took his quinine from his pocket and swallowed it, grimacing horribly at the bitterness. He heard the sound of Saint Michael's ringing the hour. "Four of the clock," called the watchman, "and all's well."

"But it could be a damn sight better," said Pinckney. He had forgotten that Lizzie was in the room. He could not quite forget that soon he would be married.

22

The next day, Pinckney felt much better. He spent a busy day at the warehouse, and by evening, he was aglow with the good effects of his productive activity. He came home to a scene of hubbub. His mother was scuttling around like a classic mother hen. It was Wednesday, Stuart's dancing school night, his bath was ready and he was not. "It's only six o'clock, Mama, he'll be home in time," Pinckney said. Mary ignored him.

"Where is that boy? He's never here when I want him. Stuart? You come here this minute," she called up the stairs.

But Stuart was far beyond reach of his mother's voice. The early darkness of the winter skies had led to ever-widening forays for the Club. Hiding in the ruins of burnt-out buildings or the incomplete structures of the new ones being erected, they moved their operations farther and farther uptown toward the center of Union military activities at The Citadel. Alex had led them, as always, but it was Stuart who had invented the Plan. As he peered down from the scaffolding of what a gaudy sign promised would be "The Finest Dry Goods Emporium in All the Carolinas," he shivered with proud excitement. Their route over the roofs of the last block was almost complete. This night's exploration should find the last hidey-holes they needed to reach the Square undetected. Then they would spy on the sentries and time their rounds on Alex's watch. That would end the agonizingly slow period of preparation.

Tomorrow would be his, Stuart's, moment of leadership. He would hang around the Arsenal as usual. He couldn't remember who would be on guard, except that he knew it wasn't Pinny. Stuart would act like a little boy and pester whoever it was. Then, when the Club made a distraction in the grounds, he'd steal the gunpowder while the guard had his back to him.

They'd be waiting for him at the Clubhouse, waiting for him, not Alex. There'd be time to make the bomb before they all had to go home for supper. And then, it would be time. They'd follow the route they had scouted, wait for the moment the sentries were farthest away, and run to the window of the armaments room and throw the bomb. There was no cover on the Square, but everything would happen so fast that the Yankees wouldn't have time to react.

"Stuart! Hurry up. People coming." Alex tugged at his ankle. Stuart pulled himself away from his daydream of heroism and looked down. Alex was already at the bottom. "Come on!" he said; then he turned and ran.

The sound of singing made Stuart swivel his head. Almost directly below, a raucous group of black men marched to the rhythm of their own bawling voices. "John Brown's body lies amould'ring in the grave . . ." The flaring torch carried by one of them threw grotesque shadows behind and around them. Stuart froze.

"Hey! What's that?" The torchbearer stopped. "Look like a bird with a red head." He lifted his arm. The light reached up to Stuart. He began to back away.

With a feral growl, the black men crashed through the thin hoarding of the construction site after him. His feet had barely touched the ground when one grabbed him around the neck with one arm and dragged him to the light. The torch was held up over his head.

"Lookee here what we got," said his captor, grinning. "A little buckra for sure. What you doing up here, white boy? Don't you know nighttime is for us nigger? Ain't your momma done told you to stay home after dark?"

"He don't listen to he momma," said another, leaning close to the struggling boy. "Too disrepectful. He poppa ought to give he a whipping for that."

"Maybe he poppa dead in the War," the torch holder said with chilling relish. "Maybe the Army catched he poppa and barbecue he." He pushed the flame next to Stuart's head. Stuart felt a searing pain along his right cheek and ear. The man holding him pushed the fire away.

"Don't burn this boy, Toby. I think this buckra need a little whipping, that's all. A little chastisement. All of we can help teach him he place. Same like the buckra used to teach we." Stuart staggered into the center of the milling men, propelled by a blow on the back of his head.

Fists fell on him from every side, hitting his raised arms, his chest, his face, his ears, his kidneys, his eyes, his mouth. The hollow sound of knuckles on flesh changed rapidly to a sickening spattering noise. Drops of blood made a random pattern on the pale new lumber of the construction site. Stuart heard a new sound through the ringing in his battered ears. Feet, running feet, and shouts. The blows stopped. He was released and fell to the ground. Rescued. He was being rescued. He forced open his swollen, blood filmed eyes. The torchlight fell briefly on a face he seemed to remember. It was blurred and strange, but he found comfort in it.

"Alex," he tried to say. Then a piece of two by four came down on his skull, and the world went dark.

Elijah entered Archer Hall with a quick step. He noticed that it was twice as crowded as usual, and he was pleased. Lots of new members to sign up tonight. He had been a member of the Union League for over a year, and he was proud of the steadily increasing strength of his chapter. The buckra weren't getting any stronger. Elijah had listened carefully to the political talk at the Tradd dinner table since Mister Pinckney and Miss Julia were home. They had already given up hope of any of their people doing anything to stop the new South Carolina constitution that would be written in Columbia in January. Elijah knew what it would say. The black man was going to get the vote. Then the black man was going to make the laws. The black man would never go to jail again. All he had to do was vote Republican, like the Union League told him.

He greeted some friends he had made at the meetings, and they told him the reason for the crowd. Daddy Cain was going to speak tonight. Elijah clapped his hands. He heard the name everywhere, but Daddy Cain had been going all over the state making speeches, and Elijah had never seen him. He pushed farther into the meeting room. As always, there was an altar draped with the Stars and Stripes holding an open Bible and copies of the Constitution and the Declaration of Independence. Elijah got as close as he could. Daddy Cain would stand behind the altar to speak.

He heard the doors close and lock, and his heart beat faster. The secrecy of the meetings was thrilling, the private signs that one member made to another on the street, the whispered date and time of the next meeting that came through his window during the night. But best of all was the moment that was coming. He could feel the excitement running through the tight-packed audience. Then it happened. All the lamps were turned out at once. And behind the altar, someone lit the Fire of Liberty. Everyone clapped and stomped and sang. "John Brown's body . . ."

A voice higher and stronger than any in the crowd soared from the shadows near the fire. And then a tall man in brilliant red robes leapt from the shadows into the light. It was Daddy Cain. He held his arms up, the full sleeves waving like flames.

"Blessed Jedus," Elijah moaned. He stared until his eyes felt that they would roll down his cheeks.

"Brothers and sisters," shouted the strong voice. It was pitched lower now. "Do you know who I am? I say, do you know this brother?"

"Yes, yes, yes, brother," screamed the crowd.

"They call me 'Daddy Cain'; do you know me?"

"Yes! Daddy Cain!"

"But I have other names, names no one knows. Do you want to know them?"

"Yes! Yes, brother."

"My name is vengeance. My name is blood. My name is death. All these and more. Do you want to know them?"

"Yes!" The response was a roar.

"My name is nigger. My name is slave. My name is boy."

"No! Never! No, no, no." There was sobbing.

"My name is blood." The clapping began.

"Yes!" Clap . . . clap . . . clap . . .

"My name is death." Clap . . .

"Yes!" Clap . . . stamp . . . stamp . . .

"My name is vengeance." Stamp . . .

"Yes!" Stamp . . . stamp . . . stamp . . .

"My name is Daddy Cain! Say it!"

"Yes! Yes, my Lawd, yes! Daddy Cain!"

A thunder of drumming feet.

Daddy Cain snatched a brand from the fire and held it over his head. His other hand moved, sweeping the crowd into silence. "Brothers and sisters," he moaned, "see the mark of Cain. The mark of Cain is on me. Even as Cain slew Abel and was marked by the righteous wrath of the Lord, so am I marked by the Lord to be a symbol of the wrath of my people. Look at me. Look at this face. My brothers, my sisters look and pity. This is a white man's face. This is the face of sin." The blazing torch lit his pale skin and aquiline features. It reflected in his pale eyes, making them look red. The crowd groaned and began to sway from side to side.

"Pity me, I say!"

The groans and sobbing filled the room. Somewhere a woman wailed.

The red arm swept them into silence. "Do you know how I got this face, this mark of Cain? You know. You all know. Did I get it from my father? No! Did I get it from my mother? No! I got it from the white man. I got it from the white man's father. I got it from his father's father.

"How? You know how. I know how. We all know how, and it is our shame. When the white man took my mother, did he ask did she want him? No! When his father took my mother's mother, did he ask did she want him? No! When my father and my father's father had to see the white man take their women, what could they say? Could they say 'No'?"

"No!" The response was a howl.

"Could they say, 'Leave my woman alone'?"

"No!"

"And when the baby come, the mulatto baby, the quadroon baby, the baby with the mark of shame in his skin, could they say, 'White man take this baby; he ain't none of my making.' Could my father say that?"

"No!"

"Could your father say that?"

"No!"

"Brothers, sisters. Can we say it now? Can we say, 'Leave our women alone!'?"

"Yes. Praise God. Yes!"

"Yes. We can say it. We do say it. We say to the white man, here is vengeance. Here is your shame. He will see his shame in the Mark of Cain. He will see it in the light of the torch. Same like you see it now. He will see it, and he will know. He will never touch your women again. He will see Cain in the torchlight, in the fire from the torch. Fire will purify. Fire is the sign of the Lord. The children of Israel followed the pillar of fire. Fire! Fire will burn away the shame. Fire! Burn. Burn the white man's walls. Burn the white man's crops. Burn the white man. I tell you. I promise you. I swear to you. The day of judgment is near. The day of fire. The day of purifying our shame. The day of blood. The day of death. The day of vengeance. The day of Cain.

"Follow me, my brothers. Follow me to the Fire of Liberty. Follow me."

The crowd followed, chanting, crying, stamping, shouting the secret words of the Union League.

"Liberty!"

"Lincoln!"

"Loyal!"

"League!"

They cheered until they were hoarse. Then Daddy Cain raised both hands in benediction. And they followed him in the oath, swearing to vote Republican.

Elijah was swept into the street by the crowd packed around him. He could barely walk alone. The shock he had received was still paralyzing him. The face of Daddy Cain was a face he knew. The skin was darker, and it was older. But otherwise, it was the face of Alex Wentworth.

He took the streetcar home, too shaken to walk. "Please Gawd," he mumbled, "don't let Mist' Pinckney ask me where I bin. Let me go to bed sick."

No one asked where he had been or even noticed him when he came in. The servants were all in the kitchen, crying and praying. Lizzie was in the study, being rocked back and forth in Shad's arms while he sang a wordless lullaby. Mary and Pinckney and Julia were all at the hospital where Dr. Perigru was struggling to keep Stuart alive.

For three weeks, Stuart balanced on a wavering line between life and death. He was in a coma most of the time; when he was conscious he was in such pain that he had to be kept drugged with laudanum to prevent his thrashing around and dislocating the splints on his arms and broken leg. He was brought home two days before Christmas.

By then, Julia had already made a decision and an announcement. "I have to be back at the Barony by New Year's Day," she said in her old imperious manner. "I will take the children with me. The boy needs to get away from the company he has been keeping; Lizzie needs some proper training, which she will never get from her mother." Mary wept and protested, but Pinckney overruled her. He remembered his own golden youth on the Tradd plantation. If he could not give the same thing to his brother and sister at Carlington, Julia could provide the nearest thing to it at the Barony. It was their birthright.

BOOK FOUR

1868-1875

23

The Tradd children spent the entire year of 1868 at Ashley Barony. For Stuart, it was a year of healing, for his body and for the invisible wounds of his spirit. He had known plantation life at Carlington until he was eight. Then the War started, and his father and brother left him to a fragmented world of women and falling bombs. Life at the Barony was dominated by the seasons, the river and the cycle of growth and harvest. It was a union with nature; it was what Stuart remembered from a time when he was happy and loved and safe; it was a return to Eden.

Carlington was not even a memory for Lizzie; she had been taken from it before she reached her second birthday. The world of the rice plantation was new, a magical kingdom of far horizons and the shimmering colors of the peacocks that roamed the acre of clipped lawn between the house and the river. When she learned that she was being sent there, away from home, she was torn between her fear of Julia and her terror of Sophy. On the slow trip upriver, she sat, with her eyes closed, frozen by the winter air and her conviction that the Barony would be just like the Orphan Asylum, wondering why she was going there when she had tried so hard to be good. When the barge bumped gently against the landing dock, she opened her eyes and saw the warm brick house in the distance. Two peacocks, disturbed by the noise and activity, strutted angrily across the lawn, dragging their plumage. Then they stopped and simultaneously spread their jeweled fans. Lizzie realized that she had entered an enchanted land.

Julia's hoarded gold had managed almost to stop time on the Barony. There were differences, but they were of scale, not substance. Ashley Barony was still, in fact, a small island of orderly beauty, the only plantation on the Ashley that had not been burnt and pillaged by Sherman's Army.

The morning after their arrival, Julia announced the regime they would follow. "Lizzie," she said, "will meet a regular schedule of lessons in the accomplishments that her mother has not taught her. In addition, she will do the schoolwork that she would have had at Mistress Allston's. And she will learn to behave like a lady.

"Stuart will spend his time outdoors, healing and strengthening his body. His mind can be disciplined later."

And the year began.

Julia took Stuart and Lizzie with her on her tour of her domain. It was a slow progress. Because of Stuart's injuries, he had to ride in a cart instead of on horseback. Lizzie asked to ride with him. The four horses in the front stalls of the hundred in the stable building looked huge and frightening to her. Julia granted the request. "You can learn to ride after your habit has been made."

They went first to the pine woods, where Julia inspected the simple calcimined frame summer house and pointed out the boxes hung on the tall tree trunks. "Yankees bleed their maples for sugar," she said. "We get turpentine from our pines. Also fatwood for kindling and lumber for building. We have maple trees, too, but they're a different kind. You'll know them in the spring; they put out pink new leaves that turn green when they're adult."

From there, they followed a track through mixed woods to the swamp pond. The water was black and still. It reflected the great circular pads of the lilies that clustered at one corner of the irregular ellipse and the ghostly gray bark of the cypresses with their grotesque bulging knees. Long thick beards of Spanish moss hung from the high branches of the trees, gray and unmoving in the hushed air above the dark water. The beauty of the eternal quiet mirror was eerie. Julia's brisk voice did little to dispel the aura. "Don't come here alone. There are moccasins that drop from the tree limbs sometimes. The cypresses make waterproof shingles for the cabins and dugout canoes like the ones the Indians used to have. Eight men can fit in one. We also use them for kitchen work. I'll show you. The wood cures as hard as iron. As long as you wet it often enough so that it never cracks, it will last forever."

They rode next past fenced fields; partridge and snipe flew up, startled, from the low mounds of stubble in them. Julia pointed to them with her riding crop. "We could live on our game," she said complacently. "There are deer and wild turkeys and bob whites in the woods, and when the ducks and geese fly over, all you have to do is point a gun in the air and pull the trigger. They're so thick, you always hit one or two.

"The streams are rich in food, too. We keep nets on two of them all winter for the shad, and fish the others for Virginia perch and bream and trout. In the spring, the trout have a delicious roe." She looked over her shoulder and smiled at Stuart and Lizzie. It made her look like a stranger. "Is anyone hungry? I think we'll stop at the flat-house for elevenses. That's what the English call a morning bite."

They devoured the cold ham biscuits and milk in the basket that was tucked into the cart; the sharp sunny air had made them ravenous. Then they ate the sweet Kieffer pears while the cart rolled through the orchard that had produced them. A sweet, rotten smell did nothing to ruin their pleasure. "That's the cane shed," Julia told them. "We have a stand of sugar cane for molasses. All the scrubbing in the world won't wash away the reek of bagasse."

They passed a long double row of white-washed cabins and a frame building with a square turret-like bell tower. Smoke was rising from a few of the buildings. "The servants' quarters and church," said Julia. "All the Barony's workers are Ashley people who never left or who tried the city and decided to come back. Most of them refuse to live on 'the Street' now, though. They want to be free men, and free men have their own homes. So I built more cabins, down near the carriage road to town and Summerville. They have ten acres each for growing their own food crops and keeping their stock, and they pay me a dollar a month in rent. I pay the man, sometimes the woman, too, to work for me. It's not much different from the old days except that there are fewer of them and they don't eat as well and dress as well. The Yankees—who know everything—set the wages for a fieldhand at ten dollars a month. It's cheaper for me than it was when I had to support the whole family. Their freedom is costing the darkies dear. For some reason, they say they don't mind . . . Over there are the barns and the smokehouse and the smithy and so forth. We'll look at them another day. Now we'll go to the rice fields. That's what everything else is here for."

When they approached the river, a terrible stench made Stuart and Lizzie cover their noses. "You'll get used to it," Julia said. "City folk relish their salt-water tidal mud perfume. Planters prefer fresh-water mud. The fields are drained now for plowing. Stand up in the cart so you can see."

Ahead of them a deep ditch ran straight to their right and left as far as they could see. On the other side of it great squares of shiny blue-black mud stretched to the river in the distance. It looked like satin. Their aunt squinted up at the pale blue winter sky. It was cloudless. "If the weather holds," she said, "the fields will be dry enough to start plowing next week. This big ditch is called 'the drain'; those small ones that crisscross the field are 'quarter drains.' The drain goes around three sides of the field. The fourth side is the river. Do you ill-educated children know anything about Egypt?" They admitted that they did not. Julia snorted. "Of course not. What could I expect? Egypt is a very old country which once had a great civilization. It depended on the river, too. They didn't manage their river the way we do, though. Their river managed them." It was clear to Stuart that his aunt thought the Egyptians should have asked her how to improve their lives.

She took them back to the house. Stuart had to rest before dinner.

His young bones had knit, but he was still weak, and he got blinding headaches when he was tired. Julia's migraines were a thing of the past and the city, but she remembered them and she was sympathetic to the boy. A fractured skull was, she supposed, an exterior equivalent of the interior kaleidoscope of bright-colored pain that she used to feel. The Barony had cured her; it would cure Stuart, too.

The main course at dinner was a delicious brown roast fowl. Stuart pronounced its gravy the best he had ever tasted and poured a ladle-full over a small white mountain of rice for a second helping. Lizzie was about to do the same when Julia told them they were eating peacock. Then her throat closed. "Don't be silly, Lizzie. We eat the hens. The males are still there to strut their plumage." But Lizzie wasn't hungry.

That afternoon, she was started on her lessons. Julia's beautiful long fingers danced among the ivory and ebony keys of the enormous square pianoforte; Lizzie was enchanted. Then Julia taught her the C scale. "Practice for a hour," she said. "First right hand, then left. Tomorrow we'll add the metronome, and the day after, you'll do both hands together." Lizzie's little hands stumbled erratically. "Come along, Stuart. We'll test the seed rice now."

The bowls of water-soaked cotton were ready. Julia sprinkled kernels on it and sighed. "If this doesn't work, I'll have to buy some, and heaven knows where I'll find any. It was hard enough to find this batch last year, and then the rain ruined it. Damn Yankees." She shook her head. "Cross that bridge when we come to it. Now let's go look at the stock." Julia was, as Stuart and Lizzie quickly learned, indefatigable.

In the mornings, she set Lizzie's schoolwork for the day, then took Stuart on her rounds of inspection. While he rested before dinner, she gave Lizzie her piano lesson and training in household management. In the afternoons, she taught Lizzie embroidery and took Stuart riding while Lizzie practiced the piano. Back home again, while Stuart rested, she gave Lizzie her lessons in French conversation while the little girl prepared and served tea under her supervision. During supper, she talked to them both about the history of Charleston, the Barony and the Ashley family. In the evening, she read to them from books on travel and European history while Lizzie patiently replaced the stitches on her sampler that her aunt had torn out because they were not perfect. When Stuart and Lizzie went to bed, Julia turned to her account books, correcting Lizzie's homework and making out the list of things to be done the next day. Lizzie was confident that her aunt never slept at all.

While the little girl labored over her schoolwork and the drudgery of becoming "accomplished," Stuart was becoming daily more enthralled by the operation of the plantation. He had nothing to do with any of the black workers except Solomon; the near-fatal beating had left him with a deep, burning fear and hatred of Negroes. Solomon was different. Stuart knew him too well to regard him as part of his race; Solomon was his friend. While Julia dealt with the hands, Stuart spent his time in the carpentry shop and smithy where Solomon was king. He emerged only when the work was underway, and he could sit on his horse next to his aunt's to observe and learn. Throughout January and February, he watched the plowing of the fields for produce and for rice. He inspected the levees with Julia and noted the condition of the "trunks," the wooden flood gates set into them. He watched the sowing of oats and peas, and even rode one of the horses that pulled a bush on a long rope behind it to cover the seed. He saw spring creep through the woods, bringing out the peach-colored leaves of maples and the tender yellow-green of water oaks, gray-green of poplar and black gum, pale grass-green of cypresses and the sharp blue-green of new growth on the tall long-leaf and loblolly pines. In March when dogwood blossoms filled the woods like falling white stars, he and Solomon dipped nets heavy with the herring that filled the streams on their migration and lifted roe-shad from the nets that had been waiting to trap them, while in the house, Lizzie learned how to sew the velvet winter curtains into bags of homespun with packets of camphor and watched Dilcey bake the shad for six hours until the tiny sharp bones were dissolved.

On the fifteenth of the month, the rice-planting began. Lizzie was excused from her various lessons to join Stuart and Julia on a platform in the barn to watch the claying. "If the kernels aren't weighted with a covering of clay, they will float up from where they're planted when the water gets to them," said Julia. "Those big barrels outside are filled with half field mud and half water. Ancrum will keep stirring it so that it's thick as molasses." As she spoke, the spout from the loft where the seed rice was stored rattled, then whooshed, and the full ochre kernels poured in a stream onto the washed floor of the barn. In one corner, three men grinned and tried out their banjoes and fiddle while from another, a group of laughing young black girls ran out to spread the rice across the floor with their bare feet while they adjusted their long full skirts and petticoats of calico above the sashes tied diagonally across their hips so that their legs were bare and free to move.

Four little black boys ran in carrying the long narrow carved cypress buckets called piggins and dumped the clay-water onto the floor. Then the music began. Around the edges of the floor, men and women clapped to the happy rhythm of the banjoes while the girls danced the rice in the clay-water with their feet. They threw their arms up and out, and their legs flashed in the moted sunlight that poured through the open doorway. The piggin-boys ran in and out, dodging the dancers, adding clay-water to the slippery mass of seed on the floor. From time to time, the spout released more rice to be added to it; the kernels rained on the shoulders and bright bandannaed heads of the dancers like a shower of gold. The gaiety and the music were infectious. Soon Lizzie and Stuart and Julia were laughing and clapping. Lizzie tried to whirl and dance like the claying girls, clapping her hands above her head. When she fell off the platform, one of the girls picked her up and, still dancing, lifted her to her brother's reaching arms. No one cared that she was sticky with wet clay, but Julia carefully picked off the kernels that were stuck to her clothes and threw them back onto the floor.

At the end of an exuberant hour, the rice was clayed. The music continued while men shoveled the rice into a tall, wet, shiny pyramid. Then the musicians led a dancing parade of all the blacks to the pine-plank tables of food set up in the courtyard. "Come along, Lizzie," said Julia. "You need a bath."

The next day, the soaked, clayed rice was measured into long narrow sacks tied in pairs. While Julia and the children watched, the first field was planted. Men steadied the rice drills while other men led the two pair of oxen that pulled them to make deep, even, close rows of furrows. Behind them followed women with their skirts tucked up over the pair of sacks tied around their waists. They bent low to escape the breeze that fluttered their petticoats and scattered the rice seed with a rythmic dip cross-handed into the sacks then a flutter of their fingers to dislodge the sticky kernels. As they worked, they sang; the men's deep voices mingled with the women's sopranos in the old spiritual that marked time for their slow steps.

Every hour throughout the long day, the teams of sowers and drillers changed. The released women rubbed the kinks out of their backs, and the men flexed their tired shoulders. Then they left. "Where are they going, Aunt Julia?" asked Stuart the first time it happened. "It's early yet, and most of the field still to be planted."

"Oh, they'll be back this afternoon," Julia answered, "I pay extra for rice planting and give prizes to the best team."

Stuart scowled. "I wouldn't do that. You're paying them for a day's work; they should work a full day."

"You sound like a Yankee, Stuart. These people are still working by the old system, and being freedmen isn't going to change that. We always had too many people on the place. All the planters did. They kept having babies, and the babies grew up. There was plenty of food for everybody and it was easy to build new cabins, so the population just kept growing. After a hundred years or so, the problem was that there wasn't enough work to keep them all busy; idle people are restless people. So the system of 'tasks' grew up. Every man and every woman who worked in the fields was required to do a task a day, whether it was sowing or weeding or harvesting. A task is a quarter acre. They'd take all the time they wanted, and they could pretty nearly fill up the day with a task. It didn't matter, because we had more than two hundred hands. Now I've got twenty-eight. But they still expect to work a task a day. If I want more from them, I've got to persuade it out of them. We taught them the task; we're stuck with it."

"Lazy niggers."

Julia slapped him across the mouth. "If you ever say that word again, I'll whip you, healed or no healed. Only white trash say 'nigger.' These are colored people or Negroes or field hands or servants. In the old days, they were just called 'our people.' A gentleman is known by the way he takes care of his people. Don't you forget it."

"No, ma'am."

In late afternoon, the planting was finished. Julia gave a signal with her arm, and Ancrum lifted the trunk. Water poured from the river into the drain. For over an hour, it worked its way into the dried earth, then filled the deep ditch higher and higher. By the time the level reached the shallow quarter-drains, the sun was setting. It dyed the sky and the water a deep crimson. When the water spread into the channels, it looked like veins of life-giving blood. Dusk fell as the quarter-drains filled. Julia called to Ancrum to adjust the flow. She sent the children to their supper and beds. Then she and Ancrum, invisible in the dark, waited until the moon rose. He lifted the trunk part way and the two solitary figures watched the silvered water creep gently across the wide field until it covered it by three inches. "Good work, Ancrum," Julia called. A mockingbird woke somewhere and gave a muted song. "I'll see you tomorrow." Overhead, stars danced in the moon-stained sky. It was not long before dawn. Julia walked back to the sleeping house; her skirts left a dark trail on the glistening silver dew on the path and the lawn. She swung her arms and smiled happily. The first rice was in.

Planting continued at a steady pace for a month. There were other crops to get in, too, but always rice came first. It required a special combination of time and weather. There had to be enough dry days first so that the heavy drills would not be mired in mud, and the tide had to be going out to the sea when the planting was done so that fresh water would enter when the trunk was opened. When conditions were less than ideal, vegetables and fodder had their turns. Lizzie mastered the scales of D, E, F, G, A and B and started on Bach's "Two Part Inventions"; she also passed inspection on cross-stitch and began an interminable struggle with satin stitch; Dilcey taught her how to make browning for gravy and how to scrape chainey briar, the tender wild asparagus that the workers' children found in the woods; she struggled with long division and failed totally to remember that *il faut* always takes the subjunctive. She fell off her horse six times and developed a hatred of riding that never left her for the rest of her life.

In mid April, planting stopped while the field hands harvested the strawberries and green peas. Lizzie and Pansy walked to the cypress swamp every day that it did not rain to pick flags, the wild iris that made sheets of blue along the edges of the black water. The woods were full of the heady scent of jasmine, and tiny violets made cushions of velvet color near the trunks of the trees. Overhead, birds swooped from tree top to limb then soared in looping flights after insects or in preparation for the songs they sang on landing. "Showing off," said Pansy scornfully.

On May first, Julia moved the household to the simple small establishment in the pine woods. Traditionally, the tenth was the day that whites had always left the plantation, and the eleventh was the beginning of fever season. But Julia's shrewd eyes had recognized the signs of malaria in Pinckney, and it had made her more cautious. No one knew what caused swamp fever, but in two centuries of low-country living, they had learned that it attacked whites, but not blacks, that it came between early May and first frost in October, and that pine woods were a protection against it. The mysterious cause added to its own mystery by infecting only those whites who exposed themselves to the outdoor air at night. Even the great house at the Barony would have been safe if they had closed all the windows, doors and chimney flues when the sun began to set. But with a pine woods nearby, it was safer to move. And they could have a night breeze to make sleeping more comfortable.

Lizzie loved the airiness and simplicity of the woods house. The furniture was of pine, made in the plantation carpenter shop. Chairs had muslin-covered seat pads instead of silk and velvet upholstery. Best of all, the deep porch that extended around three sides had a rope hammock and a wide settee-like swing. She hated to leave after breakfast every day to ride over to the Barony, with its piano and the schoolbooks waiting.

During the last two weeks of May, there was no planting at all. The fields were full of May-birds looking for seeds. Julia concentrated on checking the condition of the stock and the wide assortment of tools and equipment that always needed sharpening and repair. Stuart was trusted with the trunks. He was so pleased with his position of responsibility that he measured the water level in the eight planted rice fields four or five times every day, delighted when he could open a trunk and let more water trickle in. He was getting brown and strong. But he wasn't growing, which dismayed him. Lizzie's wrists had already appeared at the end of her sleeves, and she was still only eight years old. At fifteen, his breaking voice had settled itself in a low register that Stuart rather fancied. Unfortunately, his body seemed to have settled itself, too, at five-foot-two. He compensated by building his muscles and his sense of manhood. He poled one of the heavy flatboats for a mile against the tide every clear day, then let the current bring it back to the flat-house while he steered with the big oar in the stern. He also set his horse at every fence and fallen log he could find, remembering Pinckney's exploits from the days at Carlington.

Fortunately, the Barony horses were no longer the thoroughbreds that had made the Ashley colors famous at races before the War. Stuart's horse refused more often than he jumped, and Stuart's skull suffered no more fractures.

The first part of June was fine. The remaining rice fields were planted and covered before the tenth. But Julia did not seem as pleased as Stuart had expected. She roamed around the edges of the earlier fields every day before breakfast, peering down at the corduroy ripples that the morning breeze made in the flat sheets of water. "It should be sprouting," she said, "down deep. Any day now, we should start to see green through the water. If that seed was any good."

"It tested out all right, Aunt Julia."

"I know that." She was snappish. "And I planted three bushels of seed an acre instead of two and a half to allow for dead kernels. But testing isn't growing, is it? I want to see it growing."

"She nearly bit my head off," Stuart complained to Solomon.

"Miss Julia, sometime she worrisome same like a old cooter," the black man chuckled. "Must be cooter season for sure."

It was. The river was dotted with the prehistoric shapes of yellow-bellied terrapin swimming heavily to their nesting places. Solomon took Stuart out the next moonlit night. They concealed themselves in a tangle of brush near a sloping bank and waited. Occasional clouds scudded across the moon, and they heard the terrapin before they saw it. Then the moonlight returned, and they watched the lumbering progress of the glistening creature up the incline. It turned ponderously and began to dig in the soft earth above the water mark. Solomon leapt down and flipped it over. "Cooter, say your prayers," he chortled, "they'se a soup pot with your name on she."

The wrinkled elliptical head with its dangerous pointed beak moved erratically from side to side, while the semi-webbed feet thrashed in the air. The moonlight bleached the yellow shell of the exposed belly, making it look pale and vulnerable. Solomon darted agilely from side to side, wrapping sacking around the shell, tangling and immobilizing the feet, avoiding the vicious, loud, clacking beak. "Scipio, he lose four finger for love of cooter stew," he said gleefully, "but this old cooter ain't going to get no taste of old Solomon, no, sir." With a final swirl of the sack, he covered the head and jaws. "Hand me that rope, Mist' Stuart; now we tie she and tote she home. Dilcey got work to do tomorrow."

The next day Julia whipped them both. Stuart should never have been on the river at night in June. Then she supervised while Dilcey taught Lizzie how to make terrapin soup. Lizzie wished she could have gotten a whipping instead.

Dilcey cut the rope around the wrapped cooter and flipped it on its feet. When it struggled to extricate itself, it thrust forward and the sack fell away from the evil-looking head. Its neck was long, with thick folded skin which stretched and folded like a grotesque, misshapen accordian. Dilcey watched carefully. When the head extended to its farthest reach, she shouted "Ho, cooter!" and chopped it off with an ax. A dark, thick liquid spurted from the neck. Lizzie felt sick at her stomach.

Dilcey and Solomon strung the terrapin carcass up by its back feet, then she sent him for more wood chips to heat up the fire under the huge laundry cauldron in the kitchenyard. By the time the terrapin had drained, the water in the cauldron was boiling. Solomon lifted the cooter from the hook and plunged it into the water. Five minutes later, at Dilcey's signal, he pulled on the rope and removed it to the table nearby. Then he tapped neatly with a hammer and chisel from his carpentry shop until the heavy carapace was cracked all around and lifted it off, exposing the mound of soft, round eggs. "Good," said Julia, "there must be close to three dozen." She lifted one, blew on it to cool it, and gave it to Lizzie. It was rubbery, with a dent that she could push from one place to another.

While she poked at the curious egg, Dilcey deftly cut out the front and hind quarters and the liver. Julia touched Lizzie, and she watched while the cook peeled the ugly thick skin from the meat, washed it, then threw it into a bucket of cold water, which she carried into the kitchen. "Next one, you can do she, Miss Lizzie," Dilcey said with a broad grin.

"I couldn't," said Lizzie. But two days later, she did. Julia did not permit squeamishness. Lizzie also completed the transformation of the hideous beast into a thick, savory soup, boiling the meat for hours until it fell from the bones, then discarding the bones, cutting the meat into tiny pieces with scissors, and simmering it with spices and onion and potato. She was not confident enough to make the thickening, but Dilcey let her put in the whole eggs and, at the end add the sherry and ladle it into the big porcelain tureen.

Her experience with the cooter stood her in good stead on the Fourth of July. Julia had provided the food and fireworks for the workers' celebration; someone else provided a quantity of white lightning. In the fight that ended the party, two men were shot and one got a tremendous gash in his head. Ancrum came running to the house, where Julia was teaching Lizzie to make tomato catsup. Julia let the servants celebrate the Fourth, but she always found work to do. The Ashleys had been Tory in the Revolution.

Ancrum carried the medicine box, Lizzie a clean sheet and a box of washed cotton, Julia a bottle of brandy. "They probably drank all of whatever liquor they had," she said serenely. The rice had sprouted well.

At the scene of the fracas, she dispensed paregoric to the bruised and poured alcohol on assorted cuts. "Now go home," she ordered. "Let's have a look at the wounded, Lizzie." The bullets had gone all the way through the respective shoulder and leg of the two men who had offended the owner of the pistol. "That's a relief," said Julia, "I hate digging them out. You wash them off. Use the strong soap and see that it stings. These two won't be at work for weeks." She soaked cotton in turpentine and slapped it on the entrance and exit wounds. "Now cut the sheet in strips and bandage them, Lizzie. I'll have a look at Reuben's head." The little girl's work was clumsy but adequate. Julia noticed that her determined child's face was pale. She cleaned the head wound herself.

But she did make Lizzie watch when she dipped cotton into the brandy, then into powdered alum, then stuffed it into the gaping hole in Reuben's cranium. It took almost all of the cotton she had brought and every drop of the brandy to fill the cavity. Some alum was left. She wrapped a turban of linen strips while she educated her niece and her groggy stableman about the funerary practices of Ramses the Great. "The thing to remember about head wounds," she told Lizzie on the way home, "is that they bleed out of all proportion to their seriousness and that the brain has no sensation. Reuben didn't feel any pain at all." She maneuvered the buggy around a hole in the track. "You were a good girl, Lizzie." The small white face lit up with a smile of exquisite joy.

The summer heat soon became Julia's worst enemy. The early rice fields had been drained as soon as the sprouting rice was visible, and every day was a battle to keep the workers hoeing the weeds around the rice and to maintain just the right amount of moisture so that the clay would not dry out but also would not be too wet for the feet of the weeders. Between weedings, the water had to be put back on the rice. The trunks had to be manipulated with great delicacy. So did the field hands. It was not a question of persuading them to do more than a task. She had to cajole, bully or bribe them into finishing even one task a day.

She did not want Stuart around when she was dealing with the workers, so she took him off his job with the trunks. He was angry at first, a classic Tradd rage, but it made no headway against Julia's Ashley intransigence. Then one of Ancrum's sons provided the solution. Stuart was roaming the woods looking for some squirrels to shoot when he saw a small brown figure running along a deer path. "Halt!" he commanded, feeling like a Rifle Club member. The little boy stopped in his tracks. "Where are you going?" Stuart demanded.

"Please, God, Mist' Stuart, let me get out of here. My daddy'll take he hand to me iff'n he catch me. I is supposed to be minding the baby, and I done snuck off for a jump in the river."

Stuart laughed. "Go on, then, I won't tell on you." Why hadn't he thought of that? He remembered the wisteria vine at Carlington. The cold water had cured him of copying Pinckney after one glorious swing over the river, but this was July, not April. The water would feel good even if it was cold.

In fact, it was warm, with deliciously exciting ribbons of cold current that rose and fell in an unpredictable pattern of their own. He swam for hours every day. After a week, he persuaded Solomon to give him some rope, and he fashioned a launching swing just as good, he told himself, as Pinckney's vine.

Maybe better, he boasted to Lizzie. "Why don't you try it?"

"Because I don't know how to swim."

"Then learn. I'll teach you."

"I don't want to."

"Sissy."

"I am not."

"You are, too."

Lizzie stuck out her tongue and stalked away. She had her own allotment of Tradd temper. In this case, it was exacerbated by the knowledge that Stuart was right. She was terrified of the river. She imagined it full of cooters lurking in its depths for tribal revenge and of water moccasins waiting to wrap sinuously around her arms and legs before they bit her. She never went near it if she could avoid it.

Two days later, she could not. "Go call Stuart, Lizzie," Julia said. "I want him to ride over to the woods house for me."

"But I'm practicing the piano, Aunt Julia."

"I can hear that for myself. Your left hand is muddy. Bach requires clean, fresh notes. Now go get Stuart."

"Yes, ma'am." Lizzie closed the cover over the keyboard. "Come on, Bear, I'll take you for a walk." Bear, she believed, was a great music lover.

It was midafternoon, the hottest part of the day. By the time Lizzie trudged across the lawn, her dress was sticking to her back, and her feet were sliding on the perspiration in her buttoned kid boots. She shouted to Stuart, then looked back at the house. "Ladies don't raise their voices," was one of her aunt's many commandments. A loud splashing was her brother's response. He was invisible, hiding under the landing dock. Lizzie marched out onto it and stamped her feet. "Come out of there. Aunt Julia wants you."

"I can't get up on the dock. The tide's too low."

"It is not."

"It is so."

"Don't be a goose egg, Stuart, you can get up easy. I'll throw you down a rope. Now hurry up. Aunt Julia's mad about something Dilcey left at the woods house."

"All right. Only you'll have to hand me my breeches. I'm in my birthday suit."

Lizzie was shocked. Julia insisted that Stuart wear a bathing costume.

"Well, come on." The voice rose through the hot wooden planks.

"Where are they?"

"At the end of the dock. Hand them to me and close your eyes."

Lizzie put Bear in the landing's middle, away from splashed drops and walked on to the end. She stretched out on her stomach, screwed her eyes closed and lowered her arm over the side, dangling Stuart's shirt and breeches. She felt a tug and let go.

"Keep your eyes closed."

"I am."

Beneath her, she heard a series of splashes, then silence. "Stuart?" She was still blind.

"Here I am." The voice came from behind her.

She turned her head. "Are you dressed?"

"Yep. You can look."

The sun hurt her eyes when she opened them. Stuart seemed to be behind a screen of dancing red and blue and yellow dots. Lizzie blinked, her vision clear. "Stuart!" she shouted. "Put Bear down. You'll get him all wet." She scrambled to her feet.

Stuart cavorted around, holding Bear up out of her reach. "Stuart, stop teasing me. Stuart! Give Bear to me. Stuart, don't be mean. Stuart, give me my Bear." She could not catch him. "Stuart!" She stopped running after her brother. "Stuart Tradd, I'm going to tell Aunt Julia you were swimming nekkid!"

Stuart stopped, too, a few feet from her. "You never would."

"Oh, yes, I would, too. If you don't give Bear to me."

Stuart's red face became redder. "Nasty tattletale," he said, "take your damn bear." He threw Bear with all the strength in his arm. The little animal hit Lizzie in the chest, knocked the wind out of her, then ricocheted into the swift water at the end of the dock.

Lizzie tried to scream, but she was still winded, and no sound came out. She ran to the edge of the dock, whimpered, and leapt after the brown and white body that was bobbing away downstream.

She flailed and windmilled her way to Bear. Then she clutched him to her with both arms. The current pulled them under.

Stuart dived off the dock and swam underwater for speed until he reached Lizzie. Her eyes and mouth were open in terror. He grabbed her braids and pulled her up to the surface, then to the bank. The current had taken them down to the rice fields. His hand found the trunk and gripped its sturdy wood frame. "Help!" he shouted.

There were three women hoeing weeds near the riverbank. They dropped their hoes and trampled the green rice as they ran toward Stuart's cries.

He handed Lizzie to them, then climbed over the trunk and dropped into the field. One of the women had Lizzie draped across her shoulder like a baby. Her callused fist beat rhythmically on the little girl's back. Lizzie coughed, sputtered, choked and threw up. "That's all right, lamb, you just get your breath," the woman crooned. Her fist uncurled, and she patted the child soothingly.

Lizzie coughed and gasped for several minutes while Stuart and the other women hovered anxiously. Then she spoke. "Phew, I hate the smell of this old rice mud."

Everyone laughed.

Julia whipped Stuart with a leather strap and spanked Lizzie with a wooden spoon. Both endured their punishment stoically. They had told her that Lizzie had fallen into the rice field when she was helping Stuart over the trunk. Their sin was against the rice, in Julia's eyes. With the solidarity of children against adult, Tradd against Ashley, they agreed without discussion that Stuart's disobedience and Lizzie's recklessness had best go unmentioned. The women in the field, they knew, would never tell on them.

When Julia was doing her accounts that night, Lizzie tiptoed into Stuart's room. "Are you awake?" she whispered.

"Of course I'm awake. Aunt Julia sends me to bed at baby hours. What do you want?"

"I've been thinking about it. I've decided to learn to swim."

Throughout August, the heat grew more and more oppressive. It was what Charlestonians called "gummy" weather. Julia watched the sky constantly, afraid of the eerie dull yellow-green cast that would mean a hurricane was approaching. That was the only thing strong enough to ruin the rice now. It was tall and clean, with the kernels beginning to plump up to the perfect stage "in milk." Stuart was in charge of half the trunks again. Ancrum manned the other half. Every afternoon when the tall white clouds that built up in the burning sky grew heavy and black on the bottom, they poised themselves on the bank. If the thunderheads opened, releasing wind and heavy rain, they ran like men possessed, opening the trunks to flood the fields so that the wind could not whip the rice. Lightning struck the river at their backs, but they ignored it. The rice was more important than their fear.

Lizzie watched the storms from the deep porch of the woods house. Paradoxically, the timid little girl loved the crash of thunder and the sharp, exciting smell of ozone after the lightning. She was conscientious in her duties: when it was not raining, she tended the tiny fire in the living room that brought a draft in the windows and up the chimney, and, she thumped the big barometer in the hallway every hour to be sure that the glass was not plummeting suddenly to warn of a hurricane. Secretly, she thought a hurricane would be a great adventure and looked down on Stuart. He had always said it would be fun to have one, and now he was the sissy. He had turned into a rice planter. Worried about storms. Pooh.

24

While on the Barony one half of the family was worrying about storms, the other members on Meeting Street were thankful that their own storms were over. The year had been overfull of drama.

After Julia took the children away, Pinckney rushed to Carlington to sign up the workers. He was out with them all day, showing them what to do and testing the various ways to combine the jobs of the men for maximum efficiency.

Compared to the intricate operations of the plantation, the mining of phosphate was a kindergarten exercise. The rock had to be dug, washed, and loaded for transport. Three simple steps, which did not depend on the weather or the perversity of nature. Rock could be handled in the rain, and it was subject to neither cutworm nor rot.

It turned out not to be that easy. Because all the work was done by hand by men. And they were as diverse and as variable as nature. The first problem was to determine the task. The old plantation expectations were deeply engrained, and the men expected the task to be easily done in half a day or less. Pinckney was used to leading men. Persuading them was much more difficult. He had to establish his authority, but he also needed cooperation. A half day of work was not enough.

For weeks, he tried one method after another while he learned about the workers: which ones were strong, which were the most intelligent, who could issue orders, who had to be led. He identified the troublemakers early and fired them. At the end of February Carlington had less than a thousand pounds of phosphate ready to ship—about seven dollars worth—and Pinckney had paid out nearly two thousand dollars in wages. But the period of trial and error was over. The system had been found. On March first, he put it into operation.

The men were divided into teams of four, with strengths and weaknesses offset by the assignments of personalities. Each team was given a task, an area four feet by six feet. When the task was started, all members of the team shoveled away the "overburden," the layer of earth that covered the rock strata. It was usually two to four feet down. Then the first member of the team got down in the excavation and attacked the rock with a pickax. When enough was broken, he threw the pieces of rock up to the surface with a shovel. The second team member loaded it into a wheelbarrow and pushed it to the cleared area next to the river, where he dumped it into a pile. The third and fourth members of the team shoveled it into a cypress box with iron grates in the sides, attached the lid and swung the box out on a pulley over the river, where they lowered it into the current to be washed. After ten minutes, they hoisted the box and swung it over to a waiting barge. They lowered it, opened it, and dumped it. And the teams were paid by the bargeload, not by the hour or day. As Pinckney had expected, a competition grew up among the twenty teams, and the strongest men on each team helped the weaker ones so that the team would be competitive. There was some grumbling, but Pinny had gauged the men well. Everyone had to concede that the assignments and the system were fair.

By the end of March, Carlington had shipped a hundred tons of phosphate. Another month, and the Tradd-Simmons books would switch to black ink. Pinny rode his horse through the breathtaking spring beauty of the woods, away from the noise and dirt of the mining, and wondered why he felt so miserable.

In his house on Meeting Street, his mother was asking the same question. "Why do I feel so miserable?"

Lucy Anson patted Mary's soft hand. "You don't have anybody to do for, Cousin Mary, that's why. You're the kind of lady who likes to take care of your family's comforts, and your family's gone right now." She watched Mary's eyes well over and patted her hand again. She always was impressed by Mary's tears. They were so becoming.

"You're such a sweet girl, Lucy. I don't know what I'd do without you." Mary had become very dependent on Lucy in the three months that Pinckney and the children had been gone. It was one of the oddities of the intricate social rules which governed their world that Lucy, as a married lady, was an acceptable chaperone for a widow like Mary, who was more than twenty years older. She had become a regular figure at the Tradd house since Pinckney's departure; twice a week, she came for tea. Her presence made it possible for Adam Edwards to be there.

When Mary first asked her, Lucy was annoyed. She had her hands full; Andrew needed attention and companionship; Little Andrew was five and as noisy and demanding as every other little boy that age; Lavinia had invited herself to stay on Meeting Street when her parents moved up to their house again, and she got on Lucy's nerves; and Emma Anson had taken her servants with her so that Lucy had only Little Andrew's dah, Estelle, and one maid to help her. She now did all the cooking herself as well as the mending and the clever cutting-up of Andrew's old clothes into new ones for their son. Josiah Anson was supporting them, and Lucy knew that it was a burden on him. She did everything she could to keep their expenses to a minimum. And she did it quietly. Lucy was unobtrusive in her activities and in her person. People tended to overlook her.

Which was the reason she agreed to Mary's plan. It was the only invitation she had received in a long time.

Once she decided to go, she began to look forward to her outings. She had never known Mary Tradd very well; Lavinia was the one who visited Mary all the time—to make plans for as big a wedding as possible and to talk about how Pinckney neglected them both. She was not eager to become Mary's accomplice or confidante, but she was curious to see if there was any truth to the rumors that Adam Edwards and his daughter were leading the Tradds, mother and son, down the primrose path to abolitionism or worse. The rumors were conflicting and confused. Lucy never heard the spicier ones; people did not repeat such things to young ladies, married or not.

When the teas actually began and she discovered that Mary and Adam Edwards were blameless to the point of boring her half to death, Lucy was not really disappointed. She had a genuinely kind heart, and the middle-aged couple touched her by their obvious pleasure in each other's dull company. After the first week, Edwards brought Prudence, and Lucy's boredom was over.

The two girls were about the same age, and so different that each found the other exotic. Also, each, in her own way, was lonely. Prudence knew no one in Charleston except the Tradds. Lucy knew everyone, but she had no close friends.

She had been born many years after her parents had given up hope of having a child, and they were so protective that she was hardly allowed out of the house and the walled garden around it. Her mother was terrified that Lucy would be exposed to the diseases that took so many infants and children. Ironically, Lucy lost her parents to the yellow fever epidemic that decimated Charleston's population in 1858. She survived it, alone in a house with the yellow isolation flag on the door and the bodies of her mother, father and fourteen servants inside. Her father's elderly bachelor brother sent her to live with equally elderly cousins in Savannah, brought her back to Charleston to present her at the Saint Cecilia and gratefully turned her over to Emma Anson when Andrew asked for her hand. He also converted her inheritance to Confederate Bonds which he delivered to Andrew as her dowry. Then he died, confident that his niece would be taken care of for life. Like all Charlestonians, Lucy had dozens of relatives, but none of them were as much her family as the Ansons were. She hardly knew them. She had hoped that Lavinia would be a sister; she had always wanted a sister. She tried not to admit to herself that she did not like Lavinia. The truth was, she detested her.

But she liked Prudence Edwards very much. And she offered her friendship with such openness that Prudence could not doubt her sincerity and could not fail to respond. Soon she, too, looked forward to tea at the Tradds. The strangely assorted quartet was a happy gathering. Lucy could not really understand why Mary Tradd should be miserable. She just comforted her as best she could, wishing all the while that Mary would stop seeping those flattering tears. The Edwardses had left a half hour earlier, and she had to hurry home to fix supper. But she couldn't leave until Mary felt better. She patted the older woman's hand again, wondering how everything was across the street.

It was almost a copy of the scene at the Tradds'. Josiah Anson was uncomfortably trying to soothe Lavinia, who was crying and talking much like Mary. "I'm so miserable, Papa. I'm ashamed of myself, and you're right to be so mean to me. I was just horrid when Pinny came back from the War. I felt so frightened and confused, and I said terrible things, and I had terrible, horrid thoughts. I didn't know what was happening. First we were in our own home, then the awful Yankees just pushed us out, and then we were all crowded in here not knowing what awful thing was going to happen next, and then you came home, and you were so tired and busy and not the happy, loving papa I missed so much, and then Pinny was different, too, so cold and unloving. And I know that war does terrible things to a man, Papa, but I'm only a girl; I can't really understand about all that. So I get all mixed up, that's all. And I was very bad, I know that, and I'm sorry. But, Papa, really, I'm older now, and I understand things better, and I value Pinckney, and I do respect him, just the way you say I should. I do, Papa, truly I do. And I love him so much. If you forbid the marriage, it'll break my heart. Oh, Papa, please don't be mean. I promise, I was just upset and angry at Lucy, and I only said those things to make her mad. I'll just die if you tell Pinny. Papa, I love you so much. I can't bear it when you're angry with me."

Mr. Anson sighed. He looked at her wide eyes, brimming with tears and saw, in his memory, the little girl who always ran to papa for comfort whenever she was hurt. He had never been able to refuse his daughter anything. He wanted to believe her. "I'll write to Pinckney," he said slowly.

Lavinia looked at him, trembling.

"And ask him to call on me to make the arrangements. It will have to be a small wedding, you understand."

Lavinia threw her arms around his neck and pressed her wet cheek to his.

Pinckney dutifully returned to the city when he received Josiah Anson's summons. He arrived in the middle of one of his mother's teas. Although he was there only long enough to greet the guests, kiss Mary and excuse himself to go and change, the effect on Prudence was instantly apparent to Lucy. It was not visible, more a charge of energy that made the tiny hairs on Lucy's neck stand up. She recognized it; she had felt that way about Andrew. And she knew that it was a reaction to experienced passion, not a girl's dreamy, amorphous longings. My, my, she said to herself, I never heard any rumors about that. And I won't spread any, either. Prudence is my friend. Damn Lavinia, anyhow. And there's not a thing I can do.

Pinckney dreaded his meeting with Lavinia's father, but as soon as he saw Josiah Anson's familiar, worn face, he felt that he was with his godfather and that Josiah was only incidentally the father of the girl he was reluctantly going to marry. Mr. Anson experienced much the same thing. His affection for Pinny drove his apprehensions about the marriage to the back corners of his mind. He put his arm around Pinckney's shoulders and walked him into the library.

"Not too early for a small glass of something, do you think? It's good to see you, Pinckney. You're looking fit. Here, sit down. Tell me all about things at Carlington."

"Thank you, sir. I believe we're on the way now. I wrote you about the tonnage for March, I think."

"Yes, you did. Very impressive. Have you heard anything from your buyers? Have they paid you?"

"I don't know. I got into town yesterday afternoon, and I found that Shad was gone on one of his forays upcountry. I think his father must be sick again; Shad didn't say. He just told Mama that he'd be back in a few days. I don't even know where he keeps the correspondence or the bank records."

Mr. Anson looked worried. "Is that wise, Pinny? A man can save your life and still steal your money."

"Never, Cousin Josiah. I'd stake my life on it." Pinckney grinned. "I guess I did stake my life on him once. That worked out all right."

Mr. Anson turned the conversation back to the mining operation. Pinny was eager to talk about it; with his godfather's approving comments, he even allowed himself a little boasting about the system he had devised. "The only weak spot," he concluded, "is in washing the stone. Sometimes they don't fasten the tops tight and lose half the load. Other times, they lose hold of the rope and lose the whole thing, load, washing box and all. Charleston Mining has a big wash house with machinery to do the whole thing. But then, they've got all that Philadelphia money to spend."

"I know where there's money in Philadelphia if you want some."

"I don't want Yankees on Carlington, Cousin Josiah. Or Yankee money, either. They'd end up owning the whole place."

"Come on, Pinny. Philadelphia isn't New York."

Pinckney had to admit Mr. Anson had a point. Charleston had always recognized Baltimore, Philadelphia and Boston as real cities, almost equal in history and tradition. Nothing else was worthy of notice, regardless of population, because it wasn't old enough to have any civilization. Before the War, all Charlestonians had guests from the "real" cities for the festivities in Race Week.

"Why don't we have a talk about it when Shad gets back?" Josiah said, rising. "Right now, I've got a meeting with our latest General about some damage claims. I'll ride downtown with you."

"Fine . . . oh, Cousin Josiah, about the wedding."

"Oh, yes. The ladies want to make plans. Let's see. We're in April now. You'll be busy getting your washing machinery lined up. And summer's too hot anyhow. Shall we tell them to plan on January next? Everybody will be coming into town for the Ball, and no matter what Emma promises, I know she's going to want to fill the church. She and your mother can stake the wedding date gamble to make Lavinia the bride who leads the opening cotillion at the Ball. Give them something to think about."

Pinckney agreed with alacrity. First things first, and worry about later when later came.

During the next month, Josiah Anson skillfully used his knowledge of the law and of human nature to guide Pinckney and Shad without their realizing that they were being directed. By June first there was a hired overseer at Carlington, Pinckney and Shad had offices on Broad Street, and a bank in Philadelphia was sending a representative to examine Carlington and the account books of the Tradd-Simmons Phosphate Company, preparatory to making a loan for capital asset improvement.

Pinckney was much happier. He did not have the daily ordeal of watching Carlington's fields being torn up, and he did not have to share quarters with Jim Riggs, the tobacco-chewing former sharecropper who ran the company store.

Shad was pleased to the bursting point. He liked the feeling of having his own office with his name on the door. He also admired Mr. Anson for securing the promise of a loan at a reasonable interest rate. The businessmen Shad knew were happy to lend money, but they charged at least 20 percent for it. He had been prepared to invent another anonymous investor and put up his factoring income again, but now it would not be necessary. In addition, the bank loan would provide money to repay the original anonymous investor. With that and the proceeds from the factoring of this year's record cotton crop, he would have enough to start construction of his cotton mill.

In Philadelphia, Edward Pennington was perhaps the most delighted of all the parties. He knew the loan would be good. He and Josiah Anson had been friends since they went to Princeton together. He and his wife had often visited in the house on Charlotte Street. Now his son, Ned, would have a chance to see Charleston, as the family bank's representative. He would have no North/South bitterness to worry about. Edward Pennington had bought a substitute for his son's draft call. Ned had been at home in Philadelphia throughout the whole war. Mr. Pennington knew he could trust his old friend to protect Ned from any embarrassing encounters.

25

Mr. Anson met Ned Pennington at the North-Eastern Railroad depot on Chapel Street. He eyed the young man's two trunks and three valises with alarm. He looked at Edward Pennington III with well-concealed dismay. "How do you do, Ned. You don't mind an old friend calling you Ned, I hope. I held you on my knee plenty of times when you were still in dresses. Now you just hold on a minute while I arrange for a wagon to cart your baggage. You and I'll walk. Just a block to the house and shade trees all the way."

Privately he wondered if he should put the boy in the wagon, too. It was ninety degrees according to the big thermometer on the depot wall, and young Pennington was wearing a wool suit and a beaver hat. His starched collar was unwilted, which meant that he must have changed it just before the train pulled in. It was also tight, which meant that his neck would be covered with prickly heat before an hour passed. He didn't look exactly robust under the best of circumstances; he was a bit plump and his face was pale between his long blonde sideburns. Ned mopped his shiny, wet brow and chin with a silk handkerchief and agreed politely to wait where he was.

In the broad sun, when there's shade under the shed, Josiah Anson thought with disgust. He's not only a momma's boy, he's also a fool. Well, he won't be here long. I'll get the loan papers executed before the heat kills him.

But this time, all Mr. Anson's wiliness had met its match. Ned Pennington was excessively aware of his responsibilities. This was the first time he had been trusted with any of the bank's business by himself, and he was conscientious to a degree that depressed Mr. Anson. He wanted to know everything about phosphates, said Ned, including the chemical composition and the theories of what geological events had resulted in their deposit in the Charleston area. After he learned that, he would go over the company books and investigate each entry. Then he would examine each item represented by each entry. Of course, he would need to observe the operation at Carlington for a number of days. And then he would want test holes dug to assess the extent of the deposit so that the bank could be confident that the mining would not peter out during the period of amortization. His father believed that a month of dedicated work would be adequate. Ned was not so sure.

By the time they arrived at the Anson house Ned had damp patches on the back of his coat, and his collar had collapsed. Josiah looked at the boy who was leaning weakly on the front gate and reminded himself that he was the son of an old friend. "You'd best add another item to your agenda, Ned," he said. His voice was kind. "Tomorrow I'll find you a tailor to make you up some linen suits. Summertime in these parts can melt a man's flesh right off his bones."

"I don't know how we can afford to feed him," Mr. Anson said to his wife after dinner. He had sent Ned to his room to rest and recover from his trip. "Did you see how much that boy ate?"

"He'll eat what we eat," Emma said, "and when we run out, he'll go hungry with us. It wouldn't hurt him any."

"Emma, we've got to keep him happy. Pinckney's counting on that loan."

"Then let Mary Tradd feed him. I'll call on her tomorrow morning and tell her."

Mary was delighted. She invited Adam Edwards to dinner, too. "You have your Yankee, and I'll have mine, Emma. Then neither one will feel left out. Besides, Mr. Edwards' daughter is a very pretty girl, and the Pennington boy will like that. Let's see—you and Josiah, Pinny and Lavinia, the Edwardses, me, Mr. Pennington. Oh, fiddle. I need a lady. I know Pinny will expect Shad to be here, and that makes my table come out wrong. I know, I'll ask Lucy. She's such a sweet girl, she'll help me out."

After the initial party dinner, the senior Ansons excused themselves. Ned's business was with Pinckney, after all, not Josiah. And they had to put up with Ned every evening. Shad and Lucy also pleaded other priorities. The Tradd dinner table settled into a regular routine of six. Mary worried happily about menus, flowers, her dresses and the condition of the napkins which had already been mended once. She was too preoccupied to notice the charged atmosphere that surrounded the young people at the table. Prudence tormented Pinckney and herself by touching his leg under the table while she was talking to Ned Pennington on her right about the properties of lime salts. And Ned hardly heard her because he could not take his eyes off Lavinia's dimple whenever she smiled at Pinckney or, increasingly, at himself.

Ned Pennington was twenty-six years old. Many young ladies in Philadelphia had smiled at him; he was well-bred, well-educated and the only son of a rich banker. But none of them had a smile like Lavinia Anson's. Her soft, pouty lips somehow developed three corners when she smiled, and there was something special about them, and the indentation to one side of them and the wide blue eyes above them that tantalized him and made a promise that he did not even recognize as a promise or have any idea of defining. Ned had never been exposed to a soft, Southern voice before, or to the heady wire of a Southern girl's awe-struck admiration for the superiority of men. Neither had Edward Pennington III ever been away from home alone before. He had been educated by tutors and had toured Europe with an elderly clergyman. He was bewildered by what he considered the indolent way these Southerners lived, the undisciplined schedules for business offices, the emphasis on amusement. Pinckney had apologized because he could not invite him to any of the parties that they always seemed to be having, and Lavinia had insisted that they have one of their own to make up for it. In the middle of the afternoon, Mary Tradd had played the piano while the "young people" danced. It was shocking. His thoughts—when he had his arm around Lavinia's tiny waist and a sweet scent rose from her hair and her fingertips brushed the side of his neck—embarrassed him.

At least he was getting his work done. He had studied all of the books Miss Edwards lent him, and he was confident that he knew enough about the mineral properties of phosphate to have good judgment when he went to Carlington. That would be very soon. Ned closed the last of the company account books and looked at his heavy gold watch. He was at Pinckney's office desk and expected Pinckney any minute. Then they would make up a schedule for going to the plantation. Pinckney wanted to wait until after July 4. The workers all had a holiday then, he said, and they would be more willing to stop work and answer Ned's questions after they had had their celebration. But, Ned thought, that was typical Southern dilatoriness. Today was only June 29. No point in wasting five days. He opened his watch again. Pinckney was late.

Two blocks away, Pinckney looked at the clock in the office of the warehouse. He was annoyed that Ned was late, but not disturbed. He probably got lost, Pinny said to himself. Poor fish has to do everything six times to get it right, and he's only been here twice so far to check the shipping arrangements. He wondered why Ned had changed his mind about meeting at the office. His note hadn't said. Not that it mattered. Pinckney leaned against the wall and crossed his long legs and tried not to think about Prudence Edwards.

Josiah Anson's buggy stopped in front of the entrance to the small office building. "You wants me to deliver another letter, Miss Lavinia?" asked Jeremiah.

"No, thank you. You just wait awhile. I'm going upstairs to see Mr. Tradd."

"But Mist' Pinckney, he at the Arsenal. I left that letter just a hour ago, and the gentleman at the door told me Mist' Pinckney was inside."

"You let me worry about where Mister Pinckney is, Jeremiah." Lavinia giggled. "Just you wait until I come back."

"Miss Emma, she going be mad iffn I keep this buggy out too long. She say I is to take you to a tea party. She don't say nothing about going to no offices."

"Hush up. What Mama doesn't know won't hurt anybody. You just wait, that's all." Lavinia smoothed her hair and stepped onto the carriage block. She pulled up her openwork mitts while she climbed the stairs to the offices of the Tradd-Simmons Phosphate Company. Then she licked her lips and opened the door.

"Is Mr. Tradd here? Why, my goodness, if it isn't Mr. Pennington. What a pleasant surprise." Lavinia offered her sweet-smelling, half-bare hand. Ned lifted it and felt his face grow warm. He bowed over the fingers which had curled around his own, then straightened. Lavinia waited for a carefully timed moment before slipping her fingers just a bit slowly from his. She lifted her fan and let it fall open, then fluttered it in front of her nose. "It must be warm in here, I can't imagine why I feel so flushed." Ned hurried to open a window wider, hitting his leg painfully on the corner of the desk.

While his back was turned, Lavinia moved three steps. It placed her between him and the visitor's chair. When he turned, the movement of the fan was more agitated. "You're too kind, Mr. Pennington," she said in a weak voice. "I'm sure that fresh air is just what I need." She swayed gently. "If I could just sit down for a tiny minute?"

Ned almost ran. What if she should faint? He was a brute not to have seated her at once. "Please," he tried to say, but he choked; he gestured toward the chair as he rushed toward Lavinia. She moved at the same instant, and, to his horror his hand brushed against her breast. Thank heaven, she did not seem to notice. With a rustle of petticoats, she sank gracefully into the chair and leaned back. Ned's arm was still there, holding it steady for her. Lavinia gasped. "Forgive me," he stammered. "I didn't mean to—"

She sat forward, and he was able to step away. His arm seemed to tingle, and his hand had a life of its own, throbbing, fighting his will, wanting to reach out and touch again the rounded softness that was imprinted in his senses.

"Oh, don't you apologize, Mr. Pennington. It was all my fault. Pinckney—Mr. Tradd, I mean—he's always fussing at me for being so clumsy."

"But that's not so, Miss Anson. I remember dancing with you was like floating on a cloud."

Lavinia looked at him with wide eyes. Then she looked down at the fan in her lap. The dimple near her mouth appeared with the tiny, upturned smile that made Ned Pennington's knees melt. Oh, my God, he thought. I want to put the tip of my tongue in that dimple. I must be a degenerate. The sound of Lavinia's tinkling laugh penetrated the fog of self-denial that surrounded him.

"You mustn't talk that way, Mr. Pennington. You'll turn my head." She looked quickly at his damp temples and anguished eyes; then she looked down again with a tiny flicker of her lashes. "If I told Mr. Tradd you were flirting with me, he'd be very cross." The dimple again. "After all, even if we *are* engaged in name only, there are still rules to follow." The heavy lids rose slowly, giving Ned time to assimilate her words, then her eyes were fixed on him, huge and innocently blue.

"I—but I thought—I've never heard—" Ned stammered.

"You mean you didn't know? Of course not, how could you?" The great eyes filled with tears. "It was the War, you see. There was a boy—I was much too young, still in pigtails, but I worshiped him. And when he was killed, my heart just broke. Even very little girls have hearts, after all." The tears brimmed, then spilled two heavy, shining drops. One rolled slowly down to the corner of Lavinia's trembling mouth. She smiled a small, brave smile; the tear was trapped, shimmering in her dimple. Ned's mouth felt desperately dry. "I suppose you think I'm very silly. I was. But I just couldn't bring myself to think about boys after that. Later, after the War, I was old enough to be presented. But that would have meant people could ask to call. It would have been dishonest to allow that. I took my troubles to Cousin Pinckney; he'd always been almost like a father to me." Lavinia clasped her hands and held them to her bosom. "He gave me his protection. I promised, naturally, to release him whenever he wanted to marry. I didn't believe that I would ever want to." She raised one hand to her mouth and opened it to bite on her index finger. Ned could see the glimmer of her teeth and the warm pinkness behind them. He found it difficult to breathe. His mind searched desperately for something to say.

Lavinia sobbed. Tears poured from her eyes.

"Please don't." Ned held out his arms in supplication. Then they were full. They closed automatically around Lavinia's quivering body.

"Comfort me," Lavinia whispered into his ear.

Ned lost all control. His mouth explored the tear-drowned dimple near Lavinia's lips, then moved without volition to her mouth and inside. His hands touched her wet face, her soft hair and then the forbidden hemispheres of her breasts. He was unconscious of anything but his senses.

"Say you love me, Ned."

"I do, I do. I love you."

"Say you're crazy about me."

"Yes. Oh, God, yes."

Lavinia's three-corner smile kissed his ear. "I'm so happy," she said.

Later, when Pinckney arrived, Ned was gone. Lavinia's plea for understanding and forgiveness was impassioned. Pinny's response was all it should be. When he told Shad that Lavinia and Ned were going to be married, Shad only nodded acknowledgment. But when Pinckney left, he laughed until his stomach hurt. He had been in his office, unnoticed by the couple, even though the door was open a crack. "A neater job I've never seen," he roared. "That little number should be in politics. Those fat swindlers could learn a lot from her."

Josiah Anson felt no qualms at all about giving Lavinia and Ned his blessing. He didn't like the boy and, he admitted to his wife with a sorrowful smile, he didn't like Lavinia very much either. Her heartless duplicity was too glaring for any more excuses. While Ned was still dazzled by his good fortune, Mr. Anson arranged for Adam Edwards to marry them in the drawing room of the Charlotte Street house, bought their tickets to Philadelphia and got all the signatures on the loan agreements. "Now, dear Emma, I think we'll go visit that cousin of yours in Savannah. Even if we have to stay at a hotel. Let things cool down a little. Our daughter will give people something to talk about for a month."

On Meeting Street, Mary retired to her room with a cool cloth on her head and was "not at home." Pinckney went to Carlington to test the currents at the half-dozen places along the river where the washhouse could be built and to get gloriously drunk for a week.

Shad's father got sick again.

And Lucy Anson invited Prudence Edwards to tea. She hoped to find a tactful way to offer her assistance in promoting a match between Pinckney and her friend. With Lavinia out of the way, there was no reason that they couldn't be married. A Tradd could marry Abe Lincoln's daughter if he had one, and she would be accepted by everyone the minute her name was changed.

After her first tentative opening, Prudence interrupted her. "Pinckney and me? You're crazy." She broke into tears. Yes, she loved him, she said, and she poured out all her pain and despair. She had never believed she would love anyone, she had not loved Pinckney in the beginning; wanted him, yes, but not love. She did not even know what love was. Until it was too late.

"But Prudence, Pinny must love you. He would never have—I mean, his feelings must have been overpowering or he would never—" Prudence's harsh laughter cut short Lucy's floundering. Then she outlined her career before Pinckney. And since.

"I lie down for any red-haired man who'll have me. Or any man with only a left arm. I can pretend that they're Pinckney. I imagine the Archangel will catch me any day now and kill me. I've been having them in the church."

Lucy drew in her breath with a moan.

Prudence looked at the revulsion on her only friend's face. "No matter what you may think of me, Lucy, I think worse. I was raised with a steady diet of the sinfulness of man. Everything I ever did, starting with killing my mother when I was born, was a sin. All of them—laziness, greed, envy, gluttony, not honoring my father, not loving God—I did them all. I guess I developed a taste. Fornication came naturally to me.

"So you see, now that I love somebody, the best thing I can do for him is to leave him alone. And I love him so much, I can't even do that. What am I going to do?"

Lucy put her arm around her, and they wept together. When they had no tears left, she took Prudence's hand in hers. "You told me that your school was half empty," she said.

Prudence nodded. "Not just mine. All of them. We were so sure we knew everything. Strike the shackles from the black man and he'd want an education first thing. Give it to him, and he'd be just like us. Plus he would love us a lot. Well, they did send their children. But they stopped coming when we got past learning to read 'cat' and print their names. And the gangs on the streets beat up any white, Yankee abolitionist missionaries included. Who did we think we were, to free all those poor devils with no provision made to take care of them. We were criminally stupid. And unfair. Even the Archangel is beginning to doubt himself. That's a miracle that makes parting the Red Sea look like nothing. Oh, God, Lucy, everything I do is wrong. And I'm so angry. I want to hurt the whole world."

"Even Pinckney."

"Most of all Pinckney. Because he's too noble to go to bed with me anymore. He'd still like to, although not the way he used to, but he won't. He's too much a gentleman. I hate him."

Lucy was silent.

"All right," Prudence cried, "I don't hate him. I love him, and I want him, and I can't have him. What shall I do? Throw myself from the steeple after that fool watchman bawls out his 'all's well'?"

"The best you can do is to get away. As long as it's possible, you'll torture yourself with wanting him. When it's impossible, after a while you accept it, and then after a while longer you even stop wanting." Lucy's voice was steady and very sure of what she was saying.

Prudence's eyes looked up at the ceiling for an instant. She felt a new and different kind of shame. She had forgotten about Andrew. "How could I talk to you this way, Lucy? I am deeply sorry. Can you forgive me?"

Lucy smiled. "There's nothing to forgive. As long as you listen to me. I've grown very fond of you, Prudence, and I hate to see you suffering. Please learn something from my experience. That will help give it some value. And if I can believe that it has value, it won't seem quite so unfair."

This time it was Prudence who held her friend in sympathy. "You know," she said softly, "I once told Pinckney I wouldn't get involved with him because I was too fond of him. At the time, I was being clever and flippant. Now I guess I'll have to practice what I preached." She withdrew and stood. "I'll miss you, Lucy."

"I'll miss you. Will you write to me?"

"No. And I don't want you to write to me. It would make me want to come back."

"Where will you go?"

"I don't know. The church has missionary schools in the most unlikely places. I'll see you again before I leave. It will take time for them to arrange a new post for me."

"I'm almost always here. If you need a friend."

"God bless you, Lucy." Prudence laughed. "Listen to me. I sound like the Archangel. But I do mean it." She kissed Lucy's cheek and left quickly.

Six weeks later, Mary Tradd gave a farewell dinner for Prudence Edwards. The scandal of Lavinia jilting Pinckney was no longer being talked about. People were more interested now in discussing the new Governor the Yankees had appointed. Robert Scott was a former Colonel of an Ohio regiment and subsequently an official of the Freedman's Bureau. It was said that he was usually so drunk he had to be carried to his office, and that even the black majority in the state House of Representatives was already talking about impeaching him.

At least the man the newly franchised blacks had elected for U. S. Congressman was more colorful than a sloppy drunkard. Bowen was a professional gambler and card shark from Rhode Island.

At Prudence's dinner, Mary daringly teased Adam Edwards about this politician from his home state. Edwards laughed. His daughter looked astonished.

"I might faint," she whispered to Lucy. "He laughed. He actually laughed."

She left the next day for Baltimore where she boarded a ship bound for the Sandwich Islands and the Anglican mission there.

And the Tradd house resumed its sleepy summer schedule behind the shutters that kept out the heat. Mary and Pinckney were both glad for a quiet restful time.

26

At the Barony, there was little time to rest. It was getting close to harvest time. On September 10 the fields were drained to allow the clay to dry. Every time a heavy rain required flooding them, Julia cursed with impressive fluency in several languages that Stuart and Lizzie did not recognize. And the hurricane watch was still in effect.

At the same time, the pea vines were cut and dried, and the hay stacked. The pale yellow-green scuppernong grapes were also ready to be picked. Lizzie loved them: the round fat shape of them, a single one almost filling her mouth; the spurting sweet center pulp that squirted into her cheek when she bit down; the strange thick bitter skin that made her eyes water and her nose sting. She wished she could eat them all. Still, making the scuppernong wine was fun. Dilcey let her cork one of the bottles she filled with wine. A half day later it exploded with an exciting bang. She also taught Lizzie to make peach leather, the delicious little rolls of candy made from the peaches they had dried in the sun a month before, and benne brittle, which was great fun to break into pieces after it had hardened in the long, shallow pans. Julia, passing through the kitchenyard in a great hurry, stopped long enough to tell her an abbreviated version of *Ali Baba and the Forty Thieves*. "Sesame and benne," she said as she went on her way, "are the same thing." The next day, the hands picked the peanuts. Lizzie and Dilcey boiled some and parched the rest of the household allotment in the oven. Most of the crop was kept for the pigs. That night Stuart and Lizzie gambled on how many "pops," empty shells, they could find. Lizzie won Stuart's penny, and had a terrible stomachache from eating too many nuts. She lost the penny back to him in a race down the river the following morning. She had become an enthusiastic swimmer; she even enjoyed swinging off the rope and falling into the water with her nose pinched between her fingers; but she did not like to put her head in the water. Stuart could always outrace her because he swam underwater, only surfacing for a quick breath at long intervals.

And then it was October. The danger of a hurricane was over. The nights were getting cool, and the days were no longer hot and sticky. The family moved back to the big house, Julia declared an end to the swimming season, and started Lizzie on her schoolwork again. She was excused from her lessons only for the three most important occasions about the harvest: the first reaping, the flailing and the first fanning.

The reaping was, Lizzie thought, like a beautiful slow dance. Men and women moved through the tall golden rice as if they were wading in a sea of sunlight. The rice moved like waves, away from them, then closed behind them with a reverse undulation. The small reaphooks were almost invisible in their hands, except for an occasional glint of reflected light. It looked as if they were removing the long golden heads of the plant by magic. They moved with a steady, tireless step, singing. Everyone did at least two tasks. The crop was in heavy milk, the weather was good, the year's labors had produced a bounteous harvest, and there would be a celebration when all the rice was safely reaped.

The heads were laid on their stubble to dry, and the next day the work was divided. The women gathered the rice into thick handfuls and wrapped each sheaf with a wisp of rice. Their practiced movements were quick and graceful. Then the men stacked the sheaves in cocks.

The harvesting took almost two weeks. Most of the cocks were transferred to the long flat-bottomed boats and put in the flat-house ready for shipment. She'd have them roped together and pulled to the city by a tug, Julia told Stuart. The straw in the fields would be cut and stored to feed the cattle in the winter. Julia was jubilant. The quality of the crop was superlative, nearly two hundred grains to a head. It should weigh in at about forty-seven pounds to a bushel. Average was forty-five, forty-six was very good. The yield was excellent, too. "I'll bet you we get forty bushels to the acre. Top price should be close to a dollar and a quarter a bushel this year, because there was almost no harvest last year. That will pay out fifty dollars an acre. Even Papa didn't do any better."

"Will we be rich again, Aunt Julia?"

"No, Stuart. I doubt if we'll ever be rich again. But we'll be able to cover last year's losses and this year's costs. And we'll have good healthy seed to plant. That seems like riches to me right now."

"What next, Aunt Julia?"

"Tomorrow the flailing. We always hand-whip the seed rice. Milling might break it."

Lizzie was happy to leave the table with her books on it and spend the day in the barn. She watched the women whip the sheaves over the long log in the center of the floor and shrieked with delight when the kernels flew off and spattered on the floor. She begged to try, and all work stopped while a broadly smiling woman with a gold tooth showed her what to do. It was a lot harder than it looked. She was disconsolate when she trudged back to the platform. After the sheaves set aside for seed had been whipped, the woman drew back, and the men moved in with heavy wooden flails. They beat the heads to free the rice that had been too stubborn to be whipped off. This time, Stuart wanted to try his hand. He was more of a failure than Lizzie. She felt much better. Julia sent them both home for supper. She did not move until all the rice was safely stored in the overhead loft to wait for next year's claying.

On the following day, Dilcey fanned the first rice of the crop and they ate it for dinner. Whenever Lizzie thought about her year on the Barony, it was fanning that she remembered best.

It was a simple, primitive ceremony. The rice kernels were poured into a deep mortar made of a hollowed cypress trunk, then pounded with a long-handled carved cypress pestle. After the husks were broken, it was dipped out and put into an enormously wide, round, shallow basket. Dilcey then sang to the rice while she moved the basket from side to side and in a slow circle, tipping it up and down in short jumping motions to flip the rice into the air. The breeze blew the chaff away, and the rice showered down again into the basket which had moved to catch it.

On the plantation as in the city, rice was eaten every day with dinner. Dilcey usually fanned enough for a week at a time when the breeze was just right. The hypnotic spell of the moving basket and the gleaming silvery rice falling away from its chaff had fascinated Lizzie the first time she saw it and every time thereafter. Dilcey had promised to teach her, but her arms were too short to hold the huge basket. She knew she was growing, and she measured herself by stretching her arms across the fanning basket.

At the first fanning of the new crop, she could almost reach. In November, she had her ninth birthday, and Dilcey gave her a basket that Solomon had woven for her. It was very big, but not too wide for her arms. It was the best present she had, even better than the illustrated Atlas Julia gave her or the antlers Stuart sacrificed. They were the largest of any from the bucks he had shot. The kitchen had more venison than it knew what to do with.

True to her word, Dilcey devoted an hour or more every day to teaching Lizzie how to fan rice. Julia noticed, but she did not stop them. It was almost the end of the year. Let the child enjoy the plantation while she could. She had worked hard, and if her piano practice lost a little time to the joys of the kitchenyard, there'd be no harm done. Lizzie was far from gifted musically. And she did show signs of promise as a cook. The way the world was outside the Barony, she might need that more.

In the middle of December, Julia took Stuart and Lizzie home to Meeting Street. Stuart was silent, fighting the tears that kept trying to break through his guard. Lizzie sang Christmas carols to Bear. In her trunk, she had the riding habit Pansy had made for her, which she hoped she'd never have to wear again, a book of pressed flowers and leaves which she had labeled and sewn in calico covers for Shad, a pen-wipe for Pinckney with his initials embroidered on it, her sampler for her mother and some strawberry preserves that didn't look as if the paraffin seal was tight for Sophy. She had learned to play the piano badly, to murder a terrapin without screaming, to embroider laboriously but well, to speak a little French, to "turn" the dinner table after each course, to swim fearlessly, and two important facts: rice was to be worshiped as well as eaten and boys were more important than girls. Her aunt Julia had taught her.

Eleanor Allston made Lizzie a one-day heroine when she returned to school in January, allowing her to show off her skills in tea-pouring and French. Then it was back to normal. The following morning she had to stand in the corner for passing a note to Caroline Wragg during arithmetic class.

Stuart's celebrity lasted much longer. He was in school now, too. No more classes at the Wentworths'. In 1867 the Reverend Doctor A. Toomer Porter, a prominent Charleston clergyman, had opened a school with support from the Episcopal churches of the Massachusetts Diocese. It was called the Holy Communion Church Institute and was especially planned for the sons of planters; it provided dormitory accommodations as well as an education. The fees were minimal; few planters could afford to buy luxuries like schooling when they were trying to find money to rebuild the wasteland Sherman had left behind him.

By the time Stuart arrived, Dr. Toomer had persuaded the Federal Government to give his school an unused Arsenal a block away from his church. It was a large brick building with room enough in its three stories to house students and classrooms. In front of the Arsenal, there was a half-block square parade ground with a flagpole in the center. The boys soon began playing soldier instead of ball, marching with sticks on their shoulders as if they were rifles. When Julia, as a planter, enrolled Stuart in 1869, the school had already become known informally as Porter Academy. The educational standards were demanding, and Stuart was put into classes with boys two years younger than he was. But it did not bother him. He was the lion of the campus. Everyone had heard about his beating by the notorious Daddy Cain, and the boys listened wide-eyed to Stuart's bloodthirsty vows of revenge. "As soon as I'm old enough, I'm going to finish what that high-yellow started," Stuart said again and again. No one doubted that he would do it. He was only fifteen, and small for his age, but no one doubted.

Dr. Porter was an important figure in Mary Tradd's life that year, as well as in her son's. He officiated at her marriage to Adam Edwards. Ned Pennington's visit had resulted in more than one romance. Adam Edwards had never known such happiness as he had found at the Tradd dinner table during the weeks Ned had been in Charleston. It was not so much the excellent food; the way to Edwards' heart was not through his flat stomach. Rather, it was the feeling of comfort and ease in a well-run household. Prudence had never cared what they ate. Certainly there were never flowers on the table. Mary Tradd's dinners were a revelation. When they ended so abruptly and Mary was "not at home" for weeks, Adam Edwards felt as if he had been cast out in the cold. And he realized that Mary had all the warmth that had been missing in his life. He proposed in a long, stilted speech. Mary cried prettily and put her hand in his. They were married in May.

Mary consulted Pinckney first, of course. He was head of the family. He gave her his blessing, thought about Prudence's accounts of Adam Edwards as a father, and urged her to leave Stuart and Lizzie in Charleston. Edwards was going to accept a call to a church in Bryn Mawr, Pennsylvania. Mary wept some more, but even Pinny could tell that she was happy to agree. "I never did know what to do with children," she said in a rare burst of self-assessment.

Lizzie enjoyed the flurry of activity that surrounded her mother's "trousseau." Julia lent Pansy to sew. No one in Philadelphia was wearing bell hoops anymore. Gowns now had extra fullness in the back and sweeping trains of skirt. All Mary's clothes that still had any wear on them had to be remade. The ones that were too threadbare were cut down for Lizzie. She found herself the owner of five new frocks, with sleeves long enough to cover her wrists and skirts long enough to graze the tops of her boots. She showed them off to Pinckney and Shad, turning elegantly without ever losing the book balanced on her head.

Best of all, Mary took Sophy with her when she left. Lizzie confided to Shad that it was the happiest thing that had ever happened to her. When she artlessly added details of Sophy's methods of child care, he sat her on his lap and held her close.

When Mary left, Lizzie automatically became the lady of the house. It was a heady position. She sat at the end of the table, was served first, rang for Elijah to change courses, planned menus, presided at tea, and ordered everyone around.

It made an eccentric household, two young men under the small thumb of a little girl, but Charleston had always been tolerant of eccentricity. And it worked well. Julia's rigorous training had been more demanding than anything Lizzie actually had to handle; as soon as the servants saw that she knew what she was doing, they gave her the respect she deserved without diminishing the affection they had for her. Pinckney and Shad still considered her a baby; they had no comprehension of what she was doing.

Both of them were too busy with their own concerns to wonder why Lizzie so often sought the sanctuary of childhood in one of their laps. Pinckney made frequent trips to Carlington. The new washing shed increased efficiency so much that he was expanding operations. Also, he was deluged with invitations. A twenty-six-year-old bachelor with a prosperous business and the Tradd name was a prize to make the mothers of marriageable daughters quiver. The girls themselves paid attention only to his tall, muscular frame, flashing smile and gallant manner. They were more eager than their mothers. Pinny knew the rules: he was careful not to concentrate on any particular girl or girls. Too much attention would lead to expectations of a declaration, and he had learned how entangling an impulsive action could be.

He would not have said that he was longing to get married. But he accepted the invitations.

As for Shad, marriage never entered his mind. He was building his mill and the town around it. He called it Simmonsville, and it made him feel like a king. So did the girl he had installed in one of the first completed houses. Her name was Garnet Pearl Chester, Shad called her house the "jewelry box," and she considered that the most elegant thing she had ever heard.

Garnet had the lush, dark, early-blooming beauty that was so often found in the mountains where she had been born. She had run away from home with a man who abandoned her after a few months, and she had drifted down state, ending up in the line of people looking for jobs at the Simmonsville Cotton Mill. Shad plucked her from the line, bought her some clothes, put her in the jewelry box and told her he'd kill her if she let another man touch her. She considered herself very lucky. His wants were simple and he never beat her; both were qualities she had not found in the men she had met on her travels. Besides, he spent most of his time at the mill building, learning about the machinery that was being tested after installation. He was hardly any bother at all when he came over from Charleston.

Stuart, who might have argued with Lizzie's assumption of authority in the Tradd house, was hardly a real presence in the family. He spent his vacations from Porter at the Barony, except for Christmas when Julia came into town and took over Lizzie's role. Those weeks were the only clouds in Lizzie's life. She found her schoolwork easy; she and Caroline Wragg were inseparable best friends; she considered her household duties no more than an extension of her Barony training; and if things got to be too much for her, she could always turn to Pinny and Shad for some pampering or she could complain to the elaborate doll Mary had sent from Philadelphia. "Clarissa" was a good listener.

The oddly assorted household jogged along happily, timing itself by Charleston tradition and the chimes of Saint Michael's. In common with the rest of the people south of Broad, they were pleased by the streetlights installed in 1869 and largely unconcerned with the boom in building and business that was going on uptown. That was the affair of the

New People, not the Charlestonians. Although many of Charleston's men found employment in the offices of the new businesses, they came back downtown for dinner and after the work day was over; they did not allow the two to overlap.

With his mill to worry about, Shad paid more attention than most people to the reports of the bizarre organization that was growing upstate. In general, everyone laughed at the ridiculous name, the KuKluxKlan, and the idea of grown men wearing sheets over their heads. The Charleston newspaper seldom mentioned it, or the black state militia Governor Scott formed in response. They did grumble when he got more Union troops from Washington in 1870, even though none of them were sent to Charleston. In fact, the Yankee presence in the city was shrinking somewhat. The Freedmen's Bureau schools all closed the same year.

In 1871, Scott was impeached. His party regulars did not mind that he had run up a state debt of more than fifteen million dollars. They did object when he signed an over-issue of yet another state bond without sharing the proceeds with them. He left in disgrace, escorted by the troops he had imported the year before. He was replaced by Franklin Moses, who stole with more finesse.

"Pinny!"

"Yes, ma'am. Are you going to fuss because I didn't eat all my dinner? It's too gummy to eat."

"Pinny, don't tease. I have something important to talk to you about."

He put down the newspaper and tried not to smile. Lizzie's "bossy fits" always amused him, but he knew she took them seriously. She fussed about the house like a little old lady. "What is it, Baby Sister?"

"Look at my arms." She held them out to him. Pinckney sat bolt upright.

"What is it? Do you have a rash? Did you hurt yourself?"

"No, silly. I'd be able to take care of that. What's wrong is that my arms are right there. Hanging out. Pinny, I'm growing like crabgrass."

He realized with a shock that she was right. How could he not have noticed? Her skirt was practically up to her knees, and her thin arms extended three inches from the cuffs of her dress. The cuffs were frayed. "Sweetheart! How old is that frock?"

"I got it when Mama had her wedding."

"But that was more than two years ago. Haven't you had any new clothes since then?"

"Boots. That was all I really needed. But I'm growing too fast all of a sudden. I need everything."

"And you'll have it . . . The only trouble is, I don't know anything about things for little girls. Do you know where to get them?"

"No."

"How about Cousin Lucy Anson. She'd know. Let's go see her, would you like that?"

"I'll have to think about it. She doesn't dress very pretty herself."

"She dresses like a lady."

Lizzie's eyebrows knotted. Pinny knew what that meant. He waited for her to decide.

"How soon can we go?" Lizzie said. "And Pinny, one more thing . . ."

"Right away. What is it?"

"I want big girl frocks, not baby things. I'll be twelve soon, you know."

"Yes, ma'am, Miss Tradd, ma'am."

Lucy answered the door knock. "Go away," she cried. "Don't come any closer. Andrew's ill. Dr. Perigru thinks it might be Yellow Jack."

Pinkney scooped Lizzie up like a sack of flour and ran across the street. He shouted for the servants as soon as he was in the house. "No one is to leave this house until I tell you. And no one is to come in. There's Yellow Jack." Clara and Hattie threw their aprons over their heads and wailed. "Elijah, take them in the kitchen and talk some sense to them."

Lizzie sat in the chair where Pinckney had dumped her. Her eyes were wide and her lips trembling. Pinny knelt next to the chair. "I'm sorry I frightened you, baby. I had to act fast. Do you know what Yellow Jack is?" Lizzie shook her head. Pinckney took her hand in his. "It's a kind of fever, a terrible kind. It comes all in a rush sometimes, nobody knows why, and it makes a lot of people very sick. Some of them die. I don't want you to get it, that's why I ran. If Andrew has it, anybody who goes in his house might get it."

"Why didn't Lucy run?"

"Lucy already had it. She can't get it again. I had it, too, before you were born. So I can't get it. Now there are things we have to do."

"Do we have to run away?"

"I wouldn't know where to run. Once it starts, it can jump up anywhere. The safest thing is to stay in the house, I think. I'll go to Dr. Trott's and get some pyrethrum powder. You'll have to put a handkerchief over your nose and mouth and sprinkle it all over the house. Wear gloves, too. If the servants have stopped weeping and wailing, you can get them to help you."

"Why can't you help me?"

"Baby Sister, this is a grown-up thing to understand. I have to go help Lucy with Andrew. She wouldn't be answering the door if she had any servants there. Andrew's my oldest friend, and he needs my help."

"Suppose I catch it, Pinny?"

"Dearest Lizzie, if you catch so much as a sneeze, you wave your hand out the window and I'll be home before you quit waving."

"Really, truly?"

"Cross my heart."

"That's fair. You'd best hurry, then, Lucy looked all at sixes and sevens."

Pinckney hugged her hurriedly and left.

27

"This is a hell of a note," said Andrew when Pinckney entered his room. His voice was weak, and fear was poorly masked by his attempt at hearty jocularity.

"I haven't been to visit for a week. Can't you say hello?"

"Hell, I'm not complaining about that. Lucy told me you're busy dodging debutantes. What I'm mad about is being so weak. Cold, too. In July. And, Pinny—my legs ache. How the hell can I go for years not having any feeling, and then when I get it, it's a damned fever ache."

Pinckney took Andrew's hot hand in his. There was nothing to say. Already Andrew was squinting; his face was flushed, and his lips were red. When he opened his mouth, Pinny could see that his tongue was scarlet. All the signs of yellow fever. Lucy had told him that Andrew's temperature was up to one hundred and two. It would, Pinny knew, go higher.

Lucy came in quietly, carrying a basin of water. "Pinckney, would you please step outside for a minute? I'm going to give Andrew a sponge bath."

"Let me do it."

"No. I know how he likes it. I always give him his sponges. You could crack some ice if you'd be so kind. It's in the cooler on the back stoop."

Pinckney was gone no more than fifteen minutes. Lucy met him at the top of the stairs. "Hundred and four," she whispered. "He's getting delirious."

For the next two days, Pinckney and Lucy tended Andrew together. They put chips of ice into his mouth, sponged his thrashing body and held him down when convulsions ravaged him. In his delirium, he did not know Pinckney. At first, he stared at his red hair, lit by the lamp at night, and thought he was the devil. Then he screamed piteously and burrowed his head into Lucy's breast begging her to save him. Lucy cradled him against her as if he were an infant. "It's all right," she murmured over and minute she steadied and took a deep breath. "I'm all right now." She had dropped the bowl. Now she picked it up and washed it, pulling away from Pinckney.

"That has to be the end of it," she said, "or he will die." She stood up shakily. Her skirt was stained. "I'll change my frock and get the sheets. There's brandy in the dining room. Bring two glasses, please."

The cognac brought a touch of color to Lucy's face. "I can see why you men all drink spirits all the time," she said. "It's very inspiriting."

Pinckney poured more in their glasses. Soon they would know if Andrew was going to live or die. He looked as if he were dead already. His yellow skin sagged from his jaw and lay in folds on his neck. His breath was so shallow that it was imperceptible.

I should say something, Pinckney thought. Anything, just to make the waiting easier. "What do you know about fossils, Lucy?"

"Like arrowheads, you mean?"

"No. Fossils. Old bones. Strange creatures." He found himself crying. He told her about eohippus. He was so tired. "Forgive me," he said. "I don't know why I'm crying."

Lucy touched his hand. "I do," she said.

Andrew groaned. His body stirred. They ran to him. Lucy turned back the covers. All around him a dark stain of urine was spreading. He was going to live. Lucy turned to Pinckney, her eyes blinded with tears. She sobbed against his chest while he patted her back. "We saved him; he's going to be all right. Oh, Pinny, I'll be indebted to you all my life."

While the bells of Saint Michael's marked the hours and the watchman called his message of comfort, Lucy and Pinckney changed the sheets and bathed Andrew's shriveled legs. The blood-dark urine stopped shortly before dawn, and his breathing became natural. His pulse was weak but regular, and he was in a deep, restoring sleep.

Lucy smoothed the fresh linen cover over his shoulders. Then she smiled wanly. "I'm starving. Would you like some supper?"

Pinckney realized that he had not eaten for three days. "I could eat an entire family of horses," he said. "Where's your larder, Mistress Anson?"

The tender ash-rose of dawn filled the yard between the house and the kitchen building. Their footsteps sounded supernaturally loud on the dewy brick. Lucy stumbled from fatigue but caught her balance. "Do you think I'm drunk?"

"No. But I recommend it."

They ate mightily. A whole capon in its own bed of gelatine, a bowl of cold left-over snap beans and bacon, a pecan pie and a demi-john of buttermilk. When they finished, the sky was a pale lemon color. It was morning. A bird in the fig tree outside saluted the sun with a rippling song. Lucy looked at Pinckney. "I never knew your beard was brown," she said. A tortured bubble of laughter broke from her throat, and she keeled over onto the littered table.

Pinckney left her to sleep. He climbed slowly to Andrew's room and took up the vigil in the tall chair near the bed.

The yellow fever epidemic ravaged Charleston for five and a half weeks. When it was over, almost three thousand people in the city had died. Among them were two hundred and twenty-seven Charlestonians, including Eleanor Allston and four of her students.

Lizzie took the loss of her friends very hard. It was her first encounter with the death of anyone she knew. Pinckney tried to console her, but when she refused to go to the funerals, he became firm. "You must go, Lizzie. I'll go with you, but I cannot take your place."

"What difference does it make? They're dead. They won't know I'm there. I won't go."

"You will. Out of respect for your friends and their families. And you're wrong. Mistress Allston and the girls will see you. They'll be looking down from heaven."

Lizzie's dark blue eyes searched his face. "Do you really believe that?"

"I do."

"Really truly?"

"Cross my heart."

Unexpectedly, Lizzie's mouth twitched. "I bet you Susan Johnson isn't looking down. She's more likely looking up. She was so mean she'd sour milk."

Pinckney tried not to laugh, but he failed.

On Lucy's recommendation, Lizzie went directly from the Allston funeral to the Robinson dry goods store on King Street. Pinckney spent an uncomfortable two hours as escort while Lucy introduced Lizzie to the mysteries of fabrics, ribbons, laces and buttons. When they left, Lizzie was the proud owner of an ecru net-work reticule stuffed with swatches and samples.

The days and nights of shared dedication and revelations had created a profound intimacy between Lucy and Pinckney. Without any need to put it into words, each felt a trust in the other and a closeness neither had ever known before. It was natural for Pinckney to turn to Lucy for help with his little sister and for Lucy to call on him for everything he could do for Andrew. All of them found their lives enriched.

The traffic back and forth across Meeting Street was constant. The two houses were like twin, reciprocal annexes. In a sense, Pinckney became the head of both families; the added responsibility was not burdensome, because with it he found a complementary half. Lucy was like a mother to Lizzie and a sister to him. When Shad returned from Simmonsville, he was irritated that Pinckney had made Andrew the legal consultant for Tradd-Simmons. But he approved the wheeled chair and desk Pinny had added to Andrew's room. Altogether, Andrew was more alive than Shad had ever seen him. He was busy, and he was supporting his family himself. And, if he really knew very little about contracts, Josiah was there in the background.

Shad suggested the next big step for the Ansons. Lucy had to go out more, he said. He had not forgotten how happy she had been at the Cotillion Club Ball. He and Pinckney insisted, Andrew did not object, and Lucy finally agreed. She hired a cook, got two new dresses and began to pay calls. She even gave an occasional small supper party after Andrew mastered the mechanics of his chair and could act as host.

"It's a whole wonderful new life for me," she said gratefully to Pinckney. "I always wanted a brother or a sister. Now you and Shad are two brothers, not just one, and Lizzie is a combination little sister for me and big sister for Little Andrew." The extended family went out frequently together. The most popular expedition was to Van Santen's Bazaar, a lavish ice-cream parlor that had a tempting array of toys to fascinate eight-year-old boys and a special section with stereoscopes and slides of foreign cities which made them all exclaim in wonder and, sometimes, horror.

Lizzie began classes on October first at Mrs. Hopson Pinckney's Boarding and Day School for young ladies. The fees were higher than Eleanor Allston's had been. Mrs. Pinckney was shrewdly earning her living from New People with daughters. But Tradd-Simmons was shipping almost a hundred tons of phosphate a month. Pinckney could afford the fifty dollars a year and also the twenty dollars for painting and drawing lessons and twelve for French conversation. He offered to pay for music lessons, too, although they cost forty dollars. Lucy and Lizzie conferred, Lizzie played a Mozart sonatina, and they decided not.

She liked her new school well enough. Caroline was going there, too. But it was confusing that she was not allowed to accept invitations from the girls she met there, and it made her angry that she could not have as many frocks as they did or a coat with a fur collar and muff. It was almost a winter uniform for the girls from uptown. Pinckney was relieved to be able to refer the problem to Lucy.

"But all the other girls have muffs, Cousin Lucy! I told Pinny that was the only thing I really wanted for my birthday. When a person's twelve, she should have a special present. A hairbrush, that's what he gave me. I already had a hairbrush."

Lucy, who had selected the severely simple silver-backed brush and comb for Pinckney, wished that she could use it on Lizzie in an old-style manner of persuasion. Instead, she tried to explain, afraid that twelve was not old enough to understand.

"Lizzie, not 'all the other girls' have muffs, and we both know it. The Charleston girls do not. They are not necessary, for one thing. Our weather never gets cold enough for furs. Perhaps where the families of those girls come from, they need more than gloves to keep warm. I'm trying to be generous in my opinion, because that's what a lady does."

"You sound like Aunt Julia. 'Ladies do' and 'ladies don't.' I hate that."

Lucy smiled. "I always did, too, but that's how we all have to learn. There are reasons for all the do's and don'ts, and they're the same reasons you can't have a muff. Now stop pouting and pay attention. The whole thing about being a lady—or a gentleman, for that matter—is that you think first about the feelings of other people. You chew with your mouth closed because seeing the mess in your mouth is sickening to the other people at the table. You don't interrupt because the other person would be upset if he couldn't finish saying what he wanted to say. You stand up when someone enters the room as a sign that that person is welcome to your chair if he wants it. Do you see? The other person, the other people have to be considered first."

"That's a bad bargain, I think."

"No it isn't. Because ladies and gentlemen only associate with other ladies and gentlemen. Each of them is giving first consideration to the others. It all comes out to everyone getting a fair share. It also comes out to not thinking about things in terms of bargains. I don't want you ever to use that phrase again; it's vulgar."

"There you go. Aunt Julia always says things are vulgar. Mama used to do it too. Nobody ever says what it means."

Lucy sighed. "Oh, goodness, I'm getting into deep water. I really don't think you're quite old enough yet for us to talk about good taste. I know twelve is very grown up, but I'd rather wait a few years. Let's go back to the muffs."

"All right. I know what we'll do. I'll offer to let anybody who doesn't have a muff use mine. That's thinking of them first. But they'll say no because they're thinking of me first. So it will all be just fine." Lizzie was triumphant.

"No, honey, no. You can't have a muff because it would be a constant reminder to other girls that they don't have one of their own. Furs are very costly. There are lots of families who can't afford furs."

"Silver brushes are costly, too."

"Yes, Lizzie, but no one sees your hairbrush. You can enjoy it in private without anyone knowing you have it. You certainly wouldn't tell anyone about it."

"I already did. The girls asked me what I got for my birthday, and I told them."

"Did you say a hairbrush?"

"Well of course I said a hairbrush. That's what it is."

"I mean, you mustn't say a silver hairbrush."

Lizzie rolled her eyes. "Honestly, Lucy, I do know a few things. That would be bragging."

"Exactly. And so would wearing a fur muff. All right?"

"I suppose so. What matters is that I'm not going to get a muff, even if I throw a fit. I know when I'm licked."

Lucy settled for that.

Seven months later when Stuart graduated from Porter, Pinckney had to make a similar compromise with the single-mindedness of the young. He, too, won his point without winning understanding.

Stuart had just turned nineteen, and he was sure that he knew everything and that Pinckney knew nothing. It was a stormy confrontation. As a young boy, he had worshiped his flamboyant older brother and wanted nothing more in life than to grow up and join Pinckney's cavalry troop, carry a saber, ride a hot-blooded horse and slaughter Union soldiers. The War had ended too soon for him. He would have rushed to fire on Fort Sumter and start it again if he could. Stuart was full of anger. It vented itself against Pinckney.

"You surrendered," he cried, "you deal with Yankees, you go to their stores and eat ice cream, you speak to them on the street, you belong to the Chamber of Commerce. You're a traitor, Pinny."

All of Stuart's accusations were hits on what Pinckney considered failures in his life. He had learned to face reality, but he had never learned not to hate it. "For God's sake," he said wearily, "the War has been over for seven years. We can't change facts, Stuart."

"I never took the oath. I don't recognize them."

"Hurrah for you. You haven't had to recognize them because you had me to support you." Pinckney's temper matched his younger brother's. They glared at each other, blue eyes against blue eyes, red hair flaming. Pinckney saw the trimmed moustache that was Stuart's proud badge of adulthood and felt a towering rage. Stuart's facial hair was red. He could grow a beard if he wanted to.

"You keep telling me you're a man," Pinny bellowed. "Then you'll have to act like one. You don't want to go to college, all right. But, by God, you'll go to work and earn your keep."

"I won't work for your Yankee-loving phosphate company. You're raping Carlington's rice fields so that Yankee farmers can grow wheat."

"I wouldn't have you. I suppose you'll go running to Aunt Julia. You love that. She runs the plantation while you play in the river and shoot does."

Stuart paled. He had told the story on himself about how he mistook a doe for a buck. It was underhanded of Pinckney to use it against him.

Pinny was ashamed. His temper had made him go too far. Stuart's skill as a hunter was his only real accomplishment. He had done poorly at school, Julia allowed him almost no responsibility during his summers at the Barony, and he had lost his dominance over the younger boys in his class at Porter when, one by one, they all grew taller than he. "I'm sorry, Stuart, I'm a cad," Pinckney said. "It's the Tradd temper. Will you forgive me? I wouldn't have a prayer to out shoot you if you called me out." He held out his hand.

Stuart glowered, but he took the hand. "I'll find work," he mumbled.

"I'll help you if you let me. I had planned to take you in the company, but if you're dead set against it, I'll back down. I hope you'll let me take you in the Dragoons, though."

Stuart forgot his manhood. "Oh, boy, will I!" he yelped.

He became an assistant to the captain of one of the ferry boats across the Cooper River. Within two years he was captain of his own boat, with Billy as an assistant, and a lieutenant in the Dragoons. He was never out of some sort of uniform except when he was in dress clothes for parties, the Saint Cecelia and the Cotillion Club. He was very handsome with his sun-tanned face and neat, clipped beard. And his lack of stature was an advantage in the cramped wheelhouse of the *Dixie Tradd*.

He lived at home, but the family hardly saw him. He would dash in, eat supper and change clothes for a party or for night patrol. As far as Pinckney could tell, Stuart was a young man contented with his lot in life.

28

Pinckney had only a few months of tranquillity after he and Stuart arrived at their settlement. He had been expecting trouble with Stuart. When it was over, he was lulled into a dangerous complacency. He was jolted out of it with the force of an explosion.

In October 1872 Lizzie started her second year at Mrs. Pinckney's and her first year at dancing school. The preparations were like a small hurricane. Lizzie was getting her first long dress, and she involved everyone in the decisions about color, sleeves, trim, sash, number of petticoats, and what to do about her hair.

"I hate it! I wish I wasn't a Tradd. It's like wire. Nasty, rusty, red, old wire." She stormed one minute, and whirled gleefully the next, when she saw her new slippers or a bit of ribbon. Pinckney tried to find sanctuary at the Ansons', but Lucy was almost as wrapped up in the event as Lizzie was.

"It's terribly important, Pinny. She's becoming a young lady. The first long dress is more exciting to a girl than anything else in her life, including her wedding gown. Besides, you might as well get used to the commotion. Your house won't be peaceful again for a long time. If you think she's mercurial now, just wait until she falls in love."

When the great evening came, Lucy helped Lizzie get ready. Then she came downstairs first to alert Pinckney and Shad. Her eyes were shining with emotion. "She's lovely," Lucy said. "For pity's sake, tell her so." They made a group at the bottom of the stairs. The servants peered around the dining room door.

Lizzie came down the stairs as if she had a book on her head. Instead of her pigtails, she had a cloud of wavy red-gold tied back from her forehead with a wide bow of pale blue satin. Her dress was also blue. It was made of fine muslin, as light as a summer's breeze; the long skirt floated around her. A tiny border of white lace edged the square cut neckline and short puffed sleeves and swirled across the skirt in loops from the hem to the waist and the wide white satin sash that circled it. Her thin arms and neck were pale; light reflected from her collarbones. She looked heartbreakingly vulnerable and young and innocent. Pinckney's heart lurched painfully. He wanted to weep.

"You look beautiful, Baby Sister," he said. "Will you allow me to escort you?" He crooked his arm and extended it.

Lizzie giggled. She looked at Lucy. "You would think," Lucy said, "that a gentleman would see that a lady needs her wrap." Lizzie giggled again.

She tossed her ribboned head. "I reckon he doesn't have any manners," she teased.

Shad took the little navy-blue wool cape from the chair near the stairs and bowed awkwardly. "He's just dazzled by your beauty, ma'am. Allow me the honor."

"Why, sir, you are *too* gallant," said Lizzie with an airy manner. She chortled and turned her back for Shad to settle the cape on her shoulders. "What fun this is." Her voice was ripe with self-satisfaction.

She curtsied to Pinckney, tucked her white-gloved hand under his elbow, glanced at Lucy, grinned at Shad and departed, leaving a faint scent of honeysuckle behind her.

"Isn't she darling, Shad?"

"What? Oh, yes. She'll be the prettiest one there."

Lucy shook her head. "No, she won't. Caroline Wragg will be the prettiest. But our Lizzie feels pretty, and that's all that matters."

Pinckney delivered Lizzie to the chaperones at the South Carolina Hall and was home again in five minutes. "What have you been up to, Lucy? That child was flirting with us." He was laughing, but his eyes were angry.

Lucy poured him a glass of Madeira and pushed him toward a chair. "You're sore as a boil because you're jealous, that's all. Of course I've been teaching her to flirt. It goes with dancing. You can't be the only man in her life forever, you know. You, either, Shad. Stop scowling like that. Let's have some supper. I promised Lizzie I'd wait for you to bring her home. She wants to tell me all about it."

At a quarter to nine, Pinckney called for Lizzie and followed her home. She ran ahead of him, eager to tell Lucy her news. She was in love, and He had asked her to dance three times.

The introduction of romance into the Tradd house was like letting the snake into the Garden of Eden. Peace departed. Lizzie forgot to order meals, overlooked dust on the furniture, failed to remind Hattie to double-starch Mr. Pinckney's dress shirt, gave up darning his socks altogether and invited Caroline to come home from school with her almost every day. The girls shut themselves in Lizzie's room where they sat on the bed and talked about boys instead of doing their homework.

Lucy had to withstand tears, pathos, temper, and threats of suicide because of what Lizzie called her "orphan's wardrobe." She also was the recipient of shy confidences and requests for advice.

Shad came under the most persistent attack. Lizzie insisted on teaching him to dance so that he could help her practice. He resisted as long as he could. But one evening after supper, Lizzie plopped herself on his lap, wrapped her arms around his neck and begged him. He stood up quickly and set her on her feet. "You're a young lady now, baby. You can't go sitting on men's laps, not even mine. If you're going to pester me to death, I'll let you teach me." Before long, the practice sessions were an established routine. Lizzie's pigtails flew behind her and her black stockinged legs with their sturdy school boots followed Shad's enthusiastic lead in riotous waltzing. The thumping in the drawing room over his head made it impossible for Pinckney to read in the study.

"Things can't get any worse," he complained to Lucy and Andrew.

If he had remembered those words, he would gladly have eaten them a few months later. At the Saint Cecelia in 1873, he glanced over the crowd when he entered the ballroom and was stabbed to the heart by the serenely beautiful face of one of the debutantes. First love had come late to Pinckney; it hit him harder than it would a younger man.

"What am I going to do, Lucy?" He turned instinctively to her quiet sympathetic understanding. Lucy was taken aback by Pinckney's wild, staring eyes. He had told her that he was subject to barely controllable anger and despair, but he had made the remark in a cool, easy voice. She had not suspected the real capacity for passion in his nature. Now she saw it.

"Dear Pinny. You know as well as I do. You pay your attentions. Dance with her. Talk to her. Send her flowers. Make some pretty speeches. Get to know her. A pretty face is the least important thing about a girl. You have to find out if she's worthy of you."

"Worthy of me! Lucy, what am I for someone to be worthy of? A crippled old soldier who makes fertilizer. I'll be thirty in June. Dear heaven, I'm like a father in her eyes."

"How do you know that? Did you talk with her at the Ball?" He confessed that he had been afraid to approach her. "Well, then, you are a great booby. Pinckney Tradd, you are a man any woman would be proud to love and be loved by. You're strong; a woman can lean on that. And you're sensitive; a woman can talk to you and trust you to understand and care. You're a man, Pinny, not a boy. She will be flattered to death to be noticed by you. For heaven's sake, every girl in Charleston has been swooning for you ever since you got out of Lavinia's clutches."

Pinckney had to admit that he had been sought after, but he concluded that it was only for the financial security he could offer.

"Don't be a jackass," Lucy snapped. Her vehemence startled him. "Sorry," she said gently. "I don't like to hear you talking so ugly about yourself, that's all." To herself, she said that the money certainly wouldn't hurt, but if the girl didn't appreciate him for more than that, she, Lucy, would snatch her baldheaded. She realized that Pinckney was talking. He had buried his face in his hands; she could hardly hear him.

". . . living like a monk for years," he was saying, "I don't know how to cope with all this emotion. I didn't sleep at all last night. I feel as if I'll never be able to sleep again. She haunts me. I've never felt like this before."

Lucy's hand went toward his bowed head, then she withdrew it. That wouldn't help. "Why don't you talk to Shad? Maybe another man—"

Pinckney threw his head up. "Shad!" he spat. "What does Shad know about love? He has his doxy at his cotton-mill town for his softer moments, but the only thing he loves is the string of zeroes in his bank account. He doesn't think about anything except making money. Cotton! I couldn't believe it when he told me."

"I won't let you talk ugly about Shad, any more than about yourself. He's my friend, and yours, too."

Pinckney groaned. "You're right. I don't know what I'm saying. This whole thing is driving me crazy. Dear God, I should never have told you about—"

"The 'doxy'? Don't be a goose. I know about the world a little bit. Tell. Have you seen her? What's she like? Does she wear paint on her face?"

"You shock me, Lucy."

"I do not. Don't pretend with me. Will you tell?"

"No. I want you to forget I mentioned it." His eyes twinkled. "I'll tell you one thing. If, and only if, you give me your word that you will never say a word about it to a living soul."

"Word of honor. What is it?"

"Well, her name is Garnet."

"Is what?"

"Garnet Pearl."

"You're making that up."

"Could I invent such a thing?"

Lucy crumpled with laughter. Pinckney joined her, and for a minute his face lost its agonized expression. Then it returned. "*Her* name is Ann," he said.

"That's a lovely name," Lucy responded.

"Without an e." He made it sound like a unique and miraculous thing.

"Miss Lucy, I need your help."

"Shad, if you tell me you're in love, I'll hit you with something. I've had eight months of Ann Guignard leading Pinny a merry chase, and it's made me an old woman."

His eyes crinkled. "Nothing like that. I need your advice on what to do about this." He handed her the square white card in his hand.

It was an invitation to a tea dance at the home of Mr. and Mrs. Wilson Saint Julien. Lucy studied it. "What do you want to know, Shad?" She did not look at him.

"I want to know what it means. I haven't noticed that my name has lost an m in the past few weeks." His voice was bland, humorous. Lucy looked up then. She smiled. In old Charleston circles, the name pronounced "Simmons" was spelled "Simons." The Saint Juliens were one of the oldest and proudest families in the city.

"I'll tell you," Lucy said. "The Saint Juliens have three sons; the eldest wants to be a doctor, the middle one is good for nothing, and the youngest is the apple of his mother's eye. They also have a very pretty, well-behaved daughter who'll be presented next January."

Shad nodded. "Blue-blood breeding stock at a high price."

"Something like that, only never said out loud of course. In a way it's a compliment; they want to show her to you before she goes on display at the Ball. Are you interested?"

"I might be."

Lucy's jaw dropped.

His mouth stretched its widest. "Not in buying the little girl. I just wonder what will happen when the one-m Simonses see me at the party."

"Shad! Don't tell me you want to climb into Charleston society."

"It depends. How high can a fellow climb if he's got a thick skin and doesn't mind being a laughing stock for a few years?"

"If he went slow and easy, watched every step he took, maybe a third of the way by himself—two thirds if he married well. But I can't believe that you want to play those games. Pinckney told me that you wouldn't let him take you anywhere and he finally quit asking."

"I look at it this way. I need to be beating something, to keep moving. I've got the mill going. There's a two-m town I built out of the dust. I'm opening my own bank in Edisto County this fall. I can't do any more with phosphates. Pinckney doesn't want to put in our own refining plant the way First Charleston Mining has done, and it's his show, so I can't push. I'm at loose ends."

Lucy looked into his amber eyes. They were veiled, hiding something which she knew questions would not uncover. "If you want it, I'll tell you how to go on."

"Let's give it a try. Should be kind of funny."

"All right. I'll get some letter paper for your R.S.V.P. You send Elijah to deliver it, and on the morning of the party you send cut flowers to the hostess with your card. Do you have any cards?"

"Of course not. In my crowd, all a man needs is a handshake to introduce himself."

"You'll have to go to Walker, Evans and order some engraved . . . Here's the paper and the pen. I'll tell you what to write. 'Mister—' Shad, what is your real name? Were you baptized 'Shad'?"

"My name is Joe."

"Fine. Then it's 'Mister Joseph'—have you a middle name?" He shook his head. "Then we'll give you one. How about 'Shadwell'? That sounds very prosperous."

"Downright pompous."

"So much the better. You know, this is sort of fun." Lucy smiled mischievously. "All right, then, let's go. 'Mister Joseph Shadwell Simmons accepts with pleasure the kind invitation of . . .' "

When the social season was well underway, Lucy and Shad plotted strategy like generals in the field. The hours were filled with laughter.

They were a needed antidote for Lucy's time with Pinckney. Ann Guignard refused him. She was going to marry a third cousin from Savannah, who was in his final year at the College of Charleston.

"Methuselah Tradd," said Pinckney bitterly. Lucy did her best to cheer him up.

"The girl's a fool," she said to Shad.

Pinckney recovered from his heartbreak, as people always do. But when he saw Ann lead the Grand March at the Saint Cecelia in her wedding gown, he felt as if he had the wind knocked out of him. He felt a light touch on his arm and looked down at Lucy. "Let's have a brilliant smile for Cousin Lucy," she said through her teeth. "All the disappointed mothers are hoping you'll look stricken." She held her fan to her cheek, stuck out her tongue behind it and crossed her eyes.

Pinckney was startled into laughter. "At the Ball, Mistress Anson, and your father-in-law the President. Have you no shame?"

Lucy looked demure. "Not enough to fill a thimble," she said. "That was nicely done, Mister Tradd. Could you favor this fallen woman with another before Miss Emma catches her?" Her gray eyes rolled together.

Pinckney chuckled. "Enough. You're a jewel among women. I feel fine. Let's join the other old folks and make merry with decorum."

"Better than that, let's find out what horses to back tomorrow. Andrew and I intend to win a fortune."

After thirteen years, Charleston was having Race Week again. The Washington Race Course was scheduled for a gala reopening. None of the horses would be wearing Charleston colors, the boxes would be filled with New People, the long trip uptown would be made on the streetcars, but it was still Charleston's Race Week. Everyone would be there, and everyone would gamble a little, and everyone would have a glorious time in the grandstand. As for the New People, they would provide sport, too. There was a new pastime among Charlestonians; it was known as "politing them to death."

Meeting Street was up early the next day. Providence supplied one of the surprising springlike days that made January the traditional month for camellia japonicas. Elijah, dressed in the new suit of old-fashioned livery that he had received as a Christmas present from the family, walked majestically to the starting point of the streetcar line at the Gardens. He rejected the first two cars. The third met his qualified approval. He conferred with the driver. Then he balanced on the wide step that ran along the side of the car and directed the driver to a point opposite the Ansons' front door. All traffic waited while Billy laid planks from the street up into the rear entrance of the car, and Shad rolled Andrew in his chair up the ramp. Billy put the planks into the car, attached a bright green flag to the roof and stood back while the rest of the Tradds and Ansons entered. Little Andrew was wild with excitement, but his father shushed him. Lizzie and Lucy settled themselves, then Pinckney, Shad and Stuart. Elijah was last, carrying a large palmetto basket with a white linen cloth across the top. He deposited it on a seat and signaled the driver. The streetcar could proceed.

It filled rapidly as it moved uptown, but the Meeting Street party was neither crowded nor disturbed. Elijah stood in the aisle in front of Andrew's chair and intimidated any passenger who seemed interested in moving toward the seat with the basket. The chair blocked the rear entrance. The car proceeded slowly up Meeting, across Broad, then up Rutledge Avenue. The sun made sequins on Halsey's Mill Pond as they passed it. It took almost an hour to reach the end of the line at Shepard Street, then another half hour for Shad to push Andrew's chair in Elijah's wake to the huge marble pillars that marked the entrance to the flag-bedecked grounds and the mile-long oval track. Lucy and Lizzie held fast to Stuart and Pinckney as they walked behind Andrew. Little Andrew kept hold of his father's hand. The crowds filled the street, but there was no shoving, just happy anticipation.

When a late-afternoon chill warned of sunset, the Anson-Tradd procession returned the way they had come. They waited for the green-bannered car with Andrew's ramp, then watched with admiration while Elijah cowed the driver into turning away all passengers. He would not, they knew, demean himself by handling the planks. Stuart and Shad put them in place and moved them. They were all happy and tired from excitement. Andrew had wagered three dollars and won five. Pinckney had bet four and lost it. The cold dinner was delicious, the horses fast, the cheering contagious, the day a total success.

The car was empty except for them when they arrived at Meeting Street. A lamplighter touched his flame to the streetlamp as they turned the corner from Broad. Above their heads, Saint Michael's chimed. It struck six while Shad and Stuart took Andrew down to the street. Lucy jostled Little Andrew to wake him. "Six of the clock and all's well," cried the watchman. Pinckney handed the ladies down the step.

"And it could hardly be better," he said.

29

"Mist' Pinny!" Elijah's voice was a howl of pain. Pinckney dropped his pen and went running to the front door.

The black man's eyes were bloodshot from weeping. His face looked gray from pain and shock.

"'Lijah, what is it? Where are you hurt?" Pinckney put his arm around Elijah's bent shoulders. For answer, the suddenly old man held out a tiny red-leather-covered book in a shaking hand.

"They's closed, Mist' Pinny. I got some gennelmens to read me the words on the door. Closed tight shut. All my savings is gone."

"There must be some mistake, 'Lijah. They must have read it to you wrong. Maybe the bank's closed for lunch. I'll go see. Now don't you worry."

But the National Freedman's Savings Bank and Trust Company had closed its door forever. In response to wires and letters, the United States Treasury Department issued a brief statement. The bank had failed. Depositors would recover none of their money.

"Goddamn them," Pinckney raged. "It was sponsored by the Federal Government, and they've cheated all the poor darkies who trusted them. First they gave them land and took it away. Then they gave them schools and took them away. Now they've stolen their money. They were almighty concerned for their black brothers when Lincoln wanted to get reelected. How can they treat them like this now? It makes me ready to go back to Gettysburg and try again."

"Not me," said Shad. "How much money did Elijah have in his account?"

"Over eight hundred dollars. He'd saved practically every penny he earned for nine years. And I opened the cursed account for him. I'll have to empty my own account to pay him and the taxes. The rates are up on Carlington again."

"I'll give the old man his money."

"I can't let you do that."

"I won't miss it."

"But Elijah's my responsibility, not yours."

"Don't be a mule, Cap'n. Have you ever charged me room and board? If I can accept that, you can't not accept a few greenbacks."

It was the "Cap'n" that did it. Shad had not used that title for years. Pinny clapped him on the shoulder. "Thanks. I'll tell Elijah."

"Don't tell him it's from me. Elijah is a snob, and calling cards don't fool him. White trash I was, and white trash I always will be to him."

Pinckney grinned. "That's only because you never ask him to dance. The young ladies think you're Sir Lancelot if not Arthur himself." Shad had come far socially since Lucy had leaked the information that he owned a bank—which was true—and that his mother was from the old Virginia family that had once owned Shadwell plantation. The latter was a spur-of-the-moment fabrication for her partner and hostess at a whist party. She had not invited Shad to the party, and she revoked, making Lucy miss a pretty score. The information made her turn green, Lucy reported with satisfaction.

Pinckney tried to put the incident out of his head. He worried about Shad's and Lucy's machinations. If they went too far, the entire close community might turn against them. It probably wouldn't matter to Shad, he thought, but it was the only world Lucy had. The specter of her private life with Andrew rose in his mind, and he resolutely forced it away. He had to think about Elijah. The old man seemed broken.

"I thanks you, Mist' Pinckney, but I don't deserve it," Elijah said when he heard about the money. "I been taking your money with the one hand and swearing against you with the other for too much time." Tears spilled from his eyes, and words fell from his mouth in near gibberish. Pinckney was able to make out "Union League" and "Daddy Cain."

"'Lijah," he said, "that's all past. You had your meetings and listened to some speeches, but you never did anything but good for us. We'll just forget it."

Elijah would not be silenced. He told Pinckney about the secret rituals, he named the servants who had sworn to burn their masters' houses, and he revealed Daddy Cain's identity. "He face same like Mist' Wentworth, Mist' Stuart friend, only more years on him. He the one crack Mist' Stuart head. He speechify 'bout him. He say next time he going bust it in two. He laying for that boy, Mist' Pinckney."

"I'll take care of it 'Lijah. Don't you worry. But you'd best stop going to the meetings."

"I done stop. The Yankee gennelmen what come, they all time saying how they is the only friend we colored folks got. I ask what kind of friend steal a poor old darky treasure what he have save. No, sir, Mist' Pinny. Me and the League is separate for good."

Pinckney nodded. "You'll be glad of it. Tomorrow I'll take you to the white man's bank where I go. They'll keep your money safe."

Elijah took Pinny's hand in his. "I thanks you. You always was a good boy."

Pinckney laughed. "You old liar. I was a terror, and you know it."

"High-spirit, Mist' Pinny. That's all it ever was. Except maybe two, three time." Pinckney embraced him and left. He felt much better.

The incident with Elijah forced Pinckney to pay more attention to the political power struggle in South Carolina and, by extension, the country as a whole. He had escaped it by ignoring it, avoiding confrontation and telling himself that it all had nothing to do with him. He expected Shad to be more aware because he was in frequent contact with carpetbagger businessmen, but he was amazed to learn that Stuart was deeply involved in the Democratic Club.

"In two more years," he told Pinckney, "there'll be elections for U. S. President and for the South Carolina state offices. We've already started preparing, and we aim to win, no matter what it takes. Ulysses Grant will be out of Washington; he can't run again. We're going to run the last of his Army out of our state."

"How?"

"Tarred and feathered and on a rail, if need be. But they're going. They pulled out of eight of the Confederacy states long ago. They've stayed in Florida and Louisiana and South Carolina for almost ten. That's too long."

"It's going to take some pushing," Shad commented. "You know what our honorable Senator said." Stuart snorted.

"I don't know," said Pinckney.

"It was J. J. Patterson. You've had your head so deep in the sand you probably didn't notice when he came here from Pennsylvania in seventy-two to buy the election. A fellow asked him the other day if he was going to do anything about reforming the cesspool in the State House. Patterson nearly laughed himself sick. 'Why, there are still five more years of good stealing in South Carolina,' he said. He's not going to leave unless somebody persuades him real hard."

"We intend to," said Stuart. "We just have to wait until seventy-six to make our move."

"What happens until then?" asked Pinny.

"We keep busy and keep quiet."

"And Daddy Cain? I told you what Elijah said."

"He's looking forward to seventy-six, too. He's the Republican's favorite boy. Don't worry about Daddy Cain. I'm looking out for him."

Pinckney was reassured. He had no inkling of how many eruptions that year would bring to the quiet of Meeting Street.

He slipped back into the easy routine that had developed over the years: reading the newspaper with breakfast at the long table, then escorting Lizzie to school before going to his office; calling for Lizzie and home for dinner; afternoons at the warehouse supervising unloading of the barges from Carlington; home for supper; an occasional party; church on Sunday; duty at the Dragoons on Tuesday, Chamber of Commerce meetings once a month; family Christmas celebrations, with the tension that always accompanied Julia's visits; the Season of balls, races, teas and dances. Rarely, he had a recurrence of swamp fever. When he did, he allowed Lizzie and Lucy to fuss over him, sent Elijah to Dr. Trott for some quinine and used the few days of discomfort as a justification for leaving the work at Carlington in the hands of the overseer. Shad accused him of negligence, his mother's letters complained that her children mistreated her because they would not come to see her in Pennsylvania, Lizzie scolded that he was a regular fuddy-duddy. He had the sense that life was passing him by, but it did not bother him. He had known war, worry, riot, privation, passion and despair before he was thirty. Now, at thirty-one, he was content to live in a tranquil torpor.

In 1875 Pinckney gave in to Lizzie's persistent hints and bought a lot on Sullivans Island. The spring was busy, with conferences with the building contractor and incessant advice from everyone. Lizzie changed her mind at least twice a week about the location of the door to her bedroom and the number of shelves in the pantry. In spite of all the conflict, the house was finished before Mrs. Pinckney's school closed for the summer on June thirtieth, and it was exactly like every other house on the Island.

Before the War, the Island had been an elegant small resort for Charlestonians who did not want to travel to Saratoga or Newport to escape the heat. It was known as "Moultrieville" then, named for Fort Moultrie at the southern end. Big hotels offered every luxury, and several hundred families had large houses with stables, kitchens and servants quarters behind. The hotels offered orchestras for dancing at tea time, and the elevated promenade in front of the long hotel verandas was full of strollers taking the sea air. It had all been destroyed by the guns of the blockade fleet, but the people who had loved the salt-flavored summers had begun to rebuild in the seventies. There were no hotels, no orchestras, no promenades, no elaborate houses; only the wide sand beach and the ocean were the same. That was enough.

Lizzie loved the Island house. Its simplicity reminded her of the woods house at the Barony, but it was much better because the wind blew through it day and night. It sat on tall creosoted pilings so that the air circulated under it and the house was taller than the sand dunes that lay between it and the beach. A long narrow room paralleled the line of the water; it served as both sitting room and dining room. At each end of the room, a wing of smaller rooms ran back toward the road made of crushed oyster shells. One wing had a guest room and bedrooms for Lizzie, Pinckney and Stuart. The other held the pantry, kitchen and a bedroom for Hattie and Clara. Shad came to the Island once or twice during the summer; Julia used the guest room for the month of August, when there was little to do at the Barony except watch for storms.

Around three sides a deep porch provided access to the rooms and, except during the heaviest thunderstorms, was the real living room. It had long cushioned chaises, chairs and tables made from the bamboo that grew wild in parts of Carlington. Best of all, according to Lizzie, it had the biggest rope hammock she had ever seen. When Julia wasn't visiting, Lizzie took her pillow and blanket out to the porch and slept in the hammock, swaying in the chilly night wind.

From the porch a boardwalk crossed the dunes and led down steps to a roofed platform on the hard sand at the top of the high tide mark. It provided shade between the periods of bathing in the ocean. In spite of its protection, and her long-sleeved poplin bathing dress, and the deeply flounced hat that hung down over her face when it got wet, Lizzie was spotted with freckles within two days of their arrival. She moaned and applied buttermilk every evening to bleach them out, but she was having too much fun to let them matter. The Wraggs had a house nearby; she and Caroline scuttled back and forth like the darting tiny sand crabs that lived in the shallows of the tide.

Before dawn, Pinckney and Stuart took the new streetcar to the ferry slip at the south end of the Island. There Stuart took command of his boat. His crew had already fired the boilers and washed it down. Pinckney was usually the only white passenger. When the ferry stopped at Mt. Pleasant, it filled up with Negroes taking wagon loads of produce to the City Market. From the wharf on Market Street, Pinny walked the six blocks to his office on Broad. Lucy gave him dinner. Shad, too, if he was not in Simmonsville. At the end of the day, the trip was reversed. Stuart made his last crossing at six, and they arrived back at the house in time for a quick swim before supper at seven.

The family seldom lit the kerosene lamps in the house. After supper, they usually sat on the porch, talking quietly in the dusk, and watched the last colors die out of the sky, then lit their way to bed by candles in hurricane shades. The steady, rhythmic breaking of the waves and the whispering patter of wind-borne sand on the painted board floors sang them to sleep within minutes.

In the hottest part of the afternoon, Lizzie and Caroline stretched out across the hammock and planned their futures while their bathing dresses dried on their bodies.

"I'm going to marry a millionaire, like Mr. Simmons, only taller," Caroline said. "And have a dozen babies and a hundred new frocks and a carriage with velvet seats."

"I'm going to marry someone brave and handsome, like Ivanhoe, who'll rescue me from some terrible doom."

"Like what?"

"I don't know. A passel of wild horses, maybe. He will have seen me in passing and fallen in love but not have dared to approach me because —because something or other—but then these horses will break free from the livery stable and race in a pack down Meeting Street, and I'll be coming from Cousin Lucy's where I did a good, noble deed like keeping Andrew from setting the house on fire, and he'll be walking up and down, hoping to catch just one moment's glimpse of me, and—"

"My turn, my turn. I'll be a famous singer in the Opera, and the Queen of England will beg me to come sing for her, and because I'm so nice and not stuck up at all, even though I am the best singer in the whole world, I'll go to make her happy. And the prince will—"

"Grab your shoe and run with it!"

They rolled about like puppies, making the hammock swing and creak, while they shrieked with delight at their own imaginative genius. They were both almost sixteen years old, and they knew no more about the world than they had at six.

Sometimes they tried to unravel the mysteries that fascinated them most. They exchanged theories of how people had babies. Caroline was confident that she had the answer.

"You can look at your belly button and see that it's all pulled up by a drawstring. Now, it wouldn't be like that unless there was a reason. So it must be for babies. The doctor cuts the drawstring, the tummy opens up, and he takes the baby out." Caroline was the authority. Her married sister had given birth the year before, and she had learned then that her sister's shape was changing because she was carrying a baby in her stomach.

"Does that mean boys don't have belly buttons?"

"I guess so. I don't have any brothers. You're the one should know that."

"Well, I don't. They don't run around with no clothes on."

"Why don't you ask one of them?"

"I couldn't!"

Caroline snickered. "You could ask John Cooper. He'd be glad to show you his if he's got one."

"Caroline! You're terrible. Take it back." Lizzie pinched her friend's arm.

"Ouch! I take it back."

They gleefully discussed the shortcomings of John Cooper. He was Lizzie's nemesis, the only tall boy at dancing school, and her doggedly devoted admirer. After three years of weekly waltzes, he still stepped on her feet and blushed when he tried to talk to her.

"Well," said Caroline, "you won't have to worry about him this year.

He graduated from Porter last June, and he's going to Virginia to learn to be a preacher."

"That doesn't get me through the summer." Somehow John always seemed to appear in the water wherever the girls were swimming, even though the Coopers' house was almost a mile away. "For that matter, what will I do at dancing school next year? John Cooper's better than nobody."

"Maybe Billy Wilson will have grown. He's almost tall enough, and you used to have a crush on him."

"Ugh, he's awful. He smokes. You can smell it on him. What's going to happen to me, Caroline? I'm taller than everybody I know except Pinckney. I can see the top of Stuart's head, and he's a grown man. I'm even taller than Shad."

"Don't worry. We'll be coming out year after next, and we'll meet all the older boys. They're bound to be taller. Do you think Stuart even knows I'm alive? You're so lucky to have such a handsome brother."

"Pooh. He doesn't do anything but talk about politics. If you like old men, you should set your cap for Pinny. He's as sweet as he can be."

"No, if I'm going to be a comfort to my husband in his old age, I'll marry Mr. Simmons. He'll be so happy to have a young person in the house, he'll give me a new ballgown every day . . ." And they started all over again.

When dancing school reopened, Lizzie found that Billy Wilson had not grown at all, but that Henry Simons and Ben Ogier had turned into skinny giants. Try as she might, she could not manage to persuade herself that either of them was crush-worthy, but both were good dancers, and Friday night became the climax of every week.

On her sixteenth birthday, Lucy pierced her ears for the tiny pearl dots Mary Edwards sent from Philadelphia, and Lizzie felt like a grown lady.

BOOK FIVE

1876-1877

30

"No more lectures, Pinny. Do you want to buy my boat or not? You could convert it to a tug for your ore barges and stop paying fees to Bracewell."

"But it makes no sense for you to quit, Stuart. You can just cut down your schedule or take her out of the water for a couple of months."

"I'm a Tradd, too, big brother. I don't make half-hearted commitments. I told you this year was coming, and now it's here. I'll be for Hampton and the Democrats day and night, every day and all day, from now until we win."

"And after you win?"

"That's a long way off. I'll see about that when we get there. You can't stop me, Pinny, and I don't thank you for trying. I just wish you'd join us. You followed the General once; come again."

"I have responsibilities."

"So you say. I think your state is more important than fertilizer."

"I'll buy the damned boat. Name your price. Then get going before I hit you . . . And I wish you well."

The election for Governor of South Carolina would be held on November seventh. On February seventh the campaign began.

The state had been under the oppressive control of the carpetbagger Radical Reconstruction Republicans for ten years. They were years of taxes that went into the pockets of the legislators and their associates, years during which more than a million acres of land were confiscated from owners who could not pay the taxes, and another million were sold for two dollars an acre—or less—to raise money for taxes on what the owners could keep. Judges appointed by the legislature ruled against any white man who had served in the Confederate Army, regardless of the evidence or the charge. So-called "elective offices" were for sale to the highest bidder, and the only native South Carolinians in office were former slaves who could neither read nor write. When the Governor lost a thousand dollars playing cards on a Wednesday, the legislature passed a bill on Thursday giving him a bonus of a thousand dollars "from the citizens of South Carolina, grateful for his dedicated services to the state." The phosphate deposits which could have rebuilt Charleston were parceled out to friends of the Governor under a law that gave the state a monopoly on dredging rights in the harbor and the rivers. The friends made millions while the scars of War stayed untreated and mansions became slums in the beautiful old city.

Everything depended on the black vote and on the presidential election.

Black voters numbered almost two to one compared with whites, and the Union League had been working to organize them for ten years. But there were many like Elijah who had repudiated the League; there were many thousands more who nourished a feeling of resentment that the Yankees and the Republicans had not done enough for them; as always, there was a mass of potential voters who did not understand, did not care and did not want to be involved.

The Democrats meant to get a majority of votes, by persuasion if possible, and if not by persuasion, then by force. The Republicans were determined to hold on to the gold mine of corruption that had enriched them for a decade. As Stuart Tradd had predicted, the stage was set for bloody conflict.

General Wade Hampton, who had led the cavalry troops of South Carolina's men, had retired to Mississippi after the War. Now he returned, to lead again as Democratic candidate for Governor. He was fifty-seven and a romantic figure, still trim and straight, with a mane of snow-white hair and a full, curving moustache. Across the state, two hundred and ninety Saber Clubs organized to follow him. The KuKluxKlan offered to support Hampton, but he spurned them. "My men have nothing to hide their faces for. They are proud to rescue South Carolina from the vicious foreign hands that have been squeezing her life's blood. We want everyone to know who we are." It was a requirement for Hampton's followers to be visible. They all wore red shirts and were soon known by that name.

As opponents, the Republicans had the black state militia, which controlled all the arsenals of arms. But, fearing that the militia was perhaps not securely Republican, they added two groups of black strong-arm thugs, the "Hunkidories" and the "Live Oaks."

The average black man had the misfortune to be caught in the middle. He was the pawn both sides wanted to capture.

Throughout the spring months, tensions escalated. Pinckney was suddenly back on the old routine of the years immediately after the War. The Light Dragoons patrolled the city on horseback every night, riding in groups and carrying torches to illuminate corners that the street lamps did not reach. During the day, an armed squad stayed at the Arsenal, ready to ride at a moment's notice. The Red Shirts rode out in the countryside, in groups of ten privates led by a lieutenant. They stopped at cabins and in the small crossroads settlements, talking to black and white about voting Democratic, which they called "crossing Jordan." Sometimes the Hunkidories had been there before them; sometimes they followed. As yet, there were no direct confrontations, and there was little violence.

Fuses were shorter in the city. There were no riots, but sporadic outbursts of fighting kept the Rifle Clubs and the city military police on the move.

Pinckney returned from night patrol as the sun was rising one morning in mid-May. His patrol had broken up three fights that night on Bay Street, and his arm ached where a thrown rock had hit it. He had left his horse at the Dragoons' stable, and it was a long walk home. He was debating the advisability of sleeping for the hour before breakfast when he unlocked the front door and pushed it with his knee. It opened only about eight inches. Alarm dispelled his fatigue.

Elijah was sprawled on his back just inside the door. His breathing was stertorous. Pinckney forced the door and crouched near the old man. When he lifted Elijah's head, he felt the unmistakable warmth of blood run between his fingers. "Oh, my God." He shouted for Clara and Hattie.

Lizzie reached the piazza first. She gasped, turned and ran back into the house. When Pinckney and the women carried Elijah into the house, Lizzie had the lights turned up in the study and had put a quilt on the settee. "Lay him down here," she ordered. "Hattie, you bring me some warm cistern water and some soap. Clara, fetch the alum and a bowl from the kitchen. Pinny, I'll need your razor to shave his head and a bottle of your brandy."

Pinckney stared. "I know what to do," Lizzie snapped. "It'll take an hour to get Dr. Perigru here, he sleeps like the dead. Get me what I need, and then you can go after him. All of you, move! I'll get the bandages and cotton." She did not look like an authoritative figure. Her nightgown and cotton wrapper were too short; her ankles and feet were bare; her hair coming unbraided. But no one considered disobeying the note in her voice.

When Pinckney brought the doctor, he pronounced Lizzie's treatment as good as anything he could do. But he held out little hope for recovery.

Elijah floated in and out of consciousness all day. He told them what had happened: the Union League was urging all the fallen-away members to return to the fold. Two men had come to the door after curfew. Elijah rejected their invitation, and they hit him with an iron bar.

"Mist'. Pinny, I wants my savings from the bank now. I wants gold pieces. I wants to see the gold, I can't make out them number in the book to mean nothing."

Pinckney brought it to him. When Elijah was conscious the next time, he ran the coins through his fingers and smiled widely. "Ain't that a pretty sight?" His eyelids drooped. "I speculate on some gold teeth same like Toby got, but I too glad I change my mind. I going have the finest funeral my Burial Lodge ever seen." He smiled again, then drifted off. Pinckney held his hand.

Lizzie had just lit the lamps when Elijah woke for the last time. "Look at that big baby girl, Mist' Pinny. She too sensible. Now I is going. Don't fret. I is all paid up for everything. I got them here, right by me, a bag of pure gold on one side of me and Jesus Christ on the other, and now I is going to the wedding supper." His lips turned up in a smile, and his hand relaxed in Pinckney's. Pinny put Elijah's hand on his breast and closed his eyes. Then he held Lizzie while she cried.

"Mist' Pinckney, best you don't go to the funeral. All kind of people going be there and none of them white."

"Thank you, Clara . . . I appreciate what you're saying. But you came to us a few years ago, and you might not understand. Elijah was a part of my family. I didn't have a chance to walk with my father to his grave, but I can go with Elijah."

And so Elijah Tradd had the biggest funeral any of his friends had ever seen. Wreaths covered the glass-sided hearse and the polished mahogany coffin within which Elijah lay on white satin in his velvet suit. The horses which pulled it were black and shiny. On their heads black ostrich plumes danced, and their harness was trimmed with rosettes of black silk. In front of the hearse, the choir of the African Methodist Episcopal Church wore new robes and carried new tambourines. They sang hymns of joy and their feet danced. The procession was led by the congregation's minister riding in an open carriage pulled by a white horse. Buggies and wagons filled with men and women dressed in white mourning stretched out for blocks between the carriage and the choir. Behind the hearse, Pinckney Tradd walked with his bowed head glinting copper in the sunlight.

At the graveyard, he admired the marble stone Elijah had had waiting for the final date to be carved. He threw in the first clod of earth and waited until the grave was filled. Then he said good-bye to Elijah's other friends; he did not stay for the feast that was Elijah's final celebration with them.

At the end of June, Lizzie graduated from Mrs. Hopson Pinckney's Boarding and Day School for Young Ladies. The ceremonies were held in the garden. The eleven graduates looked fresh and happy in their long white dresses and wide-brimmed straw hats. Pinny and Shad sweltered in the sun, but Lucy managed to stay unwilted by holding a parasol in one hand and fanning herself with a palm-leaf fan held in the other. Mrs. Pinckney's speech of exhortation to the girls was interminable. Lucy took pity on her escorts and pushed a puff of air at them from time to time. When the ceremony was over, Pinckney and Shad flustered Mrs. Pinckney with compliments. Pinny, claiming his distant cousinship-by-marriage, kissed her wizened cheek and made her blush. Shad knew several of the fathers of the girls from among the New People. He introduced them to Pinny and Lucy, then watched with twinkling eyes while Lucy "polited" them to death. Afterward, the Charlestonians all went to an ice-cream party at the Wraggs'.

The following day, Pinckney and Shad transported Clara, Hattie, Liz- [illegible] Lucy, Andrew, Little Andrew and his dah to Sullivans Island. Pinny promoted Billy to captain of Stuart's ferryboat. For this trip they had [illegible] to themselves. There were armed guards at the ferry slip on the Island. No one would be allowed on the Island who didn't belong there. It should be the safest place in South Carolina during the trouble that was coming.

The move came none too soon. On July Fourth, celebrations all over the state ended in fighting between black Republicans and black Democrats. A few days later the tiny town of Hamburg erupted in a pitched battle between the Red Shirts and the state militia. Hamburg was in Edgefield County, the home of Wade Hampton, and its predominantly black population had been among the first to "cross Jordan." In response, a new "militia unit" of Live Oaks was brought in, with Commander Adams as their leader. It consisted of eighty men armed with Winchester rifles, headquartered in an armory in the old brick jailhouse.

The fight began in the courts. The leader of the Red Shirts, General Matthew Butler, demanded that the militia unit be disbanded and prevented from intimidating Hamburg's citizens. The black judge refused. He was himself a Major General in the legitimate state militia; his ruling conferred legal status to the Live Oaks.

On July eighth, a company of Red Shirts rode into town, firing revolvers in the air and giving the Rebel Yell. In their midst rumbled a caisson with a small-bore cannon. The windows of the armory spat fire, and one of the Red Shirts fell. The subsequent battle became known, in the Northern press, as The Hamburg Massacre. The armory was almost leveled, six blacks were killed in battle, and the balance killed after they surrendered.

Governor Daniel Chamberlain appealed to President Grant, and he dispatched Federal troops immediately.

Before they arrived "Black Indignation" meetings trumpeted the news of the Massacre throughout the state. In Charleston, the meeting was held at Market Hall. The speaker was Daddy Cain.

Informers from within the Union League warned their white employers, and the Charlestonians prepared themselves. "Thank God," Pinckney said fervently, "Stuart's Red Shirts company has gone up to Columbia. He's been looking for Daddy Cain. Hamburg wouldn't be worth mentioning compared with what Stuart would try to do here." The Light Dragoons and the other Rifle Clubs moved quietly into the streets around the Hall while the meeting was in progress. Through the open windows, the voice of Daddy Cain and the cheers of his listeners mounted in intensity for more than two hours. The message was chilling. "There are eighty thousand black men in the States who can use Winchesters, and two hundred thousand black women who can light a torch and use a knife." The crowd roared, the double doors flew open, and excited Negroes rushed out onto the high portico of the Hall. They stopped when they saw the five hundred white men below. Then they walked quietly down the tall stairs and dispersed. Daddy Cain went out the back door.

After it was all over, the Commander of the Dragoons broke the tension. "How come they've got so many more women than men, I wonder. Thank the Lord they can't vote; Hampton wouldn't have a prayer. Let's toast the non-franchised, gentlemen." He offered his flask.

No political news reached the group on the Island. They did not even receive the daily newspaper. Lizzie was, at first, annoyed that the Ansons were staying at the house. Andrew made her nervous. Years of inactivity had transformed the handsome young officer into a mountain of flab; the steady descent into listless depression had been accompanied by intemperate drinking, and Andrew's fat was enlarged by bloated, soggy tissue. He looked, Lizzie thought, like a huge white toad. His flesh bulged through the spaces under the arms of his chair, and he had a habit of blowing out his cheeks before he spoke. Little Andrew, at thirteen, was too young to be considered an equal by an almost grown-up lady of sixteen. He was also too old to have a dah. Lucy had long since changed Estelle's duties to general housework, but Estelle considered Little Andrew her charge nonetheless, and her attentions to him irritated Lizzie almost as much as they did the boy. "Eat your vegetable . . . wear your hat . . . don't go in the deep water . . ."

Little Andrew avoided Estelle as much as he could. Lizzie didn't blame him, but she was jealous. Boys had so much more freedom; they could ride on the back of the ice wagon and make themselves snowballs from the barrel of chipped ice and bottle of cherry-flavored sugar water that the driver kept there. They could take the streetcar from one end of the Island to the other all alone. They could, if they didn't have a penny for the return fare, hitch a ride on the wagons of vegetables, bottled water and seafood that made the rounds every morning. Best of all, they could go swimming as much as they liked without worrying about freckles.

Lizzie's swimming was restricted to early morning and late afternoon. She was in training for her debut. "I'm sorry, honey," Lucy said, "but if you spent all fall in a tub of buttermilk, you'd still have freckles in January. Last summer's didn't go away until spring was over. If you want to be beautiful, you have to suffer."

Lizzie agreed that it was worth it. All her daydreams were now concentrated on the Prince Charming who would see her at the Ball and fall in love at first sight.

"That does happen sometimes, doesn't it, Cousin Lucy?"

"Yes, dear, it really does." Lucy's voice sounded strange, Lizzie thought.

"Tell me again about the Ball, please, just one more time."

"Well, let's see. Pinckney will hire a carriage—"

"With a slam door."

"With a slam door. It makes a special sharp bang when the doorman closes it behind you, and everyone knows that a special person is arriving. There'll be a long, striped canopy from the portico to the carriage block, just in case it rains, and a white canvas runner, very wide, across the sidewalk and up the steps so that your skirts won't get dusty."

"Because they'll be white."

"Oh, yes, the whitest white ever. And your gloves will be, too. This year, all the girls will have new gloves. The Managers are giving them to each one as Christmas gifts from the Society so that everyone can accept them."

"Pooh on the gloves. Tell about the dance cards."

Lucy smiled. "I've promised, Lizzie. I won't forget. I'll see to it that Mr. Josiah puts all the tallest gentlemen on your dance card."

"Not just John Cooper, either, or I'll die. Oh, bother. Speak of the devil." Devoted John was home for summer vacation, and he had discovered a brilliant maneuver to see Lizzie every day. He took Little Andrew swimming each morning and afternoon, calling for him and delivering him to the house. Lucy was glad of his help. The undertow was unexpectedly strong some days, and her son was not accustomed to the ocean. Lizzie considered John a pest, and she got no sympathy from Lucy.

"You treat him awful, Lizzie, and you've got to stop it. You're too used to bossing men around. Pinckney and Shad think it's cute, but the gentlemen you'll meet when you come out won't like it at all. They expect girls to act a certain way, and you'd better learn it. I'll teach you, if you're not too pigheaded to listen. Now start practicing on John. When he gets up the boardwalk to the porch, act surprised and say, 'Why, John Cooper, how nice to see you.'"

"That's dumb. I'm not surprised, and it's not nice at all."

"Never mind. And smile when you say it."

"Oh, shoot . . . My goodness, Cousin Lucy, look. It's John Cooper. How nice to see you."

Poor John was so surprised that he stubbed his toe painfully.

Stuart cursed furiously when he heard that he had missed Daddy Cain's presence in Charleston. "He's slippery as a raw egg, that black bastard, but I'll get him yet."

"Careful what you say, Tradd. There's a sensitive spot under this red shirt." Alex Wentworth laughed at Stuart's stricken expression.

"Oh, Christ, Alex, I beg your pardon. I forgot."

"I was only joking. Don't make too much of it. Come on, let's go have a drink in the tavern and eavesdrop on the Republicans."

The two old friends had met by accident on the street in Columbia. Alex's mother had sent him to her family there after the scandal in Charleston about Daddy Cain's parentage. He and Stuart had not seen each other for more than eight years. Alex, like Stuart, was now twenty-three and an ardent Democrat. He was newly married to a Columbia girl, but he spent most of his time with his troop of Red Shirts rather than with his new wife or his partners in the insurance company owned by his uncle. Stuart was a lieutenant, Alex a captain. Still the leader.

"I want to hear all about Charleston," said Alex. "I still miss the old place, but my dear mama positively refuses to invite me home. She likes to pretend that Papa never lifted any extracurricular skirts, I guess, and I remind her otherwise. Lucky for him he died a hero's death at Bull Run. She sanctifies his memory; if he had lived, she would have made his every day a waking hell. Women are so narrow-minded. I intend to train Helen better."

"I've missed you, Alex. Why don't you come back to Charleston with me? Your mother needn't know. You can stay in my house."

"No. I owe her better than that. Besides, Columbia really is home for me now . . . Listen, I've got a better idea. The General is putting together sort of an honor guard to travel with him around the state. He'll start campaigning next month, after the Democratic convention makes him the official candidate. I'll get you on it with me. What do you say?"

"What can I say? It's such a surprise. Could you really do it?"

"Helen is a cousin of the Hamptons. Consider it done. Now, how about a little bourbon and branch?"

Alex was as good as his word. On August fifteenth, General Wade Hampton was named Democratic candidate for Governor by acclamation. The guard was already assembled in Columbia as escort for the General. The next day, they began the tour of the state.

31

Pinckney reported Stuart's elevation to the uninterested ladies at the Island house. Andrew and his son would have liked to hear it, but they were both asleep. Andrew always went to bed immediately after an early supper, and Little Andrew was down with a summer cold. Lucy and Lizzie were both preoccupied with Lizzie's lessons in management of a hoop skirt. She had been wildly disappointed that she couldn't have one of the new gowns with a bustle and train in the back, but Lucy had vetoed any such suggestion. "No Charleston lady would wear such a thing; it shows the body too much. We aren't able to wear hoops anymore because the skirts take too much fabric, but the girls always come out in the old bell hoops. They're much the most becoming thing a girl can wear, and it looks lovely, like the old days. It's the same sort of thing as playing the 'Blue Danube' for the last waltz."

Lizzie found the lessons discouraging, but very exciting. Pinckney, on one of his rare visits, had difficulty keeping his face composed. Lizzie was in her bathing dress. Over it she wore one of Lucy's old sets of stays, with a shirtwaist over them and the hoop covered by a petticoat on top of all the layers.

"I feel like an elephant," she complained. But she had confided in Lucy that her suddenly small waist and almost-respectable-size bosom were thrilling in spite of her inability to breathe or bend.

"You're doing just fine," Lucy encouraged. "That's it. Little steps, one in front of another, and turn your feet out like a duck. The skirt sways from side to side, not to and fro. Good. Oh, very good, honey, much better than yesterday. Now, walk alongside the settee, that's it, right to the middle. Wrists resting lightly to the front and side. Good. Now turn, slowly, not too fast. Good. Slide the wrists back to the side. Very good. Now cup your fingers and catch a band of the hoop. Got it? All right, now all at one time. Tilt the hoop with your thumb, step back with one foot, and sink onto the settee."

Lizzie sat. The hoop flew up and hit her forehead. Underneath, her bathing bloomers flashed bright blue. She burst into tears.

Pinckney fled. "That's all right, Lizzie," Lucy said. "It happened to me a million times before I learned." She went to Lizzie and pushed the skirt so that it collapsed onto her lap. "Come on, sweetheart." She tugged on Lizzie's hand. "We'll do it one more time with my hands on yours to do the tilt. Then we'll have supper." Lizzie stood, walked off, walked back and, with Lucy's assistance, settled on the seat in a froth of ruffles. "You look like a beautiful flower," Lucy said, kissing her. "I'll tell the kitchen we're ready to eat, then I'll help you settle yourself at the table. Now dry your eyes. This is the last lesson for today. When we all wore stays and hoops, all young ladies had reputations for eating next to nothing. You'll see why. There's no place for the food to go with stays on. Take teeny little bites and get one all swallowed before you try another one. When you're out of room, we'll take off the stays and you can have a proper meal."

Pinckney and Lucy stayed on the dark porch long after Lizzie had gone to bed, reclining on the comfortable chaises. Neither spoke for a long time. It was almost high tide; the waves broke softly, as if the ocean were tired after its steady march up the sloping sand of the beach. Fireflies blinked green in the patches of hardy sharp weeds on the dunes. Pinckney's cheroot glowed red in response as he smoked.

He laughed abruptly, stopped himself, then surrendered to a long series of chuckles. "I've never in my life," he said, "seen anything as funny as those bloomers under that cage. Did you really go through all that when you were a girl?"

Lucy's soft laugh was almost inaudible. "Shhh," she said, "she may not be asleep."

"Of course she is. It's very late. You didn't answer. Did you whack your nose with your hoops?"

"A thousand times. I was living with a bachelor uncle. I had to learn by trial and error, and it was mostly error. I gave myself a black eye once." She began laughing and could not stop for several minutes. It was infectious. Pinny's sides began to ache, but he continued to laugh uncontrollably.

"Shhh," said Lucy, then caught the fit from him, and collapsed into helpless giggles. They were both weak when they finally recovered.

"Dear heaven," Pinckney moaned, "I'm in pain. I haven't laughed like that in I don't know how long."

"Me, either. I'm practically crying from it. What a treat." Lucy stopped talking, her breath drawing into her throat. "Oh," she whispered on a long exhalation.

On the horizon, an impossibly large globe of red-orange rose quickly, as if thrown up by a giant, invisible hand. They watched in quiet disbelief while it climbed the sky, changing to a golden orb, erasing the stars that had been so bright before it appeared.

"I've never seen the moon rise before," Lucy whispered. "I've never known anything so beautiful."

"Not like that," said Pinckney quietly. "I've known moonrises, but not over the ocean. It's hard to believe."

They were silent again, watching the gold fade to yellow then to white while the full moon climbed. It seemed to smooth the water. The waves broke in low, lazy, dark rushes, with only a thin, lacy edge of pale foam. Across the quiet ocean a wide silver path stretched from the glimmering beach to the horizon.

"It looks as if you could walk on it," Lucy said. "I wonder where it would take you?"

"I was just thinking that."

"I know."

A shimmering silence surrounded them for a long moment. Then Pinckney looked at her. The pale, unreal light glimmered in the tears on her cheeks. He took her hand in his. "Lucy."

"Shhh. I know . . . I always know what you're thinking."

"You know that I love you?"

"Yes."

"But I just discovered it myself."

Lucy's lips turned up at the corners.

"You knew before I did?"

"Shhh." Her hand tightened on his. She turned her head to meet his puzzled gaze. "It's just one of those mysterious things that happen. I feel what you feel, and I know what's in your mind. Not always, and not everything. Just the important things.

"Right now, you're afraid that you've made a fool of yourself. Don't be. You've made me happier than I ever believed I could be. Dearest Pinny, I've been in love with you for five years. Exactly. It's five years today. Isn't that strange?"

"When, Lucy? I don't understand."

"When you told me about the horse, the eohippus. And I felt my heart hurting with yours."

Pinckney bent to kiss her hand. It was rough and worn; he felt a surge of anguish. "What are we going to do?" he said, knowing the answer.

It came. "There's nothing we can do." Lucy touched his hair, then kissed his bent head. "I've wanted to do that so often. Oh, Pinny, don't you think we can make this be enough? It's so much, just the sharing and the knowing. I can live on it and be rich."

He lifted his head and looked at her pleading eyes. "Of course we can," he said.

He left before daybreak. Lucy found his note in her sewing box: "I had to take the first ferry. Guard duty starts at six. I do not know when I will be able to return, but it will be as soon as possible. Yours. P." She held it tightly in her hand. The realization of how her life would be from now on washed over her and left her weak. Every conversation, every note would be guarded, full of double meanings and therefore dangerous. She would have to learn deceit. Her mouth felt full of bile. But he loved her. And she could hold that to her breast. She had no need of declarations or love letters. She tore the note in half and tucked it under the scraps in the wastepaper basket. Then she fixed Andrew's breakfast tray and took it in to him.

The procession was nearly a half-mile long. The Cheraw County companies of Red Shirts rode first, waving to the people they knew in the crowds that lined the road. Their horses pulled at their reins, and curvetted, confused by the cheers from the crowd and the noise behind them, but the riders held them to a walk.

They were followed by a band of Negroes, with red ribbon-hung drums and brightly polished bugles. The cannon came next, as shiny and glittering as the horns. The horse that pulled it was immense. Its black mane and tail were braided, tied with red bow knots, and its sleek brown coat was brushed to a mirror gloss.

The honor guard of Red Shirts rode behind the cannon, buttons, leather and mounts all gleaming. They were in two companies. Between them the General sat tall on a pure white horse; he waved his hat to the crowds, and his hair blew in the wind like the horse's mane. His suit was gray, the gray of the uniform he had worn for South Carolina when he was wounded three times at Gettysburg but kept on leading the charging cavalry.

The procession marched around the dusty square in the center of Cheraw, then drew up in formation around the raised platform that had been erected in the middle. It was draped with swags of red bunting. On it, a bowed figure covered in mourning crepe was bent low under the weight of polished black chains. At the figure's feet, signs on all four sides read "South Carolina."

Wade Hampton swung his leg across the saddle and stepped directly onto the platform. He strode slowly toward the figure. At his approach, the chains slid to the floor, and the bent figure straightened, threw off the black mourning and was revealed as a young girl in a shining white long-sleeved choir robe. The cannon boomed, and the crowd went wild. South Carolina had been set free.

"Never fails," Stuart said out of the side of his mouth. He kept his eyes straight ahead.

"Let's hope not." Alex stifled a yawn. "I thought there'd be more fighting and fewer speeches. Still, if the General can take it, we can. Look at him. Fresh as a daisy, after one of these shows every day for three weeks."

"And two months to go. There can't be that many towns in South Carolina."

"Almost. He's saving Charleston and Columbia for last. They get two days each."

"Whoops. Look interested. The leading Democrat of Cheraw is about to say how wonderful we are."

Julia Ashley visited the Island house for the first week in September. She had refused to come at all when she learned that the Ansons were going to be there, but Pinckney made a trip to the Barony and persuaded her to change her mind. She would never admit to fatigue, but he knew that she was nearing sixty, and the daily rounds of the plantation were grueling in the heat.

She never swam, but she walked the length of the beach twice a day, carrying an enormous black silk umbrella over her head like a cloud. As always, Julia was an imposing figure. In the house, she criticized Lizzie's posture, Little Andrew's boisterousness and Clara's cooking. She was icily polite to Andrew and distantly approving of Lucy's industry. She cast a pall on them all.

Poor John Cooper was terrified into stammers by Julia's inquisitions about his studies at the university and her humanistic pronouncements on theology. But he persevered in his twice-daily calls; he had a commitment to Little Andrew, and he was aching with love for Lizzie. Her new, charming treatment of him gave him inchoate hopes and dreams. But on this afternoon, she was at Caroline's house, and he was trapped with her aunt.

"Martin Luther was a libertine," Julia said with relish. John was desperately trying to remember what he had learned about Luther when Estelle ran onto the porch. Lucy looked up from her sewing.

"Scuse me, Miss Lucy, but they's a soldier at the back door asking for Mist' Cooper."

John leapt to his feet; he was pale under his tan. Anything out of the ordinary always alarmed him. "I'll go with you, John," Lucy said. She took the boy's arm and pushed him gently toward his visitor.

They returned in a few minutes, accompanied by a young, blonde Hercules in the familiar, hated uniform of the Union Army.

"Miss Ashley," said Lucy, "may I present Lucas Cooper. He's John's cousin." Lucas bowed to Julia. She did not offer her hand. Lucy gestured, and everyone sat down.

Lucas was the only one of them who seemed to be at ease. He was, he explained, in the most uncomfortable position possible. He had been a cavalry lieutenant out West, but injuries had returned him to the East. When he was fit for duty again, he was assigned to one of the regiments that Grant had sent to South Carolina as support for Governor Chamberlain. "Naturally I resigned my commission at the same time I reported to my commanding officer. I would take no part in acting against my own state. But the Army red tape takes time. Until the papers come through, I'm still officially attached to the regiment. The Colonel's a good fellow; he gave me a two-week leave. By the time it's up, I should be a civilian again. In the meantime, I'm in regulation dress, but hiding out with old man Porter. He suggested I come out to Fort Moultrie and have a swim. I didn't know there'd be guards at the ferry asking for references. Thank goodness Cousin John could vouch for me."

Lucy tried not to look at the red scar that ran from his browbone back into his corn-colored streaked hair. "Will everyone take some tea?" she said. He had older scars, too, but they were smaller, only short white lines, one at the left corner of his mouth, another slashing a diagonal through the thick brows above his left eye and the longest running across the sharp line of his chin.

Little Andrew came out from the shadowed living room. "Did the Injuns do that?" he said.

"Andrew! Mind your manners."

Lucas Cooper smiled. "That's all right, ma'am." He beckoned the boy to him. "You guessed it. One of the Sioux almost lifted my scalp. Yellow hair is a great prize to them. Lucky for me I had a knife in my boot."

Andrew was enchanted. "Did you kill him?"

Lucas put his finger to his lips. "Not in front of the ladies. I'll tell you another time. It turns out the savage did me a favor. I was with General Custer's Army. If I hadn't been in the sickroom at the fort, I wouldn't be here today. I've always had Luck riding on my shoulder."

Even Julia was impressed. The battle of Little Big Horn on June 25 had stunned Charleston as much as the rest of the country. She was almost genial as she put Lucas Cooper over the hurdles of questions about his family and background. It was irreproachable. He came from one of the Wando River plantations, his father was invalided in the War, his grandmother was a Lucas before she married, and he had been one of Dr. Porter's first students when he founded his school. "I'll always be grateful to him," Lucas said. "He secured my appointment to the Military Academy. I'd never have gotten a college education any other way."

Estelle came out and whispered to Lucy. "Supper's almost ready," Lucy said. "Will you gentlemen share it with us?"

John blushed. He had never been invited before, and he should not accept now. But surely Lizzie would come home for supper.

Lucas decided for him. He stood. "Thank you, Mistress Anson, but we cannot. John here has promised to lend me a bathing costume and give me a swim before the last ferry into town. I still have to live in barracks." He bowed to Julia. "Your servant, ma'am." Then he shook Little Andrew's hand, kissed Lucy's and was gone. John trailed along the boardwalk after him.

It was almost seven o'clock. Caroline and Lizzie bobbed up and down in the gully between the two lines of breakers. "Lizzie, look! John Cooper just came out of your house with a Yankee soldier. Do you think he's being arrested?"

"I don't know, and I don't care."

"Well, I'll say this. I'd commit a crime if that soldier would arrest me. He's the handsomest man I ever saw in my life."

Lizzie looked, but their backs were to her.

In the house, Lucy echoed Caroline's verdict. "That was the handsomest man I've ever seen. He looked like something out of a story book."

Julia chuckled. "He looked like trouble, that's what he looked like. Apollo with a violent past. If that rooster stays in Charleston, the fathers had better lock up their chickens."

32

While Stuart was making ceremonial marches and longing for a chance to fight, Pinckney was wishing for the peace of the Island house and Lucy's quiet company. The city was beset with small battles. They broke out in alleys, on street corners and in the busy saloons along the waterfront near the Market. On the night of September sixth, the Dragoons were on escort duty for the black Democrats of Ward Four. They were holding a rally in Archer Hall.

The late stragglers were just going in when an organized mob of Hunkidories and Live Oaks came out of an alley onto King Street. They were armed with pistols and clubs, and they out-numbered the Dragoons by six to one. Captain Barnwell fired his rifle into the air and shouted. "Halt!" The mob kept coming. "Tradd, ride to the Guard House and get the police." Pinckney spurred his horse.

He raced back in advance of the troop of policemen. When he was still a block away, he could hear shots and the blood-chilling chant of the mob. "Blood! Blood! Blood!" He cursed his missing arm, put the reins between his teeth and took out his sword.

The heavy muscles in his thighs and the pressure of his knees guided his horse into the mass of struggling men. All the Dragoons had been dragged from their horses. Many of them were down, with the fight raging over their unconscious bodies. Pinckney rode down a crowd of blacks that was clubbing one of the Dragoons against the wall of James Allen's Jewelry Store. Then he pushed back into the melee, striking right and left with the flat of his sword. Black hands grabbed at his legs and at the horse's bridle. His right boot lost its stirrup.

There were shouts and shots from the arriving police. Pinckney's horse reared. He slipped, and eager hands pulled him down. As his back hit the street, he automatically raised his sword for shelter. Someone kicked his exposed left side, and he heard the crack of his ribs breaking. Then there was the noise of running boots. The Hunkidories and Live Oaks were retreating.

Pinckney got slowly to his feet and looked around him. Twelve Dragoons were down, one dead. The rest showed the marks of the conflict in bruised and bloody faces. There was one dead Hunkidory sprawled across the steps to the Hall. "How are you, Pinckney?" asked Commander Barnwell.

"Fine. I hope my horse is all right."

"He must be. I saw him running down King Street for home. If he could keep that pace at the Race Course, you'd be a rich man."

The police had disappeared up King after the dispersing mob. The Dragoons stayed on duty at Archer Hall, then escorted the Democrats out of the area on foot. They learned the next day that the mob had torn apart an eleven-block stretch of King Street, from Wentworth to Cannon streets. They broke every street level window, looted stores and beat every white owner who came from his upstairs living quarters to try and stop them.

The orgy of violence continued for hours in the blocks next to the Federal barracks at The Citadel, but the soldiers stayed inside. Lucas Cooper was not one of them. His discharge papers had arrived that morning. He had left an hour later to join the Red Shirts in the county where his family lived.

Hampton's triumphal campaign tour was making the Republicans nervous. Chamberlain appealed again to Grant. On October seventeenth, the President issued a proclamation giving the Red Shirts three days to disband.

Martin W. Gary, Hampton's campaign manager, sent a message of formal compliance. He also helped with the arrangements for organization of the "social clubs" that took their place. Stuart found himself a member of the "First Baptist Church Sewing Circle." Down on the Wando, Lucas Cooper cut a dashing figure in the "Hampton and Tilden Musical Club." The weather was chilly enough for jackets now. If the club members happened to unbutton them, and if they all wore their old shirts under them, no one dared say a word.

The voting would take place on November seventh. The Hampton campaign reached its culmination with his appearance in Charleston on October thirtieth and Columbia on November fourth. Stuart had the day off on Halloween. Lizzie had been planning a celebration dinner ever since she returned to the town house on September thirtieth. It was not just for Stuart, although she had not seen him in four months; she was accustomed to not seeing Stuart. Caroline had talked her into it. "He'll never notice me at the Ball, Lizzie. This is a chance for him to see that I've grown up." Lizzie thought Caroline was crazy to be interested in Stuart, of all people, but she enjoyed the plotting and the fancy cooking. Caroline had a pragmatic reaction to the menu. "If you're going to have all that much food, why not make sure Mr. Simmons will be home, too?

He won't be at the Ball, so I'd better make an impression while I can." Lizzie told her she was awful and that she knew Shad would be home. They were all looking forward to General Hampton's speech.

The newly erected bandstand at White Point Gardens was festooned in red. A crowd of ten thousand excited people, black and white, filled the park and the streets around it. The Red Shirts had discarded their jackets; they made a brilliant show. Lizzie had to admit that Stuart looked very romantic. When the General liberated South Carolina from her grief and bondage, she cheered wildly with the rest of the crowd. Shad, who had seen the pageant in Simmonsville, smiled fondly at her flushed cheeks and sparkling eyes.

He also tried to comfort her the next day when they were the only two at the dinner table. Caroline's mother had forbid her to "make a spectacle of herself" by throwing herself at Stuart Tradd's head. Pinckney was called to duty at the Dragoons. And Stuart was roaming the city, chasing down a rumor that Daddy Cain was there.

"Don't fret, Lizzie," Shad said. "They're the ones should be upset. This is the best dinner I've had in my whole life. Tell me how you did it."

Lizzie blinked back her tears and instructed him in the preparation of preserve of fowl. "First you have to talk Aunt Julia into sending the game down from the country. That's the hardest part. I must have written ten mealy-mouthed groveling letters.

"Then you clean them and cut the bones out. That's a mess, but after that it's fun. You stuff a strip of bacon in the dove; then you stuff the dove into the partridge. That goes into the guinea hen. Then the whole thing into the duck. By now it's getting kind of sizable. You cram it into a big capon. And then the goose and finally the peacock. It t-t-takes two whole days to fix it and roast it." She cried into her napkin.

Shad went to her, knelt and held her head against his chest. "There, baby, don't. I'll eat every bite of it for you. And the feathers, too, if you want."

Lizzie wiped her eyes. "You'd get powerful sick." She sat up very straight. "And I'm not a baby. I'm sorry I cried."

Shad went back to his chair. "We won't even think about it. I believe I'm ready for some more, if you'll ring for Hattie."

Lizzie giggled. "Maybe I'll get you some feathers. What kind do you prefer, duck, goose, or peacock?" In spite of the coronet of braids on her head, she looked little different from the pig-tailed child who had so recently sat in the same place at table.

"Lizzie, I have a kindness to beg you."

"No feathers?"

Shad shook his head. "Not a joke favor, a real one. I want you to call me by my real name."

She was instantly interested. "I didn't know you had any other name. What is it?"

"Joe."

"Just Joe? Not Joseph?"

"My cards say 'Joseph,' but it's really just Joe."

"Well, all right if you want me to. But it's like meeting a whole new person. I'm not sure I'll remember. Why do you want to change?"

"I already have changed. Don't you remember when I couldn't even read and write?"

"That's right. I had forgot. That was fun, doing lessons together. Remember playing school?"

"You made me stand in the corner."

Lizzie clapped her hands. "That's right! What a good sport you were, Shad. I mean, Joe."

His eyes were lost in their laugh wrinkles. "I enjoyed it myself. But it was a long time ago. Now you're grown up, and I'm a genius at balance statements. So I'll try to remember not to call you 'baby,' and you try to remember that I'm 'Joe.' You might also remember that I'm waiting for some more of this excellent dinner."

"Ooops. I'll ring. Do you really like it?"

"Stuart doesn't know what a fool he is for missing it."

Stuart knew what a fool he was at the end of the day. He was tired and frustrated by his unsuccessful search. He'd been a fool to try and penetrate the wall of self-styled ignorance that the blacks used against questions from a white man. He also felt that he was a fool ever to have joined the honor guard. While other Red Shirt units raced across the countryside accomplishing something useful, he had been watching a sideshow and listening to speeches. Even Pinckney had seen plenty of fighting. Stuart had seen close to a hundred girls throw off fake chains and dyed sheets.

He stayed out after curfew, hoping that a military patrol would stop him and give him a chance to argue about being on the streets. The only people he saw were a couple of Dragoons who complimented him on the extravaganza at the Gardens.

His mood was sour when he climbed to his room in the sleeping house and little better at breakfast the next morning. Then he left for the early train that would take Hampton and his entourage to Columbia.

"I'm glad he missed dinner," Lizzie said. "He would have soured the cream on the pudding."

The entire state of South Carolina waited anxiously for the results of the election. On voting day, Shad joined the white men of Charleston in watching the polling places for the Democrats. He saw several of his acquaintances from the Charleston Hotel. They were voting Republican, and he managed not to recognize them.

On the day after the voting, there were riots in every major town in the state. Stuart finally got his wish. He knocked four Negroes flat before he was felled by a gunshot wound in his thigh.

It was not serious. He was up and about the next day. After a week he was able to stop using the walking stick the doctor had prescribed. Helen Wentworth told him his slight limp was very distinguished. He was staying with Alex while the honor guard was still on duty with Hampton in Columbia. They expected to wait a week. It turned out to be months.

The election results showed more votes than there were voters. While the two parties wrangled in the courts, Chamberlain and his supporters camped out behind the locked doors of the State House. Hampton, who had won by just over a thousand votes according to one method of counting, set up a rival government in nearby Carolina Hall.

Simultaneously, the national presidential election was the same kind of impasse. Rutherford B. Hayes, the Republican candidate, and Samuel J. Tilden, the Democrat, were at a standoff until the disputed votes could be settled from the three Southern states still under Reconstruction rule. A great deal of money and a great many patronage plums passed from hand to hand as alliances formed and shifted.

While the citizens of America and the people of South Carolina waited until the politicians decided who was going to rule them.

There was very little violence anymore. It was too late for crossing Jordan to make any difference. In Columbia, Stuart fluttered hearts at the parties given by friends of the Wentworths and tried to buy information on the whereabouts of Daddy Cain. In Charleston, Pinckney and Shad tried to catch up on the neglected affairs of the Tradd-Simmons Phosphate Company. They alternated escort duty for the dozens of trips Lucy and Lizzie made to the shops on King Street.

"Haven't I been through this before?" Pinckney demanded. He looked at Lucy with his heart in his eyes. Her tiny frown warned him to be discreet.

"A girl's coming out gown is the most important one she'll ever have," Lucy said, trying not to laugh. "It's even more important than her wedding gown."

"Somebody told me the same thing once about a girl's first long frock. I wonder who could have said such a thing?"

Lucy's eyes widened. "I can't imagine." They were very happy.

"Do you think this lace is prettier than that one, Cousin Lucy?" Lizzie was single-minded.

In early December, Pinckney received a letter from his mother that threw the house into an uproar. She was coming home to be with Lizzie when she made her debut. "It will just be me and Sophy. Mr. Edwards will be too busy to leave Bryn Mawr. Tell Josiah Anson to put me back on the list for invitations."

"It can't be done," Pinny said. "When she married an abolitionist, she knew she was giving up Charleston and everything here."

Lucy disagreed. "She's Lizzie's mother, and she won't have Edwards with her. Let me talk to Mr. Josiah." She responded to Lizzie's tug on her arm. "Yes, honey, the white silk for the bloomers, just this once. Then it's back to cotton . . . Don't worry, Pinny. You look frazzled half to death. I'll hurry Lizzie up, and you take us home. Then go on to the office and get a little peace while we practice walking up and down stairs."

Pinckney leaned back in the big chair behind his desk and lit a cheroot. The quiet was unbroken except for a squeak in the chair's swivel mechanism. He felt his tension begin to unwind. Lucy always knew what he needed. If only—he tried not to think of what his life could be if Andrew did not exist. He welcomed the diversion of the quiet knock on the door. "Come in."

It was Shad.

"Come in, man. I need some company. How about a glass of something?"

"Maybe later. I've got something to tell you—no, to ask you. Hell, I'm jumpy as a cat."

Pinkney was intrigued. He had never before seen Shad without his cloak of imperturbability. "I don't know what it is, Shad, but it looks to me as if you could use a glass in your hand. Get the sherry out; it's in that cupboard right behind you."

Shad's hand shook, and some of the wine spilled. "Damn," he said under his breath. He spun to face Pinckney. "It's not going to get any easier. Pinckney, I want to ask Lizzie to marry me."

Pinny's jaw dropped.

"I know it'll take some getting used to," Shad said quickly. "But I'd make her a good husband. I'm sure of it. I can take good care of her. I've got plenty of money. If the mills are an embarrassment, I'll sell them. There's nothing wrong with owning a bank. Or, if that won't do either, I'll get rid of it."

"You're old enough to be her father." Pinckney made the first objection he could think of. Everything in him was crying "No!"

He was not consciously aware of the reasons for his horror at Shad's proposal. They were a confused mixture of aristocratic pride, of long-buried jealousy from the time that Lizzie trusted Shad instead of him, of a refusal to admit that his baby sister was turning into a woman. Before he could acknowledge any of the causes for his revulsion, Shad's voice demanded his attention.

"I'm twenty-seven, and she was seventeen last month. Miss Lucy said once that a man should be ten years older than his wife." Shad was pleading.

"Wife? Lizzie, your wife? No. Shad, no. It won't do."

"Pinckney, be reasonable. You can't keep her a child forever. You can't keep her to yourself. She's grown. She's going to marry somebody. Do you really prefer one of those pimply boys she goes to dancing school with? This isn't something I decided last night; I've been preparing for it for a long time. Why else would I go simper and bow to all those starchy old women all these years? It was for Lizzie, so that she could still have all the Charleston parties, if she wanted them. People know me. She wouldn't have to explain or make excuses for me."

Pinckney's eyes blazed. "You opportunistic, self-serving bastard. Accept hospitality, allow Lucy Anson to risk her own social life, all so that you can carry out another one of your plans for *your* life to get what *you* want. Who knows where Lizzie fits into some other scheme of yours. You take advantage of everybody."

All the incendiary pride of his poor-white background surged up in Shad. It was fueled by the slights he had suffered from Charlestonians, insults that he had swallowed for Lizzie's sake. It was fed by his feeling of betrayal at Pinckney's hands. He had made Shad feel at home, had made him part of the Tradd family, had accepted Shad's help and advice. Without Shad, the Tradds would have starved. He fought to keep his anger under control. "You've got it all wrong. I love Lizzie. I've loved her since she was a baby. I'd do anything in the world for her."

Pinckney looked at Shad's livid face. All the veneer of politeness that had built up in the past ten years was gone, burnt away by Shad's rage. His eyes were narrowed, glittering like a fox's; his mouth was drawn back in a snarl that exposed his small, stained teeth. Under the quiet, well-tailored gray suit, Shad's body was crouched, muscles straining. He looked as if he were wearing borrowed clothes. A kaleidoscope of memories raced through Pinny's mind. Shad, spitting tobacco juice in a wide arc onto the rose bushes; Shad, shoveling food into his mouth with a spoon; Shad, jingling the coins he had stolen from another man's pocket; Shad, plunging into the maelstrom of carnality in Mulatto Alley; Shad, coming home time after time stinking of cheap whiskey and some whore's cheap perfume.

"You'd buy her a house, I suppose," Pinckney said slowly. His drawl was offensive. "You'd be good to her, just the way you are to your trollop Ruby, or whatever her name is."

Shad's lips bleached white, and he lost control. "Goddamn you, Pinckney. You insult Lizzie. If you had two hands, I'd beat an apology out of you."

"I only need one to hold a pistol. It's your dirty affection for my sister that insults her. I'd shoot you for your presumption—but a gentleman only fights a gentleman. That is something you'll never be and never understand, Trash. I was a fool to take you into my house. Now get out of it."

Shad's mouth moved, but no words came out. He slammed his right fist into his left palm, found that inadequate, turned and shattered the pebble glass of the office door with his fist.

His chair's steady squeak, squeak told Pinny that he was shaking with rage. He threw his head back against the tall leather chair, cursing fluently.

"Where's Joe?" said Lizzie over supper.

"Who?"

"Shad. We're having spoon bread, and it's one of his favorites."

Pinckney crumpled his napkin in his hand. "He's gone, sweetheart. On business. He'll be gone a long time." All of Shad's things were gone. His wardrobe had nothing in it except the torn pieces of an invitation to a supper dance.

"Oh, shoot. I wanted him to help me practice waltzing in my hoops."

"Don't say 'shoot,' it's vulgar. I'll waltz with you. You'll be my lady at the Ball, you know."

"Oh, Pinny, I can hardly wait. Only a few more weeks, and I'll be at the Ball. You won't forget the slam-door carriage?"

"It's already reserved."

"And you're sure Cousin Lucy arranged about my dance card?"

"You'll be courted by giants."

"Pinny, do you think I'll look pretty?"

"You'll be the most beautiful lady there."

"Oh, Pinny, I do love you."

"And I love you, Baby Sister."

Pinckney looked at Lizzie's radiant face. She looked about ten years old. The leaden sorrow he felt about the scene with Shad dissolved in the warm flow of his protective affection for her. I did the right thing, he thought. I'll have to face it one day—losing her to a husband. But at least I can see to it that she marries a gentleman.

"Mama, please don't poke at my hair. Cousin Lucy spent hours on it." Mary Tradd Edwards' visit was proving difficult for everyone. Her sister Julia kept referring to her as a cowbird; Lizzie resented her attempts to make changes in all the plans for her Ball gown and accessories; Lucy told Lizzie she was being rude; Stuart was still in Columbia; Mary regarded his absence as a deliberate affront; Pinckney thought he would go mad if his mother shed one more tear.

"Very well, Lizzie. I just wanted to give you a little softness around the face. You look so severe."

Lizzie studied herself in the long mirror of the ladies' cloak room. Lucy Anson had talked her out of all the laces and ruffles and satin sashes that the other girls were wearing. "Scrooching down with your knees bent might make you a few inches shorter, Lizzie, but you'll have to stand up some time, and then where will you be? You're a tall girl. We'll make the most of it. When everyone else is being cute, you'll be regal. And if you hunch your shoulders, I'll kill you." The mirror showed Lizzie a stranger, an elegant young woman.

Her hair was light auburn. "Henna doesn't count," Lucy had said, loving the conspiracy. It was pulled back from her face, exposing her lovely small ears with their tiny pearl dots, and twisted into a Psyche knot with a single half-opened white Christmas rose barely showing in the center. Her gown was made of watered silk. It shimmered like the ocean under the full moon. A wide, curved collar bared her throat and shoulders. Under it was a layer of flat rose-point lace. The enormous skirt was made in petal-like panels. They overlapped so that when she was still, they looked like an etheral inverted tulip. When she swirled in the circles of the waltz, they swung apart to reveal a rose-point lace underskirt. A white lace fan hung from her right wrist on a silver cord. In her left hand, she held a bouquet of Christmas roses nestled in paper lace and a silver filagree bouquet holder. Her long kid gloves reached to the collar, which covered her upper arms and the tops of the snowy white gloves.

"I could pass for nineteen, or even twenty," Lizzie said to herself. Her cheeks flooded with color.

"Quit hogging the looking glass," Caroline said. "Did you see him?"

Lizzie moved aside. "Who?"

"You didn't see him, or you wouldn't ask. Do you remember last summer when John Cooper came out of your house with the Yankee soldier? Well, he's here. In the vestibule. And he's not a Yankee at all. He's John's cousin, named Lucas. And so handsome you could die happy just from looking at him. If he's not on my dance card, I'll kill myself."

"Lizzie, it's time to go up. Good evening, Caroline. You're as pretty as a picture."

"Thank you, ma'am."

"Lizzie!"

"I'm ready, Mama."

"Good evening, Miss Tradd."

"Why, John Cooper, how nice to see you."

"I believe I have the honor of the first waltz after the opening."

Lizzie did not pretend to consult her card. She already knew that John Cooper was on it three times, and she didn't mind at all. At least she was familiar with his dancing after all those Friday evenings, and the array of names she hardly knew was a little frightening. "I'm looking forward to it with pleasure, Mr. Cooper."

John blushed. Oh, good grief, thought Lizzie. I'll bet he still steps on my toes, too. "If I might beg a favor," he stammered.

Lizzie looked over the top of her half-open fan. "Anyone can beg," she said. She felt at least eighteen.

"Might I put my name down for the sixteenth dance?" He was scarlet.

Lizzie forgot to be grown-up. Her fan fell from her hand and swung on its cord. "Don't be silly," she said, "you know as well as I do that only sweethearts and married people dance the sixteenth. I'd just as well paint 'Property of John Cooper' on my back." She saw the pain on his face and felt mean. "I don't want to hurt your feelings, John, but I'm not about to get spoken for at my first real Ball. I'll tell you what. You can sit it out with me. That doesn't mean anything except that we're old friends." And it's a lot better than sitting with Mama and Aunt Julia, Lizzie said to herself.

John agreed happily. She called me "John," his heart was singing.

"Psst, Lizzie. Is he on your card?"

"No. Is he on yours?"

"No. Nor Annabelle's, nor Kitty's. They already told me. Do you suppose he's married?" Caroline and Lizzie—and every lady in the room—stole glances at Lucas Cooper whenever they thought no one would notice. "Gracious, Lizzie, he's bowing to your Aunt Julia. Heavens, she's going to dance with him. I never thought I'd be jealous of Miss Ashley. Why her, for heaven's sake?"

But Lizzie was already taking her place next to Pinckney in the cotillion. She refused to ruin her first Ball by wishing for the moon. Lucas Cooper would never notice her.

"Miss Tradd, may I escort you to your chair? Where would you like to sit?"

"By a window, don't you think? Are you enjoying the Ball, Mr. Cooper? It's hard to believe it's already the sixteenth dance."

"I enjoyed it most when you called me 'John.'"

Lizzie grinned. "I know. It feels so dumb to be saying 'Mister' and 'Miss' after ten million years in dancing school and Sunday school and throwing mudpies in the Park. Let's pretend that we're not grown up while we're sitting out, anyhow. Then it'll be a real rest."

"I'd like that."

"Lizzie."

John's smile transformed him. "I'd like that, Lizzie."

"The breeze feels good, doesn't it? Do you know, John, I think I really am going to dance my slippers through. Cousin Lucy says that that's the sign of a perfect ball."

"Excuse me, Cousin."

Lizzie looked around at the source of the words. It was Lucas Cooper.

"You're being very unfair, John," he said, "trying to hide the loveliest lady at the Ball off in this corner. Aren't you going to present me?"

John was looking at Lizzie. The expression on her face made his heart sink. She had never looked at him like that. "Miss Tradd," he said, "may I present my cousin, Lucas Cooper. This is Miss Lizzie Tradd, Luke."

His bow was flawless. "Honored, Miss Tradd. But surely Miss Ashley told me you were called Elizabeth? A beautiful name to match its owner."

"How do you do, Mr. Cooper." To her own amazement, Lizzie's voice sounded perfectly calm.

"Did you have a good time, Baby Sister?"

"It was heaven, Pinny. Heavenlier than heaven."

33

"I've gotten six bouquets this morning," said Caroline. The Wragg house was the setting for the day-after-the-Ball rehash. All four debutantes were there, to compare memories and dance cards, to retell what who had said to them and what they had replied, to exchange bits of gossip they had overheard and to share the excitement of being "out" and therefore grown up.

Kitty Gourdin made a sad face. "I only got two. I knew nobody would notice me."

Lizzie shoved Kitty off Caroline's bed, where they were all sitting with their legs tucked under them. "That's for being a goose egg. You were over here two minutes after breakfast. How early do you expect people to be sending flowers? You've probably got a dozen at home by now. I heard Cousin Josiah telling Mama that he'd probably have you on his arm next year as the bride to open the Ball."

"Did he really say that, Lizzie?"

"Really, truly."

Annabelle Brewton helped Kitty back onto the pillow-strewn meeting place. "I won't be any competition," she said. "David and I are getting married in October." The other girls screamed. There was an outbreak of hugs and kisses.

"Tell, Annabelle!" Caroline demanded. "What did David say? Did he go down on one knee and put his hand on his heart?"

Kitty giggled. "Did he kiss you?"

Annabelle shook her head. "He hasn't said anything to me. Papa told me this morning that David had called on him and asked his permission. I guess he'll speak to me this evening. He's coming to supper."

"How thrilling. What are you going to say?"

"Yes, of course. It's always been planned that I'd marry David."

The girls all exclaimed and made much of Annabelle's good luck, praising David Mikell's handsomeness and charm. Privately, they all thought he was old and fat, but Annabelle was their friend, and it was important to help her convince herself that she was happy.

Caroline found the perfect way to change the subject before Annabelle could cry. "I'll bet Lizzie got flowers from Lucas Cooper. She was the only one of us he even talked to. I'm so jealous I could die. Tell, Lizzie. Tell every single little thing."

Lizzie told as much as she knew. Her Aunt Julia had supplied the dry facts about who he was. "But," Lizzie said, her eyes gleaming, "I popped in on Cousin Lucy before I came over, and she said that he was a *dangerous*, adventuresome man." The other three girls wriggled closer to her. The account of life in the Wild West and near-scalping left them all goggle-eyed. Lucas' repudiation of his career for the sake of South Carolina misted those same wide eyes.

"Just like General Lee," sighed Caroline. "He went to West Point, too, but he turned his back on it for the South."

"Why didn't he dance with any of us, though?" said Kitty. "I think the managers are too mean for words."

Lizzie knew the answer to that, too. "He said he had decided to come to the Ball at the last minute, so the Managers didn't know he was going to be there. He's with the Red Shirts, and he didn't expect to be able to get away."

Caroline sighed. "You just *know* he'd be a Red Shirt. Imagine how he must look, on a horse, with his collar open and that hair shining in the sun."

Annabelle's approaching engagement did not prevent her joining in the chorus of shrieks and moans.

Then they all returned their attention to Lizzie. "You're the luckiest thing in the world, Lizzie. He sat out the sixteenth dance with you."

"Oh, he was really sitting more with John than me. He just wanted company."

"Nonsense. There was plenty of company if he just looked." Kitty lowered her voice to a whisper. "Did you see Mary Humphries? She was positively throwing herself at him. My mama said it was scandalous."

Caroline added a morsel. "My mama said Mary was wearing paint on her face."

"Who would notice?" Lizzie said. "Did you ever see such a low-cut gown in all your born days?"

"What can you expect, poor thing," Annabelle said. "She's been out for three years, and she's not married yet." Her smile was smug.

"Bother old Mary Humphries anyway," said Caroline. "Lizzie caught his eye. Maybe he'll send a bouquet, Lizzie."

"No. I kind of hoped. Cousin Lucy told me that lots of men send bouquets to the girls who come out. Just to be polite, sort of. They don't have to mean that they're really taken with you. But John Cooper's flowers were on the front steps before daybreak. Lucas Cooper was staying with John. He could have put his card in too, if he wanted to, with no trouble."

Kitty tried to comfort her. "Maybe he left right after the Ball, Lizzie. My cousin's in the Red Shirts, and he never gets away. Lucas Cooper might have had to go back."

Stuart Tradd was fuming. "I might just have well gone to the Saint Cecelia and the Races. We aren't doing anything here at all."

Alex Wentworth smiled lazily. "I rather like doing nothing at all. If you were in the insurance business like me, you'd appreciate having months off to be a hero." He raised his wine glass. "To General Wade Hampton, the Governor of South Carolina. More or less."

The interplay of political give and take was still going on between the opponents in Columbia and Washington four months after the disputed election. Rutherford B. Hayes had finally been inauguarated as President a week earlier, on March first. But Chamberlain was still occupying the State House in Columbia, even though Hampton himself had told his men that Hayes, a Republican, had agreed to support Hampton and to remove the military troops from South Carolina in return for Hampton's releasing the state's votes in the Electoral College and making Hayes President.

"Hayes's people must have gulled the General," said Stuart. "We'll be having parades up and down State Street until our damn red shirts are in rags while the carpetbaggers and the darkies keep right on stealing us blind."

"Don't be an ass, Stuart. Haven't you see the other parades? Our dedicated legislators are streaming to the railroad station all day every day to load their booty onto cars to take to their new homes up North. You couldn't have missed that scene this afternoon. That black face grinning with a complete set of gold teeth, and the yellow wench with him wearing the year's tax revenues in jewels. You don't think they were headed for prayer meeting, do you? Not with three baggage wagons behind them."

Stuart emptied his glass. "We shouldn't let them get away. Daddy Cain's probably in Boston by now."

"Give it up, Stuart. You're so obsessed it's making you sick. And poor company, to boot."

"He didn't almost kill you."

"No, but you know he swore to. He's bitter because the Yankees got my father before he could . . . I guess I should say 'our' father."

Stuart's fist crashed down on the littered tavern table. "How you can laugh about such a thing—"

His wrist was suddenly caught in an iron grip. Alex's face looked murderous in the flickering light of the smoky lamp on the table. "I laugh because I have to. If you weren't so full of your own grievance, you'd spare some thought for how I really feel. My family is dishonored, my father cursed in public by some high-yellow fanatic, my mother ashamed to show her face in public, my own home closed to me since I was sixteen. You think you have a reason to kill this Cain because he tried to kill you. I have a million reasons. But I'm not about to make a fool of myself the way you do, looking for him. I laugh first before people can laugh at me. God willing, he's gone from South Carolina, and maybe my grandchildren will be able to live without wondering if every private conversation around them is about their relatives from the wrong side of the blanket. By then, maybe people will have forgot."

"Christ, Alex, I'm deeply sorry. You're such a good actor, you even fooled me."

Alex freed his wrist. "Let's forget it. We're both behaving odd. I never talk about Cain, and you're never sorry for anything you do. Let's get something to eat. Helen's gone to visit cousins in the country to bore them about the baby instead of us. There won't be any supper for us at home."

Stuart smiled. Helen and Alex would be parents in six months, and Helen was already worrying about whether the child should be allowed to go away to college and risk meeting unsuitable companions. Her conversation was sadly lacking in variety.

They saw the flames as they turned into the street Alex lived on. Then the fire was gone; both men thought they had been mistaken, and neither said anything to the other. Then the flames flickered again, darting out of a ground floor window like a dragon's tongue. Alex began to run. "It's my house," he shouted. "Get the fire brigade." Stuart turned and sprinted for the alarm bell on the corner behind him.

He returned from the bell on a zigzag course, beating on the door of each house with the butt of his revolver to arouse the sleeping inhabitants. It was long past midnight.

When he arrived at Alex's, the front of the house was intact, but through the windows he saw that the interior was a solid mass of flame. Stuart bolted down the driveway to the rear, shouting for his friend. If Alex was inside, he might be able to get to him from the back.

The brick-paved rear courtyard was bathed in erratic, pulsing crimson light from the windows of the house. Stuart stopped, panting to regain his breath. There was Alex, his face distorted with fury, eerily lit by the shimmering red heat. He was standing on the carriage block near the rear door, too close to the licking flames. Stuart started forward. He had to get Alex away. A hand grabbed his arm.

Stuart turned and saw—Alex.

He looked from one Alex to the other. In the hellish light, their faces were the same. Their skin was neither white nor brown, but an eerie, glowing red reflection of fire. Shock made Stuart's sense preternaturally acute. He heard the cries of the man on the carriage block near the house. "Betrayed," he was screaming, "all the promises, all the hopes, all gone. They have sold me and my people as surely as if we were still in chains. Gone. All gone. For a thief to sit in the White House. The *White* House."

Stuart realized that he was moving toward Cain, propelled by Alex Wentworth's grip on his arm. "It's the first time I've ever seen him," Alex muttered.

Daddy Cain saw them. His body jerked as if he had been hit in the spine. A horrible laugh came from his throat. "Too late, white man," he taunted. "Nothing here but Wentworth ashes come dawn. Go ahead. Arrest me. I'm proud I did it." His eyes narrowed and he crouched forward to see through the smoke that was pouring from the window near his head. "You ain't the police," he said. He jumped down from the block and stepped free of the screen of smoke. The attic window exploded from the heat, showering ruby-glitters of flame-lit glass onto the pieces that already crunched beneath their feet. Stuart heard them hitting the ground in a rapid, brittle staccato. Time was distorted. Everything seemed distant, somehow, and slow.

Alex Wentworth and Daddy Cain stared at each other; twenty paces separated them, but neither moved or spoke. Inside the house, there was a prolonged ripping crash as the staircase fell into the hungry flames below.

Stuart snapped out of his trance. He raised his arm and aimed the revolver at Cain, concentrating fiercely on the tiny target area between the eyebrows. His heart pounded with victorious elation. Slowly, relishing every split second, he tightened his finger on the trigger.

There was a blur of movement near him, and the revolver hit the ground, discharging. The sound of the shot seemed louder than a cannon.

"Leave it," Alex commanded. His hand was still on Stuart's wrist where he had hit the revolver from his grasp.

"That's Daddy Cain, you fool. I'm going to kill him." Stuart fought against Alex's hold.

"I won't let you," Alex said. "Are you blind? That's my brother. I won't let you shoot my brother."

Stuart's cry of rage was lost in the greater cry that burst from Cain's lips. He lifted his hand from his side to reveal a long, curved pistol, pointed at Alex Wentworth. Then he threw his head back. The long tendons in his throat stood out like rope. "No!" His cry was a howl of unutterable despair.

Stuart lunged for Cain while the wail still filled the air. Before he was halfway there, Cain inserted the barrel into his mouth and fired.

"No!" cried Stuart in grotesque echo. The revenge he had lived for had been snatched from his grasp, and he did not know whom to blame, Cain, his enemy, or Alex, his friend. A paroxysm of rage shook him and departed, leaving him with nothing, no emotion, no identity. A brand fell from the roof onto his shoulder; for the first time since he recognized Daddy Cain, he felt the intolerable heat of the flames. He turned to Alex, who seemed to be paralyzed, and pulled him away toward the clanging bells of the fire trucks on the street.

Stuart and Alex managed not to meet again for the five weeks Stuart stayed in Columbia. They had nothing to say to each other. On April tenth Daniel Chamberlain gave up the State House and went to Massachusetts. His remaining supporters dispersed. Governor Wade Hampton moved his supporters from the Carolina Hall and began the business of returning South Carolina to the South Carolinians. The Red Shirts, who had devoted almost a full year to Hampton, were not forgotten. Alex Wentworth's company was given the job of insuring all state buildings against fire, flood and windstorm. Stuart Tradd was named magistrate for the lovely little town of Summerville, twenty-five miles from Charleston. He received an allotment for the purchase of his robes, in addition to his stipend and the title of Judge.

"Pinny, a wire came this morning. Stuart's coming home today."

"That's fine, Lizzie. Do you think he'll be able to get through the crowd of your callers?"

"Stop teasing. I hardly have any callers at all, and you know it."

"That's not what I hear."

"Oh, Cousin Lucy exaggerates." Lizzie's cheeks were pink. In fact, she did have at least three and often more admirers every Tuesday afternoon, which was her "at home" day. Lucy chaperoned and reported to Pinckney that Lizzie was being remarkably level-headed about her success.

"Of course," Lucy said, "it does help that there are only four girls this year, three, really, with Annabelle already spoken for. It gives each of them a day to be at home without any conflict."

"Why aren't those boys out working?"

"Most of them are, Pinckney. They visit after work. There are only two who call early, and they aren't boys. Charlie Johnson and Harold Courtney."

"Charlie's older than I am. That's disgusting."

"More pathetic than disgusting. He was the 'debutantes' darling' the year I came out, and he's trying to hold on to the title."

"Who's the D.D. this season?"

"Frank Coming, by default. If the dashing Cooper ever comes back, Frank is automatically dethroned."

On April seventeenth Frank became a has-been. Stuart Tradd brought Lucas Cooper with him from Columbia.

"Pinny, this is Lucas Cooper. He was at Porter when I was."

"How do you do. I believe we met at the Ball. My aunt, Miss Ashley—"

"Yes, of course. I hope Stuart's not causing trouble by being so free with invitations."

"Not at all. Let me call my sister. She'll have to alert the servants." Pinckney was clever enough to know that Lizzie would want advance warning that the D.D. was a guest in the house. He went to find her.

Lizzie clapped her hands when she heard the news. "Caroline and Kitty will be *green*." She smoothed her hair and walked demurely down to the library.

She was perfectly composed until Lucas bowed over her hand. "Your servant, Miss Elizabeth," he said, and kissed it, against all the rules of conduct. Lizzie's fingers tingled from the exciting wickedness of it, and she blushed scarlet.

Lucas seemed not to notice. He did not precisely ignore her, but he talked to all of them equally, almost, Lizzie told Caroline later, as if she were Stuart and Pinckney's brother, not sister. Mostly, the conversation was political. Lizzie could contribute little except to say how proud she was to have a Judge for a brother.

"What did the General offer you, Lucas?" Pinckney asked. "Are you going to dispense justice, too?"

Lucas shook his golden head. "He gave me his blessings and a letter expressing his gratitude. I was just a private Red Shirt, I'm afraid, not an officer." His smile was lopsided because of the scar in one corner. "It was a good joke on me, I suppose. I quit being a paid cavalry officer to ride twice as hard as an unpaid private. And my captain had never been on anything but a mule in his life."

Lizzie thought that was very unfair, and said so.

Lucas turned the full force of his magnetism on her. "Military life is never fair, Miss Elizabeth. It's based on rank and seniority, not on skill. If you ladies made the promotions, we'd probably be a lot better off."

Stuart hooted. "You'd have the generals picked for how well they could dance."

"I don't know that that's so much worse than what we have now. Look at that poor devil, Custer. He was made General when he was younger than I am because of a clerical error. And once it was done, it couldn't be undone, even though he nearly failed out of the Point. So he led hundreds of men who were better soldiers to a senseless slaughter. It makes my blood boil.

"Please forgive me, Miss Elizabeth, for raising my voice. My whole company, all my friends, were killed."

Lizzie made a soft sound of sympathy. Lucas looked grateful. It was a very intimate look.

Then he turned his attention to Stuart. "Enough soldier's beef. When do you start giving us a little law for the white man?"

Lizzie listened through a haze.

34

That evening was the beginning of a period of alternating ecstasy and torment. Lucas Cooper stayed with the Tradds' for only three days, and during that time, he was not exceptionally attentive to Lizzie. But when he did focus on her, the rest of the world became dim. And when he turned his attention elsewhere, there was a luminous after-effect. Colors were brighter, light was almost tangible, smells were sharper, and all emotions were heightened. She imagined that she could even feel the vibrations in the air when he breathed, and she could not sleep, knowing that he was under the same roof.

"It's not because he's so good-looking, Cousin Lucy," she said. "Really, this isn't some kind of crush. I don't understand it. When Lucas talks to me or looks at me, I feel as if some kind of energy is pouring into me. I'm more alive, I'm more me. The whole world is more itself. Am I making any sense?"

Lucy took Lizzie in her arms. "My angel child," she crooned. Julia Ashley was right. Lucas Cooper was a dangerous man. He had the same effect, Lucy knew, on almost everyone who came in contact with him. There was some inexplicable hidden vitality in him that affected the people around him like an electric storm in the offing. She knew that Lizzie's were not the only fingers that tingled at his touch. Even hers did, although she loved Pinckney with all her being. Lucas' attraction was elemental, not sexual.

I wish he'd go away and stay away, Lucy thought, holding Lizzie's trembling body.

It seemed for a while that she would get her wish. Lucas went home when Stuart left for Summerville. By the middle of May, Lizzie had returned to her old self. She and Pinckney went to see the small house Stuart had rented and she came back from a week's visit full of enthusiasm for Summerville, Stuart's house, his impressive offices in the Dorchester County Court House, and Stuart himself.

"He's like a different person, he's really nice. Pinny says it's because he was eaten up by hate for ten years, but then, when that man died, he could start to live again. He's got all sorts of pretty things. Aunt Julia furnished his house with things she had in storage from Charlotte Street. And he goes to the Barony a lot. You know how he always doted on the Barony. He's not awfully busy in Summerville. It's quite small. And lovely. Millions of pine trees everywhere. It's against the law to cut a pine there. The whole town smells like Christmas decorations."

Lucy told herself that the crisis was past. And then, a week later, Lucas appeared when Lizzie was "at home," and it all began again. He was, he said, in and out of town, looking for work. "My father is still angry that I resigned my commission. He can't understand that there was no future in the Army. I've got to find something that he'll consider equally respectable for a gentleman." He stayed with his cousins this time, John Cooper's parents, and Lizzie saw him only once, but it was enough to reinfect her. When she heard that he had called on Kitty, too, and had gone to three supper parties, she was despondent.

"He only called here to be polite," she sobbed to Caroline. "He called on Kitty because he wanted to. And the Humphries gave one of those parties. I'll bet Mary wore that half-naked gown or something worse." Caroline was sympathetic. Lucas had never paid her any attention, and she had no hopes for herself. She preferred Lizzie to Kitty because Kitty, the acknowledged belle of the season, already had too many beaux anyhow.

She entered into avid plotting with Lizzie, what to wear, what to say, how to act the next time she saw Lucas. For weeks they played pathetic little games: Caroline would say the things they invented for Lucas, and Lizzie would reply with wit or disinterest or daring flirtatiousness. But it was all futile. Lucas did not reappear.

Early in June, Lizzie abandoned the make-believe. "We're going to the Island early," she cried. "Pinny says the air is good for Cousin Andrew, so Lucy is taking Little Andrew out of school two weeks before the end of the year. Now I'll never see anybody at all, not just Lucas. I might as well get freckled."

"You'll see John Cooper. Is he still writing you?"

"All the time. It's sickening. I don't care what he's studying at the University or what he's going to do at the Seminary."

"Maybe Lucas will visit them at the Island."

"Hardly likely. He's looking for work, and nobody works at the beach. It's going to be a miserable summer!"

Lizzie was wrong. The summer was the best she had ever known. Pinckney was home every night by supper time and all day on Sunday. He was in perpetual good spirits, laughing, playing games, generous with his time, attention and affection. Lizzie had never seen him so happy. If she had been less preoccupied with herself, she would have noticed the same phenomenon in Lucy. The hours together were a richness to Pinckney and Lucy that made them love everyone and everything around them. The dark porch, the steady beat of the surf and their clasped hands when they were alone—they asked no more. It was so much more than they had been able to have before.

In July John Cooper came home. He asked Pinckney for formal permission to court Lizzie. Pinckney granted it with a benevolent smile. It would be four years before John graduated from the Seminary. If Lizzie wanted to marry him then, he would have a noble profession and Pinckney would gladly give them his blessing. "I have to warn you, John, that I don't think Lizzie is thinking about marriage. She's still enjoying being a flirt. Don't let her break your heart."

John ignored the warning. He continued to swim with Andrew, but he also made a separate call on Lizzie on the days she would allow it. Which was often. John was easy to be with because she had no interest in him. After she cut off his first stammered declaration of love with "don't act crazy in the head," he wisely never mentioned it again.

Pinckney brought his horse over to the Island the first week in August. He boarded it at the stables that housed the ice and water wagon horses. Within a week, the manager of the ice plant built on additional stalls. A dozen other men had horses to be boarded.

"The Charleston Club is sponsoring jousting at the Race Course in October," Pinckney said, "and I intend to ride. The Tradd colors will be there again, even if I lose in the first round."

Lizzie, John and Little Andrew listened with fascination to Pinckney's description of the jousts. "We had them every year before the War. Every family entered at least one rider. You've read about King Arthur's knights and how they jousted. This isn't as dangerous, but it requires the same skills. Instead of fighting each other head on, man to man, we draw lots for two teams. Then we ride team against team for one sally. The idea is to strike the man opposite you in the chest and push him off his horse. Everyone has a padded breast plate and a padded lance.

"Usually close to half the riders are downed. The team that wins is victor for the morning; the one that loses has to serve the feast at midday.

"Then, in the afternoon, it's individual jousting. Only the men who were not unhorsed can compete. We ride with pointed lances then, lifting rings from three 'trees' that are built next to the track. Those who get all the rings in the first round come back for the second, when the rings are smaller. There's a third round if more than one man survives the second. It seldom happens. When no one has a perfect three rings, the ride-off is between the men who got two. It keeps narrowing down. Eventually, there's a winner."

"What does the winner win?" Little Andrew asked.

Pinckney smiled. "Ask your mama," he said.

"Your papa won the year we were married," Lucy said. "We had just come back from our wedding trip. It was all so terribly exciting, the crowd cheering, and the suspense when the horses started galloping down the field. They go very fast. Your papa and Cousin Pinckney both made it to the third round. Everyone was wild. Then Cousin Pinckney rode. Like the wind. He picked off the the first ring, then the second. But the third bounced off the tip of his lance.

"Your papa started, and everything was dead quiet except for the thunder of his horse's hooves. He got the first ring. Then the second. And then the third. The clapping and shouting was so loud that all the birds in the trees flew away. He rode up to the judges' stand and held his lance up to them. They put a wreath of flowers on it, and your papa brought it to me. He put it on my head, and I was the Queen of Love and Beauty. We led the Grand March at the Ball afterward. Oh, it was lovely." Lucy wiped her eyes with the hem of the napkin she was darning.

"I wish I had a horse," John said.

"Me, too," said Lucy's son.

"You're not old enough this year, Andrew," Pinny said, "but you can use mine, John. For practice. You'll have to find your own for the joust if you ride. I'll only have time to work him on Sundays. It would be a favor to me if you'd ride him during the week. I've got a lance coming this Saturday. On Sunday I'll tell you how to hold it. Then I have to devise something special for a left-handed knight."

"May I watch?" Lizzie's eyes were shining.

Pinny looked at John. "I don't think we should let the ladies see us at work, do you, John? They can be all atwitter waiting for the joust. What say we meet at your house?"

John agreed gratefully.

"What about me? I'm not a lady!" cried Andrew.

"You'll go with me, Andrew. During the week you'll have to make your arrangements with John."

"He must get up before dawn," Lizzie said to Caroline. "Poor John. He still takes Andrew swimming, but when he calls for him, he can hardly walk. And one day he had a big lump on his head. I hope he doesn't kill Pinny's horse."

"I thought you said Andrew was going to ride, too."

"They do that in the afternoon instead of swimming. Then John brings Andrew home, takes the horse to the stables, gets all dressed up and comes to call. I don't know why he's not dead."

"How's your brother doing?"

"You can never tell with Pinny. He seems as cheerful as ever, but he's good at hiding what's going on inside his head. He didn't tell me until the other day that he took that nasty medicine because he had swamp fever. I thought it was a digestive."

"He's so romantic, Lizzie. Do you suppose he'll ever marry?"

"Pinny? Heavens no. He's thirty-four years old. I guess Lavinia Anson broke his heart and now it's too late. He'll be one of those nice old bachelors who are charming to wallflowers. At least he's not creepy like old Charlie Gourdin. I'd die of shame."

The girls were swinging in the hammock. Lucy heard their conversation in the kitchen. She would have smiled at the intolerance of the young, but she was too worried about Pinckney. He had suffered a bad attack of malaria, which he fought all alone in town. And his clumsiness with the lance was breaking his heart. The wooden spear was almost eight feet long; five feet had to be supported and balanced by the jouster's grip on the two-foot length behind the circular guard. The weight was bad enough for a man with two arms. Pinckney had no counterbalance at all. He could guide his horse with his knees; there was no better rider on earth. But the lance was almost defeating him. One day a week was not enough. Maybe she could persuade him to go in to the office only on the days the barges were due from Carlington. That would mean four full days every week on the Island. Her heart beat faster. Thank goodness Julia Ashley was visiting Stuart this summer instead of coming to the Island. Her eyes were a lot sharper than Lizzie's. Lucy poured Andrew's laudanum and put it on the tray with his supper. He seldom used his chair anymore; he preferred the dreams the laudanum gave him. Lucy was unrepentantly glad it was so.

Pinckney refused to follow Lucy's suggestion about changing his schedule. She was trying to reason with him when she saw the glimmer of his smile in the dim starlight.

He lifted her hand to his lips. "You didn't read my mind this time," he said into her palm. "I'm closing the business for the whole month of September. The ore can pile up at Carlington."

"It will be the happiest month of my life." Lucy was cruelly mistaken. Pinckney rode back from John Cooper's on the first morning of his vacation with Lucas Cooper on a tall bay next to his sorrel. Within two weeks, Lizzie was hollow-eyed and pale.

John's schedule was still the same. But on some days he was not alone. Lucas would work his magic, John would lose all the relaxed ease that had grown up over the summer, and Lizzie would be lit from within. Then Lucas would not come. Or he would come with Pinckney. Or he would shout a greeting as he rode past the house on the beach. Lizzie tried to busy herself with a book or a new recipe for dinner, but she could not. With a mesmerized look in her eyes, she always went back to the porch to peer up and down the beach, looking for Lucas.

"You're making yourself sick," Caroline told her.

"I can't help it. I try. It's as bad as when he stayed at our house that time. I can't sleep now, either."

"What are you going to do?"

"What can I do? Lucy says I should go stay in Summerville, but I couldn't bear it."

"What does Pinckney say?"

"Are you crazy? I wouldn't tell Pinny. He'd probably go after Lucas with a shotgun. Lucy told him I was having female trouble, and he's so embarrassed he just doesn't look at me."

"Maybe he'd make Lucas marry you."

"He couldn't. I've never been alone with Lucas. Nobody could say I was compromised. If I knew how to do it, I'd be glad to have him ruin my reputation so that he *would* have to marry me."

"You'd do anything?"

"Anything."

"Even if it was scary?"

Lizzie nodded vehemently.

Caroline's voice dropped to a whisper. "Do you know what a conjure woman is?"

"A witch." Lizzie whispered, too.

"There's one out at our plantation. Papa's there for the month, digging holes looking for phosphate. I could tell Mama we want to take the excursion boat ride that goes up the river and pay a visit to Papa. We could sneak off one day and could go find her. She sells love spells. Do you have any money?"

"Mama gave me some when she was here. I'm supposed to save it for my trousseau clothes."

"Well?"

"I'll do it."

Caroline giggled. "I've always wanted to go see her, but I was always scared. It'll be so exciting."

Lucy gave her whole-hearted approval to Caroline's invitation. Lizzie's forlorn vigils over the wide beach were tearing at her heart; it was Lucas' unpredictability that was torturing Lizzie. At the Wraggs', there would be no Lucas to watch for.

Pinckney had to be persuaded. He was afraid of swamp fever. Lizzie promised not to set foot out of the house after dark. He did not approve of her going to visit when Caroline's mother wasn't there. Lucy reminded him that Lizzie's own mother had been absent for eight years, and he had not questioned her safety.

Then he relented and gave his permission. "Who's going to take the girls on the boat?" he said. "They can't go alone. I could accompany them and check on the overseer at Carlington. I might ask Lucas Cooper to come along. He's been asking me about phosphate mining. He's an engineer, you know. Some of his ideas sound interesting."

Lizzie smiled radiantly.

"No!" Lucy said too loudly. Pinckney and Lizzie stared at her. "I mean, it's not practical. You wouldn't have time to show him all over Carlington in one day, and I need you here in the evening. To help me with Andrew."

Pinckney knew she was making an excuse, but he responded to her plea, no matter what the reason. Lizzie could not sway him.

The separation from Lucas did Lizzie a world of good. The excursion boat was outfitted with comfortable padded seats, and they had a hamper of food that Pinckney swore would feed a regiment. Lizzie ate scuppernongs and watched the hypnotic sway of marsh grass in the boat's wake. It was her first river trip since the year at the Barony, almost ten years past. The boat made a special stop at the Cosway Hill landing. Caroline's father was there, waiting for the girls.

Caroline was in a fever of excitement for them to go looking for the conjure woman, but it rained for two days. Mr. Wragg put on oilskins and pursued his fruitless quest for phosphate, leaving the girls to themselves to roam through the dusty house. The old crone who acted as cook and houskeeper for Mr. Wragg did not bother with any rooms except his bedroom and study. The dining room and Caroline's room had been hastily swept, but that was all.

In the attic, the girls found three wardrobes, covered with cobwebs, that were full of fragile old ballgowns. They carried them all down to the ballroom and played dress-up before the long mildewed mirrors. The sight of themselves sent them into childish giggles. They relaxed from the pressures of being considered grown women by society and recaptured the mindless delight of the days when ballrooms and beaux were only make-believe games.

When the rain ended on the third day of the visit, Lizzie felt that her infatuation for Lucas was over, as unreal as her shadowy reflection in the old mirrors. "I must have been cuckoo," she told Caroline. "He's too old for me, anyhow, and he's not going to pay any mind to a skinny girl like me, so I might as well stop thinking about it."

Caroline was outraged. "You can't just give up like that. He's too wonderful. And he comes to see you all the time."

Lizzie shrugged. "He comes to see Lucy or Pinny or to keep John company. I just happen to live there, that's all."

"Oh, Lizzie, don't be a spoilsport. You said you'd get a conjure, and you've got to do it. Come on; it'll be fun." Caroline tugged at her arm.

"Oh, all right. But you'll have to get one, too." Caroline promised.

"I think we should turn back, Caroline. It's going to rain again."

"So what? The trees will keep it off us." Lizzie looked up at the moss-hung branches of the ancient trees. They shut out all sight of the sky and made the air below seem close and clammy. A twisted root caught her toe, and she stumbled, crashing into a thicket. When she pulled away, thorns caught her skirt.

"Caroline? Hold up. I'm stuck." She began to disentangle herself, careful not to tear her dress. Above her head, a mockingbird sang a raucous song. She imagined words in the bird's cry. "Go back, go back." If she told Caroline, she'd just laugh at her. But she had a chilly feeling that the woods and its inhabitants were warning her. This adventure was no full at all. A twig cracked nearby; it made her jump. Then she heard Caroline's giggle.

"Did I scare you?"

"Of course not. Help me get away from this awful thornbush."

After a few minutes, they came to a clearing. Lizzie felt ashamed of her silliness in the wood. Overhead the sky was still blue although thick gray clouds were gathering to the left. A gust of wind tugged at the wide-brimmed hats that she and Caroline wore, lifting Caroline's from her head, sending it bouncing and rolling like a hoop. Lizzie held hers on while she and Caroline ran after it, laughing.

Caroline's right, she thought, this is fun.

When they caught the hat, they collapsed on the grass, gasping and giggling. They carried the mood with them back onto the wood path. There was only a short way still to go.

The tiny cabin was made of unpeeled logs. It was barely visible under the towering pine tree that seemed to hold it in its drooping branches. They might have missed it except for the smoke that eddied from its clay-daubed chimney. It had a peculiar acrid odor that caught their attention and wrinkled their noses. The girls stopped. Caroline took Lizzie's hand.

This indication of her friend's nervousness made Lizzie feel much braver. "Shoot," she said, "it's not even made of gingerbread." They muffled their snickering laughter with their hands.

"Are you going in, Lizzie?"

"Well of course. Aren't you?"

"Definitely. You go first."

"Let's go together."

Their voices had dropped to a whisper. "What should we say?" Caroline's grip had tightened.

Lizzie bit her lip. "It's very quiet. Maybe she's not home." Her spirits were noticeably less high.

Caroline made a face. "Scaredy-cat."

"I am not. Let go my hand, I'm going to knock on the door." Lizzie stepped forward boldly.

The door opened before she touched it. Inside the cabin it was green-dark from the little light that filtered through the pine fronds that covered the windows. There was also a red glow from coals in the small low fireplace, but Lizzie did not see it until the woman behind the door reached out, seized her wrist and pulled her in.

"Caroline," Lizzie called.

"She must wait," said the woman. She swung the door closed.

Lizzie felt the closeness of the walls and the low herb-hung ceiling and the darkness. She began to gasp. The woman took something from her pocket and threw it on the fire. "Sit down, child," she said, "till you can breathe."

A thick smoke rose from the coals. Lizzie's hands went to her throat. She panicked. The smoke was in her eyes, her nose, her mouth. There was no air. She choked.

Slowly she became aware of a peculiar sensation. Her locked throat was opening, drawing the smoke in avidly. It was soothing, relaxing, strangely cool and fresh. She sank onto the low stool the woman showed her and inhaled a feast of the wonderful smoke.

"That's so good," she said. "What is it?"

A deep, rich chuckle was her only answer. She peered through the smoke at the woman. She was enormously fat with arms like hams and a pyramid of quivering chins. Her skin was the color of black coffee. She wore a garishly patterned draped garment that seemed to be alive, twisting streaks of yellow and red around her grotesque huge body. She smiled, flashing five glittering gold teeth.

"Why you come to Maum' Rosa, honey?"

Lizzie could not answer. Her mind told her that the woman was friendly. But her heart was pounding with fear.

Maum' Rosa's chuckle reverberated through the small, close space. "Cat got your tongue, eh? Lemme guess. You wants a bit of conjuh, maybe." She began to hum tunelessly.

"Yes, ma'am," Lizzie blurted.

Maum' Rosa threw up her hands. The pale palms glimmered in the dim light. "Do, Jesus," she squealed, "listen to the little white lady. Calling old Maum' 'ma'am.' That *too* respectful. Very pleasing. Maum' be happy to do a little conjuh for she. What your trouble, honey? You wants Maum' to talk off some wart? A lotion for them freckle?"

"No," Lizzie whispered, "not exactly."

The fat woman's teeth flashed; her elephantine body shook all over.

"Maybe," she chuckled, "maybe you wants a curse on somebody. Maum' don't curse without they's a good cause. Who done you ugly, honey?"

Lizzie blinked. Curiosity overcame her fear. "What kind of curses do you do?"

"You wants to buy one?"

"No, I just wondered."

"Maum' don't like question-asking, missy. You got business, you speaks up." The friendliness was gone.

"I'm sorry," Lizzie stammered. She gathered her skirts together. She should leave. But she couldn't, not without what she'd come for. Caroline would never let her live it down. She had to ask, at least. "Please, ma'am," she said, "I heard about a girl, she was in love, and you helped her." She waited apprehensively, feeling foolish. If the woman laughed at her, she would run.

"Oh, honey," crooned Maum' Rosa, "I done help more young girl—and boy, too—than you got years. More wants love than curses. Oh, yes, Lawd, I knows all about love."

"Then will you help me?" Lizzie's voice was eager. Suddenly she believed in the woman absolutely. The smoke swirled in the dark corners of the room. Lizzie saw shifting forms, fluid, vague shapes that could be fantastic animals or people. Inside her mind, Lucas Cooper's scarred lips and laughing eyes teased her. She felt a twisting longing to hear his voice and see the sun on his streaked hair.

"Oh, please," she said.

"Missy, they is a cost for conjuh." Maum' Rosa's round face was blurred by smoke.

"I have money." Lizzie dug in her pocket. "In gold." She held out the coin.

"They is two cost," said the mounded figure. "One in gold. The other in the stars. Conjuh always cost more than you think." She held her hand under Lizzie's, her fat palm upward.

Lizzie's fingers clutched the glittering gold. "What do you mean?" she quavered.

"What I say. You pay more than you know when you buy magic. Be sure you wants it."

Lizzie dropped the coin. Maum' Rosa's hand became a tight fist. "Go, then," she said.

I've been cheated, Lizzie thought. "Hey!" she said angrily, "you could at least ask who it is."

Maum' Rosa held the coin up at a safe distance. She laughed. "This the color of he head," she said. She leaned close to Lizzie and traced a line on her forehead, into her hair. "With the knife mark on it." Lizzie shivered at the witch's touch; Maum' Rosa laughed again. "Go home to Meeting Street," she said, "and let this old woman cook her dinner."

"How did you know?" Lizzie demanded.

"Go," said Maum' Rosa. She dipped her fingers into a gourd and threw something on the fire. The room filled with a sickening, rotten smell. Lizzie fled.

When she opened the door, smoke and stench poured out around her. Caroline pinched her nose with her fingers. Lizzie grabbed her other hand and began to run. "Did you do it?" Caroline panted.

"Yes," said Lizzie, "but it was all a cheat. She took my money then skunked me out. She didn't do a thing."

Later, she told Caroline all about it. "Do you suppose she really is a witch? She knew about Lucas' scar, and she knew where I lived."

"I do hope so, it's so exciting." Caroline bounced on the bed. "But," she said with sudden glumness, "you know how darkies are. They always know all the white folks' business. Papa says they have jungle drums to gossip on."

35

Pinckney lifted the lance from its loops on the saddle and tilted it forward. The hilt fit into the bend of his narrow waist and rested against the pressure of his bent arm. His hand gripped it tightly. Too tight, he said to himself, you'll break your wrist when you hit something. He relaxed his grip; the point dipped toward the sand. "Dammit!" he said aloud, clenching his hand again, pushing the heel of it against the polished wood. His neck and shoulder muscles strained, and the tip of the lance rose.

"That's got it," he said. "Now attach the weight, John." John Cooper clipped a narrow sandbag onto the strap over Pinckney's right shoulder. Pinny's knees urged his horse forward a few steps. "Much better," he said. "Let's try it with both." John rode up alongside and attached another bag.

This time Pinckney put his horse into a run. The afternoon sun behind him made the shadow of the lance seem a mile long. Near the end of the beach, Pinny leaned back, pulling on the reins tied around his neck. His horse, confused by the uneven weight and jerking pull of the reins, ran on into the water. A wave hit his chest, and he reared. Pinckney dropped the lance, tore the reins up over his head and brought the animal under control. Another wave caught the lance and tossed it up in the air. Pinckney rode up onto the sand and swung himself out of the saddle. He put his cheek on the horse's quivering neck and stroked him. When he was gentled, Pinny mounted and rode back to John Cooper.

"I can't do it," he said. His calm voice gave no hint of the dejection he felt. "The weights help me balance the lance, but they're too much of a shift when it comes time to stop. I guess I'll be a judge after all."

John made an inarticulate sound.

"Thanks, John," Pinckney said. "You'll have to be my alter ego. That's what pupils are for, to make their teachers look good. Get rid of that hack and get back to work on Caesar, here. You've only got another week to practice."

On the day of the joust, Stuart had driven his surrey over from Summerville. Lizzie felt very grand riding on the front seat next to him. She bowed elegantly to everyone she knew or thought she knew. Pinckney and Lucy sat on the back seat, smiling at her foolishness. Stuart and the ladies stepped out at their box, and Pinckney took the reins. He left the surrey with a groom and joined the other judges in the elevated reviewing stand.

There was a brisk wind off the river. It snapped the pennons on the bright-colored tents for the riders and brought the sharp smell of pluff mud to the eager spectators who filled the boxes. Washington Race Course belonged to the Charlestonians today. Only members of the Charleston Club and their guests had been invited to the joust.

At ten o'clock precisely, three heralds rode out into the broad lawn of the garden in the center of the oval track. They raised their long, brass horns. The thin sweet notes brought the crowd to their feet cheering. The bright warm light bounced from the distant lake in the garden, reflected off the gleaming horns and lit the golds of the massed chrysanthemum borders into tiny suns. It was a glorious day.

The competing riders came onto the track one by one. Over his padded chest guard, each wore a tabard in the colors that had once represented his family's stables in the races on this track. They were made in bold designs, like the heraldic banners of the Middle Ages. A herald announced each man: "Sir Edward of Darby . . . Sir David of Legare . . . Sir Malcolm of Campbell . . . Sir Charles of Gibbes . . . Sir John of Cooper . . ." Ned Darby, David Legare, Malcolm Campbell, Charles Gibbes and John Cooper rode at a dress walk past the boxes, doffing their plumed hats to the ladies.

". . . Sir William of Heyward . . . Sir Alan of Stoney . . . Sir Julius of Barnwell . . ."

It was a brave and foolish pageant. The "knighthoods" had begun long ago as a spectacular game that reflected the Southern love of the ideals of chivalry. In those days, they wore tunics made of silk embroidered with rich golden threads, and the titles were the names of the majestic plantations owned by the riders. Now the majority of them had no land. But they still had their proud family names. They gave richness to their patchwork tabards and validity to the unspoken claim that here were *parfit gentil* knights.

"If I had known Pinny wasn't riding, I would have made time for it myself," said Stuart. "The Tradd colors should be here."

"But they are," said Lucy. She directed Stuart's eye to the judging stand. Above it, the flags of the judges flew like banners of old.

"Which one's ours?" asked Lizzie.

"The green-and-gold one," Stuart replied.

The banner bore a silhouette of a cradle with a mast and sails. Lizzie laughed with delight. She knew the story. The first shipload of adventurers had come to South Carolina in 1670. They had numbered only thirty-six, including Charles Tradd and his young wife, Elizabeth. Shortly after the palisade was built around the tiny settlement, Charles had been killed in an attack by Indians. Elizabeth never learned of his death. She died in the same hour, giving birth to their son, the first native-born citizen of Charles Towne. The child was raised by the community. It named one of its first paths Tradd Street, in his honor.

". . . Sir Harold of Pinckney . . . Sir Louis of Ravenel . . . Sir Lucas of Cooper . . . Sir Robert of Rhett . . ." Lizzie's heart leapt. When she returned to the Island after her visit with Caroline, Lucas had been gone.

He was wearing a stark geometric black-and-white tabard. His crest was a broken bow and arrow in red. The full sleeves of his white shirt fluttered in the wind. Tall black boots made his white breeches look even whiter. As he rode by the boxes, he made his horse curvette. He swept his red-plumed black hat from his head, looked directly at Lizzie and brought it with a flourish to rest over his heart. She felt dizzy. The heralds continued their announcements, but she was deafened by the beating pulse in her ears.

"How dare you," said John Cooper to his cousin when Lucas joined the riders grouped at the end of the lawn.

"What are you talking about?" Lucas was laughing.

"You made Lizzie conspicuous. I could kill you." John's voice shook.

"You'll get your chance. We're on different teams." Lucas galloped away. The procession was over. It was time for the combat.

There were thirty-four riders on each team. They formed long lines on the lawn, a mile between them. The crowd rose to their feet. The herald sounded the attack.

The lines moved as one man, trotting slowly, lances upright in their slings. Then the pace quickened. The earth shook from the impact of hundreds of hooves. Midway to the center, the riders lowered their lances and increased their speed. The banshee Rebel yell rose high above the thundering beat of the racing horses. In the stands, some ladies covered their eyes; others screamed, but they could hardly be heard.

The lines met, crashed lance on lance. There was a moment's wild confusion, and then the surviving riders were far down the two sides of the field, slowing their horses. Behind them, lances lay in piles like pick-up-sticks; toppled knights climbed to their feet, mimed terrible injuries and looked for their hats. It was over, and no one was seriously hurt. It seemed miraculous.

John Cooper's team, led by Ned Darby, was declared winner. They had fourteen of thirty-two riders left, compared to David Legare's thirteen. The victors still on horseback rode forward amid a shower of blossoms thrown by the spectators, and the heralds shouted: "The feast has begun."

The feast was a picnic on tables and benches that the pages hastily set up on the grass around the pond. The food was simple, fried chicken and hush puppies in a decorated paper sack for each guest. The napkins were made of calico, and the wine punch was largely iced tea. But the mood could not have been more festive if they had been dining on pheasant and champagne.

The tilting began at two o'clock. After the long, sociable feast, all the spectators and most of the knights were relaxed and convivial. There had been real danger in the jousting; people remembered instances of broken limbs and even a lost eye in the pre-War tourneys, but tilting was simply a matter of skill. No drama was expected. In the stands, some men made bets on their favorites, but the bets were small. Every young wife and engaged girl had hopes of being crowned, but they all pretended that they didn't really expect it. Lucy Anson allowed herself a reverie of fifteen-years-ago.

The beaten earth track was ready to serve as the list. Three gibbet-like structures stood on the garden side of the track, a hundred feet between them, directly opposite the stands. Boys on horseback were posted near them with bags of rings in diminishing sizes. The long arm of each gibbet already had a ring hanging at the end.

"They're six inches across," Lizzie told Lucy. She was something of an expert, thanks to Pinckney's patient explanations. Lucy nodded. Her mind was not on reality.

A herald announced the first rider, Ned Darby. Applause for the winning team leader was generous, even before he tilted.

The knight of Darby waved his appreciation, took his lance from a page, adjusted its balance and his grip. Then he spoke to his mount, kicked his heels and galloped toward the list.

"It's important to ride fast," said Lizzie. "If you dawdle, it's poor sportsmanship."

Ned Darby missed the first ring, picked up the other two. Everyone clapped politely. "I guess we'd better cheer a lot before each knight rides," Lizzie said, speaking the thought in everyone's mind. Pages replaced the rings on the two empty arms.

It was after three-thirty when the last of the twenty-seven knights completed his tilt. The gibbets' long shadows almost reached the stands. There were eleven competitors remaining.

"Now they go to four-inch rings," Lizzie announced. Stuart told her to be quiet.

The rings looked impossibly small from the stands. An excited tension made the spectators stop chatting and laughing. "This is thrilling,"

Lizzie said. She tried not to crane her neck to look for Lucas' golden head.

"Hush," said Stuart.

The heralds announced the second tourney.

Lizzie knew two of the riders, in addition to John and Lucas Cooper. She clenched her hands and strained forward to encourage them.

The tilting was superb. In their stand, the judges conferred nervously. Five knights picked off all three rings. It was the largest number anyone could remember. And it was ruining the schedule. The shadows were halfway up the stands. It was almost five o'clock.

Trumpets sounded for the third tourney.

"Sir John of Cooper," a herald shouted. There was no applause for this round, with its two-inch rings. Silence paid respect to the riders' need for concentration.

John Cooper's mouth was set in a thin line. He shifted his grip on the long lance. His left hand patted Caesar's neck. Then he tightened all his muscles, bent forward and raced along the track.

"My God in heaven," murmured a man behind Stuart, "will you look at that boy ride!"

Lizzie held her breath. John's lance took the first tiny circle, and the crowd stirred. The second, and they tensed.

The third, and they were on their feet, yelling. John's face relaxed into his wide, transforming smile, and everyone shouted louder. He waved his hat.

"Sir Alan of Stoney," a herald bellowed, trying to make himself heard. He shouted again. "Sir Alan of Stoney." People shushed each other and sat down. "Sir Alan of Stoney," the herald called for the third time. The stands became silent.

Alan Stoney missed the first ring, dipped his lance toward John to acknowledge defeat and rode off the track, followed by polite applause.

Sir Malcolm of Campbell also missed the first ring and exited like a gentleman. Charlie Gibbes picked off the first, and everyone leaned forward. The second spun on his lance's tip and the crowd drew in its breath. It fell before he could try for the third, and there was a collective groan of sympathy before loud clapping. Charlie shook his fist at the offending circle in the dust, and everyone laughed.

The sun was in their eyes now. People held their hands out from their foreheads so that they could see. "Sir Lucas of Cooper," said a herald.

The red symbol of Indian defeat blazed on Lucas' chest in the low, slanting rays of the sun. He circled his horse and launched him onto the track with no apparent preparation. Before the spectators quite realized that he had begun, he had two rings on his lance. A blur of movement, and there were three. A long "aaaah" spread through the crowd. "Jesus

Christ," said the man behind Stuart. His tone was reverent. A pandemonium of cheering exploded.

Lizzie discovered that her hands were locked together so tightly that her fingers were bleached.

Another set of rings went up.

"I'll give you two to one on the dark Cooper," said someone. "Steady beats flashy any day."

"Done!" shouted Stuart. "Who's offering to give away his money back there?" He found the odds maker and settled on twenty-five dollars. Lucas and John rode across the lawn to the starting place on the track.

The heralds sounded their horns. "The judges request," said one, "that you hold your applause until both knights have run the tilt. Ladies and gentlemen, your silent attention, please . . . Sir John of Cooper."

The marshes west of the Race Course were covered with water tinted rose. There was no wind at all. Overhead, sea gulls flew in straggling groups to their resting places. Their wings cast sharp black shadows on the glowing river. Caesar's powerful legs stretched over the smooth, dark track. One . . . two . . . three. Someone shouted and was hushed. Lucas laughed. The sound was startling. His fair hair was colorless in the weak light. One . . . two . . . three. Stunned, incredulous silence, then bedlam.

"What are we going to do?" asked one of the judges.

"What can we do?" said a second. He waved to the ring boys. They rode to the gibbets.

John Cooper spurred to catch up with his cousin. "Luke," he said, "I've never asked a favor of you in my life, but I'm asking now. This is a game to you, but I've built all my dreams into this tournament. I've got to win."

Lucas raised his eyebrows. The red light of the setting sun made his scar vivid. "Why?" he said.

John's face was pale. "When I give Lizzie the crown, I'm going to ask her to marry me. I have Pinckney's consent."

Lucas smiled. "A good idea, that. She can hardly say no to Sir Lancelot . . . You want me to lose, then."

John shook his head. "I don't think about you as losing. I just want to win."

Lucas chuckled. "Sorry, Cousin," he said, "I'm going to beat you."

"For God's sake, Luke, why? It means nothing to you."

"I'm a competitive man, Cousin John. I like to win."

John's dark eyes narrowed. "Damn your competition to hell, then. You won't win this time." He took the starting position.

The sky flamed scarlet, streaked with thin violet clouds. Then slowly, it faded into orange, apricot, peach, the blush of shell-pink. In the stands, the crowd was only a mass of shadow, immobilized by the spectacle before them. Once, the two Coopers rode, then again, and yet a third time in the growing darkness. It was almost impossible to see the rings, yet each man gathered them on his lance. The sounds of hoofbeats and creaking stirrups were loud in the suspense-heavy twilight. Ring boys lit torches and sat on horseback behind the gibbets, holding the dancing light high.

John Cooper's arm was shaking from the hours of strain. He made an awesome effort of will to steady it. Caesar shook the foam from his mouth, then responded to John's urgent voice and knees. One . . . two . . . Caesar stumbled . . . righted himself . . . three. Lucy Anson's cheeks were wet with tears. Lizzie stared, like someone in a trance. Lucy took her cold hands and rubbed them.

Lucas was no longer smiling. His tabard had darker splotches of sweat in the dark, chilly night. His body moved with his horse as if they were one creature. One . . . two . . . three.

The ring boys rode to the judges' stand for instruction.

In the stands, people talked away the tension, creating a subdued insect buzz. John Cooper rested his lance in its sling and trotted over to the judges. The buzz grew lively with speculation.

Then John and the ring boys rode together to the center gibbet. The boys' torches struck brilliant fire from the ring that John took from his pocket. It was a circle of diamonds, a wedding ring. He put it on the hook. The flames of the torches turned it into a ring of rainbows.

John trotted Caesar into the darkness at the end of the lists. "They agreed," he said to Lucas. "If neither of us gets it, the tournament will be declared a draw. It will be anticlimactic, but that's that."

Lucas grunted.

John smiled. He positioned Caesar and lifted his lance.

He was racing at full tilt when he came into view in the torchlight. His head was bare, his dark hair part of the night. He seemed indomitable. "He's smiling," Lizzie whispered, "he's going to do it." The lance tip entered the rainbow, then sped on into the darkness. Behind, the ring glittered in the torchlight. "Oh," Lizzie breathed. She felt tears filling her eyes. Before they could fall, Lucas was in the light. He had discarded both hat and tabard. He was all in white, his shirt and breeches a slash of brightness. His golden head was as brilliant as the torches that illuminated it. One moment he was there, the next he was gone. Gone with him was the scintillant circle of jewels.

The spectators were frozen, unbelieving. Then they relaxed with a shuddering sigh, suddenly aware of the tension that had gripped them. The applause was deafening. Pages lit torches around the sides and back of the stands. In the judges' box, Pinckney Tradd lifted the wreath of flowers to award to Lucas. Ladies shifted themselves amid a rustle of skirts and an excited hubbub of wondering which of them Lucas would crown. Mary Humphries' mother told her to sit up straight.

Lucas reappeared on the track, and everyone cheered. The heralds sounded a paean. Pinckney stepped to the front of the judges' stand. But Lucas rode past it, reined in and slowly tilted the long pointed lance with its sparkling tip into Lizzie's lap. The ring slid off and was lost in the folds of her skirt. She did not notice. Her eyes were looking back into Lucas'.

BOOK SIX

1878-1882

36

"Why can't I have my wedding New Year's week? That's three months. It can't possibly take more than three months to bake a cake."

Lucy compressed her lips. "I won't even talk about it if you use that tone of voice, Lizzie."

Lizzie burst into tears. She threw her arms around Lucy's neck. "I'm sorry," she sobbed.

Lucy patted her shoulder until she calmed down. "Are you ready to listen now?"

"Yes, ma'am," said Lizzie.

"All right. Now pay attention to your elderly cousin. Lucas has talked to Pinckney, and Pinckney has forgiven him for behaving so outrageously."

"It was so romantic, Cousin Lucy."

"Yes, it was. But very naughty. He should have had Pinny's consent to court you, not become engaged in front of six hundred people. Never mind. That's done. What matters now is that Lucas has to find work before you can marry. No matter what novels may say, people cannot live on love."

"Lucas said he would be glad to help Pinny with Carlington. That's work."

"Yes, honey. But Lucas can probably do a lot better. He's a college graduate, an engineer. Hardly anybody in Charleston goes to college anymore. He should be able to find something that pays a fortune. Pinny wouldn't be able to offer much of a salary." Lucy did not mention that Shad Simmons had been systematically ruining Tradd-Simmons relationships with the Northern fertilizer firms that had bought the "Charleston bone," as the world called South Carolina phosphate ore. One by one, contracts were not being renewed. Pinckney was having to lay off workers.

Lizzie sighed. "I hate to wait."

"I know you do, sweetheart. But let me tell you, being engaged is such a special time, you shouldn't try to rush through it. Aren't you happy?"

"Oh, yes!"

"Well, then."

"But I would have liked to open the Ball."

Lucy laughed. "I thought that might have something to do with it. Don't worry about missing that. Sally and Miles Brewton are coming home in January. She'll be the one everybody's looking at, not the bride."

"So this is Lizzie." Sally Brewton looked up at the tall young girl. "You have the Tradd good looks, lucky child." Her bright eyes moved to Lucas. "As for you, young man, you're too handsome to live. Count your blessings that I'm not forty years younger. I'd lock you in my closet."

Lucas kissed her tiny hand. "You'd need no lock, ma'am." Sally's bell-laugh filled the air around them. "Go on with you," she said. "I have other guests to dally with . . . Pinckney Tradd, for example. No, Pinny, I won't settle for a puff of air on my knuckles. Bend down here and give me a proper kiss on my cheek."

As always, Sally Brewton's party was An Event. The younger guests had never seen anything like it. It followed Race Day and carried out the racing theme, with waiters dressed like jockeys in the Brewton crimson and lemon silks, crimson cloths on the round tables in the drawing room, reception rooms and wide halls, and pyramids of lemons holding candles as centerpieces. The mantelpieces were piled with crimson camellias in beds of greenery, and the chandeliers held candles with a faint lemon scent. The menu cards on each table promised a six-course extravaganza with appropriate wines.

"You should be ashamed of yourself," said Sally's old friend Emma Anson. "These days, anyone in Charleston who's lucky enough to have any money also has enough decency not to flaunt it before her friends who are so poor they're practically eating dirt."

"I know that, Emma, and I admire it, and I don't give a tuppenny damn. This is my swan song. I want to be remembered as outrageous, and I want people to miss my parties."

Mrs. Anson looked carefully at Sally's skillfully rouged and powdered face. ". . . Does Miles know?"

"Yes. He moved heaven and earth to get that weasel Canby to move out of the house early. The troops don't leave Charleston until March, in spite of Hayes' promises last year. I couldn't have borne to die away from home."

"People will miss you, Sally, not just your parties. What is it, heart?"

"No. The cancer. Is yours heart?"

"Yes. How could you tell?"

"There's a sisterhood, don't you think? One just knows. I can see you haven't told Josiah. He's as gay as a boy."

"The Ball and Race Week are the biggest things in his life. I was determined he'd get to enjoy them."

"Dear Emma. I wonder if our men will be able to manage without us."

Emma Anson's laugh was wicked. "They'll marry again within the year."

"A new debutante, no doubt. Well, she'll find my ghost between her and Miles on the wedding night. Go be charming to someone, Emma. I have some business to mind."

"Whose?"

"Nosy old hag. I won't tell . . . Emma, we'll see each other again before it's over. Won't we?"

"Word of honor. Go on and meddle, Sally. I'm going to snatch Josiah from Mary Humphries' décolletage."

Sally's meddling was a disappointment to her. "You're a damn fool, Lucy Anson," she said at last. "Charleston has never been guilty of New Englandism. No one would fault you for having a liaison with Pinckney, as long as you were both discreet. As it is, I heard that you two were in love all the way in Europe. If you're going to be suspected of sharing his bed, you may as well get the pleasure of it."

Lucy surprised the older woman. "I would walk naked down Meeting Street—on my hands—and not care what anybody thought. But Pinckney is too honorable. Andrew is his cousin and was his oldest friend. I'm chaste for Pinny, because he would hate himself if it were otherwise."

"You love him that much? Doesn't your eye ever stray? You're still attractive. How old are you?"

"Yes and yes and I'm a wall-eyed thirty-one."

Sally Brewton kissed her. "I wish I had known you better, Lucy. You remind me a bit of myself. I'm going to switch place cards and put you at my table."

Later, Sally told her friend Emma that she need not worry about Josiah. "Lucy has a lot of sense, whether you'll admit it or not. She'll take care of him when you're gone."

Sally Brewton died on Easter Sunday. Her husband's body was found in a chair next to her bed. He had poisoned himself as soon as she was gone. They were buried together, as they had died, with their hands clasped.

Lizzie was furious. Her wedding was the following Saturday, and she didn't want the guests to be still mourning Sally.

"Sally is not someone people mourn, Lizzie," Lucy told her. "She's someone people remember; she's part of everyone's happiness and part of

Charleston. There never was any sadness associated with her, nor ever will be. Now let's try that table on the other side of the window."

They were putting the final touches on the house Lucas had rented on Church Street. It was a very small house. Lucas had gone to work at Tradd-Simmons after all, and he could not afford a bigger one. Lizzie loved it. She called it a doll's house. Julia had given them some furniture for a wedding present. The "rice bed," a tall four-poster with delicately carved heads of rice on each post, filled half the bedroom. Its tester grazed the old, slanted ceiling. It was much too large, but Lizzie adored it. She never tired of climbing the three steps of the stool that went with it, then leaping into the center of the cloudlike feather mattress. Even making the bed was fun. There was a long-handled mahogany paddle to beat the mattress back into a puff and beautiful linen which Julia had embroidered exquisitely with a design of white wisteria vines in bloom.

"There," said Lucy. "That's much better, I think. You'll be able to reach the table from the bed with a little stretch. You can keep a candle on it in case you have to get up in the night. So much easier than turning on the gas. More economical, too."

"Cousin Lucy . . ."

"Yes, Lizzie?"

"I don't suppose it's a proper thing to ask . . . I mean, you're not my mother. But I want so much to know what's going to happen. I asked Annabelle, and she just looked very smug and know-it-all and didn't tell me a thing. I know something important happens on the night after I'm married, but I don't know what."

Lucy searched for words.

"Never mind," Lizzie said hurriedly. "I'm sorry to embarrass you."

Lucy hugged her. "I'm not embarrassed, honey. I was just trying to think of how to tell you so that you could understand. When a husband and wife love each other, it's so beautiful and so wonderful that there's no way to express it. It's something you feel. Lucas will know how to make it happen. Men learn about these things. You needn't worry. Just love him very much and share the magic with him."

"Caroline's sister told her it hurt."

"That's absurd. You'll feel shy at first and yes, there's a moment of hurt, but just an instant, and you forget it right away because you're so happy."

Lizzie sighed blissfully. "I can't imagine being happier than I am now. I pinch myself every day to see if it's true, if Lucas really wants to marry me."

"You love him very much, don't you?"

"More than anything in the world. All he has to do is walk into the room, and all my bones melt. You can't imagine how wonderful it is."

I know, said Lucy to herself. Aloud, she suggested they look again in the sitting room and kitchen. "Now don't forget," she said, "when your maid leaves at the end of the day, look in the cupboard to see if her house shoes are still there. If they're gone, so is she. No sense waiting for her to come in the next morning. You're lucky to have a girl from right across the street. She won't have any excuse about the streetcar being late."

During the thirteen post-War years, the servants' quarters behind Charleston's big houses had evolved slowly into rental units for the black population. There were still a few, like the Tradd house, where servants of the house lived. For the most part, the domestic help preferred to work by the day and live elsewhere with their families. A kind of musical chairs shifting had taken place to allow it. The Heyward family still had a maid and a cook, but they lived behind the Wilsons' house on Tradd Street. The Heywards' extensive outbuildings were now a swarming complex with babies playing in the old kitchenyard and eleven families living in the rooms which had once housed maids and footmen.

"It's awfully crowded," Lizzie said, looking at her sitting room. "All the furniture is so big. Aunt Julia's tea table looks like a barge. I wish I could have something besides Chippendale. Pinckney has all that Sheraton stuff. He really should trade. If we can't afford anything now, at least we shouldn't have to live with all those claw feet. It's like being at the mercy of wild animals."

"Now, Lizzie, don't be ungrateful. Your aunt's gifts are in excellent condition. The furniture on Meeting Street is all in need of restoring; Solomon just glued it together the best he could."

"I'm not ungrateful; really, truly I'm not. It's just that I want everything to be perfect. And don't forget, Lucas wants me to be called 'Elizabeth.' When I'm a married lady, I'm not going to answer to baby names."

Tall candles burned on each side of the massed lilies and roses, and the afternoon sun slanted down from the gallery windows. The two Tradd red-gold heads, and Lucas Cooper's molten yellow-gold next to them, looked like precious metal in the light. Caroline and Kitty stood one on each side of the trio, Caroline holding the bride's bouquet as well as her own bridesmaid's nosegay. Mary Tradd Edwards cried charmingly as her husband performed her daughter's wedding ceremony.

"Dearly beloved, we are gathered together here in the sight of God, and in the face of this congregation, to join together this Man and this Woman in holy Matrimony. . ."

Lizzie, soon to be Elizabeth, watched Adam Edwards' lips move. She was afraid that, in her blissful, dazed state, she might forget to respond when it was her turn to speak. She wanted to look at Lucas, but it was not allowed yet.

"Elizabeth." It seemed to Lizzie that her stranger-stepfather was shouting. "Wilt thou have this Man to thy wedded husband, to live together after God's ordinance in the holy estate of Matrimony? Wilt thou obey him, and serve him, love, honor, and keep him in sickness and in health; and, forsaking all other, keep thee only unto him, so long as ye both shall live?"

"I will," said Elizabeth.

"Who giveth this Woman to be married to this Man?"

Pinckney stepped forward and placed his sister's hand in Adam Edwards', who put it into Lucas' keeping. She looked up at Lucas through the fragile lace of her veil and smiled a small, trembling smile. His hand closed tightly around hers.

"I, Lucas, take thee, Elizabeth, to my wedded wife . . ."

"I, Elizabeth, take thee, Lucas, to my wedded husband . . ."

Husband, she thought. Joy filled her heart.

Elizabeth brought her attention back to Adam Edwards.

"Hitherto ye have heard the duty of the husband toward the wife. Now likewise, ye wives, hear and learn your duties toward your husband, even as it is plainly set forth in holy Scripture."

Elizabeth concentrated her whole mind and spirit.

". . . Wives, submit yourselves unto your own husbands, as unto the Lord . . . Ye wives, be in subjection to your own husbands . . ."

She nestled her hand deeper in Lucas' strong, gentle clasp.

The wedding reception was held in the garden of the Tradd house. Late-blooming azaleas and crepe myrtle competed in bright magenta pink; paler roses covered the old brick walls; and Elizabeth's favorite scent perfumed the air from the honeysuckle vines that spilled from the tiled roof of the crumbling carriage house. Billy, now a prominent businessman in the black community, directed the dozen stewards he had recruited from the steamship line that called at the port of Charleston. He looked very prosperous in his captain's uniform. Pinckney had sold him Stuart's ferryboat when Stuart moved to Summerville.

It was not a large reception. There were no more than two hundred guests. Lavinia Anson Pennington, on her first visit in almost ten years, found it very provincial in comparison with the entertaining she did in Philadelphia.

She was even more beautiful than she had been when she left. A gloss of fashion and self-satisfaction overlay her pretty, dimpled face and shiny, massed, blond ringlets. She knew that every woman there envied her the smart bustled gown she wore, and the still-girlish figure under it.

"Yes," she said sweetly to Pinckney, "Ned and I have a little boy. Just the one." Her long lashes drooped. "The doctor said I was too delicate to go through that again." Her hand flew to her mouth. "What am I saying? I forgot that you're still a bachelor, Pinny. Don't tell me that your heart hasn't mended after all this time!" Her dimple flashed.

Pinckney smiled and was silent. If Lavinia wanted to believe that, it would be ungentlemanly to tell her otherwise. "Mama tells me that you were the belle of the Philadelphia Centennial Exhibition," he teased.

Lavinia took him literally. "Not really," she said. "The Empress of Brazil was quite the star, even though she's old as the hills and the Emperor is crazy as a coot."

Ned Pennington joined them. "The real star was that new invention they call the telephone. I've already put the bank down as a subscriber as soon as they become practical."

"Ned's so progressive," said Lavinia complacently. "But then, Philadelphia is a very advanced big city."

Pickney pretended to respond to a call from Billy.

"I feel haunted by my youth," he told Lucy later, "and I don't like being reminded that it was full of near-disastrous mistakes." Lucy smiled at him over the rim of her champagne glass. All the guests had gone, and they were standing in the midst of the debris of the wedding reception.

"I'd better go," she said, "you must be tired. And the servants have to get cleaned up out here."

"Please don't, Lucy. I don't want to be alone just yet. The house is going to be awfully quiet with Lizzie gone. Let's go inside. Then the servants can clear all this away."

They settled themselves on the settee in the unlit drawing room and sat in comfortable silence in the shadows. The darkness, Lucy knew, would make it easier for Pinckney to talk when he felt ready. She slipped her hand into his.

"I feel very old," he murmured after a long while. "It's almost as if my life is over—not in any tragic way, just as if a door had closed. That boy who fought a duel over Lavinia is a complete stranger to me. Such a fool, part of a world that allowed foolishness . . . It was all so different. Do you remember?"

"Yes," Lucy whispered.

"We didn't realize how fortunate we were. Do you miss it? It hardly seems real when I remember it, more like something I dreamed."

She held his hand tightly. "Being young and foolish is a sort of dream by itself, Pinny. It doesn't need lots of what we had. Lizzie is just as happy as she would have been if there had been no War and if she had a big house and servants and a wedding trip around the world."

"You're reading my thoughts again. Dearest Lucy. Yes, I felt my heart aching today for my baby sister. Such a paltry little wedding celebration, such brave little gifts from people who had to do without in order to buy them, such a cramped little house to live in. I should have given her more, and I couldn't."

"Stop that, Pinny! We've been over all this before. I know you would have given Lizzie your house and Lucas your company if I hadn't stopped you. But you cannot do it. They have to build their own lives, just the way their friends do. You can't give them what they have to earn for themselves. The world is different now. We'll never quite get used to it, because we're part of that other, earlier world. But Lizzie and Lucas are part of this one. They don't know anything else, they're too young to remember. They will be just fine . . . And we will, too, in our own way. We've made our adjustments. We can manage."

"I hate it," Pinckney said passionately. "I hate 'managing.' It's so spineless."

"My dear, it's the hardest thing in the whole world, and it calls for the most courage. It's not so bad for me. I'm a woman, and God designed our hearts for endurance. But you have a terrible struggle ahead of you because now that the Yankees have finally gone, all the battles are over except the hardest. Life is going to get very boring, and I don't know how you men are going to manage."

Pinny realized suddenly that Lucy had put her finger on precisely the point that was gnawing at him, without his having recognized it. Nothing was happening, and there was no promise that it would ever be any different. The long conflict was at last over. There would be no more sudden alarms for the Dragoons to respond to, no more night patrols, no more danger in every shadowed corner. The state was back in the control of the men who had always controlled it; the law was the law of the white man; the streets south of Broad were so safe that a lady could walk unaccompanied. There was no foe to conquer—except poverty, and even that had become an accepted way of life. There was nothing to fight anymore, only tedium.

"How come you're always so smart, Lucy? It's blasted irritating, you know." Pinny's voice was admiring, but petulant.

"Forgive me, dear. I try to control it." Pinckney laughed.

"I thank God for having created you, Lucy, every day of my life," he said. "You are my happiness."

"And you mine, Pinny. It's all we need, really."

"Do you think Lizzie is as happy as we are? Do you believe she's really in love with Lucas, and he with her?"

"Don't worry, Pinny. She's ecstatic. You must have noticed—she was a portrait of the radiant bride. And we must both remember to call her 'Elizabeth' from now on. She's very fussy about it."

37

"You were the most beautiful bride ever, Elizabeth," said Lucas.

"Really, truly?"

He lifted her hand and kissed the inside of her wrist. Elizabeth's heart raced. "I can feel your pulse," Lucas murmured.

The carriage stopped before their little house. Lucas stepped out, still holding her hand, and helped her onto the carriage block. Then he swept her up into his arms.

"Lucas!" Elizabeth squeaked. "We're in public."

"Let the world look," Lucas said, "at Mr. Cooper carrying Mistress Cooper over the threshold of her dollhouse."

Elizabeth felt small and feminine in his strong arms. She'd never be too tall again.

He carried her up the steep narrow stairs to the bedroom and tossed her onto the puffy feather bed. Elizabeth sank into it, feeling that she was floating. She threw her arms wide as if she were flying. "Oh, Lucas, I'm so happy!"

"Listen," he said. The sound of chimes came through the open window. Saint Michael's struck seven, and the watchman called ". . . and all's well."

"Oh, yes," said Elizabeth. She sat up and held her arms out to her golden, godlike husband.

"We'll go to bed early tonight," he said. "I'll undress in the other room. Be ready when I return."

Her fingers were clumsy. The tiny buttons on her voluminous batiste nightdress eluded her touch. When she heard Lucas' step, there were still five to do. Elizabeth ran up the steps and jumped under the covers. She was more curious than afraid.

Lucas drew the curtains, shutting out the fresh air and lingering light. Then he slid into bed beside her. His strong hands pulled her body to his own. His weight pressed her deeper into the soft mattress, and it rose above her head. In the deepest recesses of her mind, some buried darkness stirred. For a fleeting moment, a jagged kaleidoscope of impressions tried to reach the surface of her consciousness. Fear . . . flames . . . pressing bodies closing her in . . . shouts . . . rough hands pushing her away . . . no air to breathe . . . helplessness . . . loneliness . . . terror . . . Her throat began to close and she gasped. But Lucas was there. She wasn't alone. There was nothing to be afraid of. Columbia was many miles and many years away.

Lucas moved his hands efficiently. Elizabeth felt an odd kind of friction. He put his hands on her shoulders, his body jerked spasmodically, and his heaviness rolled away. Elizabeth breathed rapidly, freeing her throat of its constriction.

"Lucas," she whispered, "is that what married people do?"

"Was it too little for you?" His voice sounded angry. Elizabeth wished she could see his face. She remembered what Lucy had told her.

"It was magic, my love," she said. She waited for Lucas to say something, but the dark room was silent. After a while, she burrowed into the pillows, said her prayers and closed her eyes for sleep. I don't know why people make such a fuss about *that*, she thought. At least it hadn't hurt.

Shad folded the Charleston newspaper neatly and put it on the floor by his chair. Yesterday afternoon, he thought. I was watching the new looms, feeling proud of myself. You'd think I would have known somehow, that there would have been a pain or something. Cooper. I don't know him. The austere five-line announcement had told him nothing except that Lizzie Tradd was married.

He rose heavily to his feet and walked to the window to regard his empire. In the sixteen months since he left Charleston, he had doubled the size of his mill and tripled the size of Simmonsville. The new addition on the mill carried the processing of cotton onto a final coarse cloth. He had been thinking of building more, a finishing and dyeing plant. There was no point in it now. He had no more hope of a telegram or letter from Charleston.

"Pour me some whiskey," he said to the girl who was watching him from her stool near his chair. She was the fifth of the millhands he had tried living with after he tired of Garnet. They were all alike: young, eager to please, worshipful, grateful to escape the din of the mill and the choking cotton filaments that filled the air and settled in the nose and on the body. "Lint-heads" the millworkers were called because of it.

"Pour me some whiskey, little lint-head," said Shad. He could not remember her name.

The next day he went to the nearby railroad depot. He dispatched a package and took the train North. His only baggage was a Gladstone bag full of money.

"Another present?" Elizabeth hugged Pinckney.

"It's not from me," he said.

"Oh, I see. There's a card. Look, Pinny, it's from Shad. Imagine him remembering when he's so busy and all. I do wish he'd been able to come to the wedding. What a lot of tissue paper. Lucas, come help me. After all, it's for both of us . . . Good grief! What is it?" She held the gift up. Mary screamed, in a ladylike manner.

Pinckney laughed uncontrollably.

Elizabeth looked from one of them to the other.

"It's my wedding necklace," said Mary. "Isn't it the most gaudy thing you ever saw in your life? I didn't realize Shad had such a good sense of humor. Or so much money, either. I wonder what it cost him to buy it back from that carpetbagger."

"Thoughts of mammon, my dear," chided her husband.

Elizabeth looked at the big diamonds spilling over her cupped hands. "You mean it's real? I can't believe it. How will I ever thank him?"

"How about 'Thank you for the lovely chandelier'?" said Lucas.

"Oh, you're awful. I'll think of something. Pinny, is it really supposed to be a joke?"

"No, Lizzie. Sorry—Elizabeth. Shad wouldn't think of it as a joke. Write him a nice note and tell him you think it's beautiful."

"Well, I do. Sort of. It's just that there's so much of it." Elizabeth was unaware of all the influences that had shaped her taste. She had been surrounded by beauty all her life: the extravagant beauty of nature's bountiful gifts to the low country, the majestic beauty of the ocean and the skies, the mellow beauty of Charleston's faded walls and fabrics, the restrained beauty of line in architecture and furnishings. Showiness made her uncomfortable. It seemed unnatural.

In the months following her marriage, Elizabeth settled easily and happily into the role of a young Charleston wife. Running the doll's house was no problem for her. She had been running the Tradd house for years. It was always sparkling clean, smelling of lemon oil and floor wax and the fresh flowers she bought daily from the black women who sold them in the street. Her young maid, Delia, was an artist at ironing, and she was learning to be a good cook. Lucas declared that he was the envy of all his friends.

And he had many. Almost every weekend he was invited to go hunting at someone's plantation where his skill with shotgun and rifle soon became legendary. Elizabeth missed having him home to take her to church on Sunday morning; she always felt so proud when she walked along the street on his arm. But Pinckney escorted her, then came to the doll's house for dinner, and she enjoyed that; besides, Pinny missed her, she knew; it was nice for him. And Lucas loved hunting. He always brought home some venison or duck or marsh hens or quail or turkey, whatever was in season.

The other days of the week, Elizabeth's life had a busy routine that she enjoyed enormously. The shrimp man was the first of the street sellers to come by. He was as punctual as Saint Michael's clock. At seven exactly, she heard the rattle of the iron wheels on his cart and his "Raw Swimp" passing. Before then, if she wasn't occupied in the kitchen, she liked to go to the window and watch the neighborhood cats. They were as punctual as the shrimp man. Five minutes before he was due, they would take their positions on house steps, garden walls or the curb. They were not pushy. They had learned that the shrimp man would throw each of them one of the big ocean shrimp from his cart. Elizabeth loved to see their flashing paws as they caught their treats. She would like to have a kitten, but Lucas said no. He didn't think pets were a substitute for children. He wanted a son right away.

The vegetable man and fish man followed shortly after the shrimp man, then the honey man, in time for people to buy fresh honey for their breakfast biscuits. Delia did all the buying from the vendors, of course. She would lose face if Elizabeth did it. She darted out, carrying the basin for the shrimp or fish or oysters and the basket or bowl for vegetables or honey. The other maids from nearby houses were also purchasing the day's supplies. Delia joined in the laughing insults, or serious gossip, with glee.

She served breakfast at seven-thirty. Lucas left for the office at eight. He always kissed Elizabeth's cheek in the open doorway; she always made a *pro forma* protest about public display of affection; and he always said that he was glad to have the world envy him the most beautiful wife in Charleston. It started Elizabeth's day with a glow of happiness that never faded.

By ten, she had supervised Delia's cleaning, given her orders for any special errands, like going to the grocer, or tasks, like polishing the silver flatware that was her wedding present from Mary and Adam Edwards. Then she paid or received calls. Marriage had automatically erased her age. An eighteen-year-old wife was the contemporary of all other wives whose children, if they had any, were not yet in school. Elizabeth shared recipes and gossip with twenty young "housewives." One of them, Margaret Rivers, was already twenty-six. The new Mistress Cooper felt very grown up. The other young ladies took delight in initiating her into the sisterhood of the married. They filled her ears with dramatic stories of childbirth. She acted as if they didn't make her nervous at all.

At one o'clock she was home to supervise the dinner preparations, choose blooms from the flower woman, refill the vases and change her frock. When Lucas came home at two, she poured his sherry and relayed the bits of news she had learned from her friends. At two-thirty, Delia served dinner. Lucas told Elizabeth about his day, delivered any messages from Pinckney, and discussed their plans for the evening.

They always went out or had people in. Elizabeth spent an hour every afternoon getting her frock ready and checking on Lucas' shirts and suits. The parties were simple affairs. Usually no more than eight couples. But they required careful planning. If the Coopers were giving the party, Elizabeth had to be sure that she managed to tell all the wives who would not be invited some reason that she had selected the ones who would. It did not have to be too convincing. "We haven't seen the Alstons in ages," was adequate. After everyone was alerted, it was all right to invite the guests.

The routine was cumbersome, but it ensured that no one ever heard from a third party that she had been left out of something. Earlier generations, with the effortless hospitality of big houses and staffs of servants, would have included all of their group of friends. The post-War young marrieds had to find another way not to slight any one of their contemporaries. None of them questioned the system. It was the way things were done.

At first the parties were a disappointment to Elizabeth. After an initial flurry of compliments and flirting responses, the men all congregated on one side of the room. They stood and talked about hunting, past and future, while the host made sure their glasses were kept filled. The ladies sat in a group on the other side of the room and talked about clothes, babies and parties, past and future. It was, Elizabeth thought, exactly what she talked about every morning. But she accustomed herself to it quickly. It was the way things were done. And it was, she admitted, more exciting when an occasional burst of male laughter punctuated the high-pitched conversation among the ladies. Also, she liked to look at Lucas with the other men. He was taller and handsomer than any one of them. She caught envious glances from the ladies and warmed herself with pride.

Her free time in the afternoon was taken up with thank-you notes, notes of invitation, her household accounts, and lists of social engagements—where they were going, who they "owed," who "owed" them, what she had worn to which party and what refreshments she would serve when they next gave one. "I declare," she said happily to Lucas, "I'm in a whirl every single minute of the day."

It was true. There were also Lucas' rapid rites of marriage every morning before the curtains were opened and every night after they were closed, but they hardly counted. Elizabeth decided that Lucy had told her a well-meaning story so that she wouldn't be frightened. There was no magic in the minutes. She assumed that everyone else had the same experience. It was not done to mention anything so intimate to anyone else, so she had no way of knowing.

When the temperature began to rise, the doll's house turned into an oven. It had no piazzas, and its ceilings were only ten feet high, instead of the fourteen or sixteen feet customary in Charleston houses. "Maybe we can move over to the Island early this year," Elizabeth said one day at dinner. The roast pork and rice and gravy made her feel sick.

She was amazed when Lucas said that he didn't want to go to the beach at all. For the first time since they had met, Elizabeth questioned his decision. "We'll be as roasted as that pork if we stay in town, darling. And Pinny's going to need me to run the house. Cousin Lucy and her family won't be going, if you're worried that Little Andrew might pester you. She doesn't want to be too far from Cousin Emma now that she's so sick. Besides, it'll be my last chance to see Caroline. You know she's marrying that cousin of hers from Savannah next Christmas and she'll probably never get home. Oh, Lucas, please. I've hardly seen Caroline at all, since I'm married and she isn't. She's always been my best friend." Her lower lip trembled. She was even prepared to cry if necessary.

Lucas' response disarmed her completely. He kissed her wrist in the way that she loved and spoke against her skin. "I can't stand to share you with anyone, my Elizabeth. Not Pinckney, not Caroline, not anybody. You're my wife, and I want to keep you all to myself."

That settled it.

Until Elizabeth learned that her nausea had nothing to do with the heat. She was going to have a baby.

"A son!" Lucas shouted. "I'm going to have a son." He knelt before Elizabeth and kissed her palms. "You'll have to take it easy, now. No more racing around calling on people and going to parties. We mustn't risk your health at all . . . It's hot in here. Let me get you some cold water, some lemonade. Let me get you a fan. I'll fan you."

Elizabeth smiled indulgently. "The doctor says I'm strong as an ox. If I need anything, I'll get it."

"No, let me. I know. We'll go to the Island. It's cool there, and the sea air will be good for the baby."

Never in her life had Elizabeth known such pampering as she experienced that summer. Delia did not want to leave her family, so Pinckney sent Hattie to stay with his "baby sister." Hattie thought of her as a child, too. "She acts as if she's my dah," Elizabeth complained. "She even makes me take a nap every afternoon."

"Good for her," said Lucas. "I don't want you to lift a finger, and you should get plenty of rest. I hope Pinckney will be decent enough to leave her with you when the summer's over. He doesn't need two servants to take care of him alone."

"But he does, Lucas. That's a big house, and both of them are getting pretty old."

"Well, he doesn't need that big house either. He should give it to us. We'll need more room when Little Lucas comes."

Elizabeth sighed. The only problem they had was the baby's name. "Darling," she said patiently, "you know I don't like this business of Big Lucas and Little Lucas. The Tradds have always picked other family names for the children so you know who you're talking to. Or about."

"Everybody else names children after their parents. My father is Peter, and my older brother was Peter. I want my son to be named after me."

"I know what everybody else does, and I don't care. It just isn't fair to the poor, innocent baby. Just think how 'Little Lucas' will feel when he's thirty and still being called 'little.' Suppose he's bigger than you?"

"He won't be."

Elizabeth looked at her husband's tall, muscular form. "All right. He won't be. But he certainly won't be little. Unless he's a throwback like Stuart. That would be worse. Suppose he really is little. He'd hate to be called that."

"He won't be."

"Lucas, you really are cuckoo about this baby. But I love you for it. Let's not fuss. After all, he won't be born until March. We have plenty of time. And he may be a girl, you know. May I pick the name for the baby if it's a girl?"

"You may name all the girls, my adorable Elizabeth. But first we'll have a boy, and he'll have his father's name."

The next day he arrived home with a covered basket. "I brought you somebody to name," said Lucas.

It was a tiny, trembling gray kitten. Elizabeth was enchanted. She held the little creature to her shoulder; a tiny tongue licked her chin.

"I thought she'd be company for you."

Elizabeth almost wept at his thoughtfulness. She had been lonely at the beach. Pinckney rarely came over from the city. Being tactful and leaving the newlyweds alone, she thought. Lucas left at dawn and came home at supper time. Caroline was in the city two days out of three, having fittings on her wedding clothes or shopping for her trousseau. When she was at the beach, she was not the best possible company. She was miserable about moving to Savannah, about the arranged marriage to her cousin, about her father's refusal to permit her marriage to Malcolm Campbell whom she adored even though he was a widower with three children.

"I'll call her Mossy," Elizabeth said. "She's Spanish moss colored. Would you like some milk, Mossy?"

The kitten mewed. Elizabeth grinned a Lizzie grin. "What a little love. She'll give me practice in being a mama."

Over supper, Lucas told her his news. "We have to celebrate. Pinckney has finally given me something decent to do."

"How wonderful. Tell." Elizabeth knew how very much older-and-wiser Pinckney could act sometimes. She was sympathetic with Lucas' complaints that Pinny treated him like a clerk. After all, she thought, the reason Lucas hadn't taken an engineering job was because he didn't want someone bossing him around when he probably knew more than they did. He had been top of his class at West Point. It was unreasonable of Pinckney not to make Lucas a partner right away. There couldn't be that much to learn about digging phosphate out of the ground.

"I've been looking at the books," Lucas said. "There's no reason we shouldn't be making more profit. Well, I discovered that the biggest single moneymaker is the company store. Your friend Shad Simmons set that up, and Pinckney had never looked into it. The workers don't have any place else to buy anything. The prices to the darkies are three times what we pay for the groceries and tobacco and such."

"But that's terrible."

"That's what Pinny said. The store should be a service, not a business for profit. He's put me in charge of straightening it out."

"Oh, good. The workmen will be so grateful."

"It's not what I want to be doing. The whole mining operation should be reorganized. But it's a start, I guess I have to prove to Pinny that I'm not a child. He'll see that I can run things as well as he can."

"Better," Elizabeth said. "He didn't find the cheating, you did."

"Unfortunately, I'll have to be away a lot for the next few weeks. I have to do an inventory at the store and set the storekeeper straight."

Her heart thumped painfully. "No, Lucas. Can't it wait for fall? You might get swamp fever like Pinny did."

"Don't worry, my love. I'll leave Carlington before dark. But I won't be able to catch the last ferry. I'll have to stay in town. Delia can watch out for me."

Elizabeth fought back her tears. This was Lucas' big opportunity. "Of course," she said, "I understand. Mossy will keep me company."

"Don't let her sleep in my bed. I don't want to find a fur pillow when I come home."

"I'll keep your door closed." Lucas had a separate room at the beach house. Making love would be bad for the baby and he didn't want to disturb Elizabeth when he left in the early morning.

Elizabeth and Mossy had company in August. "I certainly won't consider going to a house with a baby in it," Julia Ashley said, "so I decided to come this year."

Elizabeth was actually glad to see her, even though Julia was as acerbic as ever. She willingly tore apart the tiny flannel sacques she had made and resewed them to her aunt's satisfaction. She even tried to speak French over tea, but Julia stopped her, declaring her vocabulary deficient and her accent an affront to the civilization that had produced Montaigne and Molière. Julia forced her to come along on her daily five mile walks. "You'll be nothing but pudding if you sprawl in that hammock until the young Cooper comes. How do you suppose your Apollo will like you then?" After the initial aches and pains in her legs wore off, Elizabeth discovered that she looked forward to the exercise. Lucas did not allow swimming, but he admitted that walking might be beneficial. In September, he was home again, and he accompanied her after Julia left. Elizabeth held his arm, looked at his golden hair blowing in the salt wind, and the rhythmic surf was like music.

They moved back to the doll's house in October. "I'll have to work fast to get Little Lucas' room ready," Elizabeth said happily. "Pretty soon I'll start to show, and I won't be able to go out to shop." She made her final public appearance at the Race Course joust. John Cooper was not there; he had not been home at all since the previous year. Lucas won easily. He crowned his wife with the wreath of flowers to the applause of everyone. Elizabeth heard the murmur of admiration for her husband and felt that she was indeed the Queen of Love and Beauty.

In November, she celebrated her nineteenth birthday alone with Lucas. The rest of her family and all her friends were at Emma Anson's funeral. Elizabeth could not go. She was almost six months pregnant.

"Kemper, I told you I was leaving early today. I can't hear any more cases."

"Yes sir, Judge Tradd. But this is a special situation."

Stuart glared at the nervous young attorney. "My cousin's funeral is a special situation. Your case can wait."

Mr. Kemper was unusually persistent. "Judge Tradd, sir, if you'll just let me tell you about it . . ."

"I'll give you two minutes."

After the first sentence, Stuart took his robes off the hook and put his arms through the sleeves. He missed Emma Anson's funeral.

The plaintiff was Mr. Albert Koger, on behalf of his granddaughter Henrietta. Mr. Koger was a small, fragile man with flowing white hair tied in a peruke. He was seventy-nine years old and looked ninety-nine. His granddaughter was a small, fragile girl of nineteen. She looked no more than twelve. The Koger family was suing the state of South Carolina for the return of one hundred and eleven thousand acres of land that had been confiscated for taxes.

"My client does not recognize the authority of the self-styled government of this state in the year of confiscation, 1873. It was not, he contends, a legitimate government and therefore had no right to impose taxes on a citizen of the state which it occupied at gunpoint."

Stuart looked at the diminutive old man. Mr. Koger was red-faced and shaking with rage. It was a reaction Stuart knew well in himself. The Reconstruction government should be declared illegal and all its actions rescinded. He agreed with the old man.

"Sir," he said, "you have brought before this court an interesting and challenging point of law. Unfortunately, I cannot rule on it from my heart. And my head tells me that you will, in all likelihood not succeed. However, I will be happy to pursue it on your behalf." He bowed from the bench. "And that of your granddaughter." Henrietta Koger curtsied.

Stuart took the train to Columbia that afternoon. This was a question of politics more than law. Before he went home to pack, he drove the Kogers to the boardinghouse where they lived. Mr. Koger was patently too weak to walk, despite his fierce protests to the contrary.

Stuart would have consulted Josiah Anson first, before tackling the Governor, but he knew that Mr. Anson would be occupied with readjusting his life after his wife's death.

He did not know that his elderly cousin was incapable of adjusting. Josiah Anson was in a state of despair. Emma Anson's long illness had drained his energies without really convincing him that she was going to leave him. He could not quite comprehend that she was gone.

"He's like a lost child," Lucy told Pinckney two weeks after the funeral. "He wanders from room to room in that big house without being able to settle in one place. It's almost as if he's looking for her. It's heartbreaking."

"Is there anything I can do? Cousin Josiah was a stay for me when things were at their worst. I feel like he's my father."

Lucy touched his cheek with her finger. "Not you, Pinny. Me. I'm moving us all up to Charlotte Street."

Pinckney seized her hand. "No!" he said, squeezing until her bones cracked. At the noise, he opened his fingers and kissed hers. "What am I doing? Forgive me." Lucy reassured him. He did not, he said, want to make things more difficult for her. His face was bleached from the strain he was under.

"For God's sake," cried Lucy, "just this once don't be noble and honorable. Hate me for having to leave; hate Andrew for being alive instead of setting me free; hate Miss Emma for dying; hate Mr. Josiah for needing me more than you do. Be human, Pinckney. Then I can be human, too."

He caught her to him, and they clung desperately to each other.

"Kiss me, Pinny," Lucy whispered.

"My dearest, I dare not. Just let me hold you."

Lucy broke away from his embrace. "This is torture," she said. Her words were bleak. "We must think what we can do."

They had been seeing each other every evening, eating supper with Little Andrew. That was less than they wanted, a poor substitute for the intimacy of the shared moonlight they had known the summer before. But it was at least an hour they could count on to be together, to close out the world of reality that stood between them. Now even that would be lost.

Pinckney felt, for the thousandth time, how unjust it was that he could not take care of Lucy, make her life easier, provide her with some few little luxuries. Lucy worried, as she always did, about his loneliness now that Elizabeth was gone. Pinny urged her to take some money, even if she could not accept his overt protection. "Hire a man to take care of Andrew at least. You do too much." She shook her head.

Lucy suggested that Pinckney open up his life. He could go hunting on weekends like the other men; he could accompany Lucas to the cockfights and boxing matches that were an ill-kept secret in the old town. He refused. He had seen enough killing and fighting to last a lifetime.

"I cannot beg you to find a nice young girl and marry her," Lucy said, "although that's what you should do. It would kill me."

Pinckney's drawn face dissolved into his familiar slow smile. "I've already found a nice young girl. I just have to wait for her, that's all."

At that, Lucy broke down. "Ah, Pinny, I'm thirty-two years old, and I feel eighty-two. I see it in my looking glass."

The next evening, their last together, Pinckney gave her a small velvet-bound book of the poems of John Donne. A ribbon marked the page with "The Undertaking." One stanza was bracketed with light penciling.

But he who loveliness within
Hath found, all outward loathes,
For he who colour loves, and skin,
Loves but their oldest clothes.

Lucy kept it on the table next to her bed in the Charlotte Street house.

Pinckney found escape in the Tradd-Simmons account books. He had been neglecting business too long. And, he discovered, he had been too dependent on Shad Simmons from the beginning. It was Shad who had negotiated all the contracts, Shad who had gotten to know all the men in the fertilizer companies that bought the phosphate. No wonder that, after the break between them, it had been so easy for Shad to convince the companies to move their accounts to the suppliers in the monopoly the state had given to the carpetbagger ring. When he left Tradd-Simmons, he implied that it was finished.

"But it's not finished," Pinckney said to his brother-in-law. "We've got thousands of tons still to be dug. All we need is someone to buy it."

Lucas volunteered to go North to find the buyers, but Pinckney wouldn't permit it. "You're going to be a father soon; Lizzie would never forgive me. I'll go." He left in February, expecting to be home before mid-March. Stuart was marrying Henrietta Koger on April second, and he was going to be best man.

As it turned out, Lucas had to take his place. Pinckney was having much more difficulty than he expected. Nor could Elizabeth be the attendant for her new sister. Little Lucas was already three weeks late and gave no signs of making his entrance. Elizabeth felt like a hippopotamus. Hattie, who came every day to check on her, just made her more nervous. Pinckney had promised the old black woman that she could leave the Tradd house in Clara's hands and go to the Coopers to be the baby's dah. Hattie could hardly wait.

Julia Ashley took the part of "history's oldest bridesmaid," as she called it. She was very much in favor of the wedding. The Kogers were a family that she knew well; they were distantly connected to the Ashleys through an eighteenth-century marriage. She gave a wedding supper at the Barony after the ceremony in the old planters' church of Saint Andrews on the Ashley. It had been closed since the War, but the bishop opened it for Adam Edwards. His voice was too resonant for the tiny space, but the windows had no glass left in them, so it was able to escape. Mary Tradd Edwards, as everyone expected, cried throughout.

"It's not ladylike, my dear," said old Doctor Perigru, "you dropped that baby like an alley cat. Now stop your crying. Be a good, brave girl."

"Lucas wasn't even here. I wanted him to be here."

"Dear child, thank your stars he wasn't. There's nothing worse than having a nervous father around. I would have been too busy with him to catch the baby when she popped out."

Delia was waiting on the sidewalk when Lucas arrived home from the Barony the next morning. "Mist' Cooper, the baby done come!" Lucas ran up the steps three at a time.

"Elizabeth! My darling wife. How could I have been away? Goddamn all weddings except ours. Where is he? Where's my son?"

Elizabeth turned back the coverlet to show him the tiny sleeping baby in her arm. Lucas tiptoed across to look. "So small," he whispered. He marveled at the perfect ears and miniature fingers. "Perfect," he said. He was awed. Elizabeth felt a mixture of pride and love that filled her veins with warmth.

"Ten toes, too," she said. "Want to see?" She opened the blanket wrapping the baby. While Lucas rubbed his cheek against the doll-sized feet, she giggled. "And wetting again, too," she said. "It looks like we'll have to string extra clothes lines for all the napkins. Call Hattie, will you, darling? She can change her."

Lucas looked up from his examination of the baby's toenails. "What?"

Elizabeth repeated herself, laughing. "Didn't you know that babies don't come already housebroken?" she added. "Mossy spoiled you."

Lucas pulled at the baby's diapers. "Don't, silly," Elizabeth said. "Let Hattie do that."

"It's a girl!" he said.

Elizabeth nodded. "I've already picked her name. That was the promise, you know. I get to . . . name . . . the . . . girls." Her words trailed off. "Lucas! Lucas, where are you going?" His feet were running down the stairs.

He did not return until late that night. By then, Elizabeth had cried herself to sleep. The baby was asleep in her basket in the kitchen where Hattie was washing her napkins. "That you, Mist' Lucas?" Hattie called. There was no answer.

He stumbled into the bedroom, slamming the door behind him. The sound woke Elizabeth. She could not see him in the dark, but she could hear him and smell him. "A son," he said, "I want a son. A man should have a son." He reeked of whiskey.

"Lucas?" Elizabeth quavered. "I'm sorry you're so disappointed. But she's a lovely baby, Lucas. Next time we'll have a boy."

"I want a son," he groaned. "You've got to give me a son."

Then he was at the bed, tearing the linens off, fumbling at her nightdress. "Goddamnit, you'll give me a boy." His body was heavy and sweaty and stinking and a stranger. His fingers prodded the flesh torn by the birth, and Elizabeth started to scream. He covered her mouth with his hand. When he raped her, she felt a series of burning stiletto stabs of pain. Her mind was a black whirlpool of fear. She was suffocated, strangling. Her fists beat at her husband's head and shoulders until they fell limply next to her head. She was unconscious.

Hattie shook her awake two hours later. "Little Miss want her breakfast," she said. She held the crying baby in one arm. The lantern in her other hand illuminated the blood that had seeped through the covers Lucas had thrown over Elizabeth's body and head. "Do, Jesus," Hattie gasped. "I go for the doctor."

Elizabeth groped at her pain. "No, Hattie, I'm not bleeding anymore. Help me to the chair. I'll feed Mary Catherine while you change the bed." I must have had a bad dream, she thought. That could never have happened.

But when the baby was fed and sleeping contentedly on the clean bed, Hattie helped her change her nightdress. And when she pulled it over her head, she could smell stale whiskey with the sickly-sweet odor of dried blood.

She cradled her child against her aching body. "Please, dear God," she prayed, "please help me."

39

Lucas strode in at midmorning, with his arms full of jasmine. His cheeks were ruddy, freshly shaven, and he smelled of witch hazel. "Good morning, Mistress Cooper," he said. He spilled the flowers across Elizabeth's lap and kissed her hand. It was as if the nightmare had never been.

Elizabeth didn't know what to do or say. She picked up one of the vines and inhaled the scent.

"You must pin up your hair, my love, and prepare to receive guests," said Lucas, smiling. "I've been sending telegrams to everyone announcing the newest Cooper. They'll be flocking to see her. Have you picked a name yet?"

Elizabeth dropped the flowers and leaned toward her husband. "I had, but we can change it if there's something special you want."

"Anything you like is fine with me."

Elizabeth sat back against the pillows. "I thought Mary for my mother and Catherine for yours." Her disappointment was obvious.

Lucas patted her ankles. "Don't be too sad, Elizabeth. You'll do better next time."

She thought about the enchanting soft creature asleep in the padded basket near the window, and the Tradd temper took hold of her. "Mary Catherine is a beautiful baby, Lucas."

"Of course she is. She has a beautiful mother. As soon as she tidies her hair."

"Lucas, I'm not in the mood for teasing. Or flowers, either." She swept them onto the floor. "I've given you a lovely daughter, and you're acting as if you aren't even happy to have her."

Lucas' jaw tightened. His scar was vivid. I hadn't noticed before how much it had faded, Elizabeth thought. She felt a tremor of fear. Don't be ridiculous, she told herself. Lucas wouldn't hurt you. Her throbbing, torn body denied her attempt to reassure herself.

"Elizabeth." His voice was cold. "I will not have a shrewish wife. It is a wife's duty to be a comfort to her husband, not a thorn. I order you to make yourself presentable before the callers arrive."

"Yes, Lucas." His coldness frightened her more than his anger.

Her capitulation changed him instantly. "That's my good girl," he said. "Shall I brush your hair for you?"

"Thank you, Lucas. I'd like that very much."

The young Coopers presented a charming picture when Elizabeth's mother and aunt were shown in. Lucas was tucking yellow jasmine stars into his wife's coronet of copper braids. Mary cooed over her namesake. Even Julia was approving. "When she gets some hair, it will be dark like her eyebrows and lashes," she announced. "There's a lot of Ashley in this child."

Lucas' mother came later that day. She was moved to tears by the perfection of her first grandchild. Elizabeth decided at that moment to call the baby Catherine, instead of Mary.

Kitty Gourdin was the last visitor that day. She, too, cried when she saw Catherine in Elizabeth's arms. "Forgive me, Lizzie, I'm making a spectacle of myself. I just want a little baby so bad it makes me all weepy."

Elizabeth was full of compassion. And self-satisfaction, although she was not aware of it. Kitty had been insufferably smug when she was belle of the year. She had gloried in being a heartbreaker. Now two years had passed. Kitty's dozens of beaux were sending nosegays to the new belle, their hearts apparently whole again. She was in danger of being an old maid.

Lucas came in with a cup of tea for Elizabeth while Kitty was exclaiming over Catherine's exquisite tiny garments. Kitty became so flirtatious that Elizabeth realized with a start that Kitty was not simply being her bellish self. She was infatuated with him. Elizabeth looked with fresh eyes at her husband. He was looking down at Kitty with half-hooded, amused eyes, his mouth quirked up on the scarred side. Elizabeth caught her breath, feeling his magnetism and the uncertainty that had plagued her in the months before the epic joust. If he leaves me, she thought, I'd rather be dead.

He escorted Kitty down to the door. The muted sound of her friend's voice and her husband's lazy laughter floated up to Elizabeth for what seemed a very long time. When Lucas came back upstairs, she made a special effort to be interested in his account of her brother's wedding.

After Catherine's night feeding, Lucas began the familiar routine of closing the curtains. Elizabeth shrank into the pillows in an involuntary reaction to her fear of the pain to come. Lucas looked over his shoulder at her, his expression stern.

"I'm sorry, Lucas. It's only that I hurt a good bit."

He shrugged his wide shoulders impatiently. "Very well," he said.

Then, looking at her pleading, apprehensive eyes, his mouth softened into a smile. "Sweet Elizabeth." His tone was caressing. "I don't want anything to hurt you ever. We'll wait a few days before we start a son."

She was very grateful.

Pinckney returned from Baltimore in May, bearing new contracts for as much ore as Carlington could deliver. He noticed that his little sister had dark circles around her eyes, but she assured him that she was just fatigued from the interrupted sleep Catherine's feeding schedule caused. "She'll be off her two-in-the-morning soon, and then I'll be fine." Pinckney agreed with her that his niece was the most delightful infant in the history of the world.

He also agreed with Lucas, later, that the Coopers would have to find a larger house. The doll's house smelled like a nursery throughout. "You'll be able to take home some decent money, now, brother-in-law. If I were you, I'd start house-hunting right away." It did not occur to him that Lucas was expecting him to offer the Tradd house. He did notice that Lucas' face was very red when he left the office in a hurry.

Elizabeth heard the door slam behind Lucas when he came home. She hurried down the steep stairs to pour his sherry. "How nice to have you home early," she said. "There's a surprise for supper."

"I'm not staying," Lucas said. "This place smells too much for a man to eat anything."

"I'll tell Delia to set the table in the garden. It'll be fresh and cool out there."

"I'll get something at the tavern. There's a fight tonight."

Elizabeth bit her lips to keep silent. She knew, from friends whose husbands had told them, that Lucas often offered to wager on himself against the victor of the bare-knuckle bouts that the tavern keeper organized for the entertainment of his patrons. He had actually been in two fights and had easily won both, but she was terrified that he might be hurt one day. The fighters were usually seamen or back-country rabble who would do anything to win the ten dollars that went to the winner.

"Lucas—" she started, but when she saw his face, she said nothing more.

It was midnight when she woke. A light breeze fluttered the curtains at the window, and the last notes of Saint Michael's chimes sounded as silvery as the light from the full moon outside. She counted the deep, resonant striking, then settled back under the coverlet to let the watchman's cry lull her back to sleep. A clumsy stumbling on the stairs made her eyes fly open.

Lucas came into the room. The blue-tinted moonlight made his scar purple. His mouth was swollen grotesquely; a clot of dried blood in its corner looked black. His shirt was stained with blood and sweat. A miasma of whiskey blotted out the ammoniac baby smell. Elizabeth began to tremble.

It had been more than a month since Catherine's birth and the terrifying scene when Lucas came home drunk. She had managed to push the memory to the back of her mind where it joined other memories too painful to face. She experienced a bearable agony when Lucas resumed marital relations after letting her rest for three days, but that was, she assumed, just part of being a wife, and it did not last long. She didn't mind, because he was her husband. But now, this drunken Lucas. He was a stranger, the cruel, torturing stranger who had hurt her so dreadfully. She was paralyzed and helpless before the anger that radiated from him.

His movements were jerky and uncontrolled. She saw the torn purple skin over his knuckles as he fumbled with his shirt buttons. When he tore the shirt open with a furious wrench, she tried to close her eyes, but she could not. They were fastened on the wreckage of his face. This is your husband, she told herself, and he's been hurt. Get up and tend him.

But she couldn't move. Lucas fell onto the chair and pulled off his boots. Then he stripped off his breeches and small clothes and turned to the washstand, where he poured the contents of the pitcher over his head.

He staggered over to the window, pulled the curtains closed and moved to the bed. There was a bruised, slurred sound to his words when he spoke. "Say hello to my dear wife." He chuckled. Elizabeth could not breathe. Lucas' hands grasped for her. "Hello, wife," he said drunkenly. "Wake up, wife."

Elizabeth began to choke from fear.

"What's that?" Lucas said. His fetid breath made her gag. His fingers moved over her face to her eyes, found them open. "Looking! You were looking." He seized her shoulders and shook her. Her throat made horrible rattles. "Stop," Lucas hissed. "Stop that laughing." He took one hand from her shoulder and slapped the side of her head. Then he pushed her into the yielding feather pillows and mattress. She gulped frantically for air, but her throat was closed. Lucas' body covered hers. "Bitch," he mumbled near her ear. "Stop it. Stop it or I'll kill you. Nobody laughs at me." His closed fist hit the pillow near her head. Elizabeth fainted.

When consciousness left her, the fear and pain went with it. Her breathing was ragged, but her throat was open. "That's better," Lucas growled. "A husband has his rights. There's nothing to laugh at when a man takes his rights. Nothing to laugh at." He pushed his small penis, with his fingers, into Elizabeth's wounded body. Elizabeth stirred; the pain penetrated even through the black oblivion that protected her.

Catherine's hungry cry called Elizabeth back from her refuge of unconsciousness. She heard Lucas snoring, and she shuddered. Then she wrapped herself hastily in her dressing gown to go to her baby.

"Miss Lizzie, is you all right?" Hattie peered closely at her.

Elizabeth nodded. "Fine, Hattie. I just missed the bed steps and fell. It shook me up a little. Give me my hungry little angel."

After Catherine was fed and bubbled, Elizabeth crept quietly downstairs. She dressed and went to sit in the kitchen chair until six. Catherine always had her breakfast in the kitchen.

When Lucas came down, he was wearing his hunting clothes. He ate only hominy; he did not have to chew that. "I'm going to the woods to shoot," he mumbled. "I'll be back when my mouth is healed." He said nothing else.

"Lucas has gone hunting with some friends," Elizabeth told her mother that afternoon. "I know he'll be sorry to miss saying good-bye."

"Give him my love," said Mary. "I'm sorry to miss him, too. But I've stayed much too long. Adam just can't manage alone, poor lamb. If Pinny hadn't been delayed, I would have gone back with Adam when he left three weeks ago. Now that you're a wife yourself, you know how helpless men really are."

"I don't know anything about men, Mama. Lucas least of all. I just don't understand him."

Mary fluttered her hands. "Don't try to *understand* him, Lizzie. Men hate brainy women. They just want to be taken care of."

Elizabeth clutched at the straw of the older woman's knowledge. "What if they want something that . . . that's horrible?"

Her mother reddened. "I hope you young people don't discuss your private affairs; it's disloyal, and it's embarrassing."

Elizabeth started to cry. "Mama, please help me. You're my mother. I wouldn't talk to anyone else."

Mary looked away. "Just remember your marriage vows," she said. "You swore to 'obey and serve.' And the scriptures tell us that wives are subject to their husbands in everything. Now, stop that crying. You're the luckiest girl in the world, to have a handsome husband and a beautiful baby. You'll just have to put aside the Tradd willfulness that's in you. Understand?"

"Yes, ma'am."

"Then kiss me good-bye. And be a good girl."

Elizabeth's wet cheek rested for an instant against her mother's soft lips.

Three days later, Lucas returned. He found Hattie hovering over a billowing black wet nurse, who had Catherine at her breast. Elizabeth was ill.

"Exhaustion," Dr. Perigru said to Lucas. "I advised her to get a nurse for the baby from the beginning, but she wouldn't listen. Now she has to. See to it that she gets plenty of rest. Pinckney's been here all day. See that he gets some rest, too, if you can. He's drawn thin as wire."

Lucas cared for Elizabeth as if she were delicate glass. For the first week, she was in a daze of fever. After that, she became a little stronger every day, but she was listless and wanted only to sleep. Hattie finally cured her. "Does you wants that little baby to have no more mother than an orphan?" she said. "You shame me."

On June tenth, the Coopers, Hattie and Delia moved to Sullivans Island. Hattie was beaming with triumph. Her rival, the wet nurse, was gone. Elizabeth was still not well, but she was happy about it. Lucas would not be back in her bed for a long time. She was pregnant again.

40

A terrible racket compounded of screeched curses, breaking glass and shouts for quiet had been invading the Anson drawing room for more than a half hour.

"Is it always like this?" Pinckney asked.

Lucy shrugged. "Seems like it. It's not too bad when the windows are closed."

"Sounds like someone's murdering somebody. Shouldn't we get the police?"

"I wish they would all murder each other. Then it would be peaceful. The police came once, but there's nothing they can do. Evidently one of your aunt's tenants beats his wife every time he gets drunk. But he never kills her."

Pinckney shook his head. It was impossible to imagine that people were capable of such things, even the poor whites who lived in Julia Ashley's former town house. "You can't be expected to tolerate this din until cool weather, Lucy. Why don't you take the family to the Island? Cousin Josiah could have my room. I'll go in with Lucas."

"It can't be, Pinny."

"But I'd get to see you every day, instead of this farce of bringing papers to Cousin Josiah. It would save my life. Every time I look across the street and see those strangers where you should be, I feel murderous myself."

Lucy put her hand on his. "Don't make it harder on us both. Please. We've been through this before. Mr. Josiah is only now getting back on his feet. You know how he was after Miss Emma died. If he hadn't had to pull himself together to run the Saint Cecelia, he might have given up, like Miles Brewton. As it was, he was living in the past for months and months; all he would talk about was the way life was before the War. Now, thanks to you, he's got to come back to the present. The phosphate contracts are the only work he's had for a year. He let all his business slide when Miss Emma was dying, and he never tried to get it back. I can't risk asking him to make any big adjustments right now."

Pinckney was stubborn. "It wouldn't be that big. He'd still have you waiting on him and catering to every whim."

"Don't be pettish. I think you're jealous."

He reflected for a moment. "I think you're right." His smile was rueful. "There are too many men in your life, and I want to be the only one."

Lucy fluttered her eyelashes. "My, sir, you'd best be careful. You'll turn my little old head."

Pinny laughed. "You minx. It's wicked to mock your fellow ladies that way. A gentleman shouldn't be privy to the secrets of the fairer sex."

"Want to see me swoon?"

"I'd be enchanted."

Lucy obliged, with a prolonged sigh. When she had achieved the maximum graceful arrangement of limp arms and curved body across the arm of the settee, she opened one eye. "How's that?"

"Terrifying."

"Applaud, please. Now do a manly stance." Pinckney stood, threw his chest forward and his head back. Lucy clapped enthusiastically.

They often played these foolish charades of boy-girl flirtation. They defused the tension between them, turning the longing for each other into a burlesque, allowing them to laugh instead of despair. Andrew was now a hollow shell mentally. He lived in a perpetual fog of opium-laced laudanum. But he lived.

Mr. Anson's cough sounded from the hallway. Lucy sat up, and Pinckney sat down. The old man walked in with a brisk step. "These inventories look fine, son," he said. "You should be able to hire more workers without buying so much as a shovel. I'll send copies to Shad Simmons' laywer. Also a copy of the current balance sheet. You know, since he isn't an active partner anymore, you don't really need to figure him for half the profits. He's not contributing anything."

"He had my word on it in the beginning, Cousin Josiah. Equal partners."

Mr. Anson nodded. If that was the case, then there were no grounds for discussion. A written contract could be broken; that's what lawyers were for. But a man's word was inviolate.

"Good thing you've got Lucas," he said. "That boy has real business sense. I've searched the title on the Russell house, and everything's ready to sign now. He's making a shrewd buy there."

Lucy gasped. "Lucas Cooper is buying the Russell house? Does Lizzie know? She'll need ten servants."

"Not Lizzie," said Pinckney. "She can run a house with nothing but a maid and a cookbook. Aunt Julia taught her to do everything but put on a new roof. And Lord knows she needs a bigger house. Two babies in the one on Church Street would be more crowded than your neighbors next door.

"Don't tell her anything, though. Lucas wants to surprise her. It's really something, the way he dotes on her. Lizzie—I mean, Elizabeth—is a fortunate young lady."

"Lucas! You didn't have to hire a carriage. I'm plenty strong enough to take the streetcar." Elizabeth was in radiant good health after three months at the beach. She had walked every day, even when her husband stayed in town, as he often did. One of the nicest things about the Island was that it was such a private Charlestonian enclave; a lady could go out unchaperoned without violating any rules.

Lucas opened the carriage door and handed her in. "Nothing but the best for my wife and my son," he said.

Elizabeth laughed. "He kicked when he heard that," she told her husband in a whisper. She had brooded about Lucas' episodes of brutality for the first weeks of her stay on the Island. For the remainder of the time, she had luxuriated in his attentiveness. It was clearly, she decided, a matter of drinking too much. Both times, he had been grievously disappointed; first by not having the son he wanted so badly, then by losing the fight to a low-class sailor; he had, as they say, drowned his sorrows. He didn't know what he was doing. He never meant to hurt her. He loved her. All she had to do was keep him from being disappointed anymore. She'd do that with all her heart. She loved him.

As for the painful "wifely duty," well, that was just what women had to suffer. Maybe Dr. Perigru would recommend a rest after this baby. He'd done it when she had the fever. If he did that, and she just had time to heal, she wouldn't really mind being a wife at all. Everything else was wonderful. Catherine was almost six months old and, Elizabeth thought, the prettiest, cleverest baby in the world. Hattie swore she was saying "Mama," and she laughed all the time. Especially when Elizabeth let her touch Mossy's soft fur, or held the purring little cat close to her ear.

The carriage rolled off the ferry dock onto Market Street. Elizabeth craned her head out of the window. She felt as if she had been away from the city for years instead of months. As they turned into Meeting Street, she saw the tall white spire of Saint Michael's. It chimed the quarter hour, and she settled back into the seat. "Now I know I'm back," she said. "There's no time on the Island, and that's nice. But not for too long."

Why did we come all the way to Meeting, she wondered. We'll have to turn at Tradd to get back to Church. But the driver did not turn. She looked inquiringly at Lucas. "We're going to call on some people," he said.

"Oh, Lucas, I'm not dressed for paying calls. You should have warned me."

"They won't mind. I'm sure of it."

The carriage stopped in front of the imposing brick mansion that still had the builder's initials in its wrought-iron balconies. N. R. for Nathaniel Russell. Elizabeth knew it better by the name of its most recent owner. The Allston house. Her old school. She was completely puzzled now. Since Eleanor Allston's death, the house had been unoccupied. No one lived there, certainly not friends close enough to expect the Coopers to call, complete with baby, nursemaid and cat.

"What on earth is going on, Lucas?" She was starting to get angry. She looked again at the house. The door opened. Delia stood there, grinning, in a fresh lace-trimmed apron.

"Welcome home, Mistress Cooper," Lucas said.

"I still can't believe it," said Elizabeth when they finished their tour of the house. "It's beautiful, but I feel like an awful small pea in an awful big pod. We'll have to beg furniture from everybody we know." Catherine's crib and Hattie's bed looked insignificant in the huge square room. Elizabeth's footsteps echoed as she walked into the hall. She leaned over the railing of the magnificent staircase that was the center of the house in every sense. It dominated the structure and the imagination of everyone who entered, beautiful, fascinating and dangerous. It had an oval shape, rising from the ground floor in a swirling pattern of gleaming shallow steps that seemed to rest on air, earning its descriptive name of "flying staircase." Its shape inspired the oval reception rooms that flanked it on the south and the oval bubble of skylight far above. Looking up from its center, the viewer felt weightless, lifted into the light. Looking down from the third floor, the spiral of steps reversed their pull, becoming a dizzying vortex, spinning to the polished floor far below. Elizabeth held tight to the railing and shook her head to break the spell.

"Do you know, Lucas, that my life's ambition when I was at Mistress Allston's was to slide down these banisters? Now that it's our very own house, nobody can tell me no."

"I can." He took her arm and pulled her away from the hypnotic ellipse.

Elizabeth hugged him. "Silly, I mean, after the baby . . . And I'll be very stern with the children. They will be absolutely forbidden to try it until they're at least twelve. But, when they're all out at the Gardens, and nobody can see me and gossip about how undignified I am—well, then I'll get my wish."

Lucas folded his strong arms around her. "I intend for you to have every wish you ever wished. And then some. We'll be the grandest Coopers of all time." He rested his hand on her slightly swelling abdomen. "This is a fine house for Little Lucas to grow up in," he said. "He'll be a prince." Elizabeth felt the baby's kick before Lucas did. When the pressure touched his hand, he smiled and tightened his arms.

"Oh, Lucas," said Elizabeth, "I am so very, very happy."

41

In the frantic hurly-burly on the Cunard pier, no one noticed the stocky fair-haired man who walked purposefully from the customs' inspection area. It was not that unusual for a trans-Atlantic traveler to return to New York with twelve steamer trunks and an assortment of hand luggage.

Shad found a uniformed Cunard representative, conferred briefly, then put a folded banknote in the man's white-gloved hand. "That's it, then. You'll take care of the porters for me and send my luggage to the Fifth Avenue Hotel. Thank you for your courtesy."

The official touched a finger to his hat. "Our pleasure, Mr. Simmons. I hope you'll travel Cunard again."

"Absolutely," Shad said, lying. He had done what he went to Europe to do, and he had no intention of leaving the States ever again.

He was not expected at the hotel, but the desk clerk glanced briefly at his Savile Row broadcloth and bowed obsequiously. "A suite, Mr. Simmons?"

"Nothing too elaborate. A sitting room and bedroom will be adequate." With a neat economy, he signed the register: J. Shadwell Simons, Charleston, S.C.

The suite was a succession of wonders to Shad. The furniture was massive, brightly varnished and upholstered in deep plush. Black-veined white marble was everywhere—on the tops of all the tables and bureaus, around the oversized coal-grate fireplaces and even forming the floor of the adjoining bathroom. Shad had lived in the finest hotels in Stuttgart and London, but they had been nothing like this.

He called downstairs on the speaking tube the bellman had demonstrated to him and ordered dinner in his room. Tomorrow would be soon enough to start working on his new life. Besides, it would take most of the evening to put his things away. He did not want to trust it to the valet service. He needed to familiarize himself with all the clothes that had been made for him during the months in London. He was, thank God, finally accustomed to the intricate bridgework that the genius in

Germany had devised after almost a year's work on his teeth. Joe Simmons stood before the long, gold-framed mirror in his bedroom and smiled. "You're a handsome devil, Joseph Shadwell One-m-Simons," he said aloud.

The following morning he presented himself at the Morgan bank, to which he had transferred a half-million dollars for credit to his new name. As he expected, the manager of the office made him wait for a precisely planned interval, long enough to indicate that the House of Morgan was not impressed by a mere half-million but not so long that he was likely to take offense. As he also expected, the man took him to his club for luncheon, observed his ease there and urged him to join. Shad accepted with just the right shade of reluctance.

For the next two months, Shad surveyed the terrain of New York in the same way that he had learned Charleston fifteen years before. He walked the streets, rode the tramways and the new elevated railroads, ate in restaurants, sat quietly in the smoking room of his club, stood casually in the ornate lobby of his hotel. And always he listened and noticed things. At the end of that time, he decided that he had been right in his assumptions about New York: It was the perfect stage for J. Shadwell Simons. Furthermore, as a bonus, he liked it. It had a hurried newness, a restlessness and a lack of sentimentality that mirrored his own nature. The beggars on the streets bothered him no more than the goats and pigeons that seemed to be everywhere. The opulence was balm to his soul. He had had enough refinement in Charleston and Europe, he thought, to last him for the rest of his life. He had made a lot of money, and he wanted to spend some of it, while making a great deal more. If that was vulgar, then he would be vulgar. Charleston be damned. New York was full of people living the way he wanted to live and doing what he wanted to do. It offered everything to the man smart enough to grab hold of it.

On a Wednesday afternoon early in November, he went down to the hotel lobby to begin his campaign. Like all brilliant strategists, Shad had reduced the elements of the battle before him to its essentials and located the weakest point. He attacked it directly.

"I need some advice," he told the hotel director, "and I count on you to justify my confidence by not repeating what I'm going to tell you."

The man responded with fulsome guarantees. He would, Shad knew, spread the news immediately. "The truth is," Shad lied, "I'm feeling homesick. We're a very sociable bunch in Charleston, and I miss our little evenings. Naturally, they're very plain now. The War left us with nothing much but good manners and old traditions. But we still have music and conversation and some small suppers. I was hoping that I'd find some cultivated folks in New York, in spite of what all my friends in Europe told me. Now I'm about to give up. Can you recommend an establishment as fine as yours in Boston? I have letters of introduction there."

As expected, Shad's confidant assured him that there was no need to go to Boston for society and no hotel there one tenth as fine as the Fifth Avenue. He begged permission to speak to some ladies he knew. Invitations would be forthcoming immediately.

Shad smiled evenly, then winked. "I've met several of New York's 'ladies,' but that's not what I'm talking about," he said, looking through the office door into the lobby. Several of the magnificently gowned, expensive prostitutes strolling in the lobby smiled demurely.

The director hastened to assure Shad that he was referring to a totally different kind of lady.

The next morning, seven cards of invitation were on the rolling table with the breakfast Shad always took in his room. He held in his chuckles until the waiter was gone. The wall was breached. Soon New York would surrender what he wanted, a place in the inner ring of financiers, the "robber barons" who controlled business, stock market, politicians. The surest, shortest route was through marriage. In Charleston, he had been acceptable to a point because he had possessed something that was in short supply. Money. In New York, his money was virtually meaningless; he had considerably more than the deposit he kept at a half-million in Morgan's Bank, but that was nothing compared to the fortunes of the robber barons. However, he could offer a commodity that was in shorter supply in New York than his money had been in Charleston. Aristocracy. The fabulously new-rich would have no way of checking his credentials. They all knew Charleston's reputation for blue-blooded snobbery; none of them knew any Charlestonians, for whom New York did not exist. His chuckle increased to a rumble of hearty laughter.

"Mr. Joseph Shadwell Simons regrets that he is unable to accept the kind invitation of . . ." he wrote to six of the seven ladies. He accepted Mrs. Mary Elliott Dalton's request for the pleasure of his company at a musical evening. She was the aunt of the girl he had selected to be his wife.

Emily Elliott was the only child of Samuel Elliott, the most private of the barons. He was a totally ruthless man with blazing eyes in a yellow, mummylike, shrunken face, and a pathological fear of imaginary anarchists dedicated to annihilating the rich. He kept his name a secret, but he was a substantial partner in the activities of Stanford, Vanderbilt and Morgan, he owned more than half of the land between the Battery and Fourteenth Street, and he was reputed to have more gold bullion in his private vault than the United States Government.

Emily was his greatest treasure. He kept her a virtual prisoner in the French château he had built on Fifth Avenue and Fortieth Street. When she went out, she was always accompanied by armed bodyguards and rode in a closed carriage. Her father's terror of assassins extended to her. It was compounded by a conviction that any man who interested himself in her must be a fortune hunter.

When Shad met her, he realized that Sam Elliott was right. No man would notice Emily for anything other than base motives. She was short and pudgy, with muddy skin and squinting, myopic eyes. Her hair was as dull as her skin and much the same color. She was wearing pearls, which emphasized her sallowness—and her father's wealth. They were enormous.

Shad bowed punctiliously over her hand. He was grateful that it was gloved; probably she had damp, clammy hands. Everything about Emily gave the impression of unhealthiness.

Until she spoke. She said only, "How do you do," and she said it very softly, but it sounded like music. She had a clear, pure soprano, like one of the soloists in the boys' choir he had heard in England.

Shad hid his surprise. At this moment, he must be polite, but distant. He intended that the Elliotts court him. He spent the major portion of his visit talking with his hostess. She was, he knew, curious about him, and he was prepared to satisfy her curiosity beyond her dearest imaginings.

Yes, he told her, he was recently returned from England. He had found it a bit too rowdy. The Prince surrounded himself, he thought, with companions that were not quite the sort of people one really wanted to associate with. As for the Queen, well, she really was lacking in any sense of style. His eyes moved appreciatively around the furnishings of Mrs. Dalton's drawing room.

He asked her guidance in finding a house suitable for a quiet bachelor, something substantial but not too large. He expected to do little entertaining.

He also allowed her to elicit his secret sadness: He had left home under a cloud after killing a man in a duel over a lady's honor. Naturally, the lady never knew anything about it. She was the wife of his best friend who had lost an arm in the War and could not fight himself. His heart ached for home, he said in his charming Southern drawl, but even if he could return with honor, he probably would not. God had blessed him with deposits of phosphate on the family plantation, but it tore him apart to see the fields; once the scene of happy, devoted, singing darkies who were the descendents of generations of "his people." Now the fields were like open wounds. He could not watch what was happening. Even before the incident which triggered his trip, he had sold the plantation where the Simons had lived for two hundred years.

"And if you'll permit me, Mistress Dalton, I'll be so bold as to correct you on one little point. My name is not pronounced Seyemons, but Simmons, just as if it had two m's. We Charlestonians have all sorts of peculiar names and spellings. It makes a ridiculous amount of difference to us, especially now that about all we own is our pride in our ancestry. I hope you'll forgive me if I seem rude in asking you to allow the correction."

Mrs. Dalton assured him that she was not offended in the least.

I'll say you're not, Shad said to himself. Your mouth is watering over the romantic duelist who knows the British Royal family, and your eyes nearly fell out over the word "plantation." If you're going to get somebody to swallow your story, my boy, go with the big lie every time.

It required only four more visits to Mrs. Dalton before Shad was invited to the sanctum sanctorum. Samuel Elliott's "invalid" wife had her sister-in-law bring him to tea. Shad listened attentively to the recital of her ailments, carefully did not react to her splendid jewels or astonishing obesity and wrote her a stiff thank-you note which did not even mention Emily, who had been silently present through the entire tea ceremony.

Now we'll whet the appetites, he thought. He regretted the next five invitations from Mrs. Elliott and Mrs. Dalton. But he sent flowers with the refusals.

On December first, he answered a peremptory summons to Samuel Elliott's musty Wall Street office. He was deferential to the old man, with just a hint of irritation perceptible. When Elliott demanded to know why Shad was insulting his wife by refusing her invitations, Shad was blunt. "Because," he said, "I believe she's trying to snare me for your daughter, and I'm not going to be thought a fortune hunter."

"Isn't that what you are?"

"No, sir. I'll make my own fortune. I've made a fair start already."

"Then what were you hanging around for? Don't tell me you like hearing about my wife's gall bladder."

"I like hearing your daughter say anything at all. It sounds like an angel singing. But I won't court her until I'm rich enough to buy her from you. That's the only thing you'll understand. Your wife would give anything for a good bloodline in a grandchild, but you don't care about things like that."

"How do you know what I care about?"

"I know. You're a businessman. You buy and sell. You can't comprehend something that's beyond price." Shad bowed and left, ostensibly insulted.

The betrothal was announced at a party on Christmas Eve.

42

Elizabeth played hostess to her family for Christmas dinner that year. She had been making preparations for weeks, and it was a glorious festivity. Julia had taken the long Chippendale table from Charlotte Street out of storage; Delia had polished it to a mirror gloss; and Elizabeth had decorated its center with sprays of the bright red cassina berries that grew in the garden of the Russell house. It looked perfect in the center of the big oval dining room. The velvet draperies in the windows had originally been claret-colored. The years had faded them to a softer, uneven red which Elizabeth thought more beautiful. She had put big vases full of cassina branches on the low windowsills and lit the fire in the large fireplace, even though the day was so warm it was not needed. "I like all the reds," she explained.

"You're so clever," said Stuart's wife. "I wish I could think of things like that." Henrietta was shy to the point of invisibility, but she opened up to Elizabeth. It was the first time they had ever had a chance to make friends with each other. Henrietta was also pregnant, which Elizabeth used to create an immediate bond between them. She put Catherine in her aunt's arms almost as soon as Stuart and Henrietta arrived. Then, while Lucas served eggnog to Mr. Koger, Pinckney, Stuart, Julia and his father, Elizabeth loaded Henrietta down with authoritative new-mother baby lore. Lucas' mother listened enviously, her hands "itching for the baby," as Elizabeth whispered to Henrietta.

The dinner was superb, the service flawless. Pinckney had lent Clara for the day. Hattie and Delia were on their mettle to prove to her that their house and their white folks were much more elegant than hers.

After dinner, everyone took a turn in the garden. The bright sky was cloudless; the sun's rays nestled in the folds of the bright camellias and touched the masses of poinsettias with fire. "I don't know how a person could possibly be as happy as I am without busting wide open," said Elizabeth.

"Bursting," Julia corrected. Stuart winked behind her back. Pinckney grinned. The Tradds had not felt so much a family for years.

After their exercise, the men went off to look at the progress on the bridge that was being built over the Ashley River. Henrietta was disappointed that she could not accompany them. Stuart had told her many times about burning the old one down when the Yankees were coming. She would have loved to see the site of his heroism with him.

"You love my brother very much, don't you, Henrietta?" asked Elizabeth.

Her sister-in-law blushed. "Of course," she said in a barely audible voice. "Besides, he's very good to me and very patient with Grandpapa. It was Stuart's idea to have him live with us. I would never had dared suggest it."

"You're good for him, Henrietta. He seems so quiet and happy now. He used to be in a rage all the time."

"Do you really think so? I try to make him happy. He's very pleased about the baby, even though he doesn't show it the way Lucas does."

Julia coughed. "Damn fool to carry on so much, I say. A gentleman would act as if he didn't notice his wife's shape, not brag about it."

Catherine Cooper bridled at the insult to her son. Elizabeth jumped in to make peace. "Aunt Julia," she said with a wicked giggle, "a lady wouldn't say anything about it at all, especially an unmarried lady. She's supposed to think babies come from the doctor's bag."

Julia retreated from the field with a bark of laughter, and all was well.

Two days later, when Elizabeth was picking camellias for a new centerpiece, she felt a slow, wide streak of agony crawl up the right side of her womb. The sensation of tearing was so acute that she imagined she could hear it, like ripping a strip of linen. Instinctively her hands went to the source of the pain. Before she could touch her abdomen, it tightened and lifted in an unmistakable birth contraction. "Oh, my God," she cried. A thick spout of blood was pouring down her legs.

At least the pain was over. She staggered to the house, calling for Delia, leaving a shiny red trail behind her.

"Honey, the baby would have died even if you'd carried full term. Placenta previa, we call it. There's no way he could have lived. Try to think of it that you were spared two more months of being pregnant."

Elizabeth could not think of it that way. "I've lost my baby," she cried. "My baby's dead. Dead. Dead. I can't stand it."

Dr. Perigru gave her some laudanum and patted her shoulder until she fell asleep. He was an old man; he had seen a hundred women or more who lost babies. Elizabeth would get over it. She was young and strong; she had a child who needed her; and she would have more children. But with Elizabeth, as with all the others, he felt a profound sorrow. Life, especially new life, was so precious, and it so often slipped through his fingers. He had never learned to accept the limits of his knowledge and skill; he still felt failure, personal, responsible failure. You should give up, old man, he told himself. You're too old, too tired, too ignorant. Elizabeth was in a deep sleep. He packed his bag and left. There was a case of croup waiting for him.

Dr. Perigru was right, as he usually was. Elizabeth recovered from her loss. Hattie brought Catherine to her, and her tears frightened the little girl so much that Elizabeth stopped crying. Then Lucas came to her room, and his grief was so overwhelming that she had to put her own aside in order to comfort her husband.

He was distraught, like a madman. "My son," he sobbed, his eyes swollen from weeping. "My son is gone, before I even saw him. It's unfair, my whole life is unfair. I've never had what I should have, never. I should have been a troop commander, not just a cavalry lieutenant; they should have begged me to be in Hampton's honor guard; I should be running the company, not Pinckney. He doesn't know half as much as I do. I haven't complained. I never complain. I'm too much a man for that. But this is too much. I won't stand for it. The only thing I ever asked God for was a son. A man should have a son, or how do people know he's a man? I won't let this happen." He shook his fist at the ceiling, lifted his chin and howled. "You can't do this to me!" Then he wailed, a primeval cry of despair and rage. It went on and on, until Elizabeth feared for his sanity.

She pulled herself out of bed and went to him. "Lucas," she said, "Lucas. Let me help you, let me hold you, let me comfort you." She pulled down on his arm. Lucas collapsed, still screaming, and she fell with him. Then she held his head to her breast and crooned the meaningless syllables that always soothed Catherine, until he was quiet.

It is said that tragedy in a family either brings it closer together or tears it apart. The loss of their son was a bond of shared suffering between Elizabeth and Lucas Cooper. They were closer than they had ever been.

Until spring.

"Charleston. April 14, 1880. I find myself again writing," ran the neat, cramped script of Colonel William Ellis, "from an island overlooking the harbor and city which I once attempted to destroy. It gives me a strong sense of history and the part one man may be destined by Almighty God to play in His immutable plan. I am now in command of a battalion, instead of a company. And our orders are to restore the ship channels which once made this harbor the center of commerce and wealth for the haughty slave owners who began the carnage now known as the

Civil War. It is beyond my limited capacity of understanding to know why the Federal Government has decided to do this or why it should fall to me to be the instrument."

Colonel Ellis was a career officer, not a politician. He had seen the reason for the Union Navy's blockade during the War. He had hailed the arrival of the twenty aged whalers loaded with rock that had been sunk in the channels from Charleston harbor to the open ocean. Now it was his job to raise the "stone fleet" and dredge the channels so that the new capitalists of the South could ship cotton, timber, produce and phosphate at lower cost by sea. Colonel Ellis had been protecting Western settlers in the years after the War. He had never heard of carpetbaggers or Northern capital or bought politicians. The Congress had appropriated $200,000 for the job and sent the U. S. Army Corps of Engineers. He was following orders.

The Colonel looked through his field glasses at the divers who were marking the location of the ships on the bottom of the channel. His gaze moved on to the low mound that had been Fort Sumter. A trim sloop was tacking in to the rickety dock there. It was, he knew, full of tourists. An enterprising Athenian had started the sight-seeing excursions ten years before. Today should be highly profitable, the Colonel thought. It is the nineteenth anniversary of the first attack on the Fort, the beginning of the War.

He swung the glasses to the left, then moved them slowly from one side to the other, surveying the city. He could not say why it fascinated him so. He thought perhaps it was because it looked exactly the same now as it had done when he first scanned it. Distance blurred details, but the pastel houses with their piazzas were still there; the skyline was a jumble of low, tiled or slated roofs, and the tall spire of Saint Michael's pierced the blue heavens just as it had when he had aimed at it. He picked up his journal again.

"When I look at the scene before me, I sometimes feel as if I had never been, as if my memory were a mirage. At other times I almost believe that this flowered city is a fantasy, insubstantial and indestructible as a recurring dream. It is having an unsettling effect upon me. I will be glad when the work is done."

Again and again, the Colonel was irresistibly drawn to the prospect of the shuttered houses and walled gardens. Their mystery became more intriguing each day. They could be hiding anything and everything—beauty or bestiality, enchantment or horror, unimaginable joys or unspeakable misery.

"Lucas! Lucas, please! Please, Lucas, don't!" Elizabeth huddled, screaming, on the floor, her arms curved around her stomach. Her husband stood over her; his foot was drawn back, ready to deliver a second kick to her abdomen.

"The hell with you, then," he muttered, "you noisy, barren cow." He threw the flimsy yellow paper in his fist onto the floor and stormed out of the house.

Elizabeth sobbed until her head hurt as much as her stomach. Then, little by little, she gained control of her body. You must get up, she ordered herself, Hattie will be bringing Catherine home from the park soon. Outside the open windows, the fantastic beauty of spring mocked her misery. She crawled, aching, to the crumpled ball of paper, then pulled herself up into a chair. She smoothed the paper into a legible sheet. It was a telegram from Summerville, addressed to Mr. and Mrs. Lucas Cooper. It announced the birth of a son to Judge Stuart Tradd and Mrs. Tradd.

"Oh, my God," Lizzie moaned. She knew how Lucas felt about Stuart. He had made too many jokes about her brother's short stature and unimportant patronage job for her to doubt Lucas' feelings of superiority. Until now. Stuart had what Lucas wanted. A son. And Lucas blamed her.

She had believed that the bad times were over. It had been four months since her miscarriage, four months of mutual comforting, four months of closeness, four months of hoping for the first signs of morning sickness, four months of repeated disappointment when she had to tell Lucas that she wasn't pregnant. Only four months. And now this. Lucas had been waiting in the dining room when she came home from a luncheon party. He had an empty brandy decanter at his elbow, and his golden head was lying on the table, illuminated by a shaft of sunlight.

When Elizabeth touched his shoulder, worried, he had not said a word. He simply stood, grabbed her shoulders, shook her until her eyes rolled, threw her onto the floor and kicked her.

What am I going to do? she cried now. Her frightened thoughts scurried, looking for an escape. Pinckney. She'd tell Pinckney . . . and he'd kill Lucas. She knew it, as sure as she knew the sun would set that night and rise the next morning. For an instant, her heart soared. Then she realized that Pinckney would have to settle his grievance with Lucas in a duel. That was what gentlemen did. And there could be only one outcome. Lucas would kill Pinckney. Elizabeth whimpered in desperation. If only she could talk to someone . . . but there was nobody. Her mother would only tell her again that a wife should be submissive to her husband . . . Lucy . . . Lucy would listen, would understand. But Lucy was already burdened with troubles of her own. And she was so sweet and quiet. What could she do against Lucas? . . . Aunt Julia, then. Aunt Julia could terrify anybody, even Lucas . . . I can't possibly tell Aunt Julia, Elizabeth realized hopelessly. She's a spinster lady. She wouldn't know what I was talking about, and she'd be furious at me for mentioning anything about what happens between husbands and wives . . . All the rigid conventions of the society in which she lived closed around Elizabeth, isolating her in desperate loneliness . . . Maybe she should just take Catherine and run away. Where? How? She had never been any place in her life except for the few miles up the river to the Barony. The realization of her own helpless ignorance swept over her, frightening her more than Lucas' violence.

The front door opened and closed. Elizabeth frantically wiped the tears from her face and turned her head, forcing a smile for Hattie and Catherine.

Lucas stood swaying in the doorway. Elizabeth felt the old terror stop her breath.

"Elizabeth—" he stumbled across the floor and fell on his knees before her. "Oh, my God, can you ever forgive me?" His face was contorted with grief. "I must have been crazy. Please, oh, my darling, please say you forgive me." He buried his head in her lap and cried.

Elizabeth stroked his beautiful thick hair. "Hush," she whispered, "hush, now. It's all right. I understand." Her body throbbed with pain and her heart ached with sympathy for Lucas. She had seen him suffering like this only once, when she lost his son. It meant so much to him. His pain, she thought, was infinitely greater than anything she could feel.

The sound of Saint Michael's chimes reminded her that Catherine's time at the Gardens was almost over. "Come on, Lucas," she said, "let me help you upstairs. You can rest in the bedroom until suppertime. I'll stay with you. Come on now, dearest, you don't want Catherine to see her papa all upset."

The bells of Trinity Church rang a jubilant peal as Joe and Emily Simons came through the door. The wedding guests threw showers of rose petals after them while they ran to the waiting carriage. Emily tripped on the long train of her gown, but Joe caught her around the waist and kept her from falling.

"Thank you, Joseph," she said gratefully.

He handed her up into the carriage. "Shoot, honey," he laughed, "a husband's got to be good for something."

Their engagement had been a very happy period for him. Emily's father had opened the doors for his entry into the world he wanted, and the challenge of the ruthless manipulations that went on there sharpened his wits and made the blood surge in his veins. He felt like the master of his own life for the first time, with his greatest goals attainable.

In addition, he even learned to like Emily. Happiness did not make her beautiful, but it made her less shy, and conversation became easy for them. Joe never tired of listening to her exquisite voice, even when she was talking about things that bored him.

Which she seldom did. Emily was an intelligent young woman, and she wanted to please him. She watched his reactions carefully and soon learned that his consuming interest was business. She could not share that with him, but she was able to participate in his passion for music. Joe had gone to the Metropolitan Opera with the Elliott family one night as a duty. He had fallen in love with the opera. Emily made it a point to learn all about the productions they saw and the ones that were not in the Metropolitan's repertoire. She became Joe's guide. When they were alone together, she would even sing softly; her light, untrained voice was, so Joe declared, as beautiful as any professional's. Emily appreciated the compliment and accepted it, although she knew it was a lie. She loved Joseph, as she called Joe, with all her heart. He was the prince who had rescued her from her lonely, overprotected life in her father's guarded castle.

Joe recognized the gift of love that Emily offered, and he treasured it. No one had ever loved him before. He was sorry that he could not return it, and he vowed that Emily would never know that he did not love her. He found it easy, and gratifying, to make her happy. And her happiness reflected a satellite happiness in him.

The Elliott mansion was packed with guests, and the reception was exhausting. The newlyweds were leaving the next morning for the wedding trip to Europe that was the gift of Emily's aunt, Mrs. Dalton. When they arrived at the suite in the Fifth Avenue Hotel where they were to spend their wedding night, Joe suggested gently that perhaps they should simply go to sleep in their separate bedrooms. "I know you're tired, Emily, and I figure we've got our whole lives to be married in."

His bride's stricken face showed him his error. And so they slept not at all that night. Joe held Emily in his arms for hours until she was no longer afraid, and then the marriage was consummated quickly. Afterward he held her again, soothing her, reassuring her, and promising her that never again would she find that love caused physical pain.

By the time they returned from their six months on the Continent, they were both used to being married, and they were comfortable with each other. They had visited every great opera house in Europe, Emily had bought enough clothes to last her for a lifetime, and Joe had decided that his initial dislike of traveling abroad had been wrong. It was not so bad, if one had someone to share the strangeness with.

43

The young Simonses arrived back in New York in October, the best month of the year for that city. There was a snap in the air, an invigorating briskness that stimulated activity and increased the tempo of movement. "I feel great," Joe announced to his wife, "ready to get going, to be doing. I love this place. Everything's in a hurry here, just the way I feel."

He threw himself into the Wall Street maelstrom with such vigor that Emily saw very little of him, but she didn't mind. She was just as busy as he was. She was supervising the building and outfitting of their house, a French château in limestone on Fifth Avenue across from the still-young landscaping of Central Park. It was an enormous undertaking, but Emily was not intimidated by it. Joe's thoughtful attentiveness for the half-year of their marriage had given her a self-confidence that made her equal to anything. She coped with architects, decorators, antique dealers and gardeners with a ruthless high-handedness that matched her father at his most tyrannical. By May, the house was finished to the last detail of the gold-plated water spouts on the green marble bathtubs. It was the talk of New York; the dinner dance that showed it to Society received a half-page write-up in every Metropolitan newspaper.

Joe accepted the compliments of his guests with genuine delight. Although he insisted on giving Emily all the credit for the dazzling display of their home, he congratulated himself silently for the deals he had managed which made all the ostentation possible. His name was already a byword in the higher elevations of the financial world.

And the name was Simmons. He explained the changed spelling to Emily on the grounds of convenience. It was easier for people to pronounce their name properly when they read it on their cards. Emily agreed without even thinking about it; she agreed with anything and everything that Joe did.

But in fact, the change was not for the convenience of others at all. It was a baptism for Joe. He was his own man now, successful on his own terms. He needed no tricks, no trumped-up background. The glimpse of a red-haired girl in a crowd still made his heart lurch, but he had learned to live with that, and he was too busy for fruitless regrets. Charleston was far behind him. And, he liked to think, beneath him, too. It became dimmer every day.

"Why the hell does your brother have to send half our pitiful profits to that scallywag white-trash Simmons?" Lucas slammed the door to his wardrobe and thrust his arm into the coat he had taken from it.

Elizabeth pretended not to notice the rage he was in, but her hands shook and she dropped the hairpin she was trying to insert into her chignon. She was accustomed to Lucas' outbursts by now, and she had learned that the best way to handle them was to keep silent. It seemed to make things better. He had not hit her again, not even when they learned that Stuart's wife was expecting another baby while she, Elizabeth, was still unsuccessfully trying to get pregnant.

I wonder whatever happened to Joe Simmons, she thought now. He was the subject of Lucas' most recent outbursts against Pinckney, supplanting his fury at Pinny's lack of interest in expanding the mining operations. He had learned about Joe's continuing partnership position when he had demanded an increase in salary and Pinckney had had to refuse.

"He's probably dead and his lawyer's pocketing the money," Lucas fumed, "while I'm wearing a suit that's coming out at the elbows . . . Well, are you going to take all day? I guess you expect the train to wait for you." Elizabeth jabbed in a final hairpin and pronounced herself ready. They were going to Summerville for the new baby's christening. It was another boy, named Koger, after Henrietta's grandfather who had died peacefully in February.

The hour-long trip was exciting for Elizabeth. It was the first rail journey she had ever taken, so far as she could remember. Also, the smooth ride was infinitely preferable to Lucas' reckless driving in the buggy he had recently bought. Because they were in public, he was charmingly attentive to her and smilingly jovial with Pinckney. He was always at his best when there was an audience. All her friends envied Elizabeth her handsome, gallant husband and her perfect marriage.

It made her wonder about everyone she knew. At the christening party, she looked closely at Stuart and Henrietta, trying to imagine what their lives were really like. Their house was small and shabby, in spite of the beautiful furniture that Julia had given Stuart. Henrietta was no housekeeper, and Elizabeth could see telltale signs of poor management in the sloppy bearing of their maid and the junglelike tangle of weeds in the flower beds along the edge of the deep porch where they were sitting. But Stuart did not seem to notice, and, Elizabeth observed, he was as well-tended as a man could be. His linen was immaculate, his boots shining, his cigars and whiskey in a prominent place near his chair. Maybe

I've been wrong all this time, she thought, worrying about Lucas' comforts too little. Because she could not doubt that Henrietta and Stuart were happy. The more she watched them, the more she was convinced of it. And the more obvious it was that Henrietta placed Stuart all alone at the center of her world. Little Stuart was secondary, Koger still an unimportant personality, and the house a negligible quantity. Elizabeth remembered with shame that she had always been called "bossy" by Pinny and Joe. Even though they had said it with affection, the epithet was ugly. She made a silent promise to Lucas and to herself that she would change.

On the ride back to town, she took the first step on her new path. Pinckney suggested that they call on the Ansons, since their house was only a block away from the train station. Elizabeth started to say no; Catherine had the sniffles, and she was anxious to get home. But she bit back the response and waited for Lucas to decide. When he agreed, she pretended to be delighted.

Lucy opened the door to their knock. Elizabeth had not seen her for months, and she was shocked by Lucy's appearance. She was thinner than ever, and her light brown hair was thickly streaked with gray. Then, before Elizabeth's eyes, Lucy became younger and brighter-looking. It happened when she saw that Pinckney was among her callers.

Elizabeth glanced quickly at her brother and witnessed an equal metamorphosis. Her mind reeled. She had never before suspected that they were in love. She had been blinded by her youthful assumption that they were too old to have emotions and by her absorption in the complicated process of growing up. Now she was twenty-one and three years married—an adult by anyone's reckoning.

Yet, she thought, I still might have missed it if I hadn't been watching Stuart and Henrietta all day. I've got to stop thinking about myself all the time. Her load of guilt grew heavier.

"I'm so glad you all came by," Lucy said, ushering them up to the drawing room. "I'm full of the most wonderful news." She rushed to close the windows that overlooked Julia Ashley's noisy tenement, then tugged on the petit-point bell pull. "Sit down, do, please. I'll have Estelle bring tea and tell Mr. Josiah we have guests. He'll be so pleased."

Elizabeth barely heard the conversation that went on around her. She was preoccupied with her discovery and with her scrutiny of Lucy and Pinckney. The manners that had been instilled in her provided her with automatic smiles and polite responses, but her mind was not on what people were saying. She caught snatches: Little Andrew's future was settled . . . The Citadel was reopening in the fall, and he had been accepted . . . Yes, the Army instead of the law . . . suitable for a gentleman, and better for Little Andrew, who was no scholar . . . Andrew was holding his own

. . . only a slight stroke, one could hardly tell . . . sleeping right now . . . letter from Lavinia . . . Ned now president of his bank . . .

She contributed a description of Koger and the party and then resumed her observer's role What she saw between Pinckney and Lucy was so quietly beautiful that it made her want to cry. They did not do anything or say anything that was not completely appropriate to two old friends who met for a cup of tea, they were more attentive to the others than they were to each other, they did not exchange any private words or glances. And yet, they were touched with magic, bound by a reciprocal caring and tenderness that overflowed onto everyone and everything around them. That's what I want, Elizabeth's heart cried silently. She looked at Lucas. His eyes met hers, and he smiled. Hope flared brightly in her breast. Perhaps, she thought, if I try harder. Maybe, in time—after all, Pinny and Lucy are a great deal older.

Elizabeth held tenaciously to her hope and labored mightily to keep her vow to become more submissive. And for a while, it seemed to her that Lucas was happier and that their life together was improving. When she moved to the Island house for the summer, he spent more evenings there and fewer in town than in previous years, and she was sure that her attempts to please him were being rewarded. They walked the beach every day after supper, and on the weekends Lucas went into the ocean with her when she took Catherine for her morning swim. She was three, now, a roly-poly child with a sunny disposition and an enchanting, gurgling laugh. Even when she cried, which was rare, her face did not redden and become ugly. She was a miniature Mary Tradd. "Thank goodness," Elizabeth said often, "she's got the Ashley coloring. With that dark hair, she'll never have to worry about freckles." She herself worried all the time. Lucas did not want a spotty wife, and told her to keep out of the sun.

But the months went by, and every month brought a fresh disappointment. Elizabeth did not conceive. Lucas sent her to the doctor when they moved back to town in October, and she went, although she was humiliated to have to talk about anything so intimate to anyone, especially a man—and a man whom she knew, besides. Dr. Perigru had retired, and everyone now went to Dr. James de Winter, who had moved to Charleston from Augusta when he married Kitty Gourdin, Elizabeth's friend since childhood. Jim was a lot older, and he was a good doctor, but he was someone the Coopers saw socially all the time. After her embarrassing session at his office, Elizabeth could never feel comfortable again with Jim or even with Kitty.

Furthermore, it did no good. Lucas returned to his old taunts of "barren bitch," and Elizabeth felt her hopes die.

Hattie and Delia knew what was happening, as servants always do, and they worried with her. It was Delia who whispered to her one day that she knew a conjuh woman who could cure her.

Elizabeth recoiled as if she had been burnt. She had pushed the memory of her light-hearted adventure with Caroline Wragg to the back of her mind, but suddenly it all returned. She could smell the foul smoke that ended her visit to buy the love spell for Lucas and see the grotesque balloon face of Maum' Rosa and hear the awful promise that conjures always had a hidden price that was more than you could dream of. "Too much," she moaned, frightening Delia into retreat. That night, after Lucas had angrily used her body, Elizabeth prayed fervently for forgiveness. "I was so young, Lord, and I didn't know what I was doing. Please don't punish me by barrenness: The witch has punished me enough by giving me my wish to marry Lucas."

Her prayers went unanswered.

"It's because you don't want my child," Lucas hissed. "You're like a lump of clay or a stick of wood. You're freezing the life out of the life I put in you." His body was heavy on hers, and his panting words were heavy with the smell of whiskey.

"No, Lucas, no. I want a baby more than anything in the world." Elizabeth willed herself not to pull away from the savage thrusting and his bruising fingers on her shoulders. He seemed to enjoy gripping her arms and legs and buttocks with a ferocity that left the marks of his nails in her flesh. At first she had showed him the weals, expecting him to be sorry. But he had said only that she need not be alarmed; he'd never touch her where anybody could see the bruises. And he had twisted the soft fold on her abdomen with such brutality that she had almost fainted.

Lucas completed the morning ritual and rolled away from her, across to his side of the big bed. Elizabeth got down from the bed, washed hurriedly and started dressing in the dark. Lucas would open the curtains after she went downstairs to see to his breakfast.

His voice was loud in the closed room. "There's a word for your problem, Elizabeth. It's called 'frigid.' A real woman isn't like you. A real woman welcomes a man. She helps him. She does things with her body that make him feel the way a man has a right to feel. I've had plenty, and I know. You're a poor excuse for a woman."

Elizabeth buttoned her shirtwaist with numb fingers. "Tell me what to do, Lucas, and I'll try to do it. I've told you that, I've begged you to tell me, but you never do. You just say the same thing over and over. That I'm no good. I'd be better if I knew how, but I just don't know. I'm sorry. Believe me, I'm sorry."

She did not cry. There were no tears left in her. The accusations had been going on ever since her birthday in November when Lucas had buried his hand in the bowl of ice cream and told her that it was just like her body. The relentless battering of his words had made her miserable at first. Then they had made her heart what he said her body was. She was cold, with no feeling anymore, only a dumb acceptance of her failure. All hope, all love for him, all pride—all were extinguished. When he was with her, she was a dead creature.

It did not show, no more than did the outer wounds he inflicted. She kept up her regular round of calls and parties, she laughed with her friends and flirted as expected with their husbands. She entertained well, corresponded punctually, arranged flowers beautifully, teased Pinckney about his receding hairline, and did everything that was expected of a busy young Charleston matron.

The only genuine moments of her day were the brief times allowed for a mother to spend with her child. She fed Catherine her breakfast, and at six she read her a story and tucked her into bed. Then she could bury her face in the sweet, soap-smelling softness of Catherine's neck and, when the round little arms hugged her close, her frozen heart could melt with a tidal wave of love. The child's wriggling embraces were the most important thing in her life. They kept her from giving up. As long as she had Catherine to love, she could resist the growing strength of the pull she felt toward the whirlpool center of the dizzying spiral staircase that dominated the house.

44

"A baby? You're sure?" Joe Simmons threw his head back and let out a Rebel yell that set the chandelier rattling. While the echoes of the outburst were still sounding in the corners of the gilded ceiling, he laughed and threw his arms around his wife. "I didn't think things could be any better, Emily. I was wrong. Now they're better than perfect."

I wouldn't have believed that things could get any worse, thought Elizabeth. What a fool I was. She flinched at the sight of the bruises on her body and turned away from the tall pier glass in the bedroom to get dressed. Stuart's third son, Anson, had been born on May 11, 1882. Lucas' drunken rage had been the most brutal ever.

She finished dressing, then went downstairs. The Coopers were having a supper party in the magnificent dining room that was the envy of all their friends.

"You're so lucky, Elizabeth," Sarah Waring said to her later that evening.

Elizabeth smiled brilliantly. "I know," she said.

On June first, Elizabeth moved to the Island with Catherine and Hattie. The first night, after everything was unpacked and put away, and the house was quiet except for Hattie's snores, Elizabeth stretched out in the hammock and let the lullaby of the breaking waves soothe her tortured nerves. It was the first time she had felt safe enough to relax; the birth of little Anson Tradd seemed to have triggered a demon in Lucas. He had not ceased his attacks on her for the entire three weeks before she left town.

He had not beaten her again. The physical violence occurred only when he drank too much. Instead, he assaulted her verbally, in a terrifying contemptuous voice. And to the earlier accounts of her failure as a wife, he added a new accusation, that she was unfaithful to him. The reason she was so cold to him, Lucas insisted, was that she spent her passion on other men.

The strong ocean winds were cold. Elizabeth woke with a start, finding herself shivering. She had not intended to fall asleep, she was cramped from head to toe, and her teeth were chattering. But she felt scoured clean of fear by the wind and really rested for the first time in what seemed like years. A tiny, irrepressible bubble of happiness broke in her weary heart. At least for the summer, she could live free of fear. Pinckney was going to be at the beach with her. I suppose I should feel guilty, she thought. He's coming because his fever has been coming back again. I should be sorry that he's sick instead of glad that it makes him take a rest. But her soul rejoiced.

She struggled out of the sagging hammock and went to the back door. "Here, kitty," she called softly. A paler gray shadow came out from the darkness under the porch. Elizabeth picked up the warm, fluffy form and held it to her. "This will be our house, Mossy," she said. "You can stay inside instead of out. Lucas isn't here to make the rules." Mossy rumbled approval.

Elizabeth had never seen an attack of malaria; when Pinckney underwent one the day after he arrived, she was sure he was dying, although he promised her that the racking chills were normal and that he would be better by morning. She spent the long hours at his bedside, and the predicted withdrawal of fever was a moment of healing for her as well as for Pinckney. She was able to cry again. The relief she felt was so strong that it broke through the shell of numbness that she had built around her emotions, and all the pain and fear and sorrow poured out in a protracted storm of weeping. Afterward she, like Pinckney, fell into a deep, exhausted sleep.

The following day, she looked at her brother with fresh eyes. He had, she knew, first contracted the disease the year the mining began at Carlington. That meant that he had been its victim for fifteen years. And in all that time, he had never complained nor had he failed, even once, to take care of the myriad responsibilities of the family. It made her feel very small and selfish to brood so much about her own problems. In comparison, she believed, they were unimportant.

"Pinny," she said impulsively, "I love you an awful lot."

He looked surprised and pleased. "Why, thank you, Baby Sister. I'm mighty fond of you, too."

Elizabeth looked at his thinning hair and the deep lines that bracketed his pale mouth. Her mind did rapid arithmetic, and she realized, with astonishment, that Pinckney was thirty-nine years old. He looked much older, which shocked her.

"You need some sun," she said briskly. "You've been shut up in that office so long you look like a fish belly." She rejected the vague, half-formed plans she had made to confide in Pinckney about her personal hell. He had to get better; he did not need additional worry.

Pinny laughed. It made him look young again. "Sometimes, Elizabeth, you sound as sweet and tactful as Aunt Julia. It's like a tonic, nasty going down but good for you. You're right. I've got to work my muscles instead of my head and let the sun and water get the poison of commerce out of my system."

He began that very morning, with a swim and a long walk on the beach. He sunburnt and peeled, and he seemed to shed years when he shed his old skin. With each passing week, he grew stronger and browner and leaner. Elizabeth watched the transformation with joy.

She, too, was undergoing a sort of rebirth, although she did not realize it. The relaxed life of Island summers made few social demands; she had almost every day to herself, and she kept Hattie busy with meals and laundry so that she could spend hours with Catherine. Together, she and Pinny spoiled the little girl outrageously. At four, Catherine was a chubby little bundle of energy and affection. She responded to the adults' attention with tinkling laughter and flowerlike kisses by the hundreds. Elizabeth, in turn, responded to the presence of unqualified love from her daughter and her brother by becoming almost as childlike as Catherine when she was with her. She splashed in the water, built sandcastles, collected shells with Catherine as if they were equals.

At the end of the day, when Catherine was put to bed, Elizabeth reverted to proper young matron. But she was a happy proper young matron. She fixed supper herself; Hattie was getting too old for such a long day. Pinckney's appetite, sharpened by salt air and exercise, was a compliment to her cooking, and she enjoyed preparing his favorite foods.

After supper they sat on the porch in the long twilight and watched the color fade from the sky. They talked a little, about Catherine, about their mother's latest letter, about Stuart and his growing family, about Julia and her remarkable stamina at sixty-five. For the most part, they simply shared a comfortable silence. The sixteen-year difference in their ages precluded any exchange of confidences or any real understanding of each other. They could share affection, and that was enough.

Lucas was in complete charge of the company in Pinckney's absence, and he used the added work as an excuse to come to the Island only on weekends. With Pinckney for an audience, he became the perfect husband, attentive and charming. And the perfect father, delighting in Catherine's company and proud of her growing skills at swimming, talking, running and drawing pictures.

"It's near scandalous the way Lucas dotes on that child," said Pinny after one weekend. "She wraps him around her little finger even worse than you used to do me."

Elizabeth smiled and agreed. But she felt a cold hand squeeze her heart. Lucas was playing a role. She knew it, and it made her uneasy. He had a strange glitter in his eye sometimes, a look of malicious satisfaction, and she did not know what it meant.

Before the summer was over, she learned; Lucas had found the way to hurt her the most. He took Catherine from her. He began by bringing presents when he came on weekends. Then he started making the trip one or two evenings a week, always with candy or a toy in his pocket. Catherine soon learned to listen for his whistle at the door, and she would run from Elizabeth to him.

Bedtime, always Elizabeth's special moment with her daughter, was no longer a quiet period of reading from a story book. Lucas played games, rode Catherine on his shoulder, tickled her, let her pummel him in pillow fights, and tucked forbidden treats of cookies or candies under her pillow. Catherine became so overexcited that she woke, screaming, from nightmares and began wetting the bed.

Elizabeth did not even try to reason with Lucas. She knew him too well. On the nights he was at the beach, Catherine would push Elizabeth away and demand that Papa put her to bed. It cut through Elizabeth like a knife. And Lucas smiled.

Pinckney realized nothing. He did notice that Elizabeth gradually lost some of her brightness, and he asked her if anything was wrong. She reassured him and set to work to rebuild the facade that had crumbled. Little by little, she ceased to feel. Even Catherine's preference for Lucas did not hurt quite so much. She had become numb again.

With the extraordinary sensitivity that animals have to the atmosphere around them, Mossy suddenly staked a claim to Elizabeth's lap. She was annoyed at first; Mossy was a big cat now, heavy, and shedding in the summer heat. But as time passed, she found the steady purring a comfort. When Lucas was not there, she took Mossy to bed with her, and she held the vibrating small body close to her breast as if it were a life supporter in a stormy sea.

Inevitably, the days shortened, the nights turned chilly, and the moment came for the move back to town. Pinckney, now strong and fever-free, supervised the transfer. When they reached Elizabeth's house, she hugged him so ferociously that he frowned. "What is it, Baby Sister? Tell Pinny."

"I just hate to say good-bye. The summer's been so wonderful."

Pinckney peered closely at her, but she looked fine. "It was wonderful," he said. "We won't let so much time pass again without being together. Remember, I'm right down the street. And I still expect to be invited for Sunday dinner." He kissed her, and was gone.

"I've found me a woman who appreciates me," Lucas said the first morning after she was home. "You're not the only one who can stray from the marriage bed." Elizabeth kept her face immobile, and she looked down so that he could not see the relief in her eyes. If he believed that his unfaithfulness hurt her, he would, she hoped, keep it up. Lucas taunted her with phrases of admiration that he quoted from his mistress and tried to make her beg him to tell her the woman's name.

"She's a friend of yours, Elizabeth, somebody you see all the time at your stupid morning tea parties, somebody you think likes you. Well, she doesn't. None of them do. She told me so." Lucas grabbed her arm. "Don't you want to know who it is?"

"Yes," said Elizabeth. "Please tell me." She tried to put conviction in her masquerade.

Lucas pushed her from him. "You'll just have to wonder," he said with a laugh. "Every time you look at a friend of yours, you'll have to wonder if she's the one who knows about you, about what a cheating, frigid bitch you are. And if she's told the others. You can think about that while I go out to meet her. She waits for me every morning. After her husband leaves for work and before you chattering harpies get together. She can't get enough of me. Sometimes she sneaks out to meet me after he's asleep. Her whole life is built on waiting until I have some time to spare for her. Think of that when you're playing cards next time. Your partner may be the one who's crazy about your husband."

Elizabeth clasped her hands and twisted them as if she were distraught. "Please don't go, Lucas," she made herself say.

He responded by slamming the door behind him as he left. Elizabeth sagged with relief.

She did wonder, of course. It meant nothing to her that Lucas was having an affair. Jealousy played no part in her distress. But her pride in herself was wounded. She had kept up a good front through all the years of increasing misery, and she felt stripped bare of her defenses. She no longer valued the envy of her friends, but she would bitterly resent their pity. Did Lucas brag about beating her? Did his mistress brag about taking him away from her? Her social life became an ordeal of trying to find hidden meanings in her friends' words and expressions. But she kept her head high and a smile on her face. If she had nothing but her pride, she would make that do. She would not let Lucas take that from her.

As he had taken Catherine. When they returned to the city, he alternated between drowning the little girl in attention and ignoring her. He would take her from Hattie when they were at the Gardens and drive off in the buggy for wild races up East Battery. Hattie could insist on her rights as dah when Elizabeth wanted to change Catherine's routine, but she couldn't argue with "The Mister." She could only complain to Elizabeth, which she did at length. "That child, she look up every time a wheel turn to see if it her papa. When he come, she near wild to go and when he don't come, she little face all broke up. It too pitiful, Miss 'Lizabeth."

Elizabeth agreed, but she could not say so. One did not discuss one's husband with the servants. Or anybody else. She had to watch Catherine's bewilderment when Lucas pushed her away and her rapture when he noticed her. She had to try to soothe the hurt when he did not come to the child's third-floor room at bedtime and she had to stand by, quiet, when he did clatter up the stairs with shouts of "Where's my Cathy? Who's keeping her from me?" And Catherine ran to meet him, forgetting her mother's existence.

Hattie disapproved of Lucas' effect on Catherine, but she boasted about his devotion. "There ain't a man on this earth," she told the other dahs, "who love he child same like Mister Cooper. He crazy for she."

"Will you look at that?" The stiffly starched nurse sniffed with outrage. "The man must be crazy." Joe Simmons was standing in the door of the hospital nursery with a uniformed, caped, and veiled woman who was unmistakably an English nanny. Superiority radiated from her.

"This is Miss Hodgkins, nurse," he said happily. "We're taking Victoria home today." The nanny looked down her nose at the cribs, the blankets, the room and most of all the staff.

"You may bring me Miss Simmons," she said regally. The nurse found herself hastening to obey.

Emily had not had an easy pregnancy or delivery. There would be no more children. But Joe declared that one baby as perfect as Victoria was already more than any human couple deserved. They would just love her enough for a family of ten. He hired Miss Hodgkins, who had never before consented to go to a family not in Burke's Peerage, and put Emily's doctor on salary, to live in the house until she was completely recovered. He would have driven through the streets, tossing gold coins out the window of the carriage in celebration, but Emily said it would embarrass her. His happiness was almost too great to be contained.

Victoria was born in November. Emily giggled to her friends that they would probably have to move to a bigger house after Christmas. Joseph was already filling up the ballroom with presents for "his girls."

Elizabeth looked at the shambles of paper and ribbon in the drawing room, and for an instant she felt a glow of pleasure. This was what Christmas should be: all the family together and a jumble of children alight with the thrill of Santa Claus. The adults—Pinckney, Julia, Lucas, Lucas' parents, Henrietta, Stuart, Mary Tradd Edwards, and her husband—looked on indulgently at Catherine and her three little cousins. They were all having more fun with the wrappings than with the toys.

But then she fell back into her customary contained resignation.

Soon they would have dinner. Then Mary and Adam would take the train to the North, the elder Coopers would leave in their wagon, and Stuart would load his aunt and his family in the surrey for the ride to the Barony, where they would visit until the courts opened again. Pinny would take the streetcar up to the Ansons', and Elizabeth would be left with Lucas. There would be a price to pay, she knew, for those bright red heads and strong little bodies now building a tunnel of tissue paper on the floor. In the past, Lucas had made her suffer for each male child born to her brother, and now they were here, right under his eye, in his own house.

She forced the thought away and entered the room. The pungent Christmas scent of tangerines and pine branches was an exhilarating perfume, worth almost any price.

She held that belief to her all through the dinner, even when she noticed that Lucas was drinking a great deal, and through the farewells. She was not sorry to see her mother and stepfather leave. They were virtual strangers to her, especially Mary. She had aged so much in the three and a half years since her last visit that Elizabeth hardly recognized her. She looked much older than Julia, although she was, in fact, fifty-seven to her sister's sixty-five. But, then, Julia never changed. Except that she had softened a bit. She obviously adored Stuart's boys, although she did not go so far as to touch them.

Mary, on the other hand, would hardly let Catherine alone. She had been smothering the child with hugs and kisses for the entire week of her visit. Catherine was, she declared, her very own most precious. She even looked like her. It was true. Catherine's dark curly hair made her look like a changeling in the room full of Tradds.

Lucas fastened on that difference when he launched into his venomous tirade after all the guests were gone. "I'm a blond, and you're a redhead," he sneered. "Where did she come from, that child you passed off as mine?"

Elizabeth was appalled. Even Lucas could not have such a sink hole of a mind. "Mama said it, Lucas, she's got the Ashley coloring. I must be more Ashley than Tradd, that's all. And your mother's dark, too. It's surprising you're so fair yourself. Usually brown wins over blond in children."

"The boy would have been blond. If he had lived. Little Lucas."

Elizabeth saw the pattern taking form. He was going to blame her again for their son's death. It was a familiar theme. She braced herself for his anger. It had become so much a part of her life that she had difficulty remembering a time when Lucas spoke without wounding. She hardly heard his words now; her responses were automatic, wooden, as lifeless as the heart within her.

Even when he got drunk and struck her, she barely felt the pain. It was simply something else unendurable which she had learned to endure. At the end, there was always the warm retreat into unconsciousness. She waited for it, welcomed it, felt her only happiness in the brief lifting moment when she began to slide into the darkness. Other than that, she felt nothing: no loathing when Lucas mounted her morning and evening, no envy when he called Catherine to him and looked triumphantly at Elizabeth's empty arms when their child ran away from her.

She continued to perform her duties as a young wife and mother, running the house, entertaining, paying and receiving calls. The structure of her role gave a pattern to her days, and she was perpetually busy. Too busy and too tired and too numb to notice that Lucas' outbursts were becoming more frequent and less controlled as time passed. She did not even feel any alarm when he dragged her out into the moonlit garden in February to present her with her "Valentine."

Mossy's soft body was lying in the center of the brick path, its shiny fur dull in death. "I broke her neck," Lucas said quietly, "and I can break yours just as easily. Don't forget that."

Elizabeth told herself that she should mourn. She had loved the little cat. But she had no tears left, and no ability to feel anything. Not even fear.

45

During the party at Sarah Waring's, Elizabeth tried not to look too often at Lucas. He showed no change at all; his step was sure, his diction clear, his laughter easy. But she knew, from his reddening cheeks and the increasing brightness in his eyes that he was drinking too much. She forced herself to pay attention to the accounts of babies teething and incompetent servants that were the standard conversational fare on the ladies' side of the room. In the distance, Saint Michael's chimed the half hour.

"Just listen to the time," said Kitty de Winter. "Who's brave enough to break up the brave hunters?" There was a flurry of giggles and rustling skirts, while the wives went in a group to claim their husbands. Elizabeth joined them, smiling brilliantly, saying the required things about the selfishness of the men and the wonders of the party. The men rallied on cue, complimenting the hostess, reaffirming the meeting place for the next hunt.

And then she and Lucas were in the buggy on the way home. He whipped up the horse when they reached Meeting Street, and they sped, tilting from side to side, over the cobbles. Elizabeth held on. If she asked him to slow down, he would, she knew, go even faster. "Damned nag," Lucas muttered. "Not fit for glue." Now that they were alone, his speech was slurred.

While Lucas put the horse and buggy away, Elizabeth slowly climbed the stairs to the third floor. The night-light flickered in the nursery. Hattie and Catherine were both sleeping peacefully, but the room was too cold. Elizabeth closed the window and pulled the covers up higher over Catherine's rounded rump. Then she made sure the doors were closed so that they would not hear Lucas, and she went down to the bedroom.

She heard the front door close, then the sound of a decanter clinking on glass in the dining room. It was going to be a bad night. She undressed, folded her clothes neatly, put on her nightdress, washed her face and sat down at her dressing table to loosen and braid her hair. Her movements were like a puppet's. When she heard footsteps on the stairs, she turned her back to the door.

"As usual, my dear," said Lucas, "you are the picture of the welcoming wife." He stood behind her for a minute, then grabbed her hair in his two hands and wrenched it back, forcing her to look at him. "Look me in the eyes and simper, like you were doing to Jim de Winter," he growled.

"Lucas, please. I was just being polite."

"I'll bet you were. I'll bet you've been polite to him dozens of times. Is he the one? Or is it David Mikell? Or Charlie Johnson? Or all of them? Answer me!" He jerked her head from side to side. She felt a burning pain and heard a ripping sound. Lucas threw a handful of hair on the floor. "Maybe I should snatch you bald-headed. Then you'd find it more difficult to distribute your favors."

He freed her hair and pushed her onto the floor. Elizabeth covered her breasts with her arms.

"Whore." He kicked her stomach, then her protecting arms, probing with the toe of his boot for the soft, tender flesh behind them. Elizabeth began to choke. She fought for breath.

"Stop that!" Lucas screamed. "Don't you laugh at me. I said stop it!" His closed fist caught her on the ear, and a great roaring filled her head. She felt a warm trickle of blood run down her neck. Her throat vibrated with spasm.

The protective layers of numbness fell away from her, then. The shell around her emotions cracked, and she felt a wave of consuming terror. Lucas had hit her on the head. He never did that, never struck her where the bruises would show. He never lost all control of himself. Never before.

"Lucas," she croaked. She put her hand to her head and held out her blood-stained fingers, imploring him.

"That's right. Beg. Beg me to forgive you." His mouth twisted with hate. "You don't deserve it. I should beat the lying life out of you." Then, as an ultimate horror, he began to laugh. "It wouldn't take very long, you know. You'd strangle yourself before I hardly got started." His mood shifted, and his expression changed to one of tender concern. "Does your ear hurt, my darling? Come here and let me kiss it and make it well. You're sorry, aren't you? You're going to be a good girl. Come show me what a good girl you can be." His hands moved over her body, caressing. Elizabeth gasped for air. How could I not have seen it, she thought. Lucas is crazy. He's never been this way before. He's completely mad.

The rug's knotted fringe pressed against her bruised back when he pushed her flat and used her. She could hear his rasping breath and hissing abuse only dimly through the pulsating roar in her ear. At the moment of his climax, he shouted. "Bitch. Icy bitch."

Elizabeth felt his weight roll off her. Now I can faint, she thought. It's over. The comforting darkness began to close over her.

"Tell me," Lucas said, far above her. "Tell me his name or I'll kill you."

She opened her eyes. The relief she had felt disappeared and with it the slide into darkness. Lucas had a pistol.

His left hand tangled itself in her hair, increasing the agony of her wounded scalp and ear. The fingers twisted. "This time you won't slip away from me, you cold bitch. You'll tell me." He turned her head and inserted the barrel of the pistol into her uninjured ear. "I'll count to three. Then I'll blow your head off."

"Go ahead," Elizabeth said flatly. "I'd count it a blessing." She could bear no more; the thought of only one more brief agony and then rest eternal was like a golden promise.

"One."

Elizabeth closed her eyes.

"Two."

She heard the sharp click of the hammer cocking, noticed that her breath was coming easily at last.

"I mean to do it, Elizabeth." She did not respond. "You're making me do this. I gave you every chance." The pistol dug deeper into her ear. "Three." She waited, but there was only silence. Then the slow ratchet noise of the trigger moving. Elizabeth thought she should pray, but she was too tired. I'm ready, she said in her mind. A hollow metallic thud vibrated against her head. Lucas had tried to fire an empty chamber.

"Damnation," he roared. He tore the pistol from Elizabeth's ear and threw it across the room. It fell with a clang on the marble hearth. "Cheated, cheated by my own pistol. Cheated by my wife. Cheated by the Army. Cheated by your Goddamn brother." He threw his head back and howled like a wild beast. "Where is my son? You even cheated me out of my son. A daughter. What man wants a daughter?"

Elizabeth heard the madness in his voice. Against her will, her mind came back from stupor, sent a wakening surge of alarm through her veins. He had not mentioned Catherine since Christmas. But he was different tonight. She opened her eyes to look for Lucas.

He was on his knees by the fireplace, scrabbling in the ashes for his revolver. Elizabeth dragged her battered body upright. "No, Lucas, no." She could only whisper.

He turned. "I'll come back for you," he snarled. "I'll find some bullets, and then I'll come back. I don't need anything but my hands for Catherine."

"Lucas!" Now she could scream. "Lucas, stop. She's your baby. You love her."

"Yes," he said. "I love her." His body crumpled into a heap, and he began to wail. "My little baby." His shoulders shook as he cried.

He lifted his head. His face was contorted, eyes and mouth dripping tears and spittle. "You're trying to trick me," he said. "You always tried to trick me. You harlot, how do I know she's mine? How did I even know my son was mine and not some other man's?" He struggled to his feet and stumbled to the door.

"Lucas! Where are you going?"

"To look at Catherine, to see if she's mine."

"You can't. Lucas!" He ignored her, struggled with the doorknob. "Lucas, stop, please, you'll scare her to death."

The door flew open with a bang. Lucas stood outlined in the light from the hall, his face gleaming with sweat, his eyes glowing with madness. He lurched toward the stairs.

Every sensation of pain and weakness left Elizabeth. She had only one idea, one reason for being alive; she had to stop him. She ran to the fireplace, seized the poker, and chased after Lucas. He was clutching the banister to steady himself as he climbed. Elizabeth pushed past him, ran up three more steps and stood between him and Catherine.

"Lucas," she said, "if you take one more step, I'll kill you, so help me God."

"Get out of my way." He rose toward her.

With deliberate attention to her aim, Elizabeth brought the poker crashing down on Lucas' upturned head, hitting his forehead in the exact center.

His arms flew out and his body tipped backward over the delicate mahogany ellipse of the staircase. She covered her ears and waited while he fell to the floor far below.

Then she looked down at the sprawled, broken body. "And may you rot in Hell," she whispered.

From above she heard a tiny sound; she looked up, terrified. It was quiet. Just Catherine kicking off her covers, she thought. I'll have to pull them up again. She felt a dangerous desire to laugh at the small, everyday concerns that were first in her mind when she was standing there, still holding the weapon with which she had murdered her husband. I'll have to think about this, she said to herself. First thing, I have to put the poker back. She stumbled into the bedroom.

Her mind worked with extraordinary clarity, sifting appearances, consequences, arriving at what she had to do and what she had to say. First, the pistol. She hid it on a shelf.

Then she washed the blood from her ear and neck, put on a fresh nightdress, brushed and braided her hair. She added the clump that Lucas had torn out to the covered jar of loose hairs on her dressing table.

I'm done, she thought. Now I have to look at Lucas. Her throat constricted. Stop that, she told herself. Later you can choke to death if you want to. Now you have to arrange an accident. Catherine cannot grow up in a world that whispers that her mother killed her father.

She crept downstairs to the sprawled obscenity of death. I can't look, she whimpered in her mind. But she did. Lucas seemed to be asleep, except that his eyes were open. Don't stare at me, Lucas, I had to do it. Don't stare at me like that. She turned her head to escape his eyes.

The door to the dining room was open. Elizabeth knew, when she saw it, what she should do. She sniffed the air. Yes, Lucas reeked of whiskey. She got the near-empty decanter and the glass he had used and carried them back to the hallway. She pressed the glass into his outflung hand. It was still warm; when she touched it, her heart pounded terribly and her ear began to bleed again. She covered it with her hand to stop the blood before it could stain her nightdress.

Then she crept up to the landing on the second floor which led to their bedroom. She placed the decanter, on its side, on the step just below the landing. The smell of whiskey and the pounding in her ear made her dizzy. Almost finished, she told herself. You can do it.

She staggered to the bedroom then to wash away the fresh blood. She needed both hands. She found her scissors, took them to the stairs and used them to pry up a corner of the landing's carpet. I'll have to get that nailed down again right away, she thought. A person really could trip and fall. Again, she felt a desire to laugh. "Stop it," she whispered aloud.

The sound snapped her back to reality. She went to her room and closed the door. Delia would arrive before anyone was up. She would wake Elizabeth and Hattie and keep Catherine from seeing anything.

Done! She thought. The three steps up to the bed suddenly seemed as high as a mountain. The pain in her head and back and stomach seized her, returning with added force now that the immediate crisis had passed.

I'm not going to make it, she thought. She felt dreadfully weak.

You must, she told herself.

She fell into the enveloping softness of the cloudlike mattress and sank down, down to oblivion. Before the welcome darkness blotted out everything that had happened, Elizabeth fought back to momentary consciousness. "Dear Heavenly Father," she said, "forgive me."

At the funeral, everyone remarked on Elizabeth's remarkable composure. She was as still as a statue. Catherine squirmed in her arms until Pinckney lifted her down and held her hand. Then she leaned against his leg and sobbed.

"See how she misses her papa," said Kitty de Winter to her husband. "Lucas was such a good father. He doted on that child."

Several months later, when it became known that Elizabeth was expecting, everyone agreed that it was a tragedy that the new baby would never know his devoted father.

BOOK SEVEN

1882-1886

46

"Cousin Josiah, I need your help." Pinckney put the iron box he was carrying on Mr. Anson's desk. "And I'd like Lucy in on this too, please, sir. I need her advice."

"Of course, son. Anything we can do, we will. I'll call Lucy. Sit down."

Pinny collapsed into a chair. "I think we might want to have a bottle of something handy, too, Cousin Josiah. That strong box is full of strong surprises."

Pinckney's prediction was right. Before the afternoon was over, even Lucy was filling her glass with Madeira.

The box had belonged to Lucas Cooper; it contained the documents and correspondence that were too private to be kept in the office safe. They made up a sordid picture of debt and dishonor. There were past-due bills from his tailor, his bootmaker, the butcher, the grocer, the wine shop, the livery stable, the Charleston Club, and Dr. de Winter. Lucas had not paid anyone for almost a year.

But he had paid the rent on a house on State Street. "I went to see it," Pinckney said. "A young woman lives there in fine style. Including these." He pointed to receipted bills from the jeweler and a women's clothing store. "Lucas moved her there from Chalmers Street."

The mortgage payments on the house where he lived with Elizabeth were also overdue, close to default.

"This," said Pinckney, "is the worst." He picked up a battered pasteboard square. "It's the pawn ticket for Elizabeth's diamond necklace. Lucas bought the house with the money he got for it. He didn't mortgage it until later, when he had the other household to run. That was my mother's wedding necklace. To think of it in a greasy pawn shop! My father gave it to her."

And Shad Simmons gave it to Elizabeth, thought Lucy, but she said nothing. Shad was a subject Pinny refused to talk about, even with her.

The money was not the main problem, said Pinckney. He'd find some way to meet Lucas' obligations, no matter how many years it took him. What he was chiefly worried about was Elizabeth. She could not be shielded from the knowledge that her husband had left her penniless, because his parents were demanding an accounting. "He borrowed money from them, you see, and they want it back. They refuse to believe that he died in debt. At least they refuse to believe me. They're threatening to sue Elizabeth. They blame her for the accident, say she drove Lucas to drink. I just don't know what to do. She can't take much more, poor thing. She's like a ghost now. She moved back with me right after Lucas was found, just took Catherine by the hand and walked down the street. She stays shut up in her old room on the third floor, rocking in a chair from the piazza. It reminds me of the time when I came back from the War. She's all locked up in herself."

Lucy set her glass down with a bang that almost broke its stem. "That won't do," she said. "It's bad for her and bad for Catherine and bad for the baby that's coming." And for you, darling Pinny, she thought, it's much harder than for Elizabeth. "I'll talk to her. Tell her I'll call tomorrow."

"You're an angel, Lucy," Pinckney said. "You always were closer to her than anyone. But what are you going to tell her?"

"Leave that to me. It's women's work. You two men do whatever you have to do about the business part."

"She wants you to sell the house and everything in it," Lucy said when she came down from Elizabeth's room the next day, "and she invited me to stay for dinner. She's going to be all right."

Then, seeing Pinckney's pleading eyes, Lucy told him about her marathon talk with his sister. At first Elizabeth had seemed not to hear what Lucy was saying. She was like a statue. "I suppose she didn't want to give up her mind's picture of a hero husband. I thought I wasn't getting through to her at all. I have to confess, Pinny, it made me hopping mad. After all, she's not the first young woman to be widowed. Grief is a luxury when there are other people to be considered. So I just snapped at her. 'Your husband was keeping a woman,' I said, 'a high-yellow fancy woman. He spent all his money on her, and yours, too.' Well, I'll tell you, Elizabeth's head swung around as if I'd slapped her. I was sure I'd gone too far.

"Then she started asking questions about the woman, and it was just like a spring thaw. I don't know why, but she seemed to feel better. I guess jealousy killed some of her grief. She was positively smiling when we got to talking about the necklace. So I took a chance and told her the story about it. She actually laughed. She's going to be all right, Pinny, she really is."

"What story?"

"Come on, Pinny, you know."

"No, I don't. Tell me."

"Good heavens, everybody in Charleston knows that story. Miss Emma told me ages ago. Your papa hung it around your mama's neck and said it was big enough so she wouldn't need a nightdress to cover her and heavy enough so she couldn't get away when he came after her. She used to wear it to bed with nothing else on at all . . . Why, Pinny, you're blushing. Wait till I tell Elizabeth . . . All right, all right, don't scowl like that. I won't tell."

Upstairs, Elizabeth sat in her chair with her brows knotted in concentration. So it wasn't a friend of mine after all, she thought. I don't have to go on thinking that everyone is laughing at me. There's no need to laugh and laugh like a baboon to convince people that I'm happy and that I don't care what they're saying. They're not saying anything. That's a burden gone . . . . I don't suppose I'll ever be free of the weight of having done murder, but I can learn to carry that. At least I carry it alone. If Lucas had ruined us, if we'd been turned out of the house, everyone would have been shamed, Pinny, Catherine, the whole family. I'm glad he's dead. I'll go to Hell for it, but I'm glad. Thank You, Dear Lord, for sending Lucy to tell me. I'll be grateful to You and to her for the rest of my life.

Elizabeth took Catherine to the Island that year earlier than they had ever gone before. The little girl was shattered by her father's death; she cried for him constantly, and when she passed her old home on the way to the Gardens, she became so upset that Hattie could not console her. The beach, Elizabeth hoped, would act as a healing agent. Catherine loved to play in the sand and the water; also Lucas had been at the beach house so little that it bore no real traces of him. "I'll make it up to you, Catherine," she whispered after Catherine cried herself to sleep at night. "I promise. I'll make it up to you."

While she devoted herself to mending the damage Lucas' death had done to her daughter, Pinckney and Josiah Anson busied themselves with patching up his financial ruin. Saint Finbar's Cathedral bought the Russell House and turned it into a convent. An antique dealer from Baltimore took the furnishings. With the proceeds, Pinckney was able to redeem the necklace, which he locked in the office safe. Lucas' creditors agreed to take interest-earning notes, which Pinckney could pay when he was able. The only real difficulty was with the Coopers. Josiah Anson was in daily battle with their lawyer.

"He's wearing himself out," Pinckney said to Lucy. "I should never have gotten him involved in this."

"Nonsense," she replied. "It's the best thing you could possibly have done for him. He's got fire in his eye and color in his cheeks. The past few years have been bad—after Miss Emma died, he was like a lost soul; then, when he was himself again, he discovered that he had almost no work to do. Some of his clients found other lawyers when he wouldn't help them, others died, most of them turned all their affairs over to their children, and of course the children go to their own friends who are practicing law. Mr. Josiah's generation is just about at an end. He's seventy, after all.

"Now you present him with a good, wild fight. It makes him young again. I haven't seen him this lively since the last Saint Cecelia. He still brightens up when it gets close to time for the Ball. It's good he's President. The other Managers have to come here for the planning meetings. It keeps him from feeling so far away from everything."

Pinckney felt a familiar pang. He hated the idea of Lucy's isolation, and he privately thought that Josiah Anson was wrong to stay in the house on Charlotte Street just because his wife had begged him to. But he knew that Lucy would allow no criticism of her father-in-law. And he would never dare speak to Mr. Anson. The old man's erect carriage was supported by his pride, and if the pride made him touchy, it was, nevertheless, a support that no one wanted to see collapse.

At least he had Little Andrew. The boy was happy at The Citadel, away from the sickroom atmosphere of his home and the rapid deterioration of its neighborhood. He had just completed his second year, and he was feeling his oats as an upperclassman, with an officer's stripe on the sleeve of his uniform. He was a handsome boy, too, likely to become a debutante's darling the next season.

While his father was slowly dying, almost totally paralyzed now by a second stroke. Pinckney tried not to think about it, but Andrew's death was an inevitability. When Lucy and I finally marry, we'll move Cousin Josiah downtown with us whether he likes it or not, he had decided. Now, with Elizabeth back home, there would be a problem about space. But that could be solved. Somehow.

Lucy was talking to him. Pinckney started. "I'm sorry, dearest, what did you say?"

"I said that you're losing a button from your coat. Shall I sew it on before it falls off forever?"

Pinckney smiled. It made him extremely happy when some small domestic act provided a preview of the life to come for them. "I'd appreciate it, ma'am," he said.

Lucy's heart flooded with warmth. She knew what he was thinking.

The battle with the Coopers was over before Elizabeth moved back from the Island in October. When Pinckney told her that there would be no law suit, she just nodded; clearly she was not very interested. "They're no longer part of my life," she said. "I want nothing to do with them."

Elizabeth was no longer the wan, zombie-like creature who had departed the city in May. She was brown as an Indian, with a sunburnt nose and a thousand freckles. She had spent as much time as she wanted in the sun.

Catherine, too, was tanned. And she had recovered from her tempestuous grief. Her mother's undivided attention had gradually blotted out her longing for her father. The two were inseparable. Even Hattie did not try to assert her authority. Catherine needed her mother. Even more, Elizabeth needed her little girl.

Elizabeth resumed her old role as lady-of-the-Tradd-house. Clara was not happy about it at first; she had been running the house and running Pinckney all alone since Hattie went to be Catherine's dah, and she had grown used to doing things her own way. But Delia flattered her, and she took over the housework. Clara soon found that the new routine suited her very well, even if Elizabeth did invade her kitchen too often to bake sweets for Catherine. "That child going be fat same like a blow fish," she grumbled.

Delia cackled. "Trying to keep up with she mama, must be."

Indeed, Elizabeth's pregnancy was quite apparent. She could not have gone out in public even if she wanted to. Which she did not. Catherine was her sole interest.

In November Adam Edwards telegraphed the startling news that Mary was dead. Suddenly, from a heart attack. Pinckney notified the family, and there was a flurry of telegrams, arguing about the funeral and her place of burial. Julia was the most vehement. Her sister was an Ashley, she said, whatever her faults. She would be laid to rest in the family vault at the Barony. And she would be buried after a funeral at tiny Saint Andrews Church. It had been opened for Stuart's wedding; it could be opened again for his mother's funeral.

Stuart supported his aunt's position, at the top of his lungs.

Pinckney acted as peacemaker, intermediary and message boy. At the end of a long day and night, a compromise was reached. The family would travel to Bryn Mawr for Mary's funeral, then bring her home for burial.

Elizabeth, of course, could not go because of her condition. Thank goodness, she thought privately. I don't want to go. I hate funerals, and I hardly know Adam Edwards. For that matter, she realized, I hardly knew my mother, and I don't miss her at all. How terribly sad. I'll never leave Catherine the way she left me. I must have been a horrible child if my own mother would go off without me. But that doesn't mean I have to be a horrible mother. I'm going to be the best mother in the whole world.

She repeated her vow on December twentieth when the baby was born.

It was a boy, a fat, yelling, bald-headed, red-faced, little boy. "I suppose you'll name him after his father," said Dr. de Winter.

"Little Lucas?" said Elizabeth. "No, doctor, I'm not going to do that. Look at those tiny little two-hair eyebrows. They're the color of a new penny. This baby's name is Tradd."

47

"Now hold still, angel, and smile at Cousin Andrew," Elizabeth said for the fifth time. Young Andrew Anson clicked the shutter on his camera.

"I think that one will be just perfect," he said.

"May I stop smiling now, Mama?" called Catherine in a voice that was beginning to show a whining edge.

"Yes, sweetheart. You were a very good girl. We'll cut the cake now, and you get the first piece." Elizabeth hurried across the lawn.

It was Catherine's fifth birthday, and it had fallen on Easter Sunday this year. Two reasons to celebrate. The entire family had gone to church together and come back to the Tradd house for the birthday party. Lucy Anson brought her son and his camera to record the event. Everyone was fascinated. Photographs made outside of a studio were a new and marvelous thing.

Before the day was over, the whole family had been captured on film. Andrew had a real talent for photography. He managed, in spite of their stiff poses and self-conscious faces, to record them all in moments faithful to their personalities. For generations to come, Tradds would be able to look at their forebears and know what kind of people they were.

In the pictures, Pinckney and Stuart were toasting each other with the end-of-Lent toddy beloved of Charlestonians. The brothers were a study in similarity and contrast: the elder, taller, leaner, more supple, lounging against one of the columns on the ground-floor piazza; the younger, short and stocky, immovably planted in position, leaning forward with pugnaciousness even when he raised his glass. One clean-shaven, one bearded, but both with the Tradd thin, high-bridged nose, small, close ears and springy hair.

Julia Ashley was seated, her still-beautiful hands resting easily in her lap, thumbs touching index fingers as if they held invisible reins. She was thinner than ever, a thinness that came from tempering, like a rapier. Her face was all planes, the skin clinging to the prominent bones, defying the softening of time and the pull of gravity. Her hair was still dark, in spite of her sixty-seven years, and her back was as straight as a young tree. Only her eyes were old; they were old with the wisdom and endurance that enters the souls of those who live with the endless cycles of the earth and the trees.

Henrietta Tradd was a small, valiantly smiling figure barely visible behind the stair-step heads of her healthy little boys. The children all bore the imprint of the Tradd hair and ears.

Catherine was posed behind her birthday cake; she looked important, the birthday girl, conscious of her starring role and anxious to live up to the occasion. She was a pretty child, with dark ringlets that almost reached the lace-edged straps of her starched pinafore.

Elizabeth alone was not clearly etched. She had moved in response to some need of the baby in her arms, and her face was blurred. Her body, clad in a high-necked black mourning frock was soft and rounded with the exaggerated femininity produced by corset-nipped waist and the full breasts of the nursing mother. Tradd was almost invisible in cap and long-skirted baby dress. His tiny fist rested on his mother's shoulder.

They were a handsome, healthy family, with the Tradd energy and distinctive appearance dominating the Ashley imperiousness in numbers, but not in strength. Young Andrew Anson photographed them with love and admiration, pleased to be included by invitation and cousinship in the warmth of the simple festivities. After his duties with the camera were done, he joined Pinckney and Stuart for a toddy. He was twenty, now, and a man. Even in a family gathering like this one, in Charleston the men went off alone to talk about masculine things while the ladies saw to their comforts from a distance.

Later, when the children had been sent off with their dahs for their morning naps, Andrew was astonished by his cousin Pinckney, who deserted the conversation about the eight-point buck Stuart had shot to go talk to Lucy.

Lucy was surprised, too. "Joining the ladies?" she said. "Stuart must be talking politics."

"No, hunting. I got bored."

Lucy knew that Pinckney had not been bored at all; rather, he had experienced one of the infrequent agonies of loss that struck him when his guard was lowered. A man with only one arm could not fire a shotgun. For an instant she was furious with Stuart. Then she reminded herself that he could not be blamed. Pinckney's false arm in its sling had become so much a part of him that people forgot that he had not always had it. She tucked her hand under his good arm. "Walk me to the carriage house," she said. "I want to sniff the honeysuckle." They moved away from the ladies.

They did not need to talk. It was spring, they were together, that was enough.

Elizabeth looked at them over Henrietta's shoulder. Yes, she thought, the special thing I saw before is still between them. It was only a casual observation; she no longer hoped for any similar magic for herself. She no longer hoped for anything. It took all her energy to get through the days and nights with an outward appearance of normalcy. She had no strength left for emotions.

She concentrated on Henrietta's prattling. She was saying something about Little Stuart's birthday party. Her voice seemed to come from a distance. Elizabeth smiled mechanically and tried to listen. If she worked at it, she could bring the outside world close enough so that her withdrawal was not obvious. She had learned that in the year since Lucas' death. She could fool everyone. They all talked about how well she was recovering. She was the only one who knew that she had given up; at twenty-four, her life was over.

Sometimes, when it was such an effort of will to swallow the food that her body needed, she daydreamed about giving up altogether. It would be so easy, just to stop eating. But she couldn't do that. Catherine and Tradd needed a mother. She had to hold on until they were grown.

The children were her lifeline. Not only were they her reason for living; they were also her reward. Once in a great while, a consuming rush of tenderness would fill her when she was with them, and she would know, for a moment, what it felt like to be alive.

The days passed, and the weeks, and the months, blurred, blending into each other, all the same. Saint Michael's marked the hours as the spring flowers reached their peak, faded, and the roses took over the garden. The days grew longer, and then it was the season to move to the Island, where there was no time at all, only the slow tide moving up the beach, retreating, moving in, going out. The heat came and with it the crashing thunderstorms and the sharp rattle of rain on the tin roof.

The storms stirred Elizabeth's lethargic senses; she laughed, and she comforted Catherine's fright with songs and stories about quarrelsome cloud children throwing the lightning bolts that were their toys onto the floor of their room that was the earth. Tradd napped serenely through even the most violent storms.

In mid-September, the Island was evacuated. Elizabeth was annoyed. "Those sissy Yankee soldiers," she grumbled, "a little breeze and they start to shake." She had not experienced a hurricane in her lifetime. Hattie, who was thirty-five years older, was trembling so much that Elizabeth took Tradd from her arms. "We'd be a sight better off in the house, Hattie," she snapped, "than bouncing around on the ferry." She took Catherine's hand and marched out to the streetcar on which the Army Signal Corps had mounted the two red triangular flags warning of a gale. It was already crowded with other islanders. The officers in charge were up ahead, knocking on doors to alert the inhabitants.

"Good morning, Elizabeth," said Big Caroline Wragg. "Hand me the baby. Looks like you'll have to stand."

Elizabeth forgot her irritation. She could, at least, hear some news about her old friend Caroline from Caroline's mother.

The irritation returned, however, when the gale blew itself out that evening. "That miserable trip, Pinny, with Hattie moaning and carrying on the whole way, and for what? A few twigs blown off the trees. The whole thing is silly."

She pretended to listen to Pinckney's patient explanation of wind velocity, the Robinson anemometer and the danger of being isolated on an island if the wind had increased to a whole gale or hurricane. What really upset her was that she was losing two precious days at the beach. There was no way to make them up. Catherine was starting school on October the first.

She could not acknowledge the truth, even to herself. School would take Catherine away from her, and she was afraid of the loneliness.

For the first weeks, the separation from her little girl was not too painful. Catherine clung to her, unwilling to let go when Delia called that it was time to leave for school. But then, inevitably, Catherine began to care more for the companionship of her classmates. She darted away from Elizabeth as soon as Delia was ready to leave. Elizabeth gradually slid deeper into the shadows of apathy that were always waiting to claim her.

Pinckney asked Lucy what to do.

"She needs to be busy," Lucy said, "and she needs people. By the time the Season starts, she'll be out of mourning. There'll be invitations. Make sure she accepts them."

Pinckney commanded, and Elizabeth obeyed. She attended all the receptions and teas and card parties to which she was invited, functions suitable for a young widow. Pinckney escorted her. The two red-gold heads made a stir whenever they entered. Everyone said how nice it was to have the Tradds circulating again and admired Pinny's attentiveness to his smiling, pretty sister. Elizabeth's frozen heart began to thaw in the warmth of everyone's kindness. Her smiles became less forced. When at last the Saint Cecelia came, she genuinely enjoyed it.

She laughed when she saw that her dance card had been filled by the Managers, just as if she were a debutante again. Her partners were all old friends, and they made extraordinary efforts to be gallant. Their thoughtfulness was touching. She played her well-learned role of harmless flirtation, teased her friends about their handsome husbands stealing her heart, and scolded Josiah Anson because he was only on her card for one dance. "I know you're responsible for the cards, Cousin Josiah. As President, you could have taken as many waltzes as you wanted. You're just being cautious because you know I'm planning to set my cap for you."

Lucy and Pinckney, standing nearby, shared a glance and a smile. "She's really having a good time," said Pinckney.

"Mr. Josiah has that effect. He loves the Ball so."

It was apparent. Mr. Anson's cheeks were flushed, his eyes shining, his handsome elderly face alight with pleasure. His dress suit was nearly threadbare, his white gloves and patent dancing pumps cracked with age, but none of that was noticeable. He carried himself with such erect pride, and he danced with such youthful grace that anyone looking at him saw only the picture of a gentleman in the finest, truest meaning of the term.

"You know, Lucy," Elizabeth said, "I was joking with Cousin Josiah about trying to throw a net over him, but I declare I'm almost truly tempted. He's the most charming man here tonight." They were sitting in gilt chairs next to the wall while the debutantes formed the figure for their presentation.

Lucy smiled. "You'd have to get at the end of the line," she said. "Practically every lady in Charleston who doesn't have a husband has already had that thought, even some who aren't much older than you."

"Really?"

"Just watch. The Anson men are notoriously charming. For that matter, look at Andrew. If the Waring girl doesn't stop cutting her eye at him, she's going to step on her own feet."

"Is Andrew the D.D. of the year?"

"Unquestionably. He's hardly had an hour's sleep since the parties started."

"He is a good-looking boy. Especially in all those buttons." Andrew was wearing his Citadel full-dress uniform, a blue-gray jacket that clung to his wide chest, stopped at his narrow waist in front and extended into swallow-tails in the back. It was resplendent with rows of brightly polished brass buttons, gold epaulets and rows of gold braid on the sleeve. A wine-colored sash with deep fringe was knotted around his waist; it hung below the knees of his long legs in their trim pants.

"He's gorgeous," said Lucy smugly, "and not one of them stands a chance. He's already asked his doting mama to dance the sixteenth."

"Doesn't he have a partiality to any one of them?"

Lucy sighed. "It wouldn't do him any good if he did. He graduates in June, and then the Army gets him. It will be years before he can afford a wife. I'll be awfully old before I get to be a grandmother. I might kidnap Tradd one of these days."

"You'd pay me to take him back. He's toddling now, and he gets into everything!"

The Grand March began. Elizabeth and Lucy were quiet, watching the nervous young girls in their beautiful, billowing skirts. Both were smiling unconsciously. Lucy was remembering Elizabeth when she was a debutante; Elizabeth was imagining Catherine when her turn came.

"I'm so glad they still wear hoops," they whispered at the same time. They looked at each other, and their smiles widened.

The city's streetcars were lined up on Meeting Street, waiting, when the Ball ended at two A.M. Although they normally stopped running at nine o'clock, the Managers had managed a special final run. During the twenty years since the War ended, Charleston had experienced a kind of survival unique even for its long history of disaster and rebirth. The traditions of the Charlestonians had become a treasured source of pride even for the new, wealthy inhabitants who had moved in during the Reconstruction years to ravage their homes and possessions. These new people called themselves Charlestonians because they lived in Charleston, and they valued the civilization that the real Charlestonians had succeeded in saving, even though they were excluded from participating in it. Perhaps because they were excluded.

They had fallen under Charleston's spell. Of course the streetcars would be there for the Managers of the Saint Cecelia and their guests. And of course no one else would be allowed to ride on the special trip. There was something particularly noble and particularly Charlestonian about the circumstance that the favored group invited to the Ball were too poor to own or rent carriages for anyone except the debutantes and the infirm. Everyone was proud of the fact that not even a million dollars could buy an invitation to the Ball. Except the old Charlestonians. They did not even think about it.

"Let's walk home, Pinny. It's hardly more than two blocks, and it's too pretty a night to be shut up in the streetcar."

They strolled slowly, waving to their friends in the lighted cars as they passed, enjoying the quiet that settled afterward.

"I'm beginning to understand it, I think," Elizabeth said when they crossed Tradd Street.

"What do you understand, Baby Sister?"

"I'm going to start calling you 'elderly brother' one of these days." Elizabeth pressed his arm to tell him she was teasing. "I mean," she said, and her voice was soft, hesitant, thoughtful, "the whole thing about tradition. I used to get impatient when Lucy or Aunt Julia or you would tell me that something was important because it was traditional, that I was fortunate because I was a Tradd, that I had to live up to all sorts of standards because it was expected of me. I thought it was all just a lot of trouble, that it was silly to do things the way somebody else had done them a long time ago. . . . Tonight, though, at the Ball, it made me feel very safe and very happy to see the girls in their old-fashioned gowns and to remember that I was just like them and to know that Catherine will be just the same, marching the same figure, curtsying at the same spot in the same ballroom. It's nice that the last dance is always "The Blue Danube" and that long after I'm gone, my children's children and their children will be dancing to it. . . . It's hard to put into words . . . It's sort of—not lonely. Do you know what I mean?"

Pinckney stopped walking, which halted Elizabeth's steps. He moved his arm to release the hand she had tucked under his elbow; then he picked up the freed hand and bowed over it. Still holding her fingers, he smiled down at her upturned, puzzled face and kissed her forehead. "I know what you mean, Miss Elizabeth. You're a grown-up Charleston lady . . . Wait a minute, now. Look around you, and listen."

The three-quarter moon washed the peeling house fronts with soft, flattering light. A vagrant breeze rustled the leaves of the towering magnolia tree in the garden next to them. Then Saint Michael's bells chimed the half hour.

"Those bells chimed the day you were born, the day I was born, the day our father and our grandfathers and great-grandfathers were born. They rang for Catherine and for Tradd, and they'll ring for all the generations to come. We hardly notice them, unless we're wondering what time it is. But they're there, always, for you and for me and for all those we care about. You needn't feel lonely ever. All the people, past and present and future that those bells reach are part of you and are with you. Every quarter hour, they remind you of that . . . You belong."

Elizabeth put her arms around his neck and held herself to him for a moment. "Thank you," she whispered. "I do love you, Pinny."

48

After the night of the Saint Cecelia, Elizabeth found that her life was no longer a burden to her. It was as if the old city itself were sharing the weight of her guilts and sorrows, incorporating them into the fabric of its history, with all the other instances of human frailty and failings that had occurred behind its high walls. She still felt that her life was, in a sense, over. She had no enthusiasm, nothing to look forward to. She was still removed from the world—as by a curtain of fog—a spectator, not a participant. Nothing mattered very much.

But now she didn't mind. She was part of the slow current of time, and she was content to float on it. She could even let Catherine go, knowing that she was not losing her, that Catherine was in the same current, only a generation away. One day she went to the study in search of a book to read and found the little girl painting the mantelpiece with the watercolors she had received for her sixth birthday present.

"I wanted the ladies to look nice," Catherine said defensively when Elizabeth scolded her for the overturned cup of water on the floor and the streaks of paint on her pinafore. "They're so pretty, Mama, but they're all pale."

Elizabeth looked at the smeared blue and yellow robes and blotched pink cheeks that Catherine had applied to the delicate, carved dancing nymphs, and her anger disappeared. She took the sniffling, sticky child on her lap and dried her tears. "Let me tell you a story about when Mama was a little girl and tried to dance like those ladies," she said.

When the story was over, and Catherine had examined the crack in the inkwell on the desk, mother and daughter held hands and danced before they mopped up the puddle and washed the paint off the mantel. Elizabeth felt the presence of the father she could not remember in the room with them and was sharply aware of the comforting continuity of family.

She moved, as if in a dream, through the round of her days, calling on friends, receiving their calls, attending the parties that were big enough so that even widows were included. She did not miss the busier social life that she had known when Lucas was alive. That round of supper parties and dances was only for couples. It was the way things were done; she did not question it.

Her own summer schedule was different this year. With Catherine in school until June thirtieth she would not be able to move to the Island until the first of July. At first, she was annoyed; she had become accustomed to leaving the city before the days became hot. But then Lucy Anson enlisted her aid in preparing for a big party, and she was too busy to notice the weather.

Little Andrew was graduating from The Citadel on June twenty-third. Then he would receive his commission in the Army and his orders for posting to wherever the Army chose to send him. It would not possibly be close to home. The Federal military officials were still uneasy about the specter of armed Southerners, particularly in South Carolina. The memory of the Red Shirts was still fresh in their minds.

"There hasn't been a party in this house since Miss Emma died seven years ago," Lucy had said with a moan, "and I don't know where to begin. We'll have to turn the place inside out."

Elizabeth rolled up her sleeves, resuscitated the organizational skills she had learned from her Aunt Julia, and pushed away her perpetual listless fatigue. She shuttled to and from Charlotte Street on the streetcar two and three times a day, accompanied by Delia and boxes full of china, glass, linens, vases, cooking utensils and serving platters. The unwritten, unspoken rules were that things could be borrowed, with no damage to pride, but that nothing could be accepted as a gift by the Ansons. Because they were unable ever to repay. Josiah Anson had almost no work. The Yankee occupation had left little of any value. Those few things had been sold to pay for Andrew's education.

For two weeks, Elizabeth directed Delia and Lucy's Estelle while they washed windows and woodwork and waxed floors. She and Lucy polished furniture, mended rents in upholstery and devised recipes to utilize the supplies of the Anson vegetable garden and the game that Josiah Anson had shot and cured over the winter. On the day before graduation, they boiled and picked twenty pounds of sweet, tiny creek shrimp and made shrimp paste. Then they baked bread for the finger sandwiches they would spread with the paste in the morning. Elizabeth spent the night on Charlotte Street so that she could be up at first light to strip the garden of flowers while the dew was still on them. By ten o'clock, everything was ready, the pantry full of the food on platters covered by cool, damp cloths, the house shining and sweetly scented, the ingredients laid out for the punch that Mr. Anson would mix. She kissed Lucy good-bye and hurried home to bathe and dress. She wasn't tired at all.

But she was glad that grandstands had been erected for the guests of the graduating class. The ceremonies dragged on and on. The first graduation since the reopening of The Citadel inspired a great deal of oratory. Elizabeth looked at the Corps of Cadets standing at attention in their wool uniforms and marveled that none of them fainted. The noon sun was pitiless, striking from above and reflecting from the ochre colored walls of the fortresslike building in the center of the packed earth parade ground.

A sudden chill ran down her spine and she remembered the Union soldiers marching where the cadets were standing now. She could feel again the press of the crowd around and above her when she was a child and Sophy dragged her past Citadel Square to show her the Orphan Asylum and threaten her with banishment to it. She forced the memory back into its dark closet in her mind. All that was past, thank heaven. And Hattie might be getting old, too old to keep up with Tradd's boundless energy, but at least she loved him. She was the way a dah should be, not cruel like Sophy.

The speeches ended at last, a cannon boomed, and two cadets marched to the empty flagpole next to the one flying the flags of South Carolina and the United States. While the crowd of watchers cheered, and drums rolled, they pulled on the flagpole's rope to hoist a tattered Stars and Bars, the emblem of the Confederacy. The small band, its brass instruments shining like gold, broke into the infectious, happy music of "Dixie." The spectators in the grandstand stood. Elizabeth felt tears on her cheeks; she was moved beyond caring about the taboos on public emotional display. They were so young, the boys in their defiant uniforms, so straight and proud and brave. The last body of Citadel cadets before them had marched off to war in 1863, some of them only sixteen years old. They had never come back. Now their courage and their flag were at home again, undefeated. We won, she thought, and her heart pounded; they couldn't beat us, not with their armies, not with their taxes, not with their torches to our homes. We're still Southerners. We have our pride and our heritage. No power on earth can take it away. She turned to Pinckney and saw that his eyes were glistening, and that his posture was that of a soldier, a leader of men. His head was high, his tears a badge of honor. Her gaze moved over the crowd. They were all the same, proud, lean faces wet with tears. She loved them all and knew that they loved her. They were sharers in a beautiful world of grace and graciousness that had been cut off at its highest glory. But the essence of it would never die. The South did not need the luxuries that had made it envied throughout the globe in order to survive. It needed only its people and their refusal to accept shoddiness of materials or morals. Things did not matter. A civilization was built on beliefs and standards, not on things. The grace lived on in the hearts and souls of them all, and it would continue in their children and their children's children. The music ended, and the cheers of the crowd reached into the heavens. It was a shout of victory.

The echoes of the shout were still rolling across the broad, open square when one of the cadets stepped forward from the group, turned to face it and called out a command. The shiny black feathers that crested their shakos quivered as the cadets began to march.

"Now they'll get their diplomas," Lucy murmured to Elizabeth. "Look at Andrew. He's at the end on the right. Doesn't he look handsome?"

Elizabeth agreed. In fact, Andrew was indistinguishable from the tall young man next to him. The straps of the shakos crossed their faces just below the mouth, and the brims shadowed their eyes. Their faces could hardly be seen at all. She hoped the ritual of giving out the diplomas would not last too long. She did not want to lose the proud euphoria she was feeling in a prolonged wait under the scorching afternoon sun.

Oh, Lord, she thought, more speeches. The Commandant was unrolling a sheet of parchment. Her mind drifted to the party to come, wondering if the sandwiches would have dried out and started to curl. The shaved ice around them must have melted long ago. Lucy pinched her arm.

"That's Andrew!" she said. A tall cadet was saluting the Commandant. He accepted something from his hand.

The applause went on for four minutes. Elizabeth joined in, wondering if each diploma was going to cause such a furor. She was relieved when they did not.

Later, Pinckney told her what the Commandant had read from the scroll while she was worrying about the life-span of cut bread. A month before the firing on Fort Sumter which most people considered the beginning of the War, a ship that was bringing supplies to the Union garrison on the Fort was turned back by artillery fire from a Confederate battery on Morris Island. The name of the ship was *The Star of the West*, and those first shots of the War were fired by Citadel cadets manning the guns. Starting with this first graduating class, the Military College of South Carolina was instituting a new tradition to commemorate those cadets. From now on, all cadets would strive for the medal which would be awarded to the member of the graduating class who, by his integrity and qualities of dedication, most nearly epitomized the spirit of The Citadel. The medal was called "The Star of the West," and Andrew Anson was its first recipient. It was the highest honor any cadet could ever win, even if he went on to become the General of all the Armies of the United States.

Elizabeth was impressed. She congratulated Andrew and his mother and grandfather with extravagant enthusiasm, as did all the other guests at the party.

None of them ever knew how much more the medal meant to the

Anson family. After all the guests had left, Josiah, Lucy and young Andrew spent a long, happy hour at the side of Andrew Anson's bed. While his father and his wife held his lifeless hands, Andrew listened to his tall young son read the proclamation that accompanied the medal. Then the boy unpinned it from his uniform and attached it to the blanket over his father's heart. "I want you to have this, Papa," he said. "I won it for you." He kissed Andrew's paralyzed cheek, stood tall and saluted.

Andrew Anson's lips could not speak. But his eyes could. They told his son of his love and his pride and the peace that had finally entered his heart. Until that moment, Andrew had never forgiven himself for the undelivered dispatches entrusted to him twenty-two years before.

49

"No, ma'am, Miss Elizabeth, I ain't going take that baby to no Sullivan Island. They a big trouble coming going bust up every thing."

"Hattie, don't talk such foolishness. There's not a cloud in the sky. Now get to the packing. I don't want to stay one more day in this oven. We're going to the beach this afternoon."

"No, ma'am." Hattie's lower lip jutted out, and she planted her wide feet as if she were nailing them to the floor.

Elizabeth put her fists on her hips, matching Hattie's stance. She frowned fiercely. "I say 'yes,'" she hissed. Hattie had never seen her so angry.

But her fear was greater than Elizabeth's wrath. "No, ma'am," she said. "The conjuh women say trouble coming. I ain't going to meet it on no island."

Elizabeth stamped her foot. She was speechless with rage. And, if she would admit it to herself, unnatural fear. No matter how many times she told herself that conjure women were a senseless Negro superstition, she still shivered when one was mentioned.

Her conversation with Pinckney did little to ease her jitters.

"You'll have to speak to Hattie," she said when she stormed into the study. "She's talking crazy, and she won't do what I tell her."

Pinckney listened calmly to the details of Elizabeth's complaint. He looked thoughtful. "Maybe you'd better change your plans," he said. "When is this storm supposed to be coming?"

"Pinckney! You can't be serious."

"Yes and no, Elizabeth. You didn't grow up in the country the way I did. I spent most of my time with colored people when I was a boy, and lots of times they knew more about things than we could understand. I don't believe in conjures, or ghosts, or reading the future by tossing bones. But I don't not believe, either. I just don't know . . . and Lord knows we're overdue for a hurricane. There hasn't been one since I was a boy. We're on borrowed time.

"Still, there's never been any such thing as a hurricane in July. Hattie's jumping the gun. Do you think she's just talking storm to cover something else? She's getting pretty old, after all."

"Maybe that's it. She's been complaining about her feet for months, and she claims to have 'the sugar blood.' I don't believe it. She's not thin enough to have diabetes, and I don't notice her drinking much water. I think it's just the fashionable illness for servants these days. A lot of my friends say that their cooks and maids claim to have it."

Pinckney smiled. "Never try to fight fashion. We men learn that in the cradle from seeing how you ladies tog yourselves out."

Elizabeth laughed. "Well done, brother dear. I'm over my tantrum. I have to admit that bustles and trains are silly. I can't sit down, and I can't walk without collecting the landscape. But that doesn't solve my problem."

They conferred seriously for almost an hour. Then Pinckney went to talk to Hattie while Elizabeth talked to Delia. That afternoon, Hattie and Elizabeth took the children and the boxes of summer clothes to the beach house. Hattie helped her open the house, put away the dust covers and sweep out the sand that had seeped in during the months it had been closed. For the rest of the summer, Hattie stayed on Meeting Street, doing Delia's housework. Delia commuted to the beach by ferry. She would not spend the night.

"Conjuh always come in the dark," she said authoritatively. "Long's I home before dark, don't make no never mind where I spend the day." Elizabeth didn't even try to convince her that there was no reason to believe that anything terrible was going to happen. She was content that the succession of beautiful, sunny days cured her own mind of its shadowy superstitions.

As it turned out, both Elizabeth and Delia were mistaken. The storm came, and it came in the daytime.

Elizabeth was on the ferry, returning from a long, hot day of shopping in the city. She looked hopefully at the dark clouds piled up on the horizon. Maybe there'd be a thundershower when she got home. They always excited and revived her. The lightning seemed to tear through the fog that lay between her and the world, and the crackling electricity in the air made her feel truly alive.

The clouds spread over the sky, blotting out the punishing August sun, and a wind sprang up from nowhere. She wished she could take off her hat. The breeze would feel wonderful.

"Look at that!" said the deckhand. Elizabeth turned her head to the direction of his pointing finger. Over the harbor, the bottom of the clouds was moving down, trying to touch the water. The dozen passengers crowded to the starboard rail to watch.

The cloud moved down, then folded back up into itself, then reached out, up, down again until at last a curved dark column stretched between sky and water. At the instant they were joined, everyone heard a distant, hollow roaring.

"Bless Jesus," breathed the deckhand, "that the biggest waterspout I ever see in my life."

Elizabeth was fascinated. She had heard of waterspouts, but she'd never seen one. It seemed to be dancing. With awful, gargantuan grace, it swayed, undulated from top to bottom. Then it began to move, still swaying, across the harbor. The noise grew louder. The deckhand fell to his knees and shouted prayers. My God, Elizabeth echoed silently. The waterspout was racing toward them, and she saw that it was tremendous. The noise of it warned of its immeasurable strength. If it hit the boat, it would crush it. She tried to close her eyes and pray. If she was going to die, it should be with a plea for forgiveness of her sins. But she was transfixed. She stared, not breathing as the cyclone of water moved toward her, pushing a tall wave of breaking water before it.

The spume from the wave touched her lips and her eyes; her mouth fell open, and she was conscious of salt on her tongue.

Then the waterspout turned. In ponderous flirtation, it danced away, leaving the boat to a terrifying broadside wallow in the trough of the flanking breakers. Elizabeth clutched the rail and drew a long, shuddering breath into her starved lungs. Now she could pray. Her face wet with sea water and tears of relief, she thanked God for their escape.

In the city, people heard the cyclone before they saw it. The crossing guard on the spur tracks that ran past the warehouses on Bay Street looked desperately for the locomotive that was racing out of control, but the rails were empty. And the sound was behind him, past the end of the track at Stolls Alley. He turned just in time to see the swirling column strike the sea wall on East Battery. In a futile, automatic reflex, he held out the black and white paddle in his hand, signaling Stop. Chunks of masonry from the wall battered him to the ground. He was unconscious when the tons of water rushed through the torn wall behind the twister. He never felt his drowning.

The tornado ripped a jagged-lightning path across the unaware old town, exploding windows, scattering roof tiles like bullets. It was capricious in its destruction, like an enormous horrible child at play. It flicked the golden ball from the top of Saint Michael's steeple, then hop-scotched up Meeting Street flattening some buildings and leaping over their neighbors. At Calhoun Street, the funnel touched down in all its strength to suck up the massive Romanesque steeple of the Citadel Square Baptist Church. It dropped the pinnacle stone inside the depot of the South Carolina Railroad, then it raced away along the tracks with its roaring locomotive noise until it tired of the game and swirled back up into the clouds that had given it birth. Four miles of twisted iron rails littered with debris marked its departure.

The whole thing lasted less than three minutes. Before anyone understood quite what was happening, it was over. Most of the city only learned about the visitation when people read their evening paper.

But in the narrow old streets south of Broad, the waters were inexorably rising. The sea wall had a gap forty feet wide, and the combined currents of the Cooper River and the incoming tide were pouring through, flooding East Battery, spreading into the heart of the old city behind a foot-high crest. Within an hour, it had climbed the steps of the tall old houses and was inching under the doors of the piazzas. On Broad Street, the ground level offices were full of ludicrously bobbing desks and chairs, floating on wainscot-high water.

Men and boys waded through the flooded warehouses on East Bay Street and hauled out sacks of grain, bales of cotton, anything they could find to try and seal the widening gap in the broken wall. When night came, they worked by torch-light. After eight back-breaking hours, the tide turned. By morning, it was lapping at the lowest rank of sodden bales, and the sun was shining on the line of wagons bringing sandbags to replace them. Ladies stood in water above their ankles in their houses, thanking Providence that the flood had happened in the summer, when all the rugs were up in the attic waiting for cool weather.

It took five days for the water to return to the sea. By then, the sea wall was repaired, window panes and roof tiles were replaced, the golden orb was back in place on top of Saint Michael's, and the trains were running on new tracks. The Citadel Square Baptist Church repaired the jagged edges of its truncated steeple, and the congregation talked about the best way to raise the funds to erect a new one. The church was intact, so there was no great urgency to rebuild. In Charleston, in August, it was too hot to do anything in a hurry.

That was the disturbing thing about the tornado, everyone agreed. It had hit so fast. With a hurricane, one had time to board up windows and get in extra supplies of food and water; the winds got stronger at a reasonable rate. Everyone knew how to deal with hurricanes. Cyclones were not a part of the Charleston way of life. It was disquieting to have unprecedented calamity. Still, the city had survived. It always did. People prided themselves on their resilience and admitted that in a way it was rather nice to have something new to talk about. Nothing ever happened anymore. For those who had lived through the tempestuous years of battling the Yankees, life often seemed too tame.

Elizabeth Tradd Cooper did not share their attitude. She had been badly shaken by the fragile ferryboat's narrow escape. When life returned to a featureless succession of days and nights, she slowly relaxed again, grateful for their safe changelessness. The misty lassitude that enveloped her was a familiar, reassuring comfort.

In October Andrew Anson died. It was, everyone agreed, a blessed release for him.

And for his family, too, they all knew, although no one expressed the thought. The church was crowded with people attending his funeral as a gesture of love and respect for his father and his wife and their long, long years of uncomplaining care. Second Lieutenant Andrew Anson, USA, on duty in the territory of New Mexico, could not be present. He sent a telegram, followed by a long, youthfully incoherent letter. Lavinia Anson Pennington sent flowers.

"Cousin Josiah, with no disrespect to your grief, I would like your permission to ask Lucy to marry me as soon as the year of mourning is over."

"Sit down, Pinckney. You're stiffer than young Andrew in his uniform. I appreciate your deference to an old man, but don't overdo it."

Pinny relaxed his shoulders, but he remained standing. "You have no objection, then?" he said.

Mr. Anson smiled. "If you didn't marry that sweet girl after all this time, I'd horsewhip you. Go on. I'm not so old that I can't guess what's on your mind. Go on, I say. You're engaged. Collect your kisses . . . And God bless you, my boy."

Pinckney and Lucy had pledged their love more than ten years earlier. In all the months that followed, they had needed nothing more than a meeting of their eyes or a brushing of their fingertips to reaffirm it. Their two hearts were one.

And now the years of waiting, the strictures of circumspection, the necessary distance between them were all past. They found themselves suddenly shy, nervous, awkward with each other. Pinckney was the first to acknowledge it.

"I'm scared," he blurted. "I don't know how to act."

Lucy's face, pale and pinched-looking, softened before his worried eyes. Color crept up from her throat. "Thank heaven you said that, Pinny. I've been so frightened. I had lost the path to what you were feeling. I felt so alone. I thought you had stopped loving me."

"Lucy!" Pinckney strode across the wide drawing room, his fears submerged by his concern for her. He circled her waist with his strong arm and held her close. Lucy's head nestled in the hollow under his shoulder as if she were returning home.

The terrifying brief period of estrangement made them both preternaturally aware of how precious was the bond that linked them. And how fragile is love. Without needing a single spoken word, Pinckney and Lucy knew that they must take slow, careful steps into the intimacy that was now permitted them, discovering each other's hearts anew without damaging the special communication that they had created in past years when they could admit to no more than friendship. Even Lucy, who would have defied society's laws and become Pinckney's mistress any time in the past, now appreciated the conventions that prevented consummation of their union. She had thought they were as close as two people could ever be, but she discovered that there were still the deepest parts of their souls to be opened to each other. The deepest, and the most vulnerable. There was time for gentle, caring exploration. Time and necessity.

They began the period of engagement with a saving sense of humor about the ludicrous aspects of courtship at their age. They were both past forty; Lucy's light brown hair was streaked with gray, Pinny's red-gold head now darkened and thinned. Their faces were marked by the years and the difficulties they had faced and overcome. Yet, they were in many ways more innocently amazed by their emotions than any young boy and girl ever were. They were quite convinced that love was a miracle that only they had ever found. There was a sweetness between them that made Josiah Anson's wise old eyes sting. He had observed that life seldom rewarded those who deserved it most. But at last it was blessing the two who had earned a full measure of happiness. It made him believe again in a just and merciful God.

Everyone who knew them shared Mr. Anson's reaction to some degree. Because she was in mourning, Lucy could not go out socially. But she and Pinckney were able to see each other at home and to take long walks, to ride the streetcars, to attend church services. People who saw them together immediately felt happier themselves. There was a magic aura about them that touched everyone around them.

Elizabeth felt it, too. She had no envy of their love, even though it was something she had never known herself. She was so happy for them that she did not think of herself at all. Except for her children, Lucy and Pinny were the two people she loved best in all the world. When Christmas-time arrived, Lucy and Mr. Anson joined all the Tradds for dinner at the long table, and she felt that at last the family was complete. Everyone she cared about was there, together. When Saint Michael's watchman called ". . . all's well," they all lifted their glasses in a toast.

"Evenin', Captain."

"Evenin', Matthew." Mr. Anson loosened the tie at the neck of his dark wool cloak and turned so that it slid off his shoulders into the waiting gloved hands of the old black man who had greeted him. Matthew folded the cape over one arm, then took the cane and top hat Anson handed him.

"Fine evenin' for the Ball, Captain."

"That it is, Matthew. More like springtime than January. You won't have many cloaks to tend. Just a few from old bones like mine." Mr. Anson put a brown paper-wrapped parcel on a long bench topped with cracked leather and sat down next to it. He leaned forward and began to unlace the heavy boots that he wore.

Matthew squatted quickly in front of him. "I'll do that, Captain."

Josiah Anson straightened with a relieved wheeze. "Thank you, Matthew. I don't know how you stay so spry. You're as old as I am."

The black man chuckled. "I don't have so much of me to bend as you do, Captain."

Mr. Anson laughed, patting his belly. He was definitely putting on flesh. "Miss Lucy's been spoiling me, Matthew. You'd think I was a turkey gobbler with Thanksgiving a week away."

"Looks fine, Captain."

"I thank you, Matthew."

Mr. Anson carefully untied the string around the paper parcel and unwrapped it. He placed the string in a pocket. The package contained a pair of yellowed kid gloves and a pair of worn black dancing pumps. While Mr. Anson worked the gloves over his hands, Matthew expertly tore and folded the brown paper wrapping into lining for the shoes. He examined the often mended soles closely then slipped the shoes onto Josiah Anson's knobby old feet. "They'll do you for a while yet, Captain, if you don't try to dance every dance."

"Not likely, Matthew. I'm too old and too fat." And, they both knew, too tired. Unable to afford the five-cent car fare, Mr. Anson had walked the three miles from his house to the Ball. He pushed himself up onto his feet and checked the perfection of his necktie in the mirror. "Well, Matthew, I think I might break a few hearts tonight."

The two old men laughed together.

Stepping gently, Mr. Anson began his tour of the building to check the preparations for the Ball. He crossed the wide hall to the ladies' cloak room, knocked on the half-open door and entered.

"Everything ready, 'Sheba?"

"Yessuh, Mis' Anson." Josiah Anson smiled at the corpulent black woman who was enthroned in a shabby wing chair in the corner. "Queen of Sheba" she had been named by her father who was both butler and preacher on the Rutledges' plantation, and queen she had become. Everyone knew that after the War she had used her quick wits and organizational ability to establish a house of prostitution in Mulatto Alley. She named it The Gold Mine, and it was. When the Union troops were moved out in 1878, Queen of Sheba was rumored to be worth more than a million U.S. dollars. No one knew what she had done with it. She lived in a small, neat house and worked as a dressmaker for selected clients, including Mrs. Rutledge and her daughters. She had been a fixture at the Saint Cecelia for over ten years, directing the terrified young maids at her command and, with a flashing needle, repairing any tears that a misplaced foot might cause in a hem or ruffle.

"Do you want me to speak to your girls, 'Sheba?" Anson's offer was part of the ritual.

"That would be very generous, Mist' Anson." The queen raised her voice. "You gals!"

From the back retiring room, where even Josiah Anson did not dare go, two neatly capped and aproned black girls appeared and bobbed awkward curtsies. "This here is Viola and Rosalie, Mist' Anson. They works at the hotel, but they is really Celie's daughters what is cook for Miss Josephine Grimball." Josiah Anson nodded at the identification. "Your mother makes the best oyster stew in Charleston, girls. We use her recipe for the breakfast after the Ball. Now, be sure you don't disgrace her. You mind what 'Sheba tells you."

"Yessuh," quavered the girls, half-strangled by responsibility.

Having added another weapon to 'Sheba's arsenal, Mr. Anson's work was done. His eyes passed quickly over the table which held a supply of handkerchiefs, hairpins, toilet water, combs and hairbrushes and a large vial of smelling salts. On a windowsill a single candle stood next to a small basket full of duck feathers. If the price of a tightly laced waistline was occasional faintness, a singed feather waved under the nose would effect an instant cure.

Josiah Anson's next duty was the one he liked best. As he left the ladies' cloak room, he took the long bamboo rod that rested by the door. A single candle was attached at its end, perpendicular to the rod. Mr. Anson lit the candle with a match and walked into the soaring shadows of the entrance hall. One by one, he touched the flame to the candles in the gilt and crystal sconces on each side of the huge windows that faced the portico and the street. For the Saint Cecelia, the gas jets were closed off and capped with candle holders. The prisms threw out rainbow refractions that danced and fell into the deep green of magnolia leaves fanned behind them. Mr. Anson climbed slowly up the semicircular flying staircase on his right, lighting the candles waiting on the wall. At the top of the stairs, a wide balustered gallery crossed to the matching staircase on the opposite wall. A tarnished gold rope held a massive brass chandelier close to the gallery. Josiah Anson passed by it and moved through the open paneled doors into the ballroom. The smell of fresh-picked greenery washed over him, and the old man stood straighter.

Each year when he reached the ballroom, he had the same moment of excitement. The slightly acrid living darkness was exactly as it had been twenty-five years before when he had served his first year as President of the Society. Only fifty-two he was then; it seemed very young to him now. Each year at this moment, he felt that youth again. The years between dropped away, with all the changes they had brought, and for a fleeting moment, he was young and strong again and ready to dance through the soles of his shoes in one night. Mr. Anson allowed himself one very quiet sigh. Then he went about his business.

When he left the ballroom, he paused again in the doorway, taking a last critical look. The dozens of candles in the chandeliers and wall brackets cast a warm, soft light on the elegant old room. Five huge fluted columns stood on either side, four yards away from the walls and twelve yards away from each other. Thick garlands of smilax twisted around the columns, hiding the flaking paint. At regular intervals, the green was jeweled with waxy white Alba Plenas, most perfect and unobtrusive of all camellias. Sprays of white camellias also nestled in the banked ivy around the raised platform for the musicians and in the soft ferns that marked the places where punchbowls would be on the tables flanking the orchestra. The familiar gilt chairs were lined up against both side walls, their repairs and chipped gilt mercifully invisible in the gentle light. The parquet floor seemed to have an inner life; reflections of the flames rose from the lowest of six layers of freshly polished wax, deep and mysterious and alive. Mr. Anson narrowed his eyes. The flames danced, and the ballroom was exactly as it had been. Before.

He checked the placement and polish of the gleaming brass bolts that held the doors open. Then he waited. In a few moments, he heard the four-toned chime of Saint Michael's clock. It was repeated. Then again. He was right on schedule. He lit the twenty-four candles of the chandelier anchored to the gallery. As he finished, he heard the steps of Barnwell Gibbes with the kitchen staff behind him.

"I hope you haven't ruined the punch, Barney," said Mr. Anson, as he did every year at 9:47.

"Well, Josiah, as President, you have an obligation to test it," Gibbes said in countersign. The procession of waiters marched past the two old men with trays of punch cups, benne wafers, salted toasted pecans, shrimp paste sandwiches and fragile curled cheese toast. The last two men stopped, holding out the huge, deeply engraved silver punchbowls. Mr. Anson lifted the full ladle of one, tipped half the contents into his mouth and swallowed.

"Ahhh. Henry's brandy gets better every year."

"Brandy has a way of doing that, Josiah," Gibbes said dryly. "Do you approve?"

"My, yes." Mr. Anson waved the waiters into the ballroom.

With Gibbes' help, Mr. Anson untied the gold rope and slowly played it out until the spidery globe of brass hung suspended in the center of the entrance hall.

Barnwell Gibbes moved into the ballroom to check the perfection of the serving tables, and Mr. Anson went downstairs. The musicians passed him but did not pause to speak. They were four minutes late.

Josiah Anson took his place at the foot of the stairs, ready to receive his friends. The top-hatted doorman, as old and as black as Matthew, touched his hat brim in salute, then snapped to attention.

Saint Michael's steeple rang sweetly. It was ten o'clock. A slam-door carriage stopped in front of the stone carriage block on the curb before the entrance. There was a rustling of skirts as a gentleman handed down his ladies. Mr. Anson stepped forward to bow over the hands of the debutante and her mother. The young girl's wide, frightened, happy eyes were just as debutantes' eyes always were. Her delicate white gown floated over her wide hooped crinolines just as it should. For Josiah Anson, the moment was as fresh and marvelous as it was for each shy young lady he greeted. "Welcome," he said with a smile.

Up on Charlotte Street, Lucy whirled around the huge, cold drawing room, dancing alone to the music of her own humming. She did not mind that she could not go to the Ball this year; next year Pinny would escort her and Elizabeth. And they would dance the sixteenth together, proclaiming their love and accepting the congratulations of their friends on their marriage.

In the meantime, she had the immeasurable happiness of seeing the transformation in Pinckney. She closed her eyes as she waltzed, seeing his dear face. It had changed in the ten weeks they had been engaged. His eyes had an inner fire and there was an incandescent purity in his smile and in the line of his profile. He looked, Lucy thought, the way she had always imagined angels looked. Lit from within by a spiritual burning.

Pinny smiled when she told him he reminded her of an angel. Far from it, he promised.

He was, he agreed, burning within, but what she saw was energy and excitement. "I have something to look forward to now," he was simply. "I didn't before. I worked every day at a job I hated and came home to a house more lived in by ghosts than by me. I made no plans, I just waited. Now there's so much to do, so much to work for. I even like the fertilizer business because soon it will be giving you an easier life."

Pickney had plans now, so many that they often conflicted with each other. He poured his dreams into Lucy's lap like gifts. She matched them with her own. Throughout the months of profligate flowering—the most beautiful spring of all time, they agreed—they played with their dreams. By the time summer came, all the make-believe had been refined into one perfect blueprint for their future life. Then they shared it with Josiah Anson and Elizabeth, who were part of the perfection. Like all true lovers, Lucy and Pinny wanted to wrap their happiness around everyone who was close to them.

Pinckney was the spokesman. "We've thought it all out," he said, "and we won't allow argument from anybody. Especially not from you, Cousin Josiah." He smiled at Mr. Anson to remove any possible sting from his words. "We are going to be the happiest family in Charleston."

Mr. Anson would, of course, live with them. He would have the big bedroom on the second floor where Pinny slept now. Elizabeth would stay in her third-floor kingdom with Catherine and Tradd.

Pinckney held up his hand to forestall questions until he finished. "While Elizabeth is at the Island with the children, Lucy's going to show me how she wants the old servants' quarters over the kitchen fixed up. We'll have our sitting room and bedroom there. The summer months will be plenty of time to get it done while Tradd's not around to eat any nails left lying around.

"We'll be displacing Hattie and Clara, of course, but Hattie's past due for retirement, and we can raise Clara's wages so that she can live with one of her daughters and come in by the day. I've already spoken to her, and she's pleased as punch. Estelle will be coming with Lucy. She already lives out, so that's not a problem."

Elizabeth's mind was busy with alternatives. Estelle had been Little Andrew's dah. She might be fine for Tradd. But Delia had priority if she wanted it. In any case, she'd be rid of Hattie, and she'd be glad. The old woman was complaining more and more. Tradd was just too much for her. Her pension would make her a queen among her relatives on James Island. That was certainly where she would go to live . . . She realized that everyone was looking at her, waiting for her to say something. "I think it's a wonderful plan," she said.

They all did.

Elizabeth and the children moved to Sullivans Island on July first. As she always did, Elizabeth vowed not to leave the cool ocean breezes until time for the ritual return to town at the end of September. But this year, she seemed to have more urgent errands to run in the city. On her third trip, she admitted with a laugh that she was really making excuses to see what was happening with the work on the kitchen building.

She also had a special project of her own that the workmen were doing. Pinckney had agreed that, "as long as the carpenters were there anyhow and there was so much lumber lying around," the men could build a joggling board for Catherine.

"I was always so envious because Caroline Wragg had one. Stuart broke ours before I was old enough to play on it." The construction waited while Catherine's surprise was built. The joggling board was a fixture on the piazza of every Charleston house with children in it. It was a simple object, a long, flexible pine plank suspended between two sturdy upright supports. Thick pegs kept it from sliding out of the roomy openings cut for it in the supports. The space around the plank in the openings allowed it to move freely up and down, making a clatter loud enough to satisfy the lust for noise characteristic of all young children. The plank sagged slightly in the center, low enough for a child to sit on and joggle, bouncing higher with each rebound until the board threw the child into the air to land triumphantly on the board again or ignominiously on the floor. It was no more dangerous than any running game, and on rainy days it provided an outlet for pent-up energy that had no outdoor arena.

The workmen did an excellent job, sanding the board to a silken finish and painting the joggling board the traditional dark green. Four coats. Catherine's small bottom would be safe from splinters.

When no one was looking, Pinckney and Lucy took turns trying it out. Both had been champion jogglers in their youths.

Elizabeth examined it on her next trip into the city. "It's perfect," she announced. "Just listen to the racket it makes. Catherine will be in seventh heaven . . . Wasn't that a good idea I had? I do love making suggestions."

Pinckney chuckled. "You don't have to tell me," he said, "I remember when we were building the beach house."

Lucy shushed him. "I'm so happy to have Elizabeth's help," she said. "You men don't know anything at all about what makes a house livable anyhow." The look she gave him with the insult was so rich with affection that Elizabeth wanted to hug them both.

The renovations were interesting, but she really came to the city just to be near them. They made her feel good. Lucy and Pinny were more like parents to her than her own. They had raised her. Now, when her own life was in ashes, she felt an echo of her girlhood when they shared their happiness with her. For a little while she was Lizzie Tradd again, safe and cared for, with a future full of possibilities.

She did not, however, allow herself to understand her own motives too well. She would have had to condemn her own selfishness and leave them alone to watch their dream taking form in brick and plaster. She convinced herself that she was only trying to be helpful, and she offered advice on every decision.

At the end of August, she came up with an idea that Lucy hailed as brilliant. Josiah Anson had offered any or all of the furniture left in the Charlotte Street house. The new rooms were finished, two bright, fresh, big chambers created from the six servants' rooms that had been there before. But they were unlike the huge spaces in the Anson mansion. The ceilings were lower, windows and doors smaller, all proportions quite different.

"I don't know how anything would look," Lucy wailed. "I have to choose; there certainly isn't room for everything. I don't know where to begin."

"Summerville," said Elizabeth. "Aunt Julia furnished Stuart's little house for him with things from her Charlotte Street house. There must have been the same problem. And Stuart's house looks just fine except for Henrietta's housekeeping."

"Elizabeth!"

"Oh, don't 'Elizabeth' me, Pinny. You know it's true. We don't like Henrietta any less because of it. And there's no need to preserve family loyalty. Lucy is family, too. She might as well know all."

"All right," Pinckney said, "I surrender. I'll write Stuart today and ask when we can come."

"You'll do no such namby-pamby thing, brother dear. You'll go to Broad Street right now and telegraph him. No reason to waste time."

Lucy and Pinckney took the morning train to Summerville two days later.

Stuart met them in his sparkling green new surrey. He kissed Lucy's cheek as though she were already his sister-in-law, and her holiday mood became even more exuberant. She did not really know this grown-up Stuart very well. Henrietta was almost a stranger. She wanted to see the house; even more, she wanted to make friends with this branch of Pinckney's family. They would be her family, too, in three months.

Stuart's next words deflated some of her eagerness to know Pinny's relatives better. "Aunt Julia's at the house," he said, "and sore as a boil." Lucy, like most people, was thoroughly in awe of Julia Ashley.

"Oh, Lord," said Pinckney. "You should have warned me. We would have changed the day. What's she mad about this time?"

"Poor soul has an abcessed tooth. She rode over from the Barony at daylight to go to the dentist. And he was away on a fishing expedition. He's due back at dinner time. He's the one needs warning. You know Aunt Julia's views on a man and his work. They don't include closing your office to go after fish."

Lucy felt her holiday spirits shrivel.

She underestimated Julia Ashley. Although her cheek was swollen, Julia gave no indication that anything was wrong with her. She greeted Lucy with a smile and concentrated her full attention to the challenge of furnishing the new rooms. Julia also had decided views on the power of self-discipline in regard to physical pain. Lucy was still awed, but she was also charmed. Julia's approval was apparent, and her incisive opinions about decorating were exactly what Lucy needed to know. She began to think that Julia wasn't terrifying at all.

Then she was witness to one of Julia's rages.

Stuart drove his aunt to the dentist while the others had dinner. Julia's self-discipline did not extend to the point of trying to eat. They returned before the first course had been cleared.

"Isn't he back yet, Aunt Julia?" Henrietta's inquiry was quavering with fear. Julia was livid with anger.

"He's back. And he's the biggest fool God ever made. Incompetent jackass. He wanted to pull my tooth. I'm going to Charleston. The man there is a fool, too, but he has just enough sense to do what I tell him instead of trying to argue with me. I am sixty-nine years old, and I still have every tooth in my head. No jackanapes with a pocket full of catfish is going to touch one. Lancing's what I need, not a pair of rusty pliers."

"Ice is what you need until it's time for the train, Aunt Julia." Pinckney was firmly sympathetic. "You're not going to ride your horse twenty-two miles, no matter what you say."

Julia agreed to take the train. She rejected the ice bag. "I'll have some wine, Henrietta. It cools my nerves better than ice. Stop fussing over me and eat your dinner before it gets cold."

Everyone ate as quickly as politeness allowed. After dinner they were chagrined to learn that there was still an hour to fill before the train left.

"Why don't you take the folks to see the funny hole, Stuart?" said Henrietta.

Pinckney and Lucy declared themselves fascinated at the prospect. Julia was not so easily led. She demanded a definition of "funny hole."

"It's right in the middle of Main Street," Stuart explained. "Strangest thing you ever heard of. Yesterday afternoon it just popped up for no reason. Clarence Elgins, a sort of simple fellow who hangs around the Court House looking for handouts, came running into the building hollering like the devil was at his heels. Being Clarence, nobody put much truck in the wild story he was telling. But then the bailiff looked out the door, and by the Holy, there it was. Clarence was telling the truth. A spout of water and sand was shooting fifteen feet up in the air, right from the middle of the street.

"After twenty minutes or so, it died down. There's a hole there now, not very big, but deep as a well. You know Summerville; we don't get much excitement here. The whole town is visiting the hole, hoping it'll shoot off again."

Julia snorted. "I don't believe I'll join them. I've seen wells before."

Stuart rolled his eyes at Pinckney. Until train time, Lucy and Henrietta filled the silence with animated conversation about anything at all.

51

The smoke from Pinckney's cheroot rose straight up. There was no breeze at all, not even on the second-floor piazza where he and Julia were sitting. It was dark, which gave an illusion of coolness, but the air was gummy. He thought of removing his collar and necktie, but abandoned the idea. Julia, he knew, would not approve. He tipped his chair back against the balustrade. That much informality was permitted.

Saint Michael's chimed the three-quarter hour. "Almost ten," said Julia. "Past my bedtime." But she didn't stir. It was too hot to move.

"Why don't you go spend a week or two with Elizabeth at the beach, Aunt Julia? It would do you good."

"Don't coddle me like an old woman, Pinckney. Nothing wrong with me, now that I've got the abcess drawn. I'll get a boat to the Barony at first light. September starts tomorrow, and I've got crops to get in."

Pinckney smiled to himself. As Julia got older, rice had become increasingly central to her life. She would not relax for a moment, he knew, until it was harvested and stored away. She had been on edge all day. Not so much from the pain of the tooth as from the need to leave her fields when the rice was in milk.

"Aunt Julia," he said, "tell the truth. You think the rice stops growing if you're not there to encourage it." His voice was warm, gently teasing. He was tremendously fond of his indomitable aunt.

A rusty chuckle answered him from the darkness.

Pinckney's chair slid forward an inch from its precarious angle and he shifted his weight to balance. "What was that?" said Julia.

"My chair legs went for a stroll."

"Tipped against the rail, I suppose. You probably have your collar off, too . . . lax . . . You'd better look for dry rot in the street-floor columns. The whole piazza shook when you slipped. You can't let your house fall down while you're honeymooning in the servants' quarters."

"Yes, ma'am." Pinny was meek.

"I like that young woman."

"Lucy's very special. I'm a lucky man."

"Well, you deserve it. Ask her what she wants for a wedding present. No sense giving you any more furniture."

Pinckney was so astonished to receive a compliment from Julia that he sat bolt upright. The chair legs crashed against the floor with a loud thump.

The impact seemed to release a terrifying, shuddering energy. The piazza swayed, then made a convulsive heaving motion that threw him from his chair onto the creaking long boards of the floor. He felt them crack under him, heard them tearing. Above the noise of splintering, he heard Julia scream. Behind her piercing yell, Saint Michael's bell clanged discordantly. Pinckney heard himself shouting, but he could not recognize any words. Then all other sounds were lost in an overpowering deep rumbling; the walls of the house were shaking.

The whole city was groaning as if it were a living creature in unbearable pain. The church spires that were the only tall structures on the skyline swayed from side to side, their bells calling an angry protest. Wooden buildings creaked in an agonized high screeching, brick chimneys tumbled like children's blocks, sending up clouds of mortar dust and a crashing din. In Saint Michael's, a crack ran like a live, scurrying thing straight up the center of the main aisle. The floor opened, the galleries swayed downward, and the great, soaring white steeple settled with a giant, reverberating sigh, sinking eight inches into the quaking earth.

In the belfry, the watchman clung desperately to the sill of a window, deafened for life by the great bronze bells. His disbelieving eyes saw the columned arcade of the Court House across the street topple like dominoes. Then the stone walls buckled; with a slow, curving movement, they curled away from each other. The cornice rolled outward, like a breaking wave, and the building collapsed in a grinding roar.

In Summerville, the mysterious hole was gone, swallowed up by the chasm, twenty-five feet wide, where Main Street had been. The tall, treasured pine trees fell across streets and houses, their deep roots shrieking as they were torn from the black earth.

The age-old rhythm of the surf on Sullivans Island stopped, replaced by a confused mosaic of choppy, towering white-capped waves to the horizon and beyond. The tall support piers of the houses tilted and everything in them slid drunkenly toward their porches and the shivering sands around them.

At 9:52, the shock ended as abruptly as it had begun. It had lasted for only seventy seconds.

In Charleston an uncanny quiet fell, broken only by the eerily distinct noises of individual bricks clattering onto the rubble of the mounds that had already collapsed. Then the sound of thousands of stumbling, running people filled the city. They had been asleep, most of them, and they were like sleepwalkers now, dazed, uncomprehending, fleeing the homes that had ceased to be shelters, searching for safety away from the shaking walls and falling ceilings and exploding glass windows. Instinct told them to run, and they did, too shocked to speak, or to scream. Only an inarticulate, involuntary low moan of terror could be heard. And the shuffling, slapping sound of naked feet across the rubble- and glass-strewn streets.

Downtown, they streamed toward the wide lawns of White Point Gardens; Meeting Street was filled with figures, ghostlike in long white nightdresses and nightshirts. They stumbled, arms outstretched against the darkness that added to their fear.

In the garden of the Tradd house, Julia Ashley lay amid the wreckage of the fallen piazza, her dead eyes glaring angrily at the moonless sky. None of the passing survivors could see her. Or hear Pinckney Tradd's fading voice calling "Lucy, Lucy, Lucy," until his body had no more breath.

Uptown, the fleeing people found open space in parks and in the broad yards of the railroad depots. Lucy Anson pushed against the current, trying to go to Pinckney. "Please," she said again and again, "please let me by." But the unhearing throng pressed her backward. She struggled for endless minutes, and then her heart became a lifeless weight in her breast and she knew that Pinckney was dead. She let the crowds take her, then, not caring what happened to her.

The second shock came at exactly 10 P.M., and the populace found its voice. People threw themselves onto the quaking earth, screaming, and covered their heads with their arms. The ground rocked under them for less than half a minute, completing the destruction that the first shock had left undone. The enormous columns that fronted the Hibernian Hall toppled across the torn streetcar tracks in Meeting Street, and the roof of the deep portico crashed to its polished marble floor. The church bells repeated the horrible cacophony of the first shock. On Broad Street, the gas main exploded, and a column of fire illuminated the huddled forms of the screaming crowd.

When the tremor ceased, they staggered to their feet and continued running for the Gardens, still screaming.

There was no park on Sullivans Island. Elizabeth held her sobbing children to her, her body across theirs on the gritty sand in futile protection, waiting for the bottomless ocean to be thrown from its bed.

Henrietta Tradd tried to comfort her little boys. "There, there, it's all over," she lied. "Now help me with Papa." Stuart's heavy body was heavier in its unconsciousness. His head was ghastly, bloody from the wound made by a falling roof beam. The children pulled on his legs while

Henrietta cradled his head to her breast, and they dragged him into the center of the garden.

Throughout the night, the earth resettled itself into new alignment of its torn masses eight miles beneath the surface. Seven more shocks battered weakened walls, adding to the ruin. They were followed by the same palpable silence as the first one. People had no strength left to scream. When the sun rose over the restless angry waters of the harbor, the crowds in the parks stared at the light from wild, burnt-out eyes. Many had believed that the world was coming to an end in the darkness of groaning earth. It was full daylight when the last major tremor came at 8:30. The sun moved across a mockingly beautiful clear blue sky as the hours passed until the stricken people found the courage to leave the safety of space, praying that the earthquake was over.

They were alive, and the knowledge filled them with awe. They had survived the assault of the earth itself. Nothing in the history of catastrophe that the city had known could match the upheaval that had torn at the foundations of their homes and their lives. They rediscovered their voices then and greeted their fellow-survivors with unrestrained joyful thanksgiving, marveling that they were still able to embrace each other and to express their happiness at finding their friends and family among the living.

Then they hobbled out into the streets on their cut, bleeding feet to see if they still had homes.

In upper Charleston the people straggled, staggering, from the parks and railroad yards. All were in a dazed state, and they did not notice the pale woman among them whose eyes looked as if she had seen the deepest pit of Hell. It was Lucy Anson. She was gripped by a private fear so great that the terrors of the shaking night could not penetrate it. Her heart told her that Pinckney was dead. The mysterious bond between his thoughts and hers was broken; there could be no other explanation.

Still, she had to find out for sure. In the deepest recesses of her soul, her spirit refused to accept the loss. It prodded her onward, whispering a sweet serenade of promises . . . He's hurt, but he's alive. His mind cannot reach yours because he is unconscious. Not because he's dead. He can't be dead. He can't be.

She mumbled the words aloud, setting a beat for her stumbling feet. "He can't be, he can't be, he can't be, he can't be . . ." The syllables lost all meaning, but she continued to speak them until her mouth was dry and her lips cracked. Then she said them in her mind while she covered the long, painful miles, cutting and bruising her feet on rubble, tearing her nightdress and her hands when she had to climb over treacherous mounds of shifting, tumbled walls. Masonry dust settled on her head and body, coating it with white except for the dark splotches of blood from her wounds. She looked like a ghastly specter, an embodiment of her own fears, and other survivors shied away from her and let her pass.

It was late afternoon when she turned in through the sprung iron gate to the Tradds' garden. A slanting ray of sun rested on Pinckney's dust-filled red hair. Lucy sagged against the frivolous iron curlicues. "No!" she shouted to the heavens. "No," she whispered to the evidence of her own eyes.

She could not relinquish hope. Repetition had made her believe her own hollow words. "He can't be dead," she cried, and she lunged toward Pinckney, unaware of Julia Ashley's body even when she stumbled against its outflung arm. Pinckney's eyes were closed, and his face looked young and peaceful, like a sleeping child's. Lucy hurried to him, heedless of the ruin around them. "Pinny, my darling, it's Lucy. You'll be all right now. Wake up, my love." She fell to her knees at his side and took his hand in hers.

The cold lifelessness struck through to the core of her being, but still she refused to accept the truth. Murmuring endearments, she rubbed his hand between her own, trying to warm it.

At last, the terrible limpness penetrated her consciousness. She recoiled, throwing Pinckney's hand from her, and stared at his tranquil face.

A searing sense of loss burned her soul, followed by an explosion of agonized rage. "Wake up," she shouted. "You can't leave me like this after I've waited all these years. You cannot, I say." She threw herself across him, her bleeding hands beating against his stony chest until exhaustion stopped her.

She was able to weep, then, holding his unblemished head against her rag-covered bosom and kissing the dust from his hair into her own parched mouth.

When she had no tears left, she laid his head gently on a patch of grass from which she swept the dust and splinters with her hand. She sat quietly by his side, unmoving. All her fury and grief were spent for the moment; she felt nothing except a boundless emptiness.

Dr. de Winter found her there. "Leave him, Lucy," he said. "I'll see that he's taken care of. We need you to help us with Mr. Josiah."

Mr. Anson was standing amid the rubble of the Hibernian Hall. His eyes were vacant and confused. "I have to light the candles," he said in a childlike voice, "but the steps are gone." He held his worn old dancing pumps in his trembling hands.

Lucy put her arms around him. "The Ball isn't tonight," she said. "I guess you mixed up the time. Come along, Mr. Josiah. Let's go home."

Dr. de Winter had found a horse somewhere. A black man passing by stopped and helped him lift Mr. Anson onto its bare back. "I can't take the time to lead him, Mistress Anson," de Winter said. "There are injured people who need a doctor. Can you manage alone?"

"Yes, Doctor, I can manage." Lucy's voice was harsh. "I have a lot of practice in managing."

The horse plodded slowly uptown, detouring around the obstacles that Lucy had climbed over. It was an old horse, and it gave no trouble. The only time it showed any skittishness was when a piercing whistle tore the air as they passed Market Street. Even then, it only sidestepped a bit, then resumed its lethargic pace.

The whistle announced the arrival of a ferry from across the Cooper. It was riding perilously low in the choppy water, overloaded with evacuees from Sullivans Island. Among them were Elizabeth and her children. Like the other passengers, they were hollow-eyed and jumpy. Catherine and Tradd had slept fitfully during the afternoon, but they were tired from the long walk to the ferry slip at the end of the Island and the uncomfortable, crowded trip across the river. Elizabeth was drained. She had not closed her eyes for thirty-six hours.

When they saw the destruction in the city, the children began to cry. Elizabeth dug deep into the supernatural stamina of mothers and found a bright, cheerful voice. "Such fussbudgets," she said, crouching down between them. "Catherine, you climb on Mama's back to play horsey. Tradd, I'll make a kangaroo pouch for you in my skirt. Then we'll just scoot home in no time at all." Lumpy with giggling children, she staggered to her feet and set out for Meeting Street.

Oddly, her exhaustion helped her. She was too numb to feel the children's weight or to comprehend the catastrophe that had transformed the once-familiar streets into an alien landscape. She thought of nothing except putting one foot in front of the other and supporting her precious burdens as she trudged toward the beacon of Saint Michael's white spire in the thickening darkness.

She was ready to fall down when Dr. de Winter saw her passing the church. "Elizabeth!" he called, but she didn't hear him. He ran out into the street holding out his arms to stop her. She looked blindly at him while he scooped Catherine and Tradd from her. "Follow me," he said. "It's not far."

De Winter took them to the improvised camp in the grounds of the Scots Church. Ladies were serving coffee and hot soup from pots hung over small fires. The men, who were working in teams to clear the streets and test the safety of the floors in the houses, lined up for mugs of steaming liquid, gulped it down, then returned to their labors. Scattered around the yard, children and old people were sleeping on long pews that had been dragged from the church building.

"Here's a bench for you," Dr. de Winter said. "You rest with the children while I tell Kitty you're here. She'll bring you all some soup."

"Thank you, Jim," said Elizabeth. She did as she was told, too tired to ask questions.

"I brought you some coffee, too," whispered Kitty de Winter. "Look at the babies, sleeping like angels. They can have their soup later. You should get some rest, too, Elizabeth. There's room on that pew by the fire."

Elizabeth touched her old friend's arm. "Thank you, Kitty. I'll just find Pinny and tell him we're all right. He's probably worried half sick. Then I'll sleep as I've never slept before."

The quality of Kitty's silence cut through Elizabeth's fatigue. Suddenly she was wide awake.

"What is it, Kitty? Is Pinckney hurt?" Elizabeth leaned close to Kitty, trying to read her face in the dim light from the distant fire. What she saw there made her shudder. She leapt up.

"Wait!" Kitty found her voice. "There's nothing you can do." She started to run after Elizabeth, but Tradd cried out in his sleep. Kitty looked from her friend's disappearing back to the little boy. Tradd whimpered. She sat down by him and patted his small shoulder.

Someone had improvised biers from saw-horses with doors across them. Pinckney and Julia were decently laid out, their bodies covered with curtains. A big black man sat on the joggling board near them. He held a torch and a club. When he saw Elizabeth, he rose ponderously to his feet. "Ain't no varmints going to get these dead," he said. "Don't you worry, missus."

In the shadows away from the circle of light, something scuttled. Red eyes blinked like fireflies. Elizabeth screamed.

And screamed again. Then again and again, until the guard shouted at her. "Please, missus, please stop."

Elizabeth stared wildly at him. He was near tears, and she reacted with automatic compunction. "I'm sorry," she stammered, "I didn't mean to upset you. Do I know you?"

"No, ma'am. I is Manigo what drives for the doctor."

"Thank you for sitting with my people, Manigo." Her gratitude was genuine. The big man, she knew, was more frightened by the presence of the dead than she was by the presence of the scavenger rodents outside the small island of light. She could hear Julia Ashley's voice in her mind: "It is your duty to be strong and to set an example for the servants. They depend on you." Elizabeth managed to smile at Manigo, hoping that the grimace was reassuring. Then she glanced at her aunt's face, to see if Julia approved.

It was only at that moment that Elizabeth understood that Julia was dead. That she would never again nod shortly in acknowledgment of proper behavior, never frown in terrifying censure. Julia Ashley, who had never been beaten by war, by storm, by time itself. Julia Ashley was dead.

Elizabeth had never thought about how important her indomitable aunt had been in her life. But now, her loss carried with it all the certainty that Julia's presence had guaranteed. If Julia Ashley could be defeated by Death, then there was no safety in the world, no strength that was enough, nothing standing between Elizabeth and all the unknown terrors of life.

Her teeth began to chatter. In the midst of the oppressive, sultry heat of the night, she was gripped by a chill that shook her whole body. Aunt Julia was gone.

And Pinckney. Elizabeth's frozen heart could not even mourn her beloved brother. She stared at his calm face and felt nothing. He was finally going to be happy, she thought, and now he won't. It's not fair . . . Why, I'm thinking like a child. Not fair. This is death, not a game. Fair has nothing to do with it.

I should feel something. I should cry for poor Pinny, for Aunt Julia, for Stuart, who's probably dead, too. But all I feel is so terribly, terribly cold. Please, God, help me. I need to feel something so that I'll know I'm not dead, too. She wrapped her arms about her body, trying to stop the shaking.

"Is you sick, missus?" Manigo's voice seemed to come from a great distance. "I'll fetch somebody for you. I'll find the doctor or somebody. Who you want Manigo to fetch, missus?"

Elizabeth held herself closer. "Nobody, Manigo," she said. "There's nobody you can find. They're all gone. I'm all alone."

Emotion came, then, desperate grief and fear. It raced through her, hot, making her cold limbs tingle, exposing every nerve. Alone. There was no one to turn to, no one to help her, no one to stand between her and the unnameable dangers that lay in wait. "Aunt Julia!" she cried. "Pinny! Don't leave me. What will I do?"

The big man seized her hand and closed it around the torch. "Hold this, missus," he begged. "I got to gets somebody." He disappeared into the darkness, not heeding Elizabeth's pleas to stay.

"Oh, my God," she moaned. Her own voice frightened her. There was no one to answer. She looked around her, holding the torch high. It reflected redly off eyes watching her. Elizabeth made a last, small sound, then sat down, pulling her feet up from the ground. Under her, the joggling board quivered, trying to throw her into the darkness. She buried her head in her skirts to blot out the world.

Something touched her shoulder. She smelled scorching, felt hands slapping at her skirt.

"You dropped the torch. Fool. Stop that mewling. Look at me."

Elizabeth forced her eyes open. Kitty de Winter and her husband were on each side of her, holding her arms. Kitty shook her roughly. "There are really hurt people who need Jim, Elizabeth. You've got to pull yourself together. He can't be running to tend you every minute. Now come on back to the churchyard and stop carrying on so. You scared Manigo half to death."

"Leave me alone." Elizabeth tried to pull away from them.

"Elizabeth!" Kitty shook harder.

Dr. de Winter's deep voice stopped her. "Kitty, don't. She's in shock. Hold her head while I give her some laudanum. Then I'll carry her back to the camp."

Kitty did as she was told, but she muttered audibly while her husband ministered to Elizabeth. "I'm sorry for her and all that, Jim, but I can't take on Elizabeth's duties. I'm tired, too. We're all tired. She's not the only one. Who's going to take care of Tradd and Catherine when they wake up hungry and cranky? Nobody offered me any sleeping draught. I can't watch out for everybody."

Elizabeth slipped deeper and deeper into a welcoming darkness. She tried to speak, but she had no strength. "I'll do it," she wanted to say. "My children. I'll watch out for my children."

The Great Charleston Earthquake was front-page news in every newspaper in the western world. Joe Simmons folded the New York *Journal* and picked up the telephone to order his private railroad car brought from the yards.

"Emily, I've got to go down to the mills," he said. "Nobody knows how far the damage reached, and all the telegraph lines are down. I have to see what happened."

"You aren't going to Charleston, I hope. The paper says there may still be more shocks."

"Don't worry, honey. I don't want any walls falling on me. I'll stay far away from the place."

Simmonsville had been shaken enough to terrify people, but there was no real damage, except for broken windows. Joe could have left for New York after a day.

But he stayed. He used the pretext of going over past years' activity with the lawyer who handled all his South Carolina affairs. In fact, he was held by a totally unexpected nostalgia. This flat, baked land was the countryside of his birth; the decrepit, sagging shacks and stunted cotton plants he passed were identical to the farm where he had spent his childhood. The mill, ugly and weathered to drabness, was the beginning of his fortune. The straggling mill town bore his name. He looked around him and saw the squalid poverty he had escaped, and he vowed never to forget it again. He had come to believe in Joseph Simmons of Fifth Avenue and Wall Street, New York City. He had become complacent, even a little dissatisfied with his life. "I'm the luckiest devil in the world," he told himself now, "and I'd best remember it."

When he told Emily he would stay away from Charleston, he meant it. But now that it was so near, he felt it tug at him. His memories were softened by time. Now he saw the Tradds at Christmas, filling his first-ever Santa stocking, sharing the little they had with him. And he was ashamed of the anger he had felt and the damage he had done to Pinckney. Perhaps, he thought, he should go and apologize. That would be another first-ever for him. But his pride would not let him.

Until his lawyer told him that he had received a bank draft from the Tradd-Simmons Phosphate Company every six months for all the nine years he had been away. "Damn it all," Joe exploded, "you should have let me know. They can't afford to send me money." And he made up his mind to go to Charleston. I've got to see Pinny, he thought. And Lizzie, even if it tears me to pieces.

The manager at the Charleston Hotel was "delighted" to accommodate Mr. Simmons with a suite of rooms and a wealth of information. Mr. Pinckney Tradd, he said, was dead; the funeral had to be held at graveside because Saint Michael's was closed until it could be repaired. Mr. Stuart Tradd was still in the Roper Hospital with a skull fracture, but he was expected to recover. Mistress Elizabeth Tradd Cooper? No, she was not hurt. As a matter of fact, everyone was still talking about how bravely she had managed her brother's interment. Her aunt's, too. They said she had practically poled the barge up the Ashley River herself. The old lady wouldn't rest easy, she had told everybody, unless she was in her own land. Yes, sir, that Mistress Cooper was a fine little lady. She hadn't broke down once. Reminded folks of when her husband had that accident a few years back. She had gone through his funeral the same way, holding in her grief.

Joe threw a twenty-dollar gold piece on the man's desk and shot through the door.

"Like the sheriff was on his tail," the manager told the desk clerk. "Wonder what the Tradds are to a rich Yankee like him."

52

"Miz Cooper, they's a gentlemans asking for you." Delia rolled her eyes to indicate that the gentleman was a stranger, that she was impressed by him and that he would overhear any comments she might make aloud.

Elizabeth looked over her shoulder to the stocky, well-dressed man in the hall. He was staring at her. When their eyes met, his disappeared in a cross-hatch of deep wrinkles.

"Joe!" She ran past Delia and threw her arms around him, bending to put her cheek against his. "Oh, Joe. I'm so happy to see you. You look wonderful. Come sit down." Elizabeth led him to the settee in the library. She kept hold of his hand while they sat and talked. Joe hid his shock at her appearance. She was frighteningly pallid. Her deep blue eyes and red-gold hair looked garish in contrast to her colorless skin. Beneath her eyes and cheekbones, hollows held shadows, so that she seemed to be bruised. She was as fragile and frightened as the little girl he had first met twenty-three years before.

"How long has it been, Joe? It seems like an age."

"It has been an age. Ten years," he said. And not a day of that time, he said to himself, that I didn't think about you. What have they done to you, Lizzie? Why are you so battered? So nervous? His deepest senses told him that the earthquake alone could not account for her condition. She was dangerously near the breaking point.

Joe talked, then, his deep voice slow and soothing. He told her about Victoria and her tea parties; he told her about New York and its mushroom growth; he told her about the opera and its exciting stories; he told her about his trips to Europe, including the first one, and he exhibited his fine teeth. He even told her about his masquerade in New York when he impressed everyone with the single m in his name. By the end of his long, relaxed account, Elizabeth was laughing. Joe had an uncanny sense of having gone back in time to the days when he alone could make the solemn little pig-tailed Lizzie smile. He longed to take that child in his arms and protect her from a hostile world.

But that child and those easy remedies were long past. He had to discover who this woman was and what she needed; then he would know what to do for her, and thus for the Lizzie that was still part of her.

During the weeks that followed, Joe Simmons learned a great deal about Elizabeth and about himself and about Charleston. The city literally pulled itself back together. All the buildings had been affected, but frame structures had been able to take the conflicting stresses with only the loss of their brick chimneys. The houses and stores and warehouses that were made of brick had all cracked, and their walls were not safe. The city called on its ironworkers, the inheritors of the skill that had produced the majestic gates and intricate balconies of the beautiful old buildings. Long threaded iron rods were inserted into the houses; they ran under the beams that supported the floors and staircases. Once in place, they were like tremendous nuts. Bolts were then put on each end and tightened until the walls were returned to nearly their original dimensions. Rebuilt chimneys and fresh mortar in the cracks completed the restoration. Decorative iron caps over the bolts transformed necessity into beauty.

"It's survival with style," Joe said appreciatively. It was, he thought, the story of Charleston from its earliest days. He compared it with New York; the raw energy and passion for progress that had excited him suddenly looked like wasteful destruction. Old things and old people were despised by everyone he knew in the expanding city he now called home. In the contracting world south of Broad, they were cherished.

Joe valued them, too. It was an aspect of his nature that he had never realized before. When he had leisure moments, he spent them investigating himself, making other discoveries. It was a fascinating study.

But he had little time to pursue it. His primary concern was Lizzie. Or, as she preferred, Elizabeth. He did not question her now, just as he had not questioned the little girl he had known. But he felt, as he had felt then, that she was the victim of unnameable horror. And she was in retreat, though not as obviously as the silent child who rocked in her little chair. Elizabeth smiled and talked and supervised the constant cleaning of the plaster that was still drifting down from the ceilings and walls. But it was an act, and Joe knew it. With every day that passed, she was going farther into some world inside herself, some fortress of non-life where nothing and no one could reach her.

He thought long and hard about how to help. He decided, at last, that he had to take the biggest chance of his life, to risk losing the trust she had in him and the affection she had given him with all the openness of their first friendship. His heart wanted to take care of her, but his love for her made him push her away. She had to come back from that fortress or she would be lost to herself. After dinner one day, he pushed his chair back, controlled his voice and his face to seem natural, cleared his throat and spoke.

"You'll have to run the phosphate company now, Elizabeth. There's nobody else. Stuart inherited the Barony and is going to move there and be a planter. Pinckney left you this house and the business. If you want your children to eat, you'll have to earn some money."

"But it's your business too, Joe. I just assumed you'd take over."

"Nonsense, I've got much bigger fish to fry. I'll stay long enough to break you in, but then I've got to get back to New York."

"I can't do it."

"Of course you can. I saw you running this house when you were still in short skirts. A business is a lot easier. And a lot of fun. You were a bossy little miss. Now you can be a boss again. You'll like it."

"But, Joe, ladies don't go into business. Everyone would be scandalized."

"Don't hand me that applesauce. The finest ladies I ever knew were in business after the War. How about Mistress Allston and Mistress Pinckney and their schools? Do you think they put up with the likes of you because it amused them? There are ladies today doing mending, taking in boarders, teaching piano and giving dancing classes. All to keep a roof over their heads. You're a Tradd, my child. You can do anything you please, short of murder, and no one will say a word."

He couldn't imagine why she looked so startled. "I'll have to think about it," she said.

Joe smiled. It was going to work. "You always used to say that when you were a child," he said. "Your face did what it's doing now, too. Eyebrows crunched into the middle. It makes me feel young again."

Two days later, Joe rented a boat and crew, and they went to Carlington. It was deserted except for one ancient black man, who hobbled out from the wreckage of the derelict old house. He introduced himself as Cudjo, making an arthritic bow to Elizabeth. "Must be you is Mist' Pickney sister, ma'am. Ain't nobody else could have them sunrise glory hair. My heart done broke to learn he gone. Don't seem hardly fitting the good Lord take him and leave a old, bent-over nigger like me." Tears made a dark path over his sunken cheeks.

Elizabeth put an arm around his shoulders. "You mustn't weep, Daddy. The good Lord has his reasons. I need your help; maybe He spared you to take care of another Tradd. Mr. Pinckney told me how you took care of him."

Joe watched the old man become younger before his eyes. He had forgotten, during the years in New York, the subtle interaction of responsibility and dependence between the old Charleston families and their former slaves. It was summed up in the Charleston habit of addressing old black men as "Daddy" and black women as "Mauma." To a white child of the family, they were almost like parents, and the child owed them the respect due to parents. In return, the "parents" were expected to provide guidance and unquestioning concern for the well-being of the child, even when that child was a grown man or woman. It was a system that had never been codified in law, and Emancipation had affected it not at all. No outsider could hope to understand it, so Joe did not even try. He simply accepted the fact that Elizabeth was now in territory she knew and that Daddy Cudjo would take care of her. He followed the two of them, his sharp eye noticing the patched, antiquated equipment and general atmosphere of laxness. Pinckney had been no businessman.

The diggings had extended, through the years, to cover an area of more than a mile along the riverbank. Many of the pits had been refilled with earth from the next pit dug. There were still, however, dozens with mounds of overburden next to the eight-foot-deep holes. They were rank, with pools of scummy rainwater at the bottom. Elizabeth said something disapproving to Daddy Cudjo, and he cackled. The housewife will be making some changes here, thought Joe. Wait until she sees the flies in the company store.

On the trip back down the river, Elizabeth was abstracted. Joe noticed that she had some color in her cheeks and that she had not remembered to put on the mourning veil that was on her shoulders. It looked as if the cure was working already. "The old man said he'd call all the workers back by a week from next Monday," Joe reminded her. "If you're going to sell the company, there's no point in having a payroll to meet in the meantime. Any new owner will want to modernize right away."

"Modernize how?"

Joe pointed to the plant they were passing. "Like that," he said. "That's a real phosphate company. What you've got is just a bunch of holes in the ground."

Elizabeth ordered the boatmen to slow down. While the current held them almost in place, she stared at the tall smokestacks that sent up streams of violent yellow smoke and listened to the clangor of heavy machinery and rattling railroad cars. "What's that foul smell?" she asked Joe.

"I don't think it's foul, honey. Superphosphates, the chemists call it. I call it money." He gestured to the boatmen, and they speeded up. While the city grew nearer, he gave Elizabeth a quick education in the development of the fertilizer business in the twenty years since the discovery of the Charleston phosphate deposits.

"First thing," he said, "everybody just dug up the ore and washed it and shipped it off to Baltimore or Philadelphia for processing. The chemical companies up North paid around fourteen dollars a ton at their plants. Shipping costs were paid by the producers.

"It wasn't long before the smarter producers started crushing the rock because they were paying by the carload, and a car could hold a lot more crushed rock than lump ore.

"Then First Charleston Mining, which had heavy northern financing and considerable northern management, got their own sulphuric acid vats. That's the basis of the refinement, you see. Crushed rock goes into the acid, and it converts the phosphate to several products: a calcium salt and a soluble phosphoric acid and a residue called superphosphate. All three of them have a separate market value that's higher than the phosphate ore by itself. Are you following me?" Elizabeth nodded.

"Good. Well, the local processing started about the end of 1870. Several of the bigger companies were converted to manufacturing by seventy-one. They imported so much sulphuric acid that they could have had practically a river of it. Risky stuff, too. It'll burn a man's hand right off if he's not careful handling it. That's the main reason Pinckney wouldn't have anything to do with it. He figured the workers couldn't hurt themselves much with a pick and a shovel and a wheelbarrow."

"Wasn't he right?"

"Maybe. Maybe not. I disagreed with him. You can't protect grown men like they were children. We lost a lot of our best workers to the other companies because handling acid pays higher than shoveling ore. It can afford to; the income from the same amount of phosphate is more than tripled, even when you figure the cost of the acid."

"How much does it cost?"

Joe hid his elation. His pupil was beginning to think like a businessman.

"That was the next step," he said. "The acid came from northern chemical companies, many of them the very same companies that were happy to buy the ore and process it themselves. They weren't exactly dying to sell acid and put Charleston companies into competition. They would only sell F.O.B., which meant the local boys had to pay the freight. Shipping costs can make or break a manufacturer. The railroads set the rates, and the rates for acid were mighty high."

Elizabeth's eyes were sparkling. "I don't suppose," she said, "that any of the chemical people were cousins to any of the railroad people."

Joe slapped his knee. "God help some of my best friends if you ever got turned loose on Wall Street. You hit the nail on the head. Except that we're not talking about the South. These businessmen aren't related by blood, just by money. Interlocking directorships, they call it. It's a tight club, and heaven help the non-members."

"Come on, Joe. You haven't changed so much that I can't tell when you're saving the best part of the story. What happened next?"

"How's your geography?"

"Pretty good for any place Aunt Julia ever went. Otherwise, not so hot."

"Did she ever go to Sicily? Or Italy?"

"Italy. She loved it. She said Florence reminded her of Charleston."

"Sicily is nothing like South Carolina. It's an island, a great big one, near Italy. It's maybe the only place on earth where people are poorer than the Charlestonians were in the seventies. And it's got so much sulphur that sometimes a mountain opens up and spits it out in a rain of fire."

"I don't believe you."

"Okay, don't believe the volcano. But you'd better believe the sulphur because that's where the fertilizer plant you just saw gets it from. They import it direct by ship, and they make their own sulphuric acid. With their own acid, they make fertilizer from their own rock. And then they ship the fertilizer by ocean freight direct to England. Finished product. No railroad shipping costs, no waiting for supplies or empty cars, no fighting the directorships. They're completely independent."

Elizabeth smiled. "And they didn't even have to fire on Fort Sumter. The Yankees must be awful mad."

"They're not happy."

"Could Carlington do the same thing?"

"It could. It would take time and some very close management. Also some capital investment, but I could supply that. What do you say?"

Elizabeth looked thoughtful. "How hard is it to learn bookkeeping? That's what you mean by management, isn't it?"

"There's a little more to it, but understanding your books is where you have to start."

"Then we'll stop at the office on the way home. We'll pick up the books, you'll stay for supper, and after the children are in bed, you can explain them to me." Bossy Lizzie was back. Joe looked away to hide the emotion in his eyes.

Saint Michael's had just rung two when Elizabeth closed the big ledger and rubbed her eyes. "My goodness," she said, "I haven't been up this late in I don't know how long. Why don't you just stay the night, Joe? I'll keep the children quiet in the morning so you can sleep."

He thought of being under the same roof with her, of having breakfast with her, of spending the next day and the next and the next with her. There was a special intimacy to the gas-lit room in the sleeping city. Joe felt as if they were alone in a world apart, where nothing could touch them. But they weren't. The sun will rise, he told himself, and the room will be only a room, a tiny corner of a very large world. The sooner you return to it, my friend, the less it will hurt to say good-bye. And there is no alternative. Good-bye, it has to be. There are Victoria and Emily and New York. All waiting for you.

He stood and stretched. "Thanks, Elizabeth, but I can't stay. I've got a satchel full of papers at the hotel and letters to write. I really should go back down to Simmonsville and see how things are going. I think the best thing is for you to study the books for a few days, think about all the things you've seen and learned. I'll be back on Saturday night. After church Sunday, I'll come over, and you can tell me what you've decided." He was talking rapidly, and his voice was harsh. Elizabeth looked at him with a hurt, confused expression that wrung his heart. She had no way of knowing that he was being rough to keep himself from saying all the things he wanted to say, declarations of love that would alarm her more than his rasping, businesslike tone ever could.

"Joe?" His name was a question, meaning "why?"

He closed his arms around her in a quick, convulsive embrace. "Everything's going to be all right, baby," he said. Then he tore himself away, in proof of his promise. He walked slowly to the hotel, feeling the night air on him like an intolerable weight.

Two weeks later, Joe arrived back in New York. He entertained his friends at his club with the amazing story of his ladylike little business partner. "I tell you," he said, "we'd just better keep women out of business. I've never seen anything like it. I went away for three days, and when I got back, I had been squeezed right out of the picture. We think we're pretty smart at putting deals together; there's no cartel in the world to match the cousins of Charleston. When I think about it, I hardly know whether to laugh or cry."

"This is what I've done, Joe," Elizabeth had told him. "I thought it over and made up my mind, so I got started without waiting for you."

Tradd-Simmons had been shipping three thousand tons of phosphate a year, for a total income of forty-two thousand dollars. The company's expenses were nearly thirty thousand, of which six thousand was the cost of shipping the ore and one thousand the cost of renting office and warehouse space in the city. Elizabeth had called on her cousin Aggie who was married to one of the owners of Planters Fertilizer and Phosphate, the plant Joe had pointed out to her. Aggie's husband was happy to help Elizabeth out. He would pay only a dollar a ton less than the Baltimore chemical company; then he would process the ore in his plant along with his own. "He'll make a fortune, which is nice, and we'll save six thousand in shipping costs at a cost to us of only three thousand dollars. Plus he'll split the cost of putting in a spur track from Carlington to the North-East Railroad track that hooks up to his spur. Everybody comes out better off. Naturally, we won't need warehouse space then, and that'll save us some. Also I'm closing the office. A lady can't come and go on Broad Street business blocks. I'm converting the carriage house to offices for me and for Nat Wragg. He's been working for the Pringles, and I just stole him. He knows everything there is to know about the fertilizer business. Mr. Pringle is furious."

Joe had asked her how she managed the theft. Nothing to it, she had replied blandly. Nat Wragg was a cousin of Caroline's; they had all been in dancing school together. And his wife was a Pinckney third cousin. Besides, Elizabeth was going to pay him half again as much as the Pringles gave him.

"Which is still," she said, "a thousand a year less than Pinny was paying Lucas. No wonder we lived so high on the hog. Pinckney was keeping two thousand and giving Lucas four. I'm planning to make your share less, too, Joe. We'll each contribute four thousand to improvements. That will leave three thousand in profits for you and for me." The improvements, she figured, would take eight years.

The Carlington half share for the spur track would use the 1877 budget. Then in eighty-eight they'd build a shed and machinery to crush the rock. By eighty-nine they'd be able to replace the worn washing drums and enlarge the shed. The next year they'd build the big plant which would contain the refining and separating machinery. Two years, ninety-one and ninety-two, would be needed to buy the machinery and the vats for the sulphuric acid. "Then we can really start to recoup. Edward Hanahan will sell us acid from Planters' plant for our processing. With the profit we make in ninety-three, we'll be able to build our own acid plant and start importing our sulphur in ninety-four. It's perfect. Catherine will be fifteen that year, and, as I remember, that's just when a girl wants a new gown for every party. I'll need to be rich."

Joe had wanted to put up the capital at once. There was no need for Elizabeth to scrimp for eight years. But she begged him not to. "I'd really like to do it all from Carlington, Joe. It would make me feel good to build something. I've had a lot of destruction these past few years and no building at all." He could not refuse. It was exactly what he wanted for her, although he wished it was somehow possible for him to give it to her instead of her working so hard for it.

BOOK EIGHT

1887-1898

53

"Charleston. June 11, 1887 . . . Dear Joe. Such excitement here! Our own little Carlington railroad opened yesterday. Edward Hanahan lent us one of his tiny locomotives and a flatcar. He really is the dearest creature. The engine was polished to a fare-thee-well, and the flatcar was fresh painted and trimmed with bunting. Stuart brought his boys in from the Barony in his surrey and carried me, Catherine and Tradd out to Carlington. It was a long trip for us, longer for him, but the children behaved pretty well, and I had the foresight to pack lots of sandwiches and lemonade, so it came off all right. Little Stuart was disappointed that we didn't have a golden spike in our track, but he forgave us when he was allowed to ride in the cab and pull the whistle. Then, of course, nothing would do but to let each of the children have a turn. A noisy outing. We had our picnic on the flatcar, riding forward to the main line, then backing up to the Carlington loading platform. Then forward again, and so on, until every crumb of food was gone. I had forgotten my parasol, and I'm afraid I will be freckled as a mockingbird's egg for the rest of my days. But I don't care. It was a marvelous day, and the first step on the Master Plan has been taken.

"As I told you, there was a lot of talk when I opened the office behind the house and became a businesslady. It has all died down now. President Cleveland and his wife came to see the gardens in the spring, and people are still so busy criticizing their manners that they have forgotten all about me. I'm not very visible, anyhow. I bought one of those Remington Printing Machines and am teaching myself to use it. It makes letters that look just like the pages of a book. But I suppose such fancinesses as 'typewriting' are no novelty in New York. My 'new' machine is actually over ten years old. The man who sold it to me was embarrassed that it was such an antique. I didn't tell him that I'd never even known such a thing existed. Pinny always did his correspondence at home, and I remember him at the desk, dipping his pen into the funny old inkwell our papa gave him.

"I still forget sometimes that Pinny is gone. Yesterday, Stuart and his boys looked like a row of copper pennies with the sun on their hair. In the midst of all our happiness, I felt a terrible pang of missing that other Tradd redhead that should have been there.

"But then my nasty, selfish inner voice reminded me that I was there, and that I'm a Tradd, too. A secret between you and me, Joe. I'm beginning to believe I'm a very good Tradd. I simply adore putting neat lines of numbers in the account books and writing snippy letters signed E. Tradd to the crooks who try to charge us too much for store supplies and such. I catch every 'mistake' and have saved the company more than twenty-seven dollars already this year. Ned Wragg is an absolute saint about taking orders from a lady. He calls me 'Mister Tradd, ma'am,' but there's no malice in it. He has the work at Carlington well in hand, with mountains of ore ready to go over to Planters. I suppose it's actually in route today.

"Please forgive me for not writing the last two months. I didn't have much to say except that the track was being laid. We move to the Island for the summer next month, and I won't have much to report from there, either, unless you find sunburn and scraped knees fascinating. Tradd is two and a half now, and I plan to teach him to swim. Catherine is already like a guppy. It will mean more freckles for me, I suppose, but I love the ocean too much to worry about it.

"My fondest regards to Emily and Victoria. I hope we will have an opportunity to meet one day. And to you, dearest Joe, a heart full of love from your phosphate partner . . . Elizabeth."

Joe folded the letter and put it in the drawer with the others he had received from Elizabeth. She wrote almost every month; he read each letter until he knew it by heart.

"How are things in Charleston, dear?" Emily Simmons was a shrewd woman. She never interrupted her husband when he was looking at his mail, particularly not when there was a letter from Elizabeth Cooper.

"They've finished the spur track at Carlington," Joe said. "The children had a picnic on a flatcar while they rode on it."

Emily shuddered delicately. "How unsanitary. I'm glad we have our own railroad car with a proper dining table. Victoria would never survive anything so rough."

Joe looked pensive. "Charlestonians can survive just about anything," he murmured.

"That's nice," commented Emily. "You'd better get changed soon, Joseph. We're dining with Father and Mother tonight. You'll have time to tuck Victoria in if you hurry."

The letters continued to come, month after month, until they filled three drawers of Joe's desk. He waited for them, and if one was late, he had to exert all his willpower to keep from telegraphing an inquiry about Elizabeth's well-being. He hated himself for what he admitted was an unbalanced clinging to an outgrown dream, but it made no difference. He was in love, as he had been ever since the skinny little girl appeared on the staircase in her first long dress.

Emily's devotion ceased being something he took for granted. It became, in his mind, an unspoken demand that he was conscious of never answering. While Elizabeth's letters reflected her growing self-confidence, Emily seemed more and more dependent upon him for her opinions, her happiness and her every decision. Joe was mired in guilt because he could not love her and because she loved him too much. He became much more attentive and considerate than he had ever been. We're in the same boat, Em and I, he thought, loving on a one-way street. At least I can sympathize and try to make it easier for her. He succeeded magnificently. Emily glowed with happiness; the Simmonses were acknowledged to have the "most perfect" marriage any of their friends had ever seen.

Joe stayed away from Charleston and Elizabeth for more than five years. He answered her letters with brief, encouraging notes; he involved himself in ever-more-daring manipulations of the market and raids on competitors; he took his wife and daughter to Europe to buy art and furniture under the guidance of an impecunious Italian nobleman; he made and spent millions of dollars. And all the time he was haunted. Not by Elizabeth; he knew he could not have her. He was haunted by Elizabeth's city. In London, the chimes of Big Ben rang identical to the chimes of Saint Michael's, and he could not sleep. In Florence, he looked everywhere for the similarities Julia Ashley had found to Charleston. In Nice, the pastel walls, the riot of flowers, the raised promenade along the water, the wind in the palm trees—all said Charleston to him. Even in New York, he walked for hours along the narrow streets of Greenwich Village. Forgotten now by the city which had spread all the way up to Seventieth Street, the old area was quiet, like Charleston, its Federal houses sleeping, like Charleston, its atmosphere like a tiny world under a sorcerer's spell, forgotten by the hurrying years. Like Charleston. Joe was homesick for a life where people spoke slowly and softly and cared for each other.

In the spring of 1892, on one climactic day, everything came to a head. His office was in a furor when he arrived. Someone, or a group of someones, was dumping tens of thousands of shares of a stock that he had taken a large position in. If he wanted to support the investment he had already made, he would have to pour more than a half million into buying the shares that were flooding the exchange. It was a classic raid. On him. The only men capable of that kind of manipulation were his friends. His preoccupation with other things had made him careless, therefore a suitable victim. And, Joe realized, he didn't care. The thrust and parry of finance was no longer a challenge. "Stop buying," he told his floor broker.

"We'll take the loss." He watched the tape while he lost more than three hundred thousand dollars. Then he went home.

There was a letter from Elizabeth, reporting a frustrating delay in delivery of the sulphuric acid vats and, for the first time, asking his help with a personal problem. ". . . In a way, I brought it on myself. I've been bragging so much about how well Carlington is doing that it must sound as if I'm wallowing in greenbacks. I'm much too proud to admit to anyone that I miscalculated the way the price of everything would rise. The fact is, I have the house and the plant mortgaged to the chimneys to pay for the machinery. It will all be taken care of when we start doing our own refining, but Stuart has asked me for a loan right now. He has been having nothing but trouble at the Barony since the day he moved there. Henrietta says it's just bad luck, but I'm afraid it's because he treats his hands so badly. He acts as if he owns them, and they don't work for him. So the fields are full of weeds, the rice is poor grade, and the stock is half-starved. I've tried to talk to him, but he won't listen. He'd rather blame everything on Abe Lincoln for freeing the darkies. Anyhow, he's now two years behind on his taxes, and even a former Judge can't keep that up. He admitted that he's already sold a thousand acres of land just to have money to keep operating. He'll have to sell another four hundred if I can't help him. The Barony is huge, but I hate to think of any piece of it being cut off, no matter how insignificant. Could you possibly wait six months for your share of the company's income? That two thousand dollars will save Stuart's life. I cannot promise that he will ever pay it back, but I give you my word that I will.

"Enough gloominess! It's sinful to whine, especially in the spring. The honeysuckle vine has gone wonderfully crazy this year. It has grown right through the window and is trying to eat the ore samples on the file cabinet. The smell is heavenly, especially after a shower of rain . . ."

Joe put his head in his hands. Only two thousand dollars. He spent ten times that much for each statue he had bought for Emily's garden. He reached for pen and paper to draft a telegram, then noticed the bulky packet addressed to him in an unfamiliar feminine hand. It had come from Charleston.

When he opened it, a stained fragment of faded yellow silk fell out onto the desk. Folded inside it was a letter from Lucy Anson. His first thought was that she was telling him of some trouble that Elizabeth was too proud to admit. He scanned the tiny, cramped writing quickly.

" . . . kept up with your news from Elizabeth's reports . . . happy to hear about your success . . . exciting travels . . . lovely family . . ." His eyes slowed, then filled with a hot stinging.

"Mr. Josiah died peacefully in his sleep. He was seventy-eight, and it was time for him to rest. He had been very feeble and confused ever since the earthquake, but his last weeks were like a return to happier days for him. His appetite was good, and he was perfectly lucid. He knew he was going, and I did not insult him by denying it.

"We spoke of you, Joe. Mr. Josiah was pleased and not at all surprised when I relayed the news I had from Elizabeth about you. He said he had always known you had a lot to you, that you had saved Pinckney's life in more ways than one. He wanted to leave you something of his, as a token of his affection and respect. His watch was for his grandson, and he had little else. But he climbed up to the attic by himself and rummaged through all the things put away up there. He found this. It's the remnant of his Confederate uniform sash. The squirrels took most of it, I'm afraid. They must have used it to decorate their hideyholes. But Mr. Josiah said that a token was what counted. I was to tell you, he said, that if you had been in his company, he would have made you an officer and given it to you on the field. He added that God had made you a gentleman, and you had no need of insignia for that . . ."

"Joseph!" Emily's beautiful voice begged for his attention. He blinked his eyes clear so that he could see. "Victoria wants to show you something."

Joe looked at his daughter. Her pale hair was arranged in geometric tiers of shining ringlets, pinned up by gold clasps. Her frock was calf length, made of gleaming blue silk with cascades of lace at the ends of the elbow sleeves and lace ruffles around the hem. The back was an extravaganza of folds and velvet bows, a bustle larger than the child. Gold bracelets set with sapphires circled both wrists, and a necklace of sapphires glittered on her throat.

"Do you like my frock, Papa?" Victoria twirled to show it off.

"You look beautiful, sweetheart. Who's having a party?"

Emily shook her head. "You're so absentminded, Joseph. Victoria starts dancing school today. I told you a week ago."

"I thought you meant ballet classes."

"Heavens no. She's been going to ballet since she was five. This is ballroom dancing. Our little girl is becoming a young society lady."

"She's too young, Emily."

"She's ten. All the children start their ballroom at ten."

Joe looked at his child, dressed like a fashion plate, coiffed and jeweled like a woman. "No," he said. "I won't allow it. It's too much and too soon." He picked up the scrap of yellow silk and waved it like a banner. "Do you know what this is?"

Emily put her arm around Victoria. The two of them stared at him as if he were mad. Joe felt that perhaps he was. His heart was pounding and he was filled with a terrible angry pain. "This," he said in a barely audible voice, "is a reminder that I am a Southerner. I almost forgot for a while. But that's what I am, and that's what I want for my child. I want her to have more than the things money can buy. I want her to have a good life. We're going to move away from this noise and show. I'm going to take my family to Charleston."

Emily Simmons looked out of the window of the carriage that took the family from the train station to the Charleston Hotel, and her heart sank. The street was reasonably busy and prosperous-looking, but everything was so small, and so low. Not one building was more than four stories tall. Their house in New York was larger than most of them. She had not been present at the tempestuous meeting where Joseph told her father they were moving, but her father had made his views known to her later. The words rang in her head now. "Provincial . . . depressed . . . backward . . . slow . . ."

The impressive facade of the Charleston Hotel reassured her somewhat; the lavish dimensions of the rooms in their suite made up for the old-fashioned furniture. Emily looked for things to like. She wanted so much to please Joseph, and she knew that Charleston had a special importance to him, even though she could not understand it.

She praised the dinner, which she called luncheon, that they ate in the cavernous dining room behind the lobby. Victoria had to be reprimanded for staring at the black waiters. She had never seen a black man close before; neither had Emily, and she was equally fascinated, but she managed to act natural. She had no idea, she wrote her father that evening, that Negroes came in so many shades.

After dinner, they drove downtown. Emily remarked on the beauty of Saint Michael's church, and Joe ordered the carriage to halt. At that moment, the chimes rang. Emily's face brightened with genuine delight. "What a sweet tone," she said. "They're lovely bells." Three o'clock struck, and the watchman called. Victoria doubled up with giggles. Her mother shushed her. "It's charming," she said, "so quaint."

For an hour, they moved slowly through the old streets that Joe had learned twenty-five years before. Emily's smile stiffened, but she was determined to be agreeable. Victoria was a problem. She commented on everything and asked artless, awkward questions. "Look how narrow the streets are, Mama . . . that house is blue. What a funny color to paint a house . . . why are there so many boardinghouses, Papa . . . why is all the paint falling off everything . . . what is that dead smell . . . where are all the people . . ."

They ended the tour at the Battery, the promenade along the harbor. Joe handed his ladies down, and they walked beside the water. For the first time, Emily was truly pleased. "It's as nice as the waterfront in New York," she said. Two small black boys ran up to them and jabbered incomprehensibly. Joe laughed and nodded. They exploded into frantic dancing, rolling their eyes and singing. When they stopped, Joe flicked a coin into the air; the tallest of the boys caught it, both bowed with flashing grins, and they scampered off.

"That's called 'cutting a wing,'" Joe said. "Every pickaninny in town earns pennies from the tourists that way."

"Could you understand what they said, Papa? What foreign language was that?"

Joe swooped her up in his arms and kissed her. "That was black folks' talk, Princess. It's called 'Gullah.' You'll pick it up fast enough. All Charlestonians talk half black; babies learn it from their dahs. You won't hear what New Yorkers call a 'Southern accent' here. In Charleston, everything is different from any place else."

Emily looked at her proud, happy husband and renewed her determination to like this strange, shuttered, shabby place.

Joe set Victoria down. "Come along, Simmons ladies, we'll walk to the Tradd house. Let's enjoy this special day. Do you feel that breeze? Let me tell you about what that breeze means to this city. You'll notice that all the houses are trimmed like sails to the wind, at an angle . . ." He talked non-stop until they reached Elizabeth's house.

Elizabeth answered the door herself. Joe had written to tell her that he was bringing his family to visit, and she had been busy for days preparing for a partylike tea. The floors and furniture were gleaming, a coconut cake waited on the tea cart, and Catherine and Tradd were dressed in their Sunday best.

"Come in, come in," she cried. "I'm so happy to see you." After a confused babble on introductions, she led the way upstairs to the drawing room where Tradd and Catherine were hovering around the cake.

"Do sit down, you must be exhausted after such a long trip," she said. "Not that chair, Joe; the legs are a little wobbly . . . Children come and say how do you do to the Simmonses. The cake is for later, so you needn't make eyes at it now."

Catherine and Tradd were introduced, then allowed to leave, with Victoria in tow. "We're going to play earthquake on the joggling board," Tradd explained to Emily. "Victoria will love it."

Emily's heart turned over.

"Do you know, we had another tremor just last week?" said Elizabeth. "Tiny, of course, but we all feared for our cups and saucers. Hardly anyone had any china left after the big one."

"Joseph has spoken of you so often, Mrs. Cooper. It is a real pleasure for me to meet you."

Elizabeth took Emily's hand in hers. "Do, please, call me Elizabeth. I intend to call you Emily if you don't object. I feel as if we're practically family. Did Joe tell you that he saved my brother's life? No? Too modest,

Joe. You're allowed to brag to your very own wife. Emily, you must make him tell you. It was really heroic."

Of all the things in Charleston that Emily had made up her mind to like, the one she had feared most was Elizabeth Cooper. She had read all Elizabeth's letters; Joe did not lock his desk. But their innocence had not reassured her. They had an intimacy of shared experience, goals, planning that frightened her. She had become convinced that Elizabeth must be a great beauty with the proverbial helpless Southern charm. Now that she saw her, Emily could relax. True, Elizabeth was younger than she was, but she looked older. She had little wrinkles at the corners of her eyes and a spray of freckles across her thin nose and protruding cheekbones. She was too thin, Emily thought happily, not soft and rounded, and she was too tall, taller than Joseph. She did have breathtaking eyes, large and a blue so deep that they looked like the Mediterranean Sea. But she did nothing to accent them. Her frock wasn't even blue. It was a faded pink, certainly the wrong color to wear with red hair, and it wasn't even modish. It had a plain gathered skirt without so much as a hint of bustle. Frumpy, thought Emily comfortably. I was a fool to worry. Joseph is just being kind because she's the sister of his old friend.

Joe had been anxious about the meeting, too. He knew Emily was jealous; he was a perceptive man. He also knew that she had every reason to be jealous. When Emily relaxed, he did, too. His secrets were safe.

And Elizabeth, his precious Lizzie, was fine. She had a deep self-assurance, a self-confidence that made her a profoundly beautiful woman. I did this for her, he thought, no one else. I believed in her and helped her believe in herself. He found it the most satisfying accomplishment of his life.

"I do hope you're going to make a nice, long visit, Emily, even though Joe is a ninny to bring you-all down in June, just when it's starting to get hot. We'll be moving to the beach next month, and you'll have to come with us. Victoria can sleep with Catherine, and you and Joe can have the guest room. It's lovely and cool there, and we'll have lots of time to get to know each other. Before then, we've time to go out to Carlington. Joe, just wait until you see the plant and the new sheds. They're so impressive you won't believe your eyes."

Joe held up a hand. "Slow down, boss," he said. "No need to rush anything. Emily and I have to look at some houses. We're moving to Charleston. There'll be lots of time to see and do everything."

"Oh, Joe, Emily, how wonderful!" Elizabeth's enthusiasm was genuine, even though she wondered how such exotic creatures as Emily and Victoria would like the quiet pace of the old city. Their clothes and jewels were, she could tell, the very latest fashion; Victoria looked more like a princess than a little girl. Joe was dressed to the nines, too, but she didn't worry about him. He was still Joe.

"News like that," she said, "calls for immediate celebration. Let's call the children back and cut the cake."

"They're all too run down, Joseph," said Emily when they were alone that night. She had been appalled by Elizabeth's house; it had visible cracks in the ceiling plaster. "I don't want a used house, anyhow. I want my own, designed for me." Joe agreed. They'd hire a New York architect, too, if that would make her feel more at home. But it would take a year or more to build. Would she object to buying a house to live in while theirs was being built? The lawyer was already scheduled to meet them at breakfast and take them to look at some.

"Well, I'll look, but no promises."

Joe had to settle for that, even though he saw his plans for moving to Charleston in danger of slipping out of reach.

The next morning, Barnwell Smith, Esq. sized up Emily Simmons at a glance and breathed an inaudible sigh of relief. He was a Charlestonian, and it made him feel much better when he realized that this was not a Yankee lady determined to modernize an old house downtown. He took the Simmonses directly to the Williams mansion on Wentworth Street; it had such a staggering price on it that the estate would pay a huge fee to get rid of it. Emily made up her mind immediately. They'd buy it.

Joe was so grateful that he promised her the forty room "cottage" in Newport that she admired, as an extra little present. Emily would, he knew, never be content with a Sullivans Island house. She was also, he realized, making him a gift of her willingness to give up New York. The cottage was small recompense for her very real generosity.

The Williams mansion was a gigantic, imposing red-brick structure patterned after the Tuileries. It had been built by a Georgia entrepreneur who managed to come out of the Civil War with a million dollars. That was not a circumstance that made him popular among Charlestonians. He had built his house in a manner to suit his tastes, and to revenge himself on the people who snubbed him at the same time. Everything in the house was imported: Italian marble for the fireplaces, with Italian artisans to carve it; rare woods for the exquisite parquet floors and paneled walls; splendid French crystal chandeliers and gold-framed mirrors. The double drawing rooms were larger than the ballroom at the Hibernian Hall, where the Saint Cecelia took place. Next to the formal gardens at the rear of the mansion, the stables for the carriage horses were precisely situated so that the prevailing winds carried their odor across the invisible barrier that had defeated him. It was directed at the neighborhood south of Broad.

"Shad, how wicked," said Lucy Anson with glee. "Buying the Williams mansion. You could just as well have hired a battalion to stand on Broad Street and thumb their noses. You'll never be invited anywhere, you know."

Joe rocked back in his chair. "Emily liked it, Miss Lucy, and this move isn't easy for her. Besides, we could live in the steeple at Saint Michael's, and we still wouldn't be invited. No sense pretending to be what we're not. We're rich Yankees, and we're not ashamed of it. We'll be invited by other rich Yankees, and that'll keep Emily occupied. Victoria will be in school with the Charleston children, and she'll behave by Charleston rules. I want her to grow up a Southern lady."

"What about you, dear friend? What will you derive from this move? You've been thinking of your family first, and that's fine, but you should find some happiness for yourself."

"I'm already happy, just being here. It's a better life, even for a non-Charlestonian. I like the rhythm, the sense of proportion. I'm forty-five now, more or less, and I've wasted most of my life making money. A friend of mine in New York—well, as near a friend as I have there—just died the other day. Fellow name of Jay Gould. Ever hear of him?"

Lucy shook her head. Joe smiled.

"He sure would have been unhappy to know that. He figured everybody in the world knew who he was because he was probably the smartest money man ever lived. Anyhow, Jay was only about ten years older than me. He just burnt out. And for what? Another pile of dollars he couldn't spend if he tried. I don't want that to happen to me. I want something better for me and for my family. And I want to quit pretending I'm something I'm not. No way to fool the people who knew me before I got in the habit of wearing shoes, and no need to try. You and Elizabeth are the most comfortable friends I ever had. It's worth the move just to be here with you now."

"It makes me very happy. When are you going to bring Emily and Victoria to see me?"

"Soon as they get back from Rhode Island. They high-tailed it up there as soon as I told Emily to buy the cottage. I'm going to join them next week. We'll all be home at the end of September."

"I hope you won't find you've made a mistake moving here. It might open wounds that have healed up."

Joe looked in her eyes. She knew.

"They never healed," he said, "but that's not the reason I came back."

Lucy kissed his cheek. "You didn't have to tell me that. As Mr. Josiah said, Shad, you've got a true gentleman's soul. I pray this change will be good for you."

It turned out to be very good for Joe, indeed. The following year, 1893, a catastrophic financial panic hit New York and spread throughout the country, with repercussions in every part of the world. Banks failed, the stock market crashed, fortunes disappeared, and a crippling depression settled on America. Emily's father died of apoplexy and was spared the realization that he was bankrupt. Joe had liquidated all his holdings when he moved. He was, therefore, richer than ever because his money was worth more.

In Charleston, few people had fortunes to lose; the panic had little effect on the quiet life south of Broad. Elizabeth was wryly philosophical about it. "I wouldn't have known how to be rich anyhow. I count my blessings that I had the taste of it on paper, at least." The phosphate company's new refining plant had gone into operation the previous autumn, with the fabulous profits that she had been building toward for six years. They had come in for enough months to pay off the mortgages on the plant and the Meeting Street house. Then, with the panic, phosphate prices had plummeted world wide. Carlington was producing even less income now than it had in the days of simple digging and washing ore. She could get by, but there was nothing extra for luxuries.

And she would not even consider letting Joe supplement her income.

He carried the problem to Lucy. "Do you know what she did?" he sputtered. "Not only did she stick her nose up in the air and say that she could manage very well on her own, she even tried to give me back the necklace that was my wedding present to her. Said she thought it would be more suitable if I gave it to Emily."

Amusement replaced Lucy's irritation. Being everyone's confidante had become tedious years ago. The enormous diamond necklace was so spectacularly awful that she would well understand Elizabeth's desire to get rid of it. Joe must have wondered why she never wore it; she had been to several elaborate dinner parties at the Simmonses' house.

"You mustn't be so cross," she said in a soothing voice. "You know Charleston well enough to understand that we take a sinful pride in our ability to stand any blow that fate deals out. Poverty is downright fashionable. As for the necklace, Elizabeth was right. It's the kind of gift a man gives his wife, not a wedding present for somebody else's bride. She would probably have returned it to you long ago, except it was pawned."

"Pawned? Elizabeth took it to a hock shop?"

"No, Lucas did. Pinny told me all about it. Don't tell anybody I told you."

"Well, I refused to take it, and I told her I was insulted by her offer. That was her mother's necklace; it's right she should have it."

Lucy managed not to laugh.

Until she next saw Elizabeth. "I understand you couldn't rid yourself of the jeweled albatross," she said. The two of them collapsed in unladylike guffaws.

"You know I'll have to wear it now to Emily's parties."

"You'll fit right in with the uptown ladies."

Their malicious snobbery was a wicked pleasure to both of them.

"We're terrible," Elizabeth said. "Isn't it fun? I'll be punished, though. Retribution is laying for me. Catherine thinks the horrible thing is beautiful."

"She's only fourteen. You were completely barbaric at that age, too."

"I hope you're right. I don't seem to be able to get through to her at all. About anything. She radiates disapproval at me. I can feel it through the walls."

"She'll outgrow it. It's just a phase."

54

"Why can't you be like the other girls' mothers? It's awful for me. I feel so left out. Their mothers all go to parties, and they call on each other, and they play whist, and they go shopping together. They're all friends of each other's. You're not anybody's friend, except dowdy old Cousin Lucy and that horrid Mistress Simmons. What's wrong with you?"

Elizabeth was staggered by her daughter's angry outburst. "Catherine, darling. I had no idea you felt this way."

"You never have any idea how I feel about anything. You don't care how I feel."

"That's not true. I care about you more than any thing in the whole world."

"No, you don't. I wish I was dead!" Catherine threw herself on her bed and sobbed into the pillow. When Elizabeth touched her shoulder, she jerked away. "Leave me alone," she cried, "just leave me alone."

Elizabeth went out onto the piazza and sank onto the deep seat of the porch swing. She was in a daze. Unaware of what she was doing, she pushed against the floor with the toe of one shoe and set the swing in motion. Back and forth, back and forth. The chains that suspended the swing creaked, a high note when it swung back, a low note when it went forward. The steady rhythm was hypnotically soothing to her jagged emotions.

Her mind filled with hurt, angry cries of self-justification: I've done everything for that child; she should be grateful. I haven't had a decent frock in years so that she could be well-dressed. I gave her Pinny's room and stayed on the third floor myself. I gave her my pearl ear bobs, and she lost one the first time she wore them. I've worked like a dog so that she could have a nice home and go to a good school. She's old enough to realize it hasn't been easy on me. She's seen me up late at night working on the account books and worrying myself sick over paying bills and taxes. How dare she be embarrassed because I don't frivol around at tea parties?

The swing moved faster, with louder creaking. It sounded angry.

Elizabeth luxuriated in a moment of Tradd rage. I should go break a hairbrush on her bottom, she thought. Then her imagination reproduced the sound of a blow on flesh. It was a sound she had once known too well. Dear God, forgive me for what I was thinking. Her throat constricted. She forced herself to breathe slowly and deeply, fighting off memory. She discovered that she was trembling. The swing slowed to a comforting motion.

She thought about her own childhood. Had she been proud of her mother? Mary Tradd was hardly real to her. She had married and gone away when Elizabeth was only nine. The year before that, Elizabeth had spent at Ashley Barony. I was proud of Aunt Julia, she thought. Even as a little girl, I knew she was remarkable. She could do anything. I was terrified of her, but I admired her. I don't think Catherine is terrified of me; she must know that I love her. On the other hand, she obviously doesn't admire me, either. I've done everything wrong.

Her mind became mocking, tormenting. She doesn't love you, it said; no one loves you, nor ever has. Your mother, your dah, your husband, your daughter. Because you don't deserve to be loved. A failure.

"Tradd," she said aloud. "Tradd loves me."

But what kind of love does an eight-year-old boy know? He loves the word "Mother" because he's supposed to. He doesn't know you. When Catherine was eight, she loved "Mother," too.

"Mama?" Tradd's voice called from the top of the stairs. "Mama? It's late. Aren't you going to tuck me in?"

Elizabeth wiped her face with her skirt. "I'm coming, darling," she called. "I'll be right there."

She did not sleep that night. Saint Michael's chimes marked the steady passing of the quarter hours, and the watchman's ". . . all's well" made her want to scream. At last, when predawn was giving a misty definition to the windows, the sleepy voice of the watchman ("Five of the clock, and all's well.") reminded her of Pinckney's old answer.

"But could be a whole lot better," she muttered. And she smiled. Her thoughts stopped their desperate spiral of defeat and fell into place. Catherine has some right on her side. Elizabeth nodded. She had, she admitted, withdrawn from the world more than was really necessary. Charleston's strength was its close society, and she had rejected that strength, relying only on her own. Neither had she worked so hard just to take care of the children. She liked working, planning, commanding. She need not have made it the whole of her life. It was, in many ways, an excuse to avoid the reality that society would force her to face: the truth that she was alone. She had let herself go to seed, too. As long as she was clean and neat, she considered it sufficient. Lack of vanity was another form of pride, like her refusal to accept help for her loneliness or her poverty.

I am entitled to be proud of much that I have accomplished, she decided. I am not a failure. But it is wrong to be proud of my weaknesses, and hiding from the world is a weakness, a fault of fear. So what if people have caused me pain? They have also given me joy and laughter and help —when I would allow it. It is a fair exchange, to know some pain in return for all the good experiences. The important thing is to be open to life, not to run away from it.

And love? She permitted herself a single, self-pitying sigh. It unlocked the constriction around her heart, and energy flowed through her veins. The world was full of people who never knew love, and it kept on spinning, with moonrises and flowers and sunlight dancing on the water and ten thousand other things to gladden the soul. That was more than enough for happiness.

"Catherine," she said at breakfast, "I have been thinking about our discussion last night."

"I'm sorry, Mama. I was rude." Catherine's truculence gave the lie to her apology.

Don't get angry, Elizabeth told herself. "Yes, you were," she said calmly, "but we won't discuss it further. The fact is, I have been extremely preoccupied with Carlington, and you were right to call it to my attention. I intend to change."

"Did you and Catherine have a quarrel, Mama?" Tradd was avid for information.

Elizabeth pinched his nose. "That's what happens to little boys who mind other people's business. Now eat your hominy before it gets cold."

After the children left for school, she looked through her wardrobe, noting the many gaps in every department. Then she went to her desk and wrote a short message to Joe Simmons, asking him to call.

"I'm climbing down off my high horse," she told him the next day. "You're richer than King Midas, Joe. I'd like to ask you to vote me that raise you keep talking about. You know it'll have to come out of your share of the profits."

His face lit with happiness. Elizabeth laughed. "It's mighty strange," she said, "that when I do something selfish, it turns out to be the nicest thing I've ever done for one of my dearest friends."

"Like I always told Pinckney," Joe responded, "you Tradds are a thick-headed bunch."

By the time the Christmas party season arrived, Elizabeth was back into the round of festivities that were considered suitable for a widow. She was astonished and pleased by the welcome she received. She was also amused by the attention paid her by several gentlemen, including one who was a spry eighty-three and one who should have been horsewhipped for neglecting his wife. She gave Delia instructions to declare her "not at home" to any masculine callers except for the Carlington supervisor Ned Wragg and Joe Simmons, blessing the conventions that allowed for protection of unmarried ladies. She was enjoying her return to society, but she had no desire to try a rebirth of debutantism.

On January first, she went, as usual, to Carlington for the "powwow" with the workers. A table and three chairs had been put on the loading platform for the contract ceremony. Joe handed her up the steps; Ned stood behind her chair, ready to slide it forward when she sat down. The workers, a hundred strong, stood in a rough semicircle at the foot of the platform; their wives and children were some distance behind them. There was an electric tension in the air. Since the previous powwow, the panic had changed everything, and everyone knew it. Many businesses had closed, throwing men out of work. There were rumors about more closings, and predictions that salaries would be cut in half, for those lucky enough to keep their jobs. Ned Wragg had begged Elizabeth to make a decision about how large the salary cuts would be, and to make it early, so that he could start convincing the men that they were being fairly treated. He was afraid there might be violence. But she had refused to have him speak for her. "It's my decision, Ned, and my responsibility. If anyone's going to get mad, let him get mad at me, not you. You have to be able to walk Carlington without looking over your shoulder all the time; I'm in town, safe behind a desk." She had also refused to let Joe hire guards to encircle the crowd. That would, she said, just be a match to the fuse. He had concealed two boatloads of armed men in the tall marsh grasses around a bend in the river, anyhow. There had been rioting and attempted arson at the mills in Simmonsville, and he was not going to take any chances with Elizabeth's safety.

The plant had closed down for vacation on the day before Christmas, and the sharp blue air was free of the acrid chemical odor that usually hung over Carlington. The sun was warm. Elizabeth took off her short brown wool cape and walked to the front of the platform instead of taking her chair. She was wearing a brown, trailing skirt and a stiffly starched white shirtwaist with huge leg of mutton sleeves. Joe looked at her tall, straight back, thinking how slim she was and how glad he was that women weren't wearing bustles anymore. They looked more like people instead of clothes with heads attached. The clear golden light brought out the deep reds and golds and greens in the pheasant feathers that trimmed Elizabeth's wide hat. He was sorry it could not fall on her hair instead. A puff of wind fluttered the feathers and rattled her stiff sleeves, and he had a vague, confused impression of potential flight. Quit daydreaming, he told himself. His hand slipped into his pocket and closed around the small pistol there. If necessary he would fire into the air to summon the hidden men. Elizabeth began to speak.

"Happy New Year to you all." There was a rumbled response. "I'm not going to beat around the bush, speechifying about what you already know. We've been working for seven years to build this plant up, and now it's not doing what we thought it was going to do. I believe that things are going to change, to get better, but only the Good Lord knows when. Until that time comes, we've got to hold on. That doesn't mean that we've got to go hungry. The wages for this year will be the same as before for any man who wants to sign up."

A cheering bedlam broke out, and the crowd pressed closer. She held her arms up and waved for silence. "How does she expect us to do that?" Ned muttered to Joe. "Prices have gone down every month since August."

Joe slapped him on the back, laughing. "The Good Lord knows that, too, I expect. She'll do it, though. Lizzie Tradd can do anything she sets her mind to, once she's thought it over."

"Quiet down!" Elizabeth was shouting. She was laughing, too. So were all of the faces beneath her. A semblance of order muted the uproar.

"Before you sign, you'd better know that there's going to be more work," she said loudly. "We can't make do on phosphates alone, so we're going to fall back on other things. We've been mining open ground. Now we're going to move into the woods. The trees will have to be cut to clear the ground before the digging starts. And we'll sell the lumber. That means building rafts to float down to the lumber mill in Charleston. And while you're on your way down, I expect you to have some lines out in the river instead of lying around enjoying the trip. We can sell the fish, too." The men clapped and shouted. "There won't be any new equipment, either. If something breaks, I expect you to fix it. If one of you loses a shovel, he'll have to buy himself a new one out of his pay.

"A lot of you are too young to remember the time when the soldiers were running everything in South Carolina. I remember. Nobody wasted anything, not even an old bone. After you ate the meat off it, you used it for soup, and after that you made buttons out of it. We older folks lived through that time, we're sure not going to let something as paltry as a little depression do us down. Am I right?"

There were cheers and whistles and shouts. And a fusillade of excited, celebratory shots at the sun. "Jesus Christ!" said Joe. He leapt from the platform and started running to the river. He reached the bank just in time to prevent the boats from landing. "Go away," he roared, "false alarm. Everything's all right. We don't need you." He gestured hugely, waving the toughs away. An exposed root caught his toe, and he tumbled down the eroded embankment into the mud-flat exposed by low tide. His colorful cursing floated after the boats as they headed downriver.

When he rejoined Elizabeth, he was covered with thick, smelly blue mud. "Poor Joe," she said, "and you such a fancy dresser, too." Her control over her facial muscles was a miracle of good manners.

Ned was less adroit. His lips quivered. "We've got work clothes in the company store," he managed to say.

"For sale," Elizabeth added blandly.

Joe's chuckle freed them all. Everyone white, black, adult, child, had a good long laugh at the expense of the Wall Street tycoon.

It was the last whole-hearted merriment Elizabeth was to know for a long time. Even with the additional effort that the Carlington workers made, the revenues continued to drop. The following year, she stubbornly signed the annual contract again at the same rate, although she had already had to cut her own salary to half. By June, it was apparent that it would have to be cut again.

"You know, Lucy, I sometimes wish I could just come live here with you," she said one afternoon. "It's so peaceful."

Lucy Anson looked down the length of the vine-shadowed veranda. It was a cool oasis, a hundred and fifty feet long, with groups of painted basketwork chairs and tables where ladies were having tea from the trays brought by quiet, gray-uniformed maids. She had moved to the Confederate Home after Josiah Anson's death.

"It is nice," she said, "but I go nearly crazy sometimes because it's all so easy. You would, too, Elizabeth. You need to be doing."

"Doing what? I'm just sliding backward." She set her teacup down with a clatter. The quiet background hum of conversation from the other groups faltered for a startled moment, then resumed. "Forgive me, Lucy, I'll ruin your reputation," she said bitterly. "Making a ruckus. So unladylike. And complaining. I can hear Aunt Julia right now. 'Ladies don't complain.' I get all-fired sick and tired of being a lady sometimes."

Lucy refilled her cup and handed it to her. "Complain all you like," she encouraged. "Even Julia Ashley would have allowed confidences between friends. She and Miss Emma used to let their hair down."

Elizabeth's eyes widened. "I cannot imagine those two ever unbending for so long as a second."

"They did though. Miss Ashley would always come over for an afternoon when she was in town at Christmastime. I'd sit on the stairs and eavesdrop."

"Lucy! That's not like you."

"It's exactly like me. I lived most of my life through other people, listening in, watching from a corner. I was always a pale sort of person. That's what I have for my complaint. Always a Martha and never a Mary. Don't you fall into the same thing. Grab some living for yourself."

"Lucy." Elizabeth held out her hand.

"I'm all right, honey. Drink your tea and tell me your troubles. Mine are all behind me now."

But Elizabeth was too distressed to think about herself. She had never really wondered if Lucy were unhappy because she had always seemed so serene. Except for the time after the earthquake. "Do you still miss Pinckney?" she asked.

"I'll never forgive him for dying . . . You're shocked, aren't you? Love isn't supposed to be angry. But it is, of course. Love makes every feeling stronger and it has every feeling in it. Pinckney gave me the greatest, deepest happiness a woman can know. He denied me only the physical part, and that would have come. Then I would have had the whole world. Without him, I have this—peacefulness. It's a poor substitute."

"Lucy, I'm so sorry."

"Thank you . . . you see, we all complain. I feel better for it . . . Your turn."

"My troubles don't seem so important now. I don't have any big ones, just a swarm of little worries like a bunch of sand flies around my head. Catherine's coming out next year, and she's already pestering me about giving her a party. Most of the girls are doing that now, you know. They're presented at a private dance as well as at the Ball. That's so they can meet boys whose fathers aren't members of the Saint Cecelia. The crop of boys seems to shrink every year. Stuart's three are going to be absolute prizes when they're a few years older, even though their manners are just awful. Henrietta has no control over them at all."

"At least you don't have any problems with Tradd."

Elizabeth smiled. "No, thank heaven. He's my heart's delight. I wish he didn't have to be at Porter, though. All the little boys wear military uniforms, now, and I hate it. I'll never understand why men love soldiering so much. Stuart's boys are boarding students, and he's proud as punch of them. Little Stuart is already a captain, and he's only fifteen. You'd think he was Robert E. Lee to hear his father talk."

"It's because Stuart was too young to see the real war. Besides, the military has always been an acceptable profession for a gentleman. They can't all be rice planters anymore."

"Certainly not on the Barony. That's another thing. Stuart's giving up rice. I half expect another earthquake from Aunt Julia turning over in her grave."

"What's he going to do?"

"Lord knows. He's talking about breeding horses or raising strawberries to ship to Boston in the winter or something else foolish. In the meantime, he's selling more and more land every year. He never heard the word 'economize.'"

"That's what you're really talking about, aren't you, Elizabeth? Money."

"Lucy, you're just one shock after another today. Nobody says that word out loud."

Lucy chuckled.

"When do you move to the Island?" she said.

"That's one of my sand flies. We don't go this year. I've rented the house to a family I met at Joe's."

"I'm surprised he didn't make a fuss. He's still trying to give you money, isn't he?"

"In the nicest possible way, but I have to draw the line somewhere. He didn't approve of not cutting wages at Carlington, and I can't see letting him take up the slack for my decisions. Luckily, he never asks to see the books. He and Emily have already left for Newport, so he doesn't know about the beach house. Did I tell you about the party they had before they went?"

"No. Tell. I adore hearing about the rich and famous."

"'Famous' is right. There was an actress there!" They settled into a happy gossip.

55

In spite of all her contrivances, Elizabeth had to bow to reality and cut wages at Carlington in ninety-six. There was no trouble when she made the announcement at the powwow. All the men knew that, even after the reduction, they were still earning more than the workers at the other phosphate companies. They signed the contract without a murmur.

During the remainder of January, Catherine Mary Cooper was presented to Society at the Saint Cecelia Ball, danced the soles out of her slippers at the Cotillion Club Ball, attended her first horserace and Race Ball and, on January eighteenth, was introduced again at a tea dance given by her mother at the South Carolina Hall. She had a different gown for each occasion, and, she knew perfectly, she looked beautiful. Her long neck rose from her bare shoulders like a swan's, as several bold young men told her, and her dark hair framed her lovely face like raven's wings, which Lawrence Wilson mentioned in the elaborate poem he enclosed with the bouquet he delivered the morning after the Ball. Catherine was giddy with her success. Her only regret was that her mother flatly refused to let her wear her grandmother's wedding necklace to any of the balls. Elizabeth observed her daughter's happiness with a warm heart, feeling that the mortgage she had taken out on the house had been well worth it.

It had been over two years since Catherine's emotional outburst. Elizabeth had tried very hard to be a satisfactory mother by her daughter's standards and by her own. She took Catherine shopping, spent hours trying out various hair arrangements, taught her to manage the eccentricities of the hoop skirt she would wear to the Saint Cecelia; she also drilled her in the routines of household management and taught her to cook. Catherine loved the attention to her appearance, loathed the tedium of mending linen and skimming soup.

"You'll thank me for it one day," Elizabeth said firmly. "When you're married, your husband will expect a well-run house and a good dinner every day. You can't train your servants unless you know what to do yourself. Now stop fussing and hand me that jar of kerosene."

Outside, a steady rain beat down on the shining brick paving and silvery streetcar rails of Meeting Street. It was a perfect day for burning the chimneys. Elizabeth poured a large spoonful of kerosene across the crumpled newspaper waiting on the hearth of the library fireplace. Then she stuck her head into the open flue and shouted. "Fire coming."

"Now watch carefully, Catherine. You can do the chimney from the dining room next." She took the oily paper up with the fire tongs in her left hand, struck a match with her right, lit two corners of the paper, and thrust her left arm up the chimney as far as she could reach. There was a momentary whistling sound as the heat activated a draft, then the kerosene-soaked paper blazed high and lit the accumulated soot inside the chimney. It burned with a rushing, roaring noise up and up, past the drawing room fireplace, past the smaller one in Tradd's bedroom above, past the steeply sloping walls of the attic, erupting in shooting sparks that were extinguished by the rain before they could land on the roof. A nimble black boy watched to be sure none landed. If any large gobbet of blazing soot survived the rain, it was his job to beat it to death with the broom he held in one hand.

"Come on, Catherine," said Elizabeth. "I know how you feel. When your great-aunt Julia made me learn, I was sure my arm would be barbecued. You just pull out when you hear the soot catch. You don't even have to think about it; the noise is so startling, your hand drops the tongs all by itself and gets out of there."

"I don't see why we don't just hire sweeps like we used to."

"Because a roof boy costs ten cents and a piece of pie, and a ro-ro boy costs fifty cents and leaves you with a floor full of soot. All you need is a rainy day and a little nerve, and you save yourself the trouble of beating the rugs plus forty cents. Now crumple up this paper. Let me see you do it . . ."

The "lessons" took up every afternoon that Elizabeth could spare. How to open a fan, unfurling or spreading or snapping it; how to separate an egg yolk; how to tuck the fingers of a long glove up above the wrist so that one could eat; how to get water marks out of a table top; how to walk down stairs without looking at one's feet; how to manage the ceremony of preparing and serving tea. Gradually, Catherine came to realize that her mother was an extraordinary woman. When she was "out," and her circle of acquaintance widened past the half-dozen girls she had grown up with, she heard praise for Elizabeth from every quarter. "So you're Elizabeth Tradd's girl . . ." was the phrase that preceded an immediate increase in warming attention. Her mother, Catherine discovered, was considered by everyone to be the standard bearer of the tradition of Charleston's finest women: strong, resourceful, canny and charming, all at the same time. One elderly gentleman kept Catherine captive for twenty minutes while he outlined the relationship between the Pinckneys and the Tradds, then followed the Pinckney branch back to Eliza Pinckney, who, at the age of sixteen, had managed a plantation of a quarter million acres all alone when her father was away fighting Indians, and had single-handedly developed the culture of indigo at the same time. "When General Washington came to visit Charleston, he made a special trip to take tea with her. She was an old lady then, but as charming as a girl. Blood will tell!" The white-haired historian bowed over Catherine's hand and allowed her to escape.

"Mama," she said when she was next alone with Elizabeth, "did you know that you're held up as an example to every lady in Charleston?"

Elizabeth was shocked. "Whatever for? Have I been putting my elbows on the table? Or caught yawning behind my fan?"

"No, Mama, an example to follow. Everyone thinks you're grand . . . So do I."

Elizabeth's eyes filled. "Darling child," she said, "that makes me very happy."

In all the flurry of crinolines and curling irons, beaux and bouquets, poor little Tradd was like a lost soul. Elizabeth tried to think of special treats for him, but everything she came up with was somehow wrong. She surprised him with a pair of new roller skates, only to find them two weeks later still in their original wrapping. "You seemed so pleased with them, darling, I don't understand," she said to him at supper.

Tradd reddened and squirmed in his chair. "I didn't want to hurt your feelings, Mama. I'm too old for skates anymore. I'll be thirteen in December." Elizabeth then suggested that since he was getting so grown up perhaps he'd like to have a new suit.

"You'll be going to parties before you know it."

Tradd clutched his throat, stuck out his tongue and made a ghastly, gargling, strangling noise.

Oh, dear, thought Elizabeth. She consulted Joe Simmons, who suggested that she take the boy to Carlington. "After all, it will be his company when he grows up." She also asked Stuart's advice. He told her to send the boy out to the Barony for some hunting and fishing. He was only two and a half years younger than Anson, Stuart's third son.

She tried both. Tradd was politely thankful, but she knew that neither was really what the boy needed. He was too honest for his expressions of enthusiasm to be convincing. I'll just give up, she thought. Another month and school will be out. We'll go to the Island this year whether we can afford it or not. Tradd loves the beach.

No sooner had she made the resolution than the problem solved itself. Tradd burst into the office when he came home from school one afternoon. "Mama! Mama, may I go to Carlington and take a friend? Please, Mama, do say yes. Please, may I?"

"Of course you may, Tradd." She was bewildered and delighted. If he really liked the trip that much, this certainly was a long-delayed reaction. "Who do you want to take? I'll have to write a note to his mother."

Tradd grinned with triumph. "No, you don't. My friend's a grown-up. He's a new teacher at school. He doesn't need permission from anybody."

"A new teacher in June? There's hardly any school left. I don't understand."

"Dr. Porter wants him to teach next year. He's trying him out to see how he likes it. All the fellows hope he will. He's just splendid, Mama."

"I see. Does this choosy paragon have a name?"

"Mr. Fitzpatrick. May I take him? He'll take me, really, but he said I had to ask you first."

"It will probably be all right. If Dr. Porter thinks he's suitable, I imagine I will, too. But I'll want to meet him. We'll have him to tea one day next week."

Tradd's face fell, but he recognized the dismissal. His mother's voice had its "I'm very busy" undertone. "Thank you, Mama," he said. He left quickly. Elizabeth was already frowning over the account books again. She was trying to catch up on the summary balance for the year to date. All the demands of Catherine's social life had thrown her way behind, and she would like to be able to report to Joe. The Simmonses were having a gala farewell dinner party that night before leaving for the summer in Newport.

I'm glad I finally have a decent gown, she thought, as Delia hooked her up the back. I've been Dora Dowdy at every one of Emily's fancy parties I've gone to. The gown was very modish and very flattering. It had been made for her to wear when Catherine was presented, and she had been determined to do her daughter proud. I like my hair, too, she said to herself, now that I've gotten used to it. The back was arranged in three smooth rolls, the front cut short to make soft, tumbled curls. "The Lily Langtry," it was called.

Delia fastened the massive diamond necklace. Elizabeth always wore it to the Simmonses'. "I'll go down to the library to wait for the carriage, Delia. You can start supper. I'm sorry to make you late." She picked up her gloves and fan and hurried downstairs. There was still a little time; maybe she could get the books finished after all.

"Mama," said Tradd from the door. Elizabeth looked up, across the desk. "I'd like to present Mr. Henry Fitzpatrick."

She had a momentary impression of a tall, funny looking man standing next to her son. Then he moved across the room with startling speed, and was bent, one knee on the floor, by her side. "Your humble subject,

Majesty," he said. He lifted the hem of her skirt and bent his head to kiss it. Elizabeth dropped the pen, blotting her account book.

"What on earth are you doing, young man?" she said irritably. "Get up this instant."

He obeyed at once. Then he swept an imaginary hat from his head and bowed, his hand over his heart. Elizabeth could almost see the nonexistent plume of the unreal hat. She could not see Henry Fitzpatrick's face, but she knew somehow that it was laughing. She felt extremely uncomfortable. Not only because of the awkward situation she was in, having to reprimand her son's teacher in front of him, but also because of the crackling vitality that emanated from the visitor. She felt surrounded by electricity; her hair was standing away from her scalp, the way it did when the brush was static, or a storm was near. His bent head was too close. Even it seemed to give off some uncanny energy. It was covered with springy curls, so black they looked almost blue. He raised it quickly, and she found herself staring into eyes so blue they looked almost black. They were laughing. His wide mouth was still, shadowed by a Pinocchio nose.

"I am not flattered by this extravagant behavior, sir," Elizabeth said. She was angry, and it was apparent. "Do you always behave in such an extraordinary manner?"

Fitzpatrick stepped back. The corners of his mouth, the corners of his eyes, and the tip of his nose all drooped with chagrin. "I beg your forgiveness," he said earnestly. "I was quite swept away. I looked through a normal door into a normal room, and I saw—Gloriana, the Faerie Queen, Queen Bess." He stooped to peer into her face. "For the moment, I really believed it, you see. The effect is overwhelming. You want only a crown and a scepter."

Elizabeth frowned at him. "What nonsense," she said. Tradd's face caught her eye. It was a portrait of misery. She relented, for his sake. "I suggest we pretend that this charade never took place, Mr. Fitzpatrick. You have been introduced. You may return tomorrow for tea if you will promise to act more conventionally. Now, good evening to you." She extended her hand.

He placed the back of his hand under her palm and lifted her fingertips to his lips. "I promise that I shall try," he said. "Until tomorrow, then."

Elizabeth had a distinct, but unreliable, impression that he winked at Tradd when he left the room.

Before she could speak to her son about Mr. Fitzpatrick, Joe's coachman was at the door, and she had to leave. When she returned home again, all thoughts of Tradd's teacher had been pushed from her mind.

Elizabeth had met all of the other dinner guests before. She felt a wicked delight at the surprise on their faces when they saw her in the elegant blue and silver silk ballgown instead of the serviceable gray ottoman that she had worn at every previous meeting. It added to the odd restlessness that her encounter with Fitzpatrick had engendered; the result was a reckless gaiety. She laughed more than she usually did, and she flirted with all the men, verging on the outrageous. There are some things, dear Yankee ladies, she thought, that we church-mice Southerners will always be better at, even the drabbest of us. Joe watched her performance will ill-concealed pleasure. He admired her most when the Tradd love of danger in her surfaced. It happened too rarely, he thought, except in her perilous gambles on the future of Carlington.

After dinner, the ladies left the men at table with their cigars and brandy. Elizabeth felt the hostility of the women on all sides of her; it brought added color to her cheeks. But when Emily asked her to come to her boudoir for a private talk, her face drained. She was fond of Emily and sorry for her, because she realized how much Joe's wife disliked her life in Charleston. If her behavior was embarrassing her hostess, Elizabeth would regret it horribly.

She stood inside the satin-draped room and heard Emily close the door behind her; her heart sank. "Please sit down, Elizabeth," Emily said. She gestured to a gilt armchair, and Elizabeth obeyed. The room was stuffy, full of the heavy perfume Emily wore, and the light of the crystal wall sconces was harsh. Emily looked very tired, she noticed, and older than her forty years. She tried to think of what to say. Surely Emily did not expect her to offer an apology. That would be too high-handed. She would accept a gentle reprimand from Joe's wife, but she had nothing to apologize for. She was, after all, a lady and a Charlestonian, neither of which could be said for the other women, not by her standards. She felt her temper rising.

Emily coughed, a deep rasping that shook her entire body. When it was over, she took a long breath. "Thank goodness that's done," she said, "I've been holding it in all evening." Her lovely voice had a slight rough edge to it. Elizabeth had noticed it when Emily greeted her.

"I've been trying to think how to begin," Emily said, "and I haven't found a graceful way. I'll have to be blunt instead."

Elizabeth braced herself.

"I'm going to die," Emily whispered. Then she repeated her words more loudly. "I'm going to die. I don't want to, but I can't stop it. I'm dying."

Elizabeth shook her head, refusing to believe that she had heard correctly. Emily, so pampered and secure, could not have anything dreadful happen to her. It was against all reason. Denial raced from her mind to her limbs, releasing her from the numbness of shock. She leapt up and took Emily's tiny body in her arms. "Now, now, that's not so. You'll get better as soon as you're at the sea. The city air is too thick to breathe, with summer almost here." The fragile feel of Emily's shoulders and back made her doubt her own words. Under the elaborate lace-trimmed satin folds of her gown, Emily was as light and unsubstantial as a sparrow. Her bones felt hollow.

She slipped away from Elizabeth. "Please sit down," she said. "I always feel like a dwarf when I look up at you. I'll stand, if you don't mind. I can talk better if I walk at the same time." For the first time in their acquaintance, Elizabeth recognized a quality of dignity in Emily. She had been fond of her, but she had thought her spoiled and arrogant. Now, as Emily paced back and forth, Elizabeth grew to respect her, and fear for her.

"Joseph doesn't know," Emily said, "but he'll have to before the year's out. I'm finding it harder to hide every day." She had, she explained, a cancer in her throat. That was the cruelty of it; she knew her voice was her one beauty, and death was attacking her there. The doctors estimated that she had about a year left. "And I cannot bear to die in Charleston," Emily said passionately. "I hate it! I've tried not to. I really tried. But for the past four years, I've hated it more with every day that went by. It's like a witch, this place. It had Joseph under its spell all his life, and now it's enchanting Victoria. She wants to be a Charleston girl. She copies everything the girls in her school do, the way they dress, even the way they talk. This city is taking my child from me; it already had my husband. It's leaving me all alone, and I don't want to face the end feeling lonely. I will never understand why some dirty streets and peeling old houses can be such an enemy, and I'm tired of trying to understand. I just want to get away. I want to be in New York when I die. Then I'll only have death to face, not this horrible place." She threw out her hands, as if she were warding off an invisible presence. Her small eyes were wild-looking, their pupils so dilated that they had no color, only a deep black blankness.

Elizabeth shuddered. She could not understand Emily's passionate hatred, but she could not deny its strength. The tiny woman was burning with emotion. For an instant, Elizabeth wanted to cry out in equally passionate defense of the city that was her home, that meant so much to her. She bit her lips to silence herself. Emily's need was too great to be denied. "How can I help you, Emily?" she said instead. "I'll do anything you want."

Emily's blind eyes found her, then became normal. "Just leave us alone. That's all. Don't write any brave, amusing letters. Don't send any company reports. Don't remind Joseph that Charleston is here, waiting for him. I'm going to put Victoria in finishing school up North. Maybe it's not too late to save her from this place. Joseph will stay with me when he knows why I need him. I don't want it to be too hard for him; I don't want him tormented by reminders of this strumpet, seductress city." Her voice rose to a shriek at the end, and the cough took her again.

Elizabeth soothed her with promises, then bathed her temples with cologne. They rejoined Emily's other guests as if nothing had happened.

The remainder of the evening was blessedly brief. When Elizabeth reached home, she had a pounding headache and a sick feeling. The scene with Emily had profoundly distressed her. First, because Emily was dying. Although Joe's wife had never become a close friend, she was still, as Joe's wife, part of Elizabeth's life. There had been so many losses, too many, and Elizabeth felt them all again when she thought of this new one.

Then there was Joe. He would be shattered. He was, she believed, deeply in love with his wife. His constant attention to Emily's wishes was, she thought, the outward manifestation of whole-hearted adoration.

In addition, Emily's obvious jealousy of her was almost as upsetting as her announcement that she was dying. It was, Elizabeth decided, part of Emily's demented resentment of Joe's love for Charleston. True, Joe was generous and he cared about her. But that was because he was almost family, and families always took care of their own. He had never said or done anything that a cousin or a brother would not say or do. Or a particularly close friend. Joe was all those things to her—her closest friend when she was little, a stand-in for Pinckney now that he was dead, and an extension of her family. Emily's jealousy was senseless, part of her sickness.

The long hours of night passed while Elizabeth, her eyebrows knotted, sorted through her own turbulent reactions to the drama in Emily's boudoir. At last she faced the deepest source of her unrest. Emily's almost-hysterical rage was not a stranger to her. She had felt it, and more, on the horrifying night that she had murdered Lucas. She still felt it in the recurring dream that haunted her sleep, when she struck him not once, but again and again until she woke, terrified, and searched for his threatening presence in the darkness of her room. The dream had tortured her for years; then it had become less and less frequent; finally it stopped. Now Emily's passion had reminded her of her own uncontrollable fury, and she was frightened.

I cannot bear to live through it again, she said to herself. I must defeat the ghosts of Lucas and that insane moment. I can do it if I try hard enough. I can forget. She fought, her body and mind tensed, until dawn, forcing the emotions to retreat by a superhuman effort of will.

When morning came, she felt bruised inwardly and outwardly, but her demeanor and her heart were calm. She asked Catherine to prepare breakfast; then she went to sleep.

She had been up for less than an hour when Tradd arrived, accompanied by Henry Fitzpatrick. She had completely forgotten her invitation to tea. Luckily, Catherine was "at home" that afternoon, so all preparations for guests had been made. Fitzpatrick was on his promised good behavior. He said and did nothing flamboyant. But inevitably he was soon the focal point of all conversation. His comical face changed expression with such speed and contrast that it was a magnet for everyone's eyes; his forthright confessions about his background were disarming and fascinating. He was, he admitted cheerfully, nothing but a vagabond adventurer. He went where his fancy took him, stayed until he felt an itch in his feet, then moved on. He worked at anything that interested him, for as long as it remained interesting and no longer. Jack of all trades, master of none, and liking it that way.

Elizabeth brought her attention back to her surroundings. She had been thinking about Emily. So young. Only four years older than she. And, oh God, why did it have to take her voice? Distress made Elizabeth's own throat ache. She had to stop brooding . . . what were the young laughing about?

It was that absurd-looking young man. Strange when he was talking, one almost forgot his appearance. His vitality blotted it out somehow. He was a presence, not a portrait. She observed the group around the tea table. They were all spellbound by Fitzpatrick, even Catherine. Usually she became a bit sulky if she was not the center of attraction, but not today. Tradd looked puffy with pride. He had, after all, introduced Fitzpatrick into the group. Also, he had become part of it with him. Catherine had never allowed him to join her friends before.

Catherine! Elizabeth's attention sharpened. She never took her eyes off Tradd's teacher. It wouldn't do. Elizabeth looked quickly at Lawrence Wilson. He had been so attentive to Catherine. He was a nice boy, too, and already getting established in his uncle's law firm. She had rather hoped that something might develop between them. He'd make a good, steady husband, and Elizabeth liked his mother. Stupid boy! He was as engrossed in Fitzpatrick as Catherine was. Why didn't he say something himself instead of just listening to the stranger weave his magic web.

"What brought you to Charleston, Mr. Fitzpatrick?" said Elizabeth loudly. The spell shattered. Everyone looked at her, Catherine with irritation, Henry Fitzpatrick with such concentrated attention that she felt a physical shock.

"Beauty, Mrs. Cooper," he said. His wide mouth curled upward in a smile of impertinent intimacy. "I heard about Charleston, that it was the most beautiful city in America. Also the most historic. I'm interested in history, mostly English history. It would be nice to learn that my own country's history was rich, too. I'm from California. Out there, all the history is Spanish, and there isn't even much of that."

"California!" exclaimed Catherine. "How fascinating. Do tell us all about it."

"Perhaps another time," Elizabeth said. "It's getting late." Lawrence and the other two boys jumped up, stammering apologies, thanks and good-byes. Henry Fitzpatrick rose, too, but he showed no embarrassment. He stood, Elizabeth noticed, in segments. She hadn't realized before how very long his legs were. He waited until the others had made their exit before he bowed to Catherine. Then he held out his hand to Elizabeth. She put hers in it, good manners overcoming her reluctance.

"You haven't given me leave to take Tradd out to the plant yet, Mrs. Cooper. May I ask it now?" His bow was flawless, his manner suitably distant. He returned her hand to her, seemingly unaware that he had been in possession of it longer than she liked.

"Why do you interest yourself in phosphates, Mr. Fitzpatrick?" Elizabeth avoided looking at her son's eager face.

"I don't. I'm interested in fossils. Tradd showed me a shark's tooth from the diggings. The place must be a paleontologist's dream."

She had no idea what he was talking about, but she had to admit it sounded academic. Tradd took her arm and tugged. "Say yes, Mama, please." His enthusiasm was irresistible.

"Very well," she said, "but you'll have to go on a weekend. You must be back in the city before dark. I won't risk Tradd's health."

Fitzpatrick's nose quivered. "Fascinating," he said. "Are there goblins?"

For a moment, Elizabeth didn't realize he was teasing her. Then he chuckled, and she thought, Disrespectful young puppy. "There's swamp fever," she said shortly. "Good evening, Mr. Fitzpatrick."

"Good evening, Mrs. Cooper, Miss Cooper, Master Cooper. Thank you for a delightful afternoon."

Tradd showed him down to the door. Elizabeth and Catherine could hear them talking in the stairs. "Listen, you young barbarian," Fitzpatrick was saying, "go back upstairs and take a good look at that room we just left. I'll expect a report tomorrow on the importance of proportion in architecture. The rumors about Charleston are all true. Pay particular attention to the height of the windows and sills . . ."

Elizabeth and Catherine looked at the windows, then at each other. "I don't see anything," said Catherine.

"Neither do I. Fetch the tape measure from my sewing box." Elizabeth heard her own words with surprise. "Tradd's going to need it," she added quickly. "I'll see if supper's almost ready."

56

When Tradd's school recessed on July first, she had everything ready for the move to the Island. It came, she thought, not a moment too soon. She was sick of hearing about Mr. Fitzpatrick from Tradd; it seemed every other word out of his mouth was the man's name. Catherine was just as bad; no, she was worse. Her admiration was romantic. She talked about his charm and his exotic past and his curly hair. "Poetic," she described him. He came to tea every Tuesday, which was her day at home, plus other days when Tradd brought him from school to work on the fossils they had collected at Carlington. They were mounting them in a case to be displayed in the classroom at Porter.

Elizabeth could not deny that Fitzpatrick's manners were irreproachable. But he upset her, and Catherine's reaction to him worried her. The room hummed with energy when he entered it, and she felt danger. When they were settled in at the beach house, she relaxed for the first time since Fitzpatrick had entered their peaceful lives.

She was napping in the hammock one afternoon when she heard his voice ringing. She thought she was dreaming, and she smiled at the beautiful unknown melody. It sounded very old and strange.

". . . combs to buckle my hair with . . . and shoes of fine green leather . . ."

She stretched luxuriously and opened her eyes. The dream-song did not stop.

"Good heavens," she said. "What are you doing here?" She struggled to sit up.

Fitzpatrick steadied the hammock. "I came to talk to you about your son. Do you know you look like a lovely tabby when you stretch? I would offer you a saucer of cream if I knew where to find one."

Elizabeth got to her feet. She was so angry she was nearly speechless. "How dare you?" was all she could manage to say.

Fitzpatrick smiled, which increased her fury. She had thought they were rid of him, and he had the nerve to sneak into the house and make impertinent remarks, then cap his effrontery by laughing at her. Nothing in her life had equipped her to deal with such an outrage.

"A regal temper, by God," he said. "It's a glorious thing. Off with my head if you like, but first you'll hear what I have to say about the boy. If you care for him."

She found her tongue then. "You insult me with every breath, you unspeakable man. How can you suggest I don't care for my son? Say what you have to say, and get out of my house."

"But I have a lot to say, and you're not in the mood to listen. Suppose I come back another time?"

"You'll never be admitted here again."

He shook his head. "You don't mean that. You'll worry that you did the wrong thing by not listening. What's your choice? Shall I come again, or shall I make humble apologies and stay now? He'll be up from swimming soon, it's clouding up."

Elizabeth willed her anger away. "Is it important, what you have to say?"

"Extremely. He's an important boy."

"Then sit down and say it."

"Without humble apologies?"

Her temper flared. "Don't be a jackass," she said.

"I'll try," he replied, "but I can't promise." He folded himself into a chair. His mobile face became serious, and he looked older. Elizabeth had never seen him serious; she sat opposite him, all temper swallowed by her concern for Tradd.

"Tell me," she begged.

"Don't worry," he said quickly. "I didn't mean to frighten you. Everything I want to say is good. I meant it: Your son is an important boy." Fitzpatrick's voice was like a continuation of his singing; it rose and fell like music, and the words he spoke were strange to her ear. He said nothing about "brave" or "manly" or "strong," all the things people said about young boys. Tradd was remarkable, he said, for his intelligence and sensitivity and hunger for knowledge. "It makes him a misfit. He'd rather be reading than playing soldier like the other boys. He hides it, and hides it well. The others don't suspect he's different. But he knows he is, and there's a chance he'll begin to hide the knowledge from himself. Then he'll lose all the special qualities that set him apart."

Elizabeth's eyebrows were knotted. She was thinking hard, trying to comprehend.

"I don't mean that he's different in any classic Greek sense," Fitzpatrick said impatiently. "He'll like girls when he's older, if that's what's worrying you."

She didn't know what he was talking about. Her bewilderment was obvious.

"Oh, my innocent," he said. "Never mind about that. What I'm trying to convey to you is this: Your son is head and shoulders smarter than all his friends. He's smarter than most grown men. He's uneducated, but that can be remedied."

"Then what's the problem? He's in school."

"He's in a school that thinks armies are more valuable than scholars or poets. He's in a society, a world that prizes winning over striving. He's too young to choose the pleasures of the mind by himself. He still believes in the standards of the herd." Fitzpatrick leaned forward, his body taut with the effort to communicate.

"Think," he said urgently. "Do you remember when you learned to read?"

She nodded.

"Was it thrilling to you? Did you believe you had discovered magic?"

A flood of memory made her smile. "Yes," she said, "exactly that. Magic."

"When did you lose it?"

The smile vanished. "I don't know." She felt a crushing sadness.

"That's it," said Fitzpatrick. "Most people lose it. There are so many other demands, other things to do, other people to please. The excitement of learning slips away, and they don't even notice it leaving. It usually happens very early. Tradd hasn't quite lost it yet. He's lucky. I want him to keep it. Will you help? Do you care?"

"Yes!" She cared desperately.

He took her hands in his. "So sad," he said. "I understand. Don't be sad, Bess. You can get the magic back if you try."

Her fingers tingled. He was overstepping the bounds. She pulled her hands away. "We were talking about my son, Mr. Fitzpatrick, not me. What should I do for Tradd?"

"You've done the most essential thing already. You've accepted the importance of magic. Now, the next thing—"

"Mama, may I go to Roger's for supper?" Tradd's voice preceded him onto the porch. When he saw his teacher, Roger was forgotten. He and Henry Fitzpatrick began to talk about the clouds outside. Elizabeth looked at her son with new eyes. Instead of noticing that he was growing out of his bathing costume and worrying about finding the money to buy a new one, she paid attention to his eager questions about wind velocities and the cause of thunderstorms. Fitzpatrick answered them with equal excitement. "Fascinating," she observed, was his favorite word.

Catherine came home from a friend's house, took a chair close to Henry Fitzpatrick and listened with absorption to the conversation which had shifted to tales of storms at sea. Fitzpatrick had spent a year in the Merchant Marines. She echoed his comments, murmuring "fascinating" after every anecdote. Elizabeth knew that she meant the man and not his stories. It gave her a new worry. If she protected Catherine from his dangerous fascination, she would be depriving Tradd of the magic Fitzpatrick offered him. If she had to sacrifice one of her children, which would she choose?

As if it were reflecting the turbulence in her mind, the sky darkened with rolling black clouds. The air became heavy and still, the sea breeze died away. Everything waited in tense suspension. Even the ocean became flatter. On the porch, conversation ceased. Elizabeth felt an anticipatory quickening of her pulses.

A single bolt of lightning stepped down from the clouds to the sea. It seemed an impossibly slow descent. Then the thunder spoke with a ripping edge, and the rain fell in a solid curtain. "Bravo!" cried Fitzpatrick. Elizabeth laughed.

The storm was magnificent. Noise piled upon noise, the heavy assaulting rain on the tin roof, the crashing thunder, the mounting roar of the surf. Flashes of blue and yellow light hissed and crackled. Catherine stole away to cower under her bedclothes. Tradd would not admit to fear, but he closed his eyes and retreated into the cushions of a chaise. Elizabeth walked from one end of the porch to the other, reveling in the electric energy she felt in her veins. Henry Fitzpatrick sprawled on the chaise next to Tradd's, smiling to himself. Each of them was alone with the storm.

It ended as abruptly as it had begun, leaving a steady strong wind and a horizon tumbling with clouds. Elizabeth sniffed the ozone-spiced air. She felt clean and strong.

"Look." Tradd pointed to the right. A rainbow was forming off the far end of the beach.

Fitzpatrick walked to the door and opened it. He tipped his head back and shouted up at the heavens. "That's really gilding the lily, you know. The storm was quite enough showing off for one day."

Elizabeth gasped at his blasphemy. But she knew what he meant. A person could stand only so much beauty and no more. The rainbow was a burden to her exalted senses. He turned to her, the corners of his eyes and mouth tucked into tiny parentheses of laugh lines. "Better serve supper indoors," he said. "The sunset will do you in altogether."

"I shall," she said. "Can you stay and eat with us? We could finish our talk after."

"Nothing I'd like better. Thank you."

"I'll go tell Delia. She's probably still under the table. She doesn't care much for thunder."

Tradd found a thousand excuses not to go to bed at his usual time. Catherine also lingered in the living room instead of following her routine of brushing her hair a hundred strokes and rolling it up in rags. She sat next to Fitzpatrick and, Elizabeth saw with horror, touched his arm every time he made her laugh. Too often. He was amusing, but not that much.

"Mr. Fitzpatrick," Elizabeth said, "would you like to move out onto the porch? It's good dark now, the sunset can't bother us."

He stood up. So did Tradd and Catherine. "I have an even better idea, Mrs. Cooper. Let's take a walk on the beach, the two of us." He smiled at Catherine and Tradd. "You can't come with us. We're going to talk about you." Then he offered his arm to Elizabeth, ignoring Tradd's protests and Catherine's pretty pout.

She was glad for his support. The night was clear but dark, with only stars and a quarter moon for light. She stumbled on the steps from the causeway to the beach and would have fallen but for his quick reaction, tightening the muscles in his arm and closing it against his side to hold her hand steady.

"Thank you."

"My pleasure."

When she reached firm sand, she released his arm. For an instant she thought she must have been supporting him. His knees seemed to give way. "Are you all right, Mr. Fitzpatrick? What happened?" She could not see him; he was just a darker patch against the dark ground.

"I'm taking off my shoes. Lean on my shoulder, and I'll untie the laces on yours."

"Certainly not. You really are a shocking young man, Mr. Fitzpatrick. I'm afraid you're a risky companion for my son." And my daughter, she thought, the worry returning. She wished they didn't make such an attractive couple. Catherine had called her attention to the similarities between them, both with dark hair and deep blue eyes. She would love, she had said, to lead a cotillion with him. Everyone would look.

"He's at an age for risks," Fitzpatrick replied. "He's had too few. I get the impression that you've kept him sort of swaddled."

Elizabeth admitted that he was right. She was terrified of accidents and illness. It was easy to talk to the indistinct figure at her side. He was only a voice, a warm, interested voice. It was almost like talking to herself.

They walked for more than a mile, keeping parallel to the dimly seen pale scalloped edges of foam that marked the water's edge. Fitzpatrick told her things about her son that she had never known, about his interests, his fears, the pressures and confusions of life within the brick walls that surrounded the school. She was impressed and touched by his concern and affection for the boy. She would, she said, do anything he recommended for Tradd's well-being.

At the end of the Island, they turned and started back. "The best thing you can do for him is to encourage him to try his wings. He needs to depend on himself more. I'll take care of the educational part. For as long as I'm here. By the time I leave, he'll have found his own interests." Elizabeth's heart turned over. She didn't want Tradd to lose him.

"When will that be, Mr. Fitzpatrick?"

"Won't you call me 'Harry'? All my friends do."

"Harry. It suits you. Yes, I'd like to be your friend. You're being very generous to Tradd."

He waited. She took the next step. "My name is Elizabeth."

"I know. I call you 'Bess' in my mind. You are very like her early portraits, you know. Good Queen Bess. She's one of my particular favorites."

"I'm flattered."

They walked on in easy, companionable silence. The sand crunched under their feet. Elizabeth wondered idly what it would feel like to be barefooted. She had always worn bathing shoes, even in the water. Harry Fitzpatrick was definitely an unsettling influence, she said to herself.

Which brought her mind back to Catherine. She had tried to prevent her seeing him. For Tradd's sake, that was impossible. She took a deep breath before speaking.

"Yes?" said Harry.

"I have to speak to you about my other child. I don't approve of your attentions to Catherine, but I know that's unreasonable when I'm so pleased about you and Tradd. I suppose you know that she finds you attractive . . ."

"Are you asking my intentions?"

"Yes, I guess I am."

Harry laughed uproariously.

All Elizabeth's fears were confirmed. She acted on impulse, breaking into a run, running home to lock the doors, to protect her daughter.

Harry caught up easily. He seized her wrist and stopped her. "Let me go, you—" she said.

"Bounder? Cad? Varmint?" he suggested. "No, I won't. Listen to me, Bess. The idea of courting your charming daughter is absurd. Don't you realize, silly woman, that I'm in love with you?"

"You're crazy."

"So I've been told. That has nothing to do with it. I adore you, and that's that. As for Catherine, she enjoys playing games with me, but her eye is firmly fixed on the Wilson boy. You don't know your daughter. Her mind is too prosaic and her heart too lukewarm to fool with the likes of me." He paused for a long moment; his grip on her wrist relaxed, but he did not let her go.

"You, on the other hand, my queen, have a wild, gambler's heart and mind. Let me take off your shoes and blinders. We could make each other very happy." His grasp tightened; he pulled her into his arms and bent to kiss her.

In the darkness, he was only a looming, attacking form. Elizabeth forgot who he was, where she was. She panicked; she was back in the past, in the nightmare terror of her marriage. She began to choke; then she fainted.

A cool dampness on her forehead brought her back to consciousness. She opened her eyes and saw the golden-white pulsing summer stars. The sound of waves breaking was a blur in her ears. Memory returned and with it her fear. She began to shudder.

"Hush, Bess. Everything's all right. Nobody's going to hurt you." Harry's voice was as soft as a lullaby. He continued to smooth her temples with his dampened handkerchief until she was calm. Then, "May I help you home?"

She felt like a fool. Fainting like that. Men tried to kiss women all the time, she knew that. The only thing one had to do was say "no." Still, she was not about to offer any explanation. She would not refer to it at all. She allowed him to help her to her feet, and she leaned on his arm while they walked back to the house.

At the foot of the causeway, he stopped. "I'm sorry," he said.

"Please, let's not say anything."

"Just say you forgive me. I didn't know."

Did I say something, call Lucas' name? Elizabeth felt cold and frightened. "What didn't you know?" she demanded.

"How truly innocent you are. I am most genuinely apologetic. Will you forgive me?"

She was so relieved that she said yes. They started up the steps. She wanted conversation, anything to return the situation to normal. "Where are you staying on the Island?" she asked.

"I haven't decided."

"But you must be visiting someone. There's no hotel."

"I'm sleeping in the dunes. I brought a blanket."

She was incredulous. People just didn't do things like that. She said so. "That's terrible."

"Not at all. It's quite wonderful. The sky for a roof and the sunrise to wake you. A house just gets between you and the beauty."

Elizabeth shrugged. He must be insane.

But later, when she was in bed, she stared at the ceiling of her room and tried to imagine the sky. And, in spite of herself, she thought about Harry's words before he left: "I won't frighten you again, but I intend to make you love me. Nothing you do or say will stop me. If you lock your door, I'll climb in a window. If you go away, I'll follow you. I'll give you all the time you need, Bess, but I mean to have you."

He was as good as his word. He appeared at the house at odd hours, his head popped up beside her in the water when she was swimming, he jumped onto the ferry whenever she went to town to do any work. He never touched her, and he was just as attentive to Tradd and Catherine as he was to her. But the look in his tilted eyes told her he had meant his words.

For the first weeks, she was angry. Then she felt embarrassed. After that, he became such a familiar presence that she felt unsettled on the days he did not come. By the end of the summer, she admitted to herself that she liked his admiration. She had never been courted before, not even by Lucas. No one had ever left wild flowers in the icebox for her to find or strung shells on a blue cord to make a necklace for her to wear swimming or sung old songs to the family with sidelong glances at her. When she caught herself listening for clues to his age in the stories he told, she realized that she was in danger of falling in love.

Harry helped them move back to town at the end of September. Elizabeth expected, and dreaded, that everything would change. He would be teaching, she would be working and attending to her social life. Except for Catherine's at home days, she probably wouldn't see him at all. It would be too obvious to invite him to dinner or supper. She had been careful not to say or do anything encouraging to him. She was convinced that he was probably just playing a game with her. A summer game.

When they reached the house, she found that all the dust sheets had been taken off the furniture and that everything was gleaming. Every room had vases of chrysanthemums and asters in it, the fires were laid, and the beds were made. She looked immediately at Harry. He rolled his eyes upward and began to whistle.

"You are an angel," she said. "I always dread opening the house."

"Impressed with my dusting? I'm glad. I have an ulterior motive." He wanted, he said, to rent the rooms in the servants' quarters over the kitchen. He hated living in a boardinghouse. Tradd set up a clamor of approval. Catherine looked smug. She was quite sure that he was smitten with her.

Elizabeth thought of a dozen reasons to say no, then said yes.

Fitzpatrick smiled. "That's a relief," he said. "I've already moved my things in. I won't be much trouble. I'll do my own cleaning and I'll only use the kitchen when it's okay with Delia. She's already agreed."

Elizabeth shook her head. "You're awfully sure of yourself."

"I knew a kindhearted lady like you wouldn't turn a poor troubadour out into the cold."

She had to laugh with him. It was an unseasonably warm day, even for Charleston.

"But Elizabeth, you'll have him under foot all the time." She had taken the news to Lucy Anson the very next day.

"What's frightening is that I don't think I would mind. I'm losing whatever senses I had. He's so alive, Lucy, and so funny and so interesting. He's Tradd's best friend and mine, too."

"Do you love him?"

"I don't know. I don't think so. He doesn't set my heart pounding the way Lucas used to. He just makes me happy. Everything is fun when he's around."

"Then I don't see any harm in it. Enjoy the fun. It's certainly good for Tradd to have a man around. And for you, too. You look wonderful." Lucy looked closely at her. No, she didn't have that dazed, glowing expression that went with love. Too bad, she thought. Elizabeth had been without love for much too long.

As it turned out, Harry Fitzpatrick was not under foot at all. In contrast to his frequent, unannounced appearances at the beach, he waited to be invited to the house on Meeting Street. But he put flowers in Elizabeth's carriage house office every day, and he left notes inside the ledger or desk drawer or typewriter. Often they were verses of poems he had particularly liked. Sometimes they were pencil sketches of the ocean or the sea oats that grew on the Sullivans Island dunes. Occasionally they said only "Harry loves Bess" inside a Valentine heart.

He did come to Catherine's teas, where he captivated everyone. And he continued to work on special projects with Tradd. But he allowed Elizabeth to control his time with her. She forced herself to limit it. He had supper with them about once a week, and dinner on Sunday. It gave them no time alone, and that made her feel safe.

In November Elizabeth celebrated her thirty-seventh birthday. She invited Harry to dinner, telling him the occasion.

"You could have just said that you were worried about ages, Bess. I would have told you that I think that's nonsense. And you wouldn't have had all the work of baking a cake."

"Smarty cat, I bought it from Theus' bakery . . . And it isn't nonsense. You're just a boy. You shouldn't be leaving Valentines in my desk."

"You're just a girl, and I like Valentines. So do you. Is it chocolate?"

"Of course it's chocolate. I wouldn't be so extravagant for yellow cake. Can't you ever be serious, Harry? I don't think you realize that I'm serious. This crush you claim to have on me is absurd."

He looked at her, and his eyes made her breath catch. They were full of feeling, of wanting. They were a man's eyes. "I love you, my girl. I do not get 'crushes.' Why don't you ask me; I have no secrets from you. I was thirty on January sixth. And it's totally irrelevant. You are the child, Bess. The Virgin Queen. The Sleeping Beauty. The princess captive in the tower. I'm a thousand years older than you are. It's all right for you to love me. You will, you know it. Don't waste the time we could have together on silly number equations. . . . Give me your hands."

She raised her right hand. "Both of them," said Harry. She felt as if she would be giving too much, but her other hand moved of its own volition. He held her hands in his own, not pressing them or keeping them captive. "Now, my love, close your eyes and let yourself feel your hands in mine. Don't be afraid. Trust me. Take a chance on feeling."

She did as she was told. Harry's skin was warm and dry. His energy flowed through it into her palms and up her arms. She could feel it, although he moved not at all.

He put her hands back in her lap. "There," he said. "What time shall I come for the birthday dinner?"

Elizabeth opened her eyes. Harry was near her, but she did not draw away. "Two," she said. "Thank you, Harry."

He smiled and twitched his nose. "You haven't even seen your present. Thank me tomorrow." She knew by now that his ridiculous expressive nose was telling her that he was teasing her. She also knew that he understood why she had thanked him.

Looking back, years later, Elizabeth realized that her independent left hand's small movement was one of the most important actions of her life.

57

There was an unexpected guest for Elizabeth's birthday dinner. During the morning, Catherine rushed into her office. She had just received a bouquet of flowers from Lawrence. In the box with them was a letter asking her to marry him. He was too nervous to propose in person. "He's coming for my answer at noon, Mama. What shall I wear?"

"Your wine-colored challis, I think. It's particularly becoming. Are you going to accept Lawrence?"

Catherine threw up her hands. "Well of course, Mama. I set my cap for him at the Cotillion Club Ball."

The birthday party became an engagement celebration, with toasts to the young couple's future happiness and a great deal of argument about setting the date for the wedding. Catherine won. With a lot of concentrated effort, it could be done: She'd be the newest bride at the Saint Cecelia.

"Thank you, Mama. We'll go tell Lawrence's family now. May we be excused? We don't care for dessert. Do we, Lawrence?"

Tradd and Harry sang "Happy Birthday" to Elizabeth and ate prodigious amounts of cake. Harry's present was a pair of roller skates. Tradd was appalled. Until Harry made them all go to Elizabeth's office. He had moved the desk and chair into a corner. "No one will see us," he said. "We're all going to skate." He produced Tradd's unused skates, and a pair for himself. Then he knelt before Elizabeth. "Will you permit me, Madame?" he said.

"You're mad," said Elizabeth, putting her foot in his hand. When her skates were on, he told her to stay seated until he came back for her. He laced up his own skates and rolled across the floor backward. "Harry's showing off," she said to Tradd. "Don't you try that." Harry made a face. "I mean, don't try that until you get used to your new skates," she amended. She won smiles from them both.

Harry stopped in the far corner of the room, turned, stooped and opened a large wooden box that had gone unnoticed. Tradd skated across to him and shouted. "Mama! It's a—" Harry tripped him, then sat on him.

"Quiet, or I'll cut out your tongue," he said. Tradd laughed and banged his skates on the floor, trying to tip Harry over. "Quiet!" Harry roared. He had been busy with the box. When Tradd stopped, Elizabeth could hear music. Harry got up, glided away from the box and exposed the tall morning-glory trumpet of a Gramophone.

"Oh, I can't believe it." Elizabeth was overcome. She had seen a Gramophone at Joe and Emily's, but she had never dreamed of owning one.

Harry skated to her and held out his hands. "Now we'll dance on wheels," he said. "No ordinary skating for Queen Bess. She must have minstrels in the gallery."

In spite of several falls and a hundred near-accidents, Elizabeth was skating well by the end of the day. She had never had so much fun in her life.

Or such painful feet. Her shoes would not go back on. Harry sent Tradd for a pail of hot water and Epsom salts. "He'll have to heat the water," he said with a wicked smile, "and you can't walk on those feet. You're at my mercy, proud beauty."

She did not even blink. She wasn't afraid of him at all.

"What a good girl you are, Bess. Let me massage your feet before they cramp." He sat cross-legged on the floor in front of her chair. His strong fingers rubbed and flexed her arches, then her heels, then each toe. Elizabeth half-closed her eyes. She was more tired than she had thought, and the massage was luxurious.

"I could fall asleep sitting right here," she murmured.

"Do, if you like. I'll carry you to the house." He rubbed one foot between his two hands.

"Mmm. No, I can't. I've got to see about supper."

"To hell with supper." He rubbed the other foot.

"Here's the water," called Tradd from the yard. Elizabeth woke up.

She left her desk in the corner. The office became known as the rink. She still worked there every day, but she also practiced her skating. Catherine was horrified. "Suppose people find out?" she wailed.

"No one will," her mother promised. Her skirts covered her skinned knees. "I love my birthday presents," she told Harry again and again.

"I love seeing you play," he replied.

With Tradd's birthday, Christmas, Catherine's wedding and the Saint Cecelia all following each other within three weeks, Elizabeth hardly had time to sit down. Everyone agreed that the wedding and the bride were lovely. Elizabeth thanked them all, supervised the transfer of the wedding presents to the young Wilson's house on Water Street, then collapsed. "I'll never skate again," she moaned to Harry. "Every bone in my body hurts."

They were in the rink. Harry had found her there going over the neglected account books. "I don't even know whether we can meet next month's payroll," she told him. "The numbers keep running together."

"You're exhausted. That's no good. You'll get sick if you don't get some rest." He scooped her into his arms and carried her into the yard.

"Harry, put me down," she whispered fiercely. "You'll break your back, and Delia will be scandalized."

"This is Delia's day off, and Tradd's at Roger's house. No one will be scandalized, and I have a strong back."

He carried her up the kitchen stairs to his rooms. He put her on his bed, told her to turn on her stomach and took off her shoes. His bedroom smelled of soap and leather and tobacco. His bed was hard. It was all too masculine. "I've got to go," Elizabeth said.

"No," said Harry. "You know I won't hurt you." He began to knead her feet in the familiar after-skating massage. It felt very good. She began to relax.

When her feet were warm and supple, Harry picked up her left hand. "I'm going to rub the knots out of your arms and shoulders, Bess. If it frightens you, I'll stop." He massaged each finger, then her hand, then her wrist and forearm. "Are you all right?" he asked.

"It feels wonderful." She was enveloped in a delicious languor. His hands were slow and strong and gentle and skillful. She felt her arm go limp, and tension drained from her fingertips. Before his hands reached her shoulder, she was asleep. She was unaware of the massage, she did not feel his fingers on the bunched muscles at the base of her neck, she did not hear his voice when he moved to the other side of the bed and started rubbing the thumb of her right hand.

"I know where I'm going," he sang in a pure tenor, "And I know who's going with me . . . I know who I love . . . But the devil knows who I'll marry . . ."

Harry Fitzpatrick massaged Elizabeth's arms and shoulders, as he had told her he would. Then he stopped. He put his finger to his lips, then touched it to hers. "Sleep well, Bess," he said softly, "poor wounded little girl. What did they do to you?"

In the following months, Harry Fitzpatrick led Elizabeth into a terrain of freedom and happiness that made her dizzy with discovery. He taught her to play, and to see and to feel.

They walked the winter beach, relishing the private conquest of the deserted Island, delighting in the stark beauty of its bleak light and colors; they ran, Elizabeth holding her skirts like sails so that she was pushed by the rough wind; they sheltered in the steep dunes to picnic, feeling the warmth of the sand and sun. Harry put his head in her lap, talking about other beaches he had seen: the pebbled strips in the South of France, the powdery crushed coral in the Caribbean, the rocky crags of California. She put her hand on his hair and it curled around her fingers, capturing her.

When spring came, they drank honeysuckle nectar, and he told her stories of the Greek gods and how the sky made a canopy over the Parthenon that was the color of her eyes. He rebuilt Stuart's derelict tree-house and read Homer to her amid the tender new leaves that hid them from view.

They rode bicycles around the Race Course, floating paper boats of flowers on the lazy stream that ran through the garden in the center of the oval, and scurried away from the attack of the swans that lived on the pond. Harry fended them off while she ran across the bridge, waving his arms and shouting that they were the property of the Crown and were in rebellion against their Queen. Then he declaimed "Horatio at the Bridge" while they hissed their disapproval.

He cooked suppers for Elizabeth and Tradd, serving them up with stories. He gave them spaghetti and Marco Polo, bouillabaisse and the lost Dauphin, oat cakes and Mary, Queen of Scots, who was, he said, a silly, tedious woman who never deserved the forbearance shown by her cousin Elizabeth. He whittled chopsticks and taught them how the Chinese ate rice and shrimp.

He took them on walks around their city, trading bits of history he had learned from books for legends Elizabeth had inherited from her family. He showed them roof lines and balconies that they had never really looked at and speculated on the genius of those first Charlestonians who had created privacy within the cramped space behind their defense walls.

He rubbed the cramps out of Elizabeth's shoulders when she had bent too long over her books and washed the ink from her fingers with his tongue. When she received the telegram announcing Emily Simmons' death, he held her in his arms while she wept and kissed her throat to take away the pain there.

When summer came, Elizabeth could not bear to leave him. She defied Catherine's criticism and offered Harry a room in the beach house. Lucy Anson agreed to take her old room and act as chaperone. She gave up her usual vacation with cousins who had a lodge in the Smokey Mountains. Elizabeth's radiant happiness was too fragile; Lucy knew it needed her protection. Harry's magnetic charm had captivated everyone in Charleston, but he was a danger to Elizabeth's reputation, and she was so entranced by him that she did not even care.

Lucy was not immune to Harry's enchantment. She, too, soon felt that the room became dimmer when he left it, and she became wittier and more intelligent when he was there. It was the effect his vitality and consuming interest had on everyone. For the most part, the household was a joyous quartet. Lucy and Elizabeth were pupils, along with Tradd. They all gathered shells and examined their color and construction. They all wrote letters and threw them, in sealed bottles, into the outgoing tide. They all read voraciously and argued about the relative merits of Mark Twain, Dickens and Zola as an interpreter of national character.

But there were times when Elizabeth and Harry were alone. Lucy did not interfere, but she worried. Elizabeth was becoming more and more indiscreet. First she discarded her bathing shoes in the water; then she stopped wearing them on the beach. Next her hat was left behind; Harry liked freckles and tanned skin. He began swimming at night; soon Elizabeth joined him, enraptured by the strands of phosphorous that trailed away from her hands in the dark water. When she slept out with him in the dunes one night, Lucy felt obliged to speak to her.

Elizabeth was defensive, "Really, Lucy, I think I'm too old to be scolded. I'm not doing anything wrong."

"You know that appearance of sin is taken for sin itself, Elizabeth. I'm happy for you that you have Harry. Just don't be so overt. Whatever you do is fine, but be discreet."

"Be discreet about what, Lucy? There's no need to hide anything; there's nothing to hide. Harry is a gentleman. He's never tried any familiarity. Once he kissed my throat, but it was like a game—kiss it and make it well. He doesn't care about kissing and all that other stuff. It's one of the reasons I believe him when he says he loves me. He doesn't do anything unpleasant to me."

Lucy was stunned and saddened. Lucas Cooper must have been a clod if Elizabeth's marriage had been "unpleasant." Harry, she was sure, was not an asexual man. He was too alive and too masculine for any mistake about that. Perhaps, she thought, he was an idealist, like Pinckney. No, it wouldn't be that. There was nothing to stop him from marrying Elizabeth. What kind of game was he playing? She began to watch him closely.

He touched Elizabeth often, holding her hand when they ran to the water, pulling her hair in their mock arguments, rubbing her neck when she was tired, dancing to the Gramophone, lying next to her in the hammock and reading aloud from a new play that a friend had sent him from Paris. It was, he said, an amusing gift because the hero, Cyrano de Bergerac, was also cursed with an extraordinary nose. Lucy's French was very poor, and she did not understand the words. But Harry's lilting voice was not amused when he read to Elizabeth; Lucy knew that he was making love to her, even though Elizabeth did not. She felt like an intruder into a mystery she could not understand. She wanted to leave them alone, but she was too anxious for Elizabeth. When Carlington business demanded that Elizabeth go to town one day, Lucy asked Harry to stay at the house and repair a torn screen on the porch. "Tradd can escort his mother," she said.

Harry raised his eyebrows, but he agreed.

When they were alone, Lucy fussed around, puffing up cushions, moving chairs and tables, trying to think of what to say.

"If you want to drive me insane," said Harry, "you're doing a good job. Just blurt it out, Miss Lucy, whatever it is. It won't get any easier for you or for me."

Lucy swallowed. "Are you going to marry Elizabeth?" She looked at the faded pattern of stripes on the chair seat.

"No."

Lucy spun to look at Harry. "Then why, please God, are you making her fall in love with you? You'll ruin her."

Harry's mobile face twisted while he chose his words. "I'm in love with her," he said at last. "She delights me, she fascinates me, she keeps me in a state of perpetual excitement. I want her more than I have ever wanted any woman. And I want her to want me . . . See here, we'd better sit down. You're looking a bit wonky."

Lucy did feel faint. She had dreaded Harry's "no," but she had not really expected it. He held a chair for her, and she half-fell into it. He sat opposite, shoulders hunched, his expressive hands dangling between his long legs.

"Let me tell you some things about Bess you probably don't know," he said. "She is an adventurous, passionate woman who's never had a chance to become her real self. She doesn't even suspect that self is there, but I know it is. She really is like a reembodiment of Elizabeth the Queen—all the fire, all the strength, all the intelligence, all the courage. And she's a Virgin Queen, too. Forget the marriage, the children, all that. She may have had a thousand men in her bed for all I know or care, but she is a complete innocent. She's the most intriguing female since Scheherazade.

"I'm a wanderer, you know. Ordinarily I would have been gone by now. I've seen everything I wanted to see in Charleston. I thought this would be a stop like all the others. When I met Bess, I thought she'd be a woman like all the others. I fall in love with enthusiasm—with women, with places, with ideas. I love with all my heart and soul. And then, poof, one day's it's over. I like to think that no one is the poorer for having known me; no one has ever complained."

Lucy sniffed. "You haven't been there to hear them."

Harry smiled. "Touché. You may be right," he said. "At least I announce myself what I am, from the very beginning. I've never pretended to be a stable citizen."

"How does a man get to be like you, Harry Fitzpatrick? You're poison."

"Do you really want to know? Bess knows. I've told her all about me. I'm an adventurer and the son of an adventurer. Irish, as you see. My father was the third son of an Anglo-Irish landowner, more or less what you people here call a planter. He left home in 1848 to follow the call of gold found in a place he had never heard of called California. With the luck of the Irish, he survived the wreck of his ship when it rounded the Horn, was picked up by a faster one, and got to California with ragged breeches and a tongue that could charm the birds from the trees. A year later, he struck gold at a place called Sutter's Mill. A year after that, he went back to Ireland to marry the sweetheart he had left behind and take her back with him to San Francisco. It's a lovely, brawling place, San Francisco. But it's not lovely enough for a lifetime. When I was eighteen, I did what my father had done before me. I packed a few books and signed on to a ship to look for adventure. I was going to go to South Africa and make my own strike. By mistake, I picked a ship that was going to the Orient. But I liked Japan, so I stayed awhile. Then I moved on, worked and played my way around the world. I've gotten this far in twelve years. No, it's thirteen, now."

"And you intend to do that until you die?"

Harry shrugged. "I don't know. I'll do it until I want to do something else. I follow my fancy."

"Poison."

He held up a narrow hand. "Wait before you name labels, Miss Lucy. Have I been a bad thing for Bess and Tradd? I don't think so."

Lucy had to admit that he had not. "So far, at least. But what about when you leave? And what if—" She bit her lip.

"Don't be spinsterish, Miss Lucy. What if I become Bess' lover? If I seduce her? Do you believe she'd be better off remaining a virgin all her life, going to her grave having never tasted the wine?"

Lucy could say nothing.

"You'll not try to warn her, then?" Harry's voice was lilting.

Lucy was silent. She didn't know what she thought, but she knew that she would have welcomed Pinckney to her arms at any time and that she regretted their waiting more than she could measure. If Harry were to die, it would be the same waste for Elizabeth. But he would go away and leave her. That was worse. Or was it? Love had such a terrible price.

"You're a darling," said Harry. He planted kisses in her palm then went to look for the screen patch.

Lucy was in her room with a headache when Elizabeth and Tradd returned. She did not come out for supper. She still didn't know what to do about telling Elizabeth. And she had a sick feeling that, no matter what she did, it would make no difference.

"Was it very hot in town?" asked Harry. He and Elizabeth were on the dark porch. He spoke quietly. Tradd had gone to bed, and he did not want to wake him.

"Awful. It's hard to believe that it's already September." Elizabeth sighed. "It's even hot here."

"Let's have a swim. It'll refresh you."

"I don't know if I have the energy for a swim. I think I'll just go to sleep in the hammock where it's cooler."

"If you like. I'll get your pillow . . . Unless you'd like to sleep on the beach. I'm going to have a swim then go to sleep in my wet bathing costume. That will cool me off."

"Oh, Harry, what a delicious idea. Shall I, too?"

"I wish you would. I missed you all day."

"I missed you, too. Let's go change."

The ocean was as warm as fresh milk, with unexpected currents of cold water that touched her ankles or waist and then vanished. Elizabeth rose and fell with the easy swells in the gully between the lines of breakers, floating on her back and looking at the warm, close stars. She heard a splashing near her ears and felt Harry's hands supporting her head. "I can float by myself," she said.

"I'm going to feed your hairpins to the fishes," said Harry. "Your hair should be floating around you. You'd look like a mermaid." His fingers plucked at her hair, and then she had an incredible sensation of cool water trickling onto her scalp as her coiled hair unwound. It felt nothing like that when she washed it. This was a loosening and a caress; she became part of the tide, a sea creature. She laughed softly and pulled herself under the surface in a backward circle. She could feel the weight of her long, heavy tresses following her. When she came up, she took a breath and looked around for Harry. He was like a dark, shiny seal, with his black hair plastered to his neat, narrow skull.

"I've always hated to get my face wet," said Elizabeth. "Whatever made me do that?"

"Mermaids always do that. Did you enjoy it?"

"Yes. I felt like a fish."

"So prosaic. Be a dolphin, if you won't be a mermaid. I will not permit you to be a fish."

She turned her head from side to side, watching the swirl of her hair. In the dim light, it looked mysterious and alien, bronze, not copper. It could have belonged to a different person. She might be a different person. She did not feel like herself. She dived again and touched the sandy bottom. Her fingers closed around something smooth and solid. She brought it up with a geyser of glittering, phosphorous-flecked water. "I've found a treasure," she said. "Let's see what it is."

Harry swam to her. "It's a magnificent treasure, my Bess. It must be a jewel from your crown." He took two floating tendrils of hair and tied them around the pebble. Then his hands cupped her face; he looked long into her eyes. "Bess, my darling, you are so incredibly beautiful. I love you. I love to see you like this, free and slightly moon-struck and wild."

"I love to be this way. I wish I really were a dolphin. Or a mermaid."

Harry released her and floated away. "Take off your clothes, Bess. Let the water touch your skin."

"Harry!"

"I won't come close. I'm taking mine off. This may be our last midnight swim. Let's not waste it . . . There." His bare arms glimmered on the water, scattering green light.

"You shock me, Harry."

"No, I don't. You know me better than that. Go ahead, Bess. You remind me of that silly girl who wouldn't take off her shoes on the sand. Will you wait a year before you follow my lead on this, too? You're a catfish, not a dolphin."

"Move away more."

Harry obliged. Elizabeth lifted the hem of her bathing dress and felt the silken touch of water on her midriff. It took her breath away. The current flowed across her bare skin with a sinuous, thrilling pull. She was suddenly aware of her own body, as she had never been before. She tore the dress off. A wavelet lapped her bare breasts, and she gasped with pleasure.

Harry's voice came from far away. "Well, Queen Mermaid, was I right?"

"I had no idea. It's wonderful." She struggled with her soaked bloomers. They clung tenaciously to her legs.

"Are you drowning? Such a splashing. You'll wake up the sea horses."

"These wretched bloomers are trying to drown me. They're so heavy."

"I'll help you." With a small eddy, Harry dove under the water.

Elizabeth called to him, telling him to keep away. She felt a tugging at her ankles, saw silver bubbles rise and break on the surface near her. Then the ocean's embrace moved down from her waist as the bloomers slid over her feet. The sensation was intoxicating. She moved her head, wrapping her hair around her throat. Mermaids must feel just like this, she thought.

Harry surfaced behind her. "You said you'd stay away," Elizabeth said. She couldn't see him, but she knew he was there.

"I meant to," he whispered. His hands found their accustomed place on her shoulders and moved in the familiar, comforting massage. "That's not so frightening, is it?"

"No. But you shouldn't."

"I should. It's exactly what I should do. You like it. You like the touch of the sea, and of Harry. Don't you remember your Shakespeare, my love? We read Henry V together. This is 'a little touch of Harry in the night.'"

He made her laugh, and the strangeness she was feeling went away. When his hands slid with the current over her body, she gave herself up to the ecstatic pulsations they generated. It was all a dream—the soft night, the caress of the water, the touch of his hands—she was a wild, free, sea creature and this was her kingdom.

When she began to feel chilled, he carried her to the beach and wrapped her in the blanket he had left there. He took her up to the shelter of the tall dunes and laid her gently on the thick quilts they had ready for sleeping. "I am going to kiss you, Bess," Harry said.

It was a gentle kiss, the merest brushing of lips. But a streak of fire ran through her. "Harry," she breathed. Then Harry murmured her name, kissing her ears and her temples and her eyelids and her throat before his mouth found hers and took possession of it. She freed her arms from the folds of the blanket and closed them around his neck.

"I love you, Bess."

"And I love you. Kiss me again."

When she was drunk with his kisses, he opened the blanket and folded it around the two of them. She gave herself to the warm gentleness of his hands. Later, when the thin clouds on the horizon wore golden petticoats in promise of the sun, he taught her how two lovers become one. She floated in blissful suspension, as if her vibrant body were in some sea of indescribable emotion. All her memories had been washed away. She was new-born to love in his arms.

Streaks of peach and apricot stained the sky when Harry ran to the yard back of the house and took fresh bathing costumes from the line where they had hung to dry. "We'll have gone out early for a swim and come in for breakfast," he told Elizabeth. They dressed and ran into the surf, holding hands and laughing, like naughty children. In the water, they kissed and clung together while a brilliant red sun rose in glorious splendor.

Lucy was in the kitchen making coffee when they came in. She looked at them and knew that she no longer need worry about making a decision.

"Making love," said Harry, "is, at one and the same time, the most sublime and most ridiculous activity of which mankind is capable. We must not take it too solemnly or we will lose the dimension of fun. Think of it, my queen. All those elbows and knees to stab the beloved with. Not to mention my superlative nasal endowment which is a perpetual peril to your beautiful eyes every time I kiss you." He demonstrated, nudging her eyelids and then squashing her nose with his before his lips found hers. They kissed, laughing.

The hollow between the dunes had become the center of Elizabeth's life. They spent every night there. The hours until the house slept were ages of delicious agony for her, with her nerves and body screaming for Harry. She had to sit on the opposite side of the table when they ate, the opposite side of the porch when they talked or sang or read. If she were near him, she could not keep her hands from touching his arm or face or knee or shoulder. Fortunately, Tradd was unaware of the electricity that crackled between the two of them. Elizabeth could hardly believe that he could be so blind, but Harry assured her that thirteen-year-old boys were renowned for their obtuseness; she was grateful for it. As for Lucy, she was gently, silently approving.

When the time came to move back to town, Elizabeth felt a desperate depression. "Don't fret, Bess," Harry said. "We'll just be moving from Windsor Castle to St. James' Palace. Delia goes home every night. When Tradd is asleep, you'll come back to my rooms. We'll have candles and champagne."

Which they did. They also made love in the treehouse, muffling each other's cries with kisses. And they went back to the beach one day in autumn to savor its emptiness and then have a riotous hour trying to make love in the hammock, finally tipping out onto the floor to a bruised, sublime climax.

Harry introduced Elizabeth to every inch of her own body. She became so sensitive to touch that when she dressed or brushed her hair or washed her face, it was an erotic experience. Then he awakened her to the excitement of eating and drinking, so that each segment of food and sip of wine or water became an adventure of texture and taste and scent. She felt the softness of her own mouth, the sharpness of her teeth, the sinuous undulations of her throat when she swallowed, the swirling explosions of flavor against her palate. Her entire life became an exploration of sensuality.

Then he taught her to make love to him and to know his body as she knew her own.

Although the time when they were together robbed her of sleep, Elizabeth was never fatigued. She seemed to absorb Harry's dynamic vitality, and she had more energy and acuteness than ever before in her life. She needed it. There were increased demands from Tradd. His awakened intellectual curiosity made her time with him a challenge of wonder and shared learning. He was so excited by the world that he had a fever to discuss his thoughts and his discoveries.

She had also to respond to Catherine's needs. Elizabeth was going to be a grandmother in February, and her daughter came to her for reassurance about every change in her body and every fear. Like all first-time expectant mothers, Catherine was the recipient for all the age-old horror stories that her friends had ever heard or experienced. She felt, as all young women do, that her pregnancy was the most important event in the world. It entitled her to take up Elizabeth's time and to give her mother her opinion on every subject. She was horrified by Elizabeth's tanned face. "You look like a sharecropper," she pronounced with disgust. When Elizabeth laughed, she burst into tears and had to be comforted.

"Don't fret, sweetheart. Everyone says it's very becoming. Several other ladies are talking about getting tanned themselves next summer. It hides the lines, you see. Young things like you don't have to think about those things."

Elizabeth had resumed her normal, limited social life of morning calls and an occasional evening party. It was true that everyone responded with sincere admiration to her radiant appearance. She accepted their compliments with a Gioconda smile.

Her children were not the only sources of calls on her time. She still had the usual duties of running the house. And the Tradd-Simmons Phosphate Company. Money was a greater problem than ever. She could get no American contracts. She had to sell to England, which meant renting boxcars and shipping to the docks in the city for loading onto ships for export. If one of the ships were a day late, and the cargo of phosphate had to wait for loading, the costs for shunting to a siding and renting the railroad cars for the additional time could wipe out half the profit, small as it was. Workers were leaving, too, even though their contracts weren't up until the end of the year. They were following "the Glory Road" to the burgeoning cities in the North and West. Equipment was breaking down; there had been no money for replacements in the four years since the Panic, metal strain and corrosion were taking their inevitable toll. If her life had not been so replete with joy, she would have tumbled into despair.

She debated between mortgaging the plant and pawning Mary Tradd's necklace, deciding finally on the necklace. She would have to veil herself heavily for the humiliating visit to the pawnbroker, but she would get more money for it than for the plant, even when she made allowances for the higher interest rates.

Then a letter from Joe arrived. He was coming home to Charleston. "Shoot!" Elizabeth said. "It'll have to be the mortgage."

She returned the necklace to the lockbox and carried it up to the attic. At the top of the steps, she stopped. Then she giggled.

That night she tapped on Harry's door wearing a long velvet evening cape and a mischievous smile. "You're always interested in old family traditions," she said when she entered his room. "I inherited this one from my mother." She pushed the cape from her shoulders and stood, laughing, clad only in diamonds.

"Magnificent," said Harry, taking her in his arms.

"The idea is, that you're supposed to be the reluctant gentleman client, and I'm supposed to be the tempting professional harlot. You're not playing the game right. Quit hugging me."

Harry held her closer. "We'll play later," he said. "I couldn't possibly act reluctant now."

They never did play the game Elizabeth had invented. Instead, Harry threaded the necklace with thin wires and converted it to a tall, dazzling crown. "Your Majesty," he said, setting it on Elizabeth's streaming, mussed hair. "I believe I see a puddle." He spread her cape across the floor. "Our game will be 'Sir Walter Raleigh takes liberties with the Royal Person.'" He picked her up and deposited her on the cape.

"My crown just fell off," said Elizabeth.

"Who cares?" Harry said, deep in her ear.

"Not the Royal Person," she said.

"You look very well, Elizabeth," said Joe Simmons. He had gained weight and lost hair. To Elizabeth he seemed very old. And very sad. Overflowing with happiness herself, she could not bear to see her old friend so despondent. She searched her mind for something that might cheer him up.

Lord knows, he has plenty to be sad about, she thought. He had written her about Emily's death, terming it a blessed release. Her last months had been perpetual agony; Joe had never left her side. His suffering must have been, in its way, as great as hers, compounded as it was by his inability to help her in any way. He had taken Victoria to Baden-Baden for the waters and then to Paris for a new wardrobe, trying to cure the child's melancholy. She had been miserable in boarding school, and the loss of her mother as well had affected her deeply. Joe was afraid it might be permanent. Nothing seemed to penetrate the silent shell around her.

"You were like that once, Lizzie, when you were a tiny little thing. But I could always make you laugh. I can't do anything for Victoria. I brought her home to Charleston. She was happy here; she had friends at school. I'm hoping that being back will cure her."

"But school started last month, Joe. Will the Misses Smith take her back this late?"

"She's going to start again when the new term opens after Christmas. I have a governess for her now. She won't be behind in her studies."

Elizabeth shook her head impatiently. "For heaven's sake, Joe, no wonder the child's gloomy. She hasn't seen anyone her own age for months. You're a darling man, but it's not the same thing for a fifteen-year-old girl as a beau. Now you listen to me. Next Saturday is Thanksgiving. Stuart and Henrietta are throwing a big barbecue and oyster roast at the Barony after a hunt in the morning. I'll expect you and Victoria to call for me at nine in the morning to ride out there. And don't let her wear any frock from Paris. She's smarter than you about those things. Tell her to get cracking and have her dressmaker fix her a Charleston outfit. If she acts draggy about it, remind her that Little Stuart is seventeen and as handsome as the devil himself."

"Stuart won't let me serve turkey, even though we've got about three dozen of them hanging," said Henrietta with a nervous laugh. "You know how he is. Abe Lincoln named Thanksgiving a holiday, so Stuart refuses to recognize it in any way. I had to kill five of our best pigs for barbecue. Little Stuart said it was fitting because Lincoln was a swine."

"That's really dumb," Elizabeth said. "I wouldn't let them get away with it. For heaven's sake, the War was more than thirty years ago."

"Not for Stuart. And he's brought up the boys the same way. I don't blame him, either. The Yankees took everything we had, Elizabeth. I'm surprised at you that you can forget it."

Elizabeth managed to keep quiet. This was an old, old difference between her and her brother. It would never be settled, not if she talked herself blue in the face. Stuart's strongest emotion was bitterness, and he had done his best to infect his whole family. Still, he was bound by the rules of a gentleman. She didn't have to worry about any insults to Victoria, even if her mother had been from New York.

The girl looked very pretty and quite happy. She had her shiny blond hair in a woven ribbon snood, which was a little too grown up for her age, but her dark blue cashmere dress was suitably plain, and the wide white collar and cuffs were made of linen, not lace. She had a little color in her cheeks now. She had been terribly pale when Elizabeth first saw her that morning. The snap in the air was good for her. So was the activity. All the young girls were hurrying back and forth from the kitchen building to the long trestle tables on the lawn carrying plates and napkins and silverware. Elizabeth settled deeper in her chair, thankful that she was an older lady, with nothing to do but watch. She turned to Joe and smiled.

"You must feel like an Arab with a harem," she said. The men were not back yet from the hunt. Joe and four elderly gentlemen were conspicuous among the group of more than forty ladies of various ages.

"I feel very good," he said. "You've done wonders for Victoria, you know."

"Don't be silly. I didn't do a thing. Besides, I got to sleep late because you brought me. Tradd and Harry left before five to get here in time. I couldn't have stood it if I'd had to come with them. You did wonders for me."

Joe turned his eyes away. He didn't dare risk having her see the feeling in them. To his eternal shame, he had thought of her even when he was devoting himself totally to making Emily's last months of life as easy as possible. It was true that he believed a return to Charleston would be the best thing for Victoria, but he would have had to come back himself even if he had not believed it. He loved his daughter, but he loved Lizzie Tradd more. During the months abroad, he had ached for Charleston and for Elizabeth. The period of mourning would be over in six months. Then he intended to ask her to marry him. This time, he would have the answer from her, not from an overprotective brother. And if her answer was no, he would keep asking until it became yes. He could be patient. He had been waiting for twenty years.

"Here they come!" she cried. Joe looked back at her. When he saw her face, a fist closed around his heart. She was afire with emotion. There must be a man.

The hunters rode across the weed-choked lawn, cheering their triumph. Behind them, pairs of young black boys carried eight deer carcasses tied by their hooves onto long poles. One of the men dismounted and stalked away from the group toward Elizabeth. He was white with anger.

Joe did not know his name, but he knew who he was. He could feel Elizabeth's alarm without even looking at her. His eyes narrowed as they traveled over the approaching form. A comical looking fellow, he thought, and hardly more than a boy. Maybe I'm wrong.

"Bess, I'm close to murder," he said when he reached her side. "Come walk with me before I have a fine Irish outbreak."

Elizabeth stood and took his arm. "Of course," she said quickly. "Will you just meet my friend Joe Simmons first? Joe, this is Harry Fitzpatrick."

Joe got up to shake hands with him. Both said, "How do you do," and then Harry took Elizabeth away, toward the river.

Elizabeth almost had to run to keep up with him. When they reached the landing dock, they stopped. She was breathing so fast, she could barely get her words out. "What's wrong, Harry? I've never seen you like this."

"This fine old Southern plantation hospitality, that's what's wrong. Jesus and Mary! Why did you tell me I'd enjoy this? We got here at dawn and met your Squire Western brother the Judge for a few shots of whiskey with his friends and his hound dogs. I've never seen such a squalid performance in my life. Get the blood lust heated up then troop into the woods to shoot those magnificent animals. Damn it all, they should have shot each other and left the deer alone. At least a deer has a certain dignity about him. I can't say the same for the hunters."

Elizabeth put her hand on his cheek. "I don't believe that's it. You know how a group of men can be. You've told me yourself about California and men beating and shooting each other in barroom brawls. That's a lot worse than getting liquored up and killing deer."

Harry took her hand and held it, turning his head so that his mouth was in her palm. He closed his eyes. She could feel his lips trembling. "Harry, tell me. Whatever it is, tell me. Please."

He swallowed hard, pulled their hands down and looked at her. "You're right, my love. And I'm hysterical. Forgive me. Come on, let's sit down. I seem to be a little shaky."

He kept her hand in his while he talked. What was killing him was the ordeal Tradd had been through. The boy had killed his first deer that morning. As a celebration, he had been bloodied. "Do you know about that ceremony, Bess?"

"Yes. It sounds ghastly. But all boys do it, Harry. It's traditional."

"It's barbaric. 'Little' Stuart, who's as tall as I am, held the head back by the antlers. Tradd had to cut the throat. His dear uncle and cousins caught the spouting blood in their hands and wiped Tradd's face. Then they wiped their hands in his hair, and on his shirt. It made me sick. It still makes me sick."

"How was Tradd?"

"Superb. He acted as if he thought it was great. He didn't get sick until he could get off by himself behind a tree. I held his head."

"Well, it's over. Can't you forget it?"

"I can't forget that I stood there like a wax dummy instead of speaking up. I could have kicked them in the groin if they'd tried to bloody me, but I couldn't do it for Tradd. I had to let him go through it this time, or he'd just have to face it again. I knew that much. It was hell. I don't know how you can bear being a mother, letting your children go through these rites of passage."

"Is this the Harry Fitzpatrick who lectured me about protecting Tradd too much?"

Harry opened his mouth to speak. Then it snapped closed. Elizabeth waited. After a few minutes, his shoulders began to shake. He threw his head back and shouted with laughter. "A hit! A palpable hit!" he roared. "You glorious redheaded witch, you've speared my pontifical gizzard." He slid his arm around her waist and whispered in her ear. "I adore you, woman. Let's slip into the woods and play nymph and Pan. I'll whistle an antic tune while I chase you."

"Harry. Behave. People can see us."

"But not hear us. Let me talk lewdness into your shell-like ear."

"Absolutely not. Not until we get home. Then I'll whistle while I chase you."

"Bess, I love you. You are an extraordinary, majestic, perfect creature. Come on, then. I will be Celtic and charming to your disgusting brother."

"Good. And to the little blond girl named Victoria. She's Joe's daughter; I told you about her."

"Poor lamb. Yes, I'll speak to her of leprechauns and shamrocks. Shall I wear my bogus brogue?"

"If you like." Anything to make you happy, my love, she thought. The overreaction to Tradd's experience worried her. Her worry was for Harry, not for her son.

Elizabeth's intuition was not precise, but it was well-founded. Harry was growing restless. He was tired of Charleston. "Bess," he said as they walked sedately back to the party, "would you like to have London for your birthday present? I haven't chosen one yet, and your birthday is next week."

She laughed. "So extravagant, you Irish. I think I'd rather have the moon, if that's the mood you're in. I've never tasted green cheese."

Before Harry could say anymore, they were back with the other guests.

The two black men threw shovels full of oysters onto the sheet of iron that spanned the bed of glowing coals, and the party applauded. The barbecue had begun. In a few minutes, the oysters were cooked; the shells opened to release the steam that had built up inside. They were raked off onto trays, and the shovels lifted again. There were a dozen washtubs of oysters to be cooked before the day was done.

Henrietta and the girls brought great bowls of vegetables, baskets of hot corn bread and platters of sliced, spicy barbecue to the tables where her maids had already put the first trays of oysters.

"Come sit here by me, Joe," called Elizabeth. She had already placed Victoria at the family table with the Tradds. Harry was sitting next to her, spinning a tale that had her giggling. Elizabeth maneuvered Little

Stuart to the place on her other side. Tradd, his hair still damp from washing, was at the other end with his two cousins, Anson and Koger.

Stuart was next to his sister. As soon as they had filled their plates, he started talking across her to Joe. "Tell me more about what those Yankee papers are saying, Simmons. We were interrupted before by that stupid darky who couldn't find the rake I had put right under his nose."

Joe put his fork down. "This is news for you, too, Lizzie. Hard times are just about over for business. The newspaper boys are getting what they wanted. We'll have a war before too much longer. That's always good for business."

"What are you talking about, Joe? I read the paper. It doesn't say anything about a war." Her eyes found Tradd. His mouth was overfull of barbecue. He looked reassuringly young.

"The Charleston paper doesn't say anything about anything much, Lizzie. Hearst's and Pulitzer's have been screaming for a year or more. Seems the Spanish have been pretty hard on the natives in their colonies; Hearst and Pulitzer are stirring up the people and their circulation figures with stories about brutality and oppression. The other day President McKinley put the screws on Spain. Now they're giving what they call 'limited self-rule' to the people in Cuba."

"What's Cuba?"

"Be quiet, Elizabeth," Stuart said. "This is man talk. Don't spoil her, Joe. Do you really think there'll be a war? How soon?"

"I don't see any way there won't be one. Nobody's going to like Spain's concession. The Spanish landowners and businessmen won't go for any self-rule at all, and the Cubans won't settle for the limited part. The stock market's been climbing for weeks. There'll be war, all right. The place is a tinderbox. It could blow any time."

"Where does America stand?"

"Too close to Cuba not to get involved. We'll be against the Spanish and end up owning it ourselves. The factories up North are already starting to make uniforms and boots. Out of wool, too, damn fools. Our boys will probably die of the heat."

"Well, I'll tell you this. I'm not going to miss this war." Stuart's moustaches bristled. "I got cheated out of the last one, but I'll have a horse under me this time when they sound the charge. My boys and I will send up a Rebel Yell they'll hear all the way to Madrid."

Elizabeth felt sick. She looked down at her plate, trying to push the food around so that it would appear that she had eaten more of it. Joe, she noticed, kept glancing at Victoria, even though he kept talking to Stuart. What's he worried about? she thought. He has a girl child. The war could last ten years, and she'll still be alive. Tradd will be fourteen next month. If it lasts three years, he'll have to go. It'll be Pinny all over again. If not worse. If he doesn't get killed.

She did not realize that Joe's eyes were on Harry, not Victoria. I'm going to find out about you, young man, Joe was silently promising. I don't like the way you dragged Lizzie along so fast she nearly fell down. I don't like it at all.

59

"Lizzie," Joe said, "I want to talk privately with you, so I sent Ned Wragg ahead. He'll meet us there." They were in Joe's buggy, going to Carlington for the New Year's powwow.

I wish Joe would stop calling me "Lizzie," thought Elizabeth. I've reminded him a hundred times. She forced the irritation out of her voice when she answered him. "Talk away, Joe. We've got a good, long ride."

"I want to know if you're planning to marry this Harry Fitzpatrick. Don't tell me it's none of my business. I'm making it my business."

Elizabeth was stunned by Joe's question. She had honestly never asked it of herself. Harry was an all-consuming part of her life. She was his creation; she belonged to him; she followed his lead without question; she gave him her body and her love and her mind. But still, he was not the whole of her life. By day, she was the mother of Catherine and Tradd, the president of the phosphate company, the admired widow whom other ladies and gentlemen respected. It was only during the magic hours of the night and the rare moments of escape to a hidden place that she was really Harry's Bess. How, she wondered now, had she not wondered before what would happen? How had this double life come to seem so natural and inevitable? When a man and a woman loved each other, they got married. She had been raised to believe that. Why, then, had she never thought of it? Why hadn't Harry?

Joe had been talking for some time. She tried to concentrate on what he was saying.

". . . a mistake. I wasn't around when you married Cooper. I never knew him. But I know he didn't make you happy. I've got to speak up about Fitzpatrick. I don't want you to be unhappy again, honey. I did some checking up on him. He's no good, Lizzie. He's using you, living in your house like that. If he was a man, he'd be doing something steady, building some future. A schoolteacher doesn't earn enough to support a canary, much less a wife."

"I've asked you a million times not to call me 'Lizzie,' Joe. I'm not a child. I'm thirty-eight years old, and my name is Elizabeth." She was almost screaming at him. "And I'll thank you to leave my private life private." She turned so that her back was toward him. The trip seemed endless because of the silence between them.

When they neared the turn-off to Carlington, Elizabeth sat around to face him. "Joe," she said, "please don't let's fight. It makes me cry." She rested her cheek on his upper arm. "You're one of my oldest, dearest friends. I hate being angry with you. You just have to let me be grown up, that's all. If I make mistakes, that's part of it. I had to learn that about Tradd; you have to learn it about me . . . All right?"

His arm was as stiff as iron. "I've never been able to refuse you anything, honey," he said. "I don't suppose I can start now. But I can't say it's all right. I'll keep my mouth shut. Will that do?"

Elizabeth kissed his ear, a quick, light kiss whose impact she never suspected. "Thank you, darling Joe," she said. "Now, do you really think prices will go up soon? I'd sure like to be able to promise that we won't have to cut wages again."

While the Carlington workers were celebrating the New Year and the new contract with fireworks and white lightning, the island of Cuba was suffering from violent riots and fighting between anti- and pro-Spanish mobs. American businessmen and their families took refuge in their homes and offices. They also sent frantic cables to Washington.

At the end of January, the American battleship *Maine* steamed into Havana harbor to serve as a visible warning that the United States would protect its citizens and their property.

By now, the Cuban news was in the Charleston newspapers, too. Tradd came home from Porter every day, agog with the excitement that was afoot. Harry defused it somewhat by diverting his attention to a study of the days when Cuba was called "the Pearl of the Antilles" and pirates waited over the horizon for the Spanish treasure fleets that sailed from there. Pirates were almost as interesting as war-talk, particularly those pirates that had also preyed on Charleston. Harry and Tradd took several walks to White Point Gardens to see if they could find any evidence of the gibbet where Stede Bonnet was hung.

For the first time, Elizabeth did not participate in their excursions. She had too much work to do, she said, setting the priorities for repairs and equipment at Carlington. In fact, phosphate prices were going up a bit, but she lied when she said she had to work. What she had to do was think. Her mind had not been easy since Joe's unsettling question about marrying Harry. When she and Harry were alone together, she forgot everything that had been bothering her. They loved each other in every possible way. What could be wrong?

When they were apart, even the small separation necessitated by

Tradd's presence, she was torn by anxiety and doubts. She watched for indications that Harry was, as Joe had hinted, making a fool of her; she read hidden meanings into every remark he made; she searched her mirror for wrinkles and the onset of graying hair; she tortured herself with the thought that he would leave her; and she became jealous of every pretty girl at the parties he went to. Parties for the young, to which she was not invited.

She made up her mind over and over again that she would confront him, get everything in the open, learn the worst and learn to live with it. But then darkness would come, and she would be in his rooms, in his arms, and she would shut all the ugliness away and give herself over to happiness.

On Valentine's Day, Harry gave her an enamel locket, a violet-colored oval with a "B" of seed pearls on it. It was, he said, the color of royalty. Also it matched the hothouse violets that he had strewn on her pillow. "I want to see them caught in your hair," he said, "like a wood nymph. You promised me a chase through the pines, you remember."

"I promised no such thing. You threatened to chase me at the Barony."

"It will be spring soon. We'll find us a woods suitable for chasing."

Elizabeth held her arms up to him. That was a future he was planning. And in the back of the locket, he had placed a lovers' knot made from locks of his hair and hers. Everything was all right . . .

Harry pulled away and ran to open the window. "Christ! Someone's battering down the street door. Do you have your clothes here? Thank God. You answer the door. I'll go stall Tradd." He had put on his shirt and trousers while he was talking. He buttoned them on his dash for the house.

Catherine's pains had started, a distraught Lawrence told Elizabeth when she opened the door. She wanted her mother. "I'll come at once, Lawrence. I just have to get my cloak. Now, now, don't carry on so. She'll have a while to go yet. I won't be but a minute."

Harry and Tradd were on the stairs. "You're about to be an uncle," she told Tradd. "Both of you, go to bed. I'll be home tomorrow." She noticed that Harry had buttoned his trousers awry in haste, and she smiled. Not bad for a grandmother, she said to herself.

Unlike Elizabeth, Catherine went through a protracted period of labor. Her little boy was born the evening of the next day. His name, she told her mother, was Lucas Lawrence Wilson. Then she fell into deep sleep.

A "Little Lucas" at last, thought Elizabeth. I guess I can get used to it. Maybe we can call him "Luke." She was exhausted, and so was Lawrence. He walked her home, both of them stumbling from fatigue.

At first, she could not understand what Tradd was saying when he opened the door. He was incoherent with excitement. "Slow down," she begged. "And don't shout like that."

"The *Maine*, Mama. The Spaniards blew up the *Maine*. They killed hundreds of our Navy men. It's a slap in the face of America."

"I see," said Elizabeth. She was bleary. "That's very interesting, dear. I'm going to bed now, and I'll blow up anybody who wakes me."

In the next weeks, headlines and placards everywhere demanded "Remember the Maine!" It was inevitable that, because of his birthday, Catherine's baby was nicknamed "Maine." He was a lovely, fat baby, and Elizabeth discovered that the role of grandmother was pure pleasure. She walked over to Water Street every afternoon at bath time and received the clean, powdered, sweet-smelling infant from his dah for a session of baby talk and nuzzling. When both grandson and grandmother tired of the games, she turned him over to his scowling mother for feeding.

"You're going to spoil him rotten, Mama," said Catherine. "The doctor says not to pick him up so much. He'll get to expect it."

"He'll expect it no matter what I do," Elizabeth replied calmly. "It's the nature of babies." She liked the hour with the baby and Catherine, in spite of Catherine's petulance. There was something very satisfying about having three generations in the one room, in the old house, in the old city. It felt safe, right, the way things were meant to be. Even Catherine's self-righteous complaints seemed a normal part of the passage of generations. Her mother was being nasty selfish, according to Catherine. She had no need for the space in the Meeting Street house. She should give it to the young Wilsons. "We don't even have a garden here, Mama. Where is the baby supposed to run and play?"

"He'll have to learn to walk first. There's plenty of time to worry about a bigger house later." Elizabeth refused to argue. Her baby visits were her tranquil times; she would not allow any disruption of that tranquillity.

Outside of that hour, there was disruption every where she looked. Even the quiet, spring-flowered streets downtown were filled with an invisible, humming tension. Over on Bay Street, sailors from the ships were stopped to ask if they had been in the Caribbean on their last trip; the weekly steamers from the North were mobbed for the newspapers they carried. The telegraph office on Broad Street had a shifting, eager crowd in front at all hours, waiting for bulletins. And the Sunday afternoon band concerts at White Point Gardens changed their selections from Strauss to Sousa. While President McKinley exchanged "diplomatic notes" with the King of Spain, America and Charleston waited for war.

Tradd was bright-eyed with excitement. The quasi-military drilling at Porter now took up more than half the school day. He had been promoted to lieutenant, and wore his stripe proudly. Stuart's son, Koger, he reported, was organizing the bigger boys to be ready to leave at any minute. Harry was teaching Spanish now instead of history. "I don't know much," he said with a grin, "but nobody else knows any, so how can they tell?" He had spent five months living with gypsies in the caves of Barcelona, he told Elizabeth. His Spanish was more colloquial than classic. It was an episode in his past that he had never mentioned before, and it made her feel uneasy, as if she loved a total stranger. Every afternoon, he took Tradd up to Calhoun Street to watch The Citadel cadets in their close drill dress parades. The military college had already announced that the corps of cadets was prepared to volunteer en masse.

"Just the way they did in the War Between the States," said Lucy Anson. She was heartsick about Andrew. The Army had been a steady, secure life for him, and she had been happy even though it kept him away from her. Now he was writing letters about finally having a chance at promotion. Generals were made on battlefields.

The tension was almost unbearable. When Congress declared war on April 25, it was like a storm that finally broke after too long a wait. The city went wild with relief.

The Citadel shared its parade ground with recruits who poured into the city from all the farms and small towns in South Carolina. The three Tradd boys were among the first dozen to sign up. Stuart was apoplectic. "Too old? How can that stripling Captain tell me I'm too old? Forty-four is no age at all. Hell, that Roosevelt fellow in Washington has quit the Navy Department to organize troops, and he's forty. It's Goddamn Republican favoritism, that's what it is. They'll never forget we Red Shirts ran them out of our state!" He and Henrietta decided to move in with Elizabeth on Meeting Street. Stuart wanted to be on hand to badger the Army recruiters; Henrietta wanted to be near her children. They could leave the barracks for supper, but they weren't allowed time enough for the trip to the Barony.

"Hello, Catherine. You're as blooming as the spring. What's the matter, Bess?" Harry had her note of summons in his hand when he came to Catherine's house. She had left it pinned to the door of his rooms.

"I wanted you to walk me home. I have to talk to you about Tradd." Elizabeth kissed her daughter and grandson quickly. "Good-bye, darlings, I'll see you tomorrow."

"What's the problem with Tradd?" Harry asked when they were on the street.

"Nothing. It's a problem with us." She told him about Stuart and Henrietta moving in. "I won't dare come back to your rooms, Harry. Stuart would kill you if he had any idea."

"And probably mount my head on the wall with all his deer

trophies." Harry smiled at her, plucked a long tendril of honeysuckle from a nearby wall and presented it to her. "There are a few late blossoms on it," he said. "Let's drink them while we walk. We'll go to the Gardens."

They climbed the steps to the promenade along the sea wall of East Battery and strolled slowly. The tide was up, and there was a strong sea breeze. The wind lifted the spume of the waves breaking on the wall and blew it into their faces. Behind them, they could faintly hear the sound of hammers and shouted commands from the barracks. Overhead the sky was a brilliant, cloudless blue.

Harry held Elizabeth's arm close against his left side. She could feel the steady beat of his heart. "Take off that awful hat," he said. "I want to see the sunlight on your hair."

"Harry, it's not respectable."

"What has 'respectable' to do with us? If you don't take it off, I will."

"I'll do it. You'd just throw away the pins." As she lifted it off, a wave dashed moisture onto them.

"You look beautiful," said Harry. "The sun makes diamonds out of the dew on your hair. You should always be crowned this way." He freed her arm and took the honeysuckle from her hand. "Open your mouth, Gloriana, and I'll fill it with nectar." His eyes were intense. Elizabeth dismissed the thought that people she knew might be looking down from their flower-screened piazzas on the opposite side of the street. She tilted her head back and held out her tongue for the sweet drops.

When all the blossoms were drunk, Harry let the green vine fall into the waves. They walked on to the end of High Battery. Harry stopped her before she could walk down the steps to the lower promenade and the Gardens.

"I like to look from here," he said. In the distance before them, the low bulk of Fort Sumter marked the exit from the harbor to the ocean. Beyond it, over the horizon, they saw the staysails of a tall schooner waiting for the channel pilot to board her and guide her in. The wide reach of the harbor stretched off to their right, its waters dancing. "It's beautiful," said Harry.

Elizabeth felt a deep contentment. The noise of the barracks was far behind them, replaced by the sound of children playing and their dahs laughing in the Gardens. This was Charleston, as it always had been and always would be. She had once been one of those children, then Catherine and Tradd, soon Catherine's child and later Tradd's children. And her grandchildren's children, and theirs, and generations after them.

"I'm leaving, Bess." Harry's words shattered her world.

"No," she said. "You're teasing. It's one of your games."

"No game, my love. I have to go. I've been feeling the itch for some time."

"It's this stupid war, isn't it? You're just like all the other men."

"I'm going to the war. But not like all the other men. I don't care about shooting some unfortunate Spanish peasant boy who was sent out to die for the glory of Spain on an island he never heard of. I just want to see it, that's all. War is what makes history, and I've never seen one. I've lined up a job reporting it for the San Francisco newspaper. That'll get me transport and a front row seat."

"You'll be killed."

"Not this lucky Irish lad . . . But I won't be coming back, Bess. When my feet start to itch in Cuba, I'll take a ship to someplace else. I'll never forget you. I've loved you more than any woman I've ever known."

She wanted to cry, to scream from the pain, to hit the face and mouth she loved too much. But they were in public. She could not make a scene. "Why?" she said. Her voice was broken. "If you love me, then why are you going?"

"It's closing me in, Bess. This Xanadu city of yours. You know the Charlestonians' joke: This is where the Ashley and the Cooper Rivers meet to form the Atlantic Ocean." He stared at the choppy water where the currents collided. "They more than half believe it. For a while—a long while for me—I almost believed it, too. This is a place of myth and enchantment, and the home of the Faerie Queen. You and your Charleston cast a spell on me; I've never tarried this way before."

"Then stay, Harry. Be enchanted. You don't have to go."

"But I do. I never pretended to be other than what I am. I'm a vagabond, Bess. You always knew that."

She could say nothing. She had always known, but she had not believed it. Now she had to. She could not mistake the finality in his voice.

"When do you leave?"

"At midnight. We'll catch the next high tide."

There would be no good-byes, then, no final night in his arms. Stuart and Henrietta would be at the house by the time they got home. They would not be asleep until too late.

There would not even be a lingering farewell kiss. They were exposed to the world here, they could not even touch each other.

Bitterness flooded her mouth. "How well you arranged everything," she said. "You must have said good-bye often."

He did not deny it.

"I hope that Spanish peasant boy shoots you through the heart, Harry. I'll pray for it. Before you die, you'll just have time to feel what I'm feeling . . . I'll walk home alone. Don't come to the house. Take your things out after dark, through the carriage drive. I don't want Tradd to see you ever again."

Pride carried her down the stairs and through the park. At the bottom of Meeting Street, she could not keep herself from turning to look at him one last time.

Harry was gone.

60

The war that Elizabeth hated so much turned out to be a Godsend for her. Everyone was so preoccupied with news and rumors and the spurt of business activity it engendered that no one had time to notice her or her long silences. Joe Simmons would not have been fooled, but he was busy building a new bank on Broad Street, and she never saw him. Lucy Anson would have seen her pain immediately, but she was totally wrapped up in her own unexpected good fortune. Andrew had been sent to Charleston to supervise the embarkation of the troops when the time came. He had been home less than a week when he told his mother that he would never leave again. "I didn't know how special this place was until I saw it again after being away so long. When my job's done here on the docks, I'm going to resign my commission and become plain Mister Anson again."

Andrew was thirty-five. His fifteen years in the Army had made him lean and wiry and sun-baked to the color of his saddle. It had also given him the assurance that comes with the habit of command. Before he had even loaded the first battalion of soldiers, he was engaged to the girl who was the recognized belle of the year and he had a job waiting. On June fourteenth, the transport ships sailed. A week later, Andrew started working as a vice-president of Joe Simmons' bank. His responsibility was to oversee the building contractor. "I don't mind if he cheats me some, Andrew," said Joe, "but I'll be mad as hell if we don't open on time. I'll be taking Victoria to Newport when school's over. You watch him like a hawk."

When the troops left Charleston, Henrietta and Stuart left Meeting Street for the Barony. Elizabeth cried that night for the first time in the two months since Harry had gone.

Not because she missed her brother and sister-in-law. Stuart's repetitive grumbling "Who's too old?" had been a nerve-tearing refrain to her own misery. "I am," she wanted to scream. That had to be the reason she had lost Harry. She had been a fool to think that he wouldn't tire of a woman seven years older than he was. He had probably found a sixteen-year-old senorita the day he reached Havana.

She cried that night because it was the first time she could be sure that she had the privacy she needed for her anguished sobs.

I need solitude to heal in, she thought, and I cannot bear to have everything remind me of him. She offered the Island house to Catherine and Lawrence for the summer. "Provided you take Tradd," she said. "I have a lot of work to do in town, so I won't come." Delia stayed with Elizabeth. Catherine had her own servants.

On July first, Tradd loaded his things on to the ferry. Elizabeth was freed of another constant reminder of Harry. Tradd talked about him all the time. He was convinced that Harry's brief farewell note had been necessary because of an emergency secret mission that only he could accomplish.

On the Fourth of July Elizabeth climbed out on the roof with a glass of champagne to watch the fireworks and celebrate her sole possession of her house. There was no one to forbid her perch because it was too dangerous or too unladylike. She had only herself to please. "So what if I'm not a queen anymore?" she said aloud. "I'm King of the Mountain here on my own roof. It's Independence Day." A tear rolled down her cheek and fell into the champagne. So what? she thought. It was flat anyhow. She had found the recorked bottle in Harry's room, a souvenir of everything she had to forget.

On August twelfth, the war was over. The island of Cuba no longer belonged to Spain. Nor did Puerto Rico, Guam and the Philippines. The Spanish Empire was at an end, and the United States had become a major overseas landlord. There were more fireworks in Charleston, but Elizabeth did not bother to climb up to see them. She was finding her own Armistice within herself, but it was not yet time to celebrate.

When Tradd left for Sullivans Island, she was alone for the first time in her life. There had always been family—her mother, her brothers, her husband, her children. Never before had she been able to put her needs and desires first. She had had to please other people, obey other people, take care of other people. The first days she had been on a violent pendulum between defiance and self-pity. She had soared and wallowed.

Then she began to notice the peace in the house. It was so quiet. With the shutters drawn against the sun, each room held cool shadows and soothing tranquillity. The chairs, with their familiar shabby upholstery, were old friends, their simple lines so graceful and balanced that they were silent, undemanding refreshment to the eye. When the afternoon breeze came, she opened the windows, and the billowing summer curtains embraced her. "I love you, too, house," she whispered aloud. She immediately blushed for the silliness of talking to a house, but she felt the first tender growth of happiness, silly or not.

Every day that passed added strength to her sense of well-being. She still had times of wrenching despair and loss. Sometimes she would follow the path through the darkness to Harry's rooms and lie face down on his bed, breathing in the faint scent of his soap that remained in his pillow. Then her body ached for him, and her heart thudded painfully in her breast, and she wanted to be dead. But as the scented traces of him became dimmer, so did her grief.

She gave Delia a vacation for the whole month of September, and she had no need to accommodate herself to any influence at all. No more hot dinner at two-thirty every day. No more tea at five or supper at seven. No more menus to plan or shopping lists to make out. Elizabeth entered into a halcyon period of self-indulgence. She answered the cries of the street sellers herself and looked over their wares without any previous thinking. When she saw something that appealed to her, she bought it for her meals, whether it made sense or not. One day she had only melons: watermelon for breakfast, muskmelon for supper and no dinner at all. She experimented with new recipes; she bought a gallon of ice cream and satisfied a childhood desire to eat all she wanted, for once in her life. She lived by impulse alone.

It was an intoxicating experience, and it gave her an understanding of Harry Fitzpatrick that she had given up hope of attaining. How seductive it was to live this way. His entire life was like this, only on a grander scale. She need not look for faults in herself; he had not left her, he had followed the siren of hedonism. It had not been just a graceful speech, a sop to her vanity, when he marveled that he had stayed so long. Now she marveled, too.

I have a lot to thank you for, Harry, she thought. Without you I would never have imagined the possibility of breaking the rules about meals or roof climbing or going to bed every night when Saint Michael's chimes nine. I hope the Spanish boy didn't shoot you, after all.

In mid-September, the thrills of impulse living were no longer thrilling. She abandoned it with no regrets, interested now in the future more than in the present. She became engrossed in the company books, bringing them up to date, looking for patterns of sales, production, snags in refining processes, inventory turnover in the workers' store. Joe was right, as usual. Prices were climbing, orders increasing. War was good for business. She compared figures for income with and without their own sulphuric acid plant, realized that the costs for the raw sulphur must have changed since she had abandoned the project in ninety-three, wrote and posted letters of inquiry.

The garden was like a jungle. How could she not have noticed for so long? Tradd usually kept the weeds down and the grass clipped. She climbed up to the treehouse and made a sketch of a new garden design. Something easy to maintain: ivy at the base of all the shrubs to choke out the weeds and keep roots cool, a gravel center instead of lawn so that there'd be no need to mow. Tradd would be graduating from Porter in only two years. Then, if she had the money, he'd go away to college. She'd be responsible for the garden, and she didn't plan to spend her life pulling weeds. There were too many other things that were more interesting. After the years of stagnation, she could see light at the end of the tunnel for Carlington. And there were all those books she wanted to read: she'd walk up to the Library Society; the exercise would do her good. She wanted to go through the attic, too. Catherine's and Tradd's old toys were stored up there. The first rainy day, she'd get them out and see if any were suitable for Maine.

In the meantime, there was the luxury of the house all to herself, the breeze on the piazza, the reassuring voice of the watchman and the music of the bells. Summer would be ending soon, Tradd would be coming home, the round of calls and parties would begin. I'll just soak in the blissful easiness until then, she thought. I've earned it. I've learned that life is good, that I don't need Harry Fitzpatrick. She stretched out on the floor of the treehouse and let a mockingbird sing her to sleep.

Joe and Victoria returned home the last week in September. He went immediately to check on the bank. Andrew had done miracles. The building was finished, three weeks ahead of schedule. Joe awarded him a bonus on the spot. It couldn't come at a better time, said Andrew. He was getting married in January, and he was finding the price of houses steeper than he had expected. Joe laughed. "You know plenty about keeping men working," he said, "but you've got a lot to learn about putting money to work. Bring your lovely mother to supper tomorrow night. And your bride, too, if you like. The ladies can talk to Victoria while I teach you about mortgages. A smart man never buys things with his own money. I expect you to tell your friends that, too. You're going to be looking for good loans and mortgages for the bank when we open."

Joe went to Meeting Street that afternoon to invite Elizabeth and Tradd to the supper for the Ansons. Victoria would be glad to have someone near her age, and he had missed Elizabeth every minute he was away. He wanted to see her, even if it meant inviting Fitzpatrick, too.

". . . Harry went to Cuba, Joe, and Tradd's still at the Island, but I'd love to come if you'll send your coachman to fetch me."

"I'll come for you myself." Joe was puzzled. The soldiers had returned from Cuba right after the Armistice.

Elizabeth smiled. "Dear Joe. Too sweet to ask. Sit down while I get the tea things. Then you'll be entitled to one 'I told you so.' He's not going to come back. He got tired of Charleston."

"I don't need any tea. Come sit with me." They took places on the camel-back settee. Joe turned to look closely into her face; his arm hung down the back of the settee so that she couldn't see the fist which was squeezing Harry Fitzpatrick's neck in Joe's imagination. "How are you, Lizzie?"

"I'm fine, Joe, really truly." And she was, too. But the concern in his voice somehow was making her eyes sting. "You shouldn't worry about me so much. And I want some tea, even if you don't. I'll be back in a jiffy."

While she was gone, Joe paced the floor of the drawing room. His lips were compressed and white. He was ready to kill Harry for hurting her, and he knew that she had been hurt, no matter what she said. But another side of him was grateful to Fitzpatrick. Maybe now she'd let him take care of her. It was all he'd ever wanted.

It was hardly fair to take advantage of her bruised heart to try to win her for himself. She might regret it later, and the Lizzie he knew would never back out on a promise no matter how much she might regret it.

Joe stopped in front of a mirror and looked at himself. Do you believe she needs you? he asked silently. The answer was yes. Do you believe you can make her happy? The answer was yes, again. Do you love her more than any man ever loved a woman? And want her enough to take her with no demands that she love you? Yes. Yes. Yes to anything, for her sake.

Then speak to her, coward. There'll never be a time when you won't be afraid to speak. Do it now. The worst that can happen is she'll say no. But at least she'll know there's someone loving her. She has a right to know that. Maybe a need.

Elizabeth came in with the tea tray. Joe hurried to take its weight from her and put it on the table in front of the settee. She had brought two cups. He smiled. Keep it light, he told himself. Don't make it hard on her. They sat down, side by side, and she started to brew the tea. Joe cleared his throat.

"Do you remember Bear?" he said.

Elizabeth smiled. "Of course. I still have him. I was up in the attic just the other day looking over old toys for Maine, and I came across Bear. His fur is worn thin, but he's still got all his stuffing. I couldn't face parting with him, not even for my first grandchild. Funny you should remember, Joe. It was so long ago."

Joe nodded. "Sure was. You were no bigger than a baby cub yourself. You still had your milk teeth, and you were pleased as punch because one was loose." He took a deep breath.

"I've bought plenty of things for various females since then, but somehow I remember that one time the best . . . I guess I put my heart inside that bear with the rest of the stuffing. I never got it back, Lizzie." His eyes were lost in smile wrinkles, but the unconscious pleading of his open hands and forward-jutting shoulders gave the lie to laughter.

Elizabeth was stunned. "I never knew . . . I don't know what to say."

Joe shook his head urgently. "Don't say anything; just listen. I wanted to marry you as soon as you were old enough. That was the reason Pinckney and I fell out. He told me I wasn't good enough for you, and I believed him. He was wrong, though. When I saw you again, saw what that skunk Lucas had done to you, I would have killed him if he hadn't already been dead. I'd have cherished you, Lizzie. You loved me, then. Like a brother, maybe, but that would have been enough to start with. I didn't look to take from you, just to give."

Elizabeth felt tears fill her throat and sting behind her eyes. She covered Joe's hand with her own. He had been looking down at his knees while he spoke. This was no polished, poetic declaration of love. It was the exposure of a hidden soul. At her touch, Joe looked up. His face was naked pain. "You had too much suffering in your life, baby."

The old affectionate name touched off a kaleidoscope of memories in Elizabeth's mind. Joe's strength, his playfulness, his intuitive understanding. Yes, she had loved him, and she loved him still. She looked at the Humpty Dumpty shape that strained the buttons on his vest and at the bald spot under his carefully arranged hair, and a tide of tenderness caught her heart in a warm drowning.

What could she say to him that wouldn't hurt him? How could she explain that the love she felt was not the love of a woman for a man, but the love that came from long years of shared experience and gratitude for his gentle caring. She struggled for words.

"You don't have to tell me," he said. "I wouldn't put the hardship on you. I know I'm no prize. Fifty-one and fat and white trash in a fancy suit and a manicure. That's all right, baby. I understand. I just had to tell you, that's all. I've been holding it in for more than twenty years. I want you to be happy, honey. Don't be sad on my account."

She did not feel sad. Not then. She felt angry. Angry at herself for not being able to give him what he wanted, angry at the world for mismatching those who loved and those who did not love in return, angry at Joe, most of all, for having such a low opinion of himself. "You listen to me, Joe Simmons. You've got no call to talk yourself down like that. Not in front of me or anybody else. If somebody else said those things about you, I'd scratch their eyes out. I won't hear them, do you understand? You're the finest man God ever put on this green earth, the caringest and most forgiving and thoughtful and—" Then sadness came. It had no special source or reason. It was a sudden loss of strength and an overwhelming need for something unknown, unidentified, and forever lacking in her life. Her lips moved, but she could not speak. From deep inside her a primitive cry rose through her body with terrifying force, and she fell on

Joe's chest shuddering while the tears of her entire lifetime flowed from her heart through her eyes.

He held her close and rocked her.

When she had wept herself empty, Joe gave her a handkerchief. "Don't sniff, blow," he ordered.

"You sound like Aunt Julia."

"Don't you sass me, missy. Blow."

Elizabeth obeyed. "You still sound like Aunt Julia," she said with a shaky laugh.

He shifted her weight so that she was lying across his knees with her head resting in the crook of his arm. "I admired that lady," he said, "but she scared the stuffing out of me."

"You don't have to talk comfortable talk to me, Joe. We're past the point where we can get by on reminiscences. You did me a great honor a while ago; I can't forget it, and neither can you."

"I want you to forget it."

"Well, I can't. And I don't want to. A declaration of love like that is a treasure a woman can be proud of her whole life long . . . If you're thinking that you made me cry, that's not so. I don't even know myself why I was crying. It just seemed like everything in me had to get out. I never did like that before . . . I believe that I needed you with me to let it out. I'd trust you with my life. More than anybody I've ever known."

He wiped a stray tear from her face with a gentle finger. "I'll treasure that in my grave. Trusting is a great honor, too."

"I don't know what's come over me. It's like a spring flood. I couldn't stop crying, and now I can't stop talking. I want to tell you something that's been burdening me, Joe. Do you mind?" She did not wait for him to answer. There was no need. "Joe—Joe, I murdered my husband. I hit him with a poker on the head. In my dreams, I hit him and hit him and kept hitting him. Joe, I feel like I want to keep on forever, just hitting and hitting and—"

He lifted her to his chest and cradled her tight. Elizabeth pushed herself away. "No. Don't comfort me. That's not all . . . Joe, I'm not sorry I did it. I'm glad. I'm gladder about killing Lucas than I am about anything else I ever did. Ever." She searched his face for disgust and withdrawal. It was covered with tears. His mouth twisted with unspeakable pain.

It was her pain he was feeling. Elizabeth felt it leave her as he took it into his soul. She longed to comfort him, but she knew that there was no comfort for the agony of remorseless guilt. "I've done a terrible thing to you, Joe. It's done, and it's too late to beg forgiveness."

He smoothed her hair back from her temples. "Stop that foolishness,

Lizzie. You've given me what I always wanted, a chance to ease you. I am a joyful man."

She put her arms around his neck and kissed him on the lips. He accepted her kiss, using all his strength not to return it. Elizabeth felt his trembling. She put her head on his shoulder. "Hold me for a while, Joe." His strong arms folded around her.

After a few minutes, she spoke again. "I do love you. I'm sure of that. I just don't know which way exactly." Then she sat up abruptly. "I just realized something. You did mean that you want me to marry you, didn't you? You never said."

"Of course I did. I just didn't get that far in my speech."

"Oh. Good." She nestled into his embrace again. "I'll have to think about it."

Against her ear, a deep chuckle rumbled in his chest. "You always did say that, Lizzie. Take all the time you need."

61

The next day, Elizabeth felt light-hearted and also embarrassed. Not because she had shifted her burden to Joe. She believed in his assurances that he took it willingly. She was embarrassed that she had led him on with a kiss and a snuggle and a maybe, like a coquette. The emotional storm was past now. She felt a bond between them that nothing would ever diminish, but she had no romantic yearnings at all. If he believed they would take up where they left off, she would have to tell him no, and he would be hurt.

"Shoot!" she said aloud. "I hope this supper party won't be tense."

It was not the first time she had underestimated Joe Simmons. He called for her, handed her into his buggy and drove off as if nothing had happened between them. "I'm sorry Tradd's not home yet," he said. "Victoria's lip is stuck out a mile. She says she's going to feel like she's eating in a funeral parlor."

Elizabeth relaxed. "I hope you washed her mouth out with laundry soap," she said. She still had her friend.

On October first, Charleston's schools opened, and the somnolent pace of summer evaporated in a mist of invitations. Elizabeth surveyed the pile of invitations on her desk with dismay. "You can sure tell when people get a little taste of prosperity," she moaned. "I'd better pick a date and give a party myself. I'm going to owe everybody in the world."

"Parties are dumb," Tradd mumbled. He had sworn never to forgive her for signing him up for dancing school.

"I'm ignoring you, Tradd. It won't do any good to be surly. I'm not going to pay any attention."

Still, she did feel sorry for him. She remembered very well how miserable the young boys were for the first few weeks of dancing school. The girls always loved it. They got to dress up.

A few days later, the morning paper had a headline that might cheer his spirits. She passed it to him. "How about making peace and taking your old mother to see the show? I'll treat to an ice-cream sundae after."

"I'll say! I'll come home from school fast as I can."

Now that the hurricane season was past, the U. S. Navy was bringing the Spanish prize vessels home to America. The first port of call was Charleston.

Three of the big ships were already tied up to the East Bay docks when Tradd and his mother arrived. "Golly, they're big," said the boy.

"That's why they're called 'prize vessels,'" Elizabeth said.

"Oh, Mama!"

"Sorry, darling. It just slipped out. Are they letting people go aboard? I always heard that the Spanish captains have brocade and velvet furnished cabins with solid-gold door handles."

"Golly!"

"Don't say that. You sound like a frog. If you have to exclaim, at least be literary. I rather like 'Odds bodkins.'"

"What does it mean?"

"I haven't the faintest idea. But I'm sure no frog ever says it."

A smartly uniformed officer waved the group of people nearest the ship onto the gangplank.

"They are letting people on. Let's go, Mama."

The wide deck was sparkling clean. Elizabeth almost hated to step on it. Tradd had no qualms. He ran across to ask an officer about the Captain's cabin. Elizabeth followed him, then stopped in the middle of the deck. Let him do things on his own, she reminded herself. She looked about the ship. Groups of people were clustered around the guns, she noticed. War-happy to the end. She saw no one she knew. Tradd was having an animated conversation with the patient officer. She looked up the towering mast. Imagine being the lookout in the crow's nest in a high sea. It must be like the earthquake, only never ending.

"The Armada is destroyed, Bess." Her heart lurched, and her eyes traveled slowly down from the top of the mast. It cannot be, she told herself. But she knew it was. Harry.

He was on one knee, at her feet. He touched the hem of her skirt to his lips and lowered it to the deck again. Her hands wanted to reach out to the bowed curly head, but she held them at her sides. He lifted his face. "You have triumphed, Your Majesty. Long may you reign."

"Get up, Harry. You're making a spectacle of yourself and of me." She was icy.

He stood in one smooth motion. How could I have forgotten how tall he is, thought Elizabeth frantically. Now I have to look up at him.

Harry put his hand on the small of her back. It burned through her clothes. His mouth was close to her ear. It made her dizzy. "I had to come back, Bess, you witch. I've never gone back to any place. But I couldn't stay away. You haunted me."

"Please, Harry, leave me alone. I cannot go through all the grief again. Go away. If you don't, I don't know what I'll do. This is cruel, Harry."

Tradd's shout sounded very far away. I will not faint, Elizabeth said silently. I will not. Her legs were rubbery. "So pale, my queen." His voice was a caress. "Come sit down." He took her arm and led her to a bench. "Visitors" was stenciled on it. "I'll go talk to the boy until you're stronger."

She watched him stride to meet Tradd. He wore no coat. His white shirt clung to the long muscles of his back. Her palms could feel their flexing. She looked away from the raucous, happy reunion and concentrated her will. When the two of them joined her, she was in control of herself.

"You cannot stay in the kitchen building."

"Agreed."

"You cannot show up any time you please and expect a welcome."

"Agreed."

"You cannot embarrass me in public the way you did this afternoon."

"Agreed."

"You cannot put your hand on my back or any place else unless I tell you I've changed my mind about you."

"Can I kiss your hand?"

"No!"

"Not even a boring, socially acceptable, how-do-you-do-Mistress-Cooper kiss?"

"No. Nothing. I have to think."

Harry laughed. "Thinking is for cowards. Have you become a coward, then, Bess? In six short months?" He got up from his chair.

"Sit down, Harry. Stay over there. You agreed that we would talk."

"We can talk later." He crossed to the library door. Elizabeth stopped breathing. He was leaving. Again. And it was just as bad as the last time. Harry turned the key in the lock. "You cannot imagine how I've wanted you," he said. He turned down the lights. The flames turned blue, then vanished with a soft pop. "I want to see the firelight on your hair."

His steps were slow and confident. He stopped in front of her and began to pull out her hairpins. "Tradd," Elizabeth managed to say.

"Sleeping and snoring. I gave him a smuggled ration of real sailor's rum." Harry tangled his hands in her loosened hair and pulled her up to meet his hungry kiss with hers.

"I cannot live without you, Bess, so I've come back to get you. We'll go away together, we'll roam the world. I have so many things to show you, and so many that I want to see with you for the first time. We'll take Tradd with us, rescue him from the psalms of the good Dr. Porter. What an education for a boy!"

"You're insane."

"You know I'm not. You want to go. I can feel your heart racing against my hand. You're thinking about seeing the Great Wall of China."

"Fool. That's not what I'm thinking about at all."

"Glorious, bawdy Bess. I worship you."

The fire had burned to coals and gone out, but they did not know it. They made love yet again.

"You invited me to come over for breakfast. What's wrong with that?"

"We haven't changed our clothes, that's what's wrong. Hurry up. And button your trousers straight this time."

Overhead, Tradd's sleepy footsteps stumbled slowly down the stairs. Elizabeth finished hooking her frock and fumbled with her wildly disarrayed hair.

"Boys never know what clothes people are wearing," Harry whispered. "Here. Bundle it up in this kerchief." He put a brightly patterned bandanna in her hand. "Souvenir of Cuba."

Elizabeth giggled helplessly. "It'll never work, Harry."

He looked at her flushed cheeks, the dead fire, the rumpled hearth rug. Tradd was almost at the bottom on the stairs. "You're right. Lie down on the settee. You fell asleep there last night. Close your eyes. I'll unlock the door and climb out the window." He turned the key, ran silently to kiss her quickly. "I'll come calling in an hour. Don't look so slatternly or I'll be forced to downgrade you to a duchess."

Elizabeth turned her face into the cushions. She couldn't stop laughing. She felt the chilly air when Harry opened the window, heard Tradd asking Delia why she wasn't down to breakfast, and abandoned herself to muffled hysteria. "What in God's name has become of me?" she sobbed.

Elizabeth looked through the window of her office in the carriage house. It needs washing, she thought, and the rest of the windows do, too. Suddenly, the simple act of hiring a man to come and clean the windows seemed to her an insupportably heavy task. She put her hands to the small of her back to warm away the ache there. Outside the window, a blustery fall wind blew the dead leaves from the pecan tree and sent them scuttling from one corner of the walled yard to another. That's just the way I feel, Elizabeth said to herself, tossed and pushed and pressured.

Harry's return, six weeks earlier, had ushered in a period of conflicting demands on her emotions and her energies. It coincided with the beginning of the social activity that always marked the end of summer in Charleston. There were the usual invitations, calls to receive and return, obligations of duty and of pleasure. This year was busier than ever for Elizabeth because she was gently sponsoring Joe's daughter Victoria. The girl could not be a real part of the Charleston social world because Joe would never be accepted. Unless, eventually, Victoria married a Charlestonian. For an attractive heiress, it would not be difficult. In the meantime, although there would be no debut at the Saint Cecelia for her, she was already, under Elizabeth's wing, one of the members of the Friday evening dancing school at the South Carolina Hall. It made Elizabeth smile to see the age-old differences repeated: Tradd, at fifteen, scowled and dragged his feet before setting out; Victoria, eager and exuberant, fussed at him for dawdling.

In addition to the social activity, the increased business that resulted from the war made it imperative that Elizabeth devote more hours to planning for and correspondence about the phosphate business. Its steady growth had been halted by the Panic of ninety-three. The five years of depression that followed had seen income and equipment deteriorate. But now, there was optimism in the air. It was time to make repairs and replacements, to renegotiate contracts, to consider completing the final stages of the delayed plan. She had to make decisions, and each decision would lead to a different set of alternatives. If she repaired the conveyer belts into the washing shed, she could count on returning production to its earlier level. If she replaced them with newer, more advanced machinery, the capacity would be increased. But that would cost money, much more than the repairs. How long would it take for the greater volume to pay for the added cost? And what would have to go unrepaired in the crushing and refining operations if all the money was spent on equipment for the washing step?

There was also the question of the wages for the workers. They would definitely be raised at the January first powwow. How much could she afford; how much would they demand; how many new workers would she have to hire in order to dig the quantity of ore that the new conveyers could handle . . . if she bought them. Her thoughts ran in circles, overlapping as she imagined other possibilities and their consequences.

She could ask Joe's advice, of course. Probably she should consult him; after all, he owned a half of the business. But she really wanted to make the changes on her own, to bring Carlington up to a point where it could match any other mining company in South Carolina. She had stubbornly refused help when times were bad. Now that they were getting better, she did not want to stand back and let anyone else have the thrill of making the company a big success. Not even Joe. She had worked hard, pinched pennies, cut her own income to the bone, enlisted the workers in a group effort. Even when she worried herself sick over the problems, she had loved the challenges. She really liked being a businesswoman . . . and the admiration of her friends that rewarded her efforts. Still, she had an obligation to Joe. Her mind made more circles, and she tried unsuccessfully not to feel guilty.

Because it was not only the business. She also owed Joe some response to his proposal of marriage. He had said he would wait, and he had not pressed his suit. Not in words. But every Friday, he brought Victoria to the house, watched proudly as she and Tradd walked the ten steps to the Hall, and shared a pot of tea with Elizabeth for the two hours until dancing school was over. He was always relaxed, always had amusing stories to tell about Andrew Anson's adventures at the bank, always radiated affection for Elizabeth and gratitude for her interest in Victoria. They were pleasant hours for them both. The Tradd house had, after all, been Joe's home for more than ten years. It seemed very natural to have him there. Except that his expansive happiness exerted a pressure that was not made any less because it was unexpressed. He loved her with all his heart.

She could not let things go on this way. The longer she waited to tell him that she would not marry him, the more it would hurt him. Her silence was cowardly.

Unless . . . The hours with him were happy for her, too. It was luxurious to be loved the way Joe loved her. She had never known anything like it. And he was like a father to Tradd, who had never had one. There was a warm, family feeling to the after-dancing-school conversations. Victoria would confide in Elizabeth, who remembered the seesaw emotions of her own dancing-school days and could soothe or congratulate, depending on the events. At the same time, Tradd listened intently to Joe's assurances that dancing was no worse than the battle of Antietam and that all scars faded in time. The adults exchanged surreptitious amused looks. When the children went to the kitchen for the milk and cookies that were waiting for them, Joe and Elizabeth could laugh and agree that they would not be that age again for all the rice in China or all the gold in the world.

But then . . . after Joe and Victoria were gone, or after Elizabeth came home from any party she might attend or after supper on any evening she did not go out, there was always a knocking on the door. Harry.

Harry, whom Tradd adored. Harry, whose touch melted her bones. Harry, who could make her laugh or cry with his stories, who made her think about books and about the world and about dreams that might come true. He demanded that she be witty, and she was; that she be intelligent, and she was; that she be a woman, not a girl, not a lady, not a company president, not a mother. And she was lost, willingly, in a flood tide of sensation and shared ecstasy. When he left her, in the last hour of the night's darkness, it was a knife in her heart, a reminder and a warning of what she would feel if she lost him again.

He always took her in his arms for one final embrace before he departed. And, with no scruples, he whispered deep in her ear a siren song for her to dream of. "We'll laugh on the Bridge of Sighs, my Bess," he would say. Or, "We'll dance on the Great Wall of China." Or, "We'll ride elephants and listen to the lions sing in the night." Or simply, "Come with me and be my love."

And she would dream away the few short hours of sleeping until she had to wake and face the mundane responsibilities of house and kitchen before her busy day began . . .

Elizabeth looked away from the smudged window and down at the rows of figures on the paper on her desk. They blurred before her tired eyes. She was exhausted. But there was so much to do. She had promised Catherine she would come help her decide on a color to paint the dining room, but she was too tired to go. Catherine would want more than advice. She always did. She would somehow manage to coax her mother into promising to give her a piece of furniture or the gloves on her hands or the curtains from Elizabeth's old room on the third floor that "would look so sweet in the nursery." She was self-righteously selfish, and it horrified Elizabeth. But still, she was her daughter, and Elizabeth loved her. She just had to hope Catherine would outgrow her greediness. In the meantime, there was Maine, who became more enchanting every day.

Elizabeth sighed and stood up. Maybe the fresh air would give her some energy. In any case, she had promised, and that was that. She had to go. The budget for the store at Carlington would have to wait. So would the dirty windows. So would the warm bath and nap before supper. So would Tradd's shirts that needed their collars turned. So would the letter she owed Henrietta and Stuart. She had meant to do them all today, but there was just not enough time. There was never enough time anymore.

When she arrived at Catherine's, she felt ashamed of her earlier thoughts. The tea table was all set up, with the center of attraction a small, decorated cake atop a brightly wrapped package. "Happy Birthday, Mama," Catherine caroled. She joggled Maine in her arms, and he gurgled an incomprehensible series of sounds. "He's saying 'Happy Birthday, Grandmama,'" Catherine explained.

Elizabeth had completely forgotten that it was her birthday. She was moved beyond words by Catherine's surprise celebration.

And by the charming pencil sketch of Maine that was her present.

She exhibited it proudly to Joe that evening when he arrived with Victoria for dancing school. Joe had a present for her, too. "You have to wait until we leave to open it, though," he said. Elizabeth promised, but her eyes kept wandering back to the large box during their conversation. She felt as curious and eager as a child. Joe teased her about it, reminiscing about long-ago birthdays when she had rummaged through all the hiding places in the house, trying to find her presents before the day arrived.

"It's your fault, Joe," Elizabeth said. "You make me feel like a child again. When you're around, I'm not a grandmother at all."

After the children came home, after they reported on the excitement of the evening—Madame had actually slipped and fallen while she was demonstrating how to reverse while waltzing—after the cookies and milk, Saint Michael's rang ten, and it was time to break up the happy little group. Elizabeth had a sense of dismay. She wanted the close, comfortable feeling to last.

"Happy Birthday, Lizzie," Joe said in parting.

"Thank you, Joe." Elizabeth threw her arms around his neck and kissed him impulsively.

Joe's face lit with pleasure. "Thank you, honey," he said.

When the carriage drove off, Elizabeth ran back to the study and the mysterious large parcel from Joe.

"Help me unknot this ribbon, Tradd. How exciting! I do love presents."

Tradd was unexpectedly mulish. "I have a present for you, too, Mama. You don't have to carry on so about Mr. Simmons."

Elizabeth gaped at him. I believe he's jealous, she thought. How absurd. And irritating. "The more presents the better, darling," she said. "Trot it out. I'm sure I'll love it."

"We have to wait, Mama. It's a half present, sort of. Harry has the other half; he's bringing it over. He'll be here soon."

The words were barely out of his mouth when the door knocker sounded. Tradd raced to answer it.

Harry brought not only a present, but also a bottle of champagne and an exotic confection of ladyfingers and custard and glazed apricots that he identified as a French birthday cake. "We'll pretend we're at the top of the Eiffel Tower. It's celebrating its tenth birthday next year; we can pretend now and share it then."

Elizabeth frowned. Harry had promised her that he would not dangle his plans for adventure before Tradd's impressionable nature. It seemed that he had broken his promise.

The birthday present confirmed it. The dual-wrapped boxes contained a stereopticon and a set of slides of all the capitals of the world's nations.

"Temptation, Bess. You're too much woman to resist it. Imagine us in Rome, Budapest, Constantinople, Bangkok. Just think of really standing in the midst of these photos, of those streets and bazaars in color, of smelling and tasting and hearing what you're seeing."

Tradd was engrossed in the optical device, his eyes hidden by the viewing mask. He did not see his mother's rage.

Harry did, and it made him worry. He had, perhaps, pushed too far in his impatience to have Elizabeth decide to go with him. After Tradd stomped up to bed, Harry mended his fences. He apologized, with the infrequent seriousness that always defused her anger. Then he ignored her protests and took her in his arms to ignite the passion that was stronger than her indignation.

She could not withstand it. Still, when she was languid and glowing from their lovemaking, she retained enough recollection of her fury to upbraid him and make him agree to the bargain she set.

"You have to leave me alone for a few weeks, Harry. I need to think. It's not fair to either of us to have things drag on like this. I have to make up my mind, for once and for all. But I can't do it without time to think. If you really want me, you have to give me a chance to decide."

Harry's sudden anger frightened her, as hers had disturbed him earlier. "I won't submit to being kept hanging like that, Bess. It's enough that I've been dancing attendance on you for weeks now while you begged for time to think about things. If I leave again, I'll never come back."

"Threats only make me mad, Harry. I won't be bullied. Leave and be damned."

He caught her to him, and his touch made her weak. "Ah, my majestic Bess," he murmured, "don't do this to us. Don't push me away past recovery."

In the end, he agreed to her terms: He would go away until after Christmas, a little more than a month. When he returned, she would have made up her mind.

"The beginning of a New Year, Bess, and the end of a century. We'll sail away on January first, 1899, and meet the twentieth century on our way."

He knows how much I'll miss him, Elizabeth thought, and he believes I won't be able to live without him. I wonder if he's right. The room seemed terribly cold now that Harry was gone. She added a log to the dying fire and began again to open Joe's gift.

It was letter paper, a ream of it, a luxurious heavyweight, cream-colored bond. At first Elizabeth could not imagine what Joe had been thinking of. It was elegant paper, certainly, much nicer than anything she had. But it was so prosaic, such a dull, unimaginative present. She felt a childish disappointment, just like the times when she had hoped for a pretty frock and received a warm flannel nightdress. Useful, yes, but not really a celebration sort of thing.

Then she looked more closely at the discreet, small, engraved letterhead. It was not, as she had thought, her name and address. It read "The

Tradd Phosphate Company." "Dear Heaven," she breathed. She tore open the square envelope inside the box lid.

"Happy Birthday" was written on the plain white card in Joe's handwriting. Enclosed was a bill of sale transferring Joe's half share in the company to her.

Elizabeth was overcome by the gift. Not because of the monetary value. It was large to her but, she knew, to Joe it was insignificant. The meaning behind the present was what brought tears to her eyes. Joe was giving her independence. Not only would her income be greater now, but also she need have no misgivings about her desire to run everything alone without consulting him.

Joe had made no secret of what he wanted. He wanted to take care of her, to do things for her, to have her dependent on him. And he had given her the means to live without needing help from anyone, especially him. The generosity and love behind his gesture took her breath away.

She remembered Harry's angry accusation that she was keeping him on a string. She was doing the same thing to Joe. But Joe doesn't mind, she told herself quickly. He's happy with our Friday evenings.

And she knew she was lying to herself. Yes, Joe was happy on Fridays. But there were six other days in the week. He was a man who needed to be taking care of someone. Someone who could appreciate his fine sensibility and thoughtfulness. Victoria loved her father, but she took him for granted.

She needed a mother, too. She was entering the years when she would most require guidance and comforting and the pleasures of learning how to be a woman.

If I don't marry Joe, he'll marry someone else, Elizabeth thought. He'll have to, for Victoria's sake. And he'll take care of his wife and make himself happy that way. A vicious little jab of jealousy pinched her heart.

I told Harry I'd give him my decision after Christmas, she said to herself. I'll do the same for Joe. I owe him that, even if he doesn't ask it of me. All I need is time to think. And a little sleep. She put the screen in front of the fire and dragged herself up to bed.

Next birthday I'll be forty, she thought just before she fell asleep. The idea astonished her and made her more than a little afraid.

62

In spite of her resolve, Elizabeth had little time for thinking in the weeks before Christmas. Tradd made her life difficult. He was even more importunate than Harry, badgering Elizabeth about the boring sameness of their lives, reading to her from books about Europe, ostentatiously twirling the faded old globe in the study and daydreaming aloud about lands with strange sounding names. He interrupted her when she was working, irritated her when she was trying to find a quiet moment, wrenched her heart with his transparent yearning for Harry's return.

Elizabeth was longing for Harry herself; she needed no prompting from Tradd. Her dreams made her blush and left her body with a deep, frustrated aching.

She threw herself wholeheartedly into preparations for Christmas. It kept her from brooding and took her mind off the decisions that were eluding her. All the family were coming to the Tradd house; it was an annual ceremony now, and no one considered any other way of celebrating Christmas. Elizabeth loved the gatherings, even though they demanded weeks of work. She wrapped presents, checked supplies, ground spices, baked cookies and decorated the house with rising anticipation.

The day did not disappoint her. There was a warm sun to set the camellias and poinsettias in the garden aglow.

A new stocking for Maine joined the row on the mantelpiece in the study; he was puzzled, but almost as pleased as the older family members by the discoveries inside the bulging, lumpy stockings. The room rocked with laughter and shouts of surprise when the little presents were extracted. For an hour, everyone had the fun of being a child again. Then they watched, smiling, as Maine was introduced to the tangerine from the toe. He wrinkled his tiny nose comically at the sharp smell, and they all chuckled at the repetition of a scene that each child had provided in the past. At dinner, Maine gave them another show when he met his first drumstick. It was a noisy time of shared memories and affection.

After dinner, Tradd and his cousins went out into the garden, and the sound of firecrackers drove the grown-ups to closing the windows, even though it was such a warm day. Stuart and Lawrence settled down with a bowl of salted pecans and a bottle of port to talk politics. Catherine took Maine upstairs for his nap, and Elizabeth, with Henrietta's help, prepared the drawing room for the people who would be calling.

"Elizabeth," said Henrietta, "why don't you let Tradd come home with us to the Barony? The boys will be hunting, and he can shoot some game for you. We must have eaten your cupboard bare today."

Elizabeth had a flashing memory of the summer months when she had had the house all to herself. She startled Henrietta by a sudden hug and kiss. "You're a lifesaver," she said. "He'd love it, and so would I."

"Merry Christmas!" called voices from the piazza.

Elizabeth ran to the stairwell. "Come on up," she sang out to the first group of callers. "You know the way. Merry Christmas!"

When the early winter darkness began to close in, the last of the guests departed. The family stayed for an early supper of cold ham and turkey and relishes. Then they, too, were off, crowded into Stuart's surrey, shouting Merry Christmas farewells.

Elizabeth closed the door and slid the bolt across. The silence of the old house closed around her like a benediction. She walked into the library and sank gratefully into the tall chair behind the desk. The room was too bright. With an inward groan, she stood on her swollen feet and moved about the room, turning off the lights. The fire in the grate gave enough illumination for her purposes. She returned to her chair, slipped off her shoes and tucked her feet up in the corner of the wide seat. Her eyebrows met. Christmas was over; she had to decide what to do.

Her feet throbbed; she wished Harry were there to rub them. And other things, too. Her body reacted to her thoughts, swelling with secret hunger. Stop that, she told it, I have to think. Her disciplined mind took command.

You are almost forty years old, it said, and Harry is thirty-two. The familiar arguments battled inside her head, with a muted counterpoint of sexual longing. Harry was the most exciting man—the most exciting person—she had ever known. He was unlike anyone else. His adventurousness, his carelessness, his hedonism . . . they fascinated and threatened her. If she went with him, their life would be glorious. For as long as it lasted. Harry was not a man who offered guarantees. He was decent, caring; he would not desert her in some far corner of the world. But he might tire of her, send her home. She tried not to think of it, but the possibility was inescapable, no matter what he said.

I don't care, Elizabeth told herself. I can't let him go now. It hurts too much. If he leaves me later, I will hurt then. But not now.

And he might never get tired of her. After all, he did come back from Cuba. He'd never done that before. He was going to marry her.

What does it really matter that I'm older? I can watch my diet, stay slim, keep myself healthy.

They would be poor; the money the newspaper would pay Harry for articles about the places they went would not be very much. That was unimportant. Elizabeth had been poor all her life. It was a constant worry, but she had learned to cope.

Yes, it would be a gigantic gamble to marry him, to sail away from everything she knew. But the Tradds had always been daring. She had resented it all her life that, because she was a lady, she was never able to do so many things she wanted to. Not even ride on the back of the ice wagon when she was a child. That year at the Barony, Stuart got to manage the trunks, to watch the river in the rainstorms. She had had to learn to embroider. Boys and men went hunting, fishing, sailing. Girls and women wore corsets and arranged flowers. She was just as much a Tradd as Pinckney and Stuart. Just as reckless in her heart. Harry saw that, encouraged it. He had given her the feeling of sand between her toes, of moonlight and sliding water on her naked body. He wanted to give her more, the whole world, a new life, away from the boundaries of the Ashley and the Cooper, from setting an example, from being a grandmother, from being At Home on Tuesdays for the rest of her life, from being a Charleston lady. She could be a person with no labels, a vagabond, an adventurer.

"See Naples and die" . . . of fatigue, she thought. She laughed aloud. The sound startled her. There would be no silent rooms in an adventurer's life. Challenge, excitement, the thrill she felt when Harry was near, the neverending surprises she found in herself, physically and mentally, a running-over cup of life . . .

But always changing, moving, shedding old skins. There would be no room in her baggage for things saved or salvaged, for the past. They would build new traditions, Harry said, have no need of old ones.

Did she really need them? She looked around the tall, shadowed room. How many Tradds must have sat here, as she was sitting now, with a fire dying down under the mantel. She thought of Catherine painting the dresses of the carved nymphs dancing across the old wood, of herself trying to mimic the dance and breaking her father's inkwell. Probably her father's sister had had her own dream, given birth by those tiny dancers, and before her, a succession of little girls. They were all part of her, Lizzie—Elizabeth—Bess. No matter her last name, Cooper or Fitzpatrick, she would always be Miss Tradd of Charleston.

Even if she became Mistress Simmons with two m's? That would be a break greater than running off to Italy with Harry. The five blocks between Broad Street and Wentworth Street were wider than the Atlantic

Ocean. Charleston would have to forgive her for marrying Joe; a Tradd could do anything. But it would never forgive him. The disapproval would be hidden under layers of perfect behavior, gracious manners. The slights would be so subtle that they would have no definition, no name. They wouldn't bother her. She could fight back with the same delicate weapons if need be. But Joe would know. He was too intuitive. He would be hurt again by his eternal place outside. She wouldn't put him through that. They'd just have to make new friends. Uptown.

. . . That was funny. She was worried about protecting Joe, but what he cared about was protecting her. Each of them caring about the vulnerabilities of the other. Wasn't that the strongest foundation for building a life together? Wasn't that the basis of the magic that had been between Lucy and Pinny? It had been so beautiful. Maybe, with Joe, the same magic would grow. He loved her with a depth that awed her. And he knew her, in a way that Harry never could, yet still he loved her. There would be no need to keep her spine straight or her waist slim for Joe, no worry about growing older.

What luxury.

And other luxuries, too. She could send Tradd to any college he wanted, with a tour of the world afterward if he still yearned for it . . . She'd have to do some coaxing, though, to change Joe's tastes a little. Otherwise, he'd probably keep giving her overly gaudy gifts like the diamond necklace.

She smiled at a delightfully wicked thought. Joe might believe he knew her through and through, but she had learned some things about herself that she'd have to teach him. He would be almighty surprised.

Oh, God. The memory of Harry's body made it horrible to imagine sharing a bed with Joe. She remembered his heavy, bulging stomach and thin, bent legs. He would be fish-belly white, too. And he was shorter than she was. It was distasteful. No, she couldn't.

But there was that emotional moment when she confessed about Lucas. Joe's arms around her waist had been strong, and his touch on her hair gentle. He wouldn't rush her. He would know without her telling him that she had to find her own time. He already knew. He always knew what she was feeling, always had known. When his arms were around her, she felt safe. When he touched her, she felt loved. And she loved him, too. In every way except the carnal. Could passion grow from love? She thought of the happiness her kiss had given him, remembered the pleasure she had felt at the sight of his face. It was a thing of wonder, the ability to make another person so happy. What would the gift of her body mean to him?

Elizabeth discovered that she was crying, humbled by the realization of her incredible value in the eyes of the gentle man at the core of Joe

Simmons. "Yes," she whispered, "yes, it might be. Perhaps I could love him in every way. Dearest Joe."

Think of this, her mind said, you'd be pampered into suffocation.

She dried her eyes with her sleeve and considered the thought. It was, she decided, unfair. Joe would envelop her in a cocoon of wealth and ease. He would ask nothing of her, devote his life to her happiness. But he would also allow her any freedom she wanted, just because she wanted it. If she became lazy and complacent, it would be her fault, not his.

Her thoughts turned again to Harry. He would never crowd her. On the contrary, he always urged her to ever greater space, to trying new wings.

Why, then, did she still feel smothered? Nerves. Foolish. She shook her head, then breathed deeply until the serenity of the quiet house seeped into her. Quiet. She closed her eyes and savored it, inhaling the holiday scent of pine and tangerine peel. Her scurrying thoughts slowed, faded, displaced by the palpable serenity of the old, beautiful room and the old, beautiful city beyond its walls. Saint Michael's bells rang the half hour. The final note vibrated faintly in the stillness.

Can I give this up? Elizabeth mused. This little world of history and pride and cherished graciousness and beauty, even more precious now that it had proved so fragile in everything but spirit.

And her own spirit. Could she bend it to a changed pattern? She had been alone more than ten years; she was used to it; she loved it. The lonely moments were bitter, but these tranquil times of solitude were piercingly sweet. She was herself, not half of someone else, even if it were the "better half." She had met troubles and overcome them; she had learned that she was strong, that she could choose her own path. The mistakes she made were her mistakes, and the successes her successes.

She did not have to make a decision between Joe and Harry only. There were other rivals, too, the generations of Tradds and the woman who had reveled in overcoming the obstacles to business achievement.

Who am I, anyhow? Lizzie? Bess? Elizabeth? Company president? Miss Tradd of the Charleston Tradds? Who do I want to be?

She shivered. The fire had gone out. I'm tired, she thought, and I am more confused now than when I started. I need to sleep.

The room was dark, but she did not need a light. She knew it by heart. As she walked to the door, Saint Michael's rang the hour. From the lookout in the steeple, the watchman's cry floated across the roofs and piazzas and peeling walls of the proud old city. "Eleven of the clock, and all's well."

"But maybe it could be better," said Lizzie-Elizabeth-Bess. She put her sore feet gingerly on the stairs for the climb to her cold, empty bed.

Alexandra Ripley was born and raised in Charleston. She became interested in historical fiction at an early age, when tourists offered her nickels for directions to "Rhett Butler's grave."

She attended Vassar on a scholarship given by the United Daughters of the Confederacy, then lived in New York and Europe before returning to the South with her two daughters, two cats and two thousand books.

